Of

Darkness

and

Ruination

by

Rachel Fallon

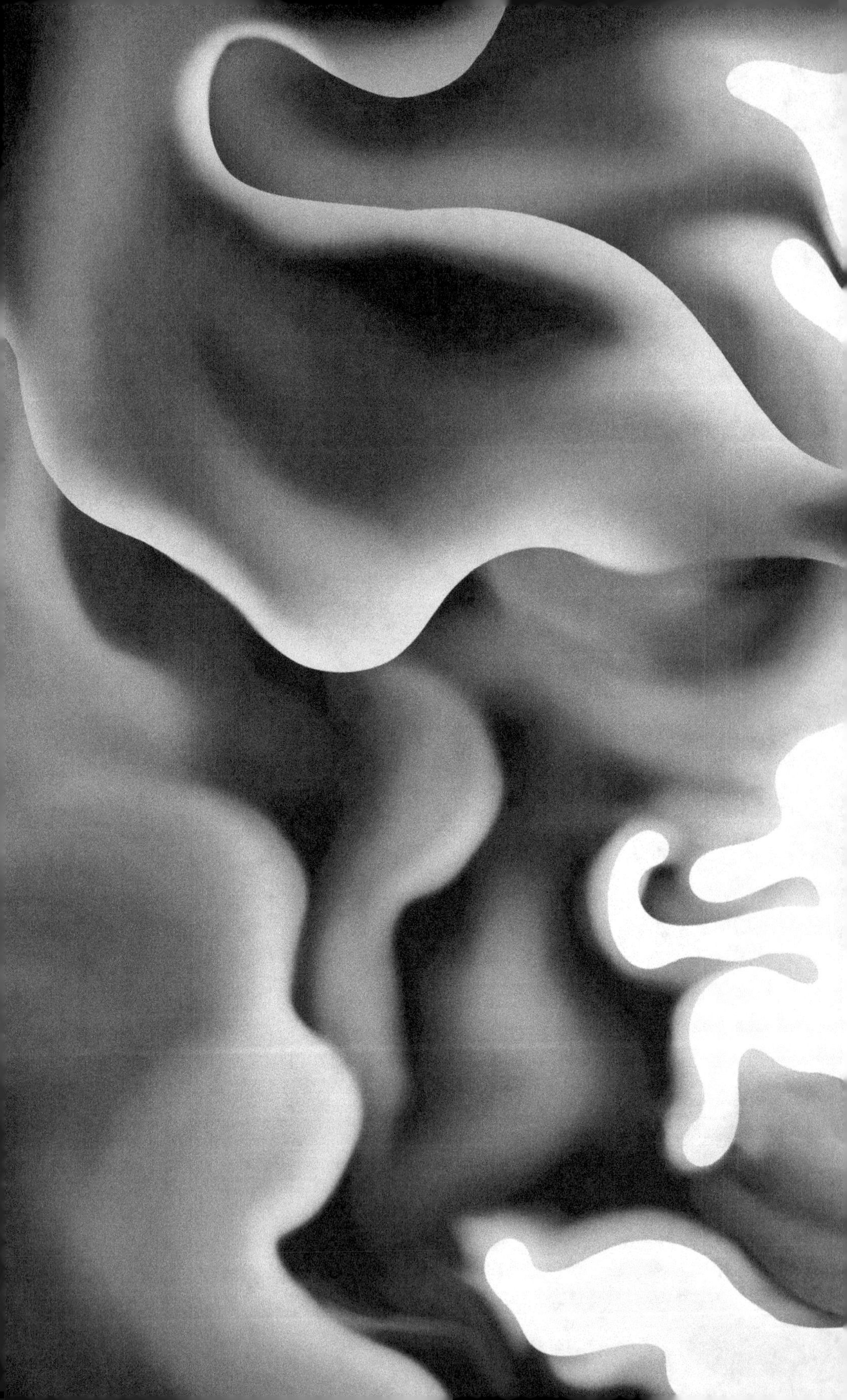

OF DARKNESS AND RUINATION

THE STAR QUEEN CHRONICLES

BOOK ONE

RACHEL FALLON

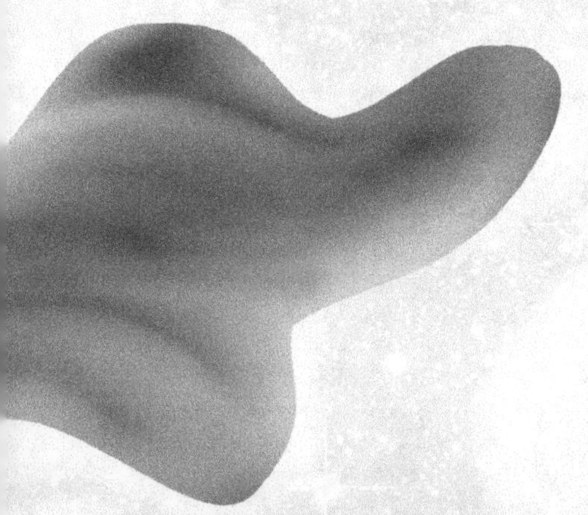

ISBN: 979-8-9894637-0-1 (Digital Online)
ISBN: 979-8-9894637-1-8 (Paperback)
ISBN: 979-8-9894637-2-5 (Hardcover)

Any references to historical events, real people, or real places are used fictitiously. Names, characters, and places are products of the author's imagination.

Front cover image by Rena Violet @violet.book.design.

Book design by Rena Violet @violet.book.design.

Editing by Loren Sorensen @lorensorensenwrites.

First printed in the United States of America.
First printing edition 2024.
Rachel Fallon
Billerica, MA 01821

To those held down in any way…may you snap your chains and bare your fangs.

Per Aspera Ad Astra

Through hardships to the stars

CELESTERRA
ARGYRE
SVA
PANCHAIA
EDEN
FRIDA
SUNRISE
SONMATHION
PIRIAWIS
KOLOR
AARU
SLIEVENAMON
TITHONUS
DAWN
EMIAN
MANU
CHRYSE
AFFARAON
NYSA
DAMACULOUS OCEAN
GWAELOD
MAGH MEALL
BALTIA
AVALON
ETHERALTA
DUN AILINNE
CANTREF
CAERSIDI
DAY
ABUZOLEAN SEA

TRITONIAN SEA
ZERZURA
DIYU
SUNSET
ARCADIA
BIARMA
BEREZAITI
SINIAWIS
IRKALLA
MOUNTAINS
MURIAS
GJOLL
EVENFALL
ASPHODEL
DUSK
ALFHEIM
FALIAS
EVENTIDE
NEUTRAL LANDS
SEGIAS
NAMMIANIAN OCEAN
RANGE
LYONESSE
EIRNE
MAEL DUIN
CORNBENIG
TAIRNGIRE
KERIS
NIGHT

Contents

Trigger Warnings

- Slavery
- Sexual Slavery/Assault (mostly alluded to but only shown in one scene where a side character is made to work in a brothel)
- Attempted Sexual Assault
- Sexual Assault (on a side character)
- Manipulation
- Dubious consent
- Whipping
- Torture
- Physical Violence
- Explicit Sex
- Infidelity (not main couple)
- Use of a drink that lowers inhibitions during a sex party
- Kidnapping
- Classism
- Arranged Marriages
- Bipolar themes in main character
- War

Guide

Human Characters:

Asteria Faelynn Zagreus
(Uh-stair-ee-ah Fae-lynn Zag-re-us)
Priscilla Tam
(Pris-cilla Tam)
Emmie Saphere
(Emm-ee Sa-ph-ere)
Eris Ventella
(Air-is Ven-tell-ah)
Soren Sevda
(Sore-en Sev-duh)
Callisto Abara
(Kuh-lis-toh Ah-bar-ah)

Night Kingdom:

Capital: Tairngire (Tear-en-gear-ah)
Ruled by: House Erebus
Shift Animal: Dragon
Colors: Black and Purple

Members:

King Calix Orpheus Atarah Erebus
(Kay-liks Or-fee-us Ah-tar-ah Ah-ree-bus)

Indirect:

Princess Ndrita Luna Nuit
(N-dree-ta Loo-na New-eet)

Princess Liviana Chandra Atarah Erebus
(Liv-ee-ah-na Chan-druh Ah-tar-ah Ah-ree-bus)

Deceased:

King Orion Dreki Ancalagon Erebus
(Oh-rye-on Dr-ek-ee Uhn-ka-luh-gaan Ah-ree-bus)

Queen Jemisha Adalina Atarah Erebus (Atarah is her maiden name - Cousin branch
of House Erebus)
(Jem-ee-sh-ah Add-ah-lin-ah Ah-tar-ah Ah-ree-bus)

Lady Kaida Azlin Atarah (Jemisha's sister)
(Kai-duh Az-lin Ah-tar-ah)

Inner Circle:

Baach Dion (Ba-ch Dy-on)
Delia Galath (De-luh Gal-ah-th)
Eryx Rownan (Air-iks Row-nan)
Harpina Anand (Har-pi-na Ah-Naan-d)
Ilta Ledanos (Il-ta Lay-duh-nos)
Lilith Karærin (Li-luhth Kar-er-in)
Titan (Tai-tn)

Other Cities:

City: Segais (See-gas)
Ruled by: Lord Rhidian and Lady Alora Asman
(Rid-ee-an) and (Uh-lore-uh) (As-man)

City Lyonesse (Lie-uh-ness)
Ruled by: Lord Kyler and Lady Aisling Daram
(Ky-lur) (Ash-ling) (Deer-um)

City: Mael Duin (Mall Dew-in)

Ruled by: Lady Jasira Hanwi
(Juh-seer-ah Hen-why)

City: Corbenic (Core-Ben-ic)
Ruled by: Lord Ciaran Tolze
(Kier-ren Toel-ze)

City: Eirne (Ear-en)
Ruled by: Lord Polaris and Lady Zillah Nyx
Khors
(Poe-lar-is) (Zi-luh Nyx) (Kh-oars)

City: Keris (Keh-ruhs)
Ruled by: Lord Sterling and Princess Ndrita Luna Nuit
(Stur-luhng) (N-Dree-ta Loo-na) (New-eet)

Day Kingdom:

Capital: Avalon (Av-ah-lon)
Ruled by: House Earendel
Shift Animal: Dragon
Colors: Gold and Purple

Members:

King Aelius Earendel
(Ee-li-us Eh-ar-en-del)

Queen Aurelia Hemera Earendel
(Ah-real-ia Heh-mr-uh Eh-ar-en-del)

Prince Arien Finn Earendel
(Eh-ree-uhn Fin Eh-ar-en-del)

Other Cities:

City: Magh Meall (Mah Mell)
Ruled by: Lord Ayden and Lady Elvi Perendi
(Ay-den) and (El-vi) (Per-en-di)

City Cantref (Can-trev)
Ruled by: Lord Freyr and Lady Eliana Dievs
(Frey-er) and (El-ee-ah-nuh) (Dee-us)

City: Gwaelod (Guh-way-lod)
Ruled by: Lord Beltane and Lady Misae Zojz
(Bel-tayn) and (Miss-ee) (Zoe-ss)

City: Caersidi (Kai-sid-ee)
Ruled by: Lord Ergun and Lady Nia Sulis
(Er-gun) and (Nee-ah) (Sue-lis)

City: Dun Ailinne (A-lin-ae)
Ruled by: Lord Kem and Lady Mererid Latobius
(Kuh-em) and (Mare-uh-rid) (Lah-toe-be-us)
City: Baltia (Bal-tea-uh)

Ruled by: Lord Dritan and Lady Clara Owilo
(Dr-it-uhn) and (Klair-uh) (Oh-we-lo)

Dawn Kingdom:

Capital: Affaraon (Aff-far-on)
Ruled by: House Bathala
Shift Animal: Pegasus
Colors: Dark Gray and Red

Members:

King Tariq Bathala
(Tar-ick Buh-thaa-luh)

Queen Oriana Bathala
(Or-ee-ana Buh-thaa-luh)

Princess Zerlina Bathala
(Zer-lean-uh Buh-thaa-luh)

Princess Sybella Bathala
(Sy-bell-a Buh-thaa-luh)

Prince Sulien Bathala
(Sul-lee-en Buh-thaa-luh)

Princess Danique Bathala
(Dan-eek Buh-thaa-luh)

Other Cities:

City: Emain (Ee-main)
Ruled by: Lord Agim and Lady Willka Kisecaw
(Ah-gim) and (Will-kah) (Kiss-eh-caw)

City Manu (Man-ew)
Ruled by: Lord Taner and Lady Aruna Lindita
(Tan-er) and (Ah-roo-na) (Lyn-deet-ah)

City: Tithonus (Tuh-thow-nuhs)
Ruled by: Lord Eos and Lady Aurora Minenhle
(Ee-os) and (Uh-rawr-uh) (Min-in-hull)

City: Chryse (Ch-rye-sis)
Ruled by: Lord Dali and Lady Elaner Paiva
(Daa-lee) and (El-ah-ner) (Pai-va)

City: Nysa (Nye-saa)
Ruled by: Lord Kiran and Lady Zorya Rusudan
(Kir-an) and (Zor-ya) (Rusu-dan)

City: Aaru (Ah-roo)
Ruled by: Lord Vihan and Lady Tala Zoreial
(Vi-han) and (Taa-luh) (Zor-ee-uhl)

Dusk Kingdom:

Capital: Evenfall (Eve-en-fall)
Ruled by: House Tynan
Shift Animal: Pegasus
Colors: Dark Gray and Dark Pink

Members:

King Astraeus Tynan
(Uh-stray-us Ty-nan)

Queen Stelara Tynan
(Steh-lar-uh Ty-nan)

Prince Cyrus Jabez Tynan
(Sai-ruhs Jaa-buhz Ty-nan)

Prince Weylin Tynan
(Way-linn Ty-nan)

Prince Kian Tynan
(Kee-ahn Ty-nan)

Princess Daneiris Tynan
(Dan-eye-ris Ty-nan)

Princess Twyla Tynan
(Tuh-why-luh Ty-nan)

Prince Vikal Tynan
(V-ih-kuhl Ty-nan)

Other Cities:

City: Asphodel (Az-fuh-del)
Ruled by: Lord Darcel and Lady Yvaine Ceirin
(Dar-cel) and (Ee-vayn) (Ker-ean)

City: Alfheim (Alf-hame)
Ruled by: Lord Aibek and Lady Siria Acheron
(Ay-beh-kh) and (Syr-ia) (A-kr-aan)

City: Gjoll (Guh-joll)
Ruled by: Lord Arrats and Lady Luna Itzal
(Auh-ratts) and (Lu-na) (I-t-zal)

City: Murias
Ruled by: Lord Oditi and Lady Asra Otieno
(Oh-dih-ti) and (Ahs-ruh) (O-ti-e-no)

City: Falias (Fah-lis)
Ruled by: Lord Visita and Lady Nisha Umbra
(Viz-ee-tah) and (Nee-sha) (Um-brah)

City: Eventide (Even-tide)
Ruled by: Lord Udaya and Lady Shirma Abital
(Uu-duh-yah) and (Sh-ir-mah) (Ah-bee-tahl)

Sunrise Kingdom:

Capital: Panchaia (Pan-chai-a)
Ruled By: House Ardit
Shift Animal: Phoenix
Colors: Yellow and Teal

Members:

King Gravadain Ardit
(Gr-av-ah-dain Ar-dit)

Queen Idalia Ardit
(Ay-dahl-ya Ar-dit)

Prince Dagur Ardit
(D-uh-g-uu-r Ar-dit)

Princess Sunneva Ardit
(Sun-ee-vah Ar-dit)

Princess Isleen Ardit
(Is-leen Ar-dit)

Prince Altan Ardit
(Al-tn Ar-dit)

Other Cities:

City: Svarga (Svar-ga)
Ruled by: Lord Baer and Lady Aditya Aferdita
(Bay-r) and (Uh-dih-tee-yuh) (Af-erd-ita)

City: Tridasa (Tri-dah-sah)
Ruled by: Lord Castor and Lady Dashinima Behrouz
(Ka-str) and (Dash-in-ee-ma) (Beh-ru-z)

City: Eden (Ee-den)
Ruled by: Lord Enver and Lady Tesni Dagfinn
(En-vaer) and (Te-z-ni) (Dag-finn)

City: Kolob (Koh-lob)
Ruled by: Lord Lairus and Lady Eadaoin Evseeva
(Lair-us) and (Aid-deen) (Ev-see-vah)

City: Piriawis (Piri-ah-wis)
Ruled by: Lord Tyr and Lady Aine Gwyndyd
(Teer) and (An-yah) (Gwinn-uth)

City: Argyre (Air-jir)
Ruled by: Lord Gunay and Lady Eostre Hina
(Gu-nye) and (Yow-str) (H-in)

SUNSET KINGDOM:

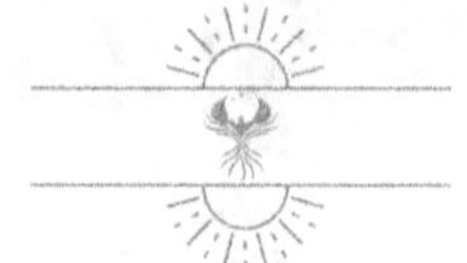

CAPITAL: BIARMA (BEE-ARM-AH)
RULED BY: HOUSE DAANAN
SHIFT ANIMAL: PHOENIX
COLORS: ORANGE AND TEAL

MEMBERS:

King Tieran Daanan
(Teer-ehn Duh-non)

Queen Eveleen Daanan
(Eve-leen Duh-non)

Princess Dysis Daanan
(Dh-ee-s-ee-s Duh-non)

Prince Vesper Daanan
(Veh-spr Duh-non)

Prince Zakat Daanan
(Zuh-kat Duh-non)

OTHER CITIES:

City: Arcadia (Ar-kay-dee-uh)
Ruled by: Lord Dimas and Lady Hesperia Nadirlo
(Di-mas) and (Heh-speh-ree-uh) (Nay-deer-lo)

City Diyu (D-ih-y-uu)
Ruled by: Lord Lycoris and Lady Amaya Morova
(Luh-kaw-ruhs) and (Ah-mah-yah) (Mor-oh-vah)

City: Siniawis (Sin-ee-ah-wis)
Ruled by: Lord Yureni and Lady Cyra Targaris
(Your-en-e) and (See-ra) (Tar-gare-is)

City: Zerzura (Zer-zur-uh)
Ruled by: Lord Sayanth and Lady Helia Kennez
(Say-an-th) and (He-lia) (Ken-nay)

City: Berezaiti (Ber-ah-zait)
Ruled by: Lord Lalil and Lady Fara Velairna
(Luh-lil) and (Far-ah) (Vel-air-na)

City: Irkalla (Eer-kal-la)
Ruled by: Lord Riluo and Lady Malina Cazriel
(Ril-uoh) and (Mah-lena) (Caz-re-el)

Pantheon of the Gods

EREBUS: God of Darkness; one of the two kings of the gods

EARENDEL: God of Light; one of the two kings of the gods

NOX: God of Night and the Moon; Patron God of Night Kingdom

HYPERION: God of Day and the Sun; Patron God of Day Kingdom

ASTERIA: Goddess of the Stars and Oracles; worshiped with Nox and Erebus as part of the Blessed Trinity in Night Kingdom; worshiped with Hyperion and Earendel as part of the Blessed Trinity in Day Kingdom

TALA: Goddess of Dawn; Patron Goddess of Dawn Kingdom

SHALIM: God of Dusk; Patron God of Dusk Kingdom

VAKARE: Goddess of Sunset; Patron Goddess of Sunset Kingdom

AUSRINE: Goddess of Sunrise; Patron Goddess of Sunrise Kingdom

ZIVA: Goddess of Love; Goddess of Soulmates

ANANN: God of War

FAUNUS: God of Beasts; twin brother of Florus

FLORUS: Goddess of Nature; twin sister of Faunus

HEDONE: God of Sex and Fertility

NAMMU: God of the Sea

ARAWN: God of Death and the Otherworld

Other Places:

THE OTHERWORLD: The afterlife where all beings go when they die; split into Elysium (paradise) and Tartarus (hell); there is a separate section inaccessible to Fae and humans where the gods live but is ruled by the two kings instead of Arawn, who rules over Elysium and Tartarus.

ADAMAH: The world in which Celesterra, Gemaria, Weathrian, and Chromatos are continents on.

CELESTERRA: Continent ruled by the Fae and blessed by the higher gods with celestial magic; kingdoms are balanced amongst each other.

GEMARIA: Continent ruled by the Elves and lesser gods are prayed to; magic is accessed via the use of crystals.

WEATHRIAN: Continent ruled by nature spirits who command magic related to their seasons.

CHROMATOS: Continent ruled by pixies whose magic is based on color.

Part One

CHAPTER 1

What did it say about me that I walked so willingly into my own doom?

Today was Placement Day, what I oh-so-affectionately called Imprisonment Day.

My duties as a slave would officially begin after the Placement as soon as I was assigned a new kingdom to serve. Freedom would forever remain a far-off dream, never given a chance to experience.

I didn't rage and fight, causing a scene as I wanted to, and instead, I found myself walking meekly into this next chapter of my life. I let myself be led to the future, where a new, unknown master would own me forevermore.

I liked to consider myself amongst the few who disagreed with the en-slavement of us humans under the Fae, but it was only now I realized just how powerless I truly am. We're just animals being corralled into their cage. The sickening thought of what would happen should I try to escape that cage, kept me from reacting outwardly.

I spent the first twenty years of my life under Fae rule with a more relaxed version of control than I'd heard other humans experienced. Jehohanan, the master of the vineyard my parents were forced to work in, gave those in our village a modicum of freedom. We kept our own little ramshackle houses. We were given time to ourselves once harvesting and bottling were completed. Children weren't allowed on the work floors, and when I was little, I never saw the punishments dealt out. My mother told me they were less harsh than most places, and the pride in her voice over that fact rankled. Still, they were allowed to raise a family in relative peace—it was a rare thing in this world.

Once I hit twenty-one, however, it was all over.

The arena loomed ahead as I stepped out of the rickety wooden wagon that brought us here—to the neutral lands where no kings held dominion. This side of the neutral lands hosted the ancient arena used for this vile event. Lore stated it was here that the agreement was forged between the six Fae kings of old, binding their celestial kingdoms with one another. The continent of Celesterra was shattered and war-torn before that historic truce. Now, the Fae kingdoms cohabited in peace and prosperity.

The smell of grass and old stone hit me as I inhaled a deep breath, trying to brace myself for what was to come. I wasn't sure there was any amount of preparation that would adequately prepare me though.

The sound of a whip cracking made me look over my shoulder to where a slew of wagons littered the grass in front of the arena. Those like me who would be assigned a new kingdom today and their families who had joined them all tumbled out of the wagons one after another. The different types of clothing made me blink rapidly. Some were dressed in what amounted to rags, while others were wearing clothing of fairly decent quality, but one and all were being shuffled into place by the Fae.

The sound of the whip cracking once more was enough to force a meek-looking boy forward, tears streaming down his cheeks. Boy was no longer an accurate term, I realized belatedly. He was like me, up for placement now that he was an adult—he was considered a man now, despite the look of him.

I winced, looking away from his struggle and focusing back on my own. I searched around the wagon I had been corralled in, hoping to spot Soren and his family, but instead, I came face to face with a burly Fae, who glared down at me.

"Move. Now." He grunted.

My mother quickly grabbed my hand and pulled me forward. Her face was scrunched in worry, with wrinkles lining her forehead and nose as she hurried me toward the entrance, my father rushing to bookend me on the other side. I couldn't catch a glimpse of his face, but I could practically feel the tension coming from him, his body ramrod straight as his hand landed on my back, pushing me forward faster.

Tall limestone obelisks lined my vision, looking especially foreboding as we made our way toward the opening that led us inside the circular arena, a large stone stage set in the back. The obelisks flanked the back of the open arena, behind the stage, and around the sides, enclosing everyone, except for the front entrance gap where we entered.

The arena was a sea of drab gray, with only splashes of green from the grass adding hints of color to the place. It felt fitting that such an uninspiring palette painted the landscape of the location where we were traded away. It deserved to be a place without color, leached of joy.

In a world of powerful Fae, humans were at the bottom of the food chain. When we reached the age of adulthood, it would be our turn to attend the bi-annual Placement Day. My twenty-first birthday passed on the Sommer Solstice, and now it was my time to be placed…whether I liked it or not.

The Fae allowed our parents to raise us until it was time for Placement, and then we would be turned over to an entirely different kingdom, never to see our families again. The Fae viewed human children like grazing cattle, allowing parents to raise the calves until it was time for slaughter. They needed humans to reproduce to make more slaves and this system had allowed the population to boom. The illusion of family life offered like tantalizing bait when in actuality, there was no choice at all.

I walked as slowly as I could, dragging my feet against the current threatening to sweep me away into a future I wanted no part of. My mother clutched my hand tightly, pulling me along and ensuring I kept moving forward. I fought against placing one foot in front of the other as other humans streamed in and around me and towards the entrance. The Fae hustled everyone in as fast as possible.

The press of humans was so chaotic that as the Fae maneuvered us forward, I couldn't distinguish one face from the next. The press of bodies was just too much. I struggled against the feeling of suffocation it brought as the mass of people surrounded me, bumping into me and my parents from all sides, stepping on my heels as the Fae kept us moving.

My mother continued to drag me through the entrance, and I felt my spirit screaming inside with nowhere to run. Causing a scene by running would result in nothing but pain—a whipping if I were lucky. Stories were still told of what happened thirty years ago to a boy from Sunrise who attempted it. He got his wish in the end, not having to attend Placement Day. Though, I doubted he rejoiced about that when the sword took his head for treason.

I sighed with a near-silent breath, taking in the space before me. The large stage towards the back was made of the same limestone as the spires surrounding the space, and chairs were set up on ornate rugs covering the grass in front of the stage. Who put down rugs over grass? I could only assume the nobles didn't want to dirty their precious feet.

The humans ahead of us began making their way up to a spot before the stage, the Fae surrounding them. The mass of people that had swarmed into the arena behind them meant we came to a standstill as we all waited to be sorted by the Fae into groups of those receiving their Placement and the families attending with them.

My father's hand landed on my shoulder, and I turned to face him. His face crinkled with age as he smiled, proof of laughter in a world determined to prevent it. His brown eyes were warm as always, but I could see his body trembling. He quickly spoke, taking advantage of the lull, low enough not to be overheard.

"Be smart. Be safe." He whispered close to my ear. I quirked a brow at him, indicating I was listening. "Mind your anger, Asteria—don't look at me like that. Listen to the Fae. And please, don't act out."

Hearing his voice tremble and crack wrenched painfully in my heart. I wanted to reach up and throw my arms around his shoulders, to feel his own squeeze me tightly to him. The mention of my temper did cause me to bristle a bit, but he was right. I couldn't risk angering the Fae. I merely squeezed his hand tightly in return. "I promise, Father. I'll do my best."

I felt his body slowly stop trembling, a sigh punctuating the release. He knew this was the best I could promise. My anger over our situation was palpable, and I'd ranted to my parents many times over the unfairness. And still, neither agreed with me, they'd long been resigned to life as it was.

Or was it just that they were simply too scared of the Fae to say otherwise? How many of us were too frightened to speak our minds or make a move toward the freedom we all deserved? How many humans would prefer to remain in the dubious comfort of what they understood?

I slowly let go of my father's hand, knowing this would be the last time I'd see him. I took a long look to memorize his face. He looked so different from me; I didn't think I'd be able to look into a mirror and see any of him staring back at me. Tanned skin from working the vineyard's fields and chocolate-colored eyes that looked back at me with a mixture of fondness and fear. His honey-blonde hair was smoothed back to tame the flyaway strands he always fought with. I inhaled his scent to remember that too, berries and whiskey invading my senses.

Before I could let go entirely, he slipped something down the sleeve of his ragged cotton shirt, which, once blue, was now nearly white from the sun and age, and paired with light tan linen pants, perfect for Sunrise's heat. I tried to hold back my emotions, the pain of knowing I'd never see him again. I was distracted as he slipped whatever was in his sleeve into my hand. His right hand quickly came up as if he were grasping my hand in both of his. My brows furrowed in confusion as I looked down, my eyes going wide with shock as what could only be an iron knife slipped up into my sleeve.

I looked up, wild eyes locking on my father's. His chocolate eyes were more severe than I'd ever seen them as he shook his head, his cue to stay silent, as I slipped the knife further up. I grabbed the edges of my dress's sleeve to ensure it was secure: If I were caught with this, I would be killed instantly.

How in the Otherworld my father got his hands on this, I'd never have the chance to find out. Nor would I have the opportunity to ask why he would give it to me when he didn't even trust me with my temper around the Fae.

My mother pulled my attention to her, so I turned and gave her all of my focus. Tears were rolling down her face as I heard the call from the podium. "All humans up for Placement, make your way to the stage!"

The announcement transformed any residual confidence I had left into pure dread as my mother and I exchanged looks. This was it, and it was now my turn to face whatever the future may hold, whether I wanted to or not.

"Individuals not up for Placement, make your way to the back." The proclamation rang around the open space, and the limestone obelisks echoed it back to us. It must have been magic, something done to make it echo sound when it hit them.

I glanced over quickly, seeing the mass of people splitting off. Those my age made their way up to the stage, funneled to where the chairs lined each side of the aisle.

In that line of sight, the spectators would sit and enjoy the show as we were left to our misery. Those older and younger quickly separated, forced to the back of the arena. The lull was over, and it was time for Placement Day to begin truly.

I took advantage of the momentary pandemonium and threw myself into my mother's arms. She held me tightly—making me flashback to when I was a small child—rocking me back and forth as she sobbed into my shoulder. I ran my hand down her curly brown hair, trying to calm her enough to say our goodbyes. I had to before it was too late. We had minutes, at most, before the line moved, and I was forced to join them.

I pulled back as my mother cupped my cheeks delicately, her green eyes sparkling with tears, staring into my sky-blue ones as her full lips parted. She spoke softly, full of love and tenderness—in a way I had never heard from her before. Perhaps it was the knowledge these parting words were forever, but I was left breathless with tears. I choked back as she said her goodbyes.

"I have loved you from the very first moment, Asteria." My mother began, tears welling in my own eyes that matched the streaks falling down her cheeks. "My little star. You were our miracle—you know that, right? I had given up hope of ever having a child when we discovered the impossible had occurred. Take this, my love." She pulled out a delicate necklace, and my jaw dropped as I took it in. "Wear it well and keep it as a memory of the parents—" I watched helplessly as my mother choked on her words. "Of the parents who loved you beyond measure."

It was…beautiful. More beautiful than they could afford. It was a precious necklace that a Fae should own. The chain was a delicate silver metal highlighted by a slight shimmer. *Silverium*, I realized. A rare metal only mined in the Day Kingdom. We were taught basic lessons in my village, Sonmathion, covering everything the Fae predetermined all mortals should know. All to ensure we could best serve our masters and not let human stupidity get in the way, according to our teacher. A crotchety old woman, but she had her uses, as she'd taught us about all the big exports from each kingdom. Silverium was a big one for Day.

The pendant was a sun, or half of one, with its rays coming off the top, and merged into an upside-down crescent moon with stars hanging underneath its curve. The stars were the only part of the pendant not made of silverium, instead made of pure star opals, the kind only mined in the Etheralta Mountains—the range that crossed from Day into Night Kingdom.

They each mined the opals from their sides of the mountain—the star opals could only be found in that one mountain range, making it the rarest gem in the world. Adamah had plenty of gems across its continents, but the star opal was special. The result of a blending of magics from Day and Night Kingdoms somehow going into the making of them, that shared mountain range making all the difference, though it was kept a closely guarded secret what exactly caused them. The star opals were named for their shine and shimmer that mirrored our stars above—those precious white gems shone with a rainbow of color inside them, making them twinkle like stars in the sky. They certainly lived up to their name, both in the sparkle of their finish, and the unique qualities that made them so brilliant.

My mother stepped behind me, moving my long, dark hair over my shoulder as she clasped the necklace around my neck. My hand immediately went up to hold the pendant as she stepped back around to face me. There was no time to ask questions about where they found such a precious item. I could only assume they must have stumbled upon it by accident, possibly dropped by some careless noble. We'd had many visits to the vineyard over the years for tours—it was the best time to get new gossip, which the ladies in the village lived for, small and cut off as we were in Sonmathion.

"Now, when you look at this, you'll remember your parents loved you more than the stars love the sky." My mother smiled tremulously, and I sniffed back the gathering tears.

"Thank you, mom. I promise I won't forget. Ever." I swore solemnly.

I stepped back, nearly running into Verin, one of the girls from my village—one of the worst.

Just my luck.

"Watch it!" She snapped, glaring at me. I rolled my eyes and turned back to my parents. I heard her aggrieved huff when I didn't acknowledge her, but my parents were more important than our never-ending enmity.

I grabbed my father's left hand with mine, and my mother's right, squeezing them both tightly. "I love you both. Thank you, for everything."

"We love you too, Asteria." My father's gruff voice shook, his eyes holding a sheen of something protective, even as he attempted to hold back the threatening tears. I looked at them both once more, preparing to go. With a deep breath, I turned around, forcing myself to walk away.

This separation had always been coming. I couldn't show the world how much walking away from my family hurt. The Fae expected us to leave without issue, and to do otherwise would not serve me well. I tilted my chin up high as I walked forward to the platform, resigned but unwilling to show the Fae any weakness. I knew better than to let feelings rule me, regardless. Any hint of them was best served being buried deep.

There was no place for love in our world. That belonged to the Fae.

Just like everything else.

I followed the clustered young humans walking to the roughly cut limestone stage—its jagged edges came off the sides in a strange irregular formation. Just as jagged and dangerous as whatever Fae I ended up enslaved to, I was sure.

Before I could step up to the large stone platform, Verin's voice rang out, and I sighed internally. She was coming for me, now of all times. I shifted to the right, stepping aside to let others make their way up to the platform. The habitual sneer on Verin's face whenever she looked at me was firmly in place as I turned to her.

"I do wish you good luck, Asteria." She smirked, clearly mocking me. "You never know what kind of master you'll have, but a whore like you is bound to find a master with no hesitation in using those skills." She was always trying to cut me with words, and I straightened up, resigned to this last battle of wills.

"A whore. Really, Verin?" I glared back at her haughty face. "You must have me mistaken for yourself."

She never forgot the man who chose me over her, despite having her pick of the men our age in Sonmathion. It was a stupid grudge Verin couldn't shake, even years later. Her capacity for pettiness would have been almost impressive if it was directed toward anyone but me. I raised an eyebrow at her, so over her and her friends trying to ostracize and hurt me. Let her make of my words what she will. I turned to go, but she stepped in front of me, clearly unable to let this rest.

"You'll get what's coming to you." Verin hissed venomously, her face turning red as her glare intensified. "I swear by the Old Gods. Some cruel master with a fondness for the whip will see that pretty little face. And he will break you. My only regret is I won't be able to see it."

That one stung—not because Verin actually managed to hurt me, but because her words spoke of the very fate I'd dreaded for years. I had no idea where I'd end up serving, and the fact that it was for life made it so much worse. If my master was excessively cruel, I had no way out—or, there was only one way out, and I wasn't about to choose death over survival. I just didn't have it in me. I straightened my spine once more, ready to tell her off. *Fuck her stupid, petty grudge.*

"Oh, come off it, Verin." Soren snorted as he appeared beside me. "We all know your aspirations to be chosen by some Fae who will take you to a luxurious castle. But if the Old Gods will it, you'll end up in some two-bit village just like ours. *Forever.*" Soren drew the last word out in a spooky tone as he winked at me. I chuckled as Verin shook in rage, before huffing and twirling around. Verin's stomping was the stuff of legend as she stormed toward the stage.

Soren chuckled and turned to me with a bright smile on his face. As much as I wished he'd let me deal with Verin, I couldn't stay mad at him when this was the last we'd see each other.

"You know she's just angry you never gave her a go?" I teased him. We both knew his decision to ignore her while befriending me was an unforgivable offense in Verin's mind. All the women in the village had wanted Soren, with his coppery red, shoulder-length hair, and sparkling emerald eyes, paired with broad shoulders and impressive height, he was considered quite the catch.

He rolled his eyes. "I wouldn't touch her or any of her hangers-on if they were the last humans on Adamah. Cruelty doesn't do it for me."

I gave him a sly smile, knowing exactly what *did* do it for him. His gaze intensified, shifting down to rake over me. My blue dress matched my eyes, a flowing fabric that clung slightly over all my curves. Soren's eyes took in each one with a hopeless want in his eyes. He was the only one in our village who tried to befriend me, and I knew I hadn't made it easy on him—but I'm fairly certain he only continued trying because he had wanted me in other ways.

I eventually gave in to him a few years ago, and we'd slept together under the stars, on one of the many nights I snuck out to the fields to stargaze. But things between us had never felt right, or permanent. We both knew it couldn't last, and a few years would be all we had. Who to let into my body was the only choice I had left in a world where all our choices were taken from us. So, I took advantage of the opportunity to make my own choice.

It was done now, Placement Day was its death knell, as we always knew it would be.

Like I said, there was no place for love in our world.

Soren gave me one last look, those emerald eyes full of emotion before he smiled sadly. I returned it as the shouts of the Fae stole our focus, and without a word, I moved forward. Soren's hand shot out to stop me—the unspoken farewell between us that I denied him before we left Sonmathion must be lingering on his tongue. I forced myself to keep walking, unable to take hearing it. Knowing something must end, and accepting that end, remained two vastly different things. It was better to close the door to that chapter without lingering on it. A quick cut of a knife was better than a drawn-out one.

As I neared the Fae directing us, I heard the whispers and titters from those seated. I cut a glance over to the nobles, and they were laughing as they pointed out different humans already up on the stage. I fisted my hands and bit my lip to force myself not to do anything stupid. It would be suicide to act. I wished I could do anything to stop what was happening, but these Fae had all the power, and I was no one.

Through my anger, I managed to put one foot onto the limestone steps, then another. I looked up above me to the bright blue sky, then down to the stone arena around me. Nature invaded it, plants bursting through the pillars. I wished the life this greenery represented would continue growing and cover this cursed place entirely. Lay waste to this stupid site and let no one else be forced to come here and throw their dignity away to the wolves.

I made my way to the waiting Fae, who was running his hand through his shaggy brown hair while his other held a list that he used to direct each human.

"Name?" He snapped out quickly, his pale yellow eyes landing on me. He must be lower in the Fae hierarchy, to be doing such a job as this.

I jolted in surprise at his direct focus, having been furious enough to not realize I was next. I quickly answered as his jaw tightened, clearly unhappy about waiting for me to speak.

"Asteria Faelynn Zagreus." I spoke clearly, not wanting to incite his ire further.

"Asteria—you'll be in group A." He shooed me over to the group on the left, and I joined the others in standing amongst a circle of Fae. Each group was fenced in by at least ten guards who scrutinized us all with eagle eyes, whips in hand as they waited for us to make one wrong move.

The guard closest to me glared down at me with narrowed green eyes, not appreciating my inspection. He was wearing dark brown armor, with the phoenix of Sunset emblazoned in the center. I gulped as he took a step closer to me, lowering my gaze as his fingers tightened on the whip. I stood as still as possible, my heart racing out of my chest.

I'd never been whipped before, and I wasn't keen to receive that particular punishment now. I was mercifully kept away from it in Sonmathion, but I knew that would change shortly. I was about to be claimed by some new kingdom and be given to who knows what kind of master. Bringing attention to myself early was quite possibly the worst thing I could do.

I stood there, choking on fear and rage; a cocktail of volatile emotions storming through me, while I prayed to the Old Gods I wouldn't be touched—with whatever power the Old Gods might have to protect against the stronger Fae gods. No one could seem to agree on how much that was, and I could only hope it was enough.

At least I wouldn't die of the nervous anticipation of waiting to be called. Being sorted alphabetically reassured me that I'd find out where my future would be sooner rather than later—whatever kind of future a slave could have anyway.

My emotions swiftly crashed, as a hopeless sense of melancholy overcame me and threatened to overwhelm me entirely. The lack of control over my life or my future is like a noose around my neck.

We'd first be presented to the Fae, who would pick through us, choosing their favorites to take home. Any humans not chosen would be assigned at random, based on each kingdom's needs and how many humans were left.

I wanted to rage and scream—or maybe cry. I wanted to shout my protests about what was happening here and why this was wrong. But instead, I forced myself to be still, quiet, and obedient.

All to ensure I live another day.

I glanced out to the crowd, knowing my parents were there, watching on from the human section. I hated that they had to stand all the way back there. Meanwhile, directly in front of us, the Fae sat in comfortable velvet chairs. The royals, lords, and ladies of every kingdom sat in comfort, judging us, measuring, and weighing us like livestock. Every kingdom except Night, of course.

When learning of the kingdoms, our teacher told us the Night Kingdom hadn't shown in as many years as we'd been alive. I heard a rumor once that the King of Night used those he deemed traitors, along with captured lesser creatures, like the Elves of Gemaria, instead of dirtying his lands with humans. The thought of a Fae powerful enough to rule over others of his own kind in such a way—gave me chills. Even the Elves, while less powerful than the Fae, were significantly more so than a mortal. I was thankful I would never have to serve such a beast.

That was the rule: you had to show up to Placement Day to get new slaves assigned to you. That decision had been made in the treaty that was forged by the six kings of old on this very spot. All the other kingdoms showed up to replace their rapidly aging human slaves. We aged and died so quickly compared to the Fae after all. We were nothing but a blip in their immortal lives.

I'd never seen Fae royalty before, and I'd dreaded this day when I would have to look upon the Fae nobility, in all their finery and freedom intact. They sat before me, judging, and deciding my fate, and all I could do was hold back screams of injustice as I stood on display, being weighed, and measured for my usefulness.

I flinched at the sound of the whip crack. A mortal fell to the floor in the group next to us. Tears tracking down her eyes as she looked to the floor. The Fae holding the whip walked over and bent down, grabbing her by the hair. The Fae were beautiful creatures, made in the image of their gods. And this Fae's blonde hair and blue eyes accented a perfectly symmetrical face, paired with shining golden armor.

His hand gripped the pommel of the sword sheathed at his side, giving the impression of a glorious being, but all I could see was the vileness of this man as his face contorted into a sneer. He dragged the girl up by her hair, looking to see which humans were watching, trying to find another target.

I looked away, cursing internally. I couldn't do anything to help. The only ones who could were in front of us. The female nobles draped themselves in their chairs, fanning themselves or leaning over one another to speak as they gossiped. Their dresses were made in the finest materials and brightest colors, covered in jewels and embroidery. One wore a bright red gown with crystals down the front. Another was a blue dress made of velvet that had extensive designs sewn in with silver embroidery, the details so fine, it was obvious it took months for the seamstress to create this one piece. A luxury we certainly never experienced.

Humans were given clothes that wore out quickly and rarely provided new ones. I looked down at my own simple dress, a light blue linen with no ornamentation. I spent months altering it in secret, making it fit me just so. What I had considered to be my best dress now seemed laughable in comparison.

I fiddled with the chain of my necklace. It felt like a small rebellion, and I was comforted by it. I owned something that was as beautiful and fancy as these noble's own jewelry. I wished I could stick out my tongue and taunt them with it, but that was courting death too closely for my liking. And I didn't want my necklace taken away when it was the only gift I'd ever received, the only physical reminder I'd have of my parents for the rest of my life. I would hide it until the day I died.

Looking back up at the Fae nobles, my breath caught in my throat. One of them stared directly at me, our eyes locking in a clash of blue on blue. I quickly looked down, showing deference as we were meant to, but my eyes peeked back up curiously and found that he was still staring. His lips rose in a lazy smirk that brought to mind the big cats roaming the jungles of Sunrise Kingdom. I couldn't help my reflexive glare, which I tried to quickly wipe off my face, terrified of being whipped for my insolence.

His smirk shifted into a smile for some reason. I looked him over and realized that based on his seating next to the king of Dusk and the crown on his head, he must be the crown prince, Cyrus.

Fuck.

I really, really shouldn't have glared at him, but he just continued to watch me, in a way that made me increasingly uncomfortable.

I gulped down my rising nerves as we stared at one another. This was definitely not what I should be doing here, and yet, he wasn't pulling me off the stage to punish me. He was just…looking at me—and I looked back, despite knowing I shouldn't.

Unlike the copper locks I was so used to on Soren, Prince Cyrus's hair was dark and slightly wavy, falling down to his shoulders. His eyes were a shade of blue deeper than mine, and they were piercing. The prince held me captive with his stare, allowing me to study his face—mocking cruelty in those smirking lips, underlined by the arrogant tilt of his chin, the slightly hollowed cheekbones, and yet he was unfairly beautiful despite it.

Our staring contest finally broke when one of his brothers, Prince Vikal, the youngest of the six children of King Astraeus and Queen Stelara Tynan, began speaking to him.

Our teacher drilled us over and over on the royals, attempting to ensure that we didn't make a fatal mistake misidentifying them. I'd have hated it then, but now, I sent her a silent thank you. I quickly looked down now that the prince's stare was elsewhere. I had no idea why Prince Cyrus should be so interested in me, but it was trouble, and I'd do my best to stay far away from it. From him.

"Kingdoms of Celesterra! Welcome to another Placement Day!" The host began, almost too cheerfully. "Today, these newly adult humans will be placed into the new kingdoms they will spend the rest of their lives serving. They will find their true homes!"

The crowd cheered, which covered my snort of derision. Though the boys next to me looked askance at me, so perhaps it wasn't totally hidden. But Placement Day wasn't sending us to our true homes, as the host tried to claim;

we were merely being handed over to our new masters, to be dealt with as they pleased.

"All kingdoms here today will have the opportunity to see the humans offered. Each will be called by name and shown for your perusal." The host continued, and I barely held back my sneer. *Shown for your perusal, indeed. Assholes.*

"The numbered cards before you are there for you to pick your human slaves. On these cards, please put the humans down in order of which you want most to allow us to decide which kingdom will receive the human if more than one kingdom wants them. Preference will go to the kingdom who ranks the human highest on their list.

Any humans not chosen by a kingdom will be sorted into equal groups to present at the end of the program and be distributed amongst the kingdoms. Once the cards have been turned in and determinations made, we will once more call each human forward, and announce their new kingdom. They will then go to the banner of their new kingdom to await transport."

The host indicated the banners with each kingdom's sigil hanging on either side of the stage on the limestone spires. His directions made me want to vomit—or burn down those banners. Old Gods, I couldn't deal with this farce. The Fae acted like this was all a merry celebration when it was them literally deciding people's fates.

Except, we weren't really people to them. We were merely objects that did their bidding. I couldn't say I was too surprised, the Fae loved celebrations and events of all kinds, with their holidays being notoriously wild. Yet, the thought of the enslavement of myself and my people being treated as such—I swallowed down the bile that rose, even as I felt my cheeks flush from the rage that hummed through my body.

"The kings of each kingdom will have full authority to place the humans in the role of their choice once you return to your territories. We will now begin, going by group. Group A!" He called, and I shivered, knowing it was time.

The nobles in front began whispering amongst themselves in excitement, sitting up and looking intently at those of us on stage. This was a spectacle to them. I'd never understood before today why they couldn't just assign us at random, but now I understood all too well. They wanted a show. An excuse to get dressed up and meet up with the other royals, to gossip and laugh.

I hated how everyone accepted that our enslavement was okay just because it was what had always been done. Humans were considered beneath the Fae just because we didn't have magic. We were cut off from the natural order, and thus unnatural ourselves.

It was ridiculous. Not being blessed with magic didn't mean we weren't connected to nature in other ways, even if we weren't tapped into it the same way the Fae were. Their magic came from gods, and the gods had imbued the land and the Fae with their magic, leaving them connected and able to feel nature in a way humans couldn't.

This ideology allowed them to keep us in our place by making humans and the Fae alike believe something was inherently *less* about us. Old Gods forbid the Fae make their own food and clean their own castles. They had magic, but it wasn't able to be used for everything, from what I understood. Humans were where they filled in the gaps.

There had to be other humans who railed against this as much as me. I couldn't be the only one. Soren was resigned to it, comfortable with leaving his life in fate's hands. My parents acted like it was only natural that we should have our free will stolen from us. Their tears for me were a surprise, as was the knife. They had spent years telling me that this was the way of things, that humans were always slaves, that we'd never been free in the history of our existence.

But that didn't mean that this was the way it should stay, or that this was all we were meant to be. I had to believe we could be *more*.

"Abbicus Donnel Reanel." The call of the first human silenced everyone. The Fae watched hungrily as the man stepped forward. The announcer took the man by the shoulders and forced him to spin in a circle for those watching, and then he walked back to us, his shoulders slumping like a weight was taken off them.

I watched and waited, nerves causing me to fidget. I had to force my feet to stay in place and not make a run for it. Biting my tongue so I didn't scream, keeping my rage in check as I tried to bury it deep inside.

"Asteria Faelynn Zagreus!" The announcer called, his green eyes narrowing on me as I took a shaky step forward. Too slow. The Fae guard who narrowed his eyes at me pushed me forward.

I caught myself before I did something instinctually foolish and reigned in my need to lash out. I fisted my hands, glaring at the floor. I didn't want to consider what would happen if the Fae saw my rage, but my anger was better than nerves and stronger than my fear. I refused to give these Fae the power, they wouldn't get the satisfaction of me quivering in trepidation in front of them.

I walked to the front of the platform and saw the Prince of Dusk immediately lean forward, elbows on his knees, all predatory grace. I ignored him as I turned in a circle, feeling like a slab of meat. This was humiliating, having all the Fae nobility in the crowd take me in like a little lamb before a dragon. They sat there, gossiping amongst themselves, judging me, and deciding my fate. I wanted to shout to the stars with my fury; let the entire world hear it.

The host nodded my dismissal to the Fae guard from Sunset. He grabbed my arm and pushed me back to the group, letting go quickly and causing me to stumble into the others. I ground my teeth as the guard smirked at me. I was shaking for a different reason now, resisting the urge to punch him in the teeth.

I would live through this experience, and I would come out of the humiliation with my head held high.

It took ages for each human to be called, but only an hour could have gone by in reality. I stood by silently as two more were whipped; one for going too slow, and the other for having the gall to glare openly at his guard. I kept my eyes down, knowing my limits, but my anger was too vast, too wild—I could barely contain it. And I couldn't afford any mistakes.

Time passed, and I watched the Fae consult the cards, watched them bicker over where the humans would be placed. I found a place inside myself to numbly observe the proceedings. Watching as my fate was sealed without my control. When the host turned toward us, stepping to the edge of the platform to announce to the Fae what slaves they'd be taking home, I knew the time had come. My life from here on out would be decided by this moment, and I was not ready.

I would never be ready.

"We shall now call forth each human and announce their new placement." The host proclaimed, turning to us with a wicked smile. "Please proceed to the banner for the kingdom assigned to you once called." We were instructed, as if we were dumb, not understanding the explanations he gave before.

I barely held back my sneer, checking it at the last moment, knowing it would do me no favors. Prince Cyrus's gaze caught mine once more and I jolted with surprise. Why was he looking at me again?

As Abbicus was called forward once more, I began to wonder where I would be placed. Technically, all the kingdoms had magic relating to the sky, since these were the celestial kingdoms. The Fae from each court drew their power from nature, and specifically their kingdom's namesake.

Day could call upon light itself, while Night could summon darkness. Dusk had lightning, while its balance, Dawn, had the wind. Sunrise, on the other hand, had water, power drawn from the dew and mists the morning brought with it. Sunset boasted fire magic, the fiery glow of a sunset come to life. Each is connected to the life beating within the land. Light and dark, wind and thunder, water, and fire.

The six kingdoms of Celesterra were split up to be balanced, as the Fae said all things in nature should be. Day and Night. Dawn and Dusk. Sunrise and Sunset. Each balanced the other, and their powers reflected that as well.

Whatever kingdom I was assigned, I would be surrounded by the magic of their land. I had felt the power of Sunrise humming in the background all of my life, like a distant morning mist. It never felt quite right to me, like I was out of place. I wondered if the magic of wherever I'd be placed would feel better. Would I ever have a chance to find that rightness? To find a balance within *myself*?

My gaze was drawn to the royals of Day Kingdom. King Aelius seemed like a severe man, not an ounce of emotion on his face. His blonde hair and blue eyes were a sharp contrast to his wife. Queen Aurelia had dark hair and dark eyes, her skin porcelain white to her husband's golden glow.

While the Fae of the northern kingdoms typically had dark skin, the Fae of the southern kingdoms had lighter complexions, and the kingdoms in between were more diverse—and of course, the humans were all over the place, sent across the kingdoms as we were. Their son, Prince Arien, seemed to be an equal split between his two parents, with the pale skin and dark hair of his mother, and the blue eyes and height of his father.

Prince Arien's eyes found me as I looked at him. He tilted his head to the side as he looked me over, and I was struck by the thought that I should lower my eyes, but I couldn't.

I felt stuck, stricken with a strange humming inside as our eyes locked on each other.

I shivered, feeling—strange. Something about him unnerved me and made me feel like a stranger in my own skin. The skin that suddenly felt too tight, as if it were made too small and I shouldn't be wearing it.

I'd grappled with that feeling all of my life, yet I had never experienced the sensation just from looking at someone. Our gazes were not of two people attracted to one another, far from it. It was something else, something inherently innocent, but I couldn't figure out what.

"Asteria Faelynn Zagreus!"

I jolted at the sound of my name being called. My eyes skittered from Prince Arien and landed somehow on his mother. To my shock, she was already watching me. Her body stiffened as she looked at the announcer and then back to me as I moved forward.

The queen gave me a wavering smile, shocking me out of my stupor. It was nearly unheard of for royals to look upon human slaves with the kindness she radiated now. Her gaze was almost soft as she nodded her head in encouragement. Could she sense my nervous agitation? I was unsure of why she seemed to care. Has Day chosen me?

If I had to choose, my hope absolutely would be an assignment with Day. King Aelius seemed no better than the other royals, but his wife and son were far superior, and I'd pick them any day—no matter how much the son's gaze unnerved me. I could work under them much easier than most of these Fae whose mere presence made me want to scream.

Just looking at them, Aelius and Aurelia being mates seemed bizarre to me. Mate bonds were rare in this world, and Fae marked with a mate bond were born with a soul mark that matched their mate's. Aurelia seemed too kind to be the other half of Aelius' soul. Unless the soul was split with one side getting all the good and one all the bad? I frankly had no idea how it worked, nor did I care enough to find out. Humans didn't have mates, so there was no point. Their ability to have soulmates, and their stupid soul marks, were only another reason they were superior, and humans were considered unworthy.

It felt like time had slowed down as I silently interacted with the prince and queen of the Day Kingdom, but only a few moments had passed. I walked to the announcer with my knees feeling like jelly from all the attention on me. I swallowed hard as I waited to hear my fate.

"Asteria Faelynn Zagreus, you will be under..."

My heart seemed to beat double time.

Old Gods, please, you may have ignored me as much as I ignored you throughout my life, but please, let me be given something good for once. Grant me this one thing.

"Dusk Kingdom!"

My heart felt like it both stilled and beat out of my chest at once. My gaze was immediately drawn to the smirk on Prince Cyrus' face.

By the Otherworld, I had a terribly bad feeling about this.

Maybe he'd forget all about this and not punish me? Perhaps Prince Cyrus wouldn't pay me any attention at all. A fool's hope as I walked to my doom. One foot off the stage after another until I finally reached the Dusk Kingdom banner. I took my place there and waited for the rest of those who turned twenty-one to be placed into their kingdoms.

I felt numb as the announcer finished declaring where everyone would be Placed. My emotions were too high and too raw and finally, they seemed to just—stop, finding that numb place inside once more.

Eyes were on me everywhere I looked. My parents, Prince Cyrus, the Day Kingdom royals—I felt all of their eyes on me.

Prince Cyrus leered at me, and I cringed internally. By mortal standards, I knew I was considered attractive. My dark hair was long, full, and shiny, with bright blue eyes that looked like the sky during a cloudless day. A light smatter of freckles crossed my nose and onto my cheeks, like little stars covering my porcelain skin, that often gained a bit of a golden glow after time in the sun. I was short, but slim, with curves I knew men appreciated, with full, heavy breasts, and a firm, rounded ass—according to Soren anyway.

He loved my body and worshiped it at every opportunity. We'd lay a blanket out by the lake near my house and stargaze, or jump in the water, and then spend the rest of the time savoring each other's bodies. He called me perfect, and beautiful, the only woman he would ever want—claiming my beauty was as Otherworldly as the Fae's, which was sweet, if decidedly untrue. His attention was a welcome reprieve from our terrible existence though, and I basked in it during the time we had, knowing that was all it could ever be.

The Fae were perfect in a way I would never be, but Prince Cyrus seemed to enjoy the look of me, nonetheless. His eyes trailed up and down my body, and I looked away, wishing he'd look anywhere else. I caught a glimpse of Queen Aurelia's sympathetic gaze. The sadness in the queen's eyes said a lot about how I'd be treated in Dusk.

Old Gods, how was I going to get through this alone? At least I'd always had my parents before now.

I paid just enough attention to realize Soren was placed in Day, and I watched as he walked off the stage, heading for the banner that hung beside the one for Dusk. Soren paused as he reached where I stood.

"Asteria." He rumbled, emotion choking his voice. I hadn't wanted an extended goodbye, knowing it was better to be done with it quickly. But the look in Soren's eyes told me he clearly had more to say. "I just—I wanted you to know—I love you. I know you didn't want feelings involved in this, so I've kept quiet. But I needed to tell you—just in case I never see you again."

I blinked in shock. He loved me? How? When? His arms came around me and hugged me tight. And for all that, I felt something for him—even if it could never be love, I hugged him right back—hard. Love or not, he'd been my best friend and lover for years.

The pain I felt at his confession was why it was wise not to get close to people. Soren was the only one I'd ever dared to let in slightly. It wasn't worth the heartache to get close to others. Part of this pain I felt was certainly because I now knew for sure that Soren had made more of us than I had.

"You were my best friend, you know," I mumbled as he kissed the top of my head, and I hugged him tight once more.

"I know." Soren laughed huskily. He pulled back and cupped my cheeks. "Be safe, Asteria." He swallowed hard, his throat bobbing.

"Goodbye, Soren." I smiled sadly, noting a glaring Fae coming this way.

He nodded once, his face forlorn, and what I now knew to be lost hopes and dreams swimming in his eyes. "Goodbye, Asteria."

CHAPTER 2

I WAS swept up with the other humans bound for the Dusk Kingdom and brought to a couple of large wooden wagons. These were much fancier wagons, with actual windows lining the sides, something the one I'd taken here had lacked. I was thankful for that, at least. It had been horrendous being stuffed into a creaky enclosed box for the ride to the Neutral Lands.

We were surrounded by guards from Dusk. Armor plate the color of nickel shone with the sigil of Dusk, proudly displayed in the center. They had swords on their hips which remained sheathed, thankfully. But the whips in their hands were curled at the ready.

I couldn't help dreading whatever might come next.

I wasn't the only one. I looked around at the other humans coming to Dusk with me. One girl's expression was completely blank, with not a trace of emotion on it. Another boy just looked resigned, eyes low and frown set. But many looked around warily, shaking, shifting foot to foot, clearly just as wracked with anxiety as I was on what to expect next.

Of course, none of the new adults here were originally from Dusk. Humans were never placed in the kingdom they originated from, and if they were, it was a human whose parents had died. The Fae wanted us split up from our families, ensuring we wouldn't be loyal to anyone above our masters.

We were herded into the wagons one by one. At my turn, I jumped in, walking down the row and taking the last open seat, so the rest could fill in behind me. Once we were packed full, the door closed with an ominous creak. I swallowed the saliva gathering in my mouth, hating that I didn't know what was going to happen, and not being able to do anything about it.

I fiddled with my necklace just to calm myself, hoping that focusing on one small thing would help.

"I hope they place me as far away from the Night Kingdom as possible." A curly haired blond girl murmured nervously to another.

"Me too." The brunette girl wrapped her arms around herself and rocked slightly, "I don't want to be one of those humans who go missing into the Night Kingdom and are never seen again."

"What?" I heard my voice reverberate around the wagon—not realizing it was me until heads snapped toward me. I sunk into my seat, but the girl who'd spoken looked at me sympathetically.

"Are you from Sunrise or Sunset?" She asked quietly. Her body was stiff, but she didn't sneer at me like the girls I was used to, so I didn't think she was about to insult me at least.

I shook my head in confusion, unsure how she came to that conclusion. "How'd you know?"

She smiled sadly, her greenish brown eyes glistening. "Dawn and Dusk's rulers have been doing their best to contain this and not let the information leak out. From what I understand, they're trying to keep it quiet so they don't appear weakened in any way to Sunrise or Sunset, being rival kingdoms, and all. It's not working very well though, because my parents worked in the palace at Dawn, and they heard a lot of whispers regarding this. But I wouldn't expect people from the northern kingdoms to be aware of it yet."

She swallowed nervously and looked around, realizing we were all staring at her, and seeming to wilt a bit from the attention.

"And what's happening, exactly?" I asked gently, leaning forward to give her one point to focus on.

Her eyes were swelled with unshed tears, hands shaking as she wrapped a finger in her dark blonde hair and pulled on it a bit with her fingers, "Night has been increasing their attacks on other kingdoms. And the king isn't just killing their Fae, he's taking humans. Any humans he's taken are never heard from again. It's been happening with increasing frequency over the past few years or so. And it's becoming more frequent lately. Neither Dawn nor Dusk has been able to figure out why, and apparently, King Calix isn't interested in negotiating."

I listened with wide eyes, my hand shooting to my necklace. My fingers tracing along the crescent moon and the stars. Night had always been the kingdom I'd wished I could know more of. I loved the night sky and the wide-open freedom of it. But if this was true, I was lucky beyond all measure that Night didn't show on Placement Day. If they were taking humans, then I needed to stay as far away from the monsters in the Night Kingdom as possible.

"Why wouldn't he just come to the Placement to get humans; why take them from other kingdoms?" A rough-looking boy in the back asked. He had clearly been living in bad conditions, with unkempt black hair, a gray shirt riddled with holes, and black pants that had faded several shades.

The blond girl nodded eagerly. "Exactly. Which is why they've assumed they're all dead. If he wanted slaves to do work, he could just show up. This is darker—something malicious. They've tried looking for them, and nothing is ever found. Not a trace."

The words landed heavily, echoing my own thoughts. The trepidation and fear it stirred in me felt like another passenger in this wagon, it was so palpable.

"What's your name?" I asked the blonde to distract myself.

"I'm Emmie. And this is Eris." She pointed to the brunette girl beside her. "We grew up together and were lucky enough to be placed together. Both our parents worked in the Dawn Kingdom's palace. We bonded over our "E" names." She laughed lightly.

Where Emmie had no problem speaking with me and the others, Eris seemed to be more cautious, looking shyly through the curtain of her light brown hair, but her gray eyes flashed with something harder—something made of granite. I knew not to underestimate that look in her eyes, not when it spoke of past experiences that shaped and molded someone into something new, something stronger. She may be quiet, but she was definitely not meek.

They'd had to deal with the royals and court for the past twenty-one years, I couldn't forget what that could do to a person. Having now seen the royals in person, coupled with the stories of how humans were treated at court, my respect for them rose. Human slaves for the nobility dealt with being used by them, frequent whippings, or even being killed for doing something as innocuous as accidentally dropping something in front of the wrong Fae. I couldn't imagine the fear of living with that hanging over my head. I've never even been near Sunrise Kingdom's palace.

"I'm Asteria." I told them, getting a smile from Emmie and a grunt from Eris, who clearly couldn't care less. "Were the people at court—" I cut myself off, biting my lip, remembering that I didn't know these people well enough to pry.

But Emmie just laughed lightly, picking up my dropped thread. "Horrible and catty and always playing some kind of game? Yes."

She bumped Eris with her arm in a playful move. Eris smiled slightly at her before going back to glaring at me. She didn't seem to like me encroaching on her friend's attention if that glare was anything to go by.

"That's terrible. I hope I'm nowhere near the palace." I shivered, an ominous feeling rising in my gut.

"Good luck with that." Eris snorted, her voice was soft yet hard, that spine of steel she possessed coming through. I flinched, but Emmie reached across and grabbed my hand.

"It'll be okay." She reassured me. "Just remember the most important rule of court."

I eyed her nervously, gripping her hand like it could somehow save me from the future. "What's that?"

"Never trust anyone." She smiled sweetly, despite her words. "Everyone is out for themselves, especially if they can improve their positions. Humans can gain favor from their masters and earn more luxuries or better duties. And you never know who is loyal to who."

A bump in the road dislodged our grasping hands as the wagon rattled, and I glanced out the window. Rain started to pour down, matching my ominous feelings perfectly. The wagon bumped again as the rain turned the dirt road to mud.

I swallowed hard, thinking of walking into the environment Emmie came from. "That sounds awful. My parents worked at a vineyard, so there was never anything like that there. The people mostly helped each other."

I looked down thinking of the girls of my village, who were always the exception. Their cattiness was mostly targeted at me, leaving me the odd one out. Verin's targeted attacks only cemented that.

"Let me guess, except for the girls around you?" Emmie asked knowingly. I looked up at her, shocked, and raised a brow in her direction.

"I grew up in court, remember? I know how to read a person." Emmie laughed casually. "And you're gorgeous. Everywhere, but especially at court, people are jealous and covet beauty. I can only imagine the girls of a small village wouldn't be any different when they saw the competition."

I groaned, putting my head in my hands, "It wasn't only that, but—I'd hoped at least that going to another kingdom would take me away from that kind of thing."

"There's no getting away from that. Use it. Beauty is a tool you can wield." Emmie smiled kindly, but there was an undercurrent to her tone that spoke of a cunning nature that lurked beneath the surface. I supposed she must have had to develop that with what she'd dealt with in Dawn.

I looked at her skeptically, but she pressed. "Trust me, a beautiful woman can get more in life from a man who's enamored with them. It's rare the Fae ever want humans, especially when the Fae are so much more of *everything* than we are. More beautiful, more magical, more experience, more education—there's no end to the list. But your beauty is comparable to a Fae, and you have this opportunity. That's rare! You could live a good life."

"It's true." Eris sniffed, looking down her nose at me, "Humans have to take whatever advantage we can. And at court? There are opportunities to rise that you would never expect. Don't turn your nose up at any opportunity you're presented with." She raised an arched eyebrow at me.

That was saying something from the girl literally turning her nose up, but I stopped to truly consider her words. Was she one of those who'd kill to have a Fae interested in them? I could only assume so.

Still, the very thought disgusted me. These Fae owned us. My body wasn't truly mine, it was theirs. I would keep whatever scrap of it that was mine. They took everything else, they couldn't have that too.

"Any other advice?" I looked up warily, hoping they had something I could actually use.

"Watch and listen." Emmie smiled slightly. "You learn all sorts of things that way. They don't expect their slaves to truly pay attention, and they'll say things in front of us they don't want known. You may see things that will give you an advantage as well. It's all about staying on top of the politics, and then spinning that knowledge in your favor."

I shook my head, feeling overwhelmed. I put my fingers to my temples and rubbed them in circles, hoping to dispel the ache growing in my head.

"It'll be okay." Emmie reached over and patted my knee. "You'll find a way through."

Would I though?

We stopped when it began getting dark to set up camp. The royals were to reside in big, luxurious silk tents for the evening, with actual furniture pulled out for them. I watched beds, vanities, tables, chairs, and sofas being hauled from a wagon by some of their human slaves. By the time they were done dragging and placing the furniture where the Fae wanted it, the poor humans were drenched with sweat and dropping onto the wet ground, fanning themselves.

The Fae had actual magic they could use for this, but still used their human slave labor to prove a point. I watched as the Fae stayed in their own, much more swanky transport. Lounging back on velvet seats and laughing amongst themselves as they drank and gossiped over the event and their new acquisitions. As the humans began to drop from their exertions, the nobility merely laughed as the guards made their way over, whips uncoiling from their belts.

I shook my head; based on the Fae's behavior here, I considered what my future might hold.

Nothing good.

That may be the only thing I was sure of at the moment.

At least they'd put up a magical barrier to keep out the rain. It blocked the torrents pouring down with what appeared to be an invisible bubble. Of course, that was done for their benefit, not ours. And it did nothing for the mud on our side of the camp either. I watched as they used magic to ensure their side was dry, but we were left to struggle through it.

A Fae did helpfully start a fire, since the logs were too wet to start one naturally. We were given simple bread and cheese for an evening meal. I could smell much more enticing scents in the air, the spices drifting in from the Fae's dinner, that had me salivating. The Fae royals and nobility remained in their own separate part of the camp; the two different sides starkly contrasted.

We were given tiny, canvas tents in a drab tan color. Meanwhile, the royals had lush flowing silk tents in a shining dark gray with bright pink both along the edges and outlining a large pegasus on the side.

We were instructed to stay in our section, with stern looking Fae guards who lined the edges. After such a long time in the wagon following a seriously stressful experience, I felt entirely too restless. I figured that as long as I remained on our side of the camp, it couldn't hurt to walk around. I started exploring around the edge of the camp, dodging puddles and the mud that stuck to my boots. When I looked up, I startled as I caught Prince Cyrus staring at me.

Old Gods, he looked so cocky, his smirk sliding into place. He didn't take his eyes off me, and I'm not sure if he understood that it was fear inducing rather than enticing.

I shoved my hands behind my back so he wouldn't see them shake. I refused to show any fear.

Prince Cyrus probably expected me to jump at the attention. I knew I should be following proper court etiquette—but what did I know of those? Before I did anything that could get me into trouble, like glaring at the pompous prince, I quickly turned away and headed to my tent, deciding that walking was far too risky, even if I was restless. I let the siren call of sleep lure me in, knowing it was the safer option.

And who knew how much sleep I'd get once we arrived at the palace and I was put to work? I'd have to take advantage on the way to Dusk. The capital was only a couple days away from the Neutral Lands, but I'd take that time to rest while I could and work on calming my nerves. I would enjoy the last bit of what almost felt like freedom, even if the royals, and their heavily armed guards, were corralling us toward our cage.

CHAPTER 3

THE next day dawned with a break in the clouds. The rain had stopped falling long into the night, and finally seemed to be over. The sun sluggishly rose into the sky as the Fae packed us back into the wagons.

Emmie was a chatterbox the entire trip. Eris seemed to be ignoring it, but I was sat on Emmie's other side today, indulging her. She was currently regaling me with all the court gossip she'd heard around the Dawn Kingdom palace or from her mother, who apparently worked for one of the queen's ladies in waiting.

"Of course, there's the scandal of the Day Kingdom's prince." She giggled in a low tone, and I remembered how unnerved I felt when said prince's eyes caught mine.

"What scandal?" I asked, cocking my head to the side curiously. I'd never heard of any scandal. We did get visitors to the vineyard fairly often, so even if we heard news much later than most, we did frequently receive word on other kingdoms.

"Old Gods, you truly are out of the loop!" She laughed, and I flushed a bit. We were in the middle of nowhere really—I knew that. The vineyard was surrounded by my village, a lake, and the mountain range—and not much else. We were near the Damaculous Ocean, so we could escape to the beach every now and again. The mountain isolated us from the capital, and it was too far for us to make any day trips when we had no horses or wagons. Those were only brought in to pick us up for Placement Day.

Life in Sonmathion had been peaceful for the most part, despite it being a prison all the same. Humans under twenty-one weren't required to work, but we still had to attend our lessons, and a strict curfew was enforced for us. If I'd been caught sneaking out, I'd have been whipped for the infraction. The Fae who oversaw Sonmathion was more relaxed, but he was still exacting in his punishments.

Soren told me about when his father dropped a bottle once. A visiting Fae noble wasn't looking where he was going and crashed into Soren's father, causing him to drop it. He was blamed for it, despite it being obvious that the accident wasn't his fault. He'd been whipped until his back was a bloody mess. Soren's parents didn't want him to see the damage and insisted on sending him out of the house, but he'd doubled back to look through the window. Even then, I'd had to swallow my rage to support Soren.

"Oh, I shouldn't tease." Emmie's voice dragged me from my thoughts. "I'm sorry. But—okay, so you know how when the king's sons are born, it's usually the first born who is chosen as the heir?" I gave her a look, clearly indicating it was a dumb question.

Everyone knew that the magic of the gods chose the next king. It was usually the first-born male, but not always. Sometimes it was a different son.

"Well, Prince Arien wasn't chosen." Emmie was far too excited by her gossip, but I nodded to encourage her to keep going. "And King Aelius and Queen Aurelia haven't had any other children. Nor does it seem they plan to with their current enmity. Some say that they've lost the favor of the gods. And if something happens to the king, rumors are that the power of Day Kingdom will go to another family."

"Can that happen?" I tilted my head to the other side as I looked at her. I'd never heard of such a thing.

Emmie shrugged, but Eris interrupted after a moment of silence, her voice rough as she scoffed. "Oh, come on. You know that won't happen. King Aelius will do whatever it takes to stay in power and ensure he has a male heir. He'd sooner slaughter any heir that wasn't a son of his. If some random male out there was born with the favor of the gods, the Day Kingdom would never admit it. They'd be cut down first."

"He couldn't!" Emmie gasped, her mouth dropping open at her friend's words. "That would subvert his own reign. The king's rule because the gods chose them, it would undermine everything!"

"Kings are kings, Emmie." Eris replied, rolling her eyes. "They do what they want and care little about who says otherwise. You know that."

She huffed and shifted slightly in her seat. "Well, yes, but—"

"But nothing. That's all there is to it." Eris snapped, looking around suspiciously: "And stop speculating before someone hears you." She nodded to the door of the wagon, which had just come to a halt. The wooden door unlatched and swung open, revealing one of the Fae guards in their nickel-plated armor. Emmie pouted but kept quiet.

We were instructed to exit the wagon and I jumped out, exiting to a large field. I may not have been eager to arrive at the Dusk Kingdom, but I didn't want to spend another night anxiously awaiting it either. As we were herded into our side of the camp, I took the opportunity to stretch while they set everything up.

My body always ached after a long time sitting. Raising my arms above my head, I arched my back to crack it, and then shifted my head side to side to do the same with my neck. I instantly relaxed, feeling more comfortable in my body—at least until I saw Prince Cyrus. I shivered—he was watching me again. The thought of him watching me stretch, taking in my more obvious assets that were unintentionally shown off, made me want to throw something at him—or gag with disgust.

I had no way of stopping him, and I hated the helpless feeling of knowing I was ultimately at his mercy. He walked away with his stupid smug face, while I glared at his back.

"Don't do that." Emmie hissed in my ear as she came up behind me.

Surprised by her sudden appearance, I whirled toward her. "What?"

"Don't glare at him! Are you crazy?" Emmie said as she looked around the space ahead of us. She looked scared, like someone might pull me away any moment.

"He's not even facing this direction; he can't see me!" I snorted.

Emmie grew very serious when her eyes met mine. "You know better than that."

I wilted immediately. She was right, of course I knew better. Prince Cyrus owned me now—or his father did. It amounted to the same thing as far as I knew.

If anyone had seen me…

"I know. I just—hate all of it." I grumbled. Emmie reached up and hugged me, surprising me so much I went stiff.

"You don't hug much do you?" Emmie laughed, squeezing me.

"No." I admitted, slowly bringing my arms around her and hugging her back. "No. Not anyone who wasn't my parents, or—well, I only had one real friend, and that was sort of complicated."

"You didn't have friends?" Emmie pulled back and gave me an incredulous look, questions overflowing in her eyes.

"The girls in my village all hated me anyway, thanks to Verin, and with life the way it is—" I shook my head, then shrugged. "I figured it was better not to get attached to people."

"That's a sad way to live, Asteria." Emmie looked at me sadly, but brightened quickly. "We're going to change all that." She set her shoulders, and I had a sinking feeling in my stomach at the sight. "We're friends now, after all, aren't we?"

She didn't give me a chance to respond, hooking our arms together and walking me to the fire now blazing in the middle of camp.

I didn't do friends. I couldn't afford to care about others who would eventually be taken away.

But I had a feeling I didn't have much of a choice in this friendship when it came to the bubbly blonde.

We spent the rest of the night getting to know each other by the fire. It was a new experience for me, but not one I hated surprisingly. Eris was quiet most of the night, only chiming in occasionally, but still, getting to spend a night talking with other girls my age was novel.

The next day, the wagon bumped along the road, and I curled up on the bench seat to look out the window, drinking in my first view of the capital of the Dusk Kingdom—Evenfall. The palace was on the horizon, and it was bigger than anything I'd ever seen. I tried not to let myself be intimidated, but I'd never even seen Panchaia, the capital of Sunrise, during all my years living there. I'd heard about it, of course, about the palace that was half in and half out of the jungle. But this…

The palace was made of black marble with veins of red, pink, and purple shooting through it like the colors of dusk itself. It was stunning, even if intimidating. Its dark color felt ominous, even with the brighter colors imitating a dusky sky. It stood high above the rest of the capital, with the middle section standing taller than the two sides buttressed against it. Pointed arches lined the palace, with spires shooting to the sky, interspersed with columns. Some of the columns started farther up, circling around towers where giant marble pegasuses reared up from either side of the small landings.

The palace was the most colorful building in sight, in spite of its darkness. The highlights of red, pink, and purple were a flash of color in a sea of dull tones. I knew that's where we were heading, and the thought of having to walk into a palace of all things sent my heart racing and hands shaking.

I opened my mouth to ask Emmie for any other advice, hoping to relieve my panic, but we turned onto a long drive leading right to the black behemoth of a palace I had been staring at. I swallowed hard, trying to prepare myself.

"You'll be fine, just calm down." Emmie patted my hand, a merry smile firmly in place.

I looked at her incredulously as Eris snickered.

I was about to respond when the door of the wagon flew open, revealing one of the Fae guards I recognized from the Neutral Lands.

"Everybody out!" He bellowed. The Fae's brown hair was shaved, leaving him looking every inch the soldier he was with that nickel-plated armor. His eyes were a strange color, blue with a ring of pink in them. His eyes weren't narrowed and glaring either, unlike many of the others.

I departed the wagon quickly and followed after Emmie and Eris as we walked to our destination. I looked up at the palace in wonder. Seeing it this close, I could make out the massive arched door opening. I lost focus on it as I got a look at the marble for the first time up close. My eyes began tracing the veins of pink, then the purple, and I was about to get lost in the red marbling when I realized my feet were leading me into the palace itself.

I flushed and made myself pay better attention. We were marched through the halls by the guards who'd been with us this entire trip, but my mind was too busy being boggled by all the wealth on display. I knew, in theory, that the Fae had much more than we did, but—I don't think I ever truly understood that disparity until now.

A familiar rage rose inside me as I gritted my teeth. I balled up my hands in my skirt as I kept my eyes low to hide all the feelings I was sure were written on my face. I kept them high enough to still study the excessive wealth the Fae hoarded while we went hungry because there "wasn't enough to go around", or our clothes fell apart as we wore them day after day, year after year, because "there was no material left over".

I spied gold and obsidian bowls and vases along with crystal and bronze sculptures. Paintings lined the hallways that had ornate rugs laid upon them. One hall seemed to be full of Dusk's ancestors, their faces and names immortalized on the walls. Velvet and silk chairs were sporadically added, purely ornamental and not practical for sitting.

An impulsive, completely irreverent feeling swirled through me as I wondered what would happen if someone actually sat on the ridiculous chairs. The urge to do so left as fast as it arrived, as we were ushered through the grandeur of the palace.

I couldn't believe this. A lifetime's worth of money we would never earn was in this hall, and I positively seethed with anger at the injustice of it all. Merely one of these stupid ornamental bowls could have fed my family forever. Yet here they sat, doing nothing but looking pretty, while back home, I knew my parents would be back in the fields picking grapes from sunup to sundown—until my father's back was near breaking and my mother's hands curled up with pain. Why would the Fae bother to give us decent working conditions when they could just do the bare minimum to keep us alive after all?

Weapons of all kinds graced the next hall we entered. Swords, specifically. It seemed every ancestor had their sword mounted here after death, with placards containing their names under the swords, just like the paintings in the previous hall. Why they would memorialize weapons, of all things—someone would have to explain to me the point of that someday.

We continued walking through the halls until we came to a broad two door entryway. The Fae leading us turned around to order us not to speak and obey—like we were going to do anything else? I rolled my eyes at him when he turned around. Then the doors were pulled open, revealing a large throne room.

Well—that certainly explained the excessive order.

At the far end of the room two thrones sat on a dais, one larger than the other. The king's throne was gray tufted velvet, with a gray frame sitting on feet made to look like hooves. The throne was wingback style—except it fanned out to look like actual wings. The color changed to a cool pink and it looked like feathers…wait—were those real feathers? I wasn't close enough to tell.

It was possible though. The throne was clearly designed to look like their animal forms. All Fae have the ability to shapeshift, but only the royal families could shapeshift into rare, winged creatures. As the six kingdoms were paired with their balanced opposite kingdom, their animal forms followed suit. Sunrise and Sunset were phoenixes, graceful birds that could turn themselves into flames. Dusk and Dawn changed into pegasus, horses with giant feathered wings. While Day and Night shifted into dragons, massive, scaled, fire breathing creatures.

The royal's shift forms were generally two different colors: one color corresponded to their individual kingdom, and the other color was shared between the two balanced celestial kingdoms. Dusk and Dawn shared the color gray between them, but Dusk had feathered wings of a dark pink color, while Dawn had bright red.

No other Fae could summon aspects of their animal forms while in their Fae form, let alone summon wings. I had no idea why the royals were different, but I was enthralled seeing the wings the king had indeed summoned. I'd never seen the phoenix forms of the Sunrise rulers I'd lived under all my life. Seeing the feathered wings here and now, I was blown away by the beauty of them. I would have loved to see the teal and yellow phoenix form of King Gravadain of Sunrise before I'd left. To see how it compared to the teal and orange of Sunset's king. Though I had to imagine both the phoenix and pegasus would be completely outdone by the dragon form Day and Night Kingdoms shared. Seeing a dragon in person had to be mesmerizing.

I was so distracted that I hardly noticed anything else about the king and queen at first. King Astraeus had long, dark brown hair that rested against lightly tanned skin, the blue of his eyes the only thing to brighten his dark features. His charcoal gray doublet was accented by a flowing cape of dark pink down his back, a chain in front connected each side with a large button shaped like a pegasus. His expression was blank, at least until he rolled his eyes over to his queen.

Queen Stelara was a complete contrast to her king; bright where her husband was dark, with her hair the shade of berry wine and her face pale enough for me to believe she rarely left the palace. Just like the king, her eyes were the opposite of the rest of her features. Black orbs stared out, which I could practically feel oozing judgment and derision. Or maybe that was the pointed sneer on her face as she turned up her nose.

I knelt on the floor in front of the royals with the others, bowing my head as far down as possible. It rankled—*badly*. I hated showing subservience of any kind, but especially not to people like these Fae, who clearly looked down on humans. I felt the disdain pouring off them, clearly sticking their noses up at their newly acquired slaves. It was not difficult to imagine the cruelty these two could dispense if provoked, and I had no wish to taste the lash of a whip.

"Humans, you are now part of the Dusk Kingdom. You belong to me, from this moment until your death." The king bellowed, a familiar smirk tipping his lips up. Old Gods, he was just as arrogant as his son. I clenched my fists so hard I felt the press of my fingernails in the flesh of my palms.

What a welcome "home".

This asshole—he was actually enjoying this, wasn't he?

"Since I have so many newly acquired possessions, pay attention—for if you are found in the wrong area of the kingdom, and especially the palace, you'll pay dearly for it. I won't repeat myself twice as I tell you where you will be assigned throughout the kingdom, and which master you will answer to. You may be *my* property, but they will be your master on a daily basis. They will see to your care, training, and punishment when necessary."

My blood turned to ice. Jehohanan, the Fae in charge of the village, never required the children to attend the punishments served out, but I'd heard of other villages who required everyone to be in attendance, regardless of age. And though I'd never personally seen my parents or any of the villagers punished, I'd heard of humans being punished plenty. I'd personally seen the aftermath of only a few punishments and considering how much I'd still despised that—it certainly did not bode well for my sanity.

A Fae male with distinct hair, short on the sides and longer down the middle, in shades of blonde and red, walked up toward the thrones and turned to face us, holding a long, tightly rolled, scroll. He began reading off names and assigning them to their roles and the Fae who'd oversee them.

My fingers wouldn't stop drumming on my knee in my nervousness. My heart felt like it might gallop out of my chest. My whole future would be determined once more. First, it was my placement to Dusk, and now I was once again to be placed, this time within the Dusk Kingdom.

Emmie leaned ever so slightly towards me and put her hand on mine, stopping the tapping with a pointed look through the curtain of her hair. I noticed Emmie twitch as her own name was called, however.

"Emmie Saphere, Eris Ventella, and Kalida Bothorn; will all be assigned to the palace under Princess Daneiris."

Emmie seemed to breathe a sigh of relief. She'd grown up in court and was likely thankful to get assigned somewhere she understood, instead of being placed on a farm or in a village like mine, where she'd be forced to do hard labor. I was happy for her, but disappointed that the only familiar faces, the only people I'd really met, would already be leaving.

Don't get attached, Asteria. Nothing good ever comes from it.

Lost in my thoughts, it took me a moment to recognize my name being called…

"Asteria Zagreus, will be assigned to the palace under Crown Prince Cyrus."

No.

If I thought my blood had turned to ice before, it had nothing at this moment. My whole body felt frozen, ready to be smashed and broken into a thousand pieces.

I can't have heard that right. Instead of relaxing like Emmie, my body was overtaken by pure anxiety, my muscles all tightening as I visibly tensed. This couldn't be happening. *Prince Cyrus.* I knew with certainty now that all the times I caught him staring at me had everything to do with me ending up in Dusk—and with *him*. Especially when they could pick and choose which slaves they wanted. For the sake of my own sanity, I forced the connecting dots to the back of my mind. I was being watched, and if I wasn't careful, my clean record of not being whipped would be broken.

Still, I couldn't help the panic at the thought that Prince Cyrus would now have complete control of me. What did he want with me? Why single me out? And what was I to do in a palace? I knew nothing about city life, let alone court!

I risked looking up briefly and knew from the instinctive dread that flooded my system that Prince Cyrus was already staring at me again. As the rest of the humans stood up, I watched them make their own ways to their new masters.

I gulped, taking a step toward the prince. This male now owned and controlled me entirely, and I honestly couldn't think of anything worse.

"Hello, pretty little human." Prince Cyrus practically purred at me. I nearly bit through my tongue, keeping it leashed. My father was right, I needed to control my anger. I had no idea what this Fae would do to me if I snapped at him. Or rather, I *did* know the possibilities and they all terrified me.

"Follow me." Prince Cyrus turned on his heels and sauntered away. Every bit of him dripped with arrogance and privilege. I sneered at his back, at his assumption that every woman in this room wanted him, and that he could have whomever he wanted. Judging by the giggling and the staring from the females surrounding us before we'd left the throne room, his arrogance, unfortunately, wasn't totally unfounded.

Confidence in a man is sexy, I'm pretty sure any living female would agree—but this wasn't confidence. It was pure, gross arrogance, and that was a different thing entirely.

I followed the prince through the winding halls, passing more ludicrously ostentatious decor as we went, and trying not to roll my eyes at it or sneer outright. When we finally reached the East Wing, the prince turned and began climbing up a giant staircase. I dutifully followed along behind him, my footsteps near silent on the plush violet rug laid over the black marble. I wondered if he still heard them. I supposed he could also smell my scent as I followed him. Fae senses were known to be incredible, and I could only imagine all the ways those acute senses supplied him with information I couldn't even conceive.

We reached a hall at the top of the steps and turned right. I wondered if he was taking me to my new quarters, or possibly straight to whatever my new tasks were. Would I be cleaning up after him? What did princes even do that he might need me for?

It felt like this place went on forever. I was starting to feel like a very, very small ant—one about to be stepped on.

I couldn't stop staring at Prince Cyrus from where I followed behind him. He'd stared at me long enough, so it was only fair. Not that the Fae cared about fairness. I'd wager crown princes cared even less.

His body was sculpted, but he was slimmer than I expected. Not overly muscular, but he was certainly in excellent shape, like all Fae seemed to inherently be. It was obvious that he lived a life of leisure and didn't spend all his time training like some. I hated noticing his attractiveness at all.

I nearly snorted, catching myself at the last moment. Fae were beautiful, it was pointless trying to argue the point in my own head. Finding one pretty wasn't the end of the world. Almost like he could sense the tenor of my thoughts, his head turned to me, and his sharp blue eyes crackled with lightning as they stared through me. He stopped moving abruptly and wrenched the double doors he'd stopped beside open.

Inside was…it was *a lot*.

"This is my solar." The prince's arm swung wide to indicate the space before me. It was huge, both long and wide, and it encompassed several different areas meant for various functions. The walls were the black marble of the palace, but managed to look open and bright with the large windows stretching across the wall that let the sun in. A huge fireplace was accompanied by two long forest green velvet sofas and a pair of wingback velvet chairs in black to go with them. Bookcases lined the walls in several spots, paired with paintings beside them. The far side of the room had another set of huge windows with heavy eggplant-colored drapes bordering them.

There was a dining area to the left, with a giant mahogany table and chairs set around it. It was already prepared with plates and glasses for ten. To the right was an office space of sorts, with a large desk in black wood dominating that area and cabinets surrounding it on both sides.

My house in Sunrise would fill this space several times over and there'd probably still be room left to fill. I shoved down the sharp pang of loss I felt at the comparison. I couldn't afford to think of my parents or my old home—my old *life*. Not now. It may not have been what I wanted, but it was…familiar, if not safe.

"My chambers are to the right over there—" The prince pointed across the vast expanse of space that made up his rooms to another set of double doors at the far end.

"Usually, our slaves all sleep in their own quarters in a shared space downstairs, but—" He looked me up and down, then walked over to another door—to the left and opposite the expansive room from where his sleeping quarters were.

The prince opened the door and waved me in. I stepped through timidly, unsure of what I would find on the other side. I wasn't sure why he wasn't putting me with the other slaves. The very thought of staying in his quarters filled my stomach with a bubbly anxious feeling.

It *was* another sleeping quarter. The room itself was ginormous, of course, like everything here seemed to be. I could only imagine the size of his rooms if this was a spare. A large four-poster bed caught the attention of anyone entering the room. The wood was light gray, and admittedly very pretty, with scrollwork and a wide variety of details making it look regal. The walls had a floral damask wallpaper in gray and cream but was covered over in several spots with huge tapestries, showing scenes of—*Old Gods*. I blushed scarlet immediately. I wasn't a prude by any means. I liked sex—*loved* it even. But the scenes on these tapestries depicting Fae orgies were like nothing I'd ever seen before.

I forced my eyes to the floor. I noticed then the plush cream-colored carpets—that had to be awful for whatever slave was forced to clean it. My eyes shot around the rest of the room, taking in the various furniture. A seating area was set by the large fireplace with two long, light purple silk sofas facing one another on either side of it. A low table was set between them with tea service sitting out on it. The vanity seemed to be the next most ostentatious piece in the room; set with all sorts of bits and bobs I didn't recognize. The room was clearly meant for a woman, making my nerves rattle as I thought of why that was, and why I'd been brought here.

One thing I was quickly coming to realize was that Dusk Kingdom preferred its luxuries. Everything here was dripping in wealth. It was so incongruous with what I'd known my entire life, I felt like I was dreaming. I must be. No one had *this* much. *Right?*

"This will be your room." The prince drawled in an almost lazy tone, but my head whipped over, giving him a wide-eyed stare. I'd put that together already in the back of my mind, but the confirmation made me want to puke. I quickly put my hands behind my back and fisted them in my skirts, a mix of fear and anger that I could only express in one mild way.

His lips tipped up and his eyes seemed to brighten as he leaned against the doorframe. "Are you going to silently stare the whole time? Or do you plan to speak anytime soon?"

Fury spiked at his amusement. I had no idea how to behave around royalty. A fact he must know very well. My jaw worked as I considered my answer.

"I—I thought it was safer this way," I admitted, cringing slightly.

"Safer?" He repeated, raising a brow as he pushed off from the doorframe and stepped toward me. It took everything I had to plant my feet firmly and not scurry back from him.

"I've never—" I started to answer, nodding. "I've never been around royalty. I'm not sure what to do here." I hated being this nervous and showing weakness to this Fae prince who'd one day be king—if he didn't get killed first. That's often happened in the history of the ever-warring Fae.

Prince Cyrus smiled slowly, exposing too many teeth, like a wolf smiling. The crown on his head caught my attention, with the pink jewel sparkling in the center of the dark gray metal. His eyes were alight with something I could only interpret as cruel amusement—and seemed to be ever present.

"The first thing you should remember is outside these walls—" His blue eyes looked dramatically around his rooms. "You need to call me 'Your Highness' or 'my Prince', or some similar indication of my station. As you'll need to always do with my family."

Fuck. I winced hard. In my nervousness, I'd completely forgotten the most obvious and important thing. Slaves don't address Fae royalty without their titles. This was a major blunder that could easily lead to me being punished. I hated to make myself small for anyone, but that may be my best bet now.

"I'm sorry, Your Highness. Please forgive my mistake." I whispered, placatingly.

That seemed to please him, his smile immediately back in place. I lowered my head in deference, but he put his index finger under my chin, and slowly raised my head back up until our eyes locked. His eyes smoldered at me like blue fire, while I tried not to cringe while making eye contact with him once more.

"Here however, when it's just us, I'd like you to call me Cyrus." He purred as his finger moved to caress my cheek lightly.

"My Prince—I—that wouldn't be—" I stammered, my eyes wide in shock as I struggled for words.

"Please, Asteria, I'd like us to be close," Cyrus murmured, his words dripping like honey in my ears. "And we can't do that if you can't even call me by my name, can we?"

He had to be using some kind of magic on me, right? Whatever spell he may be weaving, I was transfixed by his eyes and by his mouth as it shaped the syllables of my name.

Me. A lowly human slave.

Why in the Otherworld did he want us to be close, exactly? Emmie and Eris' words came back to me—beauty drew people in, even Fae. The prince's beauty meant he likely didn't suffer for companionship. Why would he want to bother me? There had to be another reason, one I was missing, that could better explain this surreal series of events.

"Of course. Cyrus." I gave him what he was looking for, thinking it was the safest option. A smile took over his face in response. He walked over to one of the long sofas, took a seat, and reclined back, his limbs spread without a care in the world.

Cyrus waved a hand to the other sofa directly opposite him, offering an invitation to sit with him. I hesitantly made my way over and sat down in his direction. I clenched my jaw, trying to hide how uncomfortable I was.

"Do you know why I asked my father to assign you to me?" He leaned forward, blue eyes drilling into me. "Why I wish you to call me by my name, abandoning all the titles and pretense?"

I shook my head silently, and his returning grin was almost disarming, if I could forget he was Fae.

"I saw you, up on that stage. You were, without a doubt, the most beautiful human I'd ever seen." Cyrus explained, his lips curling into a seductive smile, as he remembered his first glimpse of me. "But that wasn't what intrigued me the most—no."

I tilted my head slightly, wondering what on Adamah could have intrigued a Fae prince about me.

"You were born a human, but your beauty, and your attitude, are incomparable to other humans. I've never seen another mortal more Fae-like, standing there, glaring, like the world itself offended you by placing you in that cesspit where you clearly didn't belong. The fact that you are owned by us—it drives you crazy. Doesn't it?" Cyrus laughed with appreciation, and I felt my pulse quicken.

Old Gods…

"You want to control your own destiny." Cyrus stated with confidence as he smiled widely. "So many pathetic humans have lost that fight and gotten complacent in their roles, but not you."

Uh oh. My stomach sank as my heart began to beat double time. My hand twitches, wanting to reach for the dagger from my father, but I didn't have a death wish. How in the Otherworld did he know that? Was I seriously that obvious? That can't be good. Did he intend to punish me? Break me? Until I'm like all the others broken down by our circumstances? Cyrus watched me carefully as I kept my silence. I absolutely didn't trust myself to say a word.

"By fate's decree, Asteria, you were born a human, one of the unblessed. Do you know why we refer to you humans as such?" He cocked his head, curiosity lining his eyes, trying to see the depth of my knowledge.

"Because—" My throat felt scratchy, like the words didn't wish to come out. "The Fae were blessed by the gods, given magic. But humans were not, so we don't have any of the powers or gifts, the gods gifted the Fae."

"Correct." Cyrus looked pleased as he sat back slightly. "We Fae have magic, beauty, and immortality. While you humans have been left to rot slowly over time, without a spark of magic at the tip of your fingers." He looked me over, relishing my body, but somehow looking through me, like he could sense the rage that lived inside me. "But you—*oh*, the gods might not have blessed you, Asteria, but I can."

My anger at his words raged inside me, a fire roaring out of control. I raged at the damn injustice of the gods, who had seen fit to give the Fae everything and humans nothing. My anger was too difficult to control at the best of times, and I couldn't afford to risk myself by lashing out. At least in the face of my fury, my fear burned up like ash and floated away in the wind.

"What do you mean?" I forced the words out, uncomprehending what he was getting at here. He couldn't give me magic or immortality.

"I can give you a life of luxury. A life where you may be owned, but you are also happy. I enjoy having every luxury in life, Asteria, and you are by far the most beautiful and intriguing human I have seen in my many years." Cyrus said, his fingers flexing, as if he was restraining himself from reaching out and touching me. "I want you as mine. My slave, *yes*, but I also want you in every way I could possibly possess you. And in return, you will have every luxury possible. You will never want for anything again."

Fuck. A growl underlined his words, his eyes burning as he spoke. The Fae were possessive creatures, and this particular Fae's sight was set on me. He acted like I should be oh-so-grateful for it. Absolute arrogance. He never even considered I wouldn't want this. And this choice before me—this was dangerous. Princes, and Fae in general, didn't react well when told no—especially by humans.

I wished Emmie was here. She would know what to do. Court life and games were her apparent specialty. But me—I had no idea. Was this some sort of game? Did he truly want me? A human? Why, when he had so many others at his disposal? Fae and human alike.

"And if I don't want that?" I dared to ask quietly, afraid of what his answer might be—how he might punish me if he didn't get what he wanted.

But Cyrus just sat back, putting his arm up over the sofa back, and smirked. "Deny me all you want, but eventually, you will come to my bed, little human. For now, you will act as my…assistant, of sorts. Until such time as you see sense."

I nearly snorted at that assumption. That would not be happening. I would never lower myself into willingly bedding my master.

"When you make the right decision, I will shower you with every luxury you could ever want. You will belong to me, and me alone. Think about it." Cyrus smiled, a sharp canine glinting in the light. Maybe it was supposed to be a comforting smile, or a seductive one, but all I could think of was the humans whipped during Placement.

The door to my new room opened then, and a woman about ten years my senior walked in, bowing to the prince. Her face was still unlined, but the years seemed to weigh on it, nonetheless. A weariness that spoke of hard work and days without sleep. Her curly brown hair was tied in a tight bun on her head, and her sharp gray eyes took me in with intense focus. I felt like my skin was crawling as I was looked over and judged.

The woman's tanned skin was mostly covered by a charcoal gray dress with a white apron over it. There wasn't a stain in place. Not like my mother's ratty apron, which was covered in them. Hers was immaculate. Did she even use it? Or did the king and queen demand their slaves keep spots and stains out of their royal sights.

"Ah, good." Cyrus stood up in one smooth movement, and I followed his lead, if less smoothly. "Asteria, this is Whina. She has belonged to my mother for many years now. She will instruct you on everything you need to know."

He swept out of the room, leaving me with a sinking feeling in my gut. The enchanting, beautiful, arrogant, and cruel Fae prince wanted *me*. What did I do with that?

Did I resist, keeping to my morals and sense of righteous indignation? I would be guaranteed an easier life than I could find anywhere else, and if push came to shove, I couldn't deny I was attracted to him. But he owned me, and the thought of giving in made disgust rise hot and heavy in my throat. I didn't want to give him more of me than he already had, but would it prove even more dangerous for me not to? Would he punish me for it? Was it time to kiss all my unachievable dreams of freedom goodbye forever?

Maybe it was time to grow up and accept that, now that I was an adult, there was no happy ending waiting for me. My dreams of such were inspired by tales I read so many times, I eventually grew bored of them. We'd only had one fairytale book in our schoolhouse, and it contained only a handful of them. Passed down year to year, it was in terrible shape as children fought over it daily. So, I resorted to inventing my own and making myself the princess in the tale.

What a joke I now found myself in front of a prince at last, only to find myself deciding whether or not to leave such childish hopes behind.

CHAPTER 4

I SPENT the entire rest of the day following Whina around. I knew I looked as out of place as I felt. Everything about the Dusk Kingdom was so...*other*.

The cold marble halls felt suffocating despite being so much larger than our little house. I was rarely inside at home, always under the open sky where the sun or the stars could shine down on me, and I could breathe the fresh air.

Even the people here were so much more rigid and uncompromising. Everyone hurried to and fro with some task to complete. I supposed it may have been similar inside the vineyard as well, but when the people were in the village, no one rushed around like this. And they never walked around with their chins high and noses in the air.

One lady who passed by me gave me a once over before sniffing disdainfully. She wasn't even Fae! She was as human as I was. Though, in her stiff charcoal dress, so unlike the breezy linens of Sunrise, and with her coiffed black hair, I was sure she looked much more put together than me.

I was still in the dress I arrived in, and I could feel a chill throughout the palace that caused goosebumps to rise on my skin. I could see why they didn't wear linen here. My hair was still a dark cascade down my back, as loose and flowing as my dress. Most of the women who passed by had their hair up. I assumed that it was easier for them to complete their duties with their hair out of the way, but I hated having my hair up. It always pulled on my scalp and gave me a headache.

This was going to be miserable.

Was this really the rest of my life?

Before despair or self-pity could fully set in, Whina smacked me on the arm and I quickly looked over, trying to pretend I was paying attention. Her glare made it clear I failed miserably.

Whina was a harsh taskmaster. She sent instructions flying at me. From when Prince Cyrus would take his meals, to what to do with laundry, to how to arrange meetings and visits from nobility or favorites of his Highness; the list was never ending. Though she'd assured me that I wouldn't be expected to do these tasks for long, just ensure others did as Cyrus's assistant.

"Now, what is the process for his Highness meeting with other members of nobility?" Whina quizzed me, her narrowed eyes and rising brow making me cringe.

"We're to send a letter to the other noble's assistant and request the meeting formally. Then—" I trailed off, biting my lip.

The smack on my arm came without warning—the sixth I'd received within the hour. My arm was red and sore, and I ground my teeth to keep from snapping or hitting her back. As much as I may want to, it would do me no favors. This was her duty, and she'd be the one in trouble if I failed to learn it. Well, we both would be, but I refused to let another get hurt because of me.

Even if my arm was screaming from the repeated smacks.

My parents had to pick grapes, in the heat, for as long as the sun burned in the sky. This had to be easier than the back-breaking work they did, right? But Old Gods, why did I end up in such a complicated situation? *I could do this*, I reminded myself. Working in a palace where I apparently had a big fluffy bed to return to, was hardly the height of oppression. I could be getting whipped and run into the ground as we speak for not making the "right" decision.

Cyrus's offer still rubbed me the wrong way. He wanted me to be *his*. I was already his slave, and his to do with as he pleased. Why did he demand the rest of me as well? I chafed at the very idea of it. And the more I thought about it, the angrier I became.

Soren and I had spent several years sleeping together off and on. I always pulled back when he seemed to begin reading more into it than I was comfortable with. Casual sex was all I was willing to offer. When your life isn't your own, your future isn't something to look forward to—it's only something to endure. I refused to let myself feel something for a person when that relationship would never be able to last.

Case in point: Soren was now in Day Kingdom. I would never see my only friend again. Since I kept it to mere friendship, it didn't hurt nearly as badly as it could have had I let myself become attached.

Still, I had chosen Soren—or he'd chosen me, and I'd agreed. He was attractive, and I was young and curious. It was my decision. My body. My choice of partner. That was what was important to me.

I couldn't deny that Cyrus was even better looking than Soren, I wasn't blind. It was the situation that made this ugly. Sex had always been an escape for me. Now, Cyrus was turning it into what felt more like a threat than anything—at minimum, a transaction.

Despite my initial attraction toward Cyrus, I would never allow my body to be a tool I traded away. I might be a slave, but as he said, I wasn't the kind of person who would roll over and obey my masters every wish. He knew this and hadn't punished me for it—that alone set me on edge and made me incredibly unsure of trusting his offer.

As I followed Whina into the laundry room, I found Emmie there with another older woman. Gray creeping into reddish brown hair and deep brown eyes that looked me over critically. Emmie lit up when she saw me, making her way towards me.

"Asteria! Isn't this wonderful?" She smiled widely, looking around bright-eyed. "We'll be able to see each other all the time!"

"It is!" I couldn't help returning her smile, fake as it may be. Even if I didn't truly believe this situation was wonderful, at least she was here. She'd proven to be a good acquaintance on the journey here. And I could frankly use an ally.

As much as I'd tried to resist forming connections, knowing they'd one day be sundered, this was different. Not only was I here for the rest of my life, but I was adrift. I had no idea what to do or how to act. Having Emmie, who was familiar with palace life, would be a gift from the Old Gods. And it's not like I needed her to be my friend. Helpfulness was better than friendship anyway.

"Where are you staying? I didn't see you in the slave quarters?" She asked, tilting her head in curiosity. I grimaced, but before I could answer, Whina stepped over and glared at Emmie.

"What do you think you're doing?" The older woman demanded, chin rising. "You are on the royal family's time here. You can chat when you're not working." Her eyes were glacially cold. She did not mess around when it came to the royal family, apparently.

It amazed me that any human could truly care. We were just pieces of property to the Fae. The royal family especially. Why be loyal to *them*? Of all people?

"The girl's new, Whina, give her a break." The woman with Emmie rolled her dark eyes as she leaned back against a counter. Emmie managed a small smile back at her in thanks.

"Get your charges in line, Miryam." Whina huffed, bristling. "You may be able to afford to play around, but Asteria here is to be the Crown Prince's personal assistant. She must learn everything there is so that when the time comes, she can properly direct others in their specific tasks."

Miryam's eyes widened, before shooting over to me. She looked over me once more, before her lips tilted up. "Something tells me the crown prince didn't choose her for her ability to do chores, Whina."

She rolled those eyes once more before directing Emmie to grab the basket before her feet. My body stiffened, the accusation landing hard after Cyrus's proposition. He may have chosen me because he wanted to sleep with me, but that wasn't all there was to it. Somehow, he'd seen the rage over my lack of control of my life and was drawn to it. He apparently found it entertaining to offer a girl with nothing luxuries beyond her imagination, as long as she sold her soul in the ultimate catch.

"Things are what they are, Miryam. Regardless of motive." Whina countered, letting loose a deep breath before directing me forward to the other side of the room. She quickly marched off ahead of me. Emmie and I exchanged a helpless glance. I shrugged and she bit her lip to contain a laugh.

"Talk later?" Emmie mouthed, and I nodded in response before quickly following Whina's footsteps. She began going on about the ins and outs of Cyrus's garments and the upkeep to keep them clean.

I tried to take in as much information as possible. Whina promised me she was starting me with the lower tasks to learn how everything worked, before moving up to more complex and important tasks.

There was just so much to learn. As she quizzed me on laundry types and I failed to answer her questions correctly, she sighed, looking to the ceiling like it would grant her a better student.

"I'm sorry. I promise I'm trying to understand all this." I swore to her. Frustration at myself for being unable to remember something so *seemingly* mindless bubbled up.

She softened fractionally. I was surprised, I didn't think the woman was capable of it before that moment. "I know. The prince is exacting, however, and I don't want you to incur any punishments by missing something. It will take time to learn everything. We start here at the bottom, and it will begin to acclimatize you to your new role."

I nodded, feeling defeated regardless. If I couldn't even remember laundry correctly, what hope did I have here? How long before Cyrus grew tired of my lack of skill and refusal, and saw fit to do away with me? Either somewhere worse or…in a more permanent way.

Whina brought her eyes down to mine, the woman much taller than my meager height. Sympathy like I'd seen in my mother's eyes as she comforted me after one of Verin's verbal attacks was shining in her eyes.

"The prince's attention has never been so singularly focused. He's always taken advantage of whatever girls he has serving him. It's not like they ever turned him down. Many of the younger girls here would do anything to trade places with you. Otherworld, some of the older ones too!" Whina's eyes widened in emphasis, and my heart sank.

I knew she was telling the truth. Emmie and Eris had told me what people would be willing to give to have a better life. I could well imagine many of the women here would kill for the opportunity I was turning down, while I couldn't imagine giving in to any Fae—let alone the one with complete power over me. I couldn't give him any more power than he already had.

Whina continued, her eyes growing concerned as she took me by the shoulders. "But he's never chosen one before to explicitly fill that role. I can't tell you whether his attention is good or bad for you. I am loyal to the royal family, yes, but I can recognize not all positions in life are fair. The position you're now in? Some would say it's more than fair, and others unfair—and for many reasons on both sides. It's up to you to decide what to do with that."

I blinked, forehead wrinkling in confusion. For many reasons? I knew how it was unfair to me, and I could *maybe* see how other humans may view it as more than fair, possibly even exciting to be offered a different kind of life. I was being offered luxuries I couldn't dream of before now; it just didn't sit comfortably.

It felt like I was being asked to trade away who I was for that luxury. My soul, my heart, my brain—everything in me railed against it. At the end of the day, I was only left with my convictions, and how they could guide me through this miserable life. I couldn't understand those who grow up loving their theoretical chains, even if we've never known anything different. After all, how could I be the only one to recognize how unfair and cruel this life was?

Giving in to Prince Cyrus would mean giving up the core values that make me who I am. How is that fair? He's given luxury for nothing in return, because of what he was born into—an accident of birth—or fate if you believe the Fae and their rhetoric.

The prince never had to face such a decision in his life, I was sure. I was talking myself in circles, but I knew what I had to do—I couldn't just give up. I wouldn't let him take whatever little pieces of me I have that are actually mine. We humans have never been able to decide for ourselves. I barely even know who I really am, my life has been way too limited for that. But whatever pieces of me I do know, I know I can't give to someone like him. Especially since he wouldn't even truly appreciate them. He expected them because he was a Fae prince and never heard the word *no*. He wouldn't truly *care* for the pieces that made up everything I am.

Whina and I took the prince's clean laundry up to his suite of rooms. Along the way, I was introduced to the servant's passageways, which snaked like a maze through the whole palace.

"They lead from every wing and hall into a complex system through the walls of the castles down into the bowels of it." Whina explained when I shot her a questioning look. "The royals prefer us to be out of sight when not needed. Down there is where all the other slaves spend their time when not attending to their duties. Well, when they're not in the city anyway. Their living quarters are there along with spaces to congregate during off hours. The laundry room we just came from is on the floor above."

The passageways weren't my favorite. Used to open skies, it felt a bit like being encased in a tomb. No windows, no light beyond the balls of fire that dotted torches lining the passageway. They might have been kept magically burning, but I couldn't help picturing them going out, leaving me in perfect darkness. Chills rose, and I rubbed my arms as I tried to banish the image.

The passages didn't even have the splotches of color the rest of the marble making up the palace had. No, these were pitch black, like the Fae didn't want to waste the fancy marble on this area. Combined with the lower ceilings and narrower halls, less than half the size of the halls we'd passed through before, I couldn't help feeling like it was closing in on me.

Whina looked over at me, seemingly to make sure that I was paying attention. I nodded my understanding and adjusted the basket I was carrying, trying to shake off my unease.

"Many spend their free time out in the city. As long as they don't cause any trouble, the royals don't care what they do. Even if they're spending their time shaming themselves in brothels and gambling dens, using stolen money or trading favors." Whina shook her head disdainfully.

I had never seen a city before now, so I'd only ever heard tall tales of such places from travelers visiting the vineyard, or village boys who'd never actually left, but liked to pretend they had. I could only imagine what one of those places was actually like.

A den of debauchery sounded like it might be fun, as long as I could choose what I did, and who I did it with. A night of wild fun with no consequences was definitely appealing. But if the Fae also attended, I very much doubted that would be the case. They took what they wanted and damn the mortals who disagreed.

The explanations from Whina continued, and my head was fit to burst with the constant influx of new information. "Food prep is done in the kitchens, which takes up a large portion of the back of the main floor. Because the halls frequently host lavish feasts, the kitchens must be close by. However, there are many passageways leading up to the different wings containing the castle's inhabitants."

Whina showed me all the ones leading back to the crown prince's wing. It felt like running around in meaningless circles as she took me first down one, then the next, then the next—on and on. Just constant running through these endless black mazes, nothing to see until we exited to the main palace, where color finally came back into focus. This hall was even more outrageous than the rest—expensive ornamentations everywhere I looked.

Tapestries draped from every wall, showing scenes of Fae in all kinds of sexual positions. Some actually made me blush, and I cut my eyes over to the straight-laced Whina, nearly giggling when I saw her attempting to keep her eyes forward, and not on the tapestries. Some of the scenes, however, I noted for later, they'd be fun with the right partner.

We came to an intersection that had several ornate doors with gold trim, surrounded by gold and ruby sculptures lining the walls that I couldn't help narrowing my eyes at. They were excessive to the point of being unpleasant to look at.

"This is the king and queen's wing. The king's rooms are through here—" She motioned to the left door, before turning to the right. "And the queen's. Aside from the crown prince, the rest of the children are in the next wing I'll show you."

Shaking my head at the king and queen's seeming lack of taste, I begrudgingly entered the bleak slave corridors once more. I found it curious that only Cyrus had his own wing. I wondered how his siblings felt about that.

"You'll want to be careful among those assigned to the other princes and princesses. Even the ones you may be friendly with." Whina warned me, raising her eyebrows pointedly.

"Why?" I furrowed my brows at the thought. Emmie is really the only person I know here, even if it's not very well. Eris, even less so.

"Because only one can be crown prince, the chosen heir. The gods choose, but if an heir dies, it opens a spot for another." Whina stopped in the hall and leaned down slightly as she spoke.

My eyebrows flew up at what she was insinuating, and she nodded gravely. "Yes. It hasn't happened yet, but that's because Prince Cyrus is much stronger than his siblings. They're keeping an eye out for an opportunity though, I'm sure of it. The kingdoms have had siblings slaughter one another for a chance at a crown before."

Whina shook her head, tsking at the thought of siblings slaughtering one another for a crown, before looking at me meaningfully. "They will use whatever they can to gain leverage on the prince, including you. They'll send their slaves to find out information. You can't trust any of them, even if you want to."

Her warning was heard loud and clear, but I sighed miserably. Emmie was my only shot at an ally here. Eris was too abrasive and was also assigned to the princess. So that left me with no one to trust in addition to feeling hopelessly lost. That is if I could trust Whina's words.

"Wait, they're assigned to the princess. Doesn't that mean I shouldn't have to worry? It's only males that get chosen as heir after all." I asked Whina, hoping against hope for some good news.

She gave me a pitying look in return. "Oh, child. Just because it's always been males chosen doesn't mean the females aren't all waiting for the day an exception occurs."

My mouth fell open in shock. Did they really still hope for that? I was taught they'd long accepted the gods' choice in the matter. I always thought it ridiculous. Women had just as much of a right to rule as any man, but none of my classmates had agreed.

"There's nothing to say a female can't be chosen," Whina explained with a soft sigh. "It just hasn't happened. There are all sorts of rumors as to why."

"Like what?" I couldn't help but ask. That seemed like something I would have heard. Even as remote as we'd been in Sonmathion.

Whina gave me a hard look, her lips firming into a harsh line. "Never you mind about rumors. It's getting close to dinner time. I'll show you what's done and then I believe you will be taking dinner with the Crown Prince. You may want to consider your response to his offer."

I wilted immediately, but then what she said truly registered. Dinner with the crown prince? What madness was this? Slaves didn't have dinner with princes! I had no idea how to sit at a fancy table and eat with more utensils than any one meal could ever require. What did they even use all of those for anyway? Did the Fae compete to see who had the best forks?

Actually—maybe they did. They seemed to compete about everything.

I'd already decided not to give in to Cyrus. I wouldn't. I couldn't. I didn't imagine this dinner would go very well. Prince Cyrus seemed like he'd never been told no in his entire life—and especially not by a human.

This whole situation was a mess. I was way out of my depth, and I had no one to turn to. At least back in Sunrise, I'd had Soren. He wasn't always *useful* when I vented, but he listened. If I could catch them during downtime, my parents were always willing to as well. But now, I had no one at all. I'd never felt so alone in my entire life. I'd always avoided connections to ensure I wouldn't feel unnecessary pain when Placement Day came.

Yet, the pain was there all the same, lurking beneath the surface, waiting to swallow me whole.

I followed Whina through the steps for collecting meals in a daze. We made our way back up to the prince's rooms with dinner in hand. *My rooms.* And wasn't *that* a thought?

"Ah, there you are." Prince Cyrus smiled as we walked in. I instantly noticed the table in the dining area was now set for only two. He noticed me eyeing it and his smile shifted into a smirk, "Since we have so many new people in the palace today, my parents agreed to allow us all to skip the formal dinner tonight if we chose. Tonight, we'll dine together, just the two of us; tomorrow, I must return to the formal dinners."

I forced a smile and nodded my head, hoping he couldn't scent the dread rising at the thought of us being alone. "Of course, my Prince."

Cyrus turned to Whina who took the plates from my hand and put them on the table. "Thank you, Whina. I trust everything went well today?"

I noticed the surprise on her face. I had a feeling thanking her was something he was doing purely for my benefit. As if I'd think better of the man putting in the barest smidgeon of cordial effort.

"Yes, your Highness. She's going to be just fine." She nodded, surprising me with her support after her frustration with me earlier. Whina grabbed the wine glasses from the table, motioning to me to hand her the wine bottle. I quickly leaned over to hand it to her and watched as she poured both glasses.

I didn't recognize the label. Growing up in a vineyard, you end up knowing all sorts of wine variations. The Fae would very occasionally grant barrels to their slaves and the village would throw parties. Ones that were slightly off or contained bottling flaws that meant they couldn't be sold. And my parents often spoke of their work at the end of a long day, so I'd pick up different names and types from them.

There were even a few times that Soren and I snuck in and stole a bottle from the building where they bottled all the wine. I'm still shocked to this day we never got caught and whipped. After seeing the whippings on Placement Day, I don't think I'd be brave enough to try such a thing again. I hoped wherever he was, Soren now knew better too.

"From my personal vineyard." Cyrus proudly stated, noticing me looking at the bottle. "It's a label not sold anywhere outside Dusk." That certainly explained why it was so unfamiliar.

"Do you have a lot of vineyards in Dusk?" I couldn't help but ask, anything to break the quiet that laid over the room like a shroud.

"Not too many." Cyrus raised his brows, surprised by my interest. "Sunrise and Sunset have better conditions for it. Most of the wine in the realm comes from them, however, my vineyard is along the border between Dusk and Sunset. It allows me to have the very best."

He motioned to me to sit while Whina bowed and took her leave. "If you need anything else, my Prince? Otherwise, I'll be back with dessert in due time."

She gave me a look over Cyrus' shoulder, her eyes widening in what I could only interpret as an order to behave and mind myself. I nodded my head the slightest bit. Whina looked appeased at that and made her way out of the dining room after Cyrus dismissed her.

"Do you know much about vineyards, Asteria? I wouldn't expect a slave to ask about it." Cyrus's words instantly reminded me of the disparity here. Slaves were nothing to their masters. Why would he expect me to have any knowledge of such a luxurious good?

"I grew up in a village surrounding a vineyard in Sunrise." I told him as I grabbed my wine. I swished it in the glass and inhaled it. It was sweet and fruity. My favorite type. I took a sip, and it was truly delicious. The berry flavor was underlined by something lighter, giving it a good balance.

"Ah, I should have guessed. Your dress is very much like the style those around the vineyards wear." His eyes followed the length of my body. "Don't worry, I have called for my seamstress to arrive first thing tomorrow to get you new clothes."

"Oh." I was certainly surprised by that. And was he insulting my dress? *Rude.* "I thought—"

"That I would have you wear what all the servants wear here?" He scoffed, and I couldn't help but notice he called them *servants*, like they were paid for their work. He must have noticed my reaction each time he called them slaves. Like that would change anything. I wanted to scoff in return. Calling them something prettier didn't change what was. Nor would I forget that *I* was his slave, no matter what he tried here.

"No. You're mine. You'll wear clothing fit for my—" Blue eyes lit up as they once again trailed down my body. I wanted to hide from their intensity, a shiver creeping up my body. It felt like he could see right through me and view everything I didn't want him to see. "Companion." He finally finished with a smirk.

"Won't that single me out? Among the others?" I asked him, not wanting to be separated and stand out once more in a negative way. I'd had a bit of hope with Emmie. I'd never fit in among the girls in my village, and knowing we'd eventually leave, I figured that was easier anyway. Don't get close. Don't get hurt.

But I had a new chance now. And if I was going to be here for the rest of my life, I wanted to…fit. Even if I didn't open my heart, being accepted would certainly be easier than not.

But something told me Prince Cyrus didn't want me to do that at all. He wanted me to be his and his alone. The reminder that this was indeed the rest of my life was a heavy one. Could I handle years and years of his attention and not crack? When there was a part of me that wanted to give into the beautiful Fae in front of me? A small part, *yes*, but I was fairly sure you'd have to be blind to not be attracted to the Crown Prince of Dusk Kingdom.

"Indeed. But you won't be like them, Asteria. You will be above them. As my companion, it's only natural." He insisted, proving that he had no idea what it was like to not fit anywhere. Or maybe I was right, and he wanted to ensure I only fit with him.

I took a deep breath and dared to oppose him. Hoping this wouldn't see me bleeding by the end. "But I haven't accepted your offer."

"Not yet." He agreed easily. Clearly, he was convinced it was only a matter of time and my denial of him was temporary.

We ate our meals while Cyrus added commentary about his exploits. He apparently liked to gamble himself, and frequently attended races. Once dinner was over, Cyrus retired to his room, and I sagged in place before quickly making my way to my own. I was so confused by all the changes happening in my life so quickly.

I looked out the window, at the sky I so often wished I could float away to. The city below me didn't look nearly as peaceful, with bright lights and loud noises that seemed to reach my window all too easily. My village had been quiet, and our nights saw little ambient light, making the stars shine even brighter. You'd think Dusk Kingdom would have brighter stars than Sunrise Kingdom did, given its nature. I thought being closer to Night Kingdom would mean better night skies at least, but no. I heaved a heavy sigh in disappointment.

I caught sight of a hawk circling the air above my balcony and smiled. I quickly stepped out and raised my hand towards the sky, like I could reach out and touch it. Life as a hawk must be nice; completely free and able to spend its days flying through the skies.

"You're luckier than you know." I whispered to the hawk, as if it could hear me. Foolish of me, really. My mother always said I was too fanciful and that my head was lost in the skies. But I swear, I saw its head cock in response.

I knew hawks had very good hearing, and it was right above me. Maybe it could hear me? Whether it could understand me was another question. "Fly free, hawk. For all of us unable to."

Its head turned and looked right at me then, to my immense surprise. I guess it could hear me after all. I gave the hawk a smile and it trilled at me in what I swore was meant as a compassionate noise, its eyes shining with a sad light.

I brushed away the tear that escaped, and I sniffed to hold back the rest of my tears. I couldn't afford them. Not now that I was in Dusk, ripped away from my parents and everything I knew. Everyone had their worlds turned upside down on Placement Day. I had to be strong and find a way to live my life anew. Just because I was a slave, didn't mean I couldn't find happiness in some small measure.

Things could be much worse. My master could be crueler, certainly. Someone who used the whip every time his hand moved, like some masters I'd heard tale of. My parents had been lucky, and it seemed like I might be too.

Only my luck came with strings attached, and ones I couldn't rightly live with. As I looked out at the kingdom beyond my window, I allowed myself to dream of a different world. One where I wasn't a human slave, and where I could live in a palace like this because I was born for it, as opposed to being chained to it.

A world where I could meet a handsome prince and gladly start something with him, because he didn't possess me.

But that world only existed in dreams—and reality was never fair to dreamers.

CHAPTER 5

WALKING through the gardens was a surreal experience. It seemed like something a courting couple would do. But no, it was just a Fae crown prince and his slave. And said prince, for some reason only the Old Gods understood, wanted to show me the gardens.

"This is my mother's passion. She spends a great deal of time on this garden. She's very proud of it." Cyrus told me as we entered the elaborate space.

"She gardens? I wouldn't think—" I cut myself off before I got myself punished by insulting the queen.

"No, she doesn't." Cyrus barked a laugh, picking up my train of thought easily. "She doesn't get her own hands dirty, of course. She directs others on what to plant and where."

Of course. Old Gods forbid the queen got her precious hands *dirty*. The hard work of gardening must be much easier with plenty of slaves to direct every which way.

"She had the water feature installed several years ago. Her centerpiece, she calls it." He rolled his eyes, like he found this all as ridiculous as I did. I quirked an eyebrow in response, and Cyrus grinned down at me. Old Gods help me, it was hard to remember the reasons I couldn't give into him when he gave me that playful smile.

"The sculptures are changed out every so often, to keep it interesting, she claims." Cyrus explained as we walked along the garden path. I was too absorbed in looking at the row of plants that had been shaped into animal forms. A huge pegasus was seated on an elevated marble base, taking up the place of honor in the center of the garden. It was surrounded by all sorts of animals: wolves, foxes, bears, phoenixes, deer—even a mermaid.

Sculptures lined the path that led into the next section of the garden. Here, the water feature Prince Cyrus mentioned stood tall in the middle, surrounded by all types of bright, beautiful flowers, like splashes of paint thrown over the green.

"Wow." I couldn't help but breathe out. It was intense, with all the different colors dotted around the space—a bit overwhelming, but it was also incredibly beautiful. The walls were covered in creeping ivy, and light roses bloomed wild across them. Several batches of night roses were mixed into the arrangement, though they were currently closed with the sun high in the sky. There were moonlilies, comet orchids, and sunflowers all mixed into the different arrangements surrounding the fountain.

"Come along." Cyrus chuckled lightly at my slightly stupefied look. He took my arm and led me down the path around the fountain and to the other side, where I found rows of tall hedges. I raised a brow up at Cyrus, who snorted a laugh. "My mother developed a maze. It's supposed to highlight the different flower types on each hedge apparently."

There were a plethora of different types of flowers, most of which I couldn't name. I didn't even realize there were so many different types of flowers! The realization was just another reminder of how very small I was in this world, and how little I knew of it.

"Personally—" He started walking, leading me into the maze. "I think it's nothing but a vanity project. She's competing with Queen Oriana for who has the better garden." He rolled his eyes. "Every time we visit with Dawn, the two of them are jumping to tour the other's garden. All so they can judge who is better and make sly comments disparaging the other's garden. It's a waste of time really." He sounded exasperated at the thought of it.

I couldn't think of a polite response, however. It was so absurd that I couldn't help but laugh, the bitter sound filling the garden. I thought of the years when we'd had a shortage of food due to bad crops, and we'd been left with scraps because the Fae took the food for themselves. The nights my stomach felt like it was turning inside out, and I was left dry heaving from hunger.

And these queen's…competed over who had the most over the top *garden*?

It made me want to run through this maze and rip every bloom off their vines—then set fire to the entire ludicrous thing.

I somehow managed to keep a straight face through the tour as he showed me the full maze. It was all exquisite, but only artificially. All carefully planned and plotted, but with no real love in it. Still, exploring the maze was better than being stuck inside.

As Cyrus brought me back through the castle, he stopped to show me every outrageously expensive piece he and his family had purchased, just because they could. It was a miracle I was able to nod and smile my way through it. Thankfully Cyrus seemed to just enjoy hearing himself talk, not requiring much input from me. Thank the Old Gods for small mercies.

When we finally got back to his rooms—our rooms, I supposed—there was a slave waiting. She stood patiently in the entrance way, hands clasped in front of her, wearing the uniform most slaves here did, all a drab, medium gray.

"Ah, Priscilla. Excellent." Cyrus looked pleased to see her, before he turned to me. "Asteria, meet Priscilla. She is going to prepare you for dinner tonight. You won't be able to dine with my family, obviously, but I'll have food sent up for you to eat beforehand. As my personal—" He paused, considering his words. "Assistant, you'll be expected to stand behind me like the others during dinner."

"Others?" I asked, my brows furrowing at the news.

"Yes, the others." He nodded sharply. "Other sla—mortals." I eyed him as he quickly corrected his slip. "Ones my family members use as their own *personal assistants* of sorts." He smirked at me in a way that told me I was missing something. "Each member of my house has a human who assists them and only them."

Did they also have sex with these assistants as Cyrus wished to with me? Wait—

"Now, Priscilla will ready you to the standards set for a formal dinner. You are to represent me now. I expect you to be on your best behavior and show them a united front." Cyrus instructed firmly, tilting his head down to meet my eyes.

United front? Me and Cyrus? He attempts to woo me with garden tours, and in the next breath insinuates I'm going to be his to use as he pleases. There was nothing *united* between us. I nearly scoffed out loud at the very thought of it.

He seemed to read my thoughts, my face surely giving me away. His own face slid into harsh lines. Cyrus stood directly in front of me and grabbed my chin. "Do not embarrass me. You do not want me to have to punish you in front of the entire court, do you?"

I could feel my body quake at his words, and I locked myself in place. *Do not let him see your fear*, I reminded myself. He could play the nice Fae overlord all he wanted, but he showed enough of his true self in this moment. In all the little moments he didn't realize he gave himself away. I would never fall for his deception.

There was no such thing as a benevolent slave owner.

With his threat issued, Cyrus released my chin and turned on his heel. Swiftly exiting and leaving me to nearly slump in relief. The sound of a throat clearing made me nearly jump out of my skin. I'd forgotten the girl left to get me ready for this farce.

I turned to face her, and Priscilla greeted me with a small, sympathetic smile. "Come, we have much to do."

She led me over to the door of my room and walked through it with familiarity, heading straight to the vanity, and waving at me to sit. I walked over and eased myself into the gray tufted vanity chair.

Looking into the mirror, I could do nothing but curse the face staring back at me. Would Cyrus have ever noticed me without it? If the beauty wasn't there, he likely wouldn't have been paying enough attention to me to notice the rage that piqued his interest.

"You're new to Dusk, aren't you? One of the new ones?" The girl asked curiously as she began brushing my hair.

"Yes, I am." I confirmed, since there was no point in denying it, the whole court had seen us arrive. I was surprised she even bothered to ask.

"You'll learn quickly that Cyrus has a bit of a temper. He has his moments where he's the epitome of courtly grace and charm, don't get me wrong. But he doesn't like to be seen as anything less than the best. And he doesn't like to be denied." She looked down at me and bit her lip. I wasn't shocked to hear that at all.

Priscilla seemed to be conflicted. Worrying her bottom lip as she stared at me and debated with herself. I just blinked, curious why she seemed to be so torn. Finally, she sighed, her shoulders slumping.

"I don't know exactly what he wants from you, but you should just let him get it over with and let his attention go elsewhere. It's better not to have him too focused on you." She whispered, her eyes darting to the door every other moment. I shivered, her warning appropriately ominous.

"Unfortunately, I don't think I have much choice there." I sighed miserably. "He was focused before I even got assigned to Dusk."

"It'll be easier for you if you give in, you know." She said, like I wasn't already well aware—like it was even an option.

"Maybe." I allowed, tilting my head to the side. "But I'd never forgive myself either. He owns me, and I'm not going to forget that."

She sighed, resigned that she wasn't going to change my mind, and gave me a sad look. But she thankfully said nothing more on the subject.

This is why I didn't bother with people.

I watched, somewhat fascinated, as she curled my hair perfectly and then did some strange, twisted half updo, with the strands strategically falling in the front to frame my face. She dusted my face with color, a glow appearing on my cheekbones and shimmering in the light, while kohl was lined onto my eyes, making my already wide eyes stand out more.

"You don't need much. They generally request we try to make the humans prettier." Priscilla rolled her eyes. "They think they're the epitome of beauty and that it's an insult if we don't try harder to match them. But you're already stunning, there isn't much I need to embellish upon, honestly."

Her words brought a flush to my cheeks. So often, I was noted for my beauty. Ridiculed for it. Singled out for it. To me, beauty seemed to have been nothing but a curse. What I wouldn't give to be noticed for something else, for once. To be given acknowledgment for something I did, or said, or in any way *earned*. To be recognized for…my soul. My brain. My talents. Anything but features I had zero control over.

Priscilla helped me into the dress the prince had instructed I wear for the evening's events. The dress was exquisite, with a low—almost too revealing neckline, and a bodice made with velvet and silk crossing over one another down the bodice, with a skirt of sapphire blue and silver embellishments that flowed and twirled high when I spun around in it. I laughed in delight as I indulged in another spin, testing how high the skirt could fly. Priscilla bit her lip, trying to contain her laughter, but it was a lost cause. We giggled together as she encouraged me to twirl again.

We both sobered as Priscilla came from behind me to fasten a silver necklace around my neck. She smiled when she saw my ears were pierced, and added earrings that complimented the necklace. As a final touch, she slipped a bracelet over my hand and onto my wrist.

"Priscilla—" I began to protest. "This is far too much—"

Priscilla just raised a brow at me with her lips in a stern line, clearly telling me that it was, in fact, the expectation. I couldn't believe the royal family dressed their slaves up like this just to stand behind them at dinner. It was ridiculous.

When Cyrus came back into the room, I was admittedly nervous, but when he saw me, he actually did a double take. The second look lingered for a while too. His eyes tracing every dip and curve of my body before following it up to my face and hair. He looked satisfied, and greedy. The lust in his eyes was not something I'd missed. I'd seen that look too many times.

Just never on someone who owned me before.

"You look perfect, Asteria." Cyrus came up and took my hand, kissing the back of it. In my peripheral, I saw Priscilla's jaw drop, before she quickly schooled her facial expression. It took all I had to stop my own jaw from falling to the floor.

A Fae, a crown prince at that, stooping to kiss the hand of a human?

"Thank you, my Prince." I managed to get out, with a slight curtsy. I hadn't had to do such things before and Whina gave me a quick instruction during her whirlwind of explanations yesterday.

I could tell by his reaction it wasn't perfect yet.

Whatever. He could deal with it, and his whole damn family. What did they expect? They drag humans unfamiliar with court into the heart of it and just expect us to know everything automatically?

"Follow behind me. Three steps, no closer. When I sit, you'll stand behind my chair, also three steps back. Understood?" Cyrus instructed, his face stern. I just nodded quietly, hoping to get this over with quickly.

"Good. Follow." He barked, and I sneered at his back as I made to follow along, like a good little pet. It made my skin crawl.

We wound through the marble hallways and passed some other slaves who bowed their heads as we passed, forced to show deference to the crown prince. As I would be required to do with his family. I was not prepared for this—at all. Regardless of the fancy gown and jewelry, I was not ready to bow and scrape before Fae who saw me as nothing more than cattle. I was only a temporary blip in their life, with a purpose to serve and breed more slaves.

That familiar burn of anger inside me rose up. It ached to burst out of me and rain down on all those who thought to control me. I closed my eyes, but it was like a flash of bright light exploding behind my lids—I grabbed hold of my anger, strangled it and leashed it down. Now was not the time. Cyrus may have found my glares and sneers humorous during Placement, but nothing said his family shared those views. In fact, I was rather sure they wouldn't.

Following the "exactly three steps" I was demanded to follow behind Cyrus, two humans opened a set of double doors directly in front of us. As they did, the expansive dining room within appeared.

It was just as grandiose as the throne room. The marble floor was covered by a black rug, with walls covered over with burgundy velvet. Large crystal chandeliers brightened the dark space, and the room was dominated by a massive white table, reaching from one end of the room to the other.

At either end was King Astraeus and Queen Stelara. There was an empty seat to the right of the king that Cyrus made for immediately. He dropped into his chair and lounged back in his seat. I noticed that the white chairs were upholstered with black tufted silk, and actual *diamonds* on the buttons.

Old Gods help me.

I stood rigidly behind Cyrus's chair, keeping my face tilted down to avoid eyes and ensure I wasn't disrespecting the other royals somehow. I looked around from beneath my lashes and saw all the other humans either standing behind chairs or farther away against the walls. But the humans standing against the walls were dressed in slave gray, as opposed to the ones standing behind chairs who were all as finely dressed as I was.

Princess Daneiris sat to the right of Queen Stelara. Her bright red hair, somehow even brighter than her mother's, stood out like a beacon, and a handsome blonde man stood behind her chair. Next to her was Princess Twyla, who seemed to fade into the background next to her sister. She shared the same dark hair as her father and Cyrus, and her eyes, while blue, didn't shine as bright a blue as Daneiris or Cyrus's. Standing behind Princess Twyla was her dark-skinned male companion, with black hair and stunning emerald, green eyes that immediately drew the eye.

Cyrus's brothers were seated interspersed throughout the table. Vikal, with his mother's red hair, was equally easy to spot next to all his dark-haired brothers. He was the youngest of the family, and it showed in his easy laughter and joking with Twyla as he attempted to make her laugh. When she finally gave in, she saw the woman behind Vikal give a small smile that she tried to hide. She was as pale as he was, but with dark hair and hazel eyes. She looked at him with a warmth I couldn't imagine feeling for a Fae.

I looked at the humans standing by Prince's Weylin and Kian. The broth-ers were a few spaces apart, other courtiers filling in the other spots around the table with their own "assistants" behind them. A red headed woman with amber eyes stood behind Weylin, studying the room and the other humans in it like she was better than the rest of us. She seemed to take particular exception to me, glaring at me when our eyes met across the room.

My brows twitched upward slightly, until I saw her eyes dip to Cyrus with longing, and realized she was jealous. *Old Gods.* I so wanted to be done with jealous women trying to make my life difficult. I had no wish to be with Cyrus, but she obviously did. She appeared to have settled for the second eldest prince—as if she had any say in the matter. I was so inexperienced in courtly matters, I couldn't help but wonder what intricacies I may be missing here.

The other woman behind Kian was olive skinned, with blondish-caramel colored hair, and eyes like chocolate. She gave me a sympathetic look as she spied the redheaded woman attempting to kill me with her eyes.

I spared a glance around at the other courtiers and their humans, but my attention was quickly drawn away by the conversation in front of me. The royals treated us like we were part of the wallpaper. As offended as I was by that, I would try to use it to my advantage. I refused to be helpless, and the first way to ensure that I wasn't vulnerable was to listen and observe the royal court and any conversations I could be privy to.

"Have you given any thought to the issue I asked you to look into?" The king looked to Cyrus, who made a dismissive sound in reply. The king's eyes narrowed. "Cyrus, as my heir, I expect you to take defense of this kingdom seriously."

His annoyed tone was underlined with something scathing, and it seemed to bring Cyrus around to the conversation, as he sat up straight and looked back at his father. His other brothers, particularly Weylin, zeroed in on the conversation with a strange look in his eyes.

"I do take it seriously, Father." Cyrus insisted, despite his blithe manner. "The guards have been increased, especially along the border. We've added additional armaments to the walls as well as amping up the magic in the shield barriers. There's no way Calix can get past us now. We have nothing to worry about there."

My heart raced as I realized they were discussing the attacks by the Night Kingdom. Though Cyrus seemed unconcerned about another attack, it appeared the king was worried. Apparently, there was some credence to the rumors I'd heard since leaving Sunrise. A chill ran down my spine at the very thought. I'd never been around any kind of fighting before, let alone a full-scale attack by Fae as brutal as the ones in Night Kingdom.

In the stories I used to fabricate to entertain myself, I was always some warrior princess or queen who would fight off any invaders of her land. The reality of the situation, however, was that I had no idea what to do in a fight. I'd always wanted to learn how to protect myself, but humans were forbidden from doing so. It ensured that we didn't have the ability or knowledge necessary to revolt against the Fae. They may act like humans were beneath their notice, but we had numbers, and that was a threat the Fae didn't take lightly.

"I wouldn't put anything past him, nor would I underestimate him." King Astraeus gave Cyrus a reproachful look, and Weylin's lips tipped up. He seemed very pleased with his father and brother's disagreement, but I couldn't fathom why.

"I don't underestimate him." Cyrus sighed heavily, as if the whole discussion bored him. "We've already upped all our defenses though. What else would you like me to do besides be ready for when he attacks next?"

Next? Did that mean they thought it would *definitely* happen again? Old Gods, what if he got into the palace? Would he slaughter all the humans he came across? We weren't allowed weapons, so we'd be helpless to defend ourselves. I had my iron knife from my father, currently hidden away in my room, but I couldn't just carry it around. Old Gods only knew what the punishment would be if I was caught with it. They could put me to death for such a crime. Maybe I could convince Cyrus to allow me to carry a dagger. If he wanted me, maybe I could get him to see sense in me being able to protect myself, since he placed such value on me.

King Astraeus huffed, agitation lining every inch of his face. "I'd *like* for you to make sure that our borders are secure, and that Calix does not get into our home."

"I could step in, Father," Weylin spoke up, in the too-casual tone of someone who desperately wanted something. I watched Cyrus's head whip over before he leveled an icy glare at him.

"I have it well in hand, Brother." Cyrus countered, barely holding back a growl. "After all, what do *you* know of defense?"

Weylin's eyes narrowed as he opened his mouth, but Queen Stelara cut in before he could escalate things any further. "I'm more than sure that Cyrus has us well protected from the barbarian to the South. Wouldn't you agree, my dear?"

Weylin's jaw ground back and forth, but Queen Stelara looked to her husband, who stared back at her for a moment. I was caught off guard by the looks in their eyes. This wasn't a loving couple having dinner with their children, I realized.

No, their eyes contained a calculating glint. I realized that this was a war, one of words and politics, and I was completely out of my depth here. The king and queen appeared to be on opposite sides of something I didn't understand, and Weylin clearly resented his elder brother. I thought of Whina's warning of Cyrus's siblings. Did Weylin want to take his brother's place as heir?

I was watching a game in motion, except I didn't know the rules or even the players. Was every court like this? I watched with a keener eye as the conversations continued around the table.

One of the courtiers whispered to Weylin, eyeing Cyrus all the while. Another came over and leaned down to whisper in Cyrus's ear, eyeing Weylin. Kian was watching them all, his eyes going back and forth between his brothers. Only Vikal didn't appear to be paying attention, focusing on speaking to his sister.

Daneiris, though, was focused more on whispering to the woman next to her. She and Kian both seemed to take in what was happening and were filing it away for later use.

Old Gods. This wasn't a family. This was a power-tripping bloodbath waiting to happen. I'd heard the stories before, of course. Even before Whina's warning, I'd heard the tale of what happened in Sunset Kingdom—the siblings who killed one another for the throne, attempting to usurp those they should have loved and supported, to instead grasp for power.

I'd just never seen it in action before.

CHAPTER 6

Cyrus was in a mood the next day, snapping at everyone and pacing back and forth while muttering to himself. I tried to stay quiet and out of the way as much as possible. I curled up on a chair in the corner reading a book, not wanting to draw his ire towards me. I sighed as he snapped his head toward me—clearly, it was inevitable.

"Asteria! Come here. I need you to write this down." Cyrus bit out, his beautiful face set in harsh lines, while the light coming through the window cast shadows across it. I tried not to notice how it highlighted the burning blue of his eyes as they drilled into me.

I forced myself up from the chair, stretching out the aches and pains from sitting too long, and walked over, taking the seat at his desk. I grabbed the ink and quill, ready to notate whatever nonsense he was working through.

"Write exactly what I say. Understand?" He raised a brow, and I nodded. He gave a single nod in return before he resumed his pacing.

"Weylin needs to be taken down a notch. I want to send him to the South Gate where King Calix is most likely to attack to get into Dusk. I'll phrase it as an act of trust, wanting his support. He will likely be overrun, and we can blame the defenses failing on him. He's eyeing my spot, and I will not let him take me out." He growled, sending goosebumps trailing up my arms.

I dutifully wrote down the plan as he worked through it, a plan for him to send his own brother into danger and possible death. My thoughts returned to dinner last night and the tension between the siblings. Weylin apparently wanted to be heir and didn't care who he had to step over to do it. But Cyrus—he wasn't going to let his crown go. I could see the fierce determination in his eyes as he maniacally set out his plan.

Would he really follow through with this? Maybe it was just anger talking. I had to hope that was the case and he wouldn't set his brother and people up for disaster. That would only hurt his own kingdom. Surely, he'd calm down and realize that.

I debated if I should ask, but curiosity won over my caution. "How do you know the defenses will fail? Or that King Calix will attack?"

"Oh, yes." Cyrus confirmed, looking over to me, and I swore he smiled slightly before continuing. "We've done everything we can with our defenses, but Calix overwhelms us every time. He has fierce fighters and—" Cyrus sighed, a petulant frown crossing his face.

"He's the most powerful Fae in Celesterra. Plus, he can shift into a Shalim damned *dragon*. Shifting into a pegasus won't do much against that." His voice was wry, but I could almost taste the bitter resentment under it. Cyrus clearly despised that King Calix was more powerful than he was when it came to magic. The fact that his animal was much deadlier too only aggravated him further.

I shivered, not liking that idea much either. I didn't want to be attacked or, Old Gods forbid, die, just for some cruel Fae king to—*what*? What was King Calix's goal? I turned to ask Cyrus, who gave me a pitying look in return.

"He wants what we all want: power." He speculated, though I didn't know enough to guess if he was correct. "I don't know why he's capturing and killing humans. It seems quite pointless to me." My fury sparked at his words, but I forced it down. I must have vocalized it in some unconscious way, however, because Cyrus cocked his head and studied me for a moment. Gauging the warring emotions on my face, Cyrus cupped my face between his large palms.

"I will ensure he does not get his hands on you." He promised with a protective kind of possession lining his words. "You're *mine*. And you will not be taken from me."

His words carried an unspoken threat—if I tried something to remove myself, he would ensure my failure. He didn't see me as my own person, but as something belonging to him. He would chase me to the ends of Adamah if I tried to run. I swallowed hard, trying not to think too hard about what the future held for me. Misery and ruin seemed the most likely.

"I haven't agreed to be yours." I dared to remind him, raising an eyebrow. I tried to wiggle out of his embrace, but he held onto me tightly, fingertips abandoning their soft hold in favor of digging into me. As much as I didn't desire to have his anger directed at me, I refused to yield to him.

A phantom smirk appeared on his face as he released my face and brushed the hair from my eyes. A mockery of tenderness.

"You will." He stated plainly, no doubt in his mind about it.

Old Gods damn this overconfident prince. I will not!

"Now, keep writing." Cyrus abruptly demanded, finally leaving my personal space. I returned to the desk to write out the missives carrying his directions. "King Calix *will* attack, and when he does, I will put Weylin right in the line of fire—of failure. That should get the little foal back in line. Kian and Daneiris also need to be watched. I will have several servants loyal to me assigned to them for a while, in addition to the current servants watching Weylin. We will see if I can't find out what their plans are. I've clearly given them too much latitude, but with the increased attacks from the Night Kingdom, we can't afford the liability. I need strong allies."

Cyrus paused as I quickly wrote down everything he had dictated. My hopes he was just overreacting began to fade the more he spoke. It sounded like he would do this—let King Calix come through and slaughter humans… just to get his brother in line. *No. No, it wasn't possible.* No one would do such a thing. When I glanced up at him, he seemed to be deliberating something with himself as he tipped his head back and forth lightly. "Also, take note that I may need to pay a visit to Dawn Kingdom. They generally ally with Dusk as our balanced kingdom."

That made sense, since they had to balance one another to survive, they would naturally ally with one another when necessary. While each kingdom experienced the full celestial cycle in a day, their magic came from their namesake—and just because the time of day had passed, it didn't mean their magic could no longer be accessed. Magic was in the land itself, making it available to those who knew how to draw from it at all times. For the land and its magic to remain balanced, the kingdoms must do the same. It was all tied together.

Sunrise and Sunset generally stuck together while Dawn and Dusk did the same. Only Day and Night seemed to be the exception, but that was a fairly recent occurrence in terms of a Fae lifetime. King Calix withdrew from the other kingdoms, and their long alliance with Day fell to the wayside. But despite not being as strongly allied as they once were, they weren't fighting either. And I hadn't heard of the Night Kingdom attacking the Day Kingdom at all. Whatever had set King Calix on his current path had also severed the bonds with Day, and I wondered what the ultimate result might be. Without the two kingdoms in balance, would the continent be in danger? Was King Calix putting us in an even worse position than I originally assumed?

Cyrus finally sighed, dropping into a chair and slouching low. My curiosity rose and I bit my lip, trying to stop my tongue from getting me into trouble. Like he sensed my curiosity, Cyrus's eyes peeled open and punched right through my chest, knocking the breath from my lips with the intensity of them.

"Ask." He commanded with a cocky tilt to his lips and lazily narrowed eyes like he knew I was dying to ask all of the many questions swirling through my mind.

My eyes widened and my mouth opened in surprise, but no words came out. He slowly lifted his lips into a smirk that revealed his amusement.

"You clearly have questions, so go ahead. Ask me." He paused dramatically; his eyes locked on me. "I wish there to be nothing between us, my dear Asteria."

"Is it—is it always like this?" I rasped out, then swallowed, my mouth far too dry. The overwhelming number of questions I wanted answers to were all bubbling away inside me, but for now, there was one that demanded an answer.

"Like what?" He narrowed his eyes, tilting his head to the side. I could see his genuine curiosity, and it staggered me. How could he find all of this so—so normal?

"The fighting between you and your family?" I finally managed to push the words past my lips, fearing his response, but my need to understand was greater. "Your siblings trying to outdo each other and grasp for power?"

"Shalim, you are innocent, aren't you?" Cyrus's smirk turned into a real smile at my question, his amusement clear.

Heat rushed to my cheeks, which I absolutely hated. I didn't like being out of control, having my own face betray me in such a way. Innocence had never been an accusation leveled at me before, but I felt it more in this moment than I could have anticipated. I didn't know how to manage life in court, asking questions whose answers seemed obvious to everyone else. Cyrus's brilliant smile had nothing to do with my blush—*nothing*; it was merely my own lack of understanding embarrassing me.

I narrowed my eyes at the prince and that damn smile lighting up his face. His eyes were like blue flames, burning brighter than I'd seen yet.

Cyrus began to chuckle, and I was taken aback by how open his face became. He truly was handsome when he unwound like this. It was a shame Cyrus felt he had to be so unyielding and arrogant all the time. He was so much more natural this way, and the corner of my lips ticked up involuntarily.

Cyrus reigned in his amusement at my expense, but the way he looked at me made my heart beat faster, until it was like a third person in the room. I may not be willing to give into him, but he certainly was making my resistance as difficult as possible. The way he gazed upon me was as much a weapon as the sword he normally wore at his hip.

"To answer your question, yes. It's always this way." Cyrus returned to the subject at hand, but his penetrating eyes didn't leave mine. He leaned forward on his chair until his face was level with mine.

"Everyone wants power, Asteria. If someone says they don't, they're lying, either to you or to themselves. People always want control. Especially you, I think." My breath caught as he narrowed in on my own thoughts, and he nodded as if I had just confirmed it for him.

"I can only imagine how you feel." Cyrus's tone was low, seductive, and much too enticing—like he'd wrapped his words in velvet. "You had no choice but to come here, and your life is completely at my discretion." I made a sound of protest, and Cyrus chuckled, the sound causing goosebumps to race across my arms.

"You hate that, don't you? You want the power to control your own life?" He didn't wait for me to respond, seeing the answer as clearly as if I spoke it.

"My brothers all want that power too." Cyrus looked away, his gaze turning toward the large windows like the sky contained the answers to his thoughts.

"They all want the opportunity to not be stuck under the thumb of another. By Shalim, even my sisters want that. So, they plot and plan to dispose of me, and our other siblings. They'll do anything to get themselves closer to the crown, to narrow the options down so the gods will pick them as heir. They risk themselves and choose to fight, just for the opportunity of *possibly* being selected—whether or not they're the eldest, it's the magic within our blood that's favored, so the gods could choose any of them. So, I will fight them to prevent my death." He gave me a wry look, his eyebrow peaked.

I blinked, trying to imagine living like that. Yes, I wanted power over my own life, but it wasn't as Cyrus described. I didn't want power for the sake of power. I wanted power so I never had to answer to people like him again—so I could fly free and far, towards some unknown refuge where the Fae would never bother me again. But I couldn't imagine having to constantly fight just to keep my head, especially from my own family. No wonder he was so detached, he'd had to be to survive. I could certainly understand that. I'd forced myself to do something similar, after all.

"I'm giving you the opportunity to choose power for yourself, Asteria." Cyrus stood, his long limbs stretching as he did so. I couldn't help but notice his shirt riding up, exposing cut abdominals that should not be making my mouth so dry.

He slowly stalked over to me, prowling ever closer. I stood up as he moved in, stumbling slightly and backing up a step. His smirk merely grew, and he didn't stop until he was so close that I could feel his breath on my face. I shuddered a bit as he leaned in, his lips brushing my ear.

How was it possible that he shifted into a pegasus? Surely, he should be some kind of jungle cat when he moved as gracefully as a panther slinking towards its prey.

"You will have power by my side. More than most humans could ever dream of. I offer you a life of luxury and power." Cyrus whispered, his mouth hovering by my temple, brushing the wisps of hair away as he made a mockery of the gentle and unassuming action. He was surely a master of seduction, and I had to keep myself on guard.

"You can control a portion of your own life, Asteria, instead of letting it be controlled for you. I think we both know what you'd prefer." Cyrus flicked his tongue over my earlobe as he finished speaking, then bit it delicately, scraping those teeth over my earlobe before letting it go and turning his attention to the side of my neck.

I shuddered at his touch. His teeth and tongue were a seductive invitation that worked in parallel to try to wash away my resistance. It had been two months since the last night Soren and I were together. I couldn't deny that my body wanted Cyrus—badly. I could feel arousal gathering at the apex of my thighs as his tongue and teeth moved down my neck, licking and biting lightly. Never enough to leave a mark, but enough to make my body quake with want.

Old Gods, help me—my neck has always been a weak point, rousing my desire quickly. *Why did he have to go for the neck?*

It had been too long, and I needed to find some attractive human man to slake some of this lust. *Not Cyrus.* I had to remind myself he was off limits. I refused to go down that road.

It was not only against every conviction I had, but it was risky. Fae owners were known for following their whims, and Cyrus could turn around and whip me for misbehaving if he felt so inclined. Tartarus, he'd already threatened me *today.*

"You want power, Asteria." He murmured into my skin. A silky promise, but his next words proved the lie of them. "Let me give it to you."

I stiffened, his words reminding me why this was a horrendous idea. I had to shake myself and remember these were false promises—Cyrus wanted more power over me, not less. He wouldn't relinquish any bit of that power and would instead attempt to make me *think* he was giving me power. In reality, however, he would maintain all the true control.

Still, he did have a point.

Just not the one he thought.

I raised my hands to his chest and slowly pushed him back. We were both panting, the tension so thick it felt like it could snap at any moment. His eyes were so intense, I could see his need for me inside them. A need so visceral that his own powers betrayed him, and lightning struck across those blue orbs from within. Flashes of his lust striking and lighting up his eyes. His powers summoned to the forefront by the force of his emotions, out of control as they rioted.

His hands still held my upper arms, but I kept pushing him back. Cyrus reluctantly gave up ground as I looked up at him, steeling myself.

If this court was full of plots and games, I would need to adjust to survive. My rural upbringing didn't expose me to the politics and games of court life, and that was a weakness that I'd have to correct immediately.

I could do that. Play my own game. Find my own power.

I may be new to it, but I was always a fast learner.

I smirked, raising a brow and watching as he followed the curve of my lips with rapt attention. He licked his own, and I resisted the urge to do the same. I had a point to make here. "Is it really *true* power, if it's given to me? True power, I would think, needs to be earned…or *taken.*"

"I knew I'd have my hands full with you, my dear." Cyrus chuckled softly, his voice a husky rasp.

He leaned in ever so slowly and brushed his lips against my cheek. He was far too close to my lips, and his mouth lingered, smooth and soft against my skin. My eyes fluttered for a moment before I caught myself.

"You take what power you can, *when* you can. Power is a currency we can't deny, and any bit of it we get, must be guarded against thieves just the same." Cyrus stared hard at me, hoping to impart this wisdom and change my mind. That the chance to take any scrap of power may be fleeting, a momentary opportunity in time. I couldn't deny a part of me wanted to take him up on his offer. A life of luxury is hard to turn away from, after all. But I desired *true* control over my own life, and that was something he could never provide.

"Think about it. In the meantime, we must plan for my sibling's plots, and my parent's, for that matter." Cyrus grumbled, the lightning in his eyes clearing as he returned to business as usual.

I found myself a bit sad to see it go.

"Wait—" I shook my head free of the spell he'd seemingly cast over me in the last few minutes, "Your parents are against you?"

His lips tilted up as he nodded. "Oh, yes. My father, specifically. He thinks I'm not heir material. I'm not living up to the standard he requires. My mother disagrees, so my father can't do anything to me, not without royally pissing off my mother. He instead tries to find subtler ways to undermine me, like at dinner last night. I'm sure you heard him talk with me about the defenses?"

"I did." I nodded slowly. I'd thought it was peculiar that the king would go after his own son, his heir, that way. Cyrus reached out and pushed a lock of hair behind my ear. Finally calming from the desire he'd stirred unwillingly within me, the touch felt much too intimate.

Don't get attached. It doesn't ever end well.

"I don't trust anyone outside of my direct circle. It's a small group, but powerful enough to secure my reign when the time comes. My allies work in the shadows." Cyrus stated proudly. "My family's plots are so obvious, it's actually funny. They are so distracted by their plans, in fact, that they don't see what is right under their noses."

It was actually sort of genius. Hide your allies and have them work to dismantle from within. His family wouldn't even know to look for them.

"Who are they? Other lords and ladies? Slaves? Business owners in the cities?" I found myself immensely curious.

His smile was broad now, as he neatly dodged answering my question. "See, I knew you were special, Asteria. I want you with me for this. I need you with me."

The words would have seemed almost romantic, had they been in a different context. But this wasn't that. It was something deeper. I looked at him, really looked deep into those lightning eyes trying to decipher what his words really meant.

But what I found was a lonely, frustrated male, someone who couldn't trust anyone. Cyrus couldn't even trust his own family. But he owned me, and he trusted those he owned to do as he said. Cyrus had no fear of using humans when Fae didn't suffice for the job. And he wanted me with him, by his side, plotting and planning with him.

In his bed, if he had his way.

This was…pure possession.

But if I needed to play the game—maybe giving in a tiny bit was the right move. I'd already learned so much more than I thought possible from what he shared with me today. What else would he reveal?

He wanted someone; I wanted control of my own life.

I could use his want of me and turn it around on him. I could manipulate and maybe, if I played this right, I could—*could I?* Would it be possible? Could I gain what I wanted most?

Freedom.

My heart beat double time in my chest. The thrill of possibility nearly made me shake as the desire to fly free overwhelmed me. If I could play Cyrus in the right way, I could find a way to escape. If he trusted me and let me move around the palace freely…I'd find a way. *Somehow.*

"I'm not agreeing to be yours, and I will not be sleeping with you." I told him plainly, hoping that this would be just enough to entice him into further opening up to me. "But I'm not opposed to helping you." Cyrus looked at me greedily, already ensnared. And like a Siren Spider, I just needed to spin a web around him. Perhaps at the end of it, I could scurry away with none the wiser.

"I'm glad you're finally seeing some reason. The rest will come in time." Cyrus smiled brightly as I rolled my eyes, but his arm came around my waist and pulled me into him. I gasped, my breath catching in my throat at the unexpected move.

His body was flush against mine. I could feel his chest pressed hard against my full breasts. His hips against mine. Legs twined over one another. His arms held onto me tightly, as mine involuntarily went to his biceps, steadying myself. I forced myself to ignore the firmness of his muscles. I looked up at him, and immediately regretted it. I could see nothing but ruination in the lightning flashing in his eyes—an ominous warning of what the future would hold should I not succeed.

"And it *will* come in time, this I promise. You could have everything at my side. No one can resist that type of allure for long." Cyrus whispered, wrapping me as tightly as he could within his hold. "You were meant for more than life as a toiling slave, Asteria. I knew it the moment I saw you."

His breath tickled my skin, and the hairs on my arms rose as his silken tone washed over me, as inappropriately intimate as his touch. "Do you want to know what I thought when I first laid eyes on you? I thought—this girl is a fallen star. Fallen to Adamah in a riot of destructive rage that burned out and left it stuck in a life that chained it down. Its shine smothered until only the smallest flicker remained. But I can feel it. That flicker? It *wants* to burn." The lightning in his eyes flashed once. "And I can't wait to see that happen."

His hands slid down my body, feeling my every curve and raising goose-bumps with his fingertips. "A star needs to rise, Asteria, my dear. And it's only a matter of time until you do. Then—" He smirked wickedly. "Then, I'm going to ruin you."

The smoky promise in his voice, the alluring words, were enough to make me sway toward him with want. I caught myself quickly—but not fast enough.

He saw the movement and the tremble of want that coursed through me.

Victory shone in his eyes.

I seethed at the lost ground in this battle we seemed to be waging against each other.

He may have won the battle, but he hadn't won the war. That would be *my* victory.

I would help him with the political side of things and learn how to play this game the royals knew and loved so much. I'd learn it, thrive in it, master it. And then, I would get what I wanted.

I would get what I *needed.*

Freedom.

Chapter 7

Time passed strangely here, and before I knew it, weeks had flown by. With Cyrus off dealing with the defenses along the border for his father, I was left adrift by the nothingness that comprised my current duties. As Cyrus's "assistant", I was essentially arm candy as far as the court was concerned. Cyrus wanted to use this to his advantage and position me to better assist him with his plans to ensure he keeps his crown, along with his life.

With that goal in mind, when Cyrus deems me ready, I'll be overseeing his other slaves, essentially handling his spies, and collecting information for him. Until then, however, the empty spaces left in my schedule after spending time studying to take on my duties, left me feeling a bit listless.

Slaves weren't supposed to have downtime, except at night. They worked all day, and that had been my expectation my whole life. As much as I appreciated not being forced more into a field or into the kitchens, I found myself not knowing how to handle the time I now had at my disposal. What was I supposed to do, lounge around all day?

Ugh. I knew this was going to be challenging the second I was assigned here, but this was a whole new caliber that I never could have anticipated prior to Placement Day. I knew so little about these court politics and games. If I anymore hope of surviving Cyrus or this court, I was going to need help.

Letting out a groan at my predicament, I decided I had to get out of these rooms. I'd been in here too long and needed to stretch my legs and find something, anything else, to look at. I'd go explore a bit, I decided. Cyrus had said I was welcome to, as long as I avoided certain areas, like the other royal quarters, and stayed mostly to the hidden passages when traveling to different parts of the palace.

I stood up from the chair, stretching out the kinks from sitting for so long, and made my way to the door. Once in the hall, I headed straight toward the entrance of the dank passageways that slithered through the palace. I hadn't seen Emmie in weeks, and figured a visit couldn't hurt. Whina may have warned me away from being friends, but information was clearly the currency of the court, and I knew Emmie would have been hoarding any bit of gossip she found. Maybe she'd give me something useful for my own plans.

The ache in my chest would have to shut up. Friends were not a luxury I could afford any more now than I could before.

Walking quickly down to the slave's corridors, holding up my skirts so I didn't trip, I made my way through the halls and down into the bowels of the palace. As I turned the final corner into the slave quarters, the starkness of our living situations was made abundantly clear.

Entering the common area for the slaves was a veritable contrast to the rooms I shared with Cyrus. The space was loud and crowded, with people running all over the place. I tried to find Emmie through the commotion, as I walked slowly across the edge of the room.

"What are *you* doing here?" A voice I didn't recognize demanded.

I snapped my head towards the voice, my dark hair swishing in front of my face with the motion. My eyes widened in surprise as I recognized the redheaded woman with amber eyes who shot daggers at me during the dinners we attended with the royal family.

Weylin's human.

She eyed me with obvious resentment over my position. She clearly wished to serve the heir to the throne herself.

"I'm looking for someone," I replied, taking note of her sneer, and dismissing it immediately. I kept my voice level and calm, and made an effort to not give into my rising anger over being targeted for something I had no control over.

"Oh really?" The redhead scoffed. "What someone would that be? I can't imagine anyone would want to be friends with some nobody from the sticks?"

"And how do you know where I come from?" I raised a brow at her.

She raked her amber eyes up and down my body in derision, causing me to bristle with fury.

"Prince Cyrus may have taken pity on you, but a little whore like you can only be dressed up so much. Your roots clearly show. You have no class and no education on courtly matters." She spat the nasty accusations at me while she threw her hair back over one shoulder, attempting to hurt me with words. Little did she know I had battled this front most of my life. "I don't know what the prince is doing with you, aside from the obvious, but you don't belong at court."

"Okay, first off: no one took pity on me." I laughed in her face, causing her uppity smile to drop. "I didn't want to be here—still don't." I continued coolly, rolling my shoulders back. Daring her to give me a reason, an excuse to let free the rage that had been bubbling inside me.

"*Yes*, I'm from a small village. And you know what? You remind me of all the little girls there who acted just like you; who felt so insignificant and unable to stand out that they used their jealousy to diminish others and make themselves feel better about who they are." Her eyes grew wide in indignation and impotent fury, as I kept going. Could I help the years of frustration pent up within me? I yearned to share every thought I had about these stupid, vapid bitches who continually occupied themselves with trying to put me in my place.

I'd had *enough*.

"I understand why Prince Cyrus wanted me, but it doesn't mean I'm fucking him. Unlike *you* and your prince." I continued with a sharp edge to my voice, simply because the red-headed woman was too furious to get a word in edgewise. "I may not be royally trained, but that's a trait that can be taught. I was educated in my village with the same curriculum as every other human across Celesterra. Just because I came from a small town doesn't mean I'm an idiot. I'm a fast learner, and I'm more than my looks. If that's all you're going off of to judge me before getting to know me, then shame on you. Don't let your jealousy eat you alive." The venom from years past unleashed itself onto this stranger, and I couldn't help but worry about the repercussions. I wasn't worried enough, however, to stop myself from making this bitch shut up as fast as possible.

The woman's face was now as red as her hair, her fists clenching as I stepped into her space, refusing to back down. I didn't do enough in my village to stand up for myself and look where that got me. If I didn't stop this now, she'd only get worse.

"And look, I get it, you're jealous of my position at Prince Cyrus's side, and you'd love nothing more than to be there in my place. You're jealous of my looks, my dresses, the ability to wander the castle while you work task after task." The red-head's eyebrows rose higher and higher as snickers from the other slaves surrounded us, but I *really* didn't give a damn. "I'm afraid that what you just don't realize is that I don't *care*. Your opinion means less than nothing to me." I finished with a cold glare, crossing my arms across my chest for good measure. Then I raised an eyebrow at her furious and petulant face.

"Well…what's going on here?" Emmie's chuckling voice intoned, and I spun my head toward her with a relieved smile. She looked between us and shook her head. "Let me guess, Aphra here let her jealous beast out of its cage?" I chuckled lightly as the woman, Aphra, glared at Emmie.

"Stay out of this. You're nothing but a lowly slave. You aren't the chosen companion of one of the royals, not like I am." Aphra smirked viciously at Emmie, but she just rolled her eyes, a hard glint in them.

"I'm in Princess Daneiris's service. I have no need to be her chosen companion, and I *certainly* don't need to spread my legs to rise higher than I deserve. Unlike some people. *Aphra*." Emmie's own lips tilted up in an almost smirk, paired with her raised brow, she looked more cunning than I'd given her credit for.

Emmie's blow hit Aphra where she intended. Aphra flushed, brows furrowing, before she huffed angrily and muttered. "Watch yourself, Emmie. One day, I'll be able to do something about you. And when that day comes, you better watch your back."

Aphra turned her glare on me before she finally flounced away. I watched her join a group of other girls all gathered around chatting. But I couldn't stop thinking about her words. She was Weylin's chosen companion. And she thought she'd be in a position to get rid of Emmie one day. Considering what had happened at dinner with Cyrus, Weylin and their parents, it seemed Aphra was well aware of Weylin's goals. Cyrus had been right about his brother. He wanted Cyrus's crown, and he was already working on taking it.

There could be an opportunity here, but I was distracted as Emmie laid a hand on my shoulder. I jumped, turning to her. Embarrassed, I realized she'd been trying to talk to me as I focused on court machinations. I smiled apologetically, but Emmie just returned my smile with a bright one.

"Are you alright? Aphra's one of the most entitled slaves I've ever met." She rolled her eyes as I laughed in agreement.

"That seems like an understatement." I laughed wryly. "I'm fine. Thanks for interrupting though." I laid a hand on Emmie's arm, hoping she understood my thanks were genuine. I was truly glad to get rid of Aphra, and now I had more information. I could find a way to use this to my advantage. I was certain the more I could provide Cyrus about his sibling's plots, the better my own position with him would be.

"Of course! I'm just happy to see you. Cyrus is keeping you busy, huh?" Emmie asked, offering a sympathetic smile, I cringed a bit at the assumption in that question.

"Only with trying to woo me." I replied, rolling my eyes, but I let out a laugh at her surprised expression.

"You mean—you haven't…" Her words trailed off as I nodded. Her eyes were as big as dinner plates with that information. "How?!" She hissed as she grabbed my arm and pulled me into a secluded area.

"He claims that he wants me to join him willingly. But I've explained to him that being owned by a person isn't really a turn on." I muttered, annoyed by the entire situation. "He doesn't understand that sleeping with a person that literally *owns you* is reprehensible to me, but he's also not forcing me. *Yet,* at least." The worry soaked through my tone. I knew I walked a precarious edge here. Crown Princes are used to getting what they want, not used to being told no, especially by a human slave.

"And who is this wonderful creature you've been hiding from me, Emmie?" The rough voice came from Emmie's right, and I turned to see an incredibly handsome man, especially considering he was a human, and I'd recently become rather used to looking at the perfection that was Fae beauty. His blond hair was darkened by the sun, just as his skin was tanned from working outside all day. Gray eyes locked on my blue ones, and I watched them rove over my form.

Emmie's laugh tinkled through the air as she spun to face the stranger. "Tav! Where have you been hiding yourself?!" She launched herself into his arms and he laughed loudly as he picked her up in a bear hug. I couldn't help the smile that came to my face watching them. I'd never had a friendship like that. Even with Soren, I kept a distance between us. Emmie must have just met this man since arriving here, yet she was already comfortable enough to hug him.

A part of me wondered what that said about me, but I quickly corrected myself. It made me smart. I knew better than to get attached. Emmie was just…well, she was helpful—and useful. That was all.

Emmie pulled back and smiled brightly, her blonde curls bouncing as she did. "Tav, this is Asteria." She turned her smile on me. "Asteria, this is Tavarius."

Tavarius looked at me and smiled widely. "It's a pleasure, Asteria. I don't know how I haven't seen you around before."

"My master prefers to keep me close, unfortunately." I smiled wryly, shrugging the words off.

"Shh. You can't speak that way about the Crown Prince!" Emmie hit my upper arm—hard. Her eyes had widened in alarm, but I brushed it off as I noticed Tavarius's eyebrows fly up his forehead.

"Prince Cyrus, huh?" He asked slowly, and his whole posture changed. His face turned serious as he stood straight. "Are you alright?" The sympathy on his face was gutting, and his words even more so. Why would he immediately jump to asking such questions? Unless—I shuddered, quickly wiping such mauldin thoughts from my mind.

"I'm fine. He's been…okay." I cringed at my own lackluster description, but it was the best I could offer. Cyrus was a subject I couldn't quite wrap my head around.

"Well, I'm glad for that at least." Tavarius smiled slightly, his brows smoothing. His words were quiet, but strong and honest.

"And where have you been?" Emmie asked Tavarius, as she hit his arm playfully. "I haven't seen you in over a week!"

"Aw, don't worry, girlie, I just had to go fetch some exotic ruby and sapphire roses her majesty insisted we must have in the garden." Tavarius chuckled, as he gazed at Emmie. "To compliment the roses from Pranvera, of course." He rolled his eyes skyward. "It's absurdly expensive to have them shipped in from Gemaria, even more so than the ones from Pranvera. The Elves and their crystal magic." He scoffed. "Less powerful than celestial, but you wouldn't know it with their attitude about it. How the royals waste their money on such things is beyond me." He shook his head with dismay clear in his eyes.

"You're a gardener then?" I tilted my head to the side as I inquired. He had the look of a man who worked outdoors, but I wouldn't have pictured a gardener. A stable hand, perhaps. But a gardener? It seemed too delicate a task for his rough hands and rugged physique. What did I know about gardening, though?

"I know, I don't much look the type for flowers, do I?" Tavarius shook as he laughed, then winked at me. "But as it turns out, I have the magic touch." I couldn't help the laugh that forced itself through my lips, Emmie's bubbly laughter ringing beside it.

"Now please tell me, Asteria, that you'll be around more? It'll certainly make me hurry back from any assignments." He winked again as I rolled my eyes at him. His blatant flirting was kind of adorable, I had to admit.

"You better be careful, Tav. You don't want to anger a crown prince!" Emmie's giggle was slightly forced. She tried to keep her face playful, but I could see genuine worry in her eyes.

"Don't worry about me, girlie. I can take care of myself." Tavarius bumped his shoulder into hers as he smiled down at her. He seemed all smiles, this one. It was infectious, being around someone who seemed so genuinely happy. "And if the lovely Asteria wants to be in my company, well, I won't refuse. The prince will have to learn to share." He wiggled his eyebrows up and down.

"You're bad." I shook my head, but I was smiling anyway, enjoying the more playful flirting. It was a welcome relief compared to the gross flirting and leers I'd been subjected to over the years.

"Oh, you have no idea, Asteria. But I'd love for you to find out." Tavarius leaned closer to me. "What do you say?" His tone dropped lower, and my core responded, helpless against the man's charm as it clenched hard against the nothingness inside.

It'd been so long since I'd had a release not coaxed by my own hand, and I was growing increasingly agitated by my lack of sex. Since I refused to give in to Cyrus, I was left being constantly teased into a state of arousal that made the situation more desperate. But Cyrus was a line I wasn't willing to cross, and while my moral half cheered for me standing strong, my immoral side booed loudly. I was learning to live with the duality.

Tavarius could certainly come in handy. He was ruggedly attractive, had an easy confidence that was appealing, and looked like he knew how to have a good time in bed. But was Emmie right? I considered what Cyrus would do if he found out, and a cold dread slithered down my spine. I already knew before I asked the question that yes, Cyrus would act against Tavarius, harshly at that. I sighed, my dejected eyes meeting his.

Tavarius seemed to read my thoughts, as he leaned down to kiss me on the cheek, just to the side of my lips. The placement reminded me too much of when Cyrus had done the same. My eyes fluttered closed briefly, but I opened them as he pulled back.

"If things change, you know where to find me." With a last wink at me and a goodbye to Emmie, Tavarius walked off, whistling jauntily as he did.

"Thank you." Emmie exhaled her relief. I arched an eyebrow in question, and she gave me a sad smile. "I know you were interested, but I also know what Prince Cyrus would do if you were to sleep with someone else. Tav is such a good man—" Her voice dropped to a whisper. "I hate to think of what the prince would do to him."

"It's better this way anyway." I told her, shivering at the bleak thought of what one mistake on my part could bring. "I shouldn't get close to anyone."

"What do you mean?" Emmie turned to me, confusion lining her brow. "Because of Prince Cyrus?"

"No, because of life." I chuckled wryly, shaking my head. "The Fae may be able to afford to have connections, but not us. Caring for people in this world is too dangerous." The thought made my heart feel strangely heavy in my chest, but it was the hard truth.

"You can't go through life without caring, Asteria." Emmie said softly, her hand landing on my shoulder. "Caring for people is what holds us to this world. It connects us and gives us roots. It's better to fill your life with happiness for as long as you have it, than to hold back and live a life full of loneliness and misery. That's not really living."

Her words were like a dagger, aimed straight at the heart of the little girl inside me who wanted nothing more than to fit in and belong. Her words reached that young girl who had hope, before she realized it was pointless and let her anger take over instead. The one who wanted friends and loved ones beyond her busy parents. The girl who was often alone until Soren approached her and became her friend. Even still, my bruised heart couldn't take letting someone in fully. Years went by, and still, I couldn't let go of the fear. Nor the knowledge that it was all temporary. Placement Day would come and take it all away. I'd been alone for so long, and I'd had a smidgen of hope that would change here, but that was quickly dashed.

I'd been alone this long, I could bury that little girl back down deep, and continue on. Rage was easier than loneliness, anyway.

I couldn't trust anyone in this pit of vipers. Certainly not Cyrus. Priscilla seemed genuine, but how could I trust her intentions? And while Emmie had proven to be friendly and useful, she told me never to trust anyone at court, including her. I couldn't see an ending for me that wasn't miserable. Despite being surrounded by as many people as I was now, mistrust of them all meant I felt nothing but isolation.

"I suppose we'll see." I forced a smile on my face before making my excuses to Emmie. I made my departure back to my rooms where I could be just as alone as this court made certain I felt.

Mulling over my thoughts as I walked back to my rooms gave me enough time to realize that I had been so far out of my depth since Placement Day, that I'd spent my time in the palace passively. I would never describe myself as passive, but somewhere along the way, I'd become so overwhelmed and unsure about everything, I'd let my fears rule me. Instead of fighting for myself and trying to ascertain how to make the best of my circumstances, I've been sitting back and trying to take in whatever information was offered on Cyrus and all the dynamics of the court.

Enough was enough.

Freedom wouldn't be possible without getting my hands dirty. That much I was sure of.

Cyrus was out. Where? Who knew, but he wasn't here, which was all I cared about.

It made snooping much easier.

I slunk out of my bedroom and into the common area, before heading straight to the room at the other end that I had yet to step foot in. I opened the door slowly, the wood creaking just slightly as I pushed it back. I stepped across the threshold into Cyrus's bedroom. I took a moment to look around and orient myself. A large four poster bed dominated the space, with a frame made of a deep black wood and each post crowned with a carved pegasus—its wings wide in flight. A rich, burgundy silk blanket covered the bed, while a gold rug covered the floor under the bed itself. Heavy velvet drapes in the same gold color lined the windows and two sofas upholstered with a dark burgundy brocade made up a sitting area by the fireplace.

I moved around the bed and went toward the corner where I spied an enormous black desk made of the same wood as the bed. I gently eased up the rolling top to begin searching the contents of Cyrus's desk but gleaned nothing important—only a few scattered pages detailing budgets.

I huffed and moved down to the drawers that lined the sides of the desk. The first drawer contained only standard office supplies, and I quickly moved to the next drawer, not bothering to search through the quills, ink pots, and blank pieces of parchment. I sorted through each drawer, riffling through the contents and looking for anything that would help me or give me any information.

When I hit the bottom drawer, I found a ton of files. I grinned widely as I took in my prize and started flipping through them. The first few were unhelpful for my needs—or so I thought. They were budgets for businesses, in addition to Cyrus's personal accounts. The first one stated it was for "The Den of Desire", which made me twitch reflexively with surprise. *A brothel?* My eyebrows rose to my hairline, assessing why he would own such a place. He certainly didn't need the money. Unless it was so he had full access to the girls? I snorted with disgust as I began flipping through once more.

The following pages contained the budgets for gambling houses. The 'Bad Beat Den' and 'The Get Down'. I couldn't believe it. The Crown Prince of Dusk owned and operated all sorts of businesses in the seedier underbelly of society. This was useful information to have for the future, but it wasn't exactly what I was looking for. I read through the rest of the files searching for something with a tangible use when I found a document that was worth all the time spent pilfering through Cyrus's files.

A list of his spies.

Or rather, his list of payments made to them. I read through the list of people he was paying off, Fae and human alike. I was right, he was employing lords, ladies, business owners, workers, and slaves. Most of them were employed at Dusk, a couple at Dawn, and one at Sunset, but that was it.

There was a missed opportunity if Prince Cyrus was actively fighting against the Night Kingdom, and he had no spies there. Even if it seemed impossible to get someone into the Night Kingdom, surely, he could hire one in the other surrounding kingdoms. Was the lack of spies in his network due to the difficulty of getting spies into Night, or was it due to his arrogance and assumptions that he didn't need spies there? Or perhaps he was more worried about his family and his enemies closer to home. Either way, I thought he was foolish for not hiring a spy or two for the Night Kingdom.

I read the list of names several times, trying to memorize them. Noting the many names with acronyms beside them that matched up with his brothel and gambling dens. Places where people let their guards down, drank to their heart's content, and then let their lips loose secrets that should have been kept. Then I carefully placed everything back exactly as I had found it. I stood to my feet and made my way to the bed, leaning over and feeling under the mattress. My grin was triumphant as I pulled out a thick brown leather book. I untied the closure and flipped it open. I quickly thumbed through the pages until I found something of note.

I stopped as I reached the more recent entries and found my own name staring back at me. Cyrus mentioned his "acquisition" of a new slave, one he wanted to possess fully. I felt like throwing up, but I forced myself to keep reading.

"She is willful and angry. And in truth, besides her beauty, her unyielding force is what draws me to her. I see the same rage in my own eyes when I look in the mirror. I must have her fully, but her willfulness will prove to be a problem, though not an insurmountable one. Ensuring she sees us as being on the same side will help for now to ensure her easy compliance. Her temper may prove a fun challenge, and I'll allow her to put up her little show of protest until the time comes. She is a human, after all, and her will is not equal to a Fae's. It will not take long to break her."

Reading his words made me want to burn this place to ashes. He thought he could manipulate me into siding with him? Well, the joke is on him, as I never believed the nonsense he tried to woo me with. It was just like a man to hear a woman say "no" and think he can manipulate his way around it. He thought me "willful", like a horse that needed to be broken in, but by the end, I would find a way to ensure that he was the broken one.

I closed the journal back up and put it back under the mattress where I found it. I looked around as I cracked Cyrus's door back open, hoping no one was there. I sighed with relief at the empty room and crept to Cyrus's second desk that resided in the solar. Bending down, I pulled out all of the files in the drawers. I moved over to the sofa and sat down, spreading them out on the table. It was a risk, but I was livid enough that I didn't even care.

I made my way through each file and when I saw the names on each one, I smiled. Weylin. Kian. Vikal. Daneiris. Twyla. Astraeus. Stelara. He had files on every member of his family. I opened the one on Weylin. Reading through the notes, I found observations on places he went, people he saw, things he purchased, plans he made.

My eyes lit up and my smile grew wider. A rush of energy thrummed through me as I read everything I could and rushed to put everything back in place before Cyrus walked through the door. If knowledge was power, Cyrus had unintentionally left me the key to mine.

CHAPTER 8

A COUPLE of weeks later, Cyrus informed me that he wanted me to see the city. In an effort to engender in me some attachment to Dusk, he wanted me to see more of the kingdom, starting with the capital. So today we'd be heading out into it and giving me the opportunity to explore. I knew he was just trying to find ways to convince me to give in to him, manipulating me by first trying to get me to fall for the city itself. His journal entry made that clear enough, only adding fire to my already burning instincts that told me not to trust the prince—pretty face be damned.

Regardless, he said he'd be back after lunch, so I took my time finishing up my tasks. Cyrus officially handed off the responsibility of overseeing his slaves to me, which included his spies. This put me in a perfect position, as it allowed me to gain information I wouldn't have otherwise. It also meant that everything he learned was filtered through me. I knew I must tread carefully, however. Gaining information was one thing, but I had to prove myself before I could start spinning reports from his spies. I didn't doubt he would be testing me, and I was sure there were spies I didn't know about, ones that he kept completely off his records. I was playing a dangerous game, one that could see me lost to the machinations of the court, but I was left with no choice thanks to Cyrus.

My mind was spinning, thinking of the meeting I just concluded with one of said spies, so I wasn't paying as much attention as I should have been when Emmie and I managed to crash into one another.

"Old Gods, Asteria! I'm so sorry! I wasn't paying attention, and—" Emmie began, babbling apologies.

"Emmie! I'm fine. It's fine." I chuckled, my eyes sweeping over her to ensure I hadn't bumped into her too hard. "I wasn't paying enough attention either. It happens."

Emmie sighed, relieved. Since I began carrying out my duty under Cyrus's command, I'd noticed the people who hadn't blinked twice at me before had quickly become more skittish around me. The personal slaves of the royal family were seen as being at the top of the human food chain around here, and I was now one of them. It was ridiculous. Even Emmie seemed to be afraid to displease me, as I was now considered an extension of Crown Prince Cyrus.

Emmie gave me a tentative smile, which made me hopeful that she could stop seeing everything through the lens of positions and politics as the Fae did.

"How are you doing? I haven't seen you around much. Cyrus must keep you busy." She giggled, her eyebrows rising, but her eyes told me she was putting on a show for those around us who were walking suspiciously slow down the hall as we spoke. She knew very well how I felt about the situation with Cyrus. Still, my eyes nearly popped out of my head at her insinuation.

"I—well, I'm—" I stammered out, trying to land on the right response. If it had been anyone except Emmie, I would have just glared them into submission, but she was the closest person I allowed to be anything like a friend.

The very last thing I wanted was the rest of the humans thinking I was just jumping into bed with Cyrus, the man who owned us. Then again… they didn't seem to care. The rest of the humans who were *actually* doing such things seemed to be eating their positions and their privileges up. I had no issue with people fucking whomever they want, as long as it was consensual.

But when it came to master and slave…well, the power dynamics left things feeling distinctly…vile.

"Old Gods, no, no! Not like that." Emmie giggled again at my fumbling response, but she reached out a hand and placed it on my forearm.

"Are you doing alright, Asteria? Really?" She asked as she looked into my eyes, and I couldn't help casting them down to the floor. Was I? Debatable. I knew I was being treated much better than most humans. I wasn't being forced into back breaking labor or mistreated. But I couldn't help the feeling that I'd yet to see the true Cyrus. I'd seen glimpses of something distinctly darker underneath the charming prince routine. I knew he was manipulative, but I was sure it went much deeper than that. The glimpses were so few that I couldn't get a handle on it, and it left me feeling off balance around him.

Despite how attractive he was, there was just something about him that sent warning bells off in my mind. I didn't want to test how far his patience and restraint would pull before they snapped. I was fairly certain that the other shoe would eventually drop, showing me what monster truly prowled beneath his skin.

Still, I forced a smile for Emmie's benefit. "I'm okay. How are you doing? Is Princess Daneiris treating you well?"

My eyebrows furrowed in worry. The only times I would see Princess Daneiris were at the nightly dinners the king and queen insisted on. She always seemed to be vapid and catty, but I'd also recognized there was an edge to her. One she tried to hide behind pretty smiles and dresses. She fostered an image that made her seem like nothing but a spoiled princess, one that made most overlook her as a true threat. But, unlike Cyrus, I was sure there was more going on beneath the surface.

Cyrus's files indicated that he didn't think his younger sister was anything to worry about in regard to his plans. According to him, she was flighty and temperamental, unable to be patient long enough to pull off any schemes of worth. She may indeed be all the things Cyrus said, but that didn't mean she couldn't be formidable, nonetheless.

Emmie's smile was broad and happy though. "She's wonderful! She makes sure we are all well taken care of. She doesn't take advantage or force us into anything that would make us uncomfortable."

"That's great." I replied, forcing a smile for her benefit. We chatted as we continued walking down the hall. I still didn't know Emmie that well really, but she was the only person I'd really been able to speak to in a casual manner. Plus, it was nice to have a familiar, and friendly, face beside me.

As we went our separate ways, parting with a squeeze of our hands and smiles, I ruminated on her description of Daneiris. It sounded like a completely different person than the one I saw at the nightly dinners, or even described in Cyrus's files. Emmie did spend more time with her though, so she might know better than me. Perhaps the princess was different around her family than others. With the family in question, I wouldn't exactly blame her.

Thinking again of the notes I'd found in Cyrus's files about her, I was left frustrated. Daneiris and Twyla had the least amount of intel available. While Cyrus kept a spy on each of his sisters, he didn't bother with more since he didn't consider them threatening. The list of places Daneiris went and what she was doing was far from comprehensive, riddled with holes in her schedule. I was debating the likelihood that the spy he had on her had flipped their loyalties. I couldn't think of many other logical explanations for the gaps in information, and Cyrus clearly didn't care enough about her to investigate. He was too narrowly focused on his brothers and the risk they posed.

I was determined to get to the bottom of what Daneiris was up to myself, and I would need to find a way to do so that wouldn't alert Cyrus.

It was better for me and my own goals to keep Cyrus ignorant. I would need to get another spy into Princess Daneiris's group. Someone discreet and not currently in Cyrus's network, that way both he and the spy he had on Daneiris wouldn't be aware of them. It wouldn't do to have the new spy discovered and ousted to anyone. I needed one who would work for me alone.

I walked into my rooms to find Priscilla already waiting for me. I gave her a distracted smile that she returned as I dropped into the vanity chair for her to begin getting me ready. "How are you doing today, Pris?"

The blonde groaned, her head falling back before shooting back up to look at me. "I'm exhausted, honestly. Princess Daneiris keeps me busy. And sharing me with Cyrus now means I'm stretched pretty thin."

I didn't realize she worked under Princess Daneiris. Thinking back to the plan I'd just been ruminating on, it felt like the stars had aligned for me. Priscilla was perfect for this. She was someone Princess Daneiris already knew and trusted, a person Cyrus wouldn't question going between us both—I couldn't think of anything better.

"I'm sorry." I sympathized, offering her a small smile. I wished none of us had to live these half-lives. My words felt so, so inadequate. Her life wasn't her own, and she was forced into spending this extra time with me, which pushed her to the point of exhaustion. I felt horrendous even thinking of planning to use her as a spy.

But I also didn't see many other options.

"Don't you dare blame yourself!" She sighed and narrowed her eyes at me. "You have as much control as I do." She rolled her eyes before going for her bag containing her supplies.

One side of my mouth tilted up despite myself. I liked Priscilla, as much as one could when your interactions were a result of forced circumstances. But the girl was down to Adamah and friendly, which was in short supply around here.

"That's true." I sighed heavily and Pris offered me a sympathetic smile in return as she began her work. Priscilla pulled pieces of my dark hair back and pinned them in strategic places with small pink jewels, while the rest was left to fall down my back. She used a special Fae brush designed with magic to add curls at the end of my hair. I looked with wonder at the jewels in my hair, and I couldn't help but feel like I shouldn't be wearing such grand things.

I clutched the necklace from my parents, which still felt over the top. I was learning to accept the gift purely because it was from them; the pink jewels, however, spoke of a female who was letting a male spoil her, and I wasn't. But I had no choice, even though I knew the impression the rest of the court, and the city, would get from me wearing Cyrus's jewels. I forced my discomfort down, trying to accept that this was my new reality.

"Where is the prince taking you today?" Priscilla asked, finishing my hair, and switching focus to my face.

"I'm not really sure, honestly." I shrugged lightly. "He wants me to see the city, apparently. And all its many wonders." I finished dryly and she laughed in return.

"There's a lot of fun to be had out there, if you'll allow yourself to enjoy it." She nudged me with a smirk. I raised a brow at her, and she faux glared at me for interrupting her work.

"What do you mean if I allow myself?" I couldn't help asking.

"Asteria, you are bound and determined not to enjoy life." Priscilla paused and gave me a knowing look. "You're all tied up in knots about our place in this world. If you accepted it, allowed yourself to enjoy what good you *can* have…you may have a better life than you'd expected. That's all." She smiled kindly to soften the blow of her words.

I reflected on them as she continued her work, but I didn't understand how so many could just accept the fate we'd all been handed. How did they not rage inside at the injustice of it all? Could I really just forget and let myself be spoiled by a handsome prince? Was I capable of letting myself enjoy my time here? To let life be something easy and simple, not a constant struggle.

It sounded nice, I would admit. But it also sounded like a fairytale. And the Fae adored their tales of fated love and extraordinary happiness—they were entitled to living them after all, unlike myself. So many of those fairytales filled the library here, I knew I would never run out of options to read at night as I tried to escape my overactive thoughts. Where once I sought out Soren to quiet my raging mind, now I had books. I knew those tales of love were never going to be a reality for me, but the books could capture my imagination and let me dream of a different life.

I knew I could have Cyrus if I wanted. He wasn't promising me love and happiness however, and we both knew it. He promised an arrangement where I would be his enslaved mistress. And I had more respect for myself than letting that be my life.

A part of me was jealous of those who could accept the life handed to us. I envied those who coasted through life with an ease and content I couldn't muster. That wasn't who I was, and I could only be true to myself. I had no control over so many aspects of my own life, but I could control this. My time and labor might belong to my master, but I would control my own damn body and who was given the privilege of touching it.

That didn't mean I couldn't find joy in my life, like Priscilla said. I could enjoy this outing to the city and let myself have fun. Perhaps it would help get Cyrus where I wanted him. I needed him to be trusting of me, for him to want me, but he also needed to accept the fact that he didn't have me. It would allow me to use his power for myself, without forfeiting my own to him. I would continue learning everything I could about the politics here, and I would wield that information to benefit myself.

I just had to figure out how. But I knew, just *knew*, like a promise that lived in my blood, that I would find a way. I wouldn't allow for any other outcome.

"Priscilla—" I dared to begin. "How do you feel about working for Princess Daneiris? Is she good to you?" I looked up at her in the mirror and saw she had frozen.

Her eyes shot to me, skittering and nervous, her lashes fluttering. She cleared her throat. "Why would you ask that?"

"You know I'm not happy here." I stated plainly, and she nodded slowly, brow furrowing. "I need information. Some way to arm myself against Cyrus."

"And what does information on Princess Daneiris give you against him?" Priscilla's head tilted to the side.

"More than you know." I smiled wryly.

"I have no love for any of the royals, Asteria." Priscilla's lips slowly turned up. "I'll help you however I can."

"Really? That easy?" I blinked with surprise.

Priscilla laughed, but there was no humor in it. She rolled up her right sleeve. "Do you see this?"

I nodded as I saw the scar she referred to. It was long and thick, across her forearm, like—like a lash…

Old Gods.

"Princess Daneiris herself did that." Priscilla nodded gravely. "All because I didn't curl her hair the way she envisioned it."

My mouth dropped open in shock at the blatant cruelty over something so insignificant. I wanted to throw up knowing she'd been whipped across the arm for something so minor.

It was a terrible price for such a tiny mistake.

Priscilla looked at me, tears forming in her eyes that she quickly dashed away.

"I'm so sorry, Priscilla." I replied, grabbing her hand and squeezing it. "You didn't deserve such a thing. It's horrendous what they do." My anger spiked rapidly, but I calmed myself. Anger wasn't what she needed right now.

"None of us deserve any of this." She squeezed my hand back. "Can you believe I was actually excited to come here?" She laughed wryly, and the sound of it, it was…hurt. Broken. "I grew up in Sunset, in the far reaches of the jungle. The Fae there were pretty lax as far as I could tell, but I wanted to explore cities and castles. Then I came here, and it was nothing like I had imagined. Be careful what you wish for, right?"

Her words struck me. They were exactly my thoughts upon being placed in Dusk. I once wished to be surrounded by the magic of Night, my love of the stars making it seem like a dream. I'd thought Dusk might be my closest alternative, but now I wished I'd been placed *anywhere* else.

"We need to find a way, Priscilla," I swallowed hard. "To get out and away from these Fae."

"Do you really think that's possible? Really?" Priscilla's eyes lit up even as her face crumpled in skepticism. "They have every advantage over us, and all the resources." She shook her head with resignation. "It's impossible."

"Give me time. Help me." I replied, shaking my head. My eyes widened as I pleaded with her. "Cyrus has me in charge of his spies, Pris. I can use that to our advantage. I think Princess Daneiris is up to something. I just need information. The more we can gather, the better our chances when an opportunity arises. We just need to be prepared."

Priscilla looked at me for a beat that seemed to last forever. I wish I knew what was running through her head. But the ice casing around my heart cracked a bit and I…*trusted her*. Priscilla and I had been through a lot of the same experiences, and to let her slip into that crack in my heart was a relief. It felt good to open up my heart a little—but I couldn't let it open any wider;

neither of us could afford truly open hearts, no matter how much we desired it. Not when it would end with our hearts bleeding on the floor.

Priscilla closed her eyes briefly in thought. As she reopened them, I saw the resolve and the hope filling her brown orbs.

"Let's do this then." She smiled viciously, and I let my own vicious smile curl my lips. We could do this. We *would* do this, and we would be free.

Priscilla quickly finished getting me ready as we discussed some particulars about her spying and our end goal. She grabbed a day dress for today's outing, much simpler than the lavish gowns Cyrus made me wear to formal events. As Priscilla helped me into it, the dress fell softly to the floor in a slink of light pink silk, perfectly matching the jewels in my hair.

I admired myself in the mirror once it was on. It hugged my body in all the right places and left the tiniest pool of silk behind me on the floor. The charcoal gray beading across the chest highlighted my ample breasts but wasn't scandalous by any means. The beading was shaped like an hourglass across the chest, centering down the middle and avoiding the sides entirely, then expanded out once more to dance across my hips. The sleeves were made of fine, transparent fabric with an illusion of beading transferred onto my skin, covering from my shoulders to my wrists.

"You look gorgeous, my Asteria." I heard the prince's appreciative tone coming from the doorway and turned immediately.

"I'm not yours." I raised an eyebrow at Cyrus, who was standing in the doorway of my room.

He smirked and prowled closer, his eyes raking over every inch of me, leaving my skin feeling like lightning skated across it. "Maybe not quite in the way I want yet, but you are mine nonetheless."

I ground my teeth at the truth of that statement and saw the glee in his eyes at my response. I glared at him. "Are we leaving or what?"

I could see Priscilla's mouth drop open at the tone I'd taken with the crown prince, but I didn't care. Cyrus wouldn't punish me for it, not when he wanted me to give in to him of my own volition. I could afford to let a tiny bit of my true feelings shine through.

"Yes, we are, my dear." He held out his arm and I reluctantly took it, but it only lasted until the doorway of his rooms. He couldn't be seen to be treating a slave so well, of course. I had to act subservient in public. He could talk to me, but showing affection would be unacceptable. Even the slaves who slept with their masters weren't shown any measure of affection by them in public. To do so would leave the Fae in question ostracized from their peers.

When we reached the large dark gray carriage, I only had a moment to marvel over the scrollwork surrounding it before I was helped in by the footman. Cyrus followed me as I stepped into the impressively large space and sat down on a velvet cushion; Cyrus taking a seat across from me on the other bench. I was jolted as the carriage began moving, four black horses leading it into the city.

"I've never been in a carriage before." I looked around in surprise at how luxurious a mode of transport could be made to be.

I'd only ever been in wagons, and this was much nicer than those. The velvet bench seats were a dusty violet color, while the walls were covered with a swath of dark gray that was covered in silver scrollwork. There were windows lining the sides covered by small curtains in a similar dusty violet color as the seating, with ties ending in silver tassels hanging next to them to secure the curtains back.

"You'll adjust to this life soon enough." Cyrus promised me from where he watched with pleasure at my reaction.

I moved the curtain covering the window and tied it back so I could look out at the city as we passed. Cyrus began chattering away about the capital, but I was preoccupied with watching the faces of Evenfall's citizens as we moved along the road, observing all the different kinds of people who made up this kingdom. Everyone moved aside for the royal carriage coming through. The Fae walking around the city bowed their heads with smiles on their faces. But it was the looks of fear on the faces of every human slave we rolled by that struck me.

There was true terror upon seeing the carriage. They dropped to their knees and bowed their heads to the ground. I looked to Cyrus, who saw nothing wrong with this. I shook my head and looked back out the window until the carriage finally came to a stop, worrying about what the humans here had been experiencing to cause such a visceral reaction at the mere sight of the royal carriage.

I stepped out first, as the royals were always last to disembark. I could feel all the eyes on me. The human dressed and paraded around like a Fae. Angry, or jealous, or both, eyes of humans and Fae alike devoured me as Cyrus stepped out and motioned us forward.

I met the eyes of a glaring woman with light brown hair. Green eyes barreled into me as she snarled. I blinked in surprise and turned to Cyrus when his laughter registered. He leaned down into my ear. "Don't worry about her. She's just angry she no longer graces my bed. She resents your place."

"But I'm not gracing your bed." I shook my head in confusion.

"Everyone thinks you are, though." He shrugged carelessly. "Why would you refuse me, after all?" He winked as I glared and huffed before facing the street instead. I didn't want people to think I was sleeping with Cyrus. Not because I was ashamed of my sex life, but because I didn't want to sleep with any Fae, nor did I want people thinking I would ever accept Cyrus's proposal for such. Cyrus would never understand my position as he could never comprehend the debasing of a person's spirit, of what it meant to be owned and denied freedom.

Cyrus led me down the street, showing me buildings and sites he thought important. It was all very boring. He took me to the center of Evenfall where it seemed to be bustling with people going every which way. The art installation in front of me was…*fine?* Cyrus seemed very proud of it as he espoused on its details. It was all metal and rigid. No color. No softness. No wonder or magic. It was fairly disappointing when compared to my imaginings of what a Fae city was like.

I tried to pay attention anyway, until a scream caught my attention. I whipped around just as Cyrus rolled his eyes and turned, only for a blaring sound to ring out across the city. Cyrus's eyes widened as he turned to me. People began running and screaming, heading for any building they could find to get inside. I saw a Fae pull back one screaming human, a whip cracking against their lower back as they fell down, only for the Fae to step right over them as they shouted demands.

"What is happening?!" I turned to Cyrus, my own eyes wide with dread and sick with what I'd just witnessed. He swallowed hard as he looked at me, worry actually lining his arrogant eyes for once.

"The siren means an attack. Calix must be here." He looked down at me as his guards surrounded us, weapons out. "Come. We must get back. Now!" He grabbed my arm and I had to run to keep up with his pace, holding my dress up with the hand not occupied with being dragged along by the crown prince.

The guards around us seemed to stiffen and I felt the air change as a yell reached my ears. I froze as Cyrus came to a stop, pulling his sword out. I looked past the wall of guards to see a group of men descending on us.

"Run, Asteria!" Cyrus yelled. "Run to the carriage!"

I whipped my head around to gain my bearings, recognizing where we arrived. But I was still so far away from the carriage. One of the attackers finally reached the guards, swords and magic working together, they dropped the guard almost instantly, I screamed and ran as fast as I could toward the carriage. I could hear the clash of blades behind me, screams and cries ringing out around the city as the men of the Night Kingdom descended on us.

How did they make it to the city proper? Shouldn't they have been stopped at the gates? Cyrus arranged all those defenses. Except—my heart sank. He'd mentioned making sure his brother would fail to hold them back. Was this the result? Did he really sacrifice his own people to show up his brother? The thought enraged me as I ran. Did he know it would be today? Is that why he pulled me into the city—or was that coincidence? I shook my head clear and focused on running and dodging.

Fae from the Dusk Kingdom surged past me as soldiers of the Night Kingdom came around the corner. I flew to the side and down an alley, running down it and around, hoping to loop back to the road with the carriage. I panted as I ran down the next alley, forming a U shape that would lead me back to the main road and rushed forward as I sighted the carriage in the distance. Its looming gray shape looked distinctly unsafe as the world around me grew darker before I could leave the alley. Like night was descending in the middle of the day. *Magic.* It must be. A part of me rejoiced to be touching Night Kingdom's magic for the first time, but I forced that part of me down deep.

When I looked back up, I gasped and came to a dead stop. Before me was the most indescribably gorgeous man I'd ever seen in my life. People had called me beautiful as long as I could remember, but I felt like nothing more than a hag compared to this man.

Long silvery white hair, with only a small braid on each side keeping it from falling into his face. And what a face it was. Unusual purple eyes, the likes of which I'd never seen before, with sharp cheekbones leading down to full lips. He was tall and lean, packed with muscles. Even through his armor, I could distinguish the shape of his body. His shoulders were so wide, even unencumbered with the metal plate that could make armor so bulky and heavy. Instead, his was made of pitch-black scales, patterned with purple accents. As I gazed upon his armor, my attention was taken by the sigil in the center of the moon and stars bracketed by wings. It was then I truly registered that I was standing before a soldier from the Night Kingdom.

I suddenly realized I had been frozen as I stared at him. But as I met his eyes, I noticed he was studying me just as intently as I had been eyeing him. And we were both frozen as we observed each other. A strange feeling ran up my spine and burst through my body, like bright stars filled my blood as smooth darkness danced over my skin. I found myself wanting to step closer.

Sounds of battle rang in my ears, as I discovered I'd been lost in the haze of this man. I had the good sense to let fear seep back in as I noticed the huge sword in his hand. He was Fae, with clearly strong magic, and I was completely defenseless. I cursed myself for not carrying the iron dagger my father gave me, but I was ultimately too scared of it being discovered and kept it hidden deep in my room. I backed up a step, and a smirk slowly formed on this beautiful warrior's face. My ire rose right along with it. I did not appreciate being mocked, especially as I was about to be killed.

Great, another rude asshole.

The gravity of the situation hit me as he took a step closer to me. I backed up another, but he followed right along, like a rope connected us and we couldn't get any farther than six feet away from one another. These Night Kingdom soldiers killed humans like me, and here I was alone, defenseless, and attired in a ridiculously fancy dress that offered me no range of movement to try to escape.

The warrior's strange purple eyes seemed to light up as he watched me. A breath caught in my chest at the sight of them, despite myself. And I was furious with myself for it. Feeling even the slightest attraction towards Cyrus was bad enough, but a Fae from the Night Kingdom?

I had some serious problems I needed to sort through if and when I got back to safety.

I moved my left foot backwards, ready to step away, only to see his right foot ready to mirror my movement. There was no hope of outrunning him— especially in this ridiculous dress. The curious light in his eyes, paired with that devious smirk, stopped my foot where it was. I held firm. I wasn't going to give another inch to this bastard. I may be weak compared to a Fae, but I was no wilting flower. I wasn't going to cower when I faced my death.

And what a dazzling death he was.

I raised my chin, narrowing my eyes at the man before me. His smirk only grew as he continued walking. I watched each step with dread as they brought him closer to me. And a small, teensy tiny bit of excitement to see this beautiful specimen so close rose in my chest. His interest in me thrilled some instinctual part of me. No matter what my brain told me that this was a predator in every sense of the word, and I was his prey. Even knowing that, a part of me didn't care, it just wanted to be closer. Every step he took that closed the gap between us thrilled me.

I chastised myself. These sexy Fae men were nothing but trouble. And this one came from a brutal, bloodthirsty kingdom. One where humans weren't even good enough to be cattle. I should be expecting death—and I was, but I was also too busy drooling to act on my fear. I cursed myself, only to need to steel myself a moment later as he stepped into my personal space. His sword was covered in blood, and his equally bloody fingers flexed around the hilt as he stepped right up to me. I couldn't help but take it as a warning. This mysterious soldier let out a curious hum, causing shivers to erupt over my body.

"I saw you flee from where that coward this kingdom calls a prince was attempting to make himself useful." His voice was a deep rumble, laced with darkness and death. Dreams and nightmares. He raised his empty hand and used a finger to tilt my chin up further, and those strange eyes bored into mine. "I'd heard rumors—"

The bewitching soldier raised an eyebrow at me, intrigue lining his face as he looked me over. "They say Cyrus has a new human. One he's obsessed with. That must be you."

"What about it?" I snarled at him, but he merely smirked down at me in response. I looked around for an escape but found nothing useful. The alley I was in became abandoned as the fighting took over the city. I could only see blood staining the ground and bodies laid out up and down the narrow space. The brick of the building behind me was rough against my hand as I dug my nails into it, trying to bank my anger and be smart about this.

But my eyes caught on a shining metal at his belt at that moment. I deliberated quickly and decided subduing my anger was a fool's task anyway. I reached forward quickly, sliding the dagger out of its sheath and bringing its tip up under his chin before he could stop me. His eyes lit up at the challenge, and my own blazed like fire up at him.

"What do you want?" I demanded, raising my brow at him. It felt good holding this dagger. Even better holding it to a Fae's neck. Years of pent-up rage bubbled within me.

"*Oh*, I can see why Cyrus decided to keep you." He crooned at me, somehow both mocking and sincere at once.

"Because I can stab a foolish Fae who should have stayed in his own kingdom?" I spat at him, then snorted with dry humor.

He barked a rough laugh at that. "I don't see any stab wounds, do you?"

His head tilted the slightest bit down to look over himself and dug the dagger into his skin in the process.

My eyes widened. He was insane.

"I could kill you. I should kill you." My voice hardened as anger overtook me once more. "You're here to kill my people after all. You're nothing but a monster, and this world would be much better off without you."

He seemed to sense that my sanity was at its limit before I'd tip over the edge. As an insane person, he must be quite familiar with that.

"I'm a monster?" He whispered in a voice that made too many promises.

I shivered, trying to fight my reaction. Fae were charming, alluring, and seductive. And this Fae had a voice made for sex that had my toes curling, even while he promised violence.

"How do you know, when you don't recognize the monsters you're surrounded by? You see lambs where you should see lions. And make lions of those who assist the sheep."

I scoffed, realizing he'd inched closer somehow. His body now skimming mine. I pressed myself hard against the brick wall, letting its rough bite ground me to Adamah. "All Fae are monsters, but at least humans get to *live* here!"

His head tilted to the side. His eyes swept over me again, but this time it wasn't seductive, it was appraising. I ground my teeth in frustration. "Do you *honestly* call this a life?"

His words chilled the damn blood in my veins, it hit that deep. *No.* This *wasn't* a life. Not really. Living a real life would require freedom, with the ability to make your own choices. A life where you could decide where you lived, what you wore, and whom you spoke to. Nothing here was my choice. I was living suspended in time. Continuing on with every heartbeat, but that heart was encased in ice that grew thicker every day.

"Do you like it here? With Cyrus?" Colors began to swirl in his eyes as they looked me over. His hand came up and took my chin, his fingers feeling like the soothing caress of night against my skin. I tried to ignore the heat he sparked in me in his wake.

"What's it to you?" I demanded, trying to keep my composure and not expose the reactions this man caused in me. Letting my anger speak was easier. I was used to that. I wasn't used to this. *To him.* He hummed again, letting go of my chin.

"Do you enjoy being his property? Being his whore?" His voice was soft as silk, but harsh as a blade.

"Excuse me?! I am no whore!" I jerked back at his words, my head nearly colliding with the brick wall. "And *no*! Obviously, I don't want to be anyone's property! But thanks to Fae like you—"

I pushed the dagger into his skin, watching a bead of blood trickle from it, while poking a finger into the center of his armor, hitting the Night Kingdom's sigil. It probably hurt my damn finger more than anything, but I wouldn't regret it.

"And who the hell are you to come here, invade these lands, kill people, and then accuse me of whoring myself out to the man who owns me. *Fuck. You.*" I spat my words at him with all the venom I wanted to aim at the Fae who enslaved us.

Even Cyrus. *Especially Cyrus.* Because this warrior knew exactly what Cyrus wanted with me, but I wasn't going to let him know how much I dreaded that idea. And I couldn't let my rage out at Cyrus. Not with a proverbial leash from him to me. But this man—this was someone I could rage at all I wanted, because he was nothing but a Fae enemy—a fact that remained true with all his kind. I was delighted for the chance to unleash myself on him, no matter what my traitorous body seemed to want.

His eyes widened, incredulity filling them. "Fuck *me*? Do you have any idea *who* you're speaking to? You do not want to place that rage I can see in your eyes on me. I am not an enemy you want to have. I can help you, in fact."

His voice slipped from anger to seduction in the blink of an eye. I rolled my eyes at him, there was no way I was going to believe that. The only thing the Night Kingdom helped humans with was an early death.

"Help me? I wouldn't want you to help me. The last thing I need is *more* Fae. All I'd be doing is trading one cage for another. And you, you are a soldier of the Night Kingdom. Invading the Dusk Kingdom to slaughter humans for your own sick amusement! You are the definition of a monster!"

I raged at him, trying to push him away from me, but failing in moving him a damn inch.

"A monster I may be but look at who holds your leash." Something sparked in his eyes, but I didn't have time to figure out what it was as his hands locked around my biceps and held me to the wall. He leaned in, his cheek caressing mine as he whispered. "I will never be *that* kind of monster. Bloodshed is easy. The war you're fighting, however, I wish you all the best. When you're ready, you know where to come." He winked and spun, his sword slashing into the stomach of a Dusk Kingdom soldier.

I gasped raggedly. I hadn't seen them approach at all. I had been completely absorbed in this stranger—who used his sword like it was an extension of his arm. He hacked and slashed at the soldiers of this kingdom. My… kingdom. I tested the words in my mind, but it still didn't feel right to call it that. I thought of the words of the soldier in front of me. My hand went to my mouth as it dropped in awe. Wonder and terror swirled as I watched him. He was poetry in motion with a blade in hand. His blade sang a love song to bloodshed with every swing, and though his movement across the alley was full of blood and death, it was a beautiful dance of violence all the same. He moved with grace, more so than I'd seen in any other warrior.

But as the footsteps of many more Dusk Kingdom soldiers came our way, darkness descended once more. It seeped out of this beautiful monster as I stood in shock. The darkness crawled across the grounds towards the approaching soldiers. He ran his sword through the gut of another Fae. Then he looked back at me. Our eyes locked. And he raised a hand. He brought his fingers down slowly, forming a fist. And as he did, the darkness reached out and grabbed all the soldiers by their necks, cracking them.

I gasped in horror as they all fell to the ground. Wide, blank eyes unseeing. Dead.

They may have been Fae bastards, but I didn't wish them dead.

I snapped my head around and looked at this Fae. He was staring at me with a heavy gaze, before he slowly smirked. He bowed down to me, making a mockery of it.

"Until we meet again. Let that rage flow where it's earned." With a parting look, the gorgeous soldier disappeared into the darkness.

I stood there, stupefied, for far too long. He didn't kill me. Shock was too tame an emotion for what I felt. Was the Night Kingdom not as bad as people claimed? They were attacking, which didn't lend any sort of credence to that theory.

But—but he—he didn't take me against my will, didn't kill me. He tried to convince me Cyrus was a monster, which I already knew, even if I refused to concede the point to him. But I just saw him crack the necks of a bunch of innocent soldiers. As innocent as Fae could be anyway. There was no way that man wasn't just as much a monster as Cyrus, if not more. After all, he served under King Calix, the man who hunted down and killed humans.

I swung my gaze along the street, but all I could see now was Night Kingdom warriors in their black armor, leaving. Like a wave, they disappeared as quickly as they'd come.

Cyrus appeared from further down the road, running towards me with lightning crackling at his fingertips. When he made it to me, I was still in a daze over what had happened, trying to furiously get my mind in order. He reached for me, but I flinched back. His lightning magic was still crackling around his fingers, and I didn't feel like being struck. Even so, Cyrus's eyes hardened, and his jaw ground back and forth.

The lightning intensified, and when I looked into his eyes, they were similarly flashing with sparks. I withered a bit despite myself. I prided myself on staying strong, on being able to stand my ground, but this was different. This was powerful, royal, Fae magic at use.

I had no idea what that lightning would do to my regrettably weaker human body. Would it kill me? Stop my heart?

I watched as Cyrus took a deep breath, closing his eyes. When he opened them after a few beats, the lightning was gone, and I relaxed a fraction.

Until his wings unfurled.

I jolted. One moment, Cyrus was standing before me, in his normal man-shaped form, for all his Fae features anyway. The next, giant dark pink feathered wings had sprouted out of his back. I ran my eyes along them. They were—Old Gods, I hated to admit it, but they were amazing.

I didn't have much time to appreciate them though. I hadn't thought of why he'd summoned his wings. But as Cyrus quickly took me into his arms, and I felt my feet leave the ground, I regretted not thinking that through.

I gasped and squealed in terror, somehow managing both at the same time. An impressive feat. But Cyrus didn't seem to appreciate it.

"Quiet." He snapped at me.

I closed my mouth to avoid snapping back at him and then closed my eyes against the wind as he flew us quickly back to the palace. When I opened them, I pushed the shock of the unexpected flight out of my mind to appreciate what was actually happening.

I was flying!

A huge smile took over my face at this simple fact. All my life, I wanted to feel the freedom of the sky. I sighed deeply and looked up into the sun. It shined down on me in a soft caress against my skin. It felt closer than ever before as I dared reach a hand up towards it. Like I could caress it back in turn.

It wasn't perfect, since it wasn't *me* flying. It was just the closest I would ever get. That feeling though, the one I sometimes got where I felt like my skin was too tight, too small—it felt worse than ever at this moment. Maybe because I wanted to crawl out of my skin, spread my own wings, and fly.

Ridiculous. But I couldn't help the feeling.

I looked up with reverence at the sun, thanking Hyperion, the Fae's god of the sun, for this gift. The Old Gods weren't responsible for this one. It was still too far away, of course. But I hoped he felt my genuine appreciation at being this close.

CHAPTER 9

I REACHED for the stars. My fingertips brushed against the twinkling light, straining to get closer, but it was no use. I brushed against it, but that was as far as my reach allowed. I frowned in consternation. Why couldn't I reach them? What was keeping them from me?

The sky rumbled around me, and I blinked with shock. I'd never seen it do that before. Before I knew it, the sky seemed to try to touch me back, but it hit a barrier. I reached out once more, attempting to touch. I flinched as I swore I felt another's fingers reach back for me.

I looked down and gasped—my hand looked like the stars themselves, bright, shining light emanating from me. I looked up again, seeing tendrils reaching for me, the darkness of night itself shaping itself into a hand. I forced my shock away to try to focus on what was happening and how it was even possible.

My fingers and the night sky's reached for one another, but right when I thought we'd touch, our embrace was halted. I yearned for its touch, to discover what was happening. Why was the darkness trying to reach me? What kept us apart? Whatever this barrier was, it was solid. Unmovable.

I let out a cry of frustration and the sky roared in response. I swore I could somehow feel its own frustration and desperation in that moment, shaking me to my core. I could sense it, like the darkness's emotions beat in my own heart. It wanted to touch me, more than anything, to wrap itself around me and hold me close. But something stopped it.

I was sure this wasn't the first time I'd experienced the sky's agony. I recognized this scene as one I'd dreamt of often. Only, I was the one always trying to reach the stars—and I'd never come so close to touching them as I did tonight. And somehow, that proximity let me take on the light of the stars themselves.

Something had changed.

And if this was the same dream, had the night sky been trying to reach me all this time, unable to connect with me over the years I dreamt? How in the Otherworld did the darkness of the night sky have *feelings*?

I gasped as the absurd thought woke me up. I knew I was dreaming this time. I'd never once experienced a dream where I'd actually recognized it as such. Why was this dream so different?

I shook my head. These were absurd thoughts to have. The night sky didn't have feelings, and it wasn't trying to reach me. And I certainly didn't have hands made of light. Only the rare Fae who could command light itself could claim such things, and they always wielded sunlight, not starlight.

My dreams always found me in the freedom offered by the sky, and this was no different. I'd often join the stars among the darkness and dance. But the darkness never touched me even as I twirled within it. Instead, the moon would dance with me. It would unfurl from its balled up sleeping form and stretch out, revealing a dragon that lived and breathed. The sun was the same during the times I dreamed of daylight. The two dragons often kept me company in my dreams. An old fable making its way into my subconscious, clearly.

Luna, the Moon Dragon, short for Lunathaire, was playful and fun. She'd dance around with me, her glowing scales brushing against my fingers. The Sun Dragon, Zhulong, or Zhu as I called him, would tease me with his tail. He'd whip that tail at me, but only a teasing brush along my skin would connect. I felt more at home in those moments than anywhere in my waking life.

I'd played with them in my dreams for as long as I could remember. I was too often all alone as a child and my dreams gave me solace and friends to play with. I'd always struggled with making friends, even before I grew ice around my heart to protect it. Before the girl's jealousy turned into tormenting me.

I often felt peculiar as a child, like a stranger in my own skin, I constantly felt like it was too tight for my body, and I didn't belong. Not to mention, I'd frequently look to my side, like I expected someone to be there with me, only to discover I was as alone as always. Why I seemed to expect someone, I had no idea. But those things set me apart and made it hard to become friends with other children.

As a result, I would often make up stories in my head to pass the time, even while I was awake. I'd play out grand adventures, where the heroine was free and able to fight and fly. Where she could do whatever she wanted. It gave me a way to escape my reality and take me to a place where that kind of freedom was a sweet dream.

I sighed as I fought off my blankets that had somehow twisted up around my legs in my sleep. Strange dreams or not, I had to prepare myself for today. Cyrus had barely said a handful of words to me after the attack yesterday. Beyond snapping at me, he'd dropped me in my room and commanded me to stay—like a dog. He was gone the rest of the day, but I had to hope his order didn't remain in place for today.

I knew he was angry about the Night Kingdom's attack, but I was more confused than anything. After my run in with that soldier, I wasn't sure what to think. The soldier was too much—of everything. Too alluring, too dangerous, and too intoxicating. When he had me up against the wall, half of me yearned to press closer, while my mind told me to run as far away as possible. The echo of his words, claiming that he wasn't the real monster, only confused me more. How could that be possible when he was capturing and killing humans?

The attack on the Dusk Kingdom proved they were indeed randomly attacking other kingdoms. So, I supposed there was only one real question to answer. *Why?* I kicked myself for not asking when I had the chance.

I knew deep in my bones that I was missing a key clue to this mystery. Not everything was as it seemed, and I could feel the increasing tension that filled the air around me, like the land itself was revolting against something…a fanciful notion, really. But I knew there had to be a deeper reason behind these attacks. There must be. I refused to believe the Night Kingdom had orders to randomly slaughter all those in sight. However it seemed from the outside, the words the Fae soldier spoke certainly didn't make it seem like that was the case.

I was only shaken out of my contemplation when Priscilla came to prepare me for the day. We made small talk as she worked, and our time together was just as enjoyable as always. I rarely got to speak with others outside of Cyrus and Priscilla on a day-to-day basis, the only exception being Emmie, and even more rarely Eris, in the hallways as we passed one another. And now I had another reason to be happy to see Priscilla.

"How did Princess Daneiris react to the attack?" I inquired, leaning my chin on my hand as I looked at her through the mirror.

"Her ladies were all tittering about it when I got her ready." Priscilla looked at my reflection and smiled wryly. "The princess, however, looked more contemplative. She responded to one of her lady's inane comments by saying that her brothers were clearly inept and unable to defend their kingdom." She paused for effect. "Treasonous words."

We shared a smirk.

"Did she happen to mention what she wanted to do?" I asked, my brows furrowing.

"No." Priscilla shook her head. "She only said they must look into other ways to handle the situation." I hummed in response, turning that thought over in my mind. What was the princess planning?

"I'll see if I can drop any comments later today and bring the conversation around where we want." Priscilla told me with a sly smile.

"Hopefully, we find something." I replied, pursing my lips in contemplation. "I don't like all these people plotting around us. Not when we're unaware of how their schemes may affect us."

"Humans do always seem to draw the short end of the stick in these matters." Priscilla nodded in agreement, leaning over to grab bits of my hair to tie up.

Once she finished getting me ready, we moved from the vanity to the wardrobe and the dressing screen arranged beside it. I raised an eyebrow at Priscilla when I saw the dress picked out for me, noting that it was more elaborate than normal. The top was corseted with a scooped neckline and had exquisite detail in the pink embroidery across it, flowing from the corset and down over the skirt. The pink color of the embroidery shifted from light to dark as it fell to the floor.

Cyrus did love keeping with the pink and gray colors of Dusk. Any opportunity to show off his royal station, he took it. And my wardrobe was an exquisite showcase of that fact. Whether it came from his vanity or his insecurity, I still hadn't figured out. Maybe a combination of both.

I honestly wasn't sure that either of Dusk's signature hues were really my colors. Nonetheless, I ran my hand down the full skirt of the gown, appreciating the details.

"What's with the fancy dress?" I raised a brow at Priscilla, and received a sympathetic smile in return that I knew meant I wouldn't like what came next.

"Court has been called to discuss yesterday's attack." Priscilla replied smoothly. "You'll be required to attend at Prince Cyrus's side."

"Fabulous." I sighed heavily at her explanation. Prince Cyrus had only required my presence before the courtiers a few times, primarily at dinners with the royal family.

This would be my first time attending a full court session. I suppose my luck finally ran out. Though, this could be an opportunity too. Where better to learn about the politics and plots of the court than at court itself?

Less than an hour later, I took a deep breath, staring at Cyrus's back and trying not to panic. I had no idea what to expect from a formal court session, but had no time to truly worry before servants threw open the doors and Cyrus began to strut inside.

I kept my eyes lowered a fraction as I walked three steps behind the crown prince. I could feel eyes on me—those wondering about the prince's new favored slave, his whore, as was the rumor according to the Night Kingdom soldier. I forced myself not to visibly bristle at the thought.

I tried to keep my mind off that Fae soldier—along with the other slaves, particularly the female ones who glared at me from across the room. They *wanted* to be known as the prince's whore? I nearly snorted; they could have it for all I cared—I couldn't even imagine why they would want that dubious honor.

Desperate people, I reminded myself. Ones with no concept of what it meant to be free, who tried to claw back a measure of control in their lives. And that, I could well understand.

Cyrus had explained to me that during court sessions, his place would be beside his father's throne. As he sat down, I stood back by the side of the dais, against the wall and out of the way. I was supposed to be nothing more than a piece of furniture, another layer of the wall.

King Astraeus and Queen Stelara weren't here yet. but Prince Weylin was standing next to Princess Daneiris, and I could see Prince Kian and Prince Vikal on the other side of them. While Princess Twyla hid slightly behind them.

I didn't blame her.

They were all lined up to the left of the dais. Only Cyrus got to be seated beside his parents as the heir. I could practically feel resentment dripping off his siblings. Before I could look around the ostentatiously decorated throne room any further, the king and queen were announced by the herald.

The large, dark, wooden double doors opened, and King Astraeus and Queen Stelara swept into the room. Like the rest of the hall, I dropped to my knees before them. They looked as regal as ever, with the queen dressed in an elaborate gown and the king standing tall beside her. The queen's dress was made of the finest emerald silk. It trailed behind her as she walked arm in arm with her husband to their thrones. The emerald green complemented her wine-red hair perfectly and slightly brightened her nearly black eyes.

The king was in a dark gray doublet that boasted a pegasus on the breast in the darkest pink. Gold chains crossed the front in rows, a way to showcase his station. As he turned to sit on his throne, I noticed the sleeves had the sigil of Dusk Kingdom, an upside-down crescent moon entwined with scrollwork, and two pegasuses on either side, rearing up toward one another.

As soon as they sat down, the members of the hall rose from their knees. I slunk back against the wall, hoping to go unnoticed. I needed to learn more of this court, and more of Cyrus, if I had any hope of matching him in his game. I nearly snorted at myself. I *didn't* have any hope. But I couldn't just give into Cyrus because of bad odds. I had my own plans now, and I would see it through to freedom. I would gladly die trying. Some ideals were worth the risk.

"We have called you all here today to discuss the recent attack from the Night Kingdom." The king pronounced sourly, his mouth forming a hard line of bitterness. "The increasing number of attacks are a matter of concern. Prince Cyrus, please inform the court of what you've told me."

Cyrus stepped forward, only cool confidence radiating from him as he moved with the grace of a jungle cat. "As you know, my King, we made preparations in case of another attack. Weylin was in charge of the Gloam Gate, where the Night Kingdom broke through. When they breached that gate, they took what we estimate to be fifteen to twenty humans, killing many Fae in their path. Somehow, they knew our defenses had changed, and were prepared for the new magical shields we'd put in place."

He turned on his heel and looked at Prince Weylin. "Brother, you were in charge of the defenses at the fallen gate. Why don't you tell us what happened to create such a failure?"

I had yet to hear Cyrus sound so cruel, gloating over his brother's failure. He'd told me he wanted his brother to fail in his duty to defend them, so it would make him seem like a bad choice of heir. But there was no way he'd done this, right? I hadn't heard any more of the plan and had hoped he'd realized its folly. Did Cyrus know the Night Kingdom would attack on the day Weylin was expected to man that gate? Would Cyrus truly go so far as to sacrifice his own people to make his brother look incompetent?

I didn't know nearly enough about him to answer that question, I realized. Only what he wanted me to see, and the few tidbits I'd picked up otherwise. Hardly a comprehensive analysis. A chill swept up my spine as Weylin stepped forward with a distinct limp to his gait, clearly injured from the battle. A look at Cyrus showed a gleam of satisfaction in his eyes that further set off my unease.

"The shield barrier we had in place was targeted by the Night Kingdom immediately. They had to know it was in place somehow." Weylin began, his composure barely maintained. "There was no hesitation from the Night Kingdom's armies. They were already prepared to take it down. I'd tested that defense myself, and it was sturdy. King Calix is more powerful than any of us, but I thought the shield would be able to stand up to his power. Instead, his magic pierced the shield and ripped it in half." Weylin growled, his resentment of King Calix all too clear.

"Once it was down, they came in a wave of darkness. None of us could even see to defend ourselves. The king himself tore across the city with his warriors, drenching every corner in darkness and slaying our warriors." He finished, shooting a glare at his elder brother in the process.

"So, what you're saying is that your magic wasn't up to snuff, little brother. Is that right?" Cyrus taunted. Weylin snarled and made to move forward.

"Enough!" The king shouted. Both brothers stilled, but I caught the horrible grin Cyrus sent Weylin, and the glare Weylin sent Cyrus in return.

"This cannot happen again! If our shields cannot keep Calix out now, reinforce them until they can! I will not accept defeat." The king turned to his second eldest with a sneer. "Weylin, you wanted to lead this defense, and at the first attack, you failed."

Weylin looked down, anger, shame, and frustration a swirling cocktail of emotions on his face. Cyrus stood taller, his face blanking as he turned to the king.

"Cyrus, you will fix the defenses and ensure this does not happen again." King Astraeus finished, a growl underlining his voice. His disdain for his son was clear despite his order.

"Of course, Father." Cyrus bowed, taking a moment after to whisper in his father's ear. Weylin watched with a glower, but I was focused on the glint in Cyrus's eyes as the king ground his jaw back and forth in response to Cyrus's words, nodding but staying silent.

I watched the queen sit up straighter in her throne while her husband was focused on his heir. She championed Cyrus over Weylin, and the look on her face only proved how pleased she was at this decree.

I would never understand how these royals could be so satisfied with their wins over one another, especially when it resulted in the deaths of their people. The court wanted to play their games and claim victory, no matter the cost to others. Had I been in their position, my first priority would have been to help and protect my people.

But power was the only commodity they sought, and I felt sick to my stomach knowing that the loss of their people would not even be a thought when it came to their own priorities.

I looked around the room and saw a range of emotions. Some looked pleased, others angry or worried, and some showed no emotion at all. It was Kian and Daneiris who caught my attention, however, as they looked at Cyrus and Weylin with calculation.

After discussion of the attack, some of the lords and ladies came forward with other issues, or related ones. I listened in, trying to parse any information I could. Each Fae was called before the king and queen in turn. I stood still, listening to the herald announce each one, filing away every name and city in my mind.

"Lord Aibek and Lady Siria Acheron of Alfheim." The herald called next.

I didn't think much when a Fae with light curly brown hair, baby blue eyes, and pale skin stepped forward, but I paid extra attention when I saw his wife. She had the silvery white hair that was more common in the Night Kingdom, and especially its royal family, the House of Erebus. Her dark pink eyes were usually only seen in the south as well, and her skin was even paler than her husband's.

Everything about this Lady screamed *Night Kingdom* with just a look.

I hadn't thought much of it when I met my Fae soldier, but he had the same hair color as Lady Siria, perhaps even lighter than hers. I wondered if he was related in any way to that horrid king? I shuddered at the very thought.

I subtly glanced over to the king and queen, who seemed to look upon the lady with judgment in their eyes, but not the lord she was married to.

Typical.

"Your Highnesses," Lord Aibek began as he and Lady Siria bowed before their monarchs. "Our city and lands are the closest to the border of the Night Kingdom. With the increase in attacks, we would humbly ask for your assistance in protecting our borders." Lord Aibek looked young, but that wasn't much indication when it came to the never aging Fae. Once they reached maturity, their aging came to an abrupt stop, but this lord had a baby face that made him look even younger than me.

King Astraeus sat forward on his throne, his elbows resting on each arm and his hands steepling in front of him, while Queen Stelara merely lifted a haughty eyebrow at them.

"You request our help? Against the Night Kingdom?" Astraeus asked, his tone skeptical.

Lord Aibek looked a tad uncomfortable, but his wife looked straight ahead at the king and queen, refusing to show an ounce of emotion. She held her head high, unyielding under the scrutiny and pressure of the Dusk royals looking down on them. I found myself jealous of her poise and confidence.

"Yes, my King." The lord answered. He kept his face still even as he shifted slightly, betraying his unease.

"And yet—" Queen Stelara began, a cruel look in her nearly black eyes. The color turning from mere black into an endless pit with the malevolence radiating from them, "Your wife is of the Night Kingdom. Related to King Calix himself, is she not?" That harshly arched eyebrow of hers rose once more.

"I am, my Queen. He is my cousin." Lady Siria's voice was cool and calm. Nothing to indicate the queen's words bothered her. I was curious, however. Was she married into the House of Acheron for an alliance? Or was it a love match? They must have married prior to the Night Kingdom cutting off access to the rest of Celesterra.

"*Hmm.* Are we truly your king and queen? Or do your loyalties still lie to the south? How do we know you are not working with him and attempting to sabotage our efforts?" Stelara questioned, with a skeptical brow raised in inquiry. "How do we know you aren't feeding Calix information?"

Queen Stelara shot every word at Lady Siria like a dagger.

Siria, however, looked the royals down, refusing to cower. "My loyalties are as they ever were, of course, my Queen. I do not bend just because of a blood tie. I would not be here, seeking out help for my people, if my loyalties had shifted."

The queen hummed with displeasure, but I noticed King Astraeus nodding, seemingly pleased. I thought I might finally be catching on a bit to the doublespeak happening all around me, however. It didn't escape my notice that Lady Siria did not state *who* that loyalty belonged to. Nor did she refute the claim exactly. She merely stated that blood didn't sway her. There was nothing in her words that indicated she *wasn't* siding with her blood.

Feeling sufficiently worried, I looked to her husband. Lord Aibek gazed at his wife with a smile before turning back to the monarchs. "As my Lady wife said, our loyalty lies here, your Highnesses. And to our people, who we seek your help to protect."

There was a rush of approving noises and murmurs in the hall at that. Words still vague enough that they could go either way. Queen Stelara swept her eyes around the hall, her lips tightening and her fingers biting into the edges of her throne. She was displeased, frustrated, that her questioning led to the crowd and king being won over. She hadn't believed a word, and it was clear she wanted to do something about the lord and lady, but what that was—well, I was happy enough not to have to find out.

"We will provide you with additional soldiers to help protect your lands and people, Lord Aibek." King Astraeus declared. The queen's eyes slanting over to him in displeasure, while Cyrus narrowed his eyes in rage at his father.

There was something here, but whatever it was, it was just out of my ability to understand. The division between the king and queen, and Cyrus along with her, were pulling the court in two directions. Peering around at the assembly of lords, ladies, and other nobles that made up this court, they seemed to be split down the middle. Half agreed with the king, and half with the queen.

"Of course, we will, Father. I will send one of our best commanders to lead them. We must ensure the borders are secure." Cyrus smoothly interjected.

The queen's face relaxed an inch, a smile finally tilting her lips, though it was hardly convincing. The razor thin line was too cutting and sharp to truly be considered a smile. Queen Stelara was more weapon than woman, made to pierce her enemies with just a look.

My eyes shot back to Lady Siria, and observed the most minuscule movement of her lips, turning down in displeasure. I couldn't fault her, as anything that made the queen perk up in such a way could not be good.

"Very well." King Astraeus sighed. He eyed Cyrus with a weary expression, one Lord Aibek also wore before Lady Siria grabbed his hand. He quickly forced his face into a blank slate and squeezed her hand.

I wondered if I could get Cyrus to divulge more information on this situation to me. He thought I was helping him, after all. And I suppose I was in a way—even if it was all to help myself.

Offering the ruse of support for Cyrus did in fact provide me with more knowledge and power to use on my own. But now, I had the sinking feeling that helping him at all would not turn out well. Some innate sixth sense flashed a warning of danger at me. I'd learned long ago to trust myself; there was no one else worthy of it.

Cyrus turned to me at that moment, winking. His beauty struck me like a blow before I grimaced. I hated how he could disarm me with a glance.

I couldn't afford to become distracted by a pretty face. Cyrus was as beautiful as any Fae, but he was still the one who held my leash.

And I refused to be his dog.

CHAPTER 10

I SIGHED in relief as Priscilla got me out of the tightly laced gown I was forced to wear to court. I heard a masculine chuckle from the doorway and gasped, holding the dress up to cover my chest as Cyrus appeared. Eyes lighting up with that strange spark of lightning as he entered.

"It couldn't be that bad, could it? All the ladies of court wear dresses like this." His words made me bristle. Priscilla bowed as Cyrus walked closer, though I caught the cautious look on her face.

"It is, *indeed*, that bad." I replied, my lip curling reflexively. "What are you doing in here? This is most—"

"Inappropriate?" He murmured, lips tilting up as he reached out and fondled the fabric of my skirt.

"Yes." I hissed, pulling the skirt of my dress out from his hand and stomped toward the bathing room. Cyrus chuckled once more, clearly amused by my reaction.

"Do you not think I should be able to see what belongs to me?" His tone was sultry, but his words hit me like the lash of a whip.

"I do not belong to you." I told him, even as I tasted the lie on my tongue. I most certainly did, just not the way he wished.

Cyrus walked over to where I stood in the doorway of the bathing room. I glanced around, holding my dress tight to me, hoping it wouldn't fall as I searched for another exit.

I found none, not in time. Cyrus was in my space in a heartbeat, reaching up to finger a lock of my hair. His scent, lightning and mint, filled my head as I breathed his proximity into me. He was much taller than me, forcing me to crane my neck to look up at him.

"But you do, Asteria." Cyrus murmured, tugging my hair to make me keep my attention on him. "You're merely human, and I am your master. You may not be willing to share my bed yet, but that does not mean I do not own you in every way."

Cyrus was too confusing. One minute he was cold, the next hot. Another trying to be kind, then asserting his ownership of me and my status as a slave—never letting either of us forget our positions in society.

His size consumed me, and his smell was intoxicating. I fought tooth and nail to not get lost in it. The fortifications of my walls stood tall, fighting off the seductive tone of his voice attempting to overpower me, insisting that I forget the meaning of his words. I jolted, standing ramrod straight, recognizing his intentions.

And yet, still, it truly had been too long since I'd last felt a man between my thighs. My core throbbed at the very thought, longing to be filled and forget how empty it was. Like it knew if I consented to this man's offer, it would likely be filled completely in moments. I had to shake the lust off. A beautiful, dangerous Fae was not something I needed—especially between my legs. Especially not him.

If I was going to give into any Fae, I'd rather it be one like—

Purple eyes flashed before me, silver-white hair falling around my own face as he leaned in, inviting, teasing me with his mere presence…

I cut myself off immediately. Even in my own head, there was no place for thoughts of silver-white hair and purple eyes—of a soldier who drank me in the same way I yearned to consume him. He was an enemy, one whose kingdom would see me dead if I got too close. He was a beautiful lure, right into a deadly trap. I looked up at Cyrus's blue eyes instead.

"What was that about at court today?" I demanded, glaring at him. Needing to cool things down before I lost my head.

"What do you mean?" He asked, eyes suddenly wary and full of surprise at my change in subject. He leaned back, studying me.

"You wanted me to help you, right?" I persisted, giving him a look and letting him know I was not in the mood to play games. "I've been doing my best to gather information, Cyrus, but I can't do much without the full picture—" Cyrus raised a brow, a dubious, questioning look taking over his face, but I pushed on.

"Why was your mother accusing Lady Siria of treason?" Cyrus looked ready to interrupt, but I kept on, impatiently planting my hands on my hips. "And why did you insist on sending your best commander, when it was clear you didn't agree with sending anyone in the first place?"

The more I questioned, the louder my voice rose. My frustration bubbled over from the lack of answers I'd received to the many questions I had. Cyrus glanced behind us, to where Priscilla was still on her knees.

"Get dressed. Then come talk to me." Cyrus sighed, conceding the point, then ran a hand through his hair. He gave me a lingering look, before disappearing into the other room.

I sighed with relief, turning to Priscilla, and found her to be watching me warily. I cocked my head to the side, questioning, as I walked back over to her to finish getting out of this dress as quickly as possible.

"You must be more careful, Asteria." Priscilla whispered in a voice so quiet that I barely heard her, even with her speaking directly into my ear. "Cyrus's temper is legendary. It's only so long until you push him too far, the way you go at him."

I gulped at the thought. I knew I was pushing my limits, but I couldn't help it. He drove me crazy. A part of me needed to get as far away as possible, while the other—as much as I was loath to admit it—wanted to give in to him. It would be so nice to let a handsome man take care of me and dress me in fancy clothes and jewels. It would be nice to have a man fill me up the way I desired—to feel us reach completion together.

I steeled myself in resolution, I refused to give in to those baser desires that tried to steer me around.

It was weak.

And I would never be weak. I would never be the type of person who needed another to fulfill their own happiness. I was never going to be some wilting flower, waiting for a man to take care of me. I'd never allow a man that much control over me.

Cyrus wasn't a safe choice. He had already proved to be…turbulent, to say the least. As Priscilla cautioned, his temper was apparently legendary. He was dangerous and handsome. Scheming and yet kind when he wanted to be. Always passionate, but most certainly manipulative. The good did not outweigh the bad. I would not let him own more of me than he already did. Those innermost, squishy bits, my heart and soul—those parts of me were just for me. It was all I had in this world.

Cyrus might promise a way for me to gain power, but nothing would truly change. Society wouldn't allow it. I would just be further under his thumb. He might let me hold my leash from time to time, but it would still be choked around my neck.

No power he gave me would ever compare to power I took for myself.

Freedom and the will to live an *actual* life kept me alive—drove me further when the path got harder. A pretty face and lack of sex would not mess that up for me.

Besides, I was beginning to suspect his manipulations and plans went much further than I imagined. I'd found his notes that contained facts about others—but there was nothing about his own plans.

I needed more, and I was determined to get it. I would take what I needed, starting with insisting that Cyrus tell me all he knows. I'd continue to gather information and when I had enough, I would ascertain my freedom. Even if I needed to hide out in some remote spot of Celesterra. Somewhere in all of Adamah *must* be safe. If necessary, I would flee to another continent like Gemaria or Weathrian, as long as it meant my life would become my own.

I said my goodbyes to Priscilla as I made my way out of the room. Turning back from the door, I looked around the grand living space. Cyrus was sprawled out on one of the sofas, a glass of wine in his hand. He slowly swirled his glass as I walked over and took a seat on the opposite sofa. I sank back into the plush cushions, enveloping myself in its luxurious feel. Cyrus looked me over, his gaze like a brand as it traveled over me.

"What do you want to know, Asteria?" Cyrus sipped his wine leisurely, sprawling across the couch like he was without a care in the world.

"You know what I want to know. What is going on?" I narrowed my eyes, calculating. "I can't help you if I don't know what's actually going on here."

"Surely, you must realize there is much I have not told you." Cyrus sighed dramatically. "There is always something unraveling, at all times. My father and brother constantly fight against me. My mother and I must fight fire with fire. Or—lightning with lightning." He wiggled his eyebrows at me in a playful manner, but I just rolled my eyes at him.

"Night Kingdom is our biggest problem. Lady Siria is still loyal to her cousin, despite her honeyed words. The royal family of Night have always had closer family ties than the rest of the royal families have managed with our blood and houses." Cyrus's eyes met mine, and his countenance grew more troubled as a burdened sigh left his lips. "Siria was close with Calix when they were younger, and there's no reason to suspect that's changed. Having my commander leading this group ensures I have eyes on the situation."

"The situation?" I pressed, raising a brow.

"Yes, there has to be a reason they are asking for support against supposed attacks, when Calix would never attack his cousin." He shook his head, a storm brewing in his eyes that reflected in his furrowed brow. He may act like he didn't have a care in the world, but there seemed to be a great many burdens weighing on him behind the cavalier attitude. "They are at no risk there. If they are seeing strikes against them as they claim, they are likely faked so we don't suspect them. My father was a fool to grant their request, but perhaps it will prove worthwhile if my man finds something."

"What of the king himself?" I rubbed my forehead, exhausted. This family and their machinations. I didn't feel prepared to ask about his mother. Not yet—not when just the thought of the queen made me shudder; not when Cyrus was aligned so closely with her. "Do you have a spy on him?"

Cyrus eyed me, seeming to debate something in his head. He appeared to make a decision as he leaned upwards from his sprawl, leaning towards me.

"I have tried. Repeatedly. But my father is ever paranoid. If myself or my siblings so much as speak to a slave and my father hears of it, he won't use them. He's wary of one of us killing him off to take the throne. Not that I blame him." He mused absentmindedly.

My jaw dropped. Did that mean—

Would Cyrus—

Would he attempt to take his own father out?!

The thought was incredibly disturbing—still, Cyrus was sharing information, so I swallowed my disgust and leaned in conspiratorially. Let him think what he will. Each moment of this conversation was another piece on the game board revealed, allowing me to use them to my advantage.

"If I can find a way to turn one of the slaves he takes," Cyrus continued on, not sparing a thought for the horrendous thing he just said. "I can finally get eyes on him. There's one girl you spoke to multiple times. If my father chose her, would you be able to turn her? Or at least, get her to give you information you can pass along?"

The question made goosebumps rise along my arms, as he turned considering eyes toward me.

I stared at Cyrus, unable to comprehend the way this man's mind worked. And—how did he know about Emmie? She was the only one I ever spoke to aside from Priscilla, but I'd never done so in front of him.

"Who?" I tried to play dumb, thinking that was my best option.

"The girl you met with in the slave quarters." Cyrus replied dryly, leveling a look at me. "—Servant's quarters." He quickly corrected, but it was obvious he didn't much care. attempting, *poorly*—to distract me. He seemed to think that merely not referring to humans as slaves would be enough to get me into his bed, an endgame he considered an inevitability. All it did was show his fundamental misunderstanding of the problem.

I didn't bother asking how he knew about Emmie, but I made a note to be more careful so his spies wouldn't report on me. They were supposed to be coming directly to me first. Which made me think twice, as it meant Cyrus either had one or multiple spies that reported directly to him on me and what I did throughout the castle. I twitched, holding back a full body shudder at that thought.

"I'm not sure." I replied finally, not liking the idea of involving Emmie in this mess. I didn't want Cyrus to assume she'd be interested in such a scheme either.

Of course, she likely *would* be interested, but I wanted to hedge my bets.

"How would you ensure that your father picked her?" I asked, voice wobbling. I hated how uncertain I sounded, suddenly afraid for Emmie. She was ambitious, but I didn't want to see that eagerness to rise higher backfire on her.

"All my father really needs is to have her dangled in front of him." Cyrus smirked slowly, doubling the fear I worried showed on my face. "Just a few choice words would direct his attention, and he'd be demanding to see her immediately."

I swallowed hard. I didn't want to dangle Emmie as bait for the king. I only wanted Cyrus to ultimately help me in my own plans. But I had little choice, in the end. A slave doesn't have options—we have orders. Still—

"Is there not someone else we could use?" I dared ask, wincing when a sharp glare was leveled on me. Cyrus's eyes roved over my face as he leaned towards me. I tried to hide the flinch as I waited for my question to backfire.

"I allow you to ask your questions, but do not interfere with my plans, darling." Cyrus reached out and grabbed my chin, hard. I tried to cringe back, but he held fast to my face. "I have been waiting years for a chance to get a spy that my father doesn't realize is connected to me. This is my opportunity. Do you understand?"

Cyrus's fingers dug into my chin until I whimpered, his eyes lit up with bolts of lightning as his displeasure with my slight resistance radiated from him.

If I tried to fight Cyrus on any of this…who knew what he would do? I knew of the violent punishments doled out, even if I hadn't seen any yet.

My master stared me down now. For all his ease with me thus far, I felt as if I hovered on the edge of a knife the whole time I'd been here. Sensing something dark lurking in those stormy eyes. I had yet to see it brought to the surface.

Chaos simmered beneath his exterior, and I knew without a doubt I did not want to test the razor's edge he teetered on.

Yet it began to feel more like an inevitability, for my desperate desire to be free was always on the line, and there was little chance of getting to freedom without a few bumps along the road.

"She loves to gossip." I admitted, forcing the words out. My lips didn't want to utter them, my jaw clenched hard against what felt like a betrayal. Even if Emmie was the one who told me not to trust anyone. Even if I didn't have any people in my life I truly considered friends. "If you get her in with the king, I can find out what he tells her."

"I knew I could count on you, Asteria." Cyrus's hard stare lightened as he smiled widely, returning to the charming prince once more as he let go of my chin and caressed the skin he surely just bruised. Strangely, he softened a bit, in a way I hadn't yet seen from him. "In this world and in this court, it's impossible to trust anyone. It means more than you know to have you here helping me." He leaned into me, and his hand encompassed my cheek. His thumb slowly tracing over the apple of it.

"Why do you resist me so?" He whispered the words, but I was struck by how pained, they sounded. "I can give you so much. And all I want is you."

That lightning sparked again in his eyes. Blue flashes upon blue irises, making it almost look like his eyes were cracking from within.

I closed my own eyes for a moment, unwillingly tempted to give into the gentle touch, the warmth blooming in his eyes. It felt so genuine, so full of affection, that I felt the trap of needing his embrace, of wanting it to encompass me. I sighed, as I opened my eyes, prepared for the same song and dance we kept volleying back and forth.

"You own me, Cyrus." I sighed, a sad smile gracing my lips, knowing he would never understand the divide between us. "And there's no such thing as true choice when the person holds your life in their hands. Not for me."

Cyrus looked profoundly sad at that, but I had the sudden realization that in truth, his parents did the same thing to him. Oh, he could move freely, and he wasn't punished like humans were.

But was he truly free?

I couldn't imagine having a father who worked against me constantly. Nor having the safety and love of my father twisted into something corrupted and violent. To have no love from your father must be agonizing. My heart bled a little for him, that he never experienced the love all children should have from their parents. He may be the free one between the two of us, but I couldn't help but feel sympathy for what he lacked in his life, nonetheless.

"I need you, Asteria. Your ability to speak to other humans without bringing attention to yourself will be invaluable. In fact—" He looked me over, slowly. I felt flayed open by his gaze, like it could strip away my walls and expose the bruised soul beneath. Maybe that's why he wanted me so badly. Maybe he recognized that in me, and his own bruised heart reached for that likeness. "You've already taken over meeting with my spies and passing along information, which has been immensely helpful. I'll have to introduce you to some of my business partners soon. Their own spies bring in plenty of information. You can start taking their reports as well."

"I can do that." I agreed easily. "And what of the Night Kingdom? Are there any plans in place to deal with them?" My unbidden thoughts found themselves back on the soldier I met, and the questions he left me with. I couldn't help the desire to find out more about him—about them. The Night Kingdom was a land of mystery and violence, and I yearned to crack them open and unravel those secrets.

"You know, Calix and I were once friends." Cyrus replied, his face darkening, as he changed the trajectory of the conversation slightly. There was an almost whimsical gleam in his eyes, as he thought back to his friendship with the king of Night.

My mouth parted in a surprised exhale. I wouldn't have expected there was ever anything but hate between the two royals with the state of their current relations.

"I know, you wouldn't guess that now." Cyrus chuckled, not missing a thing. I leaned in, resting my chin on my palm, and the shift gave him the encouragement he needed to continue. "I truly have no idea what happened to him. One day, things were the same as always. During events, we'd get together and drown ourselves in drink and women. And the women did love Calix," Cyrus shook his head with a slight laugh. "But all of a sudden, he went strangely quiet, and locked down his borders. A few years later, he began launching attacks on all the other kingdoms." He sighed as he picked up his wine and drank deeply.

"We only saw each other a handful of times a year, but when we did, it was always like no time had passed." Cyrus looked off to the side. "As crown prince, I can't get truly close to many people. They all want something from me: my position or wealth, my power." He laughed wryly but something in it was distinctly sad.

"I understand." I murmured, allowing a soft smile to slip free. Cyrus's gaze caught mine, looking so deeply into my eyes that I couldn't even blink while he held me captive. I saw the same impotent rage and sad longing in his eyes that reflected in mine when I looked in the mirror. It made me shudder with a tempest of emotions: terror, uncertainty, and longing. Along with an unwilling understanding—at least where this was concerned. Neither one of us let others close to us and we both felt the cost of disavowing such connections. It was isolating, often leaving us with a bitter resentment for the things we can't have.

As for King Calix, I couldn't fathom what could have happened to cause a playboy king to snap and begin attacking different kingdoms and killing their people, slave or no. I shuddered at the thought. Only a mad man could do such a thing.

All of a sudden, Cyrus was in front of me, on his knees, his hand reaching for my face. He brushed his fingers through my hair, pulling me closer to him. My breath parted, lips slightly open with shock and overwhelming emotion. His palm cupped my cheek as his thumb ran along my skin.

"You really do understand, don't you?" He murmured softly.

Our eyes were still locked, and I felt the tension between us rise ever higher. I breathed heavily, matching his. His other hand came up and cupped my other cheek.

"Cyrus," I whispered, not even sure what I wanted to say. Was I going to warn him away, or invite him closer? The moment was too charged to be sure which I meant at that exact second.

"Asteria…" Cyrus brushed his thumb across my lips, his eyes slightly glassy as he whispered my name, a sweetness to his tone that I'd never heard from him before.

A crack formed along the walls I used to keep him and everyone else out, like lightning had struck them. The damage left in its wake was unknowable in this moment, as Cyrus pressed his lips to mine.

I took a startled breath that let his tongue sweep into my mouth, and then I was lost to sensation. Our lips gently parted, our tongues entwining as we learned the contours of the other's mouth. His hands swept across my cheeks as he pressed me into him, holding me in place.

Cyrus transitioned us from a soft, sweet kiss to a more desperate, harsh one. The pressure of his lips became bruising. His teeth nipped at my bottom lip, causing a throb between my legs. It had been too long, and I sighed deeply, letting my lips match the force of his. My tongue swept in and explored his mouth.

Cyrus's hands trailed from my cheeks up into my hair, grabbing it and holding it in fistfuls, using it to guide my mouth where he wanted it. My own hands found his in return and pulled, causing him to let out a rough grunt as he smiled against my mouth.

It was that smile that woke me up. I pulled away, just enough to feel his lips lightly press against mine. I exhaled slowly as I parted from him. That cocky smile brought me back to reality as I stared at him with wide-eyed shock.

Did I really just kiss Prince Cyrus, heir apparent to the Dusk Kingdom, like we were two desperate adolescents? My heartbeat escalated, as I tried to convince myself this hadn't actually happened.

Cyrus was breathing hard, and his cocky smile formed itself into a hard line. The moment of honesty between us was lost as the desperation and sadness quickly faded from his eyes, replaced with a gleam of satisfaction and arrogance I hated.

"See, my dear? It's only a matter of time."

CHAPTER 11

PRISCILLA swept into the room after breakfast the following morning and began to help me dress for the day. We chatted over what we discovered about the happenings around the capital. While she saw more of the city than I did, I observed more of the court. She was limited in her service to the princess, so I managed gathering intel for the most part when it came to court gossip. But Priscilla could freely enter the city when she wasn't busy helping the princess or myself. By swapping the information we'd each gathered every morning, we figured we would not only have a more complete picture, but we'd have an advantage by working together as a team.

"It's insane, Pris. This family is constantly at one another's throats." I said, rather emphatically as I waved my hands around. Priscilla artfully dodged my hands, pressed her own into my hair, reminding me to still, while we shared knowing smirks through the mirror. "Cyrus wants to get Emmie into the king's service to get the upper hand on him." I gulped as I thought about what needed to be done, despondent at the very idea. "How am I supposed to send her into the king's service? I've seen what he's like."

"I don't know, Hun." Priscilla murmured quietly, weaving what must be some kind of magic through her fingers, making my hair look perfect.

"He figured that since she's a gossip, she'd tell me anything the king tells her." I explained, a crease forming between my eyebrows. "And King Astraeus apparently gets chatty when he's…sated." My face wrinkled in a grimace, then giggled when I saw Priscilla's pretty face mirror my own.

She sighed as she grabbed my hair and began brushing out the bottom half. "It could be worse, trust me. Cyrus is being fairly tame right now, by his standards anyway. I think he's trying not to scare you. But be careful. If he keeps twisting you into his plans, I'm worried what may become of you." She finished quietly, her eyes beseeching me. The warm honey brown full of worry and care I was unaccustomed to.

I could feel myself warming even more to her and struggled with how to manage it. I couldn't afford to care, to love—hadn't I learned long ago that only the Fae got that particular luxury? But I could feel my walls shaking and cracking, no matter how much I wished they wouldn't. Priscilla and Emmie were the closest to friends I'd ever had. I worried for Emmie because of Cyrus's plans, and I worried for Priscilla, a warm soul caught in a cold kingdom, one I was using to help spy on a princess. I could feel the beginnings of real connection stirring within me. I couldn't help but fear what would happen if I didn't get control of it.

I told myself not to think of how I warmed to Cyrus the other night. I tried not to remember the way his eyes softened on me when we had a moment of understanding, the desperation I saw meeting my own loneliness. I tried not to recall how generous his smile had been before it turned cruel and calculating. I tried not to want the possibility of who Cyrus could be, had he not been a monster, a Fae. I tried not to regret that, had our lives been different, the people we may have become might have had a different ending—but thinking that way led only to disaster.

The worry I allowed myself was solely for Emmie and Priscilla. But I knew I needed their help just the same. They'd proved to be my only paths of information outside of Cyrus and his own spies. And here, knowledge was assuredly power.

"I have no desire to be part of Cyrus's plans." I reassured Priscilla. Her brow raised up in disbelief, and I waved her off. "Seriously, you should know that by now. But I worry about what he might do should his plans actually come to fruition. At least this way, I'm in the know and can control my own fate to some degree." Priscilla snorted, still looking dubious, but didn't call me out on the deflection.

"Now, what is happening out in the big, wide world?" I smiled up at her and she rolled her eyes at me.

"The people are…nervous, is probably the best way to describe it."

"Well—" I stifled an eyeroll of my own. "Obviously. I saw them during the attack; they didn't exactly look at ease."

Priscilla leaned down to pull out the jeweled hair clips Cyrus had gifted me. Beautiful white and pink diamonds sparkled on the ends, which contrasted magnificently against my dark hair when Priscilla placed them in just so. Once she was done, she paused and looked up to meet my eyes.

"They know the Night Kingdom will attack once more, and they worry now that their rulers cannot protect them."

I bit my lip as I considered how right the people were. Their own rulers, those who should be protecting and defending them, were the ones leaving them vulnerable as they played their games from the safety of the palace.

Priscilla lowered her voice to a murmur as she nervously glanced at the door. Seeing it undisturbed, she continued. "They know both Prince Cyrus and Weylin have overseen defenses that have failed and wonder why the king allows them to continue. They question why the king doesn't just take over himself. They worry about their futures, and what will become of them if the royals cannot protect them."

All understandable concerns. I worried myself what would happen should Night Kingdom breach the palace walls. I couldn't count on my last interaction with my—*the* soldier, being typical of such brutish people.

"There is dissent growing throughout the city." Priscilla continued, her voice barely a whisper in the wind. "Just small pockets here and there, but Asteria, they're growing louder as time passes and nothing changes."

I took in a sharp inhale while I considered her words. The city's growing resentment wasn't really a huge surprise. Not with how Cyrus used his people like lambs to slaughter just to prove his brother incompetent. A large part of me wanted to cheer them on, despite them being Fae. But dissent could be dangerous. If they attacked the palace, or the royals attacked the people, humans would get caught up in the middle, and they would be the ones to suffer.

The creak of an opening door caused us both to fall silent. The low murmur of two voices reached us through the papered walls. Priscilla quickly finished her final touches of my ensemble, and I stepped out of my room and into the living space, looking around to see who had arrived.

I blinked in surprise at finding Princess Twyla. Her long brown hair was braided over her shoulder, a style she often preferred, whereas her sister generally let her red hair flow down her back in loose waves. Her blue eyes, so like Cyrus's—if a bit lighter, cut to me as I entered. I froze, unsure of what to do in this situation.

Cyrus seemed to notice his sister no longer paying him attention. He turned to me and instantly a small smile took over his glum face. "Ah, yes. Sister, this is Asteria. Asteria, my youngest sister, Princess Twyla."

I saw the surprise in Twyla's eyes before she hid it, her eyebrows twitched like they wanted to rise, but she controlled her expression. Frankly, I was just as surprised at being formally introduced to a royal.

"Princess Twyla." I curtsied. As I rose, I saw a gleam in her eyes that made me slightly uncomfortable, but I couldn't figure out what it was exactly that caused it.

"Asteria. You must be something special for my brother to have bothered introducing one of his playthings." Princess Twyla was cool and condescending in her tone, which only made me want to bristle. "Does your cunt do magic? How have you managed to bewitch him?"

I locked my jaw to prevent myself from replying with something scathing, as Twyla cut her eyes to Cyrus with a playful smile.

"She's not a plaything." He huffed out a reply. "Nor am I bewitched."

He walked over to the forest green velvet sofa and sat down before the mahogany coffee table. He looked up and patted the seat beside him, "Come Asteria, let's see what brought my sister all the way to my wing, especially since I've never seen her bother before."

He smirked up at Twyla who rolled her eyes. She seemed to wait for his invitation to sit as I took my place beside him, trying not to sit too close. It was useless as he pulled me closer the moment I sat down. I shifted uncomfortably, looking up to see his sister watching with a scrutinizing eye. Twyla smoothed her expression quickly as she joined us, flopping onto the opposite sofa as she turned her glare on Cyrus. Cyrus merely raised a brow at her before he rolled his eyes, taking her in like one might a bratty child who is misbehaving.

"Well, Sister? The floor is yours." He waved a hand dramatically to underline his point.

"Your slave doesn't seem to want to sit next to you, Brother." Twyla slowly looked between us, smirking slightly. "Why don't you let her run along?"

"And you should remember your place." Cyrus glared at her. "It's not for you to tell me my business."

"Always so touchy, Brother." Twyla huffed. "You know, you'd have more allies around here if you stopped being such a possessive dick."

I had to choke in my laughter. By the Old Gods, was she trying to get herself killed?

"And what, *dear sister*, do you know about that?" Cyrus smirked cruelly, leaning forward with his elbows on his knees. "You've always stated you were above such—what was it now? 'Petty squabbling for an ugly chair', I believe you called it."

Twyla seemed to sense the dangerous edge she was teetering on. As she straightened, she lowered her eyes to the floor. "You're right. I've never much cared for it. But Shalim knows that you and Weylin are causing quite the stir. The defenses failing? That *was* you, wasn't it?"

"Oh Twyla, I would never let our people be hurt just to prove my brother's incompetence." The lie dripped from his lips like poison as he confirmed my fear.

What a fucking bastard. I tried to push down my fury, reign in my need to shout in his face, and finally managed it when I dared to look at Twyla. She focused on her brother, but I caught the flinch in her expression. As I was turning away, her eyes caught mine briefly. I saw the knowledge there, the certainty and sadness. She knew as well as I did what Cyrus had done.

"What's happened to you, Brother?" Twyla murmured sadly as she played with a ribbon on her dress, one that crisscrossed the front and was finished with a bow tied at the middle of her waist. She no longer made eye contact with Cyrus. Almost like she was too afraid to look and see the truth of who her brother was there.

"What do you mean, Twyla?" Cyrus's head tilted to the side in question.

Twyla opened her mouth, but paused, unsure of speaking more. It felt as if her comment was blurted out without thought, not calculated at all on her part. A sister trying to understand who her brother had become. But I could have told her that the ground she was walking on was just as dangerous as a trapping pit filled with snakes.

Cyrus's soft question contrasted harshly with his next words as he lost his patience, nearly shouting. "Meet my damn eyes!"

Twyla jumped in her seat as her eyes flashed to his. She sat ramrod straight, and her discomfort made me want to look anywhere else.

She's Fae. I reminded myself. *No better than any of them.*

"That's better. You were doing so well, too." Disdain dripped from Cyrus's lips. "The veneer of confidence is much better than this weakness you show.

I know how you prefer to fade into the background, Sister, but truly, it's unseemly for royalty to act in such a way."

"I know." Twyla bit the words out, clearing her throat as if to dislodge the next ones. "Forgive me, Brother." Her nervous shifting made me even more uncomfortable. The confidence she'd arrived with had eroded within minutes of speaking with Cyrus. It felt like a reflection had fallen, cracking as it revealed the scared little sister she was inside, rather than the dignified princess. I found myself cheering for her to hold her own against him, even if she was Fae royalty. No one deserved to be degraded or spoken down to like that.

"Forgiven." Cyrus smiled easily and sat back, looking the very picture of a magnanimous prince. "*Now. What. Brings. You. Here?*"

Cyrus's slowly drawn-out words made me stiffen. Twyla's eyes shot around the room before landing on me. The sudden shifts of mood and temper were not a good sign. My alarm bells were ringing loud and clear.

"I'd…heard rumors." Twyla began slowly. "About you sequestering your new slave in your own quarters. I wanted to see what all the fuss was about. I've never known you to use a human more than once or twice before moving on."

Did I hear that correctly? Cyrus's philandering sounded about right, but not a royal hoarding a slave girl like a dragon hoarded jewels. Did people actually think that was what was happening here? And why would a princess even care about who her brother slept with? There had to be something else going on here, but Cyrus didn't seem suspicious of her statement. If anything, it seemed to put him more at ease. The suspicious glint in his eyes faded and his body released the tense hold it had been in.

"Well, Asteria is hardly just *anyone*." He smiled brightly, that charm of his that clouded my head reappearing, leaving me confused once more as I remembered that moment of real connection we'd shared between us. *Damn Fae allure.* They were said to be able to draw anyone to them when they wanted. The magic in their very blood akin to a Siren song—and just like the Sirens of the Namminian Ocean, they would kill when they lured their mark in. I'd never seen one in action, of course, but the Namminian Ocean bordered Dusk, so I may have the chance now if Cyrus ever had reason to make his way to the coast with me in tow.

I'd lived on the coast of Sunrise Kingdom, where the Damaculous Ocean spread wide, as far as I could see from the small beach near my old village. Occasionally, friendly Mermaids would make their way to the rocks nearby to sun themselves, waving to any people they saw and inviting them to talk and share stories about their life on land. They loved interacting with people. But despite being cousins of the Mermaids, the Sirens were ones you did not want to catch the attention of.

I thought of Fae much the same way. If humans were more like Mermaids, Fae were like bloodthirsty Sirens, luring us to our deaths with their beauty and magic. And you'd often forget that fact upon seeing and hearing them. Just as I kept forgetting what Cyrus was when he turned that smile and charm in my direction. I had to keep reminding myself of his true nature. Those glimpses of cruelty I'd seen from him were not mere tricks of the light. They were the truth, hidden beneath smoldering blue eyes.

"What makes her so special?" Twyla drawled, eyebrows rising. "I'd never known you to give humans the time of day. Let alone take only one to bed. I would think you'd rather have a harem of women to choose from."

"There's not much you do know, Sister." Cyrus laughed, husky and low. Twyla straightened at the insult, but he continued on like he hadn't just essentially called her an imbecile. "She's as beautiful as one of us, is she not?"

Cyrus reached over, fingers running through my dark hair until he took a piece of it and twirled it around his finger. His eyes shot to me as he did so, and I did my best to hide my thoughts behind a placid smile. I knew Cyrus wouldn't appreciate his sister or anyone else discovering the truth of our relationship.

"She is." Twyla grudgingly admitted, sounding disgruntled by that fact. "But by Shalim, Cyrus, she's still human." She looked at me accusingly, like I was the Siren here, luring her brother off course. I nearly laughed at the thought.

"*And?*" Cyrus replied, his tone silky and dangerous. His body stilled completely beside me, alarm bells now screaming in my ears. He eyed his sister with the stillness only the Fae were capable of, a clear warning to tread carefully. I sucked in a breath as he slowly let go of my hair, turning in his seat to face Twyla.

Twyla gulped at his demand. Her fate hanging in the balance as Cyrus baited her, wanting to see if she would continue to challenge him. The danger in his tone dared her to test him and see what happened. She looked torn for a moment, before that submissiveness I'd seen before seemed to pull back over her like a veil. *Protection*, I realized. To survive her siblings, she'd learned to don a veil of meekness.

A part of me felt furious on her behalf. In Fae society, the females were second to the males. Kings and lords ruled lands, while queens and ladies served them. A female royal had never been chosen by the gods to be the heir to a kingdom, and the Fae males took that as confirmation that females were somehow *less* than them—that they were not designed to rule, but to serve.

I took a subtle deep breath, calming the wave of rage rising within me— for Twyla, for the females of this world, human or Fae. I remembered my father's words before I was placed, that I needed to control my temper and keep my head. My fingers curled into my dress, my knuckles going white from the pressure as I tried to calm myself.

By the Otherworld, Twyla was here arguing that I was a measly human, something to be tossed away—and yet, I couldn't help the sympathy that stirred within me, nonetheless. The women of this world were all dealing with a variety of the same thing. We may be in different classes or races, but even those at the top of the hierarchy were pushed down it by the men in their lives. I barely heard the rest of their conversation, caught up in battling my own feelings, trying to remain still, and keeping a placid smile in place.

Smile and nod. My mother once told me that when a man or those of higher station spoke, to just smile and nod. That lesson had been drilled into me since my earliest memories, my mother insisting it would keep me safe.

I used my mother's lessons here, keeping Cyrus's weaponized attention off of me. *Thanks, mom,* I thought wistfully.

"Well, I wish you luck, Asteria." Twyla said, turning towards me as she and Cyrus finally stood. I followed suit as the rules and protocols demanded, giving the royals the due they thought owed to them. "You'll need it." She winked, a smirk lining her face that set my teeth on edge.

"Princess Twyla." I replied blandly, curtseying deeply as I maintained my own meek facade until her steps reached the door. I watched as Cyrus whispered something in her ear, her face paleing rapidly, but I couldn't for the life of me hear it from my position by the sofa.

As soon as Twyla turned and exited the room, I sighed and fell back into my seat. Cyrus's chuckle made me lift my head. When I blinked wearily, I opened my eyes to find him kneeling in front of me. Cyrus cupped my cheek, reminding me of the last time we did this. I tried to keep my shock in check, tried to forget how for a moment, his lips had felt gentle and sweet against mine.

"Don't worry about Twyla. She's dim, and fairly harmless." Cyrus said, in what I'm sure he thought was a soothing voice. "She prefers to amuse herself with shifting and flying off to the less populated lands to the East, where she can run in her pegasus form and fly unencumbered. She has no real ambition for anything else, least of all the crown."

I considered his words as his thumb skated down my cheek and towards my lips, his blue eyes stuck on them now. His brown hair fell to his shoulders, swaying as he leaned slightly forward toward me. His thumb ran across my bottom lip, tracing it, and I tried thinking through the shiver it caused.

Twyla wasn't dim, that I knew. It was clearly a front, and one I was shocked Cyrus didn't see through. This was vital information. A little tidbit I'd keep in my mental file and find a way to use to my advantage later. If I was going to find a way to beat Cyrus at his own game, information like that was worth its weight in gold.

I decided to keep my mouth shut and not give any word of warning to Cyrus that his sister was much more cunning than he thought. Not that he'd believe me anyway. Men always believed they knew best, and refused to discuss options once their minds were made up.

I once got into an argument with Soren, as he refused to believe that the moon was a dragon, the son of Erebus. He insisted the creation story couldn't be true, that the first moon wasn't an egg, and had never fallen and hatched into the first dragon. Despite the fact that the son of that dragon and Erebus became the first king of the Night Kingdom, while the other child became the moon we know today. I believed the myth had truth to it, but he refused to hear a word and called me silly for believing fanciful stories.

I'd always loved the tale, however. How the other king of the gods, Earendel, also had two children with the dragon to keep the balance. One child becoming the first king of Day Kingdom, and the other flying into the sky and lighting up the world as our sun. The stories of the sky always enthralled me, but Soren brushed them off, refusing to consider I was right.

Cyrus and Soren were as different as could be, but on this one point, they were in tune with one another—they didn't listen, certain that they were infallible.

Cyrus released a breath of air as he leaned in, placing the slightest brush of a kiss against my lips. He didn't linger however, perhaps sensing my mood. Instead he stood, offering me a hand up, and we went to go about our day as normal now that the interruption was over.

Cyrus worked at his desk while I alternated between reading a book and going over spy reports and budgets. When I finally grew bored of the tedium of work and my eyes began to hurt from squinting at numbers for much too long to even attempt more, I made my way to the slave's quarters. I spent time with Emmie and a disgruntled-as-usual Eris. Cyrus's plans ringing in my ears and an ominous feeling rising over what was to come.

As I fell to sleep later that night, that apprehension returned tenfold. But not about Emmie. Twyla's visit and her claim about wanting to see me, didn't sit right in my mind. Something was going on, and Cyrus was oblivious to it. My instinct told me that it wouldn't be long before whatever it was came to a head, however.

THE NEXT AFTERNOON my rising dread coalesced into a summons. For Cyrus—and me. I was personally named in the message from the king to appear before him. Cyrus seethed as he called Priscilla to quickly change my dress into an even more elaborate one. One that he considered appropriate for me to wear when we appeared before his father. Priscilla rushed over quickly, and once Cyrus was gone and we were well on the way to having me ready, Priscilla turned to me.

"Princess Daneiris is up to something." She whispered, a thread of panic in her tone. "And it's something to do with you, Asteria. She's going to be waiting in the throne room. You *must* be careful."

"Me? What could she want with me?" I asked, shaking my head in confusion. This certainly wasn't what I expected, and my disquiet increased tenfold, until I felt it in my Otherworld damned throat.

"I don't know." Priscilla's tone was so frayed, her worry coming through loud and clear. "I tried to find out but…she knows I help attend you. I think she was worried that I'd tell you, which, let's be honest, I totally would have." I giggled in response, but Priscilla was too worried, biting her lip as her warm brown eyes filled with unshed tears.

"It's going to be alright." I soothed her as I leaned in and put my arms around her. "Let's finish armoring me up for court, and I'll go find out what this is all about. "

I couldn't help the hug I gave her. She nearly collapsed in my arms, but I stiffened slightly. By the Old Gods, what was I doing? Priscilla may be helping me put on metaphorical armor for court, but she was also breaking through the armor I'd used my whole life. I needed to remind myself of the pain getting too close to others could cause, so I pulled back and gave her a reassuring smile.

Priscilla's smile was relieved as she rushed to help me finish dressing. As soon as we were done, I made my way out to the solar to meet Cyrus. He quickly ushered me out the door and down the halls, my heart beating out of control the whole way.

Why was I being called before the king? What was Princess Daneiris up to? Cyrus, sure, I could see them targeting him. But *me*? I was nobody to them. This had to have something to do with Twyla and her little visit. As we walked through the hallways, I felt the gaze of past kings bearing down on me. I looked away from the walls and down to the floor, following the lines in the marble seen around the edges of the halls, where the carpet didn't conceal it. Their elaborate lines gave me something to focus on to calm myself as we walked. They swirled in and out in increasingly enchanting patterns.

That distraction ended when we came to the grand staircase leading down to the throne room. The steps were large, and I had no desire to trip, so I looked back up and focused on Cyrus's back as I descended. When we reached the landing, I looked around the hall filled with the swords of past kings, princes, and generals. No women, of course. Women were *technically* allowed to be warriors, but they were looked down upon and didn't receive the same honor as their male counterparts.

Obviously.

I had to hold in my snort at the absolute absurdity. Injustice/absurdity— there was really no difference when it came to the rules these men put in place.

I followed Cyrus's steps around the corner as we finally came to the throne room. My heart felt like it might beat right out of my chest. Its pounding had gotten so frantic that there was no way the Fae couldn't hear it. The doors were opened for us and there they were, King Astraeus and Queen Stelara sat regally on their thrones. The clear inequality between their seats not at all lessening the intensity of the queen. Thankfully, she looked angrily at the woman standing beside the king, and not at me. Her preference for her son might actually benefit me in this situation. I prayed to the Old Gods that it might work in my favor when it came to whatever situation we were called in for.

Indeed, Princess Daneiris seemed to be on the receiving end of her mother's wrath today. She stood beside the king's throne, just as Priscilla warned me. A smile graced her face that surely spelled someone's doom. She was clearly attempting to look innocent and sweet, but the malicious smirk that kept creeping upon her lips gave her away.

I sank to my knees before the royals, hating every moment of my subservience.

"Father. Mother." Cyrus offered as he looked up at his parents. I rose behind him—staying back the standard three steps required for propriety. "Sister." He ground out. Cyrus recognized that something was clearly afoot, and Princess Daneiris seemed to be at the heart of it.

"Cyrus. During the last Placement, you requested the human behind you be placed into your service. I obliged, as I saw no issue with this." King Astraeus stated, his face blank of any emotion. Cyrus didn't seem concerned—not to other's eyes, but I knew the slight stiffening of his posture meant otherwise. "However, I've received some worrying reports from your siblings. They are concerned about your attachment to your slave." The king's booming voice echoed around me, and I flinched as I realized this was why I was called to attend with Cyrus.

Cyrus went stock still. I could practically feel the rage seeping out of his pores. This could be an opportunity to get away from him but—the danger you know is always better than danger unknown. I noticed bruises and cuts on other humans, not to mention their haunted looks, when I went to visit their quarters. I wouldn't soon forget their conditions—and as precarious as my situation was now, I had a certain power with Prince Cyrus that would not be guaranteed should I switch masters.

There were no good choices here. But I put aside my anger and focused on the next steps—on Cyrus and what he would do.

"My attachment? She is my slave, and I enjoy her talents. What is so wrong with that?" Cyrus's voice came out sounding blasé enough even I might have believed him.

"Your sister tells me that you treat the slave more like an equal than someone in her position should be treated." The king mused, a brow rising on that cold face. "That you even introduced her formally to Twyla and let her sit beside you during the conversation." King Astraeus glared at his eldest son.

Of course. No wonder Twyla's visit didn't feel right, she was spying for her sister. I felt foolish for not recognizing it earlier. I was still so new to this, trying to wrap my head around Cyrus's plots and spies and the rest of courtly politics. It felt like an impossible task, keeping up with all the members of the House Tynan and their moves in this game, but my life, my freedom, depended on it. I was determined to beat them at their own game.

Chapter 12

"Oh really?" Cyrus chuckled. Somehow, he managed to look amused, staring at his father without a bit of respect or contrition. "Little Twyla said that, did she?"

"Yes. She did. What do you have to say for yourself, Cyrus?" King Astraeus replied, barely containing his smile, his tell of how much he despised having Cyrus as his heir. "This behavior is certainly not suitable for the Crown Prince, the heir to my throne."

"You're absolutely right, Father. We must think of the crown's reputation." Princess Daneiris smiled sympathetically at her father. "Already, word is spreading of how Cyrus treats his slave as if she were Fae! Our reputation would be damaged severely should this spread any further. I think it would be best if you moved the girl into my service. A female serving among another group of females wouldn't cause others to look twice."

Daneiris turned to Cyrus and smirked viciously, clearly confident that she had out maneuvered Cyrus at this game. I had a sinking feeling she was right, and I was about to be traded to her. I thought of the scar on Priscilla's arm and knew I wouldn't last. If she whipped Priscilla for not doing her hair correctly, she could find any excuse for my work to be unacceptable. I could practically feel the air stir from the swing of the whip as she spoke. A premonition of what would come in her service.

"It's funny you mention our reputation, dear sister." Cyrus purred. I couldn't see his face since I was still behind him, but I could imagine it quite clearly. The lightning in his eyes, the smirk growing on his face. That cocky arrogance that only ever faded in place of cold anger or desire.

But Cyrus didn't address her request, one his father seemed inclined to agree with. I was truly the last concern for these people. A mortal among immortals, whose insignificant mortality was of little interest. This masquerade had nothing to do with me. We were here for the Fae to battle for control and power, to see who would emerge the winner in this game.

"My slave won't be going anywhere." Cyrus began, his voice as cool as ice and his bearing calm and collected. "You see, I discovered something much more damaging to our reputation should word get out. Daneiris here seems to think that she can grasp more power by pitting the two of you against one another." Cyrus looked to his parents, who looked back at him with furrowed brows, glancing over to where the princess stood, stiffening at her elder brother's words.

"And what exactly is that, *Son*?" King Astraeus ground out, his jaw ticking as his frustration bled through.

"It appears that she was planning to convince Mother that you fucked one of the queen's ladies in waiting. Lady Asra, to be exact. We all know how you enjoy redheads, after all." Cyrus chuckled, even as his mother's hands curled around the arms of her throne, tightening on them with each word. Her eyes flashed. The nearly black orbs were haunting ordinarily, but now they looked down-right terrifying.

"What? I'd never do such a thing. Her ladies in waiting are off limits." King Astraeus protested, eyes widening as he glanced over to his daughter. For her part, Princess Daneiris looked like an animal who suddenly realized they were caught in a trap.

"Oh, yes. Daneiris has planned it all out. I'm sure she would have made it very convincing, driving a wedge between you two, the court, and kingdom. After all, no one cares if the king fucks human slaves. But a Fae lady of the court? That would be *scandalous* adultery."

Did these Fae not realize that fucking anyone who was not their partner was actually adultery? I shouldn't be so astonished by the way the Fae spin reality to be how they want it. Slaves were fine for them to have sex with, not even counting as people in their minds—but another Fae was a line that couldn't be crossed. I clenched my fists for a millisecond as an outlet for my frustration but forced my hands open and wiped them down my skirt, so I didn't give myself away. Showing my feelings would be a disastrous idea now.

"And with Lady Asra?" Cyrus chuckled, and I felt vaguely sick at his amusement with this whole debacle. "Lord Oditi would turn from you for such a slight as you fucking his wife. One of your closest supporters, gone. The crack in the court, widened. It was a masterful plan, truly. It's only a shame Daneiris isn't better about hiding her machinations before she can put them into effect."

Cyrus turned enough toward Princess Daneiris that I could see the smirk he sent her way.

"Father, you cannot believe this. He is clearly grasping for anything to keep his little pet." Daneiris sneered back at Cyrus. Who merely raised a brow back at her.

"Is that so? Why don't we bring in your ladies in waiting? Before the king, they'll surely speak the truth, and if not, well—I can *encourage* them." Cyrus replied, a glint in his eyes that spoke of his excitement. It was moments like this that reminded me how despicable he was, anxious to force innocent women to admit to treason. I couldn't imagine they would leave here intact. Either by Cyrus's hand, or the king's when he found out their involvement in this plan.

"By all means, if you can bring me proof, do so now." King Astraeus leaned forward, looking between his two children facing off across the throne room.

"Sister? Which lady would you like to sacrifice in an attempt to save your own hide?" Cyrus smiled gleefully, raising a brow at her.

Daneiris was fuming. Her hands formed fists by her side as she glared at Cyrus. Lightning crackled around her hands as she set her shoulders back, and instead of giving up one of her loyal ladies—she sent a bolt of lightning barreling toward me. I gasped and jumped back to avoid being fried to death, but Cyrus merely waved a hand and caught the bolt mid-air, sending it back at her.

Princess Daneiris shrieked and ducked, letting the lightning hit the wall behind her. She stood in a fury and began stomping toward us. Cyrus moved to protect me, standing as a barrier between his sister and me, his own hands beginning to spark with lightning. The two began to face off, and my breath caught in my throat as I tried to think of a way to not get caught in the middle. I had no wish to die because I got stuck between Fae siblings fighting over a throne.

"Halt!" Queen Stelara shouted, and I nearly breathed a sigh of relief as both Cyrus and Princess Daneiris stopped and turned toward their mother. "Is this true, my daughter?" Her unnerving glare was locked on the princess, waiting for verbal confirmation. Princess Daneiris opened her mouth for a moment only to promptly close it as she bowed her head. Her fists shook with impotent rage as her lightning faded away.

"How dare you?" King Astraeus seethed, as he stood up, wrath lining his own expression. "You sought to weaken this court? My rule?!"

"No!" Princess Daneiris insisted. "No, Father, never. I sought only what I am owed! Respect. Authority. Power. A seat at your table as you—"

"Enough!" King Astraeus bellowed, his face turning red as he cut off her explanation. I almost felt bad for her. Was I not doing the same as she? I sought freedom, power over my own life. Princess Daneiris may seek to rise in power, but she was refusing to let men keep her down just because she was a woman. It wasn't so different, and the thought unnerved me greatly. And now, Daneiris stood before her father, shaking and with tears forming in her eyes.

"You are owed nothing. *Nothing*! You take only what I give you and you should thank Shalim I deigned to grant you anything at all. You have more than proven you are not worthy of it with your actions." The king told her disdainfully.

Princess Daneiris looked at her father with mute shock, his condescension and scorn hitting her like a physical blow. As much as I loathed this woman, even I felt sympathy at this moment. The king made it clear his children were nothing to him but another piece of his own power to use as he saw fit. Cyrus, Weylin, Daneiris—none of them met the impossible standard he set, and all of them internalized their father's words and set their sights on tearing each other apart instead. Trying desperately to claw their way to the top of the hierarchy, anything to feel like they had a bit of control in their lives, as if they could potentially measure up in their father's eyes if they just kept trying.

Daneiris looked around, her eyes sharp as she calculated her next steps. The others were focused on King Astraeus, leaving me the only one watching her for a moment. Meaning I was the only one who saw her lips twitch into a slight smirk before she let loose a scream as she fell to the floor, crying and screeching as we all stared in shock.

What in the Otherworld was she doing?

I couldn't believe it. The normally composed eldest Princess of the Dusk Kingdom, on the floor like a child having a hissy fit. This—this was her plan? What could this possibly accomplish?

"Get up." The queen hissed through the hysterics. "Now, Daneiris!" She shouted, breaking through the commotion. "That is enough. You are a damn princess of Dusk Kingdom! Act like it."

The princess slowly stood, shaky and unkempt for once. Cyrus looked incredibly pleased with himself. I wasn't sure exactly what was going on here, but I felt sick nonetheless, hating all of it. As much as I had hoped to not be transferred into her service, this wasn't what I'd wanted at all. I understood her ambition, I just didn't appreciate being targeted by it.

"Go to your room. We will discuss this later." Queen Stelara told her daughter, her voice glacially cold. Princess Daneiris lowered her head and quickly walked away. She slunk past us on her way out of the throne room, glaring at Cyrus and me both. Like this was somehow our fault.

"As much as it pains me to thank you for bringing this to my attention, I must do so." King Astraeus reluctantly nodded his gratitude. That alone was quite the accomplishment. Still, he narrowed his gaze on Cyrus, knowing full well that his son wouldn't act without further calculation.

"Think nothing of it, my King." Cyrus bowed his head to his father.

"There is still the matter of your human." King Astraeus smirked, and my heart sank. Why did I think Princess Daneiris's plan would take the attention off me? *Of course not.* My luck never worked that way.

"Oh, I'll be keeping her, I think." Cyrus's eyes danced as smug certainty radiated from him. "I have one more piece of information, if that wasn't good enough for you to allow such." I stiffened. Was he really holding information over the king's head—for me?

"What is that?" King Astraeus replied, stiffening just as I had, his glare focused on Cyrus.

The prince walked over to a Fae guard standing along the wall. The guard nodded at whatever it was Cyrus told him and left the room. Cyrus clearly had some plan in mind, and I ground my teeth in frustration at being unaware of it. The king, it seemed, was also frustrated with his son at the delay Cyrus was causing. I exhaled quietly enough that no one would hear it. The prince was treading a fine line here.

"Well?" The king snapped at him.

"One moment, Father." Cyrus responded smoothly. "I'm having the guilty parties brought forward to see judgment carried out."

Old Gods…I had a really bad feeling about this. Queen Stelara sat forward slightly on her throne, eagerly anticipating whatever was to come. King Astraeus tapped his fingers impatiently on the arm of his throne, his gaze staring daggers at me while he waited. I struggled not to shift from foot to foot from the unease filling me. Cyrus merely stood and waited, the picture of calm.

The doors to the throne room slammed open. Guards burst in, dragging along two people in chains. I gasped lightly. They were human slaves, a man and a woman. What in the Otherworld was Cyrus up to? Fear filled me for the humans, knowing this couldn't end well for them.

"What is the meaning of this?" King Astraeus demanded as he stood from his throne and walked down the dais. His face showed more emotion than I'd seen from him before. From the furrow of his brow to the crinkle around his eyes and the purse of his lips, his worry seemed to be real and true. The *king* was worried about a human slave. It was such a contradiction to what he'd just said about me. He stood before the crying female, crouching down and running a hand through her hair, so lightly and gently that I exhaled a breath in surprise. The hypocrisy when he was just berating Cyrus for treating me the same nearly made me laugh out loud. If the situation wasn't so awful, I probably wouldn't have been able to contain it.

I shifted my gaze around the room to note the expressions of the others present. No one was surprised by this show of care from the king, which told me they were all well aware of his feelings for her. Something Cyrus was surely about to use against him. I waited to see where Cyrus was directing this little play of his, and how I might be able to twist it to help myself.

"Your slave here, Despoina, has made you believe she is loyal to none but you, isn't that correct Father?" Cyrus asked as he strolled slowly up towards where the humans had been dropped before the thrones. Standing just behind them, where the king stood in front. King Astraeus looked up from who was apparently his personal "companion", as I was supposedly Cyrus's.

"Of course. Despoina has always been loyal." Astraeus insisted, a severe frown aimed at his son.

"I am—I swear! I am!" The woman cried and nodded frantically and reached her hand out to the king, who ignored it despite looking like he wanted nothing more than to take her hand. My heart hurt watching her. She was so desperate—desperate for the king to believe her. She looked at him with adoration and love in her eyes. It made me feel faintly sick. He didn't deserve that from her.

Cyrus smirked up at his father as he leaned down. He grabbed the neck of the male beside Despoina and wrenched him upwards, whispering something in his ear that made the man's head hang low. At least until Cyrus forced it upright.

"Meet Tavarius."

I gasped, covering my mouth with my hand to keep the sound muffled. Cyrus turned his head to me—his eyes dark like a gathering storm and his smirk vicious as a blade.

I inched my way up until I could see Tavarius better. That ruggedly handsome face was beaten and bloody now. My hand shook in front of my mouth, and I slowly lowered it, numb shock filling my limbs with heavy dread. Cyrus's look at me lingered in my mind as I took in the broken man in front of me. The only one since arriving that dared to flirt with me and offer to take me to bed…

A sick feeling rose in me, and I struggled not to vomit right onto the throne room floor.

"They've betrayed you, my King. He's been fucking Despoina behind your back." Cyrus explained, rather callously. I shook my head slightly in disagreement—no! This couldn't be happening! "Committing treason by touching the king's property. Defiling it. Making you look a fool. And worst of all, she's pregnant with his child."

Glee radiated from Cyrus as he put on a front of sympathy and grace. His face painted with a frown of disappointment before he pursed his lips and nodded to the king in apology. Not a spec of the gloating I was sure he was doing internally could be found on the surface.

"Is this true?" King Astraeus's face grew hard and cold, all the care from before wiped away. He turned to Tavarius, and his voice was as icy as his expression. I waited for Tavarius to deny the ridiculous accusation.

"Yes, my King." Tavarius replied through his blood-drenched mouth.

This had to be Cyrus. Whatever he said to Tavarius, he ensured he would lie to the king. That he'd believe telling the truth would be an even worse fate. I couldn't imagine any other way this could come to pass. The room was spinning, and I was beginning to feel out of control in a way I rarely allowed myself. The piece of me I let care for others was being carved into now, my heart bleeding out onto the floor along with Tavarius's blood.

"Astraeus, please. You know I wouldn't do such a thing!" Despoina pleaded, frantically shaking her head as she cried her denials. The king stepped in front of her, I watched as he backhanded Despoina so hard she fell onto her side. I winced at the motion of his hand, at the abhorrent force with which he struck her. Her sobbing increased as King Astraeus turned away from her, a clear dismissal. He turned to Tavarius, then pulled back his fist and punched Tavarius with enough force that his head flew backwards. Cyrus merely laughed as he lifted it back. King Astraeus hit him again and again, Tavarius's blood rushing and bones crunching.

I watched in mute horror. My stomach turning and tears streaming down my face. I could do nothing but shake in fear. The queen on the other hand, looked incredibly pleased, smiling down at Cyrus like he'd accomplished a wonderful feat.

I suppose to her, he had.

The sick bitch.

The king looked backwards and held out a hand. One of the Fae guards came forward and handed the king an object from his belt. He cracked his hand and…a whip unfurled to the floor.

Old Gods, no, please no…

Two guards came up to Tavarius, taking an arm each as Cyrus stepped back and ripped his shirt down the middle, exposing his chest and back completely. Cyrus prowled over to me as I watched the whip dance through the air, the hard crack as it landed and broke skin, and the heart wrenching scream of agony from Tavarius as it hit his skin. Cyrus came up behind me, his arms encircling my waist and pulling me back against his body.

His cock was hard as a rock and pressed snugly against my ass.

Old Gods, I was honestly going to be sick.

Cyrus got aroused from this? What in Tartarus was wrong with him? I watched the whip come down, again and again. I didn't even notice I was still crying steadily until Cyrus leaned down and licked a trail of tears off my cheek.

"You see, my dear Asteria?" His lips murmured against my ear, my heart shielding itself with its cage of ice. "You see what happens when you flirt with another?" My heart dropped into my stomach as the ice around my heart spread through my veins. My body frozen with horror.

"Oh, yes." Cyrus laughed lowly. He nipped at my ear, torturing me with a honeyed voice and poisonous words. "I know all about that. You considered letting him take you to bed. That is unacceptable." His voice hardened as he pressed my body back against his, rubbing his cock against my ass in the process. His fingers came up and trailed across my heaving chest. The fear and anger made my breaths heavy as I struggled to breathe through the panic.

"This is your punishment. And his." Cyrus lightly bit my earlobe, then sucked it into his mouth. He tried his best to taunt me as he worked to turn me on against my will, but my horror was too vibrant an emotion to be dulled. His fingertips against the tops of my breasts, his cock snug against me, his teeth on my earlobe. All of his motions clashed against the terror and pain of what I was witnessing. The brutal torture of a good man. One who was beaten and then stripped down to be viciously whipped. He'd committed no crime; Cyrus was obviously lying about Tavarius fucking Despoina—they were both innocent.

This was him making a space for Emmie in his father's bed. His cruel machinations lined up perfectly with punishing me and Tavarius. A happy coincidence for him when he needed a man to blame, and a brutally eye opening one for me. I realized now how quickly all of my plans could fall apart. How much did Cyrus already know about them? Was he just humoring me? If he knew about Tavarius flirting with me, he could know *anything*. Fear rose and rose, pricks of rage joining it, until—

A strike of lightning reverberated around the room. I watched as blue lightning barreled toward Tavarius. I screamed in horror and tried to run to him, but Cyrus held me fast against him. Laughing in my ear all the while.

"Oh no. You're going to watch this."

I cried as I struggled against him, but Cyrus grabbed my hair and forced my eyes on Tavarius. Just in time to watch the lightning from the king's fingers strike his chest. His whole body lit up, the lightning seeking everything inside him and liquifying it.

And poor, sweet Tavarius slumped over on the ground, dead.

All because he dared to flirt with me.

"No! Tav, Old Gods, no!" I whimpered with shock. I turned to Cyrus in my grief and rage. "What have you done?"

"What I must." Cyrus laughed cruelly in my ear, as he forced me to turn around and watch what was transpiring. To look at Tavarius and the charred body before us. Despair filled me. A good man was dead, all because of me.

No, I reminded myself. Not me, but *Cyrus*. The man at my back thought he could seduce me, yet what he accomplished was proving himself to be exactly the monster the alluring Fae soldier from the Night Kingdom said he was.

Did Cyrus know about what transpired between us as well? My fear rose. Should Cyrus discover what happened, the thought of what he might do to him struck me in the heart.

I wanted to move, to flee, to do *anything*—but I may as well have been made of stone as Cyrus held me firmly against his body, only able to watch in alarm as the king turned his attention to Despoina.

"No!" I gasped wetly; my voice strangled in my throat by my tears. I'd never felt so powerless in all my life. And that realization sparked the rage back inside me. The combination of terror and panic overwhelmed me as Cyrus began speaking once more.

"Leave her to me, Father. I know just the place for a whore like her."

King Astraeus looked over to his heir and for once, they shared a smile—a cruel one.

"Oh, yes, my son. Put this treacherous whore back to work. I think that's the perfect place for her. If she wants to spread her legs to anyone who comes by, she can do it while earning us money at least." The laugh he let out made me thrash against the bonds of Cyrus's arms, but it was pointless.

I was trapped. In his arms. In his life. In his kingdom.

The throne room doors opened once again, and I hesitated to look, hating to think of what could be coming next. I blinked, absorbing the sight of Emmie walking in. Her blonde hair was styled in a half up do with a mass of curled ringlets. Her makeup was done immaculately, highlighting her cheekbones and making her eyes pop. She was dressed in a dark gray slave's dress, but one that clung to her body in all the right places and was cut low to show off her chest.

Fuck. *Oh fuck*. This was it. The moment Emmie would be thrown in front of the king as bait.

Would my soul be damned for the choice to go along with this when Cyrus brought it up? For what came to pass because of it? The consequences of my actions when stuck in a situation with no good choice to make? Would the death of the kind Tavarius and the degradation of loyal Despoina blacken my soul forevermore?

I felt like they would. I wanted to collapse to the ground. I wanted to scream and cry until my voice gave out.

Emmie walked slowly, swinging her hips all the while. I nearly rolled my eyes, but I noticed the king's attention firmly on her ass. Fuck, it was actually working. As Emmie made for me, Cyrus finally released me. I nearly sighed in relief, my legs almost giving out from the abrupt change of now carrying my own weight—until Emmie wrapped her arms around me.

"It's okay, Asteria. It will be okay." Her voice was quiet, hushed. She must have noticed the charred body on the ground. Did she realize who it was? She must not have. I couldn't imagine her staying so calm if that was the case. Her thanks for not sleeping with him haunted me—it had been for exactly this reason.

As it turns out, the offer was enough to damn him. It hadn't mattered that I said no, I would never stop being sorry for what he had been dragged into because of me.

"Who is this?" King Astraeus asked, making me cringe. Apparently, he was as predictable as Cyrus thought. With his favorite disgraced and discarded, a spot in his bed opened up.

"A slave." Queen Stelara's wry voice answered, making me twitch. She'd left Cyrus to handle his father, sitting back to enjoy the show. And it was apparent she was truly enjoying it. Eyes lit up with malice as she watched Despoina be dragged away to her fate. I watched with devastation, my heart hurting for this woman who deserved so much better.

"Cyrus?" The king demanded, letting out a long-suffering sigh as he glanced down to quickly glare at his wife. "Who is she?"

"No idea. A slave, as Mother said." Cyrus shrugged nonchalantly.

King Astraeus glared at his son, but was seemingly assured he didn't know her, and turned to Emmie, who blushed under his attention. Fuck.

King Astraeus stepped closer to where we currently stood on the edge of the throne room. Slowly meandering over as his eyes devoured Emmie. "What is your name, little beauty?"

"I'm Emmie, my King." She giggled prettily as she answered him, before she dropped into a graceful curtsy—exposing her cleavage to him as she leaned forward. King Astraeus took the time to enjoy the view as he stepped in front of her.

My muscles twitched, wanting to reach out and pull Emmie back to me. Cyrus seemed to sense that, shifting me back against his body once more. His hands on my hips as he ground against me.

"Don't ruin this, my dear. You won't like what happens if you do." Cyrus warned in a whisper, his voice underlined with malicious threat.

His warning had me freezing in place. I couldn't imagine I would like anything he did, so I stayed still as Emmie rose and the king dragged his eyes down her body.

"A vacancy has recently opened up in my bed, little beauty." King Astraeus murmured lowly as he reached out and ran a finger down Emmie's cheek. She shivered at his touch, and I watched her melt before him. "Would you be interested in the position?" The king smirked, already assured of what her answer would be as he confidently propositioned her.

I couldn't believe what I was watching. Actually, I could. Emmie herself told me that humans had to take any advantage they could to rise. Especially in a place like this. She would jump at any opportunity. And the one she was being offered was the best she could get. The king was the highest authority in the kingdom, after all. Warming his bed would have all sorts of perks. One's I could also get if I gave into Cyrus's wishes. One's I refused.

"I would be honored, your Highness." Emmie smiled widely, matched by the king's smile. How quickly he forgot Despoina. I couldn't imagine bubbly, sweet Emmie facing the consequences of becoming entangled with the king as Despoina had just experienced. She'd already become a target for the machinations of the court and an unwitting spy.

"This meeting will be wrapped up shortly." King Astraeus assured Emmie. She beamed back at him as he called for one of his guards. "Jakal."

"Your Highness." Jakal stepped forward and bowed to the king.

"Show her to my room." He ordered, then turned back to Emmie. "I will meet you there shortly, little beauty. Then we can become better acquainted." His smile was exceptionally wolfish for a man who shifted into a pegasus.

"I'll be awaiting you eagerly, my King." Emmie winked as she curtseyed once more, giving me a quick hug, then walking off with Jakal to the king's bedroom. To be his.

"Now," King Astraeus turned back to us, sneering. "What to do about you two?"

"Father—" Cyrus stiffened immediately. He tried to begin speaking, but Astraeus cut him off quickly.

"Yes, yes." The king waved his hand. "You traded information for keeping your whore. In gratitude for shedding light on the betrayal happening under my nose, and you inadvertently helping me find a new pretty little thing to bed, I will grant your request to keep her."

I wasn't being traded. Thank the Old Gods for that. Relief swirled alongside my indignation for how the king spoke of Emmie and me—then horror was added to the mix as I realized just how stuck I was with a man who killed innocents so he could play his sick games.

"Thank you, Father. I—" Cyrus relaxed against me, his fingers squeezing my hips, a spot I didn't realize was so sensitive until he did so. I shivered despite myself, and Cyrus pulled me closer, placing a kiss on the side of my neck.

"You are far too attached to this girl, and it will not stand, Cyrus. We must present a certain image to the world, and being besotted with a human will hurt that image." Cyrus bristled as his father stepped closer, until he was standing a mere step in front of me.

I took a deep breath, looking back at him. I knew I should avert my eyes, but I couldn't. I was rooted in place, engulfed by the maelstrom of emotions sweeping through me.

"What are you saying?" Cyrus demanded, his tone dangerous and sharp. One that spoke of restrained violence, of the very storms he wielded. I was honestly surprised that Cyrus had the audacity to speak to his father as he did.

"You can keep her on the side, but you will show the world something very different." King Astraeus smiled slowly. "It is time for you to marry."

Cyrus was against my back, so I couldn't see his face. My own expression was a picture of surprise. His plan was for Cyrus to take a wife and keep me on the side? I nearly snorted, considering I wasn't even sleeping with him. But by the Otherworld, *no*! I refused to ever allow myself to be put in that position. I hadn't considered that Cyrus would marry in my lifetime—I hadn't even worried about it. Thankfully, I had no plans to ever give into him, but unfortunately, everyone already believed I had—and that was enough.

"A wife? Are you kidding me?" Cyrus spat the words out, his surprise and anger swirling together to form a vicious mixture. His hands gripped my hips tighter and my body reflexively pushed into his touch despite my desire to remain still. I couldn't help the reaction, but I didn't want to encourage him either.

"Yes, Cyrus. A wife." King Astraeus snarled impatiently. "Show me that you are worthy of being my heir. Make an alliance, secure the betrothal. Having a wife and child will shore up your position. Despite my wish that the gods had chosen someone more worthy to be my heir, you are it at the moment. Perhaps if you don't marry, Weylin will soon find himself in your place." The smirk the king gave his son was full of arrogance.

"Fine. We've always been close with Dawn Kingdom." He sniggered, making me curious to know why he *laughed* while proposing a bride. "I'm sure Princess Zerlina will be eager to take the position of future queen."

"A good choice." The king nodded begrudgingly. "You handle that, along with the traitor." He raised an eyebrow and I felt Cyrus nod, his head coming to rest on my shoulder. His chin dug into it as his cheek sat against mine.

"Of course, my King. I will get on that immediately."

"Very well then." King Astraeus sharply nodded and turned, walking out of the throne room. I was so focused on him and Cyrus that I didn't notice Queen Stelara creep up until I turned to see her standing before us. I jolted hard, but Cyrus caught me, and I quickly straightened. Not that it mattered. The queen ignored my presence entirely, despite the fact that I was pressed flush against her son's body. I was curious to know what the queen did in her own time. I knew she kept a human as well. Was she sleeping with him? It seemed like all the Fae have a human they keep as their main companion. Perhaps that was part of the reason she didn't care about her husband fucking humans.

We didn't count. It was only scandalous if he fucked another Fae. Someone who actually *mattered*.

The thought sat bitterly in my throat, wanting to be released in a wave of fury. But I bit it back. I couldn't afford to voice my thoughts in present company.

"You did well, my son." Queen Stelara smiled, more warmly than I'd seen her do in my entire time here.

"Thank you, Mother. Father is all too predictable." Cyrus scoffed. "And Daneiris stepped too far out of line. She may need a reminder why she doesn't want to fuck with me." Cyrus growled and the queen merely chuckled.

"How the gods ever chose your father for kingship is beyond me. He's clearly unfit." The queen responded, waving her hand to the side, dismissing her husband and his position. "It's a good thing this kingdom has us, or it'd likely be wiped off the map already." She glowered at the thought, or perhaps she imagined her husband as she did so.

"As for your sister, yes, she will indeed need a warning." She paused, her head tilting to the side as she considered. "Just don't do any permanent damage. She's still my daughter, despite her very wrong opinions. Your siblings are too busy trying to grab for scraps of power and influence to support you as they should." His mother huffed. I tried to untangle all these bits of information Queen Stelara unwittingly shared so I could begin to figure her out, but it was like a puzzle with all the pieces mixed up and some missing completely.

"Of course, Mother. I will ensure you still have all your children by the end of this." Cyrus's right hand released my hip and reached for his mother. "They will learn to bow to me in time. Once I sit the throne, I'll make sure they all get in line. As will you, I'm sure."

"Yes," Queen Stelara nodded in agreement. "I'll be starting with your sister as it appears. In the meantime—" Her eyes found mine for the first time and I twitched against the urge to hide. It felt unnervingly like a predator stalking their prey when she looked at me. "—Get your inclinations under control. Do not be seen to be treating this one as anything but what she is. Don't follow your father's footsteps in this. I have done what I can to minimize word of his behavior getting out, and I refuse to do it for you too. You have a princess to woo now. Focus your attention there instead."

"Don't worry about me, Mother." Cyrus replied. I could practically feel his arrogant smirk. The queen scrutinized her son, and I nearly breathed a sigh of relief, knowing her eyes were no longer on me. "I'll ensure Princess Zerlina feels the full weight of my attention."

His mother released a heavy sigh while studying him, her eyes lingering back on me for a moment. For that second she glanced back at me, I didn't breathe. After that lingering heartbeat, she nodded, then sharply spun away on her heel, stalking out of the throne room. Surely to go terrorize someone else—Princess Daneiris most likely.

"Now, you and I have some business to attend to, my dear." Cyrus spun me around to face him by my hips. My hands shot out and grabbed onto his arms to avoid falling over in the process. I breathed out heavily. I slowly brought my gaze up to his. A cruel light glinted in his eyes, but there was something else that lingered. A trace of that same man who showed me there was more depth and layers to him that he hid away. The man that kissed me so sweetly and sparked passion between us. Old Gods, had he been that man all the time, I would have struggled not to jump into his bed—despite my convictions. But that man was completely overshadowed by the monstrous act carried out only feet away—and I could not, *would not*, forgive him for the horror show he'd orchestrated today.

CHAPTER 13

"Come along, Asteria." Cyrus smirked like he could tell what I was thinking and didn't care one bit. He walked away from me, trusting I'd follow along. Because, honestly, I truly had no choice in the matter.

Otherworld damn him and his stupid expectations! And damn the fact that I had no choice in following through and proving him right.

I hurried along behind him, blinking with surprise as he led us to the main entrance where a carriage awaited us. A wagon trailed behind the carriage, piquing my interest. I narrowed my eyes at Cyrus's back as he stopped in the middle of the round cobblestone drive.

He didn't move towards the carriage, instead walking straight to one of the nearby guards. The Fae nodded at whatever Cyrus said, and the two spoke for a few moments before the guard ducked into a side door. Cyrus glanced over at me and the smile he flashed in my direction filled me with trepidation.

I was right to fear that look. A moment later, the side door opened and Despoina was dragged out. She wept softly as guards held either arm, dragging her to the wagon and loading her in. I was transfixed by the scene unraveling before me, so much so that when Cyrus touched my arm, I jumped in surprise.

"Let's go." Cyrus demanded, taking my arm and dragging me toward the carriage. I stepped up into the carriage in a haze, beginning to feel numb with all that transpired over the last hour. Cyrus watched me for the entire journey while the carriage rattled down the roads to wherever our destination was. The sinking feeling sat heavily in my gut, but the numbness spreading through me didn't allow me to dwell on it.

"It's time." Cyrus said as the carriage came to a stop, a wide smile spreading over his face. He exited the carriage and waited for me to step down before he led me toward the front entrance of the building we stopped at before.

I noticed the women right away. Several stood around out front, dressed in the most scantily clad outfits, leaving no room for imagination. Chests nearly burst out of their low necklines, while others had tiny straps barely hanging on, and high slits showed off their toned legs and thighs. I gulped at the sight of them.

The building itself was fairly nondescript, dark gray brick made it blend into its surroundings. Cyrus waved me along impatiently, and I followed him through the door, entering into a whole different world.

The loud sounds reached me first. All the yelling, screaming, moaning, and laughing. Glasses clinked, and cards shuffled. Chips dealt across tables.

The main floor had all sorts of card tables set up. A long bar ran across the back of the establishment. Men drank and gambled with women perched half naked on their laps. Some smoked a substance I could only guess was eclipse—named for its effect of euphoria eclipsing reality. I watched as several women laughed while they pulled men who were bemoaning their losses toward a set of stairs, clearly intending to lose themselves in the women to forget. Grabbing them by the hips or ass and boasting of the entertainment he'd offer her. The women were well practiced—agreeing eagerly instead of laughing at their obvious exaggerations.

I blushed, realizing now just how innocent I was, prior to this evening. It was one thing to read of Cyrus's gambling dens and brothels, but to see it in person was a surreal experience.

"Well, well, what do we have here?" Said a busty woman who eyed me over, clearly assessing my body and looks. Her dress was so short I felt my eyes nearly falling out of my head. "She's a pretty one, my Prince, she'll certainly bring in quite a lot of coin."

Was she propositioning Cyrus to purchase me? For her establishment?

Oh, Otherworld, no—I refused to allow it!

"I'm afraid she's not available, Saskia. She's mine." Cyrus replied coolly as he narrowed his eyes at the woman. His arm came around my waist and pulled my body against him.

"That's a shame." Saskia tsked as she continued to look me up and down. She shook her head with remorse. "She looks like she could keep me in business for years." I stiffened at her predatory tone, and Cyrus let loose a growl which made the woman burst out with a smoky laugh.

"Calm down, my Prince, the message has been received." Saskia continued to chuckle, her voice raspy and low. "Now, what can I do for you? Are you looking for some more women to add in? Is your girl not keeping you satisfied?"

Should I be insulted? A part of me bristled at the assumption that I couldn't please my partner—the other part was annoyed that my partner would be the prince in this situation.

"I have a new girl for you." Cyrus began, studying me with a raised brow before he turned his attention back to the older woman. "One who will need to be broken in only slightly to the job. She's experienced in sex work, but not in a brothel. She was castle-only before she became a companion."

Saskia opened her mouth to say something, but the two guards came in, holding Despoina between them, dragging her to us and dropping her to the ground. I glared at them as I yanked out of Cyrus's grip, going to my knees before her.

"Despoina? Are you—" I winced as a hand fisted my hair and yanked me back up to my feet. Cyrus used his grip on my hair to turn my head to him. I seethed, my teeth grinding as I glared at him.

"Don't test me right now, Asteria. You see this?" He forced my head to Despoina, collapsed on the ground. "This could be *your* fate. I've been so good to you, my dear. I've tried to give you everything you'd ever need, only to have it tossed back in my face. And then you flirt with some random slave, consider taking him to bed, and make a fool out of me." His words were a low hiss, only for my ears.

The din of the brothel prevented even Fae hearing from picking up his words.

"If you don't behave—" Cyrus continued with a harsh frown and a shake of his head. "You'll force my hand. I don't want to do that, Asteria. I want you with me. But I will not accept your insubordination. Do you understand?"

I could barely find my words, my rage was so intense. I forced a nod of consent. He yanked my hair back hard, and I let out a rough gasp as the pain tingled my scalp.

"Use your words." He growled.

"I. *Understand.*" I spat the words at him. Cyrus wasn't used to not getting exactly what he wanted, and I drove him insane because I wouldn't bend to his wishes. Clearly, his fragile ego would never recover from such a terrible slight.

Which led me to the conclusion that if I wouldn't fuck him, the greater punishment would be to make me fuck whoever I was told to, consent or no. I refused to let that *ever* be my fate. Cyrus was exactly the monster he tried to pretend he wasn't, today was proof of that—and I was resolved to find my way out of his domain immediately.

"Good." Cyrus purred. "I hate when we argue so, my dear. Now, be a good girl for me while we're here." I was seething, and Cyrus could certainly tell. He'd been drawn to me for that anger after all. He just smiled, satisfied, like he'd won.

"This is her?" Saskia's voice snapped me out of my tunnel vision, and I noticed she was looking down at Despoina with a raised brow and pursed lips. "She doesn't look like much."

"She was the king's favorite. Today has been a hard day for her." Cyrus chuckled. He dared to mock her, after all he put her through? "Let's get her into shape, shall we?" He turned to his guards and then Saskia in turn, commanding each. "Bring her up to my room. Send Yasmine and Finnia up with her."

"You're the boss." Saskia said, nodding her confirmation, then walked off to follow his instruction.

"Now, I hope you don't get jealous, my dear." Cyrus murmured, leaning down to speak in my ear as his arms came around me, holding me by the waist. "After all, a man has needs, and you're proving quite the stubborn one." Cyrus chuckled darkly. "But I do hope you like to watch."

Fuck. He really was going to make me watch him break Despoina in. I struggled to swallow the bile rising in my throat.

This whole environment was too much. I was clearly much more naïve than I'd thought, but I was having a hard time processing everything that had happened tonight already. My eyes blew wide with shock as I watched all the debauchery taking place.

Cyrus grabbed my hand to pull me along. Up the staircase and down several halls, each filled with screams and moans. There were several open doors that left my mouth hanging open after one glimpse inside, before we made our way up another set of stairs to a door at the top landing.

Cyrus opened it and inside was a large suite. A fairly simple bedroom with a living area and a bathing room to the left. A balcony came off the living area and oversaw the city.

"Sit, Asteria." Cyrus commanded as he pointed to a chair facing the bed.

I hesitated, and Cyrus glared pointedly. I dropped into the chair across the room begrudgingly.

"Good." Cyrus smiled, instantly appeased.

A knock sounded at the door, and then two women were sweeping inside. One was blonde with shoulder length hair and a small, thin frame, and the other was a redhead with long, curly hair and voluptuous curves.

"My Prince," the blonde purred as she sauntered over, "It's been too long."

She went up to Cyrus, but just before her hands made contact with his chest, he grabbed her hands and held them away from his body.

"I'm afraid we're not here for me today, Yasmine." The blonde's eyebrows rose at the same time mine did. He'd insinuated I'd be watching him fuck tonight, so what game was he playing now?

"Did you really think I'd make you watch?" Cyrus asked, looking at me as he smiled. My mouth parted in surprise because—*yes*, yes I did. Cyrus shook his head. "I want Asteria here to see what happens when one disobeys. Despoina is your new pupil, she'll be brought up momentarily. Asteria is to watch this first training session."

"Of course, my Prince." Yasmine sighed, seemingly disappointed.

The redhead, Finnia I assumed, slinked up, cooing. "Are you sure we can't tempt you, my Prince?"

"All you ladies do is tempt." Cyrus laughed, a silky thing that made Finnia shiver. Both of them giggled in delight while I scrunched my nose as covertly as I could, unable to reign in my disgust and disbelief. "But I'm afraid not." The apology in his tone was genuine, and I worked to stop myself from gagging.

Cyrus prowled towards the chair I sat in, picking me up from it, and then sat in it himself before placing me on his lap. I immediately tried to move away from him, but his hands locked me down, unable to move.

"Oh, no you don't." He murmured in my ear. "You're going to sit right here and watch."

I went preternaturally still, not wanting to raise his ire nor squirm on his lap.

He'd definitely like the squirming too much.

The door opened once more and Despoina walked in. My heart hurt for her. She didn't deserve this. She'd done nothing wrong, and even if she had, *no one* deserved this. To my surprise, she was holding herself more confidently than she was when I last laid eyes on her. I thought back to what Cyrus and the king had said and realized with shock that they'd both mentioned she'd done this sort of work before. I'd been too caught up in what was happening to truly process their words.

It didn't make it any better that she was being forced into this position, but watching Despoina now, her tears finally stopped and a smile started to peek out—I was forced to admit she wasn't as upset as I would have imagined.

I was relieved for her sake, even if I didn't quite understand it. I would have been livid in her position.

The two girls led Despoina to the bed, where they began going over all sorts of rules.

"You never ask the clients questions. Ever. Even if it's what they like, you wait for them to make the request." Finnia insisted, and Despoina nodded in understanding. They continued going over the extensive list of rules, and Despoina chimed in with her own questions from time to time. It started to remind me more of when Whina was training me for my duties than like we were in a brothel. All of the day-to-day drudgery of daily tasks being covered.

"You want to make the client feel like the only person in the world. They know they aren't, but we're selling the fantasy. *That* is what they are purchasing, in truth." Yasmine circled Despoina as she spoke. "Any person can open their legs and let someone do whatever they want, no one is looking to purchase a dead fish. You want to entice them, tease them. Find what they desire—and then exploit it."

"Every piece of information is something you can use, either in that encounter, or another, or even just to pass to our prince." Finnia agreed, trailing a hand along Despoina's arm. "Knowledge is key, darling, remember that."

That was actually very good advice, and it gave me a greater understanding of this work that I'd lacked before. How different was this than what I was doing with Cyrus? Was I not trying to keep him interested to exploit him for my own plans? I couldn't judge them for the work they did. It was their way to survive. We all had masters to please, and we all fought to get out from under them to some degree.

This was how they found some control in their own work. Targeting desires and twisting the situation to please themselves.

Maybe there was a way to twist *this* particular situation to my benefit. With Cyrus under me, already angry with me, I needed to do damage control. But control was the key word. I needed to maintain it and find a way back into his good graces. Priscilla and I would never be able to get out of this court if he was watching my every move.

Eventually, the two brothel workers slowly brought Despoina down to the bed and began showing her what to do. How to move, where to touch, what to say—it was all a choreographed dance to them. Yasmine laid a hand on Despoina's thigh, grabbing the material of her dress as her fingers dragged it upwards with every move of her hand. She teased the freshly bared skin, until she reached Despoina's breast, where she paused to play further. Using her fingers and tongue in conjunction, until Despoina was writhing beneath her.

Finnia was hardly idle, and as Yasmine got going, the redhead spread Despoina's thighs, trailing her nails along the skin as Despoina shivered pleasantly. She brought her fingers up to Despoina's exposed panties, and ran her finger along it, up and down and then circling her hidden clit. Finnia took her panties and made them press tightly against her—then used her tongue to lick upwards.

"What do you think, my dear? Would you like that?" Cyrus whispered in my ear, his fingers absently trailing along my own arms.

I didn't answer. I kept silent, refusing to give him what he wanted. He kept trying to tempt me, and when he grabbed my hips and pulled me firmly against his cock, I was forced backwards. I had no ability to overpower him, so I was going to need a good plan to get through this without completely betraying everything I believe in.

If I could keep Cyrus happy, without letting my own barriers down, would that be enough for him? I would never have sex with him, no matter what he believed, but it was clear Cyrus was going to escalate this dance of dueling desires between us—no matter what I wanted.

I would have to allow some play here. Make him think he's breaking down my walls and succeeding at his plans. That's what Cyrus needs to believe if I'm going to have any hope of freedom.

I flinched in surprise when a man came in through the door. Finnia and Yasmine stood up with large smiles.

"Despoina, this is Gage, he's going to help break you in." I paled rapidly. My eyes shooting back and forth between them. I could feel Cyrus's excitement below me, where I was situated on his lap. Rapidly calculating, I realized

Cyrus would expect me to fight or flee, so I tried to stand up, acting like I was doing exactly that—and Cyrus held me fast against him, just as I expected.

"Nuh-uh. You aren't going anywhere, my dear. Not after what you did." Cyrus brushed his hands across my thighs as he tilted his hips against my ass, impressing upon me his hard length. I breathed through my nose, centering myself as I accepted the part I had to play to get through this. My impulse when faced with a thick cock rubbing against me was to rub back, so I made to move like I was going to, and then stopped myself. Like I had suddenly realized what I was doing.

It had the desired effect, Cyrus chuckling as he grasped my hips hard. After all that had transpired, letting him touch me made me want to be sick. Letting a monster use me in any way went against every instinct I had. But I would press down the wild emotions I could feel bubbling beneath the surface. My emotions would sometimes get the best of me and go haywire with rage or despair—now wasn't the time for that. Now was the time for carefully thought out moves in this game.

I refused to think about how good it actually felt to have a cock rubbing against me. Cyrus was attractive, and when my brain was turned off, it was easy to be distracted by that fact. Were he a different man, this may have been a different situation entirely. I took a deep breath, pushing all of my own lust to the side to focus on what mattered.

Cyrus began kissing and nipping along my neck, as Gage disrobed and went to Despoina. Her smile at him, shy but bright, indicated her pleasure at the attention she was getting, and I took a moment to breathe through all that had happened to Despoina today. To see her genuinely smile with pleasure—it was a shock after everything.

"Did you honestly think she would dislike this?" Cyrus chuckled in my ear. "She was upset about losing the king's favor, sure." Cyrus licked the lobe of my ear, his teeth grazing it before giving the lightest nip. He used his knees to open my own legs, and his cock settled more comfortably against me. With the slightest buck, he was teasing against my core, and my body betrayed me, pressing into his touch. "But she's always been fine with falling into any Fae's bed she could. Before my father, she slept around with half the lords."

This was unacceptable. I had a plan to carry out here, one I couldn't manage when my body was a horny mess—begging for another pet, another stroke. I needed to reel myself back in and get back on track.

Cyrus wouldn't let me turn my head away from the tableau in front of me, forcing me to watch as Gage got in on the action. I couldn't help my own reaction. I'd never watched someone have sex before. Nor have I ever imagined seeing more than two people involved. But the two women were not bystanders, quickly getting into the action along with Despoina, who licked and sucked Gage's long cock as Finnia straddled his face and lowered herself onto his waiting mouth. Yasmine giggled delightedly as she got on the bed behind Despoina and began to lick her, using her fingers to bring her to a trembling orgasm. The visual, combined with Cyrus's attentions at my neck…

"Shalim." Cyrus breathed in and let out a moan. "You smell absolutely delicious, Asteria." He ground against me, adding pressure to my cunt that when combined with his movement next hitting my clit, lit me up like lightning had struck my nerves, causing my breath to hitch. My body still yearned to betray me. I was unforgivably wet from Cyrus's actions. No matter the horror of the day, my body only understood a man able and willing to please me. And his damn Fae senses told him everything—there was no hiding the dampness between my thighs from his nose. "You don't want to like this, but you do, don't you?"

I stayed quiet, not wanting to encourage him. But his hands moved slowly down my legs, and glided back up them, bunching up the fabric of my skirts when he reached my calves. My legs were fully exposed, and the touch of his fingers skimming my bare thighs had me unraveling into a pool of wanton desire. Cyrus breathed in, his fingertips trailing over my thighs, back and forth. I gasped with longing, a part of me craving his touch, even as I hated my body for reacting to it.

It had been so long, I was wound so tight, it felt hard to breathe—I couldn't catch my breath—

"Don't worry, Asteria. Just feel it. Let me help you." Cyrus's voice was begging in a way that seemed completely unnatural for him. The moans and dirty talk from the four lovers in my view charged the atmosphere around us. The heady ecstasy they were all giving themselves over to, even as they trained Despoina, it was too much. With Cyrus's fingers along my skin, his urgent demand to touch and be touched—his desire to make me feel all of the pleasure he could offer—for fuck's sake, I wasn't going to last, could barely remember why I couldn't give in to him. Why I couldn't take my pleasure. Why I couldn't demand he meet my needs for a change.

Cyrus's fingers skated down my inner thighs, and the last restraint I had snapped.

"That's it, my dear. Let yourself enjoy it." Cyrus panted in my ear, clearly as affected as I currently was. "You've been so bad, but I've been good to you, haven't I? I haven't made you do anything you don't want." His cock ground against my core, and I clenched down as I met his movement with my own, thrusting backwards and getting a gratified grunt from Cyrus. The two of us met in a rhythm created of sighs and moans, grunts and the rustle of clothing.

"Today was regrettable, I admit. I didn't want to do any of that." Cyrus murmured, his voice heavy with sensual need. "I had no choice, you understand. We needed someone in with my father, and now we have it. It was always going to take something dramatic to make that happen. But Despoina will be happy here."

He was trying to account for the horrors he created in the throne room, and a quiet, insistent voice told me to stop and protest—to fight and to resist his touch—but it was overwhelmed by the thrust of his body against mine, the moans of the others in the background. My body was craving touch—after so long denied, it had finally pounced upon the pleasure on offer and had no intention of stopping now.

His fingers ran along the top of my undergarments, down the seam of my panties, feeling the wetness that was leaking through them. He moaned and grinded against me. "I didn't want to make you witness any of it, but you had to understand that actions have consequences, my dear. You seemed to feel you were exempt from punishment, because you know I don't want to hurt you."

I didn't know any such thing, but I couldn't think of that right now. All I could think of was the fire burning inside me, and the months of sexual frustration I had been subjected to. Cyrus's fingers promised relief in this moment. I bucked up into them and his throaty chuckle sounded against my neck where he nipped lightly. I moaned as I pressed back against him. His other arm wound around my waist, pulling me further into him.

His fingers slipped into my undergarments, sliding over my bare cunt and we both moaned as his fingers finally slid through me. "Shalim, you're so wet for me. My good little girl. You're going to be good for me, aren't you, Asteria?"

His hand around my waist came up and grabbed my jaw, pulling my head to face him. His other hand stilled, not moving against my dripping folds. I whined, bucking against his fingers.

"Tell me, Asteria." His voice was rough, strained, like his restraint hurt him as much as me.

"Yes." I nodded quickly and his mouth crashed down on mine. His lips devouring as his tongue snaked out into my mouth to play against mine.

His fingers slid through my arousal, circling my clit as I pushed up into him. My tongue tangled with his as I whimpered into his mouth. I hadn't felt another's hands on me since before Placement Day. The charge it sent through me to have another do so shook my whole body.

"Such a good girl. So fucking wet for your prince." Cyrus's lips left mine as he kissed down my jaw, up to my ear. "Let's see how you like this…" He trailed off as his fingers slid lower, down to my entrance. My breath stuttered as I felt him push a finger inside me. We both groaned as I tilted my head back onto his shoulder.

"Fuck." I breathed out as he quickly added a second.

"You've been so worked up, my dear. Just think, you could have had this the whole time." Cyrus chuckled, his lips finding my exposed neck as he started to nip along the column. His fingers slid in and out of me, his thumb going to my clit and circling—dancing along the edges, making me whimper with the assault. He was driving me to the brink. He kissed down my neck as he added a third finger inside me, stretching me and causing me to clamp down around his fingers.

"Fuck." Cyrus hissed. "You're so tight, darling. I can't wait for you to finally break, Asteria. To let me finally fuck you like you need." His fingers sped up and I couldn't stop my loud moan from escaping as I writhed against him. My head tossed back against him, my eyes watching Despoina ride Gage's cock as the women took turns helping one another and riding his face.

"Yes, you'd like that wouldn't you? Feeling my cock filling you up, stretching you out." His fingers stretched out inside me at that moment, causing me to keen as I suddenly felt much fuller. Cyrus chuckled huskily. "Yes, you would. I know I would. Feeling all this tight, wet heat around my cock as I fucked into you. I can't imagine anything better."

His free hand came up and snuck under the top of my dress, cupping my breast in his hand. I pushed up into it as his fingers clamped around my nipple and pinched it. I moaned hoarsely, overcome with sensation.

"Shalim—Asteria—" Cyrus's voice cut off, strangled with desperate pleasure. He pulled his fingers out of me, and I whined in response, feeling empty and unfulfilled. "I'm sorry, my dear, just hold on."

He shifted me slightly forward and made me stand. I heard his belt clink as he let the front of my dress fall down, leaving me confused as how could he get his hands under if—he pulled up the back of my dress and then quickly pulled me down into his lap once more.

The front of my dress prevented anyone from seeing anything. And that was good because I felt—*fuck*. He'd pulled his cock out and was now sliding it along my bare cunt. My arousal covered his cock as he slid back and forth. I jumped when the head of his cock hit my clit, making Cyrus chuckle and do it again.

I was on the precipice of feeling that cock fill me up completely—feeling more than the tease of his tip hitting my bundle of nerves.

I knew there was a reason I shouldn't want this. I just couldn't remember it right now. The thought quickly flew away.

"Don't worry. I'm not going to fuck you here. I just had to feel you." A strangled noise left him. "By the Otherworld, you feel too good, Asteria." He did too, and I let my hips roll back and forth against his thick cock as he slid against me, his length between my lips, flaying me open and keeping me on the edge.

"That's it." He breathed heavily. "Fuck yourself against my cock, Asteria." I moaned and leaned against him, letting my hips move as I chased my pleasure. The feel of his cock bare against me left me wanting more, needing to be stretched out and filled to the hilt. I rode against his cock as its head repeatedly hit my clit, giving me enough friction to finally find the climax I'd been chasing. Starlight blasted behind my lids, taking me out of my mind and body for a moment—I felt myself dancing in the darkness, the night sky welcoming me with the freedom and wild joy it always had. A yawning void I would gladly fall into forever. I writhed against his cock, tilting up so that his cock was drenched in my arousal. I shook as I rode out the ecstasy washing through me, cries of gratification falling from my lips as my head crashed back against Cyrus's shoulder.

He grunted as he felt my cunt flutter against his cock, aftershocks still rocking through me. Cyrus grabbed my hips and kept me moving against him, until he was groaning, and I felt the splash of his orgasm against my folds as he came. The sticky drips of his cum against my cunt nearly had me panting for more.

Cyrus sighed and collapsed back into the chair, his arm winding back around my waist, pulling me against him. He buried his face into my hair as I collapsed against him, both of us panting and spent. Months of sexual tension unleashed unexpectedly.

When the high of carnal satisfaction faded, I tensed, remembering why exactly I *hadn't* wanted to resolve that tension between us.

Old Gods…what had I done?

CHAPTER 14

CYRUS knew the second I stiffened against him that I was regretting what happened. He sighed long-sufferingly as he lifted me off his lap, offering me a towel from the table to clean myself with. I wasted no time getting his spend off me. Despoina and Gage were similarly finished, and Cyrus grabbed my hand and led me out of the room. Not stopping downstairs, we went straight from the stairs to the door leading outside. He didn't stop until we reached the carriage, helping me inside and jumping in after me.

He had a small smirk on his face that I looked pointedly away from. He laughed lowly as he glanced at me.

"Don't worry, I won't push you for more. Not yet." Cyrus said calmly, making me look over at him in surprise. He smiled and leaned forward on his bench seat towards me. "Now that I've had a taste, I am desperate for more, certainly. But I know you'll draw further away if I do that, you can't help being obstinate—it's in your nature, and it's one of the things I enjoy about you. But this—what happened today? You've proven that under all that headstrong refusal, you do want me, Asteria. It's only a matter of time now, so I'll wait. And when you're ready? You'll be mine. *Completely mine.*"

I swallowed hard and looked away. His words inspiring both rage and fear, but also shame. Overwhelmingly, I was ashamed of what had just happened. Not because I took the pleasure from him that I'd desired in the moment, absolutely not. Regret over something that comes as naturally as sexuality was pointless. I could be disappointed in myself for succumbing, yes, but my shame lay in another direction.

I looked out the window at the bland city passing me by. He was partially right, a part of me did want him. Cyrus was beautiful and powerful—who wouldn't desire someone like that?

But I knew what he was—malicious, diabolic, nefarious, so many words, and I still couldn't find one to encompass the vile underbelly Cyrus hid behind a veneer of charm. The same man who—I drew in a shaky breath as I thought of what he'd forced me to watch today. What he had done, condemning an innocent to a hard, brutal death—and sending another to a brothel against her will. At that rotten, pitiable heart of his, he was a true monster.

I held myself shakily together until we finally arrived back at the palace. I had to stay three steps behind Cyrus as normal, when all I wanted to do was run as fast as I could away from him. When we reached his rooms, I escaped into mine as fast as I could.

I collapsed against my bed, grabbing my pillow and muffling my sobs into it. I'd let rage guide me for so long. Didn't let myself get close to people so I couldn't be hurt later. It was all for nothing. I felt *too much*.

The rigid ice I'd built around my heart cracked in an explosive rupture, sending shards of it spiraling out to cleave and slice into me. Care and desperation sunk into me. I worried desperately about Emmie. About Priscilla. About Eris, even, no matter how prickly she was.

Cyrus's actions today showed me that I was playing a game I had no chance of winning, not as things stood now. I was too inexperienced, too naïve, and had none of the resources that Cyrus had at his disposal. I worried for all of those I came to care about, as the reality of what my plans meant for them if I was discovered hit home.

Tavarius was a sweet man, and his death cut through me like a sharpened blade. He had deserved a better life, one where he could live long, free, and happily. Instead, he had died brutally. And the man responsible? I'd just let him touch me, and I felt the need to bathe and scrub my skin raw to wash his vileness away.

I couldn't comprehend his actions. What he'd done was so horrendous, I had never imagined a person could be capable of such evil. My soul felt battered and bruised from witnessing it—like an innocent layer I hadn't realized was there had been severed from my soul against my will.

I thought that I couldn't let myself care about others, but I did anyway—those around me had snuck into the cracks in my armor and settled there. It was dangerous, it could get me killed, but I didn't know how to turn it off. I thought that Soren proved that I couldn't love. He loved me, but I wasn't able to return his feelings.

Maybe that just meant I wasn't in love with Soren, not that I couldn't love at all.

Old Gods, love felt like much too dangerous an emotion.

My emotions ran rampant, a tempestuous tumult within me. My moods tended towards extremes from time to time, but they now plummeted me down farther than ever before into a black hole of depression. I felt…*lost*. Lost and unsure, my anger so far out my grasp, the only thing I could find now was desolation.

I FELL INTO a fitful sleep, my emotions pinging all over the place as I tried to sort out what had happened today in my mind. As I flew up among the stars, Luna greeted me, her shining scales glowing as she danced around me. I skimmed my fingers down her scales before she flew back to her spot. My brows creased as I looked over at her. She normally spent more time with me, and right now—I needed her calming presence more than I could express.

Tingles broke out over my skin, and the feeling of another presence impressed itself upon me. I turned, facing the dark expanse of night.

I gasped as I sensed the darkness reaching for me. I lifted my now glowing fingers, ignoring their iridescence, and tried to grasp the incorporeal. I could tell we were so close, mere inches between us as fingers of darkness became clear when my own hand neared them. My skin lit up the space before me and separated the regular darkness of night from this strange dark presence.

A bright wave of emotions filled me, coming from an external source. It's desperation to reach me, sadness, an undercurrent of love, promise and devotion. I could even feel the inexplicable desire to make *me* feel better. The ethereal darkness somehow knew the despondency I had fallen into after the harrowing events I'd witnessed.

We could not get any closer to each other, the barrier between us was still firmly intact, making me want to cry with frustration—but I had cried until I had no more tears left to shed before I even fell asleep. I yearned for the darkness to wrap me up and take away all of my pain—to make everything that had happened since I came to Dusk nothing more than a terrible dream.

The dark hand banged on the barrier, and the reverberation of it spread out in ripples across the star flecked sky. We both paused, watching for a moment as the barrier shook. Another bang and then—

A loud, shrill noise broke through the peaceful dark, causing me to gasp as the intrusion tore me from my dream in an instant. I groggily looked around, upset that I had been awoken right when progress was being made—that I had been taken away from the darkness offering me solace I could never find in my waking life. I threw my blanket off, rolled out of bed—and came to a dead stop.

The hawk I'd seen flying around before was standing on my balcony, where I hadn't bothered to shut the doors, allowing the calm winds to snake through and kiss my skin with a light, cool breeze. The hawk was standing right at the entrance to my room, staring directly at me with an uncanny level of intention.

It cocked its head, trilling slightly in what I could only interpret as a question—making me wonder if I was losing my mind. I didn't understand what made me so certain, but I couldn't shake the surety that the hawk was trying to communicate with me.

When I didn't answer immediately, the hawk began walking slowly into my room, as if it didn't want to spook *me*. I shook my head as if it would shake away the surreal image in front of me and replace it with the reality that I was alone, but the hawk was still there. It stopped when it was right in front of me and bopped its head into my hand. I blinked slowly, and brought my hand up, petting the hawk cautiously.

It trilled sadly, looking at me like it knew the emotions that whirled through me until I was left numb from the onslaught—a shell of myself all that was left in their wake.

"I'll be okay, I think." I told the hawk with a tremulous smile, my voice soft and weary, like all life had been leached from me.

The hawk made a soft noise, and I wondered at what insanity had led to me confessing everything to a hawk of all things, but I told it of all the events that occurred yesterday, and how my plans for freedom felt hopeless when up against such vile and ruthless Fae.

Tears rained down my cheeks, causing the hawk to burrow into me.

"Thank you, hawk. I don't know why you're here, but I'm very grateful." I laughed wetly as I pet its head.

It made a soft noise in response, but the sound of a door opening and people murmuring made the hawk pull away and stand up, fully alert. It looked back at me once more, trilling at me, before it flew off. Its abrupt departure left me to wonder if I had still been dreaming during that encounter, and only now was I actually waking up.

A soft knock was all that announced Priscilla before she opened my door and walked into the room, coming to a standstill when she saw me on the ground leaning against my bed, disheveled, and with the residue of tear tracks down my cheeks. She immediately knelt down next to me, taking me into her arms as she softly petted my hair back.

In the safety of my friend's arms, I let down all of my walls, the ice armor I'd kept around my heart unable to be pieced back together, leaving me to just—*break*.

My sobs returned as everything that had occurred, everything that I felt, just hit me again and again—wave after wave, leaving me drowning in their wake. I thought I'd cried myself out, but I hadn't known anything. My tears had just been renewing until I unleashed them once more.

Priscilla murmured soothingly to me, petting my head and letting me get everything out. A steady rock in the storm I felt consumed by, one I grabbed onto with both hands in the hope I wouldn't be washed away completely. My tears finally slowed, but my grief and shattered heart remained, causing me to slump into her arms.

"I'm sorry." I whispered, wiping the remains of my tears off my cheeks. Embarrassment over the state she found me in rose up, but I was so worn that I couldn't even embrace the feeling, clinging to her in a way I had never dared before.

"Oh, Asteria." Priscilla replied, her voice soft and sweet, full of sympathy and genuine kindness. "Don't ever apologize for feeling what you need to."

Her words hit me hard, my eyes closing as I took them in. I'd never allowed myself to feel what I needed to. I tried to lock emotions away that I felt were too dangerous or tried to bury them when my rage or despair rose out of my control—making it seem like they controlled me instead of the other way around. They were a fire in my soul that would catch and burn, and I feared I would be left as nothing but cinders in the aftermath.

My inclination to hide my emotions away was coming back to bite me. By the Otherworld, I had no idea how to deal with the fallout of the hopeless grief that consumed me.

It felt like the gloom of Dusk had settled into my bones, leaving me to feel the heavy weight of it in my soul. I was swallowed by a gray pall, like all color had been leached away.

"I don't know what to do." I said miserably.

"None of us do." Priscilla started, her smile full of understanding. "Life is all about living despite the unknown. Facing down the knowledge that anything could come next and moving forward despite it."

A breath whooshed out, torn from my chest at her words. The unknown—I had feared it my entire life, wishing I could fly up to the sky and escape the fate that awaited me on Adamah. But that was never going to happen. I forced myself off the floor. For once in my life, I wasn't alone. Priscilla was right here, helping me through everything. Maybe the unknown wasn't as frightening when you weren't forced to face it alone.

"I don't know how to thank you for this." I said as I threw my arms around Priscilla, hugging her tightly. My voice strangled with emotion as I held her, my friend. One I could now fully admit to myself *was* a friend.

Love wasn't as much of a weakness as the fear that always lived within me—of the unknown, of the pain caused by loss. Those fears had kept me captive in their grip, and as I loosened that grip and let them go, a lightness brightened my soul. So damaged by the past day, but I could swear stardust swept through me, it felt so sublime.

"You don't need to. That's what friends are for." Priscilla replied as she tightened her arms around me, blonde hair spilling over my shoulder as she rested her forehead on it.

I would have to learn exactly how friends, like we now were, behaved with one another. My relationship with Soren was certainly not a good template to work from.

CHAPTER 15

The next few days passed with only Priscilla keeping me company. Why Cyrus decided to be magnanimous and let me have time to myself, I wasn't sure—but I was going to take full advantage and ready myself for the inevitable. I would be forced to spend time with him again, and I would have to keep the image of Tavarius from flashing in front of my eyes every time I did.

I armored myself internally, but not from connection to others this time. Cyrus alone was the one I needed to keep at bay. I would have to play this game with him once more, and I was going in knowing how brutal my end would be should I mess this up. Getting caught wasn't an option. I *would* find a way to get myself and my friends far from those like Cyrus who would harm us on a whim.

On the fourth day, when Priscilla appeared, Cyrus was standing beside her. My reprieve from him was at an end. Priscilla's wince when she made eye contact communicated silently that Cyrus's presence wasn't going to lead to anything pleasant.

"Asteria, Dawn Kingdom has answered my proposal faster than antici-pated." Cyrus said with a smirk lighting up his face, leaning back against the doorframe. It took me a moment to register what he was talking about before I remembered his father had ordered him to find a wife. He'd mentioned asking the princess of Dawn, but it had only been a few days. It seemed unusual for a royal to answer an offer so significant within such a short timeframe. They generally ruminate over decisions for ages.

"They'll be here today." Cyrus continued, looking at me with narrowed eyes. "Princess Zerlina will be here—ostensibly to see if we are compatible, but in truth, it will be to ensure our marriage benefits her and her family. Dawn's royal family will want to ensure this union brings them enough additional power and status to make it worth their time." Cyrus scanned my body with his eyes, assessing my appearance.

"As my personal slave," Cyrus said, for the first time referring to me as what I truly am, and not dancing around the truth. "You will be representing me. While the royal family won't bother themselves with slaves, we must ensure that your presence behind me makes the right impression when anyone does look at you."

"And with your ethereal beauty, it's inevitable they will." Cyrus stepped towards me, his hand reaching out and fingering a lock of my hair. I'd never felt more like a doll being made to his specifications.

"Ensure she looks her best for this." Cyrus's voice hardened as he let go of my hair and turned to Priscilla with his instruction. He spun back to me, and his harsh appraisal left me unsure of what had changed—other than him getting a taste of what he wanted. He sang my praises for months, used my body as he wished, and now he stared at me like I offended him with my appearance.

"Get rid of those bags under her eyes, will you?" Cyrus said to Priscilla, before leaving the room entirely, silence the only thing in his wake.

"What a dick." Priscilla's voice broke the silence a moment later. I let out a surprised laugh, causing Priscilla to smile widely.

I realized I hadn't laughed since the day Tavarius died. After a few days, I was feeling a bit more put together, less like shattered glass, but I knew now I had been changed irrevocably from it. Events of that magnitude had a way of lingering in one's soul, reshaping it until you become someone else on the other side.

I wasn't sure who I was becoming, but I now recognized the folly in my prior actions. I didn't see any other way forward than embracing the changes that were overtaking me. I was currently lingering in some middling stage—between who I once was and whoever I might soon become. A part of me was even excited to see who I may be at the end. Slavery didn't offer one many choices in discovering who they truly were, so I would have to muddle through until we found our way out.

Priscilla helped me get ready, ensuring my dark circles and all evidence of my breakdown and subsequent days of wallowing were covered up. She pulled out an elegant dress with a sweetheart neckline that was created to mimic twilight with an ombre of pink, purple, and gray shifting into one another. The gray section at the bottom flared out dramatically over my hips, and I twirled in front of the mirror just to make Priscilla smile as it lifted and spun, giving a peek at the dusky pink heels on my feet.

"Remember, no matter what happens, you are Asteria Faelynn Zagreus. You are strong. You are fierce. And you will not cower before any Fae royal who thinks themselves superior to you." Priscilla said as she grabbed my hands, squeezing them as she gave me a steadfast nod, helping raise my confidence as I went to face the beasts beyond my door.

I nodded back, hardening my resolve and fortifying myself for whatever royal insanity I was bound to face. When I emerged from my bedroom and entered his solar, Cyrus immediately looked up from his work and analyzed my appearance. I repeated Priscilla's mantra internally as I straightened my back and ensured my face was wiped of all emotion, raising my chin defiantly.

Cyrus rose from his chair and sauntered over to me, play-acting at a blasé attitude, but the cracks of lightning that flashed through his eyes gave away his frustration. Those bolts of lightning brightened as they drank in my appearance.

"You look gorgeous as always, my dear." Cyrus said as he gave me a satisfied smile, forcing me to push down the urge to punch him. After everything that happened—this was where his concern lay? Worrying about my appearance and showing off to his future wife's parents that he had a slave that was up to their royal standards?

I didn't bother to answer, and Cyrus's face shifted into a stormy expression that screamed a warning loud and clear. He didn't have time to waste on me, however, and we were soon hurrying down to the throne room, where Cyrus would receive the contingent from Dawn Kingdom.

I balked as we neared the throne room, my steps ceasing as I viscerally remembered what happened the last time I was inside those doors. Taking a deep breath, I forced down my tumultuous emotions—I had to pull myself together before facing the fiends of this court, I couldn't afford anything less right now.

The throne room was packed full when we arrived, with courtiers lining the walls—an expansive selection of pink and gray gowns and doublets as the courtiers paid homage to their royals. There was the odd splash of other colors like the woman wearing a bright red gown or the yellow and blue doublet I spied on a man across the room.

Cyrus walked confidently towards the dais, not sparing a glance at his courtiers as he made for the other princes and the princesses who were in their regular positions, standing to the left of the thrones. I walked three steps behind Cyrus, counting each step to ensure I didn't get too close before so many nobles. Every lord and lady of Dusk must have been called to attend court for this momentous occasion. I ensured the sarcastic sneer that wanted to creep out was kept from my face; I certainly didn't want to experience the whip for the first time before this entire crowd. If Cyrus and King Astraeus were anything to judge by, I could only imagine how bloodthirsty their lords were.

I swept my gaze across the room to find the six lords and ladies of Dusk. It was imperative I gather as much information as I could during this event. I felt vaguely like a clock was ticking down on me, every second passing and leaving me more likely to be trapped under Cyrus's control forever if I didn't find a way to get out.

Lord Oditi and Lady Asra Otieno of Murias often attended court, as Murias lay not far from Evenfall. Lady Asra was the very redheaded lady in waiting that Princess Daneiris was going to accuse her father of cheating on the queen with, had Cyrus not exposed her scheme. Lord Oditi was particularly close to King Astraeus, so it would have been disastrous for them.

The other pair I had seen around the court were Lord Visita and Lady Nisha Umbra, who were also relatively close by. Their city, Falias, was south of Evenfall and came close to bordering the neutral lands. Lord Visita was a favorite of the ladies at court, and I certainly couldn't blame them. Had he not been Fae and had Cyrus not been a concern, I may have joined them in their efforts to get his attention. He was particularly handsome, with his dark shaggy hair, sharp features, and golden eyes. I'd collected plenty of rumors about him entertaining various women around the castle, and equally as many about his wife. Lady Nisha had luminous skin that was a gorgeous deep brown, making her pale gray eyes stand out vividly. Her black hair was highlighted with blonde—a unique feature that only added to her striking looks. Standing next to her husband with his shining, golden tan, it was no wonder these two were so popular with men and women of every persuasion.

I was surprised to see Lord Aibek and Lady Siria were here, as when they came to beg for aid, Cyrus had sent his own commander to uncover the truth of the matter—sure that the attacks were a ruse and that their loyalty was not with King Astraeus. Considering they were in attendance for the arrival of Dawn Kingdom, Lord Aibek and Lady Siria must either not be aware of the close eye their royals were keeping on them, or unconcerned about it.

My gaze shifted to the nobles I could only recognize from what I'd read on them. My gaze immediately caught on the Lord and Lady of Eventide, the coastal city that brushed the Namminian Ocean. Lord Udaya and his wife, Lady Shirma Abital, whose union was a bit controversial at the time, since Lady Shirma was the only one left of her family who could rule their city when her father died. Women weren't allowed to take up lordship however, meaning she had to quickly find a man who'd step in and marry her so she wouldn't be displaced. Lord Udaya was the fourth son of a cousin to a lord in Sunset Kingdom, hardly the noble stock the royals of Dusk prized so highly. But Udaya saved her from losing her home, and by all of Cyrus's accounts, they had grown a genuine affection between them.

Lord Udaya still looked like he had come straight from Sunset Kingdom, with his light brown skin and freckles that dotted the bridge of his nose and sprayed onto his cheeks from time spent in the sun. He had large earrings hanging from his ears, a traditional practice for men in Sunset and Sunrise that he still honored. Lady Shirma's skin was lightly tanned, and her hair flowed down her back in big, chocolate waves. Her almond-colored eyes watched the room with calculation, where her husband leaned casually against the pillar with his arms crossed and a bored look on his face.

Cyrus strutted down the aisle leading to the dais his parents' thrones sat upon, taking up residence beside it when he arrived. I cut over to the wall behind him, where the slaves of his siblings were already lined up. I could feel the burn of eyes on me, some with jealousy, but others with sympathy. They knew what Cyrus and King Astraeus had done in this very room—one of their own lost to the cruel machinations of the royal Fae.

My emotions were too raw when it came to Tavarius to allow myself to think of it now, and my eyes kept firmly away from the spot where Tavarius died.

When the king and queen were announced, they swept into the room with all the regality of their mantles. Queen Stelara was dressed more elaborately than I'd ever seen. Forgoing the pink and gray her people stuck to, she shone in a turquoise ball gown embroidered with gold across the bodice and—what seemed to be an entire garden on her pleated skirt.

Giant red roses, made out of a fabric that seemed almost life-like, were sewn into the skirt in a garish display. Gold jewelry dripped from her neck, wrist, and ears; the entire look was topped by the golden bejeweled crown sitting atop her wine-red hair.

King Astraeus, on the other hand, wore a brocade jacket in charcoal and gold, matching his mantle decorated with golden chains and pink gems. His golden crown was a shocking deviation from his usual dark gray, even I had to admit he looked the very definition of kingly. But as I watched King Astraeus, all I could see was a whip in his hand and lightning crackling along his fingers—ready to kill once more. I couldn't stop the involuntary flinch as he strode toward his throne.

I closed my eyes to take a moment and center myself while all the bowing and scraping occurred, taking advantage of my having to bow my head low to avoid the many eyes around the room.

"Rise." King Astraeus said, sitting back on his throne as he waved a hand at the room at large, giving permission for everyone to stand once more.

Muted murmurs were all that followed the king's instruction, courtiers tittered and whispered to one another as Queen Stelara drummed her fingers on the arms of her throne. Princess Daneiris was once more standing tall and confident, and I realized I hadn't thought of her at all in the wake of everything that happened.

Old Gods, I needed to get back on my game. I should have considered the political implications of how the princess was dealt with, finding out whether she was punished or not—and if she was brewing up any new plans in the destructive wake of her last plot. I had let the importance of my own plans fall away as I fell into the black hole that had opened within myself. I couldn't afford such a distraction, not when the state of the court could change in a moment, leaving my plans to crumble to ruin if something vital was missed or exposed.

Giving up wasn't an option, that was certain. I would just have to work twice as hard to find the means to escape. It was more important than ever—this past week had proven that tenfold. I refused to spend the rest of my life stuck in this Tartarus on Adamah. I would not bow to Cyrus's cruel whims, nor would I let his family use me as a disposable pawn.

I needed to thank Priscilla for lifting me back up and dragging me out of my desolate spiral. I'd underestimated friendship and the power that came from having the true support of another person. Priscilla had been there for me at a time when I needed her most, along with the strange hawk, who had offered surprising comfort. Despite the fact that it woke me from the peace and bliss the darkness had promised, if only we could break the barrier holding us at bay. I didn't understand…well, any of it. Not on a conscious level, it felt more instinctive and surreal than anything I'd experienced, leaving me with nothing I could properly compare it to.

Only that my very soul seemed to light up within the darkness.

The darkness's embrace offered a type of freedom I had never known and would spend the rest of my life chasing the feeling of. Like an addict smoking eclipse, the drug popular with those who frequented the brothels and gambling dens, who would chase the high of feeling like the world was eclipsed by euphoria.

I was distracted as the doors opened, and the herald began to call out the new arrivals, "Presenting King Tariq and Queen Oriana Bathala, and their children, Crown Prince Sulien, Princess Zerlina, Princess Sybella, and Princess Danique. Joined by Lord Eos and Lady Aurora Minenhle and Lord Vihan and Lady Tala Zoria."

I was surprised to see how many had traveled from Dawn Kingdom for a potential betrothal. Paired with the speed of their reply to Cyrus, I wondered if perhaps Dawn's royals were already looking to strengthen their alliance with Dusk. Before that doomed night with Tavarius, I had gotten reports from Cyrus's spies that there had been a particularly nasty attack on Dawn. In the wake of it, they were surely feeling more vulnerable than normal. Royals never wore vulnerability well.

The king and queen of Dawn walked down the aisle leading to the thrones their counterparts currently sat upon. King Tariq was dressed in Dawn's colors, his jacket made of red velvet with gray accents. Queen Oriana was decked out in a red ball gown, similar to Queen Stelara's in shape, only hers was encrusted with diamonds and ruffles bordered her hips. The color of her gown complimented her beautifully—the contrast against her light blonde hair stunning.

Crown Prince Sulien was younger than his two older sisters, but by virtue of being male and the gods chosen heir, he walked directly behind his parents. His chin length blonde hair and citrine eyes made him particularly striking. He was incredibly handsome, yet I found myself wishing for silver-white hair and purple eyes. I shook the thought from my head—no good would come from that. Still, I found that I couldn't help staring at the prince, though neither could the women beside me. At least until Prince Sulien's eyes wandered toward me, stopping right on me. I stiffened slightly as he shot me a small smirk.

I caught Cyrus looking over at me with a small frown. Old Gods, he'd obviously caught that little interaction. I prayed to the Old Gods that he wouldn't think too much of it. I couldn't handle his temper today.

I forced myself to look elsewhere, finding Princess Zerlina, the eldest child and the potential betrothed of Cyrus, who followed her younger brother. I wondered if that fact bothered her—that she'd have to marry outside her kingdom, to a Crown Prince, if she wanted to be queen. Was she like Princess Daneiris, who plotted against her brother to try to open a spot for herself?

I suppose I'd find out.

Even by Fae standards, I had to admit she was gorgeous, with chestnut brown hair streaked with blonde, light blue eyes, and sharp cheekbones that alone had to be the envy of many women. Her younger sister, Princess Sybella, could be mistaken as her twin, they looked so similar.

Both wore elegant dresses that showed off their wealth, with Princess Zerlina wearing a light pink in a clear nod to Dusk. She clearly thought it wise to show her willingness to become a member of Dusk through her clothing. Considering Cyrus dressed me in the colors of Dusk as well, I was sure she was correct. Despite how many courtiers wore a similar color to herself, the princess managed to ensnare the court as she walked forward.

The youngest sister couldn't be more opposite to the elder two. The twin of Prince Sulien, Princess Danique wore breeches and light armor instead of a dress, shocking the court and leaving a trail of furious whispers behind her. Her slight smirk indicating she couldn't care less. With identical blonde hair and citrine eyes to her brother, she had the cheekbones of Zerlina with the button nose of Sybella, along with full, plump lips and dramatically arched eyebrows. Her hair was pulled back into a tie at the back of head, falling like a waterfall from it.

Apparently, Dawn Kingdom didn't force their ladies to conform to the same standard that Dusk, and even Sunrise, did. I'd never heard of a female warrior before, but the sword strapped to her side and the knives across the baldric she wore told me she was absolutely a warrior.

The party reached the base of the dais, and King Tariq and Queen Oriana nodded their heads in respect, while their children bowed and curtsied. King

Astraeus and Queen Stelara nodded back while Cyrus and his siblings bowed and curtsied in turn to the foreign monarchs.

"King Tariq, my friend, welcome to Dusk Kingdom!" King Astraeus smiled wider than I'd realized he was capable. "Queen Oriana, you look lovelier every time I see you."

"It's good to see you too, my friend, but please don't encourage her." King Tariq replied with a laugh, King Astraeus joining him as their queens seemed to simultaneously roll their eyes. "And Queen Stelara, you are truly a vision of beauty. I hope Astraeus knows what a treasure he has truly found in you."

"If you think so, Tariq, you should have married me before he could." Queen Stelara gave Dawn's king a sharp smile.

Astraeus turned to her, his eyes narrowing slightly, but Tariq laughed, "Oh, if only! Unfortunately, our parents had other plans." He winked at her, and I was surprised to see Stelara actually smile in return.

"Surely, it is a shame." Oriana cut into the conversation, her voice a sarcastic drawl. "I imagine Astraeus and I could have had quite the time."

"Oh, my dear friend, everyone knows that much like your husband, my own prefers redheads." Queen Stelara smiled widely as she winked at the blonde queen.

"Oh, who can choose!" Tariq said. "I do love a blonde, especially my gorgeous wife." He smiled as he turned to his wife, uncaring that he was just flirting with another queen in front of her. She smiled back at him, but I could see now why the two queens competed over such a silly thing as a garden—they were truly competing over something else. Old hurts and grudges were buried under years of peaceful coexistence, but resentment still simmered, nonetheless.

I had to refrain from rolling my eyes at the petty games being played. It was all just so *tedious*.

"Ah, there is truly a plethora to choose from, my friend." King Astraeus said as he spread his hands, palms facing upward, as if to indicate all the choices before them. "In fact, I have a new blonde find I'm sure you'll make the acquaintance of while here!" My heart seemed to freeze in my chest as King Astraeus's words sunk in. Emmie. He was talking about Emmie.

"Oh? Well, I cannot wait to sample what you have to offer, Astraeus." Old Gods. Was he…was he talking about sharing Emmie between the two of them? By the Otherworld, these Fae were so messed up. They thought they could just share us around, make us have sex with whoever they wanted?

And—they could. Emmie would have no choice in the matter. I wanted to be sick, or perhaps curl up into a ball under my covers once more.

"I'm sure!" King Astraeus replied with a laugh, and I'd seriously never heard him so jolly. "Now, let me reintroduce my son and heir to you."

By his tone, he surely fooled everyone into thinking that he was proud to show off his heir. Many here knew better, but I wondered if Dawn's royals were aware. I couldn't believe King Tariq would be eager to marry off his daughter to a man who may be killed and usurped. I wondered at King Astraeus's intentions behind aligning the heir he despised with his friend's daughter. Was he just willing to toss her away should Cyrus fail to secure his position? Silly question on my part, of course he was. But I also wondered if maybe…maybe he wasn't as intent on getting rid of Cyrus as he made it appear. Astraeus could disagree with Cyrus, want him to change, but could all of his machinations truly be intended to mold Cyrus into the heir he desired?

"Prince Cyrus!" King Tariq greeted the crown prince as he stepped up to the two kings.

"King Tariq, a pleasure." Cyrus said as he bowed, lifting back up with a charming smile. The kind of smile that made one not realize there was a monster hiding behind it. But that was true of all of them, wasn't it? All these men seemed to have a monster inside them. They were predators, hiding their sharp claws and teeth behind charming smiles and compliments, until it was time to tear you to pieces—then they'd leave you bleeding out on the floor. Your heart and dignity torn apart in their destructive wakes.

I wasn't sure the women of this court were any better, in truth.

"Allow me to reintroduce my eldest daughter, Princess Zerlina." King Tariq directed his words to Cyrus, but his eyes went to his daughter as he held out a hand for her to join them.

The princess walked over sedately, taking her father's hand before she curtsied, directing a coy smile to Cyrus. He took her other hand when she offered it to him, pressing a kiss to the back.

"Prince Cyrus." Princess Zerlina breathed out, her voice reminiscent of wind chimes, the tinkling harmony coming through in her voice.

"Princess Zerlina," Cyrus's tone was layered with charm and invitation, a purr and a caress rolled into one. "You are more beautiful than I remembered. Truly, it is an honor you and your family have graced our halls with your presence."

"Of course, Prince Cyrus. Dawn and Dusk Kingdoms have long been allied, being one another's balance as we are." Princess Zerlina said, subtly reminding those present that Dawn was equal in power. "Those bonds cannot be broken, but they can always be reinforced. I'm looking forward to ensuring the strength of our kingdoms for many more centuries to come."

I blinked in shock as a cheer rose up from the courtiers at her words. Were people truly buying this, or was this just the court recognizing when to appease the royals?

"I concur, Princess." Cyrus purred at Princess Zerlina, whose eyes lit up in response. "I'm very much looking forward to getting to know you better while our fathers sort out the terms of our betrothal. I'm anxious to begin courting you, in truth."

"I'll be looking forward to it, Prince Cyrus." Princess Zerlina replied with a coy smile, before she stepped back to join Princess Sybella. Princess Danique remained next to their brother; twin looks of boredom painting their faces.

Court thankfully came to a close for the day, and while some filed out, others hung around to gossip, politick, or scheme. Cyrus made a beeline over to Lord Visita, the two making for an unfairly attractive pairing next to one another, and I flushed as my eyes couldn't help roving over them and the picture they painted. Until Lord Visita caught me, winking at me with a smirk before turning back to Cyrus. Cyrus immediately whipped his head to look at me, and I averted my eyes away—though I feared it was too late. I couldn't imagine Cyrus would be very happy with my eyes straying to his friend, especially not after what happened with Tavarius. I swallowed hard, needing the reminder of why Cyrus shouldn't be admired. No matter how pretty the outside, the inside was rotten to the core.

The Old Gods must have been smiling down on me, as they granted me a distraction at just the right moment. One of Cyrus's spies who currently reported to me, a Fae named Garridan, was meandering his way over. He was one of the rare Fae who didn't have any land or titles, living in an apartment in the city paid for by Cyrus, and paid to attend court so he could uncover secrets and plots by the nobility and the lesser Fae alike. His blonde hair swayed around his shoulders as he walked the room, his green eyes alight with secrets.

He casually walked by me and leaned against the wall next to me. He had a talent for going unseen, even appearing physically smaller when he wanted to. It made him an excellent spy.

"Asteria." Garridan drew out my name, smiling playfully as his head tilted toward me, not even lifting it from the wall he was leaning back against. "You may want to keep an eye on Weylin and the visiting Princesses." My eyes met his as his playful demeanor vanished, replaced by a serious scowl. "He's planning to essentially poison them against the betrothal, all in an effort to get one of them to marry *him* instead."

"Thank you, Garridan." I replied, while my mind spun with what this meant—how I might be able to use the information. "You've proven helpful as always. If you get any more intel on this, let me know."

"Of course." Garridan tipped his head in a nod. "I'll be around, but it'll be better to have multiple sets of eyes on the situation."

I nodded my agreement. Garridan couldn't be everywhere, so I would need to set a few others to the task of watching Prince Weylin and Aphra. We already had several watching the visiting royals.

"Anything you catch on the people from Dawn, bring it to me as soon as possible." I commanded, knowing it would sound like it was for Cyrus, when in reality it was to hopefully aid in my own plan. Unsuspecting, he nodded his confirmation before disappearing off into the crowd like a ghost, no one noticing his comings or goings.

I desperately wanted to keep this information to myself. Cyrus deserved to watch all his schemes crash and burn. I had to be smart about this, however, and holding back such vital information would lead to him inevitably finding out elsewhere. He would never trust me if that happened, and I needed as much of Cyrus's trust as possible if I was going to succeed in finding a way out of here.

CHAPTER 16

I took hours for Cyrus to finish socializing and collect me so we could return to his rooms. I was exhausted by that point, but it was quickly forgotten when I realized Lord Visita was joining us. On the walk back to our chambers, my nerves were fraying as I tried to figure out what this was about. After the past week, I couldn't help the dread sinking in my stomach as we walked into the solar.

Cyrus walked up to me with a gleeful smile, a giant sign that warned "danger ahead". His hands grasped my hips as he directed me toward the sofa.

"Asteria, allow me to introduce you to Lord Visita Umbra." Cyrus rumbled, waving the man over. Lord Visita prowled forward, flashing a disarming smile at me. I couldn't help the way my arousal sparked at his movements, but I could certainly resent it.

When the nostrils of both the Fae men in front of me flared, I was reminded that they could smell all sorts of things humans couldn't…including arousal.

Fuck.

"It's so very nice to meet you, Asteria." Lord Visita said, reaching over to grab my hand, surprising me with the kiss he laid on the back of it. I looked at Cyrus in confusion. He'd literally had Tavarius killed for flirting with me, how would he react to his friend doing the same?

"Since you seemed to like Vissy so much," Cyrus explained, a wicked smirk growing. "I thought I'd bring him here for you."

"For…me?" I asked nervously, my hands beginning to shake as I moved them into the folds of my dress to hide it. There was no way he meant what it sounded like.

"Oh, yes." Cyrus crooned. "I know it's been a difficult few days for you, my dear."

I nearly snorted at the severe understatement, but my nerves were too great to think of making a sound.

"I thought you deserved a reward." Cyrus continued, reaching up and skating his hands over my shoulders. I forced myself to stand still and endure his touch. "Vissy and I grew up together, we're closer than brothers, really."

I jolted in bewilderment. Cyrus didn't have many he considered friends, let alone brothers. When your own brothers were trying to kill you, however, I supposed one needed to outsource.

Cyrus's hands left my shoulders, only for him to join me on the sofa, sitting on the left, while Lord Visita—Vissy apparently—sat down to my right. The foreboding I felt only increased, bubbling up my throat it was so thick. The two males sat too close, their legs brushing mine where they made themselves comfortable.

"You see, Asteria, Vissy and I have shared many things during the years we've been friends." Cyrus lifted his hand and began to run his fingers over my skin—from my neck, over my collarbone, down my chest.

My breath caught at the action, the sensation rocking through me. I may hate Cyrus, may want to get as far away from him as possible, but my body didn't quite get the message. It saw an attractive man paying me attention. One whose cock I felt just a few days ago—his sizable cock. I'd heard Fae typically had bigger ones than humans, but I had thought it ridiculous rumor and propaganda. I was positive that Soren's size was more than enough for me.

Until the moment I realized those rumors were anything but fake, and a part of me had ached to feel the stretch of that kind of size inside, filling me up and thrusting into me until I lost sight of every single reason I didn't want Cyrus touching me.

. "And though I do prefer to keep you jealously to myself—Vissy is a special case." Cyrus's fingers continued their journey, caressing my skin and leaving goosebumps behind. Lord Visita dared to reach out and grip my thigh, startling me as I swung my gaze back and forth between him and Cyrus. "It's been a while since we've shared a woman."

My eyes widened in astounded alarm, but before I could hoist myself off the sofa and away from them, Cyrus threw his arm around my waist, laughing as he held me down. The bastard had the audacity to laugh at my reaction after that? I pinned him with a fierce glare, causing him to roll his eyes.

"Oh, Asteria, I know you're not ready for everything yet." Cyrus's tone was taunting as he continued. "I promise, not one cock will find its way inside your delectable little cunt today. No matter how much you beg." A cruel smirk lit his face as panic filtered through my body.

What was he going to do—what were *they* going to do to me?

"Oh, Cyrus, give the girl a break." Lord Visita laughed. "Let's at least help her loosen up first." He smirked as he began to slide to his knees, looking up at me as his hands slipped under my skirt. My breathing became heavy from a combination of fright and arousal as his palms slid sensuously up the bare skin of my legs, my skirt rising with them and exposing me to the cool air of the room.

"What—" I tried to ask, but my throat felt horribly tight. I cleared it—the two men beside me meeting one another's eyes as they shared a loaded glance. "What are you doing?" I knew what it looked like, but a Fae lord on his knees in front of me made absolutely no sense.

"You see, my dear friend here refuses to get on his knees for a woman." Lord Visita laughed softly, meeting my eyes with a soft smile. "He thinks it's below him as Crown Prince to kneel before another of lesser status." Lord Visita rolled his eyes, and paired with his words, it made him seem more easy going than Cyrus ever was, and that smile held a captivating quality that was hard to look away from.

"I see no need to debase myself in such a way." Cyrus said with a huff, rolling his eyes in return just like brothers would act with one another. "Besides, you're all too willing to step in to help."

"You're damn right." Lord Visita agreed, nodding eagerly. He turned his gaze from Cyrus to me, his face softening. "Let me make you feel good, Asteria. I can make this so, so good for you."

Old Gods, he was tempting. I couldn't help but believe his promise of pleasure, positive that he would make it an experience to remember. His hands were running over my thighs, and I wondered if Cyrus told him how that movement turned me on, or if he just happened upon the spot instinctively. I squirmed in my seat, unsure of what to do. My moral compass screamed to get up and leave, but I knew I was on shaky ground with Cyrus. Would doing so put me at a disadvantage when it came to my plans?

"Unless, of course, you're ready for my cock, my dear? That could be arranged instead." Cyrus whispered in my ear, his voice a seductive tenor that truly had me grasping for my sanity.

That voice made me forget all the despicable things he's done, made me wish to spread my legs wider and welcome him between them. But I couldn't—wouldn't—give myself to him. My original arguments still stood in addition to the horrors he'd made me witness.

But…Lord Visita didn't own me, did he? That gave me…a pass of sorts, right? I was so turned on that I could feel my arousal dripping down my thighs. Two attractive men touching me, no matter my feelings on either, was bound to do so. I'd never had more than one partner before. Never even considered it. But this…

I couldn't lie and claim that I totally hated it. Lord Visita's fingertips ran along the outside of my panties, hitting my clit just right, tearing a gasp from my throat as I grabbed his wrist. His filthy smirk, punctuated by the slightly elongated canines of the Fae, cemented my decision.

"No sex." I commanded; the sentiment slightly undercut by my heavy breathing. I wouldn't cross that line, but that didn't mean we couldn't play. At least as far as Visita was concerned. I would endure Cyrus's touch for the sake of my hopes and dreams of freedom, always at risk with his chaotic moods.

"Of course not." Cyrus cooed in my ear, a laugh bubbling up and releasing in a smoky exhale.

"When you cum for me, darling," Visita began, "The only thing I want to hear from those pretty lips is you screaming my name." He ran his finger along my lips as he spoke, and once he was done, he straight up ripped my undergarments away in one pull. "And none of this 'Lord" shit. You'll call me Vissy, yes?" He looked into my eyes, but his hands were busy spreading my thighs.

"Yes, Vissy." I breathed out, watching him in anticipation.

Cyrus began undoing my dress, letting the top of it pool down around my waist as he undid the clasps on my bustier, leaving my breasts on full display. I breathed in deeply, reminding myself there would be no sex, so this didn't truly count—I could maintain my dignity, my principles, and still get off.

Lord—Vissy, I reminded myself, dove between my thighs and licked straight from my center up to my clit, wrenching a moan from me as I reached down to tangle my fingers in his hair. Cyrus cupped both my breasts, fondling them with a surprising amount of gentleness, before his fingers found my nipples, pinching them hard. An action I didn't even know I enjoyed, but the feeling went straight to my center, adding to the wetness Vissy was lapping up.

My fingers gripped hard in Vissy's hair while he ate me out with enthusiasm. Considering Cyrus apparently refused to do so—*the dick*—I was surprised how enthusiastic Vissy was. He bit lightly on my clit, scraping his teeth over it and causing me to buck my hips upwards, chasing the sensation as a strangled noise left my mouth. Cyrus chuckled slightly before sucking my nipple into his mouth, sharp teeth nipping the bud, while Vissy filled me up with two fingers, beginning to thrust in and out. His tongue swirled around my clit, then back down, then back up.

I rapidly lost myself in the different sensations they were stirring from my body, my head thrown back in ecstasy. Having two men touching me at once, playing my body like a fine instrument, overwhelmed my mind until nothing was left but the feelings they evoked.

"Fuck." The word slipping from my lips in a whine, my whole body trembling as Cyrus and Vissy both bit down simultaneously. Vissy's chuckle vibrated along my skin, as clear as the one coming from Cyrus's mouth as he released my breast.

Cyrus's hand came up to the back of my neck, sliding into my hair and using his grip to pull my mouth to his. Our mouths crashed together in a fury, both of us working out our frustration with the other in a battle of tongues.

I pulled Vissy's hair when he removed his fingers, only to have his tongue enter me instead, his thumb finding my clit and circling as he lapped up the juices coming from me, thrusting his tongue in and out. My lips parted from Cyrus's, and I blinked blearily when he pulled his pants open in a rush, the buttons flying across the room.

I couldn't focus on what he was up to, as Vissy stole my attention back, lapping at me like a starving man.

"Old Gods. Vissy, please." I begged, forgetting why I never did such a thing, only focused on the pleasure I knew he could bring me. Vissy pulled back, his face covered in my juices. His smile was wolfish as he grabbed my hair, pulling me to him and kissing me passionately. Lips caressed, tongues meeting to stroke the others, and a part of me wished I'd been given to him, where I could have experienced this intense pleasure regularly. Momentarily forgetting all the reasons I denied Cyrus. If I had met him under very different circumstances, perhaps in another life, I may not have been able to deny him, Fae or not.

Cyrus was insanely attractive, just like Vissy, and I could only think of one man who surpassed them as I recalled his Otherworldly beauty. I struck the thought of the Fae warrior with silvery white hair from my mind. I wouldn't ever see him again, and dwelling would get me nowhere.

Vissy's mouth parted from mine with a final nip at my bottom lip, and I smirked slightly at him as he looked at my kiss-swollen lips. His low growl was the only warning before he was diving back between my thighs and resuming his task with gusto.

Cyrus's movement caught my attention from the corner of my eye and looked just in time to see him pull his cock out of his now broken pants. My eyes widened at my first real look at him—shocked that he had pulled it out at all, and…

Old Gods. That thing was huge.

I took a deep breath, my lips parting as I wet them with my tongue, reminding myself that was one cock I couldn't ride—no matter how much I suddenly wished to.

Vissy's tongue hit just the right spot and I let loose a loud moan, his fingers thrusting faster, harder as the moans fell from my lips. I thrust my hips up, chasing the feeling and desperately wishing something thicker than his fingers was thrusting inside me.

"No, keep that mouth open, my dear." Cyrus chuckled darkly. "I may have let you keep that delectable cunt hidden from me, but that doesn't mean you can't suck a cock."

He waved said cock in front of my face, while a shock of rage swept through me. I opened my mouth to argue with him, but unfortunately, that gave him just the opportunity he needed. The head of his cock was suddenly in my mouth, and I reflexively closed my lips against the intrusion—which only resulted in me accidently sucking the tip of his cock. Cyrus groaned in pleasure as he fisted my hair in his hand, thrusting lightly into the wet heat of my mouth.

Vissy took that moment to directly hit a spot inside of me that made me completely lose control. Pleasure swept through me and in the resulting tide, I swallowed Cyrus's cock further down my throat.

"Shalim. Fuck." Cyrus moaned as he tossed his head back, the veins of his neck standing out as I sucked his length. "Your mouth feels like Elysium."

I figured the damage was already done by this point, so what was a bit more? If Cyrus was going to demand this, I may as well take as much gratification from this encounter as I could.

I bobbed my head on Cyrus's cock with enthusiasm, my hips thrusting up desperately to meet Vissy's fingers and tongue. The excitement of having two men at once was potent. I could feel exactly how wet it had made me, certainly beyond what was normal for me, and I knew I'd only grown wetter once Cyrus shoved his cock in my mouth. It was twisted, perverse…but I couldn't deny I was thoroughly enjoying it.

I rolled my tongue around and up the shaft of his cock, following the vein, before sucking just under the head. Cyrus's sharp gasp, followed by a hard thrust into my throat, proved the method was effective. If I could have smirked in triumph, I would have, but in lieu of gloating, I just hummed around his length. When my head moved backwards, revealing Cyrus's glistening cock, my hand joined in to stroke him, only to remove it each time I sucked back down to his base.

I was so drenched I could feel my arousal running down my thighs, Vissy's chin similarly covered with the evidence of my desire. My orgasm was mounting, so turned on that I bobbed on Cyrus's cock hungrily, allowing him to grab my hair and fuck my face. His hips snapped forward, my tongue roving over his shaft and up to the head, swirling around it before sucking right at the tip. The swear that left his lips making the corners of my mouth lift in what would have been a smile if my mouth wasn't stuffed full.

"Fuck. What a good girl you are, Asteria. So good." Cyrus panted out his praise. "I knew you'd be amazing at this. So fucking perfect."

Cyrus's grip on my hair grew tighter and pulled an involuntary moan, muffled though it was, from my mouth. His words only heightened my rising desire, squirming against Vissy's face as I chased it.

"That's it. Suck my cock." Cyrus barked out, his grip on my hair verging on pain. "Harder. Let me see those cheeks hollowed out." I followed his instruction, lost in a haze of indulgence, sucking extra hard until my cheeks were hollowed out to their limit. I felt a spurt of precum hit my tongue as Cyrus let out a broken moan.

Vissy licked up and down my cunt, his fingers thrusting continuously. Sensing I was teetering on the edge of climax, he sought to push me over to the edge, adding another finger, causing me to whine at the additional stretch as he sucked my clit into his mouth and swirled his tongue around it.

The two men acted in concert with one another, playing my body like their instrument and producing a song of carnal pleasure, until I careened into the wild throws of rapture. My climax hit me hard and fast, stars exploding behind my eyes as I erupted. Cyrus pulled out of my mouth just long enough for me to scream Vissy's name, as requested.

He'd earned it.

I shook and panted, riding the storm raging through me, before a cock was shoved back into my mouth. Still riding the high, I sucked it into my mouth and bobbed on it as Cyrus chased his own orgasm. He thrust hard several times before he stilled, and I felt the splash of his spend as he came down my throat.

Cyrus waited until I swallowed everything he had to give, then pulled himself out of my mouth, slapping his cock against my cheek. I blinked up at him, confused, and he ran his head over my lips. I parted them, and Cyrus ran just the tip over the tip of my tongue, showing me what he wanted. I followed his direction, licking and sucking on his head like a piece of candy. He watched me with heavily lidded eyes and a sated smile. When he twitched, overstimulated from my continued attention, he finally pulled back, allowing me to collapse against the sofa.

Vissy chuckled as he stood, leaning down to kiss me once more. He pushed my hair back, palming the back of my neck as he explored the contours of my mouth with his tongue. No doubt tasting Cyrus as he did so. It made me wonder, when they said they shared things, had they…

Vissy's lips parted from mine and not even a moment later, Cyrus had taken his place. The abrupt return of his jealous nature was apparent as he tried to practically eat me alive with his kiss. I struggled to take in a breath until he finally pulled back, leaving me with a heaving chest as I panted, adding to my sweaty, debauched appearance.

The two men collapsed on the sofa, one on either side of me. The three of us were quiet for a moment, and I took the time to try to digest what had just happened. My orgasm had left my mind deliciously blank however, and I decided it couldn't hurt to shelve for later.

"As wonderful as that was, I didn't get to cum you know." Vissy chuckled as he grabbed my legs and swung them up onto his lap.

"Don't be a greedy bastard, Vissy." Cyrus mumbled, pulling my upper body down so my head was in his lap, and my body was completely stretched out. He began running his fingers through my hair in a surprisingly sweet action, One I had certainly never expected from him.

As Vissy began to run his fingers up and down my still bare legs, Cyrus reminded me my dress was still around my waist when he began running his hand down my neck, across my décolletage, and finally found my breasts as he absentmindedly plucked and pinched my nipples. I could only take a few moments of his ministrations before I was squirming. Cyrus chuckled, slapping my breast and making me gasp. I looked up and saw Vissy watching with hungry eyes that roved over my body. A glance upwards confirmed Cyrus was doing the same.

Neither male took things further; maybe they both realized I was at my limit for what I could take physically, mentally, and emotionally. As I calmed down from our encounter, my thoughts began circling once more as what I'd allowed to happen truly sunk in. Thankfully, Cyrus and Vissy merely stroked my skin until I went from aroused to somewhat relaxed, despite the men doing the touching. It was soothing, and I was fighting to keep my eyelids open before long. Soon enough, I was whisked off to sleep.

I DRIFTED OFF and must have slept through the rest of the night into the morning, as when I landed in my little dreamscape, excitement overcame me as I spotted Zhu. I saw him much less than I did Luna unfortunately, it being a rare treat to sleep during the day. He unfurled from the ball he'd curled himself into for sleep, his head peeking up as fiery eyes found me. He flew over, his tail skating along my arm in greeting, flame flickering over my skin.

"Hi, Zhu. I've missed you." I smiled widely at him; and the worries of my waking world were left far behind.

He made a trilling noise I took to mean he missed me too. I reached out and brushed a hand along the scales on his side. The fire engulfing his scales never burned me, even with the heat of the sun roaring through them—merely left behind a warmth that sank into my bones.

In this dream space, nothing hurt, nothing could touch me. I'd been that way as long as I could remember.

I first met Zhu when I was five or six. When I first began to understand that I was a slave, and what that meant. It was the first time I saw a human being punished, in fact. I wasn't supposed to have witnessed it, but I had snuck out of the house and wandered the village. Not that I had to actually sneak out, with both my parents slaving away at the vineyard. I'd spotted them standing in the village square and skirted along the sides to avoid being seen.

Seeing the whip cut through that poor man's back, it was horrifying on a scale my younger self couldn't process—and I didn't. I didn't even remember the event when I was awake, having buried the memory so deeply, it was as if it never happened. But here, I remembered, because it was after I had run back home and buried myself under the covers, falling into a fitful sleep, that I met Zhu for the first time. I'd met Luna when I fell asleep that night, and my dreams often contained my dragon friends ever since.

I kept an eye out for encroaching darkness, but everything was quiet. The sky was silent and bright, no desperate shadows in sight. It was possible the darkness couldn't exist here in the sun, and it was only at night it could appear. The sound of a hawk came from far away, but no matter where I looked, I couldn't find a trace of the raptor. The sound of its screech grew louder and louder, and I could feel my hold on the dream slipping.

I AWOKE IN my bed, decidedly not where I fell asleep, but more concerning than that— the hawk was next to me on the bed.

"What are you doing here?" I asked the hawk, feeling silly. It squawked at me and took off, leaving me blinking in confusion. I looked out to my balcony where he'd just flown off, seeing it was mid-morning. I was still in my dress from last night, only it was covering me fully. Had Cyrus actually bothered to dress me?

I forced myself up and off the bed, rubbing the sleep from my eyes, I stretched out my muscles, trying to loosen the tight feeling crawling under my skin. I wandered out to the solar, surprised to find Cyrus working at his desk. He looked up when I entered—*fuck*—I should have waited to come out after I had time to process how my principals had bent from a combination of logic and pure horniness. How I seemed to always lose my mind and forget why certain acts with certain people were a bad idea the moment I grew aroused was concerning.

That couldn't be allowed to happen again. I'd given Cyrus enough now to think he was winning in this battle of ours, so I wouldn't let him gain another inch. I nearly snorted as I thought of the inches he had quite literally choked me on, but I fortified my resolve.

Shoulders back, chin tilted up, eyes narrowed. Cyrus, *the bastard,* seemed amused, a smile playing at the corner of his mouth.

"Asteria, I'm glad you're up." Cyrus said, his smile fading as a storm began brewing in his eyes. "Priscilla will be coming by this afternoon to help get you prepare. We'll be holding a feast tonight to celebrate Dawn's arrival. Which reminds me, there will be a ball in a few days' time. My mother decided a masquerade would be 'just perfect'." He rolled his eyes.

At least the events gave me plenty of opportunity to gather information to use to make my escape. Gathering resources and finding a path out would be more complicated, but I would persevere, no matter how long it took. In the meantime, as much as I hated attending these affairs, they were a necessary evil.

"I have a meeting to attend, so I'll be unavailable for a couple of hours." Cyrus said as he stood and began gathering the papers before him on the desk.

I didn't remember any meeting planned for today in his schedule, but I nodded my understanding before he swept out the door. I was surprised Cyrus hadn't taken the opportunity to harass me over what happened between us last night. It was so unlike him not to dig in and try to pry for more.

I took the rest of the morning to check in with our spies and gather whispers from yesterday. With the arrival of Dawn, there were bound to be many I would have to sort through, trying to find the legitimate threads to follow amid a pile of blustering dead ends.

⚜ ❦ ⚜

By early afternoon, I needed a break, and I still had several hours until Priscilla would arrive, so I took the opportunity to go visit Emmie. Traveling through the dark tunnels always left me uneasy, but it was the best way to travel unseen. My mind kept wandering to Dawn's arrival and what that would mean going forward, so I didn't realize I had somehow wandered into the wrong tunnel until it was too late.

"Fuck." I cursed, turning around and trying to find my way back. The area looked vaguely familiar, and I was sure Whina had shown me this route when she toured me around, but I couldn't remember what part of the palace it was in.

Whispers caught my attention, bringing me to a dead stop in the dark tunnel. No, not whispers, voices some distance away. Curious, I wandered forward, the voices becoming louder the closer I got to a fork in the tunnel. Listening for a moment, I followed the voices to the right.

There—the voices were coming from an alcove within the rock. I moved into it and found a poorly concealed hole. Shifting away the cleverly designed fabric mimicking the material of the wall, my hand flew up to stifle my gasp as I realized it looked directly into Queen Stelara's rooms.

Or what I assumed was her rooms, as there the queen was, lounging back on a sofa upholstered in white silk. Directly across from her sat Cyrus, leaning forward on his elbows, his furrowed brows at odds with the ease of his mother as she relaxed and sipped her wine.

"Just because it's been forbidden for thousands of years doesn't mean we can't use it." Cyrus argued against his mother. Whatever was said leading up to it, I had unfortunately missed.

"You're talking about risking the balance of our kingdom." Queen Stelara said, raising her eyebrow pointedly.

"It's too late to worry about that." Cyrus replied as he stood, beginning to pace back and forth. Too late to worry about the balance? What were they talking about?

"It was only forbidden because others deemed it cruel and inhumane. Not to mention, if all the Fae used it against one another, we'd have wiped ourselves out." Cyrus continued, his voice rising as he began passionately defending whatever argument he was making. I was lost on what he was referring to, other than it was about something forbidden, obviously, and for good reason it seemed.

"Yes, and that remains true. If we began using it, and others followed, we would face the same issue, Cyrus." The queen insisted as she placed her wine down, leaning forward as she spoke to her son.

"It's been enough years that no one will suspect us of using it. They won't know where the power came from." Cyrus continued. "And we have more than enough slaves available to power the magic for years. Blood magic would solve all of our problems, Mother. You have to see the logic in this."

More than enough slaves? Blood magic? A horrible weight filled my chest as I realized he was talking about actually *using* a forbidden type of magic. Magic was supposed to be natural and good—a gift from the gods themselves, generated by nature. But now Cyrus was about to use a magic that apparently needed humans to power it.

"I do." Queen Stelara admitted, a belabored sigh slipping through her lips. "But we have to be careful. If we use all of our slaves to power the magic, we'll have none left to actually assist us. Nor do we want them finding out we're sacrificing them for this. The very last thing we need is the humans trying to rise up in revolt."

By the Otherworld, it felt like Adamah was spinning around me. They were going to kill us to power this magic. I swallowed down bile, I couldn't afford to be sick and give away that someone was listening. My plans for escape were more important than ever. I had to get myself and those I cared about as far from Dusk as possible.

But could I really just run and forget the countless innocent humans who would be sacrificed in the name of power? Cyrus called it a cruel and inhumane magic, and the indignity of what he planned lit my blood up from the inside out. Rage rushed through my veins until I could feel something inside me rise up, only to fall back down before I could unleash it. I shook it off; this was too important to let rage cloud my judgment.

It was said that you needed to arrive in the Otherworld with your body as intact as possible. Having pieces, even one's blood, stolen away could affect one's ability to properly enter the Otherworld, preventing them from facing judgment. Meaning they wouldn't be sent to Elysium or Tartarus and would instead linger as nothing but a spirit, haunting this world. That was worse than just killing someone, it was destroying their soul, ruining them completely, along with their chance for eternal peace.

"They wouldn't get far." Cyrus scoffed, shaking his head. "We'll be able to overpower any we need to using blood magic. Think of it. We could make iron weapons to use against Night or any other who challenged us. The plans I've drawn up will work."

I bent over, my hands on my knees as I processed this. Cyrus may be able to hold the unruly Night Kingdom at bay, but the words of the Fae soldier I couldn't seem to forget crossed my mind once more.

How do you know, when you don't recognize the monsters you're surrounded by? You see lambs where you should see lions.

He was right about one thing—Cyrus and his family *were* monsters.

How did I fight against this? So many questions flooded my mind, the overwhelming thoughts converging into a storm inside my head. I wandered back to my room in a daze. I didn't want to see anyone right now, I certainly couldn't face Emmie, who'd be able to tell something was wrong immediately.

I took the rest of the day to sort myself out. I'd have to keep this extremely quiet. I wanted to tell Priscilla when she arrived, but Cyrus wouldn't be far behind her. I couldn't take the risk. I would have to wait until I knew he was far away to update her. For now, I had to focus on the task at hand, and prepare myself for gathering more information tonight.

When Priscilla arrived, we got started and I watched as she did my hair and makeup flawlessly. I let out a large sigh when she was finished, and

Priscilla popped her head on my shoulder, gazing at our shared reflection in the mirror.

"What's wrong?" Priscilla asked, her voice a low whisper, but I heard it like an explosion in my ear. I wanted to tell her everything, but a glance toward the door leading out to where Cyrus waited stilled my tongue.

"Nothing," I met her eyes with a tired grin. "I'm just not looking forward to this. Weylin is apparently making a play at the princesses, hoping to win them over and turn them against Cyrus. It gives us some potential opportunity, but it's a chore to deal with the pampered royals trying to outmaneuver one another. It's hard to imagine Princess Zerlina ditching Cyrus for Weylin of all people." I raised my eyebrows wryly, and Priscilla laughed.

"I doubt Weylin's thought too hard about it. He's desperate to be the heir. He'll offer them whatever he can." Priscilla said knowingly. Like us, Weylin had his own goal to achieve, and we both knew how that drove one forward.

"True enough." I sighed. "Well, let's get this over with." Priscilla looked amused with my reluctance but bit her lip and kept that amusement to herself. She wasn't forced to attend these events like I was, since she wasn't the personal slave of one of the royals or lords.

Lucky girl.

CHAPTER 17

THE feast the night prior left me exhausted. Spending the night essentially spying on hundreds of people was a grueling endeavor in itself, but standing on heels for hours on end wasn't exactly the easiest either. I'd rather fend for myself in the Savitr Jungle, quite frankly. While half of Panchaia, including the royal palace, sat inside the Savitr Jungle, the bits outside of it quickly got dangerous. Inhabited with leopards, gorillas, snakes, and many other dangerous animals that would kill you in the blink of an eye.

At least the night had proven fruitful. I got word of Prince Weylin arranging a meet up with Princess Sybella. Which is why I was now skulking around the garden they'd arranged to meet in. I did have to wade through a lot of boring gossip to get to the good stuff, but I fortunately managed to catch another whisper that may prove even more vital.

I had made my way around the perimeter of the feast hall. Sticking to the wall, but slowly moving around to catch pieces of conversation, drifting to where I spied anyone I wanted to overhear. It was on my way to Prince Weylin that I overheard it.

"Did you get the message out?" The first man whispered to the second, not having noticed me against the wall.

"I did, Night was informed." The second man replied, stilling my blood. Night? As in, Night Kingdom?

"Good. When can they plan another attack?" The first man asked.

"A few days. They can certainly manage to do it while Dawn is here, no worries about that." The second man responded. My heart rapidly beating as I listened in. "I doubt it will make them think twice about an alliance though."

The first laughed, and I managed at that point to get a look at them, slightly off to the side in a bend of the wall that curved around a pillar. They likely thought themselves secluded. My eyes widened as I caught sight of Prince Kian laughing. It was him inquiring about when the attack could happen.

He tended to be quiet when his siblings fought, but his keen eyes always took in everything around him. I moved back and flattened against the wall, trying to stay unnoticed. I didn't understand why Prince Kian would be arranging for another kingdom to attack his own. His people would be the ones hurt in an attack. Was he just a traitor? Or was something more going on here?

"I don't care about that. I just want to get these people to safety." Prince Kian said, with surprising sincerity in his voice.

My brows furrowed upon hearing him. What people, and more importantly, what safety? Night Kingdom was notoriously brutal, *no one* would be safe there. He was arranging an attack that would kill his people and mine alike. What did he hope to accomplish?

Prince Kian and his accomplice moved on, leaving me with hundreds of questions and no answers. And now I was following up on the meeting Weylin planned, when what I wanted to be doing was chasing down Prince Kian and shaking him for answers. I would have to be more circumspect than that, of course. I didn't want to tip Prince Kian off, but more even importantly, I didn't want Cyrus to find out.

Whatever Prince Kian's goal, anything important that I could keep from Cyrus, I would.

Between the three brothers, I was up to my neck in secret plans and devious desires. There was hardly enough time in the day to investigate them all.

I followed the hedges in the garden and found one section where short hedges were bordered on the edges by taller ones, giving me a great place to hide and peek out to watch. I waited until I heard the steps of a large man walking by, knowing it was Prince Weylin. It was only a few minutes later I heard several sets of lighter footsteps, meaning Princess Sybella was being smart about this and likely brought one of her companions.

"Princess Sybella, you're a vision of loveliness to my tired eyes." Prince Weylin praised, and since I was hidden, I could freely roll my eyes at how thick he was laying it on.

"Oh, Prince Weylin, do you sweet-talk every girl you hope to whisper treason to?" Princess Sybella replied, raising a brow at Prince Weylin.

My jaw dropped. Princess Sybella looked sweet and innocent on the surface, but clearly that only went skin deep. She had the boldness to call out a prince for treason against his family, and I found myself liking her a little despite myself.

"Princess Sybella, I assure you, I have no plans of any treason!" Prince Weylin sputtered a defense, but she merely laughed and waved him on.

"Go on, give me your best pitch." Princess Sybella said, a small laugh falling from her lips.

This was not at all going how I expected it to. I was sure Weylin felt similarly, if for different reasons. After being stuck with this insane family for so long, I'd come to expect nothing less than secrets, schemes, and backstabbing.

"Very well." Prince Weylin nodded, sounding uncomfortable, yet undaunted from his plan. "My brother is not fit to be heir, and your sister will be shackling herself to a man who won't live to see the crown on his head. I seek to help you and your family avoid this fate."

"Is that so?" Sybella asked. "And what makes you think he won't live to see the throne become his?"

"My own father, the king, doesn't want him as his heir!" Weylin laughed incredulously, while I was shocked he admitted it so freely. I wasn't sure it was exactly accurate either, not after the way King Astraeus insisted Cyrus marry.

"Hmm. I see." Princess Sybella hummed. "And what is it you want from me and my sister?"

"Nothing." Weylin declared softly, earnestly almost. Clearly, he was doing his best to appear charming and kind to the visiting royal. "I'd like our kingdoms to work together, of course. And when I do take the throne, I will need a queen. I see no reason that the queen shouldn't come from Dawn Kingdom."

I peered around the hedge, looking for Princess Sybella to gauge her reaction. I spied her standing by the fountain, looking down at the exotic fish from Gemaria that Queen Stelara had recently added. They twinkled like green emeralds, and Sybella lowered her hand into the water, skimming her hand across their crystalline scales.

"I'll be sure to consider your—" The princess trailed off for a moment. "Generous offer. My sister and I have much to consider indeed."

"That is all I ask, Princess." Prince Weylin asserted. "I'd hate to see your family choose poorly in this. As sure as dusk comes daily, my brother will never be king." With those parting words, Weylin nodded his head to her and walked away, Sybella and her companion departing in the opposite direction. I leaned against the hedge, waiting a few minutes to ensure they were long gone before making my own way out.

Entering Cyrus's rooms, I came to a standstill upon finding the man himself pacing while lightning crackled all around him—bolts of it dancing off his aggravated form. His face was set in a scowl that made me wish to turn and back away, but his head whipped over to me before I could.

"Asteria. Tell me you got something." Cyrus demanded. I felt like a trapped rabbit before a very hungry wolf. He'd been fine before I left to spy on his brother's meeting, there was no way Weylin was who had him so pissed.

"What happened?" I asked, hoping to find out what he knew before admitting to anything I'd been keeping hidden from him—but my voice betrayed me, cracking at the end.

Way to play it cool, Asteria.

"Fucking Kian." Cyrus growled, clenching his fists tightly. My eyes widened as I realized this was indeed about Kian. There was no way Cyrus could know about what I'd heard though, so I kept my mouth shut, hoping for more information.

"I've been summoned to appear before my father in an hour." Cyrus fumed, his anger coming off him in snaps of electric bolts. "Apparently, Kian found a slave stealing from us—a slave that just so happens to be Raziel." His tone made it clear he believed this to be no coincidence.

Neither did I. I released a deep sigh, running a hand through my hair. Raziel was one of Cyrus's best human spies, trusted by many in the palace and the city—his genial nature making him the ideal spy.

"That's not good." I replied lamely, unable to voice my suspicions without giving too much away. Cyrus was more right than he knew—there was no way this was a coincidence. I just couldn't figure out how this all added up. What was Kian trying to accomplish?

"No, it's not." Cyrus snorted. "I want to know how he discovered Raziel answered to me." His eyes drilled into me, and I nodded my understanding of my new task. I would do what I could to find out. "Now, what did you discover at the meeting, my dear?"

His sharp words told me his patience was at its limit, so I succinctly informed him of what happened in the gardens with Prince Weylin and Princess Sybella. When I was finished, he stared at me for a solid minute, making me squirm a bit uncomfortably, before he let out a loud, bellowing laugh. I flinched in surprise, my eyes going wide.

"Oh, my brother is such a fool." Cyrus laughed, holding his stomach as he bent forward, it was so powerful. "I suppose I should be grateful for that fact. It makes my life so much easier."

I tilted my head to the side, considering his point. He was right, Weylin was too upfront with the princess. He laid all his cards on the table right away and proved that he didn't have what it takes to manage a kingdom in the process—spilling royal secrets to a foreign princess.

"Good work, Asteria." Cyrus praised when he finally calmed down. "We'll go deal with my father and Kian. Hopefully we can sort out this business with Raziel." I nodded my agreement before he continued. "Then I must meet with Princess Zerlina. While our fathers may agree to the official betrothal, I still need to win her over to ensure she doesn't protest it and fuck my plans up. Hopefully, some standard courting will be more than enough, considering this will get her a crown. You'll follow along behind us but don't draw attention to yourself."

I had to follow him even as he courted someone? Old Gods, how was I going to get through this without throwing up or laughing? It seemed an impossible task, really. I could only wish Princess Zerlina good luck.

"You're so beautiful, Asteria." Cyrus stated as he stood, walking over to me and caressing my hair. "And now my dreams are filled with nothing but you writhing on my cock. Watching your glorious breasts bounce as you ride me, or that perfect ass shake as I pound into you from behind." He smirked at me, and while his words might have stirred some arousal, now all I could think about was him sending his slaves to be sacrificed like cattle to the slaughter, using their blood and bone to fuel his forbidden magic. It was so easy for him to take a life, to spill one's blood and use it for his own means.

I had to focus on what was happening here and now. This bastard is going to court someone and yet speaks of dreaming of me in the same breath. *Fae*, Old Gods, they were something else. He thought I would be jealous of his courting Zerlina, but that couldn't be farther from the truth. That he tried to distract me from any supposed jealousy by playing on what happened between us…

It did give me an opportunity. Playing the jealous lover card could help keep Cyrus's trust in me if it's what he expects now. It would also keep him distracted as I investigated both his and Kian's plans.

"That's not going to happen." I said as I turned away from him, hoping I could make this believable. "You expect me to watch you court another woman and then fall into your bed? I wouldn't degrade myself to fuck a man who owns me, but I certainly wouldn't share if I did!" I spat the words at him, knowing he would expect my rage to be explosive.

Cyrus watched me as lightning sparked in his eyes, his jaw grinding as he held back the words he wanted to say. Instead, he smiled widely, unnerving me all the more.

"You keep saying that, Asteria." He murmured, stepping forward until he was towering over me. "Yet, you keep ending up with your legs spread and your cunt dripping wet."

I stared him down, glaring at him, while praying my façade didn't crack.

"I must marry, my dear. And you know I cannot be loyal to a slave of all things." Cyrus spoke quietly, in an almost-but-not-quite regretful tone.

I flinched involuntarily. I didn't even *want* Cyrus to be loyal to me, I didn't want him at all! But the harsh truth he spoke dug into that angry place inside me that had softened a bit after I was left a beaten down mess when Cyrus killed Tavarius.

"A slave, of all things."

I was not a *thing*.

Rage roared inside me, like the rush of fire from a dragon's maw, and this time, it felt *glorious*.

Things kept going from bad to worse around here. I was still unsettled and shaken from what had happened to Tavarius, from what I'd found out about Cyrus's plans. Part of me felt like I was drowning, with no surface in sight—but the other…

The other part of me was determined to rise from the ashes of the ruination he'd made of me.

I wanted to rage, to fight and scream, to let the fire sweep through and devour me until I was made anew. I was not made to drown under the waves of evil that kept trying to sweep me away. If I didn't find a way out of the darkness Dusk had surrounded me in, I might truly lose my mind.

"Now be a good girl for me today, Asteria." Cyrus crooned, tucking a piece of hair behind my ear. "You don't want to embarrass me in front of my future wife and queen. That would not go well for you, no matter how much I enjoy you."

I swallowed hard, the warning received loud and clear. I smothered my rage down to a simmer for now. I need to act the part of a jealous lover from here on out. I didn't know what Cyrus would do if Princess Zerlina requested some punishment. Would he have me whipped or flogged? Or something else, something…worse?

I thought of it the whole way to the throne room. This family never did anything that wasn't a grand spectacle it seemed. Even a human stealing was brought forward in ostentatious surroundings. When we reached the throne room, I sucked in a deep breath to prepare myself. Raziel was sweet, I didn't know much about him other than that. Nor did I know if his sweet nature was genuine, or if it was just part of a ruse to gather information. Either way, I didn't want anything like what happened to Tavarius to happen to him.

"Ah, brother!" Prince Kian called out with a smile on his face.

"Kian." Cyrus greeted, nodding curtly, which seemed to only make Kian's smile grow wider. He looked over at me then, and I flinched in surprise. The other royals never really looked at the slaves that wandered behind them, but Kian's eyes raked over me. Not in the same way Cyrus or Vissy had, or even Soren. This was different, and if he had been someone different himself, I might have called what lingered in his eyes concern.

But this was the Fae arranging for an attack by the Night Kingdom, which would result in humans being brutally taken and slaughtered, who was accusing a likely innocent man of theft—which could result in terrible punishments, just to get rid of a spy of his brother's. There was obviously no compassion within him.

"What is the meaning of this, brother?" Cyrus drawled as he stepped up to where his father sat the throne.

"Yes, let's get to the matter at hand." Kian replied, smiling at his elder brother. "This human," He paused, waving a hand at the guards, who dragged Raziel in and dumped him before us.

King Astraeus just looked on, seemingly bored with the proceedings, but there was something in that expression that made me think otherwise—a thread of excitement. Excited to get a spy of Cyrus's out of the picture, or just for a chance to assert his authority?

"This human was found to be stealing jewels from the royal family. I caught him red handed. Literally, rubies were spilling out of his hands!" Kian laughed, like this was a jolly time for all.

"Human," King Astraeus called, not even bothering to remember his name. I seethed but clamped my jaw tight and watched. Helpless to do anything to help Raziel.

Helpless. It was a feeling I was becoming more familiar with, even as I tried to fight back, to take back some bit of agency, but the helplessness still remained. I couldn't stand it.

I wasn't built to be helpless. I was created to fight, and yet this world didn't allow it of me.

I thought then of that silvery white haired Fae from Night Kingdom. Would he allow a woman to fight, or would he be more like those here who refused to allow women, or humans, the chance? No, he was a soldier in the army of King Calix, he's probably killed hundreds of humans, he certainly wouldn't help them. He called those in Dusk monsters, and yet he fought for the worst of them all.

Despite my best efforts, he was still slowly seeping into my thoughts, like a virus had infected me and now spread through my bloodstream, until it scorched deep into my soul.

What would make someone stay under a king who slaughtered humans and didn't even care about having to kill other Fae to do it? In fact, why did King Calix do this at all? What did humans do to him? They're the ones who enslave *us*! Cyrus said he used to be different, so what changed? What made a man, a Fae King, go from party boy to waging war and slaughtering humans?

I forced the questions from my mind. It wasn't like I was likely to ever find out.

"Did you, or did you not, steal jewels from us?" King Astraeus drawled. I looked at Raziel and to my surprise, he was looking straight at the king, a slight smile curling his lips.

"I did." Raziel confirmed, and my eyes nearly popped out of my head. Not only admitting to it, but not properly referring to the king by his title either? What was he doing? He definitely knew better than this.

Cyrus looked ready to lose it. I could see lightning sparking in his eyes and around his fingertips, which he swiftly put behind his back.

"Why? Why would you do this?" Cyrus demanded of Raziel, who looked over at him and shrugged. I couldn't believe what I was witnessing.

"See, Father? The human is unrepentant. It's best we place him with the others." Kian said, and I looked over to him, confused by what others he was referencing, only to find his eyes darting to me and widening. Like he was emphasizing a point, only he seemed to forget that it only worked when both people were aware of what was happening.

"That's a bit extreme." Cyrus spoke up, "Maybe—" But the King didn't let him finish.

"No, this human clearly stole from us, and he has the gall to show no respect on top of it. Would you have us let thieves run free, is that what you would do as king?" King Astraeus demanded as he turned to Cyrus, who bristled at his accusation. He couldn't say why he didn't want Raziel punished. This was bizarre, but Raziel was definitely up to something, and I had a feeling Prince Kian knew exactly what that was. I would have to get to the bottom of this.

Could it be connected to Kian's plans with the Night Kingdom attack?

"Of course not, my King." Cyrus bowed his head, grinding his teeth.

"Good." King Astraeus exclaimed, clapping his hands before he stood and walked down the dais. "Kian, take care of it." The king ordered his younger son before he walked out, leaving Prince Kian, Cyrus, Raziel, and me.

"Don't worry, Brother." Prince Kian teased. "There's always more where he came from." Kian gave a grimacing, forced smile to Cyrus. He looked over to me before his eyes shot back to Cyrus, calling over two guards to bring Raziel. "You don't mind me adding him to your others, do you, brother?"

"What is he talking about?" I dared to ask. "What others?" Cyrus looked at me, his gaze growing hard.

"Don't worry about that." Cyrus growled. "Go back to my rooms, I have to deal with this." He stalked off, leaving me behind, sure I was missing something important.

It didn't take Cyrus long to return to his rooms after I made it back, and then we were off again, but to the gardens this time. Princess Zerlina arrived not long after, looking beautiful in a purple and yellow ombré dress that had embroidered flowers down it.

"My Prince." Princess Zerlina simpered as she curtsied, a broad smile on her face.

"My Princess." Cyrus replied, bowing as he kissed her offered hand, "You look stunning today. I dare say I'm the luckiest prince in the land."

Princess Zerlina blushed prettily as she laughed, "Oh, not as lucky as I am. The other ladies are dreadfully jealous, you know."

"Is that so?" Cyrus asked with a smirk as he offered her his arm. She took it and they began walking along the garden path. I followed behind them, joined by a male with dark skin, light blonde hair, and eyes a shining shade of light green. Princess Zerlina's human was also forced to tag along.

"Oh, yes." Zerlina enthused. "You're one of the most eligible bachelors in Celesterra! My father was thrilled to get your betrothal offer." She smiled up at Cyrus as they walked, her other hand coming up to lay over his where he'd placed it on her arm.

"And what about you, Princess? Are you thrilled?" Cyrus questioned, raising a brow at her.

"Of course!" She gushed, laughing. "What princess doesn't hope to be queen one day? To have children of the royal line that can shift. I would hate for my children to not feel the joy of the skies because my husband's blood diluted mine."

It was true that while royals could shift into one of the three forms: dragon, pegasus, or phoenix— the further they got from the ruling line, the less likely their children became to inherit the gift, and would instead shift into other, less regal, animals. If a daughter was married off into another family, it was a fifty/fifty shot if the children of that union would have a royal shift animal or not.

I was jealous enough of their ability to fly that I couldn't even blame Zerlina. What I did blame her for was the inane conversation and flirting I was forced to listen to. I looked at the human who came with Zerlina, and he looked equally bored out of his mind. The gardens weren't the most stimulating place either. It didn't escape me that Cyrus brought Zerlina here, the same place he brought me while trying to win *me* over. It seemed to be his go-to spot.

Maybe he'd have better success this time.

"Yes, we should go for a flight! I haven't had the chance to shift for weeks!" Princess Zerlina exclaimed, making me look up in surprise.

Cyrus smiled at her before looking to me, "Asteria, be good while I'm gone."

I nodded in agreement, watching in awe as Cyrus shifted. I hadn't seen him shift fully before, only having seen his wings when he flew me back to the palace. It was an incredible sight. Zerlina quickly followed suit, and while Cyrus became a beautiful charcoal colored horse with bright pink feathered wings, Zerlina's wings were a deep red. The two horses ran their snouts along the others as if in greeting, before they flapped their wings and took off into the sky.

"You need to be careful." The man beside me warned, surprising me and jolting me out of watching the two pegasus fly.

"What?" I asked, my brows furrowing in confusion.

"The princess is a jealous one." Zerlina's human explained. "She doesn't wish to be second place, not to anyone—nor in any circumstance. She resents that she's not in line for the throne, that her little brother was chosen despite her being the eldest. And she's already heard rumors about the prince's *fondness* for you. I just—" He looked down at me and then back to the sky, worry clouding his peridot eyes, "Just be careful. I know you have no more say than I do in who we serve, and I've tried to remind her of that, but it doesn't make a difference to her."

Fuck. Of course, Cyrus's obsession manages to fuck me over in numerous ways. Is it not enough that I'm stuck in this Tartarus damned place with him, now I have to deal with a jealous princess too?

It was the next day that his warning proved helpful, as Princess Zerlina came to dinner in Cyrus's rooms, I was made to stand on the sidelines and watch. But when Cyrus was called out to deal with an issue, I blinked, and Zerlina was in my face suddenly. I flinched backwards but she grabbed my arm, her nails digging in painfully.

"I've heard of you. Asteria Zagreus, a little human Cyrus acquired at the last Placement Day, correct?" Zerlina cooed as she raised an eyebrow, her sharp features looking even sharper now that the fake, overly bright smile she wore around Cyrus had dropped.

"Yes, Princess." I replied, nodding. Not wanting to show her an ounce of emotion on my face or in my tone, as her nails dug deep grooves into my arm.

"Let's get one thing straight." Zerlina began, her glare fierce. "I do not share. Nor will I be embarrassed by a husband who treats his human like she's Fae. You will find a way to get dismissed from Cyrus, or you will soon disappear."

"You think I haven't tried, Princess?" I dared to snap back, letting the façade of a placid slave fall away as I glared back at her. "I don't want to be here, but Cyrus won't let me go."

Zerlina laughed wryly, rolling her eyes. "Don't you worry about that, I'll make sure he gets rid of you. And if not, well…" She trailed off as her hand left my arm, leaving me gasping at the pain left behind where her nails scored my flesh.

I tried to lift my hand to apply pressure to the painful gouges, but before I could, Zerlina's hand was around my throat. She gripped tightly, making it hard to breathe as she shoved me hard into the wall.

I tried to swallow, my hands coming up to pry her off, but she was much too strong. I couldn't budge her fingers an inch. Fuck, I hated being helpless. The Fae knew what they were doing—keeping us weak and unable to resist them.

"I'll just have to get rid of you myself if not." Zerlina threatened, a cruel smile spreading across her face. "Though, that will be a *much* more permanent end for you."

Zerlina removed her hand from my throat, and I fell to the floor, gasping for breath. She knelt beside me, gripping my chin, and forcing me to look up at her.

"It's your choice, *Asteria*." The princess spat my name like it was a particularly nasty disease as she sneered at me. "Find a way to remove yourself from my future husband, where he will no longer be able to treat you so above your station, or you will deal with *me*."

I shuddered at her words while she brought her hands together, air forming a twisting column between them. The air burst from her hands forced my mouth open, slithering into my throat where it choked me on what was somehow too much and not enough air. I sputtered and clawed at my throat, Zerlina merely watching her work with a smile.

The sound of footfalls coming closer was never so welcomed as Zerlina lazily turned toward the door before she withdrew her twister of air from my throat and let me go. I fell forward, coughing and gasping as I struggled to breathe normally.

Crazy bitch. I had to find a way out, now more than ever. I wasn't going to die here, surrounded by insane Fae, forced into acts I hated, and made to watch as humans were picked off one by one. No, I *would* find a way to freedom.

And Old Gods help anyone who gets in my way.

CHAPTER 18

"Asteria, my dear." Cyrus called. I sighed miserably as I walked out of my room into the solar. "There you are." He smiled. "There's to be a ball tonight. Priscilla is going to help you this afternoon with your dress, but in the meantime, I need you to go see what your little friend has found out from my father."

"Of course, Cyrus." I answered, and he looked me over, tilting his head to the side.

"What's wrong? Are you feeling neglected with the princess here?" Cyrus asked, as he took my hands in his and caressed my skin. I forced myself not to pull away for a moment, as if I truly enjoyed his attention. Then I yanked my hands back.

"Never." I spat out, making sure to make my voice wobble a bit. "I already told you, I will not be having sex with you, Cyrus, and especially not now. You'll soon have a wife to fulfill all your needs. I won't be your mistress, it's below me."

It was, perhaps, a bit farther than I should have taken it, and Cyrus proved me correct when storm clouds formed in his eyes, his face growing hard.

"Below you?" Cyrus growled, his voice dangerously low. "You are a slave, Asteria, *nothing* is below you." He grabbed my chin, reminding me of Princess Zerlina actions the day prior. His words were somehow even crueler than hers had been. Nothing was below me? He had to be joking.

"Just because I'm a slave, doesn't mean I deserve to be forced to debase myself." I spat back at him. While I was supposed to be maintaining the act of the jealous mistress enough to fool him, I was so over his pretentious attitude—and with Zerlina's for that matter. I was sick of all these Fae who thought they could get away with doing whatever they wanted to us.

I gasped as pain exploded across my face, my body hitting the ground before I realized what had happened. I blinked up at Cyrus, whose hand was still out from where he had hit me with the back of his hand. He looked almost as shocked as I felt.

"Oh, my dear." Cyrus murmured as he crouched down. "I'm sorry, you see how angry you make me when you say such foolish things?"

I tried to crawl backwards when he reached for me, but it was fruitless. Cyrus grabbed me, lifting me off the ground as he ran his fingers over the spot he'd just hit, causing me to flinch back as the pain flared. His eyes darkened once more, and I braced myself for whatever might come next.

"Go to your little friend." Cyrus chuckled, stepping away. "Get me the information I need. Zerlina and Sybella have already thrown their lot in with me—Weylin will be sorely disappointed once he finds out, but I've told them to wait to say anything to him, it'll be better to pick the right moment. Now run along, Asteria, and I hope you will be in a better mood when you return. You must not embarrass me at the ball tonight." Cyrus smiled and with a final brush of his fingers across my cheek, walked away.

I all but ran out of the room, heading straight for the wing where the king had moved Emmie. He kept a suite of rooms where the women he favored could live close by. I worried about Emmie being so surrounded by Astraeus, but at least I didn't have to go to the king's rooms directly, or to the common areas where I last saw Tavarius. I shivered at the thought, I didn't think I could ever look at them the same way.

I made my way quickly through the halls, keeping to the dark passageways as much as possible while I thought through my options. Which were admittedly limited. If I was going to find a way out of here, I needed more time—time I wasn't sure I had. The convergence of the many schemes being played throughout Dusk were like a web that had entrapped me, and I was being spun ever closer to the spider waiting to devour me in the center.

I knocked on Emmie's door, and she opened it after a moment with a large smile, immediately throwing her arms around me.

"Asteria!" Emmie screeched, making me laugh as I hugged her back.

"Emmie, I'm so happy to see you." I told her honestly, before pulling back and looking her over. "You're well?" She looked more than well, an expensive dress covered in jewels fell over her curves, and she looked healthier, weight filling out her cheeks and hips.

"Oh, I'm amazing!" Emmie sighed happily, and twirled around, laughing as she threw her arms out to both sides. "Look at all this, I couldn't believe it was all for me!"

I forced a laugh for her sake, but looked her over critically, checking for—and praying not to see—any signs of abuse. Cyrus's ringing slap still rang in my ears.

"And he treats you well?" I inquired with a raised brow, needing to double check.

"Of course he does!" Emmie gushed as she ushered me over to a tea table by the windows, pouring two cups of tea as I sat down across from her.

"He's so good to me, Asteria. He's much sweeter in private than public, of course, the king must maintain his authority. But he's interested in my life, my likes and dislikes, my friends."

Emmie paused to sip her tea, smiling at me when she put her cup down. "He asked about you, you know. He's more concerned about his heir than most would think. Astraeus is trying to push him to be better, and he wanted to know about those he keeps close—I sang your praises of course, and Astra seemed satisfied."

"Oh." I replied, unsure what to make of the king asking about me. He'd already tried to get me moved out of Cyrus's service, thinking he was too close to me. "Does he have any plans to push him further?" I asked her carefully, wondering if he was just telling her what she wanted to hear, but it did line up with what I'd been theorizing: that the king did want Cyrus as his heir, he just wanted him to do things his way. Having Weylin replace him as heir was a smokescreen to make him think his father had other options in mind, but in truth, he was merely a catalyst to push Cyrus in a certain direction.

Was the queen aware of this, or was she in the dark like the rest of the court seemed to be? The king played a dangerous game, turning half the court against his son—a very stupid game, really. He likely thought he could do whatever he wanted with no repercussions, not realizing the damage he was doing—not only to Cyrus's reputation and credibility, but to his son and his kingdom as well.

"Oh, yes! But—" Emmie paused and looked at me. "You can't tell him, Astra would be furious if it got out!"

I forced a smile, fighting back a wince at her familiarity with the king.

"Of course!" I promised, feeling awful about having to lie to her, but maybe it wasn't a total lie. I might not tell Cyrus if that ended up being better for my own plans. Still, I wasn't happy about the way Emmie and I were being dragged into this game among royals.

"He has plans for after the wedding." Emmie continued, smiling. "He wants to stop Night Kingdom and their continued attacks, and the only way to do that? Alliances." Emmie brightened, excited about the gossip she had to share. "Once Dawn and Dusk are tied together, he wants Cyrus to get Day on board. He'll treat with King Aelius. He doesn't have a daughter he could have married, of course, only a son, and Prince Arien wasn't chosen by the gods." Emmie's voice dropped to a hush as she spoke about the foreign Prince.

"He wants Cyrus to convince King Aelius to ally, with the promise of helping him figure out where the magic went that *should* have chosen Prince Arien. Apparently, King Aelius was told by the Oracle that Queen Aurelia carried his heir—only for him not to be chosen!" Emmie smiled excitedly, leaning towards me. "Can you imagine? Tracking down all those with royal blood in Day until he finds the one Aelius seeks? Oh." She clapped her hands together. "I can't wait!"

Shock ran through me, but I was practiced enough at this point that I could smile and nod to hide my reaction. If an heir had indeed been chosen, they had to be in hiding if Aelius knew nothing of them. Of course, that was if they existed at all. King Aelius was likely to kill any not of his own blood who were blessed by the gods, so hiding would make the most sense. I knew Aelius had kept trying for more children, but the gods had never granted him another child, and that resulted in one frustrated king. One who was apparently positive that his heir had already been chosen.

Emmie didn't seem to care about the Fae heir who'd be killed by Aelius when he found them, and I couldn't help thinking Aelius was going down a dangerous path, one against the very gods who granted him power.

Would the gods really choose Prince Arien if his father killed the heir they had personally chosen for Day Kingdom?

Or would Aelius try for another wife if his current one couldn't grant him more children? I couldn't imagine he would get rid of her, not when she was his mate. Either way, I knew Cyrus getting involved in that mess would not mean anything good.

AFTER FINISHING MY tea, I made my excuses to Emmie and left, the information she gave me sitting heavily in my heart. I couldn't decide if I should tell Cyrus or not, and I was so distracted with my spiraling thoughts that I didn't notice Prince Kian until he was practically on top of me.

"Oh!" I yelped, leaping backwards before I bowed my head. "Forgive me, my Prince." My head whipped up to look at him when he grabbed my arm.

"Come with me." Prince Kian instructed, grabbing my hand and pulling me down the hall, into the dark secret passageways.

"Prince Kian? What is—" I tried to ask what was going on. His conversation from the feast looming in my mind.

"Hold on." He demanded, and I shut my mouth, keeping silent as he seemed to wish. My nerves churned, fearing that Kian discovered I'd overheard him, and now he planned to silence me permanently—but equally hoping I might get insight on what exactly he was up to.

I followed him down stair after winding stair, spiraling downwards. This passage wasn't made of marble like the rest of the palace, but a dark, weathered stone that made the hall appear even darker, sucking all surrounding light into the stone itself. We finally came to the bottom of the stairs, and I blinked in shock.

An iron door loomed ahead. The very forbidden material was supposed to have all been melted down and sunk to the bottoms of the oceans. Some bits still illegally remained, like my dagger, but nothing this size should have survived the culling.

I looked at the prince warily. I'd never interacted with him before now, and only knew minimal bits of info from Cyrus. Was he bringing me down here to lock me up or kill me?

He took a deep breath, turning to look me in the eyes, and I was taken aback by the sympathy, the compassion, displayed so clearly on his face.

"You hate my brother." Prince Kian stated placidly, and I flinched, opening my mouth to automatically deny his claim, but he raised a hand to stop me. My mouth felt as dry as a sandpit, and I struggled to swallow as I worked to control my panic—before it could control me.

"I can see it, Asteria, and I don't blame you. Judging by that bruise forming on your cheek," Prince Kian said softly, looking at my cheek. I raised a hand to try to cover the bruise, but he grabbed my hand—stopping me from hiding it—and squeezed my hand in a strangely supportive gesture. I looked at him with wide eyes, completely confused about what was happening.

"He's beginning to escalate, isn't he?" Kian prompted; his tone still gentle as he continued. "Cyrus was fine playing by your rules at first, but the longer it's gone on, with you continuing to refuse him, the worse he gets.

I wasn't sure if I could trust he was being authentic, not with his family's track record, but I tilted my head forward slightly—just enough to confirm his words, but not so obvious I couldn't deny it later if needed. Kian breathed in deeply, nodding his understanding.

"I hate my family." Kian said, leaning against the wall opposite the iron door. "That shouldn't come as much of a surprise to you, I can see the contempt in your eyes as you look at us. Oh—" Panic struck me at his words, not having realized it was obvious, and considering all the implications of that, but his chuckle made me pause. "Don't worry, my family is too self-involved to have even noticed."

Prince Kian laughed wryly as he ran a hand through his short brown hair, tousling it out of place. "They only get worse as each year passes. I don't understand their actions, truly. I hate how they treat humans, and that may seem odd to you, coming from a Fae—a royal one at that, but I don't support slavery, Asteria. It's beyond awful, what has been done to humans, but what Cyrus and my father do—it's incomprehensible."

My mouth was surely hanging open, but everything I had learned about how to play the games of these courts since being placed here had abandoned me as Kian poured his heart out to me.

"I know you saw me the other day, and I also know you didn't quite understand what you heard." Kian peeled off the wall as he raised a brow at me, moving to open the iron door before my thoughts could spiral at his admission.

He walked through the door into a dark room, leaving me to follow— and promptly stopped short as I realized he'd brought me to a dungeon. Dank and dark, matted with blood and bodily fluids, with crumbling walls. This far underground, the crumbling rock only revealed dirt and worms, no light dared to touch this place.

Hanging from the walls, tied on racks, curled up on the floor in chains- -humans were everywhere I looked. Blood and flesh decorating the space around them. I whimpered and turned to vomit, Prince Kian holding back my hair and rubbing my back, as I processed the horrifying sight before me.

"It's alright. I'm going to get them out." Kian reassured me in a low whisper.

I wiped the back of my mouth when I regained control of myself, and turned back to face him, unsure about his intentions.

"I can't tell you much, not yet." Kian declared, raw pain on his face. "Not when there's a chance Cyrus could find out. You'll learn everything soon enough, I promise. But this—" He motioned to the tortured humans around the room. "This is what they do, Asteria, this is what I have to stop."

"I don't—I don't understand." I shook my head. "Why? Why are they doing this?" There was no reason to torture people like this, none at all.

"I don't know, truly. Whatever their current plans are, I know they're twisted." Kian sneered. "They get off on having power over people. They think of humans as nothing but cattle for them to do with as they please. My brother is worse than you have likely ever imagined, Asteria, and I'm worried for you. The way he is with you," Kian shook his head sadly. "He's obsessed, and that isn't going to bode well for you."

"I want out." I blurted out before I could control my tongue. The rage that lived inside me clashed with the horror over what I was seeing, and it rose up in a violent swell that nearly bowed my back as it swept through me—cresting into an inferno, one trapped beneath my skin, screaming to be released.

"I've held back information from him, trying to gather enough to give me leverage, or something I can exploit. Anything to get away from here—to be free." I told him, gambling on Kian's sincerity. I didn't think it was possible to fake a reaction like his. If he was truly working to help humans, then he may be my best chance at freedom.

"I'm glad to hear that." Prince Kian smiled at me, relief pouring off him, "I've seen too many humans get used to their chains—forgetting how to live without them. When I first saw you, I knew instantly why my brother wanted you, and it was more than your beauty. He saw your fierceness, your discontent with the life you were given. He desired your fight because it makes it all the sweeter for him to break you."

Remembering the words Cyrus wrote about me, his plans, I knew that was exactly what he wanted—what I would never allow him to achieve.

"What do I do?" I asked the prince plainly. Kian walked further down the hall, over the stains and torture instruments strewn about, averting my eyes before I vomited again. Kian came to a stop before a man hanging from his wrists, toes barely grazing the ground. I gasped when I recognized Raziel.

Kian clasped a hand on his bare shoulder, squeezing it lightly. I looked Raziel over, wincing at the state of his chest, completely covered in bleeding lacerations from being brutally whipped.

"Why did you do this? Get him in trouble?" I tilted my head in confusion. Kian barely managed to smile slightly back at me as Raziel struggled to open his eyes.

"He didn't." Raziel asserted, his words raspy and rough, but clear. "I wanted out, this is how. With the rest down here, we'll all be freed soon." My head spun as I locked eyes with Kian, who nodded to confirm Raziel's words. I let out a huge sigh of relief, years living with the pressing weight of slavery coming out in a rush.

"How? Can I leave too?" I begged Kian, real hope filling me for the first time.

"I can't tell you yet." Kian shook his head. "Not until you're far away from my brother. No offense, but you've never undergone torture before, nor do I wish you to." He grabbed water for Raziel, and I noticed a full glass had been left just out of his reach, torturing him with the scant inch he couldn't reach. Bastards.

"I can't guarantee you won't crack under torture, so it's not safe to reveal what's happening. Rest assured; we'll find a way to get you out, I promise. It won't be easy, not with how close my brother keeps you, but you've been busy gathering information. You know Cyrus's plans, don't you? You know who his spies are, their assignments?" Kian questioned as he focused on helping Raziel sip the water.

"I do." I nodded in confirmation when Kian looked back at me, and a large smile took over his face.

"That's wonderful news." Kian paused; his eyes boring into mine, a heavy weight burdening his gaze. "That information is incredibly important, Asteria, and it will make getting you out a very high priority. I'm pretty sure he's interested in getting you out anyway, but knowing you'll be able to blow the lid off Cyrus's plans will sweeten the deal."

I tilted my head to the side, about to ask what he meant, and who exactly wanted me out—but I snapped it shut.

"Right, you can't tell me yet." I mumbled in frustration. I didn't know who he believed wanted to help me get out, or why they would be interested in me beyond whatever information I could provide—and I had much more than anyone knew. Kian made it sound like someone was interested in getting me out before that was a consideration, however.

Kian laughed lightly at my grumbling, "I commend you, Asteria. I know it can't be easy to be in your position, with my brother trying to wear you down constantly, but you've held firm. You're not letting Cyrus, or your circumstances break you."

"I don't have another choice." I admitted, shrugging a shoulder lightly. I was a bit uncomfortable receiving praise for something I saw as a necessity—let alone something I had failed at twice now. I refused to think about the times I had given in to Cyrus, of what had happened before that first time. Going back into that headspace would do nothing but bring back all of the pain. Instead, I would focus on getting free, and then use every single skill Cyrus taught me to bring him down.

Cyrus, in all his obsessive surety, believed he could tame me—but I was too full of wild rage and indignation to be tamed. Instead, Cyrus had ended up creating the very monster that would ensure his ruin.

Kian gave me a pained grimace, looking from me to Raziel. "No, I don't suppose you do." He agreed quietly.

"What about my friends? Priscilla and Emmie? I can't leave them here." I asked him quietly.

"Let me think about it, we'll figure something ou—" Kian's words cut off as his head snapped towards the door. In a flash, he had my mouth covered and was dragging me into the back, behind a stack of boxes that blocked us from sight of the door. I made to fight my way out of his arms when I heard the iron door creak open. I went still in Kian's arms, and he squeezed me closer against him, like he was praying to Shalim for us both to disappear into the wall.

A familiar sounding pair of footsteps made a chill run down my spine. The wooden boxes had the slightest crack of light coming through where they stacked on top of each other, and I angled myself so I could see, praying the man on the other side wouldn't see me peeking through the gap. But I had to truly see, had to know, what kind of a monster lay beneath the skin of the man I once thought had something sweet and gentle inside him—even buried as it was.

"Raziel, Raziel, Raziel." Cyrus snickered as he stopped in front of the man. "I knew humans were incredibly dumb, but you've really taken it to another level." I clenched my hands into fists, watching him gloat over a bound and tortured prisoner. I wanted to spring out and land said fists directly into his face.

Raziel just looked at him dryly, not giving him the reaction he was clearly hoping for. Cyrus looked frustrated for a moment, before he picked up the whip hanging on the wall nearby. A breath caught in my throat, and Kian clamped down harder on my mouth. I couldn't even argue it was unnecessary, I wasn't sure I'd be able to keep quiet. Not when I'd be forced to watch whatever Cyrus was about to do.

The glee on his face as he struck the whip down made bile rise in my throat. He snapped it down again and again, until Raziel finally let out a moan of pain.

"There we go!" Cyrus laughed. "I was starting to worry someone else had snuck down here—" A pang of fear hit me, and Kian's arm tightened almost painfully around me before Cyrus's next words made us both slump in relief. "—And cut out your filthy tongue!"

Raziel looked up at Cyrus from where he hung by his chained wrists, bleeding from old and new wounds alike, and spat right at him. I nearly clapped in amazed pride, but Cyrus's eyes went glacially cold as he went to the cart against the wall, where all manner of torture implements rested. Fuck, would that be all it took for Cyrus to kill him? His pride was more delicate than he wanted anyone to believe, and a direct hit to it threatened him more than anything else.

Cyrus sauntered back to Raziel, twirling a sharp implement in his hand. This wasn't any mere blade—oh no, this wretched man had grabbed what looked like a dagger, but sharp spikes jutted out along the edges. If used, it would not only stab, but repeatedly rip apart a person's insides on the way in and out. I began to shake as Cyrus brought the knife to Raziel's throat, and from the way Raziel's already broken body sagged, I wondered if he gave up all hope of escape at that moment.

"Don't worry, human. There's still plenty of fun left to have." Cyrus sneered a mocking laugh, before he slowly ran the blade across Raziel's neck, not deep enough to kill him, but enough for blood to trickle down across the width of his neck. A grisly sight in an already damned place.

"Your little friends here, on the other hand, well…some of them have certainly outlived any use I may have for them." Cyrus walked over to the man hanging across from Raziel, one who looked more dead than alive. His face was black and blue, swollen beyond recognition, while his arms and legs hung at odd angles, like they'd all been snapped.

Cyrus turned back to smile broadly at Raziel. "This one stopped being any fun days ago, but now, he'll get to serve a higher purpose, one that will truly serve his masters."

Cyrus ran the spiked dagger down the man's already battered face, but as he said, the man didn't react at all. A devastating sob rose up in my throat, but I swallowed it down before it could escape. My life depended on Cyrus not finding out I was here. He may have his own plans for me, but finding me here, with his brother of all people, would quickly put an end to his games.

Cyrus released the poor man from his chains, laughing as he fell to the disgusting floor. I didn't know if it was good or bad that the human had no reaction, just sprawling where he fell. Did that mean he couldn't feel the pain anymore? That would probably be for the best, but I couldn't help but feel the instinctual wrongness of it—of a human body so far past its limits that it just gave up. With heartbreaking certainty, I realized it would be better for the man's sake if he'd long ago checked out of the body he had no control over. I didn't know what Cyrus was planning, but I was sure the man wouldn't want to be present for it.

Slow tears tracked falling down my face as Cyrus tortured the man, making Raziel watch as he cut pieces off him. I choked back my sobs as much as my fury. I wanted to run out there, steal his dagger, and drive it through his fucking skull. I wished I had the claws needed to tear his face off, or the power to burn him to cinders—but I was helpless, knowing if I tried to fight Cyrus, the only result would be my death.

If Kian couldn't get us out, we were all going to die here. Once the man had bled out completely and stopped offering any fun for Cyrus, he gave Raziel a twisted grin, spitting on him before promising he'd return. I choked on my tears, surging up to go after him without even realizing it. Thank the Old Gods Kian held me down, or I would have died via stupidity.

Once Cyrus was far enough away, Kian raced over to Raziel. I followed slowly, almost afraid to approach and see his state up close. He needed a healer, badly. But that wasn't going to happen while we were stuck here.

Kian checked on each human, helping them sip water and move into slightly more comfortable positions, promising each it wouldn't be much longer. They were all just as shaken, clearly more dubious about salvation after Cyrus's theatrics. We'd already stayed too long as it was, so Kian reluctantly led me back up the stairs, parting from me at one of the landings and instructing me to go back to my rooms like nothing had changed. To not give anything away. I did exactly that. Making my way back to my rooms to prepare for the ball tonight.

Something I truly had no interest in going to. I couldn't forget what I'd seen today. Cyrus and King Astraeus were worse than I could have ever imagined. True monsters, in every sense of the word. As vicious as any creature raised from the depths of Tartarus. My Fae soldier had been right about Cyrus. I had no idea what he might be capable of beyond what I'd seen already. Could it get even worse?

Thinking of the forbidden blood magic, I knew the answer was yes.

Wait…Kian was arranging for an attack by the Night Kingdom. Why would he do that if he's helping the humans escape? Was it to create a distraction? And where exactly were we all going once freed? Dammit, I knew Kian couldn't tell me, and I understood why, but all these questions were making my head throb.

PRISCILLA SHOWED UP not long after I arrived back, and I sighed in relief. At least she could offer a break from the waking nightmare now haunting me. I couldn't tell her about Kian, not without jeopardizing our potential escape. Nor could I reveal what I had witnessed. I couldn't let on to anyone, or everything would be doomed. I felt terrible hiding this and the information about the blood magic, but I knew it was safer for her, and that was what truly mattered. I buried everything I'd learned down deep, to the point where I could get through tonight without breaking down.

Priscilla and I instead chatted casually as she curled my hair the way Cyrus wanted it, even though I preferred it straight. My eyes widened as she pulled out a ball gown that was a bit over the top for a human slave. Old Gods, Zerlina was going to kill me sooner than later once she saw this.

The dress was a gorgeous ombré, with a dusty pink bodice highlighted with gray embroidery, a sweetheart neckline that dipped low in the front, and two tiny sleeves that came off the bodice and circled around my upper arms. The skirt faded from light blue to dark blue as it fell to the floor and was covered with diamonds that started at the bodice and grew heavier in number near the bottom.

The dress looked like dusk itself, fading from day to night. Princess Zerlina would certainly hate what it represented—as did I. Cyrus was claiming me as his with this dress, disgust fizzled through me as I tried to shake off the feeling of being branded like cattle. I took a deep breath, reminding myself I could take this dress off, that I *would* get away from him.

I just wasn't sure how changed I would be on the other side.

The naïve girl who walked into Dusk Kingdom seemed almost unrecognizable to the woman I saw in the mirror, a woman planning to circumvent the royal's devious plans with the lessons she'd learned. Maybe I wasn't so different, but I *felt* different—like Cyrus's evil had rubbed off and dulled some of my shine.

"Look at you." Cyrus breathed, and I spun around. He looked at me with wide eyes, raking over every inch of me. "You look even more magnificent than I thought you would, my dear. I'm going to have a horrible time tonight trying to keep my hands off you."

When he reached me, he ran a finger down my neck and across my chest. My breath hitched, trying to keep my emotions buried. I had to play this game to the end, wherever that may lead.

"Your soon to be wife might have some words to say about that." I flirted lightly, feeling nauseous as I did. There was finally hope, I just needed to suffer through him a bit longer.

"Don't worry about her." Cyrus chuckled huskily. I nearly laughed aloud. *Don't worry?* About the crazy princess who wants to kill me—sure, that was likely.

"Remember, tonight you need to be on your best behavior." Cyrus lectured, and I felt like a small child as he spoke to me. After what I witnessed today, I was a bit more hesitant to sass him back, viscerally aware of the monster in beautiful packaging before me—cognizant of the lengths he would go to. So, I followed him down to the ballroom without complaint, and as he was announced, I made my way silently to the wall beside the high table where the royal family and their guests sat.

My eyes widened to see Emmie there already. She smiled widely, waving me over to join her. I walked slowly, eyes roving the room to see who was here. All the usual suspects, plus Dawn's contingent. Princess Zerlina hadn't arrived yet, but aside from her, everyone else was here. She'd be the last to arrive, with Cyrus second to last, as they were the guests of honor tonight. King Astraeus really went all out with this ball for the celebration of the reinforced alliance between Dawn and Dusk.

Everywhere I looked there was grandeur and opulence. Towers of champagne glasses, tables full of every dessert imaginable, a wide array of meats and cheeses. They could feed the kingdom for a year with all the food on offer.

Tufts of fabric lined the ceiling in waves of gray, pink, and red, matching the banners of Dusk and Dawn Kingdoms that were embroidered with their house sigils and lining the walls. The sigil of House Tynan, with its upside-down crescent moon and two pegasuses rearing up toward a star, was a constant source of confusion for me. The pegasuses had strange horns on their heads that their animals didn't actually have. I'd seen both Cyrus and Zerlina in their pegasus forms, and neither had a horn. House Bathala's sigil was more accurate, with a pegasus rearing in front of a red sun at dawn.

The colors of the two houses dominated the room, with ribbons curled around columns, and the elevated stage the musicians played from was strewn with rose petals in the same colors. Thinking back to my humble village, they wouldn't be able to believe their eyes at the extravagance on display. I never believed I'd feel wistful nostalgia for a place that only ever felt like a placeholder to me, but I was.

The simple life I led there was nothing like my life here, for both good and ill. Celesterra was all about balance, so there had to be a way to find balance between the two extremes: not as simple as Sonmathion, and not as excessive as Evenfall—after all, no amount of money and excess could cover up the rot within this kingdom.

Cyrus stood, bowing to Princess Zerlina, as he offered her his hand to dance. She accepted his hand with a wide smile, and the court clapped and toasted the happy couple as they made their way out to the dance floor. Prince Weylin quickly followed suit, asking Princess Sybella to dance. The princess didn't look inclined to agree but did anyway for appearances sake. Prince Weylin would likely spend the dance trying to convince her to ally with him once more.

Prince Sulien asked Princess Daneiris to dance next, and she gave him a charming smile as she accepted, leaving Princess Twyla to be asked by Prince Vikal. Princess Danique refused to dance, declaring so loudly before anyone could ask her, making my lips curl up slightly in a smile. Other than her, only Prince Kian remained seated, swirling his drink in his hand, and chugging it back. I was incredibly jealous; I would kill for a drink right about now.

Watching royals fawn over one another was mind numbing. They all switched partners for the next dance, except for Cyrus and Princess Zerlina, who continued to dance, laughing and having a grand ole time together. They were truly perfect for one another—beautiful and cruel, just like their parents. King Astraeus and King Tariq would dance with their own wives, then each other's, then sit out a dance to talk and scheme with their heads bowed together.

The other courtiers all seemed to be having the time of their lives. Lord Visita caught my eye at one point and winked but I just averted my gaze. He was much too handsome for me to entertain his flirting, it would only lead to bad decisions, I knew myself well enough to recognize my weaknesses.

I just wanted to get out of here, take my heels off, and slip into what I knew would be a haunted sleep, but I dutifully kept an eye on everyone. I listened for any information I might be able to use, but so far, everyone seemed to be keeping their conversations light, revealing nothing of any real interest, unfortunately.

The double doors of the ballroom opened and a man entered. He looked around the room before spotting who he was looking for and letting out a breath of relief, before he ran across the room, directly to Cyrus. People gasped and whispered at the interruption, speculating about what had happened. Cyrus paused his dancing to speak with the man, his face quickly hardening, before he slowly smirked.

Cyrus sauntered over to his father, who'd been watching the interaction while dancing with Queen Stelara, but he stopped dancing immediately and turned to speak with Cyrus. The whole ballroom seemed to be holding its collective breath, waiting for the fallout of whatever was occurring.

King Astraeus glowered at whatever was said, and that was definitely concerning, as was the way Cyrus smirked, a light in his eyes I knew spelled trouble. What really caught my attention though, was Queen Stelara. Her mouth twitched, a smile growing before she caught it and snuffed it out, but her eyes shot to someone in the ballroom. I just couldn't see who from my vantage point, and I ground my teeth in frustration.

"What do you think is happening?" Emmie whispered from beside me. While we'd spoken on and off throughout the night, we'd been quiet for a bit as we observed the room. Me, hating every moment with these people. Emmie, wishing she could go and join them.

As much as I'd love the opportunity to dance and have fun at a ball, I would never enjoy doing so in Dusk, a land of blood and death, where the people enjoy torturing humans for fun. I'd forgone all my childhood dreams of living life as a princess long ago anyway.

"Nothing good." I murmured, keeping my voice low, but the man who belonged to Queen Stelara heard me, looking at me with eyes brimming with trepidation. While I hadn't interacted much with him before, I could only imagine the terrible things he'd seen belonging to the queen.

"Lord Aibek, Lady Siria." King Astraeus called out, silencing the room. He raised a hand, signaling the guards, and my heart began racing. The lord and lady stepped forward, Siria's hand on her husband's arm. They were both dressed in black, and I had to wonder if that was intentional, since black and purple were the colors of Night Kingdom. It could be a show of defiance but was just as likely a coincidence.

The guards began forming a half circle, moving through the crowd and coming up behind the Acheron's, boxing them in.

"Do you want to explain yourself?" King Astraeus asked with a raised brow, his stern jaw set in a hard line as he glared at them.

Lord Aibek shook his head, looking confused, "Your Highness, I'm afraid I don't understand." King Astraeus laughed, and the twinge of mania in it was deeply unsettling.

"You must think me stupid." The king seethed. "You came to me asking for help protecting your lands from Night Kingdom, but I had to be sure you were being truthful, considering your blood." He sneered at Lady Siria, who raised her chin defiantly.

"We sent a commander to ensure everything you said was true, and what did he find? You! Colluding with King Calix! Sharing resources across the border at a minimum, but worst of all—" King Astraeus paused in his accusations, the crowd holding their breath in anticipation, while I held mine in dread.

"You helped Calix's soldiers cross your border undetected, so they could sneak into my kingdom and slaughter my people!" The king yelled, his fists curling as lightning crackled around them.

Lord Aibek opened his mouth to say something, but never had the chance, a guard smacking the hilt of his sword hard across the back of his head. Cyrus came forward, and some magic I'd never seen before covered the lord in a net of magic, preventing him from using his own.

Lady Siria quickly raised her hands to use her own magic, but they were clapped in chains—iron chains. Her magic sputtered and died out, the iron smothering it. More iron they shouldn't have.

And the magic Cyrus used? Could that be…

"Traitors." Emmie muttered angrily, shaking her head in dismay. I closed my eyes for a moment, breathing deeply. Emmie seemed to get further away day by day, falling under the spell of King Astraeus, and everything he could offer her.

I didn't know what to think about this situation myself. I was all for working *against* Dusk Kingdom, but *for* Night Kingdom? I couldn't fathom how anyone could support them. Though…thinking of the soldier's words that day in the alley, I still had so many questions. What was Night Kingdom really doing, what was the goal? Something more was behind this, I was sure, but I couldn't see the whole picture.

Sympathy weighed on my heart for Lady Siria. King Calix was her family, her blood. I didn't know what made Lord Aibek choose as he did, but Lady Siria was loyal to her family. That was something I could certainly respect, if nothing else.

I turned to see the reactions in the ballroom. The people seemed to be thrilled to have traitors being imprisoned during the ball. Dinner and a show, I snorted to myself. My eyes found Prince Kian in the crowd, a solemn look on his face. I thought of what he'd shown me, of the humans strung up below our feet, and it dawned on me that since Fae were harder to break than humans, the Lord and Lady were facing unfathomable pain in the very near future. I swallowed down bile, as Prince Kian looked up, meeting my eyes.

Rage, dread, anguish—they sparked across the ballroom, encompassed in a single glance that held the weight of two desperate people, fighting an unstoppable force.

CHAPTER 19

AFTER the ball last night, I was growing increasingly worried about my plan to get Emmie out. I figured I had one real option, as much as I hated to consider it. But Emmie was one of my only friends, so here I was, entering the slave common rooms deep within the palace.

I looked around, avoiding the gaze of the girl who bothered me last time. *There.* I walked across the room towards her, and Eris looked up as I approached, glaring when she spotted me.

"Oh. It's you." Eris scoffed, her unimpressed tone making me roll my eyes. She went back to reading her book in an effort to ignore me.

"Don't worry, I'll skip the small talk." I assured her. "I'm worried about Emmie." Her head snapped back up. Eris looked around before getting up and tilting her head to the side, motioning me to follow her. Thank the Old Gods, I certainly didn't wish to have this conversation publicly.

Eris led me to a small, sparse room. Walls and floors the same black marble as the rest of the palace, only this room didn't have rugs and tapestries to brighten it up. She only had a thin single bed, a small table by the side of it, and an equally tiny dresser by the wall, a stack of books piled on top of it. I hadn't realized Eris enjoyed reading so much, but the books were the only personal touch to the room. Everything else was utilitarian and bland.

"Well? Are you going to sightsee or are you going to tell me about Emmie?" Eris snapped, not amused by my perusal of her space. Sighing deeply, I walked up to the dresser, absentmindedly reading the book titles.

"Emmie has gotten more and more attached to the king. More…zealous in defending him and his interests. Even when he's clearly in the wrong." I admitted, feeling way too exposed for my liking, but Eris was my best shot at getting Emmie on board.

I tilted my head, considering, "Well, I suppose as king, he's *never* technically in the wrong. But morally? Absolutely." Eris snorted and I turned to face her.

"You're right about that. And…about Emmie." Eris sighed, sitting down heavily on her bed. "She's been pulling away, more and more every day that passes." She turned her eyes away, trying to hide the glassy sheen. "I was happy for her at first. Finding a place in the court where she's safe is no easy task. But she's been so caught up in him, it's like she's obsessed. Anytime I try to remind her this is just to ensure her safety, that she needs to remember what she truly believes in, she kicks me out."

My mouth parted in surprise. The two had grown up together, were closer than many siblings, yet Emmie was kicking her out?

Eris laughed wryly and the sound was profoundly sad. "Yeah, I know exactly what you're thinking—and you're right. She's losing herself, Asteria, and I don't know what to do, how to help her."

Old Gods, the despair seeping from her, I *felt* for her. She was losing her best, and likely only, friend, slowly but surely, the longer she was here. The king was corrupt, I knew that, but now I feared that corruption spread like a plague. Infecting anyone near him.

"If I told you something, something that would help Emmie, would you promise to keep it to yourself?" I dared to ask, hoping my instincts were right here. So much was at stake here, and this could be a foolish risk…or it could be exactly what I needed.

Eris looked almost affronted at my words, rearing back, but I raised my hand, asking her to hold on. "It's dangerous and could likely either get you killed or blow the whole thing if you breathe a word." I explained with a hard tone. She needed to know how serious this was, even if I couldn't tell her everything.

I couldn't really explain the things I had seen, watched, been made to do—the time I'd spent here would likely haunt me forever.

"I promise, Asteria. I won't say a single word to even hint at whatever you tell me." Eris said, and her voice was low and raspy, but completely sincere. I knew she grew up in a similar court, that she knew these games better than I ever would, but still, I had to trust the devastation she radiated while speaking about Emmie.

"I'm getting her out." I declared with more confidence in my tone than I truly felt. "I can try to get you out too, but either way, I'm leaving." The words landed heavily between us, given life for the first time. A part of me wanted to swallow them back, like I had just ruined everything—but no, it was this place. *It* was ruining *me*. And those words? They felt like the first true breath of air I'd ever taken.

Eris's eyes were wide with shock, her mouth parted but no words came out.

"I know." I sighed, smiling wryly. "It seems impossible, but something is in the works. I just need you to trust me. Can you do that?" I beseeched her, praying to the Old Gods she would. We needed to get Emmie out before she lost any more of herself. I needed to get Priscilla out before she gained another scar. And *I* need to get out before I lose my sanity.

Eris's eyes drilled into me, like she could reach down into my soul and pull it apart to see if I was worthy of something as rare as her trust obviously was. I didn't blame her, I trusted few myself, but we were all trusting strange people these days. I trusted Prince Kian did have a reason to get me out and would do his very best to ensure the other humans and I were freed. But beyond that? I couldn't trust anything. This court ensured any trust I did have was broken down, when it was a fragile little thing to begin with.

After what seemed like an eternity but was likely only a minute or two, Eris slowly nodded her head. She stood up, crossing the room to where I leaned against her dresser. I stood up straight at her approach, and she put out her hand.

"From this point on, we are allies, Asteria. But you get me and Emmie out of here—you will have my trust and loyalty from that day forward." Eris said passionately.

I blinked in shock, not anticipating her reaction. Maybe she was as miserable as I was in Dusk, if helping to free her and Emmie clearly meant so much to her. Her offer was no trivial pledge. I reached my hand out, grasping hers as we shook on it, our agreement now sealed with brief nods from each of us.

Which meant I now had to find a wayward Prince and explain there was going to be an additional person to get free. I couldn't believe I didn't think of Eris before, especially when Emmie wouldn't leave without her. Eris was just so unassuming that it was easy to forget her. She would make a great spy, actually.

Leaving Eris to the rest of her day, I headed up the stairs, hoping to find Prince Kian. I wandered the halls for a bit, listening to servants and hoping one would eventually reveal his location. It was nearing lunchtime, so I made my way down to the kitchen, where I claimed to be getting something for Cyrus so I could listen in.

"This one is going to King Astraeus and his new little plaything. Take that up." One of the slaves commanded. I flinched, hating that Emmie was being referred to as a *plaything*. Even the human slaves weren't immune to the catty belittling of other humans.

"These to Princess Daneiris and her companion." The woman continued. Of course, the man got called a *companion*. Typical. I could feel my rage rise at the disrespect they showed my friend, but I shook it off. They weren't at fault here, not really. It was this system we lived in that kept humans beneath the Fae's boot, that forced women into situations like mine and Emmie's. It was broken—more like completely fucked, honestly—and it needed to be stopped.

Anything cracked could be repaired, but if we found a way to blow this whole system to smithereens, we could create something new, something extraordinary, from the ashes.

"This goes to Prince Kian, he's requested his meal in the library today." One of the maids smiled widely and eagerly stepped forward, patting down her hair and readjusting her dress so it was pulled down low, putting her breasts on display. I rolled my eyes, but followed the maid to the library, and once she was gone, slinked into the large space like I was here for a book. Which now that I thought about it, wasn't a bad idea. I needed to research blood magic and find out what Cyrus would be able to achieve with it. I needed to understand where the iron came into play, because my intuition told me it was all connected.

Looking at the large library, I sighed wistfully, wishing I was here to grab a new book. Cyrus's collection was small enough that I'd already finished most of the interesting books, and I was sure this library would have plenty of adventures and romances I could dive into, but no—the research had to come first.

The library was incredibly dark, the colors normally infused within the black marble were muted in the stone used to build this room. There were no windows anywhere in the space, likely to protect the books, but it left the area feeling musty and slightly dank. Dark wooden chairs and plum colored velvet sofas littered the space, along with some tables that had small lights on them so one could actually see the words on the page.

I looked up to find Prince Kian sitting at one of the tables, watching me with an amused smirk. I looked around quickly before I sped over to him, pulling out the chair across from him and taking a seat.

"How can I help you today?" Kian asked, raising a brow and trying to come across as serious, but his amusement seeped through.

"Two things. One, I need Eris to come with us when it's time. Can you make that happen?" I demanded, getting right to the point. Cyrus would expect me back soon, and I'd already spent a lot of time looking for Kian.

"Whose Eris?" He inquired, tilting his head to the side. I sighed in frustration as I explained who she was and what she looked like. Prince Kian looked uncertain, and I could only plead with him to do this for me.

"Please." I begged, and I hated begging, but the only way to get Emmie out of here was going to be with Eris's help.

Kian stared at me, his jaw working back and forth, before he finally sighed, and hanging his head forward. "It'll be complicated. There's a lot of you to get out. Including Aibek and Siria, now. But we'll figure something out."

I perked up at his words, not only insanely relieved that he would attempt to get all of us out, but I'd not heard anything about Lord and Lady Acheron since they were arrested.

"Are they…" I trailed off for a moment, feeling like it was a sincerely stupid question. "Are they okay?" Kian looked up at me, but once I'd opened my mouth, I apparently couldn't stop. "Why would they work with Night Kingdom? Why would you? They're slaughtering us!" I hissed at him.

Kian laughed wryly, with a profoundly agonized look in his eyes. "My family are the real monsters here, Asteria."

The silvery-white haired Fae soldier, and that conversation we had, ran through my mind again. He'd said the same thing, but I didn't understand how Night Kingdom could be anything but awful, not when they cut through cities killing people left and right.

"I can't explain right now." Kian continued. "But I promise you'll have an explanation soon. In the meantime, Aibek and Siria are being held in the dungeons. Getting them out is a high priority. They haven't broken yet, but my father and brother can be—"" He swallowed hard, "Inventive. We must get them out before the cause is completely exposed."

"The cause?" I pushed, tilting my head to the side, as my brows furrowed, but Kian just shook his head in response. I sighed in frustration, but jolted when he placed his hand lightly on top of mine.

"I'll do my best to get you all out. You have my word." Kian promised, his face creased in sincerity.

"Thank you." I whispered, feeling a bit unsettled by the show of genuine kindness. I cleared my throat. "The second thing I wanted to ask you about. Blood magic."

"What?" Kian pulled back, a perplexed look on his face. "What about it? Where did you even hear of such a thing?" His voice grew increasingly alarmed, and I glanced around to ensure we were still alone.

"Cyrus." I blurted out, and Kian's eyes widened. "I overheard him and your mother talking, and he's planning to use it. He said it was forbidden, and I know he's planning to sacrifice humans for it, but I don't know what it is."

"Fuck." Kian swore, running a hand through his hair as he sat back heavily. "This is bad. Blood magic is—Shalim, he could use it to increase his own power, make wards, create weapons. Blood is powerful, Asteria, it's what gives us all life, and that—" He paused, looking me right in the eye. "That kind of magic, the kind coming from the lifeblood of a human or Fae, rarely has limits."

"What do we do?" I beseeched him, my shoulders heaving as I let out a strangled breath.

"When you're out, you're going to tell—" Kian cut himself off. "You're going to tell the people you go with. I won't see them directly, we only pass messages, and this is too important to pass in a message that may be intercepted. You must tell them, and together, come up with a way to stop him."

My heart felt heavy when I left the library. I hadn't thought overly much of what I would do once I was free. Freedom itself was enough to drive me ever forward, but now...I realized this wouldn't be over once I was out of here. Too many were at risk, and what Cyrus was planning was an evil that should never be.

I couldn't just walk away from that. It sounded like Kian believed whoever was going to help us get free, was also going to be able to help stop Cyrus. I would have to wait and trust until then, when we could figure out what came next. Two things I didn't do very well with.

I STOPPED SHORT upon entering the solar of Cyrus's suite. Princess Zerlina was here, in Cyrus's lap, their mouths meeting as they kissed hungrily. I went to back out of the room when Cyrus spotted me.

"Asteria, wait." He called, and I froze in place, half turned back to the door.

"My apologies." Cyrus chuckled, lifting a scowling Zerlina off his lap. "Zerlina got a bit carried away."

Ah, she was trying to seduce him before the wedding. How scandalous of her. The royals were strange about sex, they could sleep with humans without consequence both before marriage and after, but a Fae? That was highly improper and would be a huge scandal if it got out. Ridiculous, but the Fae had bizarre rules.

"Are you apologizing to your slave?" Zerlina scoffed. "Cyrus—"

"Do not—" Cyrus growled, interrupting her, "Presume to tell me how to handle my own human."

Zerlina narrowed her eyes at him, darting to me before going back to glaring at him. "I am to be your wife and I refuse to have my husband treating slaves as something they are not."

Zerlina should have realized her error in talking back to him as lightning began to crackle around his hands, but she held firm. I couldn't help feeling admiration for her at that moment, even though she'd threatened me. I knew it wasn't easy to stand up to him.

"Let's get one thing straight, shall we?" Cyrus narrowed his eyes at Zerlina before he grabbed her by the hair, yanking it down until her knees hit the hard floor. He wrenched her head back, so she was staring up at him. "You will be my wife, yes, but not my keeper. As your husband, you will be subservient to me, just as my slaves are." Zerlina opened her mouth to argue, but he didn't allow her a moment to speak.

"You will honor me. You will *obey* me." Cyrus commanded, reaching for his belt, he snapped it off like a whip crack. I nearly flinched from the memories of Tavarius that sound brought with it. My eyes widened in incredulous horror as Cyrus whipped out his cock, shoving it into Zerlina's mouth as she sputtered and hit his thighs, trying to get a breath.

"What's wrong, my darling betrothed?" Cyrus laughed. "I thought you were trying to seduce me?"

He pumped into her mouth with harsh thrusts, forcing her to take it as he fucked her mouth. Sympathy flooded through me. No one deserved this, I didn't care if Zerlina had been horrible to me, I wanted to help her, to stop Cyrus. Knowing I couldn't help her, I tried to leave once more, but Cyrus turned his head to me with a lazy smile that I knew was hiding his savage glee in causing pain.

"Asteria, come here." Cyrus ordered, and I turned to him, my eyes pleading for reprieve. He shook his head. "*Now*, Asteria."

I swallowed at the hard tone and did as he said, slowly walking over to where he and Zerlina were by the sofas.

"You women, always so obstinate." Cyrus complained as he continued thrusting, fisting Zerlina's hair in his hand. "Let me make one thing perfectly clear here. While neither of you wants to see me with another—" I raised a brow while he wasn't looking, because he clearly had no idea how far off base he was.

I looked at Zerlina, catching her watering eyes, ones that looked completely broken. My own watered as I was forced to watch this strong, defiant Fae princess be degraded. I was sure that in her position, she'd never dealt with anything like this before.

"I'm sorry." I said silently to her, and her eyes closed in response. When Zerlina opened them, the force of a tornado whipped through her eyes, her strength rising back from the bleakness she'd fallen into. Despite what she'd threatened before, she knew I was there with her at that moment, my rage rising to meet hers in a clash of flame and air that could spark an uncontrollable wildfire. Both of us were merely tools for Cyrus to use, and she finally realized that I wanted nothing more than to get away from him. I wasn't here to get in her way or prevent her from taking a crown. I was a prisoner to his whims, and now, so was she.

Cyrus was an absolute bastard, able to bring some of the strongest people in this kingdom to their knees. I sincerely hoped the gods saw him damned to Tartarus forever. He deserved to feel the pain it promised for millennia.

Zerlina and I maintained eye contact when Cyrus resumed his little speech—after thrusting his hips several more times.

"But you both will have to adjust to the concept of sharing me with the other. I don't care about your protests; you both belong to me now. And you—" Cyrus thrust in hard, and tears spilled down Zerlina's cheeks.

"Will." He thrust again and I tried not to cry myself as Zerlina gagged horribly on his cock.

"Obey." Cyrus grunted as he used his grip on her hair to force her down harder on his cock.

"Me." Zerlina's head bobbed as his hips sputtered, finally cumming with a shout, spilling down her throat.

He pulled his cock out of Zerlina's mouth, slapping it across her face. She blinked up at him, shocked by the added insult, but I'd come to expect nothing less. Cyrus smirked back at her, wholly pleased with himself.

"You're both so obstinate." Cyrus tutted, shaking his head in dismay. "Asteria here thinks she can deny me sex forever." He moved behind me, slipping my hair over one shoulder as his arms came around my waist. He bent and nipped at my throat. "I will break her. One day very soon, I will sink into this delectable cunt and spend the entire day fucking her until she can't walk."

Zerlina appeared ready to explode, getting up from her knees in a fury. Already, she was back to looking at me with disgust, and I sighed quietly. I suppose I shouldn't be surprised; I may not be an obstacle to Cyrus for her, but I was just a slave, nonetheless.

"I am a *Princess* of Dawn Kingdom, and I refuse to be treated as a slave or whore! Your human is so far below me it's not even funny, and you would treat us the *same?*" Zerlina seethed, her fists clenching as the air around us began to grow thick and heavy, making me very nervous.

Cyrus growled threateningly, thankfully pulling away from me and stomping over to her. He took her by the neck, his hand sliding around it and squeezing.

"You *are* the same, my dear Zerlina. You will learn, that I promise you. If you want a crown on your head, you will obey me, or you will find yourself lacking a head." Cyrus spat, and lightning joined the charged air in the room, until it felt like their combined powers might create a storm strong enough to obliterate everything in the room, including me. "Now, we have a plan for the afternoon, do we not?"

"Yes," Zerlina gritted out. "We are to go into the city today, so the people can see their future *Queen*." She stressed the last bit, glaring at Cyrus, and I realized she was in denial about what had just happened. Maybe she thought if she didn't face what Cyrus just did to her, it wouldn't be real. I couldn't blame her; I'd gone through my own stages of denial. But she would eventually have to admit what had happened, and that Cyrus wasn't some fairytale prince who would make her queen—he was the monster who would see her ruined.

"Ah, good!" Cyrus smiled widely, his temper disappearing like fading wisps of smoke. "I need to check on some of my investments while we're there. Before we leave though, Asteria, file these plans away for me." He waved a hand toward the papers spread out on the table in front of the sofa. "I'll escort Zerlina back to get ready and send Priscilla for you. My kingdom may be meeting my future Queen, but despite your many protests, they'll also be meeting my future concubine."

The blood drained from my face. *What the fuck?* Horror and rage battled inside me, unsure which should take first place at that announcement.

"I will *never*." I spat at him, unthinkingly. Shock causing my ruse to vanish into thin air. I winced, hoping he would see this as me not wanting to be second place to Zerlina.

It was my turn to have my hair yanked and pulled back, and I struggled as Cyrus forced my face to his. He claimed my lips possessively, his tongue invading my mouth as he tried to dominate me. I raised my hands to push his shoulders, ineffectively attempting to get Cyrus off me. This kiss was different from the ones that came before, this one felt like a violation. Not only did I not want him touching me, but he'd just forced me to witness him assaulting Zerlina, and then announced I would be his official concubine—that he was dropping the façade of choice, and I would soon be his in every way.

I needed to be long gone by then. Kian was getting us out, and soon. I just had to get through this a little bit longer and ensure Cyrus didn't take what he wanted before that. I should have asked Kian how long before the plans moved forward, but it had to be within the week, right? I wasn't sure how much longer I could take this, not without cracking completely.

CHAPTER 20

Once Cyrus had left to walk Zerlina back to her rooms, acting as if she wasn't a grown woman who could handle it herself, I stomped over to file the papers he indicated, cursing him all the while. I needed to investigate whatever these plans of Cyrus's were before filing them away. Kian had said that whatever information I'd gathered would be valuable, and it felt like it finally gave purpose to all the intel I'd been collecting since I arrived in Dusk. I knew knowledge was power, and one of the ways the Fae kept humans powerless was by controlling everything we learned.

Shuffling through the papers, my breath caught in my throat. Intricate plans were detailed here for weapons and warfare, both for use against Night Kingdom, and any of the other kingdoms. The plans weren't ready yet, but if they succeeded, they may be able to hold King Calix and his kingdom at bay. I wasn't sure how to feel about this, not when Dusk Kingdom was just as bad as Night. Fae seemed to mostly be deplorable, though one or two good ones certainly existed, like Kian, but that was it. They were a greedy and cruel race overall.

I had been right; the iron and the blood magic *were* connected. Cyrus's plan was to use blood magic to craft iron weapons for use against other Fae. There were both offensive and defensive uses for the iron, and it seemed like he'd already started, as it mentioned having enough to cover the entire border in iron to prevent any Fae soldiers from breaking in. Those plans were detailed alongside ones for weapons, with one plan in particular detailing projectiles that shot balls of iron at long and short range., but there were other iron weapons described, like nets, swords, daggers, and arrows.

There were other plans here too, ones for the blood magic outside of the iron. Cyrus wrote of boosting the magic of the shield protecting the borders, along with using the magic to supercharge his lightning. There were a lot of theories written down, though nothing was definitive. Cyrus had only just started working with the magic, and it thankfully appeared that he didn't quite know what he was doing yet, which was a relief.

The thoughts of what he could do with this on a larger scale were terrifying. Not even considering how evil the use of this magic was, he could conquer the continent, and no one would even know what was happening. No—no, the gods required balance, and if he tried that, it would end very badly for him. Still, I didn't like what this spelled for the future of Celesterra.

I quickly read through the rest of the file, fighting down nausea as I did. I knew I needed this information, and I soaked it up like a sponge. I didn't know where this information would be going, who had the power to actually *do* something. I closed my eyes for a moment, frustration at my own uselessness rising. *I* wanted to do something. Not have some secretive third party handle it. I wanted to be able to strike Cyrus and his twisted family down. To save and free the humans in both literal and figurative chains. All throughout the continent and beyond if needed.

But I had no power, no strength, no magic. I didn't shape shift or fly. I was nothing—a useless, weak human who went along with whatever she had to in order to survive. I tried to force down the rising rage, frustration, and helplessness, but they surged together into a strange spark, one that shimmered through my veins like a rush of ecstasy—like something inside me struggled to break free.

The Old Gods knew I was struggling to break free, why wouldn't all of me want the same?

I stood back up, wiping any trace of emotion from my face and filing away the papers just in time, as Priscilla swept into the room with a new dress over her arm.

"Oh, Priscilla." I sighed, smiled truly. "You have no idea how good it is to see you right now."

"Oh?" Priscilla asked, her eyebrows rising before they furrowed, a worried crease forming across her forehead. "What's going on?"

"There's a lot happening, things I can't tell you about yet." I admitted, as I walked over to her, taking her hand and squeezing it. I wanted to give her what truth I could. "Not without putting us all in danger. I've already put one person at risk, I can't do that to you too."

"Asteria—" Priscilla's worried tone had me interrupting her.

"I found a way, Pris." I whispered, excitement creeping up in my voice. I couldn't quite contain it, and Priscilla's eyes widened as she realized what I meant.

"A way? You mean…a way…out?" Priscilla whispered back, haltingly. I smiled widely and nodded, and she squealed loudly before dropping the dress and throwing her arms around me.

We both laughed until tears came streaming down our cheeks, holding each other and swaying back and forth slightly. When we pulled back, we both laughed once more at the ridiculousness of our actions, but we had both needed the release. We'd been mistreated and suffocated under the rule of House Tynan, the mere idea of getting out from under them was—well, *freeing*.

We couldn't seem to contain our grins or the occasional giggle as Priscilla got me ready. Considering what I was about to do, I needed the distraction. I had to believe that this was going to be one of the last times I was forced to do anything by Cyrus, one of the last times I would be forced to have my hair curled and done up the way he liked, one of the last times I'd be forced into a dress he chose and not me. Silly things to care about, in the grand scheme of things, but they were choices I wanted to be free to make for myself.

I had to keep my hope alive, it was all that was keeping me going, from falling into that pit of despair I fell into after Tavarius. Well—hope…and *rage*.

Priscilla helped me into a dress that reminded me a bit of the ones I used to wear in Sunrise, light and flowy like those dresses had been, but it was also nothing like them. This was considerably more expensive, more beautiful, more everything. It cut almost indecently low across my breasts in strips of fabric, leaving me bare above and below them, my waist exposed around the sides and back, with a beaded adornment in the middle connecting the bodice and skirt. The straps over my shoulders fell down behind me in two draping bolts that swished when I moved in a swirl of lavender-gray color.

"You look beautiful." Priscilla smiled, admiring her work.

"I'm…exposed." I snorted, my nose wrinkling as I looked at my cleavage nearly spilling out, the fabric barely covering my nipples. I had no problem wearing provocative clothing, but this felt more like Cyrus had specifically dressed me for the role he imagined me in—which felt much less empowering than choosing to dress that way for myself.

"Well…" Priscilla drew out the word, her mouth screwing up on one side. "That's true, but you look amazing nonetheless!" Her bright smile and undefeated attitude had me barking out a short laugh.

"Thanks, Pris." I smiled slightly, shaking my head.

"Just remember, all of this will be over soon, right?" Priscilla said, confidently at the start, but withering by the end. Her fear was written plainly on her face.

"Right." I nodded, firming my lips into a hard line, not allowing any of my doubts slip through. Priscilla threw her arms around me, hugging me tightly, before making her way out and back to Princess Daneiris.

I walked into the solar after fiddling with my dress, trying to ensure all my important bits stayed covered. I stopped short at finding Princess Twyla waiting.

"Where's my brother?" Princess Twyla demanded, but her tone was undercut a bit by the way she bit her lip.

"Princess Twyla." I cleared my throat, curtsying. "Prince Cyrus went to—" I cut off as the door opened, and said prince entered.

"Twyla." Cyrus's surprise was given away by his raised brows. "What are you doing here exactly?" His eyes narrowed as he watched the princess shift uncomfortably on her feet. After what happened before, I was shocked she would dare come here.

"Shalim." Twyla whispered, her eyes closing briefly. "I came to apologize, Cyrus." His mouth hardened as he walked closer. "Is that so? And what, *exactly*, are you sorry for, Sister?"

Cyrus came to stop in front of her, and Twyla looked up at him, gulping at whatever she saw in his eyes. I knew his moods all too well, and I was positive lightning would be crackling in his eyes, warning anyone who looked that he was on the edge of losing it.

"I shouldn't have helped Daneiris. She threatened to—" Twyla trailed off, swallowing hard, like she was having trouble getting the words out. "It doesn't matter, I should have fought harder against helping her."

"Yes, you should have." Cyrus agreed. "Apologize to Asteria as well, and I will consider the matter over. Don't, and be prepared for the consequences, Sister." Twyla's eyes widened, and mine followed suit. Apologize to *me*? A royal Fae apologize to a human slave? Cyrus never apologized to me for anything. Why would he…*oh*. This was about humiliating her. Belittling her by making her apologize to someone so beneath her.

Twyla surely knew his intent, and she tilted her head back, looking to the ceiling like the gods might tell her what to do. When she pulled her head back, she looked right at me. Her lips pursed and she opened her mouth several times, the words struggling to roll off her tongue.

"I apologize, Asteria." She said finally. "I'm very sorry for what I did, and I hope I didn't cause you any unnecessary harm."

Unnecessary harm? Was that supposed to be different than *necessary* harm? This family, by the Old Gods.

"Thank you, Princess." I nodded, taking the path of least resistance instead of screaming at her and Cyrus both all the things she and her family should really be apologizing for.

"Good, thank you, Sister." Cyrus clapped his hands together. "Of course, due to the harm caused, it only seems fair you owe me a favor now, to be collected in the future." He smirked at Princess Twyla, who looked like she wanted to run out of the room as fast as possible. She nodded in agreement, looking defeated.

"Now, get out." Cyrus rumbled, smiling widely.

The princess wasted no time, running out as Cyrus came up to me, looking over his supposed *concubine*. His gaze made me incredibly uncomfortable, but I forced myself to stand still.

"You look beautiful, my dear." Cyrus praised, his hand coming up and cupping my cheek. "You better behave today. I won't have anything go wrong in public, understand? I already have my hands full with Zerlina, I won't accept anything but obedience from you."

I swallowed back all the things I wanted to say. Soon this would all be in the past. I repeated that thought over and over in my head.

"Of course, Cyrus." I cooed, giving him a sickeningly sweet smile. He narrowed his eyes at me but nodded before leaving to go get ready himself.

It unfortunately didn't take long, and Cyrus ushered me out to head into the city. We walked down to the grand staircase, which never failed to creep me out a bit. All the black on black and murky lighting looked like I imagined the entrance to Tartarus must, but it definitely seemed to fit the Tynan's.

Princess Zerlina met Cyrus on the landing of the stairs, taking his arm with a smile as we made our way to the carriages. Luckily for me, since the princess was here, I wouldn't have to ride in the carriage with him. It would be unseemly for their slaves to join them, after all. Cyrus ignored this before, but he wouldn't in present company.

Princess Zerlina's human joined me in a carriage several down from Cyrus's. The second and third carriages were taken up by Zerlina's ladies in waiting, and a few of Cyrus's people. Lord Visita spotted me and winked, and though I rolled my eyes, he was undaunted and smiled widely until his wife, Nisha, grabbed his attention. They were joined by Lord Arrats and Lady Luna, who followed them into the carriage.

We made our way through the streets of the capital, the gray buildings inspiring absolutely nothing. I stared forlornly at them as they passed by. Everything here was so bland and colorless, not at all like I once imagined a large city full of Fae magic would be. I wondered if any of the other cities in Celesterra were like I once imagined. Maybe they weren't, maybe the only real beauty to be found was in my dreams. I would envision shining palaces with dancing lights in the skies, all sorts of colors covering the cities thanks to buildings, flowers, shops, and people alike, magic at use everywhere you looked. Evenfall was nothing like that, in fact, one could almost mistake it for a purely human city—if the pointed ears and slightly elongated canines of the Fae weren't noticed.

Thinking of my dreams, I thought back to the dream I'd had last night. I had joined Luna in the sky, floating among the stars and dancing, and I'd soaked it all in—the peace and freedom it offered. But the darkness had appeared again, reaching for me, desperate to claim me. I didn't understand what had happened to make the darkness now seem so tangible, in a way it had never been before. Or why when I was there, I yearned for its embrace just as fiercely, my hands glowing like starlight as I tried to cross the divide between us.

The carriage came to a stop, and I jolted out of my reverie. Stepping out with the help of the footman, I looked around the square. People were lining the streets, stopping to get a look at the Crown Prince of Dusk and his betrothed. A mixture of Fae and humans surrounded us, though the majority were Fae. Cyrus and Princess Zerlina certainly looked like a beautiful couple as they stepped out and waved to the people. Princess Zerlina dressed in her house's colors, a deep red sheath with charcoal embroidery, while Cyrus was wearing a deep blue.

The two began their progress, going into some of the more upscale establishments and meeting people along the way. The rest of us followed behind them, nothing but decoration really. Cyrus wanted to check on his investments, so he made a point of visiting the gambling dens and brothel he owned. He left Zerlina with her ladies as he did so, and her face when she realized where he was going and why was priceless.

Zerlina huffed and moved along to another dress shop while she waited. I lingered outside with the other humans and about half the guards. The others went in with her, but the shops could only fit so many at a time. I was shocked out of the boredom of waiting by the blaring sound of an alarm. My head snapped up, looking around wildly.

The guards looked at one another, and half of them ran off toward the action, leaving a few behind as screams began sounding from streets away. I shifted on my feet as a roar sounded above us, freezing me in place. My blood heated, raging through me as I felt a throbbing within my chest. I was shrouded in the shadow of a beast as it flew overhead, the screams around me nothing but dull noise, unable to look away as shimmering black scales that reminded me of looking into the night sky consumed my vision, splashes of purple like the aurora across the sky.

The dragon could mean only one thing, and as it passed overhead, I sagged against the wall. Feeling I was released from a spell as my body practically vibrated. The guards were now on high alert as we waited, knowing we were in the eye of the storm. When the door to the shop flew open, we all collectively jumped—even the well-trained guards on edge. Princess Zerlina stood in the doorframe, eyeing the street as the guards sighed in relief.

"What is going on?" Zerlina demanded, the guards looking to one another.

"Princess," A fair haired guard began. "The kingdom is under attack. It's Night Kingdom. You should shelter in the shop; they won't expect you there. We can't risk them finding you." He gulped but his eyes hardened nonetheless as he grasped the hilt of his sword. "They would take pleasure in killing the Princess of Dawn, the one-day Queen of Dusk. It would be a significant blow."

Zerlina nodded, but I noticed a bit of fear now swam in her eyes. "Of course. You'll come inside with me. I'm sure the humans will be fine out here." Zerlina sniffed, her upturned nose scanning over me briefly before she turned to her own human. "Except you, you come with me." The dark-skinned man nodded silently and moved to join her inside.

The guard hesitated, "Princess, Prince Cyrus will not be pleased if something were to happen to Asteria." I jolted; not aware they even knew my name.

"I am to be his wife." Zerlina glared. "He will be much more upset if something were to happen to me."

"Of course, Princess. But—" The guard, who I had to give credit for trying to protect me—even standing against a princess to do it, started to protest but Zerlina wasn't having any of it.

The thought of being left out here to the whims of the Night Kingdom…I shivered as the reality descended on me—even as the memory of one Night Kingdom soldier in particular invaded my thoughts.

"I am the princess of Dawn and your future queen. You will obey me!" Zerlina snapped at the guard, who bowed his head submissively. "Inside! Before I have your head for your insolence."

Zerlina turned on her heel and walked back inside the dress shop. The guards entered after her, but the fair haired Fae hesitated.

"Take this." The guard turned to me, pulling something off his belt. "I'm sorry I can't stay out here to protect you. With their armor, getting a shot at the heart will be impossible. Aim for the eyes or throat, they're the most likely weak spots to be exposed. If you don't have a clear shot, then aim your knee or foot between the legs—a man will go down hard at that."

I was surprised to see him hand me a dagger, slowly reaching out and grasping the hilt. I couldn't believe he was giving this to me. It was illegal for humans to have weapons, and if he was found to have given me one, he could be executed himself. I swallowed hard and looked up, making eye contact with the guard.

"Thank you." I choked out, my voice raspy, unused to this sort of kindness from a stranger, a Fae, a guard of Dusk Kingdom. The other humans were already fleeing, and I tightened my grip on the dagger as he gave me a wry smile.

"We're not all like Cyrus." He whispered, shocking me completely, before he disappeared into the shop.

Leaving me alone. Grasping a dagger. Exposed on the street. As the Night Kingdom attacked. *Fuck*.

I prayed quickly to the Old Gods, asking them to watch over and protect me—for whatever good it might do, as I took off running. I had to get out of sight quickly and looked around for somewhere to duck into and hide. But every shop I passed had closed, blocking their doors and windows. They'd been prepared for another attack, but now there was nowhere for me to go, and the din grew louder as the fighting made its way closer and closer.

Fuck, fuck, fuck!

I was nothing but a mouse in a trap, and the cat was getting much too close for comfort. Or the dragon.

No. Fuck that. I was no mouse. I may be human and technically power-less, but I would meet that damn dragon's flames with my own.

My rage was as hot as dragon fire, that I knew. And I could feel what felt like my blood sparkling in my veins again, like my body wanted me to unleash all of the rage and fear into something tangible.

Still, I wasn't stupid. I ran into the closest alley and pressed myself against the wall, hoping against hope I wouldn't be found, that no one would come this way. I tried to calm my rapid breath, repeating that mantra to myself as I tried to get myself under control.

"Well, well, what do we have here?" A voice drawled from the other side of the alley. I froze, whipping my head toward it in shock.

Darkness surrounded him like a lover, skating over his skin like a caress. The darkness was bathed in midday sunlight that created a surreal effect, like an ephemeral night wrapped within the day's sunlight. It made him look like a god on Adamah. He was even more stunning than I remembered, with long silvery white hair that brushed over his shoulders and ended at his broad chest, with pieces braided back to keep it out of his face. I spied a tattoo on his neck and wondered absentmindedly if he had more to discover beneath that armor. His bright purple eyes were animated as they drifted down my body.

Old Gods. Had I thought Cyrus and Vissy handsome before? I suddenly couldn't understand how. Not compared to *him.*

He put his sword back in its sheath as he approached me, a smirk on his face I seriously considered trying to slap off.

"You, again." He purred, and I hated that I couldn't stop the shiver it caused. I reminded myself that this man was part of the Night Kingdom. A Fae who hates humans, who has slaughtered us in untold numbers. He must be playing some game—the Fae do love their games. Nothing else made sense.

He may have been right about Cyrus being a monster, but what he did was just as despicable. He may claim they aren't monsters, but evidence sug-gested otherwise. Case in point: he was here right now—*attacking.*

"What do you want?" I snapped, summoning as much bravado as I could muster, false or not. "Are you going to kill me this time? If so, just get it over with."

I clutched the dagger tightly, and his eyes went right to it. He smiled broadly, flashing perfectly pearly white teeth at me.

"I'm not going to kill you." He chuckled huskily, "I should be asking if you're going to try to kill me, the way you're clutching that dagger."

I scoffed, "Like I could do anything against a Fae." My anger rose swiftly, hating being talked down to.

"Don't sell yourself short. You have no idea the things you could accomplish." He said quietly, sounding bizarrely sincere.

It only served to confuse me more. My eyebrows furrowed, "What do you want?"

He stepped closer, and I brought the dagger up between us as a warning, but he merely smirked as he stepped right into it, the point of the blade hitting the hollow of his throat. I swallowed hard. I didn't handle confusion well, so I let my anger take the wheel. I should have been more afraid, faced with a Fae who I knew was here to murder human slaves, but the fear evaporated in his presence.

The moment he stepped in front of me, I felt…stronger. More centered, as all of my muscles relaxed and my mind calmed, but somehow also the complete opposite, like my body didn't know whether to relax or go into a heightened state of arousal, so it chose both. It happened last time I saw him too, and it infuriated me. That feeling like I was out of control of my own body. My body was the only thing I did have control over, and here he came, taking even that from me.

"Are you doing that?" I snapped at him.

He tilted his head to the side as he considered me, "Doing what?"

"Are you influencing my emotions?" I demanded, clutching the dagger tighter. "Making my fear fade? Making me feel—" I slammed my mouth shut, not wanting to admit to the other feelings he provoked in me with his mere proximity. His nostrils flared, and I knew he scented my arousal, as much as I wanted to deny its existence.

He drew in a deep, startled breath. "Your feelings seem altered?"

Now it was my turn to be startled at his quiet question.

"That doesn't make any sense." He continued, mumbling to himself. His head turned to the side, and I watched the flow of moon glow hair fall over his shoulder. When those purple eyes found me again, I felt trapped under their gaze. "I can't influence emotions. Now, if you'd remove the dagger…"

He went to push it away and I dropped it into my other hand, bringing it back up instantly. He caught my wrist and I grappled with him for control of the blade. Our hands weaved in and out of each other's as I tried to point the dagger at him, and he tried to lower it—until he finally bothered to exert a bit of force. The merest amount enough to overpower me, my frustration mounting as he took the blade from my hand. He held not only the dagger, but all the power too.

"What am I going to do with you?" He laughed, shaking his head.

I brought my leg up, taking the guard's advice and trying to knee him in the balls, but his hand wrapped around my thigh, holding my leg in mid-air, a teasing smirk on his lips as he raised his brows at me. I glared at him, trying to surprise him with a punch to the face, but he grabbed my fist, using it to step into me while holding our arms to the side. Trapping me between him and the brick wall.

Our bodies touched in ways that shouldn't thrill me as they did—lighting me up from the inside. My nipples grazed his chest, covered in that thin, scaled black armor. His sharp cheekbones caught my attention as I traced them with my eyes. He chuckled, his own eyes dropping downward, his tongue licking his bottom lip lightly before his sharp canine scraped over it—looking more like a true fang, the kind the now extinct Vampyres were said to have possessed than they had on any other Fae I'd seen. I was quickly distracted from that when I realized how exposed this dress truly left me under his gaze. I told Pris, this damn dress was nearly indecent.

But the heat I felt as he watched my heaving breasts? It was so, *so* wrong.

He raised his other hand and trailed his fingers down my cheek. "I don't understand what you are doing to me, but it has to stop." His throat bobbed on a gulp, and I watched the movement avidly. "Fucking Nox. You need to stop looking at me like that." His whisper sounded like pure sex, melting me like a candle dripping wax.

"Like what?" I breathed out. Our eyes locked, and colors began to dance in his eyes: green, pink, blue—all mixing with the purple. The aurora existed within those orbs, and I was absolutely enthralled.

"Like you want *more*. You *smell* like fucking sex." He groaned, and I figured it was only fair, with the way he sounded. "I can *feel* the want radiating off you—your want for me, be it my body or spilling my blood. Such a violent little thing, aren't you?" He growled, a rumbling noise I felt in my own chest, making me shiver. He let go of my hand finally, my arm falling limply by my side, but he brought his hands up, clasping both sides of my neck and tilting my head back. His lips came down, a millimeter of space between his and mine. A part of me begged for him to close that space between us.

The other part recognized this was *insane*. What was I doing?!

"Fuck! I would kill to be able to do this. But I can't. I won't." He shook his head like he was trying to clear it from a fog as he stepped back, confusing me thoroughly.

"What—" I started, but his eyes snapped back to me, and I froze.

"Still think I'm a monster?" He whispered, tilting his head to the side.

"You're still part of the Night Kingdom. You're still Fae." I whispered back, an answer, and a desperate reminder for myself of the reasons I had to grip onto my hatred with bloody fingernails.

He huffed a laugh, "So I am."

He looked me over, his eyes felt like a sweep of shadow against my skin, and my entire body hummed in answer.

"I'll see you soon." He promised, grabbing my hand and placing the dagger back in it, wrapping my fingers around the hilt—and began to walk away.

"What do you mean?" I demanded, walking a few steps after him. "This is insane! You're doing something to me. I want all of you Night Kingdom monsters dead!" All of my questions and doubts flew out of my head, nothing but rage sparking and firing through my mouth.

He stopped dead and turned to face me, smirking. Darkness began gathering, swirling into a cloud that surrounded him in a thick blanket of night, blotting out the sun. It took me a few moments to realize wisps of shadow were coming from his hands and drifting upward. I watched as those shadows reached out, strands aiming right for me until they consumed me entirely in their dark embrace.

My chest heaved as my breath quickened. It was just the two of us inside a cloud of unnatural darkness—and I had just essentially threatened him. I couldn't see a thing, and my fear came trickling back in, knowing I was at a complete disadvantage. Stuck in the dark with a Fae who could likely see everything while I was left blind. An enemy Fae, at that.

"You're right to fear me." He spoke directly into my ear, making me jump. I hadn't heard him approach at all. "I could kill you with a snap of my fingers. It would be so easy. Here in Dusk Kingdom, you're better off trusting few. Strangers even less so." I could picture the wry smile on his face at his tone.

"Why don't you feel like a stranger?" I barely forced the words out. That feeling of *knowing* had pervaded me from the moment we met, and it hadn't lessened since. Leaving me feeling off kilter and lost when it came to how to respond to him. Rage, lust, fear, peace…a swirl of conflicting emotions raced through me—all centered around *him.*

He was silent, leaving me with nothing but the darkness for a solid minute. I swallowed and tried to look around, hoping for any glimpse of light in the darkness.

"That's a damn good question, isn't it?" He finally answered, but it was such a non-answer, I had to close my eyes for a moment to try to control my reflexive anger. It was pointless, in the end. I screamed in frustration, throwing my hands up in the air.

"Maybe I will stab you! If it will get you to answer an actual question!" I raged at him, needing to let some of it out before it burned me up from the inside.

He laughed, *laughed* at me, while my rage bubbled over. He let some of the darkness dissipate, and like a veil had lifted, my vision returned as I breathed a sigh of relief. As much as I loved darkness, I didn't love being blinded by it. But I could now see *him*. The current source of my trouble and a Fae I could attack with no compunction, no consequences—aside from him killing me if I failed, of course.

I surged forward with the dagger, trying my damndest to stab him, high or low, I couldn't care less. I just wanted to let this rage *out*. It burned as it drove me forward, like flames licking through my blood and bone, consuming everything I am until all that remained was ash.

He didn't even have the decency to truly defend himself, laughing as he blocked me at every turn. It didn't stop me from trying to stab him, though. Somewhere. *Anywhere.* Until he finally got tired of dodging me and slammed me up against the brick wall of the alley.

"Are you quite done?" He asked, eyebrow raised, his lips lifting in a smirk I wished I didn't find so damn alluring.

"Never!" I sneered at him, burying that attraction as much as I could. He chuckled, giving me a glimpse of a true smile, an unfortunately stunning one.

"Good. Keep that rage." He advised, sounding completely genuine. I blinked rapidly, feeling off balance, and dropped the dagger. The sound of the fighting from the rest of his forces grew closer, and his head snapped toward the end of the alley. He looked back at me, and his gaze was piercing.

"See you soon." He whispered in my ear, his hands brushing down my bare arms and leaving chills in his wake.

He disappeared in a cloud of shadows, leaving me to sag against the wall, alone, with a thousand questions running through my mind, and no answers forthcoming. I didn't understand...so many things. My reaction to him. The familiarity I felt with him. Why he said he'd see me soon. Why he didn't kill me. I'd gone after him with a dagger, a human trying to attack a Fae was an automatic death sentence. So, why didn't he kill me? He was here with the Night Kingdom specifically to kill my kind, and I'd broken a law that would give him full rights to do so on top of that.

And he just—didn't.

What in the name of the Old Gods was going on?

CHAPTER 21

THE sounds of the attack began to fade as I wandered back in the direction of the shop, still in a haze of shock and bewilderment. I followed the few landmarks I remembered, trying to forget the chiseled face of the Fae that was *definitely* my enemy and *not* someone whose body I should be aching to feel pressed against me again.

I turned the corner, trying to shove all thoughts of him away, only succeeding because Cyrus was outside, yelling at Zerlina. Wanting to delay this, but knowing there was no point, I walked up to them, and Cyrus's head whipped towards me.

"Thank Shalim." He breathed, shooting a glare at Zerlina, who glared right back. "We'll discuss this later." He ground out, his jaw clenching.

"Yes, we will." She hissed at him.

So…that marriage was definitely going to go well.

"Asteria you—" Cyrus stopped speaking abruptly, the smile that had been growing on his face falling. His nostrils flared, and my stomach sank, knowing that spelled trouble.

"Why do you smell like—*who* was with you?" Cyrus demanded, grabbing both my upper arms in a tight grip.

"And what is this?" He seethed, letting go of one of my arms, only to yank the dagger from my hand.

"Well?" Cyrus glared down at me. I swallowed hard, unsure of what to say. I didn't want to tell him the truth. I didn't want to get that guard in trouble. Nor did I want to find myself in further trouble.

"I found it." I blurted out. "I ran for cover when I was locked out here. The soldiers came and I—I was scared." My jaw worked as I spat out the words. I hated admitting weakness, but it was the lesser of two evils, knowing that admitting the truth would lead to the Fae he gave me the dagger, a rare kind Fae, being sentenced to death.

Cyrus sighed heavily, pulling me into a hug. His head rested on top of mine with a familiarity he'd never earned. I wanted nothing more than to push him away. It felt so wrong for him to be touching me, especially after the rightness I'd felt in that alleyway.

"I'm so glad you're unharmed, darling." Cyrus whispered into my hair. "This will never happen again; I promise you that." No apology was forthcoming, of course. It was unbelievable the things Cyrus focused on. It took all my willpower to not roll my eyes. I was thankful when Cyrus finally released me and returned to glaring at Zerlina, who just crossed her arms, raising a brow at him in challenge.

After what she'd already experienced, I was impressed she would dare. Then again, she seemed to be in denial still. Once that wore off, she may not be so brave. I found myself hoping she was however—she would need that bravery if she intended on shackling herself to Cyrus forever.

"Why do you smell like another male, Asteria?" Cyrus demanded, as he turned back to me. I could practically taste the fury pouring off him, knowing that someone else had touched what he believed was his property. But I wasn't, nor would I ever be, his.

My heart, my soul, my entire body rebelled at just the thought of being Cyrus's. While every part of me cried out in burning desire when faced with the Fae soldier from Night, it did the exact opposite now in front of Cyrus— screaming to run as far and as fast as possible.

"I was cornered by one of the Fae soldiers. I managed to get away, but it was—" I gulped, feigning like I was overcome after such an ordeal. I managed to speak true, even if the sentiment was false.

Cyrus stared at me, eyes boring into me like he could burrow through and expose the lie. Finally, after what seemed like forever, he nodded in acceptance. He quickly pulled me back towards the carriages, leaving Princess Zerlina fuming behind us. He pulled me into the carriage he and Zerlina had taken, completely against protocol. The princess stopped short as she realized this, her eyes narrowing and cheeks turning red.

"Absolutely. Not." Zerlina growled.

"Get in the fucking carriage, Zerlina!" Cyrus barked back at her. She swallowed hard as a bolt of lightning cracked from the tips of his fingers—a clear sign his patience had snapped. Realizing this, she stepped into the carriage and threw herself into the seat across from us. Cyrus gripped my hand in his, refusing to let go. Zerlina's stare fastened on our hands the entire ride back.

By the time we reached the palace, the tension in the carriage was near boiling over. Before Princess Zerlina could throw open the door, Cyrus caught her hand, finally releasing mine.

"Asteria, make your way back to our rooms." Cyrus ordered, but his tone was shockingly gentle compared to how furious he still looked. "You can relax and recover after your unfortunate ordeal. I likely won't be back tonight. I'll need to deal with the fall out of the attack. Along with a princess who seems to think she can overrule me."

Zerlina froze for a moment, before her eyes widened, incredulous. Cyrus squeezed her hand in warning—and squeezed it hard, Zerlina's fingers turning white from the force of it.

"Come. On." Cyrus growled, yanking his betrothed out of the carriage with him.

I got out of the carriage and was surprised to find Lord Visita there, his wife waiting by the carriage.

"Are you okay?" Vissy asked, his brows furrowed in concern as he looked me over, like he might find some visible wound on me. His eyes snagged on my cleavage, and I again cursed Cyrus for this damn dress.

"I'm fine, Vissy." I smiled slightly to soften my brush off. "You should go take care of your wife."

He looked intensely down at me, "I'd rather take care of you." I managed to swallow my exasperated sigh before it escaped—but seriously, *these Fae men*. How did I manage to keep attracting them? Cyrus, Vissy, whatever that was in the alley with the nameless, gorgeous enemy soldier.

"I'm fine, I promise," I replied. "I just want to go to sleep, honestly."

Which was the truth. In my dreams, I was free. I could fly and float up among the stars. I could let go of everything that plagued me—all of my problems ceased to exist while I was there. And the darkness's embrace beckoned, calling me to it like a Siren Song, unable to resist the *need* to break that barrier and find out what awaited me on the other side.

"Okay, but if you need anything, send someone for me." Vissy insisted. I raised an eyebrow at him but nodded, hoping it would be enough to get him to go away and leave me to crawl into bed, alone.

I managed to slink away from Vissy and the rest of the prying eyes in the courtyard, making my way up to my room. I thanked the Old Gods Cyrus was going to be busy tonight, not having the energy to deal with him at all after everything that transpired. I wanted nothing more than to collapse into bed—which I promptly did, leaving my dress in a pool of fabric on the floor to worry about later, I let the silk sheet drape over my naked body as I fell into bed. Barely a moment after my head hit the pillow, my eyes shut and I drifted off to sleep, where my dreams awaited.

I ROSE UP among the stars, Luna immediately uncurled from her position in the sky and flew over to greet me. I smiled joyfully as she played all around me, dipping and swooping, her moonglow scales illuminating her path through the star-lit sky. I reached my hand out to trail my fingertips along those glowing scales. The luminous being trilled in response. She was a true dragon, unlike the Fae who could shift into a dragon form. Which meant she couldn't exactly speak in words, using trills and growls to communicate. I had no idea if Fae could speak in their dragon form, to be truthful, but I knew they could certainly speak in their Fae forms. Luna had only the scaled form before me. Not as sinuous as Zhu, with more bulk to her form, but just as graceful—and even more playful.

I obliged her eagerly, playing with her through the stars and the sky, dancing around her to the tune of a balanced universe. One that I somehow felt and understood. Luna motioned for me to grab onto her tail, and I followed her direction. I laughed as she took off, wings beating through the sky as I skated along the air current left behind her. I closed my eyes, almost believing that I was flying myself. Not just floating like I usually did here, but truly flying.

Nothing had ever felt so right.

Well, except for one thing—but I was certainly not thinking about *him*.

A shiver went down my spine, and I ceased playing. I could feel it once more. The darkness approached. I felt that churning, desperate desire once more—and as shadows banged on the barrier, trying to break through, I put my palms up, as close as I could reach, but not close enough. The darkness was still too far, prevented from touching me. Awe consumed me as my hands lit up with starlight, so in contrast to the vast darkness before me. I marveled at the sight even as I struggled to reach the dark fingertips stretching towards me.

I let out a cry of frustration. It was so close! Closer than before—like the barrier had shrunk. Still, we fell short, and I startled awake in my bed, aggravated at the failure.

I was relieved to find Cyrus had yet to return. I called for breakfast and ate quickly before Priscilla arrived to help me dress. I assuaged her worries that I was okay after the attack yesterday, and she hugged me so tightly I thought I may suffocate to death, but I squeezed her back just as hard. Priscilla was a true friend, the first female friend I'd ever had. Emmie was—something different. A friend, but not someone who would be there for me in the way Priscilla was. I never thought I'd have a friend like this, and it nearly brought tears to my eyes to feel that sense of comfort and support. While I'd rued the fact that my armor had cracked and let people in, I couldn't regret it when it came to Pris.

It was dangerous, to be sure, but I was certain now it had been worth it. So long as Emmie didn't prove me wrong. I made my way to see her next, but her head was so in the clouds over the king that it was like talking to a wall. I sighed in frustration and made my way back to my room.

Cyrus was thankfully still absent, so when I looked out the window and saw my hawk flying around, I made my way out onto the balcony. It landed and trilled as I pet it, but didn't seem to relax, its body tense as an alarming sound left its beak.

"What's wrong, little guy?" I murmured to it, but it wasn't as if it could answer.

I looked up to the sky, drawing in a panicked breath as I watched the day be eclipsed by darkness. Not the regular darkness of night, or maybe it was exactly that—only it was the magic of Night and not the natural kind. A cloud of pure darkness, just like I'd seen that Fae soldier of the Night Kingdom wield, began to blanket the entire city. From my vantage point, I could see it seeping down into every street between the city gates and the palace.

The hawk cawed loudly, startling me as I tore my eyes away from the surreal scene. The hawk quickly bumped my hand with its head before it took off, flying directly into the darkness. I couldn't help but be nervous for its sake. I swallowed hard and moved inside. We had to be under attack again, but it didn't make sense. Night Kingdom had just attacked yesterday, and they had never attacked two days in a row before.

It wasn't long before the door slammed, making me jump as Cyrus stormed into the room, clearly furious. Lightning was crackling all around him and he stormed towards the windows where he stood for a moment watching the darkness descend with clenched fists.

"My father forbade me and my brothers from going outside. He sent our entire army but refused to let us go." Cyrus fumed, pacing back and forth before the window. "It's too dangerous for princes, apparently. He argued that Calix has clearly changed tactics, and we have no idea what this attack will bring, but he's doing nothing but making us look weak. They will think we're too scared to go up against the Night Kingdom."

Small lightning bolts sparked off Cyrus as he spoke, and I considered carefully how to respond, but ultimately, didn't have a chance.

"Zerlina was an absolute handful yesterday, you know." Cyrus turned his head to me, and his eyes raked over me. "I hope you won't prove as difficult today. It seems I must ensure you both understand the way of things."

An ominous dread filled me, just as the darkness filled the streets outside. Cyrus going from furious to deathly calm was never a good sign. Cyrus reached out a hand and I reached out a trembling hand to take it, gulping as I tried to control my heartbeat. He led me into my bedroom, and I scrunched my eyebrows together as I opened my mouth to ask him what was going on—but Cyrus covered my mouth with his hand before I could.

"You've been quite difficult, Asteria." Cyrus murmured. I looked into his eyes and the swirling depths frightened me in a new way. "I've done everything I could, given you everything you could possibly want."

I truly feared where this was going, but the first stirrings of a deeper fear, a type of terror I had yet to experience directly, hit me when I realized what it was in his eyes that had frightened me—not just fury, but a crazed madness that was wholly new.

"You deny me your body, again and again—yet you get wet at my friend's touch like a whore." Cyrus growled, leaning in so he crowded me, and I was forced to lean backwards, putting me off balance. *Old Gods*. I knew that night with Vissy was going to come back to bite me, even if Cyrus was the one who insisted on it.

Cyrus took advantage of my lack of balance, using it to direct me backwards toward the bed. Alarm bells began blaring in my head at the direction he led me. "Cyrus—"

"You think you have control here. But you only have what I allow you." Cyrus hissed, and I realized what this was about. Control. His father took away his control, and now he wanted to prove to himself he still had it. He grasped for it in all aspects of his life. From his slaves to his family, he sought a type of control over everything—but that type of control was impossible to gain. As a slave, I had learned to seek control where I could, and not let the lack of control in other areas drive me crazy. But Cyrus never had to learn that lesson.

"Zerlina now understands her place." Cyrus declared, and my heart sank for her as I contemplated how exactly Cyrus had managed that. She may be a bitch, but she was a woman who still deserved to make her own choices and control her own body.

"It's time you do as well."

Cyrus's mouth crashed down on mine, but I refused to kiss him back. I raised my hands to push him off, but he caught them and held them in an iron grip. I dared to bite his lip, but when he pulled back, he only laughed. Chills went down my spine at the sound of it.

Dread choked me, but rage joined it—sparkling in my blood. I knew how powerless I truly was here. Cyrus had been fine playing my game and waiting until I gave permission, but now…now his lack of control was being redirected to me, and he would take mine away to assuage his own. He had once promised he would be my ruin, and the time had come.

"Cyrus! No!" I gasped as I was thrown backward on the bed. "Please— Old Gods, I—" His hand clamped down on my mouth, cutting me off.

"Shut up." Cyrus seethed, as my eyes grew wider. The loss of power, of control—it drove his actions *and* my fear, equally.

"You think you can continue to deny me? *Me?!*" Cyrus raged. I gasped as he let go of my mouth to fasten his hands on my arms, tightening them to the point of pain.

"Please, Cyrus, you're hurting me!" I begged, trying to shake him off, but it was no use. My arms felt as if they might crack in two from the pressure he was exerting. I struggled to breathe through the fierce pain, but it was nearly blinding.

Old Gods. Was this how strong the Fae truly were? I always knew they were strong, but—he wasn't even really trying, barely applying pressure, and I felt as if I might crumble under his hands—my bones an inch from flaking away to dust.

"Good." Cyrus sneered, and my eyes went wider. I knew his cruelty. I'd seen it during my time here, and when Kian showed me the humans in the dungeons, when Cyrus came down to play with Raziel, I'd realized then that I truly knew nothing of what he was capable of. But now—now he was letting that cruelty loose with me.

With the grip he had on me and the cruelty I knew he was capable of; I wasn't sure I was going to even survive this. I knew Cyrus couldn't be trusted, but I had still let my guard down. Let myself trust, even the slightest bit, that he wouldn't hurt me. Not *me*—not when he wanted something from me. For Tartarus's sake, I was a fool.

"I have endured enough. I've offered you everything you could ever want!" Cyrus seethed above me, his sneer becoming a low growl that sent chills through my body. "And what do I get? An uppity little human who thinks she can deny a Fae prince! I've acted the perfect prince, trying to win you to my bed."

His words scorched through me as I realized he truly had reached his limit of patience. While I'd known it was inevitable, I had hoped to be out and long gone by then. I renewed my fight against him, despite beginning to shake with horror. I kicked my legs out, my arms burning as I fought his hold. I tried to swing my head forward to headbutt him, but he moved before I could, yanking his head out of my reach.

No. *No.* This was *not* going to happen.

Old Gods. Please, *please.*

"Cyrus, please, please don't do this!" I grit out as I continued struggling in his arms, but it was futile. He was stronger, more powerful—there was no fighting him off. I froze as he roughly shoved me down to the bed. His fingers were like claws, digging into my arms even more painfully. I whimpered in response and watched a cruel smile take over his face.

"Yes. Beg, my pretty little Asteria." Cyrus gloated, a smirk on his face that was edged with cruelty and want. "Plead for me to end this. To not take what I want. What I'm *owed.*" What he wanted wasn't just my body, I realized, not anymore. Now, he wanted to watch me be humiliated, wanted to take from me what he wanted despite my protests. He was a fucking monster of the worst kind.

"But I think I've waited long enough. Don't you?" Cyrus crooned, sickly sweet. "After all, you belong to me. So now, it's time to take what's mine."

I let loose a scream as he ripped my dress down the middle, trying to flail and kick—anything to somehow stop him. I was so close to being free, to being far from here where Cyrus couldn't hurt me. I couldn't—wouldn't—let this happen. Not *now*, so close to freedom…

Cyrus just laughed as tears of fear and frustration began to leak from my eyes.

"You could have had a much easier time of this, but instead, you refused me. You tried to deny me what is mine. Remember that. It's all your fault, Asteria. And now…," He gave me the worst smile I had ever seen, frothing with rage and sadistic pleasure. "Well, now, I'm going to *ruin* you."

I screamed, doing everything I could to fight him off, but his hands kept ripping my clothes away until I was left in my undergarments, exposed to his eyes. Starlight flashed behind my eyes and fire scorched through my soul as I screamed and fought, refusing to submit to him. Cyrus's cruel laughter echoed in my ears as I sobbed through my hoarse screams.

I tried to get my knee up to hit him in the balls, but he caught my knee with lightning quick reflexes. He sneered, a growl coming from deep in this throat.

"You think you can hurt me? You? A pathetic little human?" He took my knee and roughly pushed it down to the bed, then did the same to the other one—until I was spread open in front of him.

"Get! Off! Me!" I roared in his face, panic beginning to overtake me. I had no way out. No one to help me. In this moment, I was reduced to nothing but another human slave, being used by their Fae master.

Cyrus just looked amused, "Don't worry, my dear, you'll enjoy this. In the end, at least. I'll show you."

"Don't you fucking touch me!" I yelled as he went to cut open the bustier holding my breasts up. I watched it open in disbelief that this was happening, not noticing his hand going straight to my throat. He wrapped his hand around my neck, holding me down with so much force I felt like my windpipe might just snap. I tried to gasp a breath, reaching up to claw at him, trying to scratch or cut, to do anything—absolutely *anything*—to get Cyrus off me.

A part of me wanted to laugh wryly—Verin was right after all. My beauty finally proved fatal, and I ended up right where she said I would: under a cruel master who would take what he wanted from me.

"Didn't your mother ever teach you when a lady says no, she means no?" A growling voice came from the doorway and Cyrus's head whipped around to see who had spoken. His jaw dropped, but a sneer quickly took over.

In a blur of movement, Cyrus was ripped off me and thrown into the wall. So fast, I barely registered it happening. But it gave me what I needed, and I gasped in a desperate breath. I reached under the mattress, grabbing my iron dagger. I wished it had been in my hand when I'd truly needed it, but I sent a silent thanks to my father for having its protection now.

I hurried to scurry off the bed and moved to the corner of the room where I could protect myself better. I grabbed my ripped dress and held it in front of me to cover myself.

I wiped the tears from my eyes so I could see clearly and found a tall Fae male standing between Cyrus and me. I nearly did a double take. This wasn't just any Fae, but the most beautiful one I'd ever seen. One who'd pressed me against an alley wall just yesterday. My jaw dropped as I realized it was *him*.

"Calix." Cyrus growled, and I jolted back—hard—against the wall.

King Calix? The King of Night Kingdom? *No.* It couldn't be. Not *him*. I'd spoken to him. Fought him. He'd let me *live*. He flirted with me, for Tartarus's sake! No one hated humans more than King Calix. I was so confused, but I couldn't focus on that—on him. Not with Cyrus still in the room.

But…by the Otherworld, could this day get any worse?!

"Cyrus." King Calix growled, a hard smirk aimed at the prince. "I would say it's good to see you again, but I'd be lying. Now, Asteria is coming with me."

Cyrus laughed incredulously, but the Fae with moonglow hair and the aurora in his amethyst eyes, the one I hadn't been able to stop thinking about—*King Calix* apparently—wasn't done.

"Or I could unman you for putting your unwanted hands on her? Which do you prefer?" Calix asked in a flippant tone, but his hand tightened on the hilt of his sword, now aimed at the manhood in question.

I blinked in surprise. What was happening? Why would he do this? It was one thing to not kill me before, but it was another to actively protect me now—and yet another to threaten a fellow Fae over a human. I shook my head, my hair falling in my face.

Why is he defending me?

"She's mine!" Cyrus yelled, his face contorting in fury as his sharp canines were revealed with his snarl. "I won't let you take her."

Cyrus sent a burst of magic at the king, but the lightning fizzled out as King Calix sent his own magic, dark as night and absolutely enthralling, shooting back at him. Cyrus went flying into the wall, the windows rattling with the force of it. He slumped to the ground, unconscious.

I breathed a sigh of relief, at least until I looked back and jumped, finding King Calix right in front of me. His eyebrows were furrowed, and his face was creased in concern.

"Are you okay?" Calix asked softly. I swallowed roughly, my mouth opening to respond when a groan from Cyrus cut me off. I looked over, wide eyed and fearful he was getting up, but his head merely slumped over.

A very soft touch to my shoulder had me frantically bringing my hands up to defend myself. Willing to burn whoever it was with the iron dagger if I must. But the Fae king took his hand away, holding both hands up as if in surrender.

"Sorry." I rasped, my voice hoarser than I'd ever heard it.

"You've been through a lot, it's quite understandable." Calix smiled gently, my confusion over his behavior rising each time he spoke. "But we need to get you out of here while he's still out. Unfortunately, killing him as I'm sure we both wish would start a war too early, so that will need to wait."

Calix looked truly apologetic about that, and I shook my head again, trying to clear it and gather my thoughts. I felt numb. The fear and anger and helplessness I'd felt while Cyrus was on top of me all freezing me in place. I tried shaking myself out of it.

I was strong.

Cyrus didn't break me.

He didn't succeed.

He failed.

I kept repeating those words in my head until I felt able to finally take a deep breath.

I looked up at the man in front of me, more gorgeous than I could handle in this moment. I was a mess of emotions no matter how much I tried to push them down—when I succeeded with one, another rose up. They kept churning until I finally swallowed and dared to ask him the questions burning in my mind.

"Why? Why protect me?" I asked quietly, my hoarse voice lessening with each word. "And why would I go with you? You kill humans, don't you? Cyrus is a monster, *absolutely*, but you aren't any better. And what do you mean start a war—aren't you already at war?"

My voice rose to higher and higher pitches as questions spilled out of me. Shock was hitting me hard in the aftermath and I felt more frazzled and unsure than I ever had. I didn't know what to do, what to think.

"I promise, things aren't what they seem." King Calix began, hesitantly taking my hand in his. "I'll explain everything later, Asteria. But the attack yesterday was just to get us into Dusk, the one today was to cover our tracks as we got you, your friends, and my cousin and her husband out."

My eyes widened as I jolted, surprise too tame an emotion to describe what I felt at his words. All of this…was to get us out?

"Prince Kian—?" I started to question but trailed off.

Calix seemed to understand though, and nodded, "Yes, I'm the way he's getting you out. You know what he thinks of his family." He gave me a knowing look. "Do you honestly think he'd send you into the care of worse monsters? And as for war, some sparse attacks aren't a war. We're not quite ready for that—not yet."

With the hand he held in mine, he helped me out from the corner I was still nestled in. I was too confused to think too hard about him helping me.

"Not yet?" Was all I could bring myself to ask.

"Not yet." Calix smiled. "Don't worry, I think you'll more than approve when I explain, but like I said, we need to get you out of here. Once we're somewhere safe, then I'll explain everything." He stepped back and went over to the armoire, pulling out a couple dresses.

"You only need enough to last you a couple of days, just until we get back to my kingdom." Calix's face gentled as he looked at me, holding my destroyed dress up in an effort to cover my exposed body. His jaw hardened as he turned and glared at Cyrus—pure fury and absolute loathing filled that stare as he sent a bolt of pure darkness into him. I flinched back, but Cyrus's body seemed to shake before slumping down further. I turned back to Calix to find him smirking, clearly pleased with whatever he just did.

"I'll turn around, but I'm not leaving you alone in the room with him." Calix assured me, before turning, leaving me gaping at his back.

This? This was the monstrous king the continent was afraid of? Something wasn't adding up. The reputation of the Fae who slaughtered humans was so at odds with the man in front of me. I quickly raced to dress, wanting to get away from Cyrus as quickly as possible. Grabbing my dagger, my necklace from my parents, and a few other little things I might need and stuffing them in a small bag.

"I'm ready. But—" I bit my lip, unsure about asking what was truly on my mind. Calix zeroed in on the motion, biting his own lip as he looked at me. His purple eyes flared with color, and I was entranced by them. I desperately needed a distraction.

"Kian said I would be free. Is that true?" I asked hoarsely. Calix slowly crossed the distance between us and cupped my cheek before he glowered at my neck, where Cyrus surely left bruises behind.

"I promise," Calix started, looking into my eyes—and he was so intense, so overwhelming, that I felt like I could barely breathe as his eyes locked on mine. "You will never be anything but free from this day onwards."

I swallowed hard, shaking, wanting so badly to believe his words, but not sure I could trust him. Fae had proven treacherous, and I barely knew the one in front of me. Rumors painted him as the worst of the worst, but my experience said something different—and my instinct said something *wildly* different. I nodded, deciding I'd work it all out later. Getting out was the most important thing right now.

Calix smiled gently and took my hand, a shock running through me as he did. The feeling of my blood sparkling returned, but not in rage this time. The realization of my freedom maybe? He led me out of the room, and I only spared a small glance back at Cyrus, elated to be leaving him and his cruelty behind.

I'd wanted nothing but freedom for so long, and now, it was possible that it was finally here.

PART TWO

CHAPTER 22

Reaching the hallway I stopped short, Calix stopping with me since he was still holding my hand in his. Three warriors in armor similar to Calix's stood in the hall, staring at me.

"We need to keep moving, before someone comes looking." Calix urged me forward, "You'll have plenty of time to meet everyone on the way."

I only got a quick glance at the three warriors, but did a double take when I noticed one was a woman. Female warriors were practically unheard of—Princess Danique being the only one I knew of. This one didn't seem much like a princess, though she was certainly just as beautiful—though I'd never seen an ugly Fae. I was fairly sure they didn't exist.

Her thick red hair was tied back, but I could tell by the way it laid that had it been loose, luxurious waves would fall down past her shoulders. Her eyes were a vibrant, intense amber that flared as she gripped a short sword in one hand and a dagger in the other. Those amber eyes roved up and down the hallway, searching for threats.

I barely got a glimpse of the other two, only seeing short brown hair and long red hair, respectively. The latter's a different shade than the woman's, more copper than wine. But the king still holding my hand quickly pulled me down the hall. I looked around, sure someone was going to pop out and stop us. My fear that had somehow quieted when Calix showed up and stopped Cyrus, ratcheted back up at the mere possibility. I couldn't stay here—I would rather die than be forced to spend another moment with that bastard.

"Here!" The man with short brown hair called, coming to a stop next to a tapestry lining the wall. We came to a stop, and I watched in confusion.

They'd seemed in a rush to get out, now they wanted to stop and admire the art? The brown-haired one moved the tapestry aside and Calix sent magic at the wall. I watched in wonder at the show of magic. I hadn't seen enough of it since coming to Dusk. I had hoped being around the Fae would mean getting to see more magic than I had in Sonmathion—the lord rarely bothered. Since arriving in Evenfall however, I'd only seen lightning and the occasional use of small other magic. Calix's magic during his attack was the largest use of it I'd witnessed. I watched, fascinated, as Calix casually flung magic at the wall. My mouth dropped open as a door revealed itself in the wall.

"What?" I whispered to myself.

"Secret door." The brunette turned to me, light blue eyes alight with mischief as he smiled. "It was meant as an escape route, but I think it's been mostly forgotten about. Thankfully, I'd felt the magic of it when I passed by."

"Yes, yes. We all know your greatness, now let's go!" The red-haired man joked before pushing the brunette forward. I blinked in surprise, not used to seeing the Fae joke around much. They always seemed so serious. I caught Calix smiling slightly at the two before he pulled me through the door, but as we stepped in, he came to an abrupt stop. Calix looked towards me warily, an eyebrow raised.

"You're not going to try to stab me again, are you?" He asked dryly. The other three broke into laughter before muffling themselves as Calix turned to glare at them for the noise. I glared back at him.

"Not if you don't give me a reason to." I huffed. He chuckled before continuing into the tunnel. The passageway was dark—very dark. It was clear no one had used this in years. None of the light available like the other passages had.

I couldn't see anything in front of me, but I realized they could all likely see perfectly with their Fae eyesight.

Calix leaned down towards me, "Just hold on to me. I'll make sure you don't run into anything." I could practically feel the smirk he was wearing and glowered at him.

"Oh, now I almost want to see what she'd do if you let her run into something." The female barked, laughing. I turned my glare to where I thought she might be based on her voice, but she only chuckled in response.

"You're pretty gutsy." She giggled. "Most humans we bring in take a while to open up to us, but you seem to not be afraid of the Fae. Especially if you tried to stab our king." Her tone was more curious than anything, so I sighed loudly, listening as it echoed around the tight space.

"I've always had an issue controlling my anger." I admitted. "I refuse to cower before the Fae just because they think themselves superior. Plus, while most Fae seem to be terrible, I've recently found out there's a couple good ones out there." Thinking of Kian cemented that fact, even if I was unsure of the ones with me.

"I think we're going to get along fantastically." The female chimed, cheerful and upbeat. Although I couldn't see her, I could imagine the smile she was wearing as she said it.

"Just what we need, another Harpina." A male voice snorted, who I was pretty sure was the redheaded warrior.

"Oi!" She protested. "You'd be lucky as shit to have another me! At least we don't have to deal with another *you*. The whole kingdom would run to the nearest shore." I couldn't help the giggle that rose up in my throat and spilled out of my mouth.

I felt Calix squeeze my hand, "Ignore those two. They're like small children, they can never stop arguing over something. *Anything,* really." He groaned. A smile twitched at the corners of my mouth, but I forced it back down. I didn't know these people, I only knew their brutal reputation. Nothing made sense at the moment, and I needed to figure out what was going on and why. That had to be my focus.

That, and finding my friends.

"My—my friends." I gasped, tugging Calix's hand. "Priscilla and—"

"We've got them." One of the men behind me answered. "One a bit less willingly than the other, unfortunately." His tone was grim, and I knew instantly that Emmie had fought them. My eyes closed momentarily, useless in the darkness. I could only hope that Eris and I could coax Emmie back from this attachment she'd formed to the king. He was no good for her— for anyone.

We walked through the cold passageways, down and down and down. A chill crept over me as we walked. Every time fear tried to take me, Calix was there—squeezing my hand, joking with the others. It somehow managed to calm me enough to make it through. When we came to the door at the end, I nearly wept in relief. The brunette man slammed the door open and we all walked out of the dark passageway.

I blinked, the lights from the city near blinding after such encompassing darkness. Thankfully, the city was blanketed by the darkness of night. Courtesy of the man beside me, so at least the sun wasn't there to scorch my eyes. I watched in awe as more darkness came spilling from Calix, surrounding us as we began to walk swiftly away from the palace.

Calix looked down at me, and *Old Gods*, I hadn't truly appreciated how tall he was before. He definitely had a foot on me at least. I was fairly short, just a couple inches above five feet, but he had to be well over six feet. Probably several inches above it if I had to guess.

"We need to get out of the city." Calix declared. "The darkness will mask our escape." The joking king from the passageway was gone, replaced with a much more determined one. "Eryx, go find Titan. Let him know we've got Asteria, and we'll meet them outside the city." The brunette, Eryx apparently, nodded sharply before he transformed into a hawk before my very eyes. My jaw dropped, not only at getting to witness another shift—but because I *knew* this hawk.

He trilled at me as he passed overhead and flew into the darkness surrounding us.

"Did you have him spying on me?!" I demanded, whipping my head toward Calix.

"I'll explain when we're safe." The king grunted in return, and I grumbled, but followed along.

Calix let go of my hand to draw his sword and covered me as we began moving swiftly out of the city, where we'd apparently meet up with the rest of his army. I knew he could fly, he was a royal after all, so if he really needed to get us out, he could. I realized that he'd have to leave people behind in that case, and I softened a bit, knowing this meant he was unwilling to leave any of his people behind at Dusk's mercy. They didn't have any, and he likely knew that well.

I tried my best to keep up with my shorter human legs, but I inevitably lagged behind. The Fae with me refused to let me get far from them thankfully. One of them was always behind me, another beside me—and when whoever was leading noticed, they slowed notably to match my pace. It made me feel sort of guilty for holding them back.

I sighed in relief as I caught sight of the city gates looming ahead. As we passed through, I paused in horror, the bodies of fallen guards littered the gates. Reminding me, I was surrounded by Fae with a brutal reputation for a reason. I was quickly moved along, and I swallowed bile as I skirted around all of the bodies.

"They wouldn't have let you go, nor would they have protected you or the other humans here." The red headed man said, recognizing my discomfort.

I glanced over at him. There was a compassionate look in his eye, one that was rare in the Fae from my experience. I was beginning to think these Fae were nothing like those I had encountered before. I nodded my understanding; well aware these guards would never have let me leave. Some of these same guards stood and watched as humans were beaten or killed. Just because there were one or two good ones, didn't mean the rest were anything but awful. Though I did say a prayer to the Old Gods that the guard who tried to help me, who armed me with a dagger, was nowhere nearby.

OUTSIDE THE CITY, several horses were waiting. Calix gestured me over to a beautiful black war horse with a silver mane and tail. It whinnied as we approached and Calix hushed it, running a hand down its neck and whispering to it.

"You'll ride with me." Calix turned to me, holding out a hand. I glanced to see the others already mounting up, so I swallowed hard, trying to bury my nerves. Calix smiled softly, one side of his mouth tipping up.

"Never ridden before?" He asked quietly.

I shook my head, looking at the giant creature he expected me to get on. It was absolutely a powerful warhorse, made for fighting with huge muscular legs that hit the ground at random intervals, making me twitch. I nearly screeched as Calix's hands circled my waist, lifting me up and putting me in the saddle. I looked around with wide eyes from my new vantage point, trying to stay perfectly still.

"Relax." Calix chuckled, mounting up behind me. "The horse can feel your emotions. If you're nervous, you'll make her nervous. You're perfectly safe."

"We'll see about that." I scoffed. Calix huffed a small laugh, while Harpina began cackling in the background. Calix's arm banded around my waist and pulled me into his body, forcing me to relax into him. Except it did the opposite of relaxing me. His body curved around mine, pressing into me as he leaned forward, gripping the reins. His breath was in my ear. His firm chest was against my back. His arms and scent surrounded me. His legs bracketed my hips and I felt a distinct hardness pressed against my backside. What felt like pure energy radiated out from every place he touched me, like sparks were going to catch any moment.

Calix snapped the reins with a kick, and the horse took off through the woods. I held on for dear life to the saddle, a plush black leather that was rapidly being marked up by the indents of my nails. A husky chuckle in my ear distracted me from tearing the leather to shreds. I turned my head to look back at Calix, and I was surprised to find his face all but pressed against mine. His mouth close enough I inhaled the breath he exhaled. Deep inside, I wanted to close that distance. Something in me sang for his darkness and wanted it closer. I didn't like not knowing why, so I shoved the strange feeling down deep.

I'd had more than enough Fae men ruining my life, thank you very much.

I scowled at him, but he just smiled wider, "What? You're not going to fall off." Calix attempted to muffle his laugh. "You'd have to somehow get both your legs over mine and fall all the way to the ground before I could catch you. You'd slide much slower than I can move, I promise you." I scoffed, scowling at him before I turned my face forward, not even dignifying that with a response.

"Oh, you have your hands full with that one, Calix. Good luck!" the red haired male howled with laughter, before he snapped his reins and took off ahead of us. Calix growled after him. The vibration of it against me, paired with our bodies bouncing and shifting against one another as the horse galloped, left me wanting to growl myself from the shiver it caused.

"What exactly is that supposed to mean?" I demanded, unsure of how offended I should be.

"Ignore him." Calix said, snapping the reins and sending the horse galloping faster. We rode for what seemed like hours, but finally, Calix began pulling on the reins, the horse slowing in turn. I looked around and saw the other two slowing as well, until all the horses were walking at a much more sedate pace. Calix steered the horse around several bends, until we came to a dip in the landscape. As we came upon it, I blinked in shock to find an army suddenly before me.

"We'll camp here for the night. Tomorrow, we will be arriving at Night." Calix rumbled in my ear.

"Tomorrow?" I gasped, a stab of excitement spearing through me as I truly registered where I was going for the first time since Cyrus's attack. "I'll get to actually see Night Kingdom?"

Calix laughed softly, "You actually seem excited about it. Most are terrified to enter my kingdom after all they've heard about me." I tilted my head back a bit to catch his eye.

"Well, I can't say I'm not a bit afraid, I'm not stupid." I admitted. "But if you went through all that trouble of saving me, and haven't killed me yet, I think I'm alright for the time being at the very least. And I—".

I trailed off, unsure of finishing that sentence. What would he think of my love for night? Of the stars, moon, and darkness? Soren had always found it strange, having hated the dark. I was sure he was happy to be placed in Day. I did love the sun as well, of course. Its warm rays brought me peace, and sometimes when I let my mind empty, standing under the sun at the height of the day, I felt a sense of home and belonging I could never find anywhere else.

I just loved the night equally to the day. If the sun was home and belonging, the night was wonder and excitement. Sunrise, sunset, dawn, and dusk, none of them could compare to the wonder of day and night. My mother loved sunrise more than any other time of day, the magic in the land of Sunrise seemed to be calming to her. While humans couldn't do magic, we could feel the natural magic of the land in some minor ways.

"What?" Calix asked, prompting me to continue as he broke through my thoughts. I sighed loudly, deciding if anyone could understand, it was probably him.

"I've always been drawn to the night. To the stars and the moon. Before I was aware of your attacks, I wanted to see Night Kingdom more than any other kingdom. To feel night magic caress my skin, surrounding me at its peak. To see the wonder that I assumed would exist there. Though, based on what I've seen of Dusk, I'm beginning to suspect none of the kingdoms match the wonder the stories often speak of."

I quieted as I realized I had rambled at him far more than required. I could feel my cheeks heat in embarrassment, but he just tightened his arms around my waist.

"Interesting." He hummed softly. He was quiet for a moment, apparently considering something deeply. "I hope it lives up to your expectations. It is nothing like Dusk, trust me. They have lost their way, and the magic reacts to that. My kingdom has not, and our magic is still wild and free."

"What do you mean?" My eyebrows scrunched as I considered his words. I knew Dusk Kingdom was certainly corrupt, but what did that have to do with their magic?

"When the balance is not maintained, the land itself starts to fall to chaos—and everything else follows." Calix explained, his entire demeanor tense. His explanation didn't make as much sense as he seemed to think it did, but I refrained from asking more questions for now, as we were descending into the sprawling camp.

We came to a stop by a row of horses tied up to stakes in the ground. A young teen boy ran up and bowed to Calix.

"My King, we're relieved to have you back among us. Please, allow me the honor of taking your horse." The boy pleaded. A gleam of hero worship in his eyes that I found surprising. I'd never seen anyone look at King Astraeus or Cyrus like that. No one had seemed to have any true sense of love for their rulers. But this boy seemed to have stars in his eyes as he watched his king dismount. Calix's whole body brushed against mine as he did, and I couldn't contain the shiver in response.

Once Calix dismounted, he turned to me, his eyes dark with heat. He closed them before I could truly appreciate it, the way they darkened to the deep purple of a night sky, flickering stars in the distance, the ripple of a dancing aurora. Calix shook his head, his silvery white hair tossing about his head slightly before he opened his eyes, and the heat was replaced with a bland look that didn't line up with the way he'd just looked at me. He held his hand out to help me dismount, and I allowed him to assist me.

A hawk cawed above us, and I watched in awe as it turned back into a man. The brunette quickly landed on his feet after shifting mid-air. The worried look on his face as he opened his mouth caught both of our attention, but he was focused entirely on Calix.

"Eryx? What's wrong?" Calix asked, and the hawk shifter—Eryx apparently—ran a hand through his hair.

"Titan needs to see you. He got Siria and Aibek, but it's—" Eryx trailed off, his hand squeezing the back of his neck as he debated what to say next. Calix seemed to vibrate with energy as he waited for a response.

"What?" Calix demanded after Eryx waited too long to speak. "Are they—"

"They're alive." Eryx interrupted, reassuring him. "Come on. Titan's with them, he'll fill you in." The two walked off, but I was relieved to learn they had indeed rescued his cousin and her husband. I hoped they were alright, but it didn't sound particularly good.

"This way." Harpina surprised me, taking my arm in hers and leading me away, down to the rows of tents set up.

"Where are we going?" I asked. I looked back towards where Calix was walking away and chastised myself as I found myself worrying about him. It was none of my business. *He* was none of my business. A few strange meetings meant nothing, and I had learned the error of trusting royal Fae even a smidge. He may have rescued me, but I was sure he only did so to use me in some way.

"To see your friends. Priscilla and Emmie, yes?" Harpina smiled at me, and I was struck but the—the *joy*, on her face. She was actually happy to have gotten us out, to be leading me to my friends. I'd never known the Fae to be happy for humans for any reason. She continued to chatter as we walked towards one of the black tents. It was set up across the field, hidden within a dip of the land. Knocking on the post outside quickly with three sharp raps, she moved the tent flap aside and I gasped as I saw Priscilla, Emmie, and Eris inside.

"Asteria!" Priscilla cried, throwing herself at me with a huge smile on her face. She crashed into me, and I fell back a step from the force of it as I laughed, squeezing her back as her arms held me tight.

"You did it! You actually did it!" Priscilla crowed, laughing and crying with joy. I laughed with her as I wiped away the tears tracking down her cheeks.

"It certainly seems that way." I mused, pulling back. I caught sight of Harpina watching with a broad smile, and it surprised me—the emotion she was willing to show to humans—that she felt it at all.

"I'm shocked you managed it. Good job." Eris grumbled, but I caught a small smile at the corner of her mouth. From Eris, that was as good as the teary, joyful hug from Priscilla.

"Of course she did!" Harpina scoffed. "I can tell from knowing her five minutes that she's a force to be reckoned with." I rolled my eyes at the sentiment and looked over to Emmie. She looked to be asleep, but Harpina put a hand on my shoulder.

"We had to sedate her to get her out. She wasn't willing to leave. Kian made it very clear you wouldn't leave without her, so we were forced to take measures to ensure she didn't get us and everyone else caught or killed. She'll wake soon."

"Thank you." I looked back and gave her a small smile. "Truly. I don't know what you guys want from me, but I'll never be able to say how thankful I am that you got me and my friends out of that cesspool." My voice cracked, the emotions I'd been trying to suppress bubbling back up.

"It's okay to cry, you know," Harpina said softly, her eyes were sad and knowing, causing my breath to catch in my throat. "What he did to you… It's a failure on his part. Not on yours. *Never* yours. You need to allow yourself to feel all those emotions to move on. You deserve to live a life free from all that held you down before, and the first step will be recognizing the pain and trauma you experienced. Trust me, you're far from the only one who's had to do that. All the humans we've rescued must eventually face their own demons to move on."

"All the humans you've rescued?" I managed to ask, holding back pathetic tears I had no wish to shed over that piece of shit.

"Later." Harpina promised, giving me a soft smile. "Calix wants to explain everything to you." I nodded, barely able to move my head without tears threatening. The image of Cyrus—over me, on top of me, holding me down and nearly cracking my bones with the pressure, the cruel look in his eyes. His words—his smug, awful words about owning me and doing what he wanted. My lips trembled as the fear and pain slipped back out from the careful shield I'd tried to lock them behind.

I fell to the ground, knees hitting the grass. I couldn't stop the sobs from wracking my entire body as they finally broke free. I hadn't wanted to cry in front of Calix—or any of the men. But now, alone with just other women around me, I let myself feel all the horrible emotions I'd desperately tried to suppress.

A flash of blonde on one side and red on the other announced Priscilla and Harpina—both reaching out to hold me. I let their arms come around me, trailing through my hair or rubbing my back, as I shook with tears. I looked up when Eris kneeled in front of me. She reached out her hand, the tear tracks down her own face showing her understanding. I reached out to meet her, and our hands clasped together. She wasn't a hugger, but she squeezed my hand tightly, supporting me in the way she knew how.

I had never had female friends, never really had friends at all—but now I was surrounded by females who were here to help and support me. To comfort me when needed and lift me back up. It felt—*precious*. I was immensely grateful to find such support in the aftermath of everything that had happened, to realize I had this wonderful thing I'd never had before. And I wanted more of it. Friendship. Comfort. Support. All of it.

I fell asleep surrounded by the females I had come to call my friends. All of us sharing a tent and crying together. We spent the night telling our stories of what had happened to each of us. Whispers in the night of lashings, food being withheld, attempts like what Cyrus had tried—all of the abuse we'd weathered since Placement Day.

We expelled every bit of it through our words to one another, as if letting the words out might also release the pain from our hearts and minds. Our souls may be rattled and dented from the Dusk Kingdom, but together, we may also be able to find some sort of peace in the aftermath.

When I finally fell asleep, exhausted beyond measure and all out of tears—the darkness was there to greet me immediately. Luna didn't even get a chance to say hello before it appeared. It seemed so much closer, so much more intense. I reached out immediately, but that same damned barrier blocked us from meeting. I looked down at my glowing hands, wondering truly for the first time what in Adamah this was—and why in Tartarus did I keep dreaming it?

CHAPTER 23

THE tumultuous thoughts of the night stayed with me when I awoke, but I was thankful to have so many distractions. The camp was being broken down and the army was preparing to move out . I decided I would help Priscilla and Eris get Emmie ready to be transported since she still slept, but Eryx appeared and asked me to follow him.

"You can ask, you know." Eryx chuckled as we weaved through the tents, having caught the glances I couldn't help shooting him. I blushed at being caught, but quickly cleared my throat and began talking to distract from it.

"Why did you come see me? Why comfort me?" I asked him, needing to know why he'd been there for me on one of the worst days of my life.

He came to a stop in the middle of the path, several people dodging out of his way with looks of annoyance that quickly changed to admiration once they saw who it was. Eryx turned to face me, his face oddly serious for such a playful, slightly boyish looking face.

"I comforted you because you needed it, Asteria." Eryx explained gently. "Because everyone deserves, and needs, comfort now and again."

I tried to swallow the lump growing in my throat, to try and get the words out to thank him, but I couldn't. His eyebrows furrowed as he looked at me sadly.

"Cyrus is one of the fucking worst out there; no one deserves having to put up with him, or his family for that matter. How in Adamah Kian is related to those people—" Eryx snorted, shaking his head ruefully.

I couldn't help the tiny laugh that escaped my lips. Eryx looked so immensely pleased at my reaction, a smile spreading over his face, that brought one to my own.

"As for why I was there in the first place," Eryx continued as he began walking again, I raced to follow behind, "I'm Calix's spymaster. I control our network of spies, but I occasionally like to get out into the other kingdoms and see what's going on myself."

We approached a large black tent, the sigil of the Night Kingdom decorating its side with the crescent moon and stars flanked by dragon wings.

"Your presence in Dusk began causing waves among the more gossip-inclined, and once Calix ran into you, he—" Eryx cut himself off quickly, startling me and wondering what he stopped himself from saying. "I thought it best to keep an eye on the situation myself. I know what Cyrus can be like, and none of us wanted to see you become yet another girl he's hurt."

I froze at those words, "Others? He's—" I swallowed hard, and it was dry and painful. "He's done—*that*—before?" I hated how meek my voice was, and the way Eryx's face dropped was answer enough. Before I could think about that too long and start crying again, *and wouldn't that be embarrassing,* I narrowed in on the other part of his sentence.

"Why would you care what happened to me? Why do any of you care?" I threw my hands up in frustration. Sick of not knowing what in the name of the Old Gods was going on.

"Perhaps I can help explain." The voice coming from the tent entrance sent a shiver down my spine. Not one of fear or terror, but something much more pleasant. The purr to his voice was back, the growling gone for the time being. I wasn't sure which I preferred. I'd seen so many sides to this man already—from flirty and playful, to seductive and thrilling, to dangerous and deadly, to threatening and serious. I wasn't sure which, if any, was the true Calix. That thought should scare me more than it did—Fae were unpredictable, and often monstrous. But I just couldn't summon fear around him for some reason, my instincts insisting that there was no danger, despite all that the Fae represented—despite what had already happened.

It was perplexing. Quite frankly, it was more than perplexing. It was a mystery I wanted solved.

I shifted to face Calix, and my breath caught for a moment. The rising sun caused his silvery white hair to almost glow, his purple eyes intense and bright. His sharp cheekbones were highlighted by the shadows cutting across them thanks to the sun's movement upwards, and his plush lips smirked slightly as he waved a hand toward the interior of the tent, inviting me to enter.

Eryx squeezed my shoulder, and I nearly jumped, having completely forgotten his presence at the sight of his king.

"I'll see you later, Asteria. I look forward to actually being able to answer when you speak to me." He winked and I laughed slightly. It would certainly be much easier than trying to understand a hawk.

I entered the grand tent before me, moving inside to find a table and chairs set up, and a bed off to the side. It was fairly sparse for the luxury the tent represented from the outside. Even if we were only staying here a night, I had thought a Fae king would demand more. King Astraeus certainly would.

I startled when my inspection revealed a large Fae male standing off to the side. His arms were crossed over his massive chest as he stared at me with shockingly bright blue eyes. His head was shaved at the sides, and he had blonde hair on top that was just long enough to flop down and frame his face, hitting high cheekbones. They were sharp in a very different way than Calix's, which highlighted the beauty of his face, whereas this man's just made him look harder, more intimidating—more so than his giant size already made him. He practically had tree trunks for arms, for Old God's sake.

"This is Titan, the general of my armies." Calix introduced. "Titan, this is Asteria Zagreus." My head whipped to him at the address.

"How do you know my last name?" I demanded, crossing my arms over my chest. Much like Titan was—the damn general of the monstrous army I'd heard so many horrific stories about.

"Eryx is very good at his job." Calix smirked, and I glared at him while he chuckled, walking over to Titan and slapping him on the shoulder. "We're good here. Can you make sure her friends make it back alright?"

A quick nod, "I got 'em here, didn't I?" His wry smile caused the king to roll his eyes.

"You did. Now get going." Calix instructed his General in a surprisingly playful manner. Titan's eyes shot over to me, and while I might have thought the blue might remind me too much of Cyrus, Titan's eyes were more—electric—ironic, considering Cyrus's sparked with actual lightning.

Titan raised a brow at me, a smile playing at the corner of his mouth. "You're not going to stab him if I leave, are you?" My mouth dropped open.

"For Nox's sake, Titan." Calix muttered, shaking his head.

"I'm not going to stab him unless he gives me a reason to." I raised my brow right back at him, lifting my chin. That twitching smile on his lips turned into a broad, full one, a sharp bark of laughter following its appearance.

"Good." Titan nodded, his eyes dancing with humor. "You'll fit in just fine then."

Calix sighed as Titan ducked out of the tent, leaving me watching him, completely flabbergasted. Calix's chuckle was…sensuous—I felt it through my entire body. Why was I having such an intense reaction to this man? A Fae king no less! I'd already learned such men weren't to be trusted. Even if he had saved me, which still didn't make any sense.

"Don't mind, Titan. He's both protective of me *and* supportive of women stabbing men to protect themselves." He chuckled again. "I'm sure you have a lot of questions. Before we leave, I'll explain everything." He waved a hand to the chairs and took one for himself, sitting down and propping his legs up on the table, crossing one ankle over another. He was so casual, so at odds with what I'd expected.

I cautiously sat down and leveled him with an expectant stare as he smirked back at me.

"I'm sure you've heard all kinds of stories about me and my people. Well—I suppose I *know* you have given what you yelled at me before." His smirk faded. "I had hoped you would be ready to leave then, but it was clear you weren't. I should have just taken you anyway, damn the consequences. At least then, Cyrus wouldn't have—" Calix looked down at the table as I fidgeted, trying not to think of what was left unsaid.

"I apologize for that. I don't believe in taking people against their will, so I held off, but—" He swallowed, clenching his fists as he worked his strong jaw back and forth. It took a moment before he collected himself, but I couldn't even speak. Just the *thought* of what had occurred yesterday left me frozen.

"My people aren't monsters. However, I myself am another story." Calix said darkly, his countenance growing severe as he continued. "I've killed many, as you've heard. I've drenched the kingdoms in blood in the name of saving the weakest amongst us. I've either personally, or through my orders, killed far too many Fae. But when they're the ones keeping people as slaves—" A loud cacophony outside had Calix shutting his mouth abruptly, his head whipping up. "Fucking Nox!" He swore as he lunged upwards, drawing his sword and charging outside.

I stood up in a rush, nerves cascading through me, but stopped myself before I took a step forward. What exactly was I planning to do here? I shifted from foot to foot, nerves driving me to move but lacking direction. I listened to the sounds of the camp, the noise of people moving and yelling. I nearly jumped out of my skin when Calix stormed back into the tent. I clutched a hand to my chest as I panted, but thankfully, Calix was too distracted to notice.

He began gathering up his weapons and storing them away on his person and as he slid a shining black blade back into its sheath, he turned toward me.

"I'm sorry for the delay, Asteria. We can continue our discussion as we fly, but unfortunately, we need to leave—now. Our scouts have alerted us that Cyrus and his men are gaining on us. The others are breaking down the camp, and your friends will travel with them, but it's you Cyrus really wants." His head tilted to the side in thought. "And possibly Siria and Aibeck, but they're being moved as we speak. You'll stay with me, I'm not letting you out of my sight."

Calix grabbed my hand and pulled me with him before I could even open my mouth. Too much was happening at once, and I hadn't even had a chance to consider what little he had said about himself, and now Cyrus was coming? *Old Gods.* I shuddered, but as I stumbled along, his words finally registered.

"Wait, fly? As in, you're going to fly me back? Why are we flying and no one else is?" I asked, both excited for the chance to fly again and nervous about leaving everyone behind.

"Because we need to get you as far away as possible so that Cyrus can't get his hands on you again." Calix growled. I looked over at him, and he looked so far from the playful Fae he'd shown before—this was the more serious, growly version. And those growls…well, I couldn't deny this version was equally attractive.

No!

No, Asteria. By the Old Gods. Stay away from Fae males. That's the new rule.

Or at least…stay anything but platonically *away from Fae males. Yes, that. That works.*

We skirted through the tents and people quickly, Calix nodding and speaking briefly to a few people as we passed. Everyone gave him a wide berth for the most part, but strangely, it wasn't based on fear, but respect. They knew their king had important tasks to see to and they were getting themselves out of his path to make it easier. It was a much different relationship than King Astraeus had with his people, that was for sure.

I was so distracted by their dynamics that it took me a bit to realize tents were folding themselves up and trunks were packing themselves. I watched in wide eyed wonder, my mouth hanging open at the use of so much magic. This was what I had initially expected the life of the Fae to be like when I left Sonmathion, not the boring, practically magic-less life they led in Dusk. I wished I could stop and watch it in action, it was incredible!

When we reached the top of a small hill, Calix finally came to a stop. In a whoosh of air, his wings unfurled at his back. My breath caught on a gasp as I glimpsed them, before the king was sweeping me up in his arms. I grumbled, wanting more time to inspect his wings—dragon wings! Actual dragon wings were right there, and I wanted time to see the differences between them and Cyrus's pegasus wings. But we were already lifting high into the air, and I was immediately distracted by the fact that I was flying again.

It didn't matter that I had done it once before, it felt brand new. A wide smile took over my face as I watched Adamah grow smaller beneath us and lifted my face up to enjoy the heat of the sun's rays.

"I promised you an explanation." Calix said, his dour tone quickly wiping the smile from my face. I looked away from the sky and glanced at his face, seeing that he was indeed still in serious mode.

"You did." I agreed softly. I knew I should have likely been more afraid before getting said explanation, but I couldn't quite work up any fear. He seemed so different from any Fae I'd met before, as did his friends. And my instincts always seemed to be pretty accurate, they had warned me about Cyrus from the very beginning.

"I know you've heard terrible things about me. It's an unfortunate conse-quence of what we're trying to do." Calix started, staring off in the distance, while I couldn't seem to tear my gaze from his face. The feel of his arms holding me tightly against him acted as a grounding force as I prepared for whatever he was about to reveal. I had questioned for so long what the Night Kingdom was actually up to, that it felt surreal to be getting an answer. "For a long time after I became King, I carried on with the status quo. Human slaves were just a thing that had always existed and always would. That is, until about ten years ago, although I admit it had been slowly creeping up before then."

"What was?" I asked, biting my lip, hooked on the words falling from his mouth. Calix looked quickly to my mouth before meeting my eyes, giving me a wry smile.

"Discontent." He explained, swerving to the left in a tilt that had me clinging to him. Despite the heavy topic, a real smile crept up for a moment as he watched me fling my arms around his neck to steady myself. "A feeling of—wrongness, anger, take your pick. All are equally true. I just couldn't stand the idea of humans being kept as slaves anymore. They were people with just as much right to their autonomy as any Fae."

My mouth dropped open, complete shock overtaking me at such a casual statement that was anything *but* in meaning. He had to realize how rare, how absolutely impossible, such a sentiment was. Especially from a Fae. Especially from a Fae *king*.

My mind rapidly spun as I tried to connect the dots, the rumors, his actions, his words—none of it truly added up to anything that made sense.

Before I could say anything, Calix continued, his eyes drifting to me every so often as I stared at him in stunned silence.

"I abolished slavery in my kingdom, but that wasn't enough. I still felt all this—rage. I wanted the rest of the humans to be free, not just those in my kingdom. So, I began doing just that. Small attacks here and there, slowly allowing us to free more and more. As for the humans, this is truly their fight. I'll never be able to understand the horror they've gone through, so I gave them a large role when forming the Resistance. Responsibility and planning are shared among us. Eventually, we will be forced to go to war to free everyone, but we aren't there yet. For now, we try to free as many as possible. Especially in the kingdoms with the cruelest masters."

I couldn't believe what I was hearing. A human resistance? Fae and humans working together towards *abolishing slavery*? Actual *free* humans! It was everything I had ever dreamed of—could this possibly be real?

"You agreed you were a monster when we met before, but now, you claim to be a savior?" I raised an eyebrow as my lips tilted up in a smirk, challenging him to gauge his authenticity. This was too important, too life changing, not to.

Calix's eyes lit up at my challenge, banishing the bleak cast they'd taken on during his explanation. "I can be a monster or a savior, but I'm usually a mix of both. I do monstrous things to save people from a life enslaved to greedy Fae kings and lords, but still—the good doesn't erase the bad, and the things I've done *are* monstrous." His eyes darkened as his hands flexed, but since he was holding me, he only succeeded in sinking his fingers into my back and thighs. He looked to me as he loosened his grip, and our eyes met with a spark I felt through my entire body. One that banished the darkness in his eyes in favor of the aurora rippling through it.

Calix quickly looked away, clearing his throat. I was left feeling like my body was strung too tight—too familiar to me from mornings spent feeling that same tightness that left me with constant aches and pains I'd learned to shove into the background and ignore.

"I have killed plenty of my own kind and even some humans who protected them. Those who refused to see the truth of things. I've used those who don't see the truth to protect those who do. Those things will forever prevent me from being any type of hero, I assure you." Calix snorted, a smirk lining his lips as he looked at me. "Besides, being a hero would be quite boring, don't you think?"

I huffed a laugh, "Sure. *Boring.*" I bit my lip in thought. "This doesn't seem real. It sounds like you somehow ripped my dreams out of my head and are splaying them out for me, trying to entice me. It's too good to be true." I finished quietly. My mind spinning with everything he'd told me.

Calix's face softened. "I know. It can be overwhelming for a lot of humans at first. Those who have dreamt of freedom for too many years with no hope of it ever being reality. But I promise you, Asteria, it *is* reality. It's also why we need you." His lips curled into a genuine smile, softening his entire face.

"What do you mean?" I questioned, tilting my head to the side. I knew they wanted the information I had collected during my time at Dusk. But what impact could that truly make when it was only one kingdom, one prince, I knew anything about.

"Dusk is at the epicenter of the chaos beginning to rise. We're dealing with dual issues, and your intel can ultimately help with both. We haven't been able to get a spy close to Cyrus or King Astraeus before, they're both too paranoid." I snorted a laugh at the understatement, and the smile Calix gave me in response caused my breath to catch. It was highly inconvenient the way my body kept responding to him.

As we broke through the tree line, I spied lights shining up ahead. I squinted, trying to make out what I was looking at.

"This is the best way to view the city for the first time." Calix said, and his smile came through in his voice as he landed us on a hill just outside the city. He put me down softly, his wings unfortunately disappearing before I could get a good look at them. But as I took in my surroundings, the sight in front of me stole my attention. I stood there, completely transfixed as shock and awe coursed through me. I truly couldn't believe what I was seeing.

"This is the Night Kingdom?" I asked breathlessly. It was everything I had ever dreamed of, and so much beyond anything I thought possible. When I first imagined Night Kingdom, *this* was what I'd hoped for. A magical place where the moon and stars reigned supreme, with beauty and wonder everywhere you looked. When I'd heard of the Night Kingdom's attacks, of Calix's reputation, I'd lost all hope that it would be anything like I'd imagined—but now I was standing before a dream brought to life.

My eyes landed on a gleaming, sparkling palace on the horizon, making it difficult to look anywhere else. It shone like a star over the land. Beautiful and suited perfectly to its surroundings, as opposed to the overbearing monstrosity that was the Dusk Kingdom's palace. When I finally was able to drag my eyes elsewhere, there was something new and wonderful in every spot. Calix's chuckle stole my attention from the splendor of his kingdom—a sound even more compelling than the sights in front of me.

"It is." Calix answered, his voice filled with pride. It was clear he loved his kingdom deeply and was incredibly proud of it. One look at the city in front of me, and I couldn't blame him in the least. There were so many wonderful sights, it was hard to know where to look first.

"This is Tairngire, the capital of the Night Kingdom. Straight ahead there." Calix's arm rose to point at the giant, glittering palace in the distance. "Is Tairngire Palace. Though few call it that. Most call it the Starlight Palace, others call it the Opal Palace, and some refer to it as the Fallen Star." He chuckled warmly; a heat I could feel radiating off him.

"Is that because…" I trailed off, but Calix nodded, easily picking up what I meant.

"Because it looks like glittering starlight? Yes, that's one of the reasons. It looks even more like starlight at night, too. Everything seems more alive at night thanks to the magic of my kingdom." Calix explained, shifting to watch me as I took in his kingdom. "But during the day, it's certainly no less beautiful. The palace is made of star opals, so it glitters and shines no matter the time of day."

My jaw dropped, "Star opals? The entire thing?" My voice rose several octaves as I gripped the necklace my parents had given me on Placement Day, which was currently hidden beneath my shirt. It had a small amount of the white and multicolored star opals, and even that was shocking to see. Star opals were the rarest jewel in all of Celesterra, only found in one single mountain range that stretched through Day and Night Kingdoms. I supposed they had full access to those mines, but still, an entire palace of star opal seemed strange when the jewel was so rare.

"The palace was built long ago." Calix smirked, nodding. "Star Opal *is* rarer now, but we still have plenty. The mines are more magic than nature, after all." I looked at him incredulously, but he just shrugged.

"It increases the value to not say otherwise, doesn't it?" Calix smiled impishly, and I couldn't stop the embarrassing giggle that fell from my lips. Calix watched me for a moment, his smile fading into something warm, before he chuckled and stepped closer. I watched in awe as giant wings unfurled once more from his back. My eyes widened as I finally got my first real look at them. They were absolutely magnificent.

Wonder and envy battled for control as I inspected them. Wishing that I could sprout my own wings more than anything, yet consumed by the beauty of the pair before me.

Unlike Cyrus and the royals of Dusk with their feathered wings, Calix had tougher, scaled wings, with thin membranes and veins that stood out on their undersides. The majority of his wings were black, but purple ran down the edges and along the veins and talons. The wings of a dragon but scaled down to fit his Fae form. They were beautiful—amazing—and if this wasn't even their full scale, then I could only imagine what he was like when shifted into his dragon form.

Calix silently watched me marvel at his wings. The pair shifting slightly as his shoulders straightened, and I realized he was just as proud of them as he was of his kingdom. He was pleased to see the awe on my face at the sight of them, preening slightly before he caught himself and smiled bashfully. A strange sight for a king.

"We'll fly over the city so you can get a dragon-eye view on the way to the palace." Calix informed me as he stepped into my personal space. His scent overwhelmed me. It was indescribable, like night personified, a moonlit-darkness, and hint of fire—perfectly reflecting his magic.

Magic that I could feel pulsing in the land on which we now stood upon. I had never been around magic much back in Sunrise, and in Dusk they barely used their magic except for offensive purposes—or Cyrus's temper tantrums. But being here in Night, with Calix, I couldn't put my finger on it, but something was just…different. It felt *right*—like the magic that was imbued in the land of the Night Kingdom was welcoming me home.

The magic surrounded us, and I breathed it in, relishing the feel of night magic across my skin. This was exactly what I had dreamt of all my life, when I used to look up at the stars and wish to be surrounded by the magic of night. Though, I had never imagined being surrounded by kings and princes, or entrenched in politics and battles, the way I seemed to be now. That was an addition I never saw coming.

Calix swept me up into his arms, his jaw clenching as his eyes hardened— so different from the playful flirty Fae who purred in my ear. Calix was a mystery, for sure, and one that I desperately wanted to unravel. Who was the real Calix? The playful, flirty Fae? Or the serious, warrior king?

My desire to figure him out had nothing to do with the fact that he was the most gorgeous man I had ever seen. No, definitely not. And I would repeat that over and over to myself if necessary, until I believed it wholeheartedly.

I wrapped my arms around his neck and clung to him as Calix took off into the air, his wings flapping as he flew us towards the shining beacon that was his palace.

"Look down." Calix murmured in my ear, shifting me slightly so I could see better, but keeping his hold tight around me so I wouldn't slip.

I followed his instruction, looking down at the glittering city sprawled below. It was made up of three huge, and somewhat circular, sections. They blended into one another at the edges, but the circular shape of each section followed the natural flow of the land.

"This is the Starshine District." Calix informed me, hovering for a moment in place so I could take the area in. "Most of the residential housing in the capital is here in this district. There is minimal housing in the other districts, mostly for those who prefer to live close to their jobs."

There were large apartment towers, containing housing for many in one building, that took up the West side of the district. The middle was filled with smaller houses and buildings in all sorts of colors. Families walked the streets, children running around and playing in yards, or what seemed to be areas set aside for them to play. With constructions I'd never seen before. There were small mini replicas of castles, something long and narrow the children slid down, strange loops the children sat in and swung upwards, and sets of bars they moved across hand to hand. They were dotted around the district, and seemed to be quite popular judging by how busy they were.

Following the river, snaking along the district on the East side, there was an area with large mansions and manors. They sat on expansive, green estates dotted with all kinds of trees, flowers, and bushes. They were beautiful and were worked into the surrounding land like they had always been there. The architecture of all the buildings contained curves and swoops of a like I'd never seen before. Making everything look elegant and Otherworldly—magical.

I noticed the change as Calix flew us above the next circular district. The colors here were even more vibrant, with bright colors in every spot I looked. The scents in the air were more varied as well. With the smell of savory meats, the sweet scent of pastries, and the fragrant floral arrangements, all reaching my nose. Music floated up, along with the chatter of those in the area who were shopping or sitting down to eat with friends. Laughter and smiles seemed to be in abundance, and a few people even noticed their king flying overhead and sent bright smiles and waves, or respectful bows of their heads, Calix's way.

It was so very different from how people reacted to Cyrus and King Astraeus.

And everywhere I looked, people were using magic. From the restaurant server using magic to bring food to a table, to the shopkeeper lighting a lantern. Using magic seemed to be a normal occurrence here.

"This is the Moonglow District. It's where our restaurants, bars, shops, and theaters are located. A lot of our public events are held here. You see that big dome in the middle?" Calix asked quietly, but I could sense the underlying excitement in his words. He clearly enjoyed having the chance to show off his city and I couldn't blame him. If this city was mine, I'd be bragging about it too!

"Yes, what is it?" I nodded, my eyes zeroing in on the dome in question. I could tell he was pleased I asked, he was so eager to tell me that I couldn't bear not to play along. Plus, I was desperate to know everything about this kingdom. It was like my dreams had come to life, complete with the shining palace. I wanted nothing more than to explore everything it had to offer. Well…maybe I'd rather continue flying—I could spend forever in the skies, and it wouldn't be long enough. It was a toss-up, really.

"That's the Moon Dome, it's the largest theater in Celesterra." Calix breathed in my ear, causing a pleasant, shivery sensation. "We host all sorts of performances there, and we occasionally use it for public events as well. Before I shut our borders to outsiders, people used to flock from all over the kingdoms to come here. I hope one day that may be possible again." We flew directly over it, giving me a closer look. I marveled as I realized the dome on top was made to mimic the moon, craters and all.

"At night, magic within the dome activates and it lights up, glowing like the moon itself." Calix continued, and I gasped at the very idea, incredibly excited to see it.

I'd never expected to see such wonders. Even at Dusk, Cyrus largely kept me to the palace and away from the city. On my few trips into Evenfall, I didn't see anything remotely like this. Whereas Night seemed built to impress, to showcase the wonder magic offered. While Dusk was bland in comparison. The people didn't stop and wonder at the sights or at the magic they literally had at their fingertips—and likewise, their city wasn't designed to impress in that way either.

"This is the Shadowgleam District." Calix's soft tone reached my ears over the wind as he flew us over the final district. I found myself thrilled to hear what other magical sights I'd find here. "This is obviously where the palace is located, as well as our other official buildings, like Nebula Hall and Cosmic Dust Stables, which is the largest stable in Night." He pointed out each as we flew above, and I was taken aback by the size of the sprawling stables to the East of the palace.

"And over in that forest?" He moved us to face the West, where a small bridge led to an expansive forest. "Deep inside resides our altar to the gods, where we go to pray or honor them on holidays." Calix smirked, and I could feel it against my cheek as he spoke closely, to ensure I could hear him. My pulse pounded, and I worried he could hear my blood rushing in reply to his mischievous tone.

"It also contains something I really want to show you in person. Words just don't do it justice." He flew us back toward the palace, pointing out the surrounding buildings. "There is some housing for public officials scattered around Shadowgleam District, along with a few bars and restaurants, but nothing like in the other districts."

I looked around at the buildings he pointed out, even as curiosity about what he wanted to show me took hold. I was immediately distracted, however, as my eyes fell on the cliffs behind the palace, stretching out over the water far below. It looked like one would fall right into the sky if they stepped off the cliff. I could only imagine how it would look at night. Probably like jumping into a sea of stars and swirling auroras rather than water. It must be a perfect spot for dragons to take off and fly from…and was probably why his ancestors built the palace here.

As we neared the palace, Calix slowed and began to dip lower and lower. I ached at the thought, holding tightly to him in silent protest. Being in the sky felt right, more so than I could ever explain. Calix looked at me, a question in his eyes, and I sighed as I looked out once more at the slowly disappearing view of the Tairngire. I reached up my hand, like I could run my fingers along the clouds and capture a bit of the sky to take with me before we hit the ground.

"I've always been jealous of those of you who could fly. I would live up here if it were possible." I admitted, filled with an inexplicable sadness, along with an aching sort of amazement. Calix's expression slowly shifted from curiosity to surprise, if not shock.

"What?" I asked, my eyebrows scrunched together as I tilted my head to the side.

"Nothing. It's just—I would stay up here forever if I could too." Calix laughed slightly, shaking his head, as if he was shaking the thought away. "I'll make sure this isn't your last time in the skies, Asteria. I promise."

The earnestness as he voiced his promise, and those intense purple eyes, caused a large smile to spread across my face. The thought of flying again was enough to buoy my spirits. Calix's mouth parted slightly as he stared at my mouth, his fingers tightening their grip around me. The hand that was curved around my thigh burned through my dress and into my skin.

The tension between us rose, and I could feel the blood rushing to my cheeks—shocking me. I wasn't normally one to blush, especially not over something so innocent. But his stare didn't *feel* innocent, it felt more like he stripped me down until I was left bare and wanting before him. I tried to pry my own eyes away from his plush, parted lips. I couldn't afford to let myself be distracted by this beautiful Fae man—I'd certainly learned my lesson about that, *hadn't I?*

"Thank you." I said softly. Hoping to break the strange tension between us. It succeeded in shattering the moment, Calix shaking his head in bafflement as he shifted his focus to landing. We came to a stop right outside the palace, landing softly on a sparkling stone walkway.

Guards were positioned outside the large doors, but I couldn't even be bothered to pay them any attention—not when I was so close to so much star opal. The palace walls sparkled in the light in the sun, pinks, purples, blues, and greens. I'd never seen anything like it in all my life. Calix led me up to the tall, wide black double doors. They were curved, and down the seam where they would open was the phases of the moon, with the full moon in the very center. They were etched in a beautiful, gleaming silver, as were the other etchings that decorated the edges of the doors, surrounding them entirely. Their meaning was lost on me, crafted in a language I didn't recognize at all.

As the doors opened, I didn't have time to focus on that mystery. Calix led me forward, guards joining us on either side. I blinked in surprise, but I supposed it made sense they would follow their king. It was a necessary reminder that Calix wasn't some boy who rescued me or playfully flirted with me, he was a Fae king. He had important responsibilities and people to take care of. He didn't have time for someone like me.

CHAPTER 24

CALIX gestured for me to follow, but I was too stunned to move. The palace was…it was remarkable. I'd never seen a more beautiful building. The entry was rounded, with shining walls, and floors of matte black, layered with a gray damask rug. A giant chandelier hung over the space with moons and stars dangling from it. Calix's laugh managed to drag my attention away from where I was gaping at the entry to the palace.

"If you're this impressed now, wait until you see the rest of the palace." Calix chuckled, and I couldn't help my blush of embarrassment, cursing myself for how easily I blushed in his presence. I probably seemed like a simpleton to him, but then again, what did he expect? I was a human slave. I cut myself off, my whole body jolting in shock.

It truly hit me then, and I locked up, not knowing how to react, or how to move forward from here. Lost—in a way I had never anticipated. I looked to Calix, imploring him with wide eyes.

"I'm…I'm *free*?" I asked softly, hesitating. "I could really—walk away? And you wouldn't do anything?" My voice stuttered, but I couldn't help it. I felt sort of faint, like I needed to sit down.

"You are." Calix responded fiercely, grabbing my shoulders as the warmth of his hands seeped into my skin, grounding me. "You are free, Asteria. You're not a slave anymore. You *never* will be again." I drew in a wet, gasping breath. "And while we would appreciate your help, it's completely up to you to stay or go. You can leave at any time. I often put humans up in apartments or houses of their own; we provide them funding until they find work and can support themselves in their new lives—in freedom. Where they can choose—where *you* can choose, whatever it is you want to do."

The sincerity in his eyes brought tears to mine, but I refused to let them fall as he continued. "If you would like to stay and help us, you can stay here at the palace. You'll be paid for your work, as all my people are. We already have a suite ready for you, and your friends will be close by. At least until they decide what they want to do themselves." Calix looked me over with a critical eye. He seemed to realize I was close to losing it, and intuited I wouldn't want that to happen in public.

He smiled at me, and it was enough of a distraction to keep my tears at bay—the beauty of it greater than I ever knew a smile could be. "Why don't you go rest for a bit?" Calix's brow furrowed as he looked at me worriedly. "I've assigned you a lady in waiting, and she will gladly assist you. Once you've rested, I'll introduce you to everyone, including the human leader of the Resistance."

That got my attention. The human leader? He'd said he shared the responsibility with humans, but still, I hadn't expected…

"Ah, Delia!" Calix turned to the woman who entered, who gave him a cheerful smile as she approached. "Asteria, this is Delia, your new lady in waiting. Delia, this is Asteria."

She turned to me, her wavy golden brown hair swinging over her shoulder, as her eyes met mine. Eyes that almost uncannily matched her hair, with light brown irises. She radiated an inherent kindness. Her pointed ears and obvious beauty though…

"Wait—she's Fae?" I questioned, my face screwing up in confusion. "Why would you assign a Fae to be a lady in waiting for a human? For that matter, why do I have a lady in waiting, isn't that just for the nobility?" I didn't understand it, this whole kingdom seemed to operate on completely different rules than the rest of Celesterra.

"Why wouldn't he?" Delia giggled. "I'm honored to assist wherever I'm needed, and I love getting to help our new human residents!" Her smile was so sincere it left me speechless. She seemed to recognize how lost I was, and she softened, walking over to take my hand. "Don't worry about a thing. Let's get you to your rooms, shall we?"

"Your Highness, if you'll excuse us?" Delia turned to her king, hand squeezing mine. Calix eyed me, looking torn for some reason, before he shook his head and smiled at Delia.

"Please." Calix nodded. "Just let me know once Asteria is ready and I'll convene the others." He turned to me, and he gentled as he stepped closer to speak quietly. "If there is anything you need, or even something you *want*, please don't hesitate to ask. We'll make sure you learn how to enjoy your newfound freedom."

"Thank you, Your Highness." I choked out. He winced at the words for some reason, but that gentle smile didn't wane, and I felt the same intensity from when we landed begin to rise once more. We both seemed to pull ourselves out of it as Delia took my arm and began to lead me away. I turned my head to look back and found his eyes following me intently. Even as others tried to speak to him, his entire being was focused on me.

Having such intense attention from not only the most powerful Fae alive, but also the most attractive by far, was a heady experience. I tried to shake it from my mind as Delia began chattering away, pointing out different areas and impressive art as we passed by. I felt like a sponge as she led me through, everything was so magical, so beautiful, so Otherworldly, and I wanted to soak up every bit of it.

But I was still unsteady, and my thoughts swirled around my head in an ever-increasing cyclone. Free. I was *free*. Calix, the King of Night Kingdom, had freed me. He was going to help me live and support myself. He would let me fight for others still enslaved. So many options and choices were suddenly laid before me, and it was entirely too overwhelming.

"This is the suite King Calix has assigned to you." Delia chimed as she finally came to a stop. "I hope you like it." She bounced on her toes as she led me into the room. I couldn't help my bewildered smile as I watched her, she was just so genuinely sweet—so opposite to the Fae I had known before.

As I walked into my new suite, however, my body locked up in shock. I was expecting something basic. If Calix gave humans he rescued rooms here, then I assumed they must be small dormitories. Like the room Eris had in the slave quarters in Dusk—but no, this was *nothing* like that. The room was circular, which was the first thing I was delighted to find, certainly located in one of the round towers. The palace had several such towers that reached toward the sky in addition to the sharper angled architecture.

The walls were done in a sapphire color that looked like the night sky, and the ceilings were domed. With sapphire as the base color that continued up to center point, and silvery white columns of some sort that started halfway up the walls and reached up to the center of the dome. It was a beautiful contrast.

Highlighted by the silver starburst shaped light, made of crystals that had little bobs of light inside, that fell from the midpoint.

The living space had pointed arched windows that went from floor to ceiling, completely taking up one rounded wall that looked out over the water. I couldn't wait to see the view at night, positive it would be a gorgeous sight. Beside the windows was a door that led out to a large balcony that was furnished with lounge chairs and a table. Flowers lining the balcony railing in a litany of colors: pinks, purples, blues, and greens—all the colors of the aurora, I idly noticed.

Inside, a velvet ivory sofa, with sapphire and silver throw pillows, curved around the space in a half-moon shape. There was a silver desk that appeared to be hand carved with celestial imagery and it made me want to inspect every bit of it. Velvet chairs in sapphire and ivory accented the space and had small silver tables beside them. The space was lavish and luxurious…and nothing at all like what I expected.

"Through here is your bedroom." Delia announced as she led me through the doorway. I felt like I had barely gotten my breath back when it was taken once more. The ceiling was clearly done with magic, to make the bright, twinkling stars spin overhead. It was absolutely astounding.

"You can turn the ceiling off anytime," Delia explained with a smile at my obvious wonder. "The magic is fixed into this switch here, so you can turn it off or increase the number of stars."

I had to have stepped into a dream, no way was this reality. Even the floor was covered in a plush ivory rug that I wanted to sink my toes into immediately. I loved everything about it, I couldn't even imagine a better room than this. One where I could look at the stars whenever I wanted.

On top of having my freedom, it sort of made me want to cry—in joy, in shock, in being absolutely wonder struck…and yet totally lost.

The bed was equally incredible, with silver head and footboards, along with the four posts coming from them. The headboard had the phases of the moon across it, while the posts had scrolling designs down them including shooting stars—and I was sure I spied several runes. The sapphire bedding looked so inviting, as if I could just fall into it and sink down like a cloud. I didn't know what fabric it was made of, but it was the softest thing I'd ever felt.

One side of the room also had floor to ceiling windows, with a door set into the middle leading to another balcony. A walk-in closet, that was larger than I thought closets could be and still be classified *as* a closet, was already filled with so many clothes I didn't know how I'd ever wear them all. Casual and formal dresses, skirts, tops, pants, even leather armor like I'd seen Calix wear, which truly surprised me. One entire wall was taken up by accessories and shoes, and I couldn't stop my mouth from falling open.

I walked out of it in a daze and continued into the bathroom. The white shining opal of the palace wasn't covered up here—it was left to shine, with a large black tub big enough to fit an orgy, a standing shower with so many shower heads, I was sure it would feel like being in a waterfall, and a black vanity that took up the back wall. It was the most elegant bathroom I'd ever seen, and it was apparently for me.

It was almost unnerving—like they'd plucked out all of my dreams and laid them bare.

"Why don't you take a bath and then get some rest? I'm sure it's been a difficult few days for you." Delia suggested, her hand squeezing my shoulder in a comforting gesture.

"What about my friends?" I asked, somewhat off topic, after the guilty realization I hadn't asked about them yet. My face creased in concern as I turned to face her.

"They haven't arrived yet, but I will let you know as soon as they have. I promise." Delia swore, and I could see why she was a lady in waiting, she had a very soothing aura that I'm sure the noble ladies appreciated.

In truth, I didn't mind it myself right now. My emotions had been jumping all over the place for the last few days, and it felt like I could take a deep breath in her presence. Especially as she got me in a bath filled with sparkling bubbles that changed color in the light. I couldn't fight the smile each time I popped one of the rogue bubbles that floated upwards. Delia washed my hair, which was something I'd never experienced before—I had been severely missing out. I just relaxed and enjoyed it,it was the best bath I'd ever experienced.

When I got out, Delia was there with nightclothes and a robe for me. She ran her hands over my hair, I watched with wide eyes as it was left completely dry and bone straight in her wake, fascinated with the magic they used here. I wished I had the ability to access it as the Fae do. Having the ability to get my hair perfectly straight, with no frizz, was enough of a marvel to envy.

Delia tucked me into bed like a child, but I couldn't even complain. When my body hit the bed, it felt like floating, and I was so comfortable that I drifted off immediately. Delia's pleasant humming was the last thing I heard before I was swept from one dream to another.

I WAS DELIGHTED to find Zhu there when I arrived among the clouds—receiving a fiery kiss from his tail along my cheek that left a pleasant warmth behind. I'd managed to be lulled into such a sense of calm before falling asleep, that I hardly felt a difference in my temperament. Today, Delia, and my new surroundings, had managed the impossible—I'd been just as peaceful awake as I was asleep.

When I slowly woke from my nap, I felt better than I had in a long time. I was always groggy upon waking, needing to stretch and feeling that awful twinge pain—of my skin feeling too small and too tight. I shoved the blankets off, wiping my eyes and forcing myself up despite the pain in my back and legs. Right—I'd been riding a horse, hadn't I? At speed too.

Everything kept hitting me in waves, and this time, I let myself truly process my new state of being. I looked around this unbelievable room that was apparently *mine*, and I let the tears fall. I couldn't even figure out why I was crying! I wasn't sad, I wasn't so angry that tears came to my eyes, I was… free. I wouldn't say *happy*, I wasn't even sure I knew what that felt like, but *free*. And I was in the Night Kingdom, the kingdom I'd dreamt of seeing since I was child, but one I'd thought an impossibility—even more so after learning of the attacks.

Once I was done crying, I surprisingly felt much better. I may not know what to do with myself, may not quite understand why King Calix was doing all of this, or why he decided to free humans to begin with, but I had a focus going forward. For now, at least. Calix said I could meet with the Resistance and make my decision then. There, that was a plan to go forward with. I didn't need to be so overwhelmed by the choices and options before me. One step at a time, I reminded myself.

"You're up!" Delia's musical voice carried in, followed by the rest of her. A wide smile that quickly turned to concern. My face was surely a splotchy mess thanks to my tears, so I quickly wiped at my eyes and cheeks to clear the evidence as best I could.

"Are you alright, Asteria?" Delia asked, her concern clear in a lowered tone and furrowed brows. When I didn't answer immediately, trying to decide *how* to answer, she continued. "I know you've been through a lot, and you don't need to talk about it, but I *would* like us to be friends, and friends are there for each other." Delia seemed unsure of herself for the first time, shifting slightly from foot to foot as she bit her lip.

"That would be nice." I told her honestly, smiling up at her. Friends may be a newer development for me, but Priscilla had proven how needed they were to me. I wouldn't make the same mistakes of the past and turn down more. "I'm okay, just a bit overwhelmed, honestly."

"Well, that's certainly understandable." Delia seemed relieved, her smile flitting back across her face. "What feels overwhelming? Maybe we can tackle it together." She urged me up as I detailed my thought process on the different choices and paths now ahead of me, helping me get ready and making sympathetic noises as I talked it out. She agreed with my plan, explaining that many others had felt similarly upon being freed, which was a relief to hear. When I asked about my friends, Delia let me know they would be invited to the meeting I'd soon be attending.

Unlike in Dusk, I wasn't told what to wear. Instead, I was allowed to pick whatever I wanted. When I just stared at all the clothes in the closet before me, Delia smiled sympathetically and rubbed my back slightly as she urged me forward.

"You will never be told what to wear or what to do, again." Delia assured me. "You're free, here. And hopefully, one day, humans will be free everywhere."

"It's surreal." I shook my head. "I dreamed of freedom all of my life. Raged against the circumstances I was born into, feeling like I was shoved into a life that was never meant to be mine. And now—" I shook my head again, wandering to the closet and touching the different fabrics, trying to figure out where to even begin when it came to just deciding what to wear.

"It's not just the big life decisions that a lot of humans struggle with when they first arrive." Delia smiled at me. "It's the little things too. But I promise, you'll quickly grow used to making your own choices. But for now, how about this?" She pulled out a pair of pants made of some type of soft leather, and a corset style top that would show off my shoulders, arms, and cleavage. The very idea of wearing pants was so bizarre, but I found myself eager to try them, nonetheless.

"These are often worn by our warriors here, and you strike me as a warrior, Asteria." Delia's words made me straighten, a warm sort of pride rising. "The leggings are made of cloud leather, as soft as the hide of the Cloud Beast. The top is armored, so if someone were to stab here—" She pointed to the middle of the corset, where it would cover my stomach and lots of important organs. "The blow would glance right off. Many prefer ease of movement when fighting, which is why there are only thin straps. There are typically pieces that go over the exposed areas when they armor up for battle, but you certainly won't need that for a meeting."

"I'm—I'm not a warrior though." I protested, feeling like it would be disingenuous to wear warrior's clothing when I had no idea how to fight.

"Only because you weren't allowed to be. You can be trained." Delia insisted, eyes alight. I took in a sharp breath, my own eyes lighting up. I'd always wanted to learn how to fight, but it was strictly forbidden. The idea that I could now actually train to fight made me eager to get the clothing on.

Delia helped me dress, and I was taken aback by the final result. The outfit was comfortable and freeing, and I felt strong. Looking in the mirror, at the dark hair I was finally able to wear straight as I preferred, at the light makeup Delia dusted on my face, not overdone, but just enough to highlight my features, I felt more myself than ever before.

WALKING THROUGH THE palace halls, I was struck again by the differences between Night and Dusk. It was so much lighter and brighter here than Dusk. It was always so dark and oppressive in that palace, but here, everything was the opposite. For a place that called itself *Night* Kingdom and specialized in darkness, you'd think this would be the gloomier kingdom, but no, everything looked inviting and wonderful.

Delia led me into a room that was dominated by a huge round table in the center, with a map of Celesterra carved onto the top and little pieces representing armies and palaces scattered across it. The room was filled with people, but I didn't get a chance to see who before I was nearly bowled over, Priscilla launching herself at me. I fell back a step trying to right myself, laughing, as I caught her.

I caught Calix smiling at us from the corner of my eye, but my focus was quickly brought back to Priscila.

"I'm so glad you're okay." Priscilla gushed, her smile beaming. "Can you believe this place? It's not at all what I had imagined!"

"It's incredible." I couldn't help matching her smile, relief filling me at seeing her well. "I haven't seen a lot yet, but what I have is amazing."

"We'll have to fix that shortly." Calix interjected, smiling at the sight of our reunion. "We'll take you ladies out tonight and show you the city, but for now, let me introduce those you don't know."

Calix cleared his throat and turned to the table, as Priscilla and I grabbed our own spots around it. I somehow ended up right next to Calix, several people helping to usher me into place in a whirlwind of movement. I only realized where I landed when I looked up, meeting his eyes. My lashes fluttered in surprise, and I turned to find somewhere else to focus before I embarrassed myself. I spotted Eris across the room, and she gave me a nod, a slight smile gracing her face to my surprise. I was worried that Emmie wasn't here, and I feared that if she still believed herself in love with King Astraeus, we'd have a battle before us to get her to see sense.

"Asteria, you already know Eryx, my Intelligence Officer, my Spymaster in short." Calix introduced, nodding at his friend. I smiled at the boyish looking Fae and gave him a nod in greeting. I could only imagine how many trusted that innocent face with their secrets.

"Yes, I believe I cried all over him already." I told Calix wryly, watching in delight as Eryx's face went bright red and the room broke into laughter.

"In my defense," Eryx drawled. "I didn't want to leave you alone if I could help it. You seemed like you needed someone." His cheeks were still pink, and I couldn't help warming more to him.

"Thank you, Eryx, truly." I said softly, and he nodded in return with a blushing smile as Calix clapped his shoulder before continuing his introductions.

"I'm not sure you were properly introduced to Baach before. He's my Master of Ceremonies—essentially, he plans all our parties." The group laughed and the redhead in question rolled his eyes. I recognized the redheaded Fae instantly as the one who helped break me out along with Calix, Eryx, and Harpina.

"I'm also a warrior, not just a party planner." Baach gave a flourishing bow, followed by a twinkling wink as he rose, and I couldn't help the laugh that burst out of me—his offended tone at Calix's description was clearly a joke, but his dramatics were hilarious.

"And of course, you know Harpina. She's my Constable." Calix added. My eyebrows furrowed at the unfamiliar term, never having heard of the position before.

"I handle law enforcement for the kingdom." Harpina told me, thankfully recognizing my ignorance. She smiled widely, if a bit wickedly, as she continued. "We'll have fun tonight, don't worry. We know just where to take you for your first night out! But first we'll get down to planning." She rubbed her hands together excitedly.

My eyebrows rose at Harpina's clear enthusiasm for both going out and battle planning, but Calix merely rolled his eyes, leaning over a bit toward me.

"Harpina lives and breathes battle, it's why I made her Constable." He confessed, and I laughed lightly at his description—it certainly made sense based on what I'd seen thus far. Calix blinked for a moment at me before he cleared his throat and turned to the large Fae male I met in his tent. He was the same height as Calix, but much wider, and while I appreciated a muscular form, Calix's was much more to my taste. Lean and muscular, like he was sculpted by the gods them—*Old Gods!* I needed to stop thinking about him that way.

"And this is Titan, my General." Calix waved a hand in the man's direction and nodded gruffly at me, but his lips tilted up briefly at the corner of his mouth before he caught it.

"This is Lilith. She's my Beastmaster, handling all the animals from horses in the stables to the ones in the menagerie." He nodded to a female Fae with long, wavy brown hair and eyes the green of nature itself. I could absolutely see her in the forest with a horde of animals at her back.

"Nice to meet you." Lilith greeted me, waving, sedate but cheerful all the same. I returned the sentiment before Calix turned to a pretty blonde Fae with big blue eyes. She beat him to the punch before he could even open his mouth.

"I'm Ilta, it's wonderful to meet you!" She bounced on her toes, a large smile showing off shining white teeth with tiny little sharpened canines, and where Calix's were intimidating, if sexy, hers were honestly adorable. "I'm King Calix's secretary. I help with all the sorts of things, basically keeping him on track. I'm so excited you're finally here! We've been talking about it for what seems like ages now."

I tilted my head to the side, confused. I glanced at Calix, opening my mouth to question him on what Ilta meant, but to my surprise, Calix had a slightly bashful look on his face. He quickly moved to introduce someone else before I could interject. Ilta smirked at Calix, not seeming to mind the quick rush past her introduction as she winked at my bewildered expression.

"This is my sister, Princess Liviana. She's a seer, so she helps us with the visions she receives." A seer, and his sister at that? She looked much like Calix, with the same silvery white hair, the same royal, beautiful facial structure with sharp cheekbones, straight noses, and plump lips. The only difference was she had luminous silver eyes instead of purple.

"I thought all the seers stayed with the Oracle?" I inquired, not sure exactly what the difference between the two was, but I did know that the seers were required to work with the Oracle. I was too embarrassed to ask those in the room for clarification.

"They're supposed to." Princess Liviana nodded, smiling slightly. "But my brother refused to let me go." She paused, chuckling. "The Oracle couldn't really argue with Calix when he threatened to hide me away forever—after burning her cavern to ashes—if they tried to take me."

My eyebrows flew upward in shock. I knew the Oracle wasn't someone that anyone, even royals, messed with. She was a direct line to the Fae's gods. That Calix fought so hard to keep his sister, obviously spoke to how much he loved her. It was refreshing after spending so much time in Dusk, with its feuding royal family, to see royals who would instead go to extremes to protect one another.

"This is Callisto." Calix introduced a woman with medium brown skin and black hair in tight curls that fell around her face and to her shoulders. Her eyes were nearly black as well, but unlike Queen Stelara's, hers had a warmth that the queen lacked. "She's one of my advisors and takes point on the Resistance." That got my attention quickly.

"It's so nice to finally meet you, Asteria." Callisto gave me a broad smile, and while I was very interested in learning more about the Resistance, I again noticed that word: *finally*. What were they talking about? "We're hoping you'll be able to help us take the next step forward in freeing humans across Celesterra." Her confidence in her role was clear, and she was clearly a fighter, a warrior, despite being human.

"It's nice to meet you, truly. But—I don't know how I can help with something of that magnitude." I admitted, not able to help fidgeting under their collective stares. It seemed like they were betting a lot on me for some reason, and I didn't know how much I could help beyond providing information on Cyrus.

"That's why we're here." Calix spoke, leaning forward with his fists on the table. "We have made efforts to get as many humans out as possible across the realm, but it's gotten to the point that the other kingdoms are now taking the attacks more seriously and beginning to counter us."

His voice was hard, all traces of the playful Fae long gone. "We need to be careful; I refuse to risk my people's lives any more than necessary, Fae or human. Prince Kian has been a good ally, but he's limited in the help he provides. He has never been in his brother or father's confidence, but my sister foresaw in her visions that the human Cyrus claimed would be the one to change everything." His eyes cut to Princess Liviana, and mine followed, astonished to find out the gods had delivered a vision of *me*.

"It's true." Liviana's smile was one that held secrets—something sly and knowing was in the tilt of her lips. Those strange silver eyes shifted between Calix and me. "I could see you would not only be the catalyst but would be the reason and the answer." My eyebrows furrowed together at her vague explanation.

"Don't mind her." Baach drawled, rolling his eyes. "Seers just love holding information on a hook. She could explain, but she won't."

The princess huffed, "Things must happen as they're meant to. I can only interfere so much before it risks changing things. The Gods were very clear." She softened a bit, looking to her brother and then me, her eyes imploring, "They only show me so much. Trust me, I wish I knew a lot more than I do, but it tends to come in bits and pieces."

"Seems like a lot of pressure." I muttered, shaking my head, baffled by her prophecy. How could I be the answer, the reason? What could I do that would ensure human freedom? It made no sense at all. *Slavery* was the reason.

"Don't worry about that right now. We don't expect you to come in and know the answers to everything. Let's start with what you know about Cyrus, Astraeus, and their plans." Calix redirected me, his voice encouraging, and his eyes gleaming.

"Alright." I sighed, trying to forget the strange prophecy. The soft smile that crept across his face in response had a tinge of pride to it.

I laid everything I'd learned out for them. It took a while—long enough that they called in food as we realized we were going to miss dinner. I couldn't believe I was watching a king, princess, and nobles of all kinds eating while standing and plotting. It was so unlike what I'd grown used to. They were so casual and laid back amongst themselves. Calix never even insisted on anyone addressing him properly. His friends called him by his name.

When I started explaining Dusk's future plans, they listened with wide eyes and open mouths, shocked at the lengths Cyrus would go to. I couldn't blame them; I was still disturbed by it myself. Using forbidden magic, creating iron weapons, sacrificing humans…

Calix looked increasingly disturbed as well, his eyebrows furrowed as his eyes clouded, the purple darkening to an eggplant shade. His shoulders stiffened, and the room seemed to darken around us, until Eryx clapped a hand on his shoulder, and Calix shook his head—the room lightened immediately, the shadows retreating.

"You managed to get an incredible amount of information. This will absolutely help us to change the course of the war going forward." Calix praised as I finished, looking at me with respect in his eyes that was hard to take. "We have enough warning to craft a defense against the iron weapons they're planning on if it comes down to that, but the best-case scenario will be stopping them before more human lives are lost."

I nodded in agreement, and the others murmured their own. It was clear none of us wanted to see more human lives lost—especially for such a nefarious purpose.

"You've also given us several areas we can focus on exploiting." Calix continued, leaning over the map as he ground his jaw back and forth in thought, moving the pieces around. "Weakening the alliance with Dawn will certainly help, for one. The other kingdoms are largely following Dusk's lead on this at the moment, given they are the ones we've attacked most—their treatment of humans was the most concerning to us, and for good reason."

Calix scowled at the map of Dusk, knocking the pieces representing Dawn off the kingdom map. "If we can get Dawn to submit and break the alliance, we should be able to get the other kingdoms in line. Especially once everyone finds out what Dusk is planning. None will accept use of the forbidden magic. If we push hard at this, we may be able to force the kingdoms into a treaty that sees every human slave freed. Though, there will likely be some bloodshed needed to achieve it still."

The king's words were fierce and passionate, and seeing a Fae with so much invested into human freedom was…it was enthralling, in truth.

"You really think so?" Hope lit my own eyes as they caught his. It hadn't seemed possible my information could help them that much, but once Calix laid it out, I could see the way the dominoes would fall. It could be possible, and my excitement at the prospect grew.

"I do." Calix nodded, his silvery-white hair swaying with the movement. "And you're welcome to be involved as much as you want. You can join the Resistance and help us directly, or you can find another job, one that fulfills you, I hope."

"I want in." I practically demanded, shaking my head. "I've spent my entire life living with this—*rage*. Rage that humans are enslaved, rage that I was a prisoner in my life, rage that other humans seemed to just roll over and accept this was our fate. Living in Dusk showed me it was more complicated than I knew—much more. But it also proved to me that change will need to be forced, kingdoms like Dusk are corrupt beyond anything I could have imagined."

It was true. All of it. But beyond that—Liviana said I was a pivotal piece in whatever was to come. The gods had sent that message, and if the gods had a plan for me—who was I to argue? Knowing that all my work spying was actually important, and that we could use it to fix the continent, it meant *everything* to me. I wouldn't squander the chance I'd been given to be a part of this—to see real change come about due to my actions.

I once thought my life would be nothing more than a gust of wind through the forest of the Fae's infinite lives—but now, I could plant roots of my own. I would make a real impact on history—and a big one, if I had any say in it.

Calix's serious facade cracked as he slowly smiled—a vicious, fangy smile that made tingles break out over my skin. His eyes sparkled, a swirl of colors sweeping into the purple and leaving me slightly breathless as I watched them, entranced.

"I'm glad to hear it." Calix rumbled so deeply that I felt it down to my bones. "The first step will be training you. Titan and I will make sure one of us is working with you each day. We meet in the afternoons every few days to discuss the Resistance and any updates unless there's something that can't wait, like today."

"Does this mean I get a weapon?" I bounced on my toes, the thrill of such a forbidden thing running through me. Titan barked a laugh while Calix rolled his eyes, but I saw the smile he tried to hide.

"Yes, Asteria, you'll get a weapon." The king confirmed. "Titan won't accept anything else, believe me." Titan rolled his own eyes back at his king, leaving me wondering yet again at how casual they all were together.

Calix trusted these people. Implicitly. They were his friends, and they saw him the same. I thought of Cyrus, who only had Vissy—and he wasn't exactly loyal to Cyrus in the strictest sense of the word. Looking at Calix now, it was hard to even recall Vissy's golden eyes, Calix just took up the entire space around him, demanding attention.

He was regal in a way Cyrus wishes he was, sexy in a way Vissy would kill for. I would need to be very careful. I didn't want anything to mess up this strange and wonderful turn my life had suddenly taken. I would have to keep things as strictly friendly and professional as possible around the king.

"Well, now that's sorted, let's show the new girls the city!" Ilta cheered, with a beaming smile.

"By Nox, yes!" Harpina yelled her approval, joining the commotion. The others began talking all over themselves and I watched on, completely bemused.

"They're always like this," Calix murmured to me, a soft smile in place as he watched his friends—his family. My heart ached unexpectedly at the sight of it. I'd never had anything like this, but he had a whole group of tight knit friends, close family, and a kingdom that loved him. I had Priscilla, but I didn't even know if I could count Emmie anymore, and Eris was barely an acquaintance. I suddenly wished I had what Calix did. I wondered if, now that I was staying here and working with them, I could maybe…*fit* here.

Friends were different from lovers. I could guard my heart against any romantic love while still accepting the love of friends. I'd discovered already that my life was so much fuller with a friend in it. Like there had been a room I didn't realize was empty until someone stepped into it and the sound echoed. Now, that one single person left the room feeling small and unused. It needed more people to fill it up and looking at the rowdy group in front of me, I had hope it would soon be quite full.

As long as I could keep Calix at a distance, everything would be fine.

CHAPTER 25

ILTA and Lilith joined Delia and I as we went up to my room to change. They both insisted on helping pick my outfit, and I'd already decided to try befriending them, so I didn't bother to fight them on it. Priscilla promised to join us once she changed her outfit, while Eris begged off to stay with Emmie. She'd refused to leave her room, crying and demanding they let her go back. It broke my heart, and I resolved to go soon to talk to her and try to help her see reason.

I was thoroughly distracted though as the three women descended into my cavern of a closet and began pulling out outfits and holding them up against me, then trying another, and another. I was a bit bewildered by the whirlwind but let them do their thing. They looked too delighted to interfere or ruin their fun.

"By Nox, this is perfect!" Ilta squealed, and we all looked at her as she held up a dress. I assumed it was a dress anyway, but—

"Why is it so short?" I questioned, my eyes going so wide, I was sure my eyes might fall out of my head. She held the dress up against my body, confirming it would hit me at mid-thigh. I'd never even considered wearing something so short before.

"It's in style here, trust us!" Delia giggled, as she browsed through my jewelry.

"We're not as stuffy as the other kingdoms." Lilith added with a sly smile. "Oh, don't get me wrong, we abide by court protocols and dress codes when needed—but for a night out…." She trailed off with a raised brow, and I sighed in defeat, taking the dress from Ilta and making her clap in excitement.

I changed quickly, pulling down the skirt as much as possible. Looking in the mirror, I stopped short at the sight of myself. I looked—amazing. The dress fell down to my thigh in a swirl of blackish purple colored fabric, the colors of the Night Kingdom—it appeared to shift from one color to the other as I twirled in the mirror. Making it look like I was wearing the night sky, which made me love it even more.

The sweetheart neckline and the inch-wide straps only added to the allure of the dress, somehow managing to be sexy, while not making me feel overly exposed—even with more skin showing than the dresses Cyrus put me in. All three women smiled at how enamored I was with the dress.

"I knew it!" Ilta proudly proclaimed as she grabbed my shoulders, meeting my eyes in the mirror. "Let's do your hair and makeup!" I couldn't help matching her smile. We all talked and laughed as we got ready. And when Priscilla arrived, bringing everyone else's outfits as was apparently requested, Delia sent for champagne.

"A toast!" She called out. The rest of us quieted and held our glasses, looking at Delia expectantly. "To new friends and freedom. To finding a home." Her words choked me up immediately. I raised my glass, and we clinked them together. Bringing it to my mouth, I repeated her toast in my mind, and drank. The champagne bubbled like happiness down my throat, like a faraway dream realized in the flesh. I brushed away the tear leaking from my eye before anyone could see it.

Priscilla bumped her shoulder with mine, giving me an understanding smile. She looked as flustered as I was.

"How are you doing?" I managed to ask her, my throat tight from emotion.

"I'm—overwhelmed." Priscilla laughed softly. "But in the best way? If that makes sense?"

I nodded in agreement, "Completely. This is all—a lot, but it's more than I ever imagined we could have. When I set out to ensure we got free, I had no idea what to do afterwards. I told myself to worry about it later." I chuckled wryly. "Thank the Old Gods for Calix and Kian, I honestly have no idea how we would have managed it otherwise."

Priscilla was quiet for a moment, before she laid her head on my shoulder, blonde hair spilling into my dark tresses. I rested my head lightly on top of hers.

"I think you would have found a way, Asteria." She said confidently. "I knew when I met you that you were a force to be reckoned with. I even thought that Cyrus had no idea what kind of woman he was trying to chain to him." I snorted a laugh, and she giggled softly. "You would have found a way and look at everything you accomplished already—you need to give yourself more credit."

I nodded, brushing my head along hers as I promised to try. We finished our glasses of champagne—watching the others get ready as we giggled between ourselves—and then made our way to the palace entryway, where we would meet up with everyone to leave.

"Is this normal?" I asked, tilting my head towards Lilith. "For the king to just—go out?"

"Calix is different from any king you've met before." Lilith chuckled, leaning back to meet my eyes. "He prefers his friends to be more casual when we're not on duty. The people love him, and unlike some of the other royals, he's able to go out into the city without worrying about any revolts from the disenfranchised because, well—the Night Kingdom doesn't have any."

"At least, not anymore." Harpina chimed in, and I swung my head towards her, my brows furrowed in question.

"Things weren't always this way." She explained, shrugging. "Calix took over as king when he was only one hundred and twenty, after his father was killed in battle. There was a war fought during that time between the kingdoms, with Sunrise and Sunset on one side and Dawn and Dusk on the other. Night and Day both stepped in to try to put a stop to it. King Orion, Calix's father, and King Diell, Aelius's father, didn't like that trade was being suffocated because of the war, but King Orion was unfortunately killed in one of the battles."

"Calix's mother, Jemisha, had died birthing Liv not long before." Ilta added softly, her eyes glinting with a sadness that seemed incongruous on the excitable Fae. "Calix thinks he was seeking death, unable to go on without his mate."

Lilith nodded in agreement, as we all huddled in a group to ensure no one else heard us. "Calix was young, suddenly king, and he had a baby sister to raise on top of everything. He had been raised a warrior, and after his father's death, he threw himself into it even more. He developed quite a reputation on the battlefield for the beautiful brutality he exhibited. Not to mention, his magic, his darkness, was more potent and powerful than anything they'd seen before. And as any young, powerful boy—" Lilith smirked, but Ilta picked up her hanging thread.

"He gained quite the ego." Ilta laughed with a wink.

"As ridiculous as they're making it sound, it is true." Harpina shook her head at them both, rolling her eyes with a loud sigh. "Calix was a bit of a womanizer. Women just threw themselves at that pretty, powerful king, either hoping to be queen or just to warm his bed." I could feel my cheeks burning harshly at her words.

I was not jealous. No. It was just—*fuck*. I couldn't even think of a justification.

"But despite everything, he was serious in his duties." Harpina emphasized. "Partying, fucking—those were the times he allowed himself to let go. There was too much on his shoulders, and he never thought further about issues like slavery because he was barely keeping his wings in the air with everything else he felt was his responsibility."

I could easily picture it. Calix had those moments when he switched between serious and playful—both parts of him were real, I now recognized, he had just compartmentalized himself to be able to take on everything he was given.

He'd been forced to take up kingship and raise his little sister all on his own. I couldn't imagine the pressure he must have felt. Could I truly blame him for not thinking of humans earlier? When he was the first Fae who ever bothered to step back and actually think about us in the first place?

"Ten years ago, he became very serious about freeing the slaves. I think it started in truth a few years before that, just little things here and there he would sit up and realize he hated, but he started to free the people within our kingdom first. It took years for us to get it right—to find what worked, how we could set them up for success in a free life." Lilith continued the tale with a large sigh. Her green eyes bored into me like she wanted me to understand something. "He would lose himself in women to take the pressure off before that, but twenty-one years ago, that all stopped."

I scrunched my brows, opening my mouth to ask why, when Harpina hurriedly began talking.

"That's not the point." She argued, glaring at Lilith for some reason. "The point is, five years ago or so, we expanded—working on freeing humans in other kingdoms. We'd finally managed to make our kingdom completely free, and all people were being treated equally. The Lords and Ladies enforce it throughout the kingdom on Calix's behalf, and it helps us keep everything running smoothly."

"I understand." I nodded, knowing they were worried about my reaction to the years before Calix woke up to the truth, but I couldn't harp on that when he was the *only* royal who did care. He worried about humans now, and that was all I could ask for. "It's honestly amazing he did all of this. Most Fae never bother to care."

"It's a shame, isn't it?" Calix's husky voice surprised me, and I whirled around—stopping short at the sight of him. Old Gods, I was in so much trouble. Black leather pants clung to him like a second skin, and I bit my lip as my eyes roved upwards, taking in the black half-tucked, long sleeve shirt that was buttoned scandalously low, exposing part of his pale, muscular chest, and the shimmering black and purple dragon scales tattooed across it. The iridescent tattoo made me want to rip those few buttons wide open and explore what lay beneath.

His sleeves were rolled up to show off his forearms, and by the Otherworld, I'd never been so attracted to forearms before, with tattooed bands of runes spun in gleaming silver around them. Purple stitching added a splash of color to his shirt—incidentally making us match as well—and crescent moons dotted each collar, which were splayed just enough to catch glimpses of the tattoo on his neck. His silvery white hair was down and fell past his shoulders, while those cheekbones I could cut a diamond on led my eyes right up to his own burning purple irises—he looked like a god come to Adamah.

Calix's eyes devoured me in turn, the intensity between us ratcheting up with so much more skin on display. His eyes traced my chest, taking in my overflowing cleavage before plunging down to the dip of my waist and caressing over the curve of my hips, before brushing up and down my legs—his stare scorching me like a brand. I could practically hear my skin sizzle in want, and I bit my lip hard to distract myself from the charged atmosphere.

"You look…" Calix growled, his tone low and reverberating, full of a wind-swept darkness that trailed off as Ilta bounced up next to me, throwing an arm around my shoulders.

"Doesn't she look fantastic? But we need to go—come on!" Ilta cheerfully redirected us both as she dragged me away, but I couldn't help looking back. Calix was still watching me, shadows circling around him, his eyes swirling with color as they dipped to watch my ass as I walked away. At least until

Eryx slapped him on the back of the head. I couldn't contain my giggle as I turned forward.

I knew better. I truly did. I was supposed to be staying away from Fae men—but Calix, he made it utterly hopeless. He wasn't just the most gorgeous man I'd ever seen; he was the one who gave me freedom, who sought to free my people from slavery. He gave me the tools I needed to let me take power over my own life, where Cyrus had sought to take and control it. He was a king, but he didn't act like he was superior to anyone around him—treating me like an *equal*.

He was entirely too tempting for my mental health. Maybe my physical health as well, depending on if the bulge I saw in his pants was him hard or not—and if not…that could admittedly be a real danger—he might break me in half.

Since what happened with Cyrus, part of me worried I would think of *that* whenever I next had sex. But I refused to let fear make my decisions for me, and I doubly refused to let Cyrus have any power over me. I'd spent too much of my life not following my desires due to outside forces. I was finally free. I could finally focus my rage on something—freeing humans and stopping Cyrus and King Astraeus from carrying out their horrid plans. I wouldn't limit myself now—not when I had the chance to finally have *everything*.

And it seemed like Calix was interested—sometimes, anyway. He was hard to pin down, and Lilith had hinted at him no longer sleeping around. I was too curious as to why. Harpina had seemed set on steering away from that conversation, so I'd have to ask later. But it begged the question, did Calix want me? Or was he just being nice? Maybe he just liked the view? Tonight, I was determined to get answers.

Which left me with the question, would *I* want to jump into something? With a Fae king no less? I wasn't sure myself—maybe it wasn't fair to Calix to need to know where he stands, when I couldn't even answer that question.

The girls looped their arms with mine as we walked down the streets of Tairngire, the boys following behind. We walked through Shadowgleam into Moonglow District, and I was able to see the city up close for the first time on the ground. It was truly beautiful, with looping, curving, and swirling architecture that left the buildings feeling whimsical, especially with the materials used to make them—the brightly painted wood and stone, mixed with shining metals. Nymph trees and Darkelm trees lined the streets, and moonlillies, starbells, and goddess dahlias were planted in the ground or hung from baskets outside businesses and homes. They lent a colorful, quaint touch to the city, along with smelling amazing. The fragrance of flowers, and a unique scent I struggled to identify, filled the air instead of the smells of sweat, dust, and smoke—like Dusk had always smelled of.

I watched in wonder as we passed different businesses, the people using magic to serve food and drinks or just for entertainment. Magic was in abundance in Night—all of it coming from the gift of the gods imbued in the land around us. That unique smell—like darkness, stars, and the cosmos themselves, underlined with fruity and floral notes—I couldn't truly describe how it smelled, only that I knew it must be the magic itself—it was how my dreams smelled when I floated in the night sky.

The girls pointed out places as we walked, showing me good spots for shopping, or eating. We turned the corner, approaching a building with a sign out front reading *"Otherworld Bar"* in bright, glowing letters that were white at the top and faded to black on the bottom. A bar named for the afterlife—*interesting.*

Inside, it was completely different from the gambling dens I'd seen in Dusk. A crescent moon shaped bar dominated one side and was lit up with a vivid glow. One side of the bar was dark, the other light, white walls contrasting against black ones—made to mimic the two halves of the Otherworld, Elysium and Tartarus.

The Elysium side contained the bar, with silver and pink sofas scattered around with low tables in front of them, and higher topped tables with standing room around them were positioned nearer the bar itself. Glowing balls of light hung from the ceiling over the tables, illuminating the space for those occupying them.

On the Tartarus side was a dance floor, where people lost themselves to the music. This wasn't dancing like at the balls I'd attended before, and I watched with wide, shocked eyes as people danced pressed up against one another, grinding as if they were having sex on the dance floor. I barely even noticed the red sections set up for more…private interactions. Instead of solid walls, alcoves were dotted around the Tartarus end of the bar. Some of them were lightly curtained for privacy, and others were completely open for the voyeurs to watch the couples inside. Each alcove was painted a deep red, and had burgundy padded benches set up for multiple…positions.

Tartarus, indeed.

"Old Gods!" Priscilla exclaimed, Ilta's bright laughter merging with Delia's as they entertained themselves watching us react to the shocking sight.

"Not like anything you've seen before, huh?" Delia giggled.

"Otherworld's my favorite place. We come here all the time. It's a place to let loose and not worry about any judgment." Ilta added as she smiled widely, revealing her small, sharp canines and lending her excited smile a slightly more devious air in this setting—none of the adorable energy from earlier. "Let's get you ladies a drink!"

I shook my head in bemusement, hearing the boys chuckle behind me. I turned around to see Calix, Eryx, and Baach watching us just as intently.

"Not what you expected?" Eryx raised his brow, a sly grin taking over his face. I shook my head, exasperated that he and Delia both felt the need to tease us, and narrowed my eyes at him.

Baach laughed, swinging an arm around my shoulders, while I tried to keep my eyes off Calix. I could feel the weight of his eyes on me, and I worried I wouldn't be able to keep my distance right now—not with the people behind me practically having sex on the dance floor.

"Welcome to our world, Asteria! Stick with me, I'll show you the ropes!" Baach cheerfully proclaimed, looked much too excited, so I gave in—laughing as I let him pull me along.

I saw Eryx elbow Calix from the corner of my eye. He was glaring at him for some reason, but I was distracted by Baach chattering at me about the different drink options. Ilta came up on my other side, handing me a drink.

"It's called a Nebulita, it's a specialty here." Ilta smiled, and I took a sip of the strangely colored drink, the pink, purple, and blue swirls pouring into my mouth. It tasted fruity, with a sparkling aftertaste—it was delicious, and I downed it before I even realized, and immediately asked for another. Baach and Ilta laughed, and Baach raised his arm to the bartender, ordering more drinks for us.

"Be careful—they're strong, and you're not used to drinking much, I imagine." Lilith warned, her face soft as she implored me to use caution.

"Oh, don't mind our Lilith. Always with the mothering! She mothers her beasts so much, I think it just spills out on to us." Eryx teased with a twinkle in his eye. Lilith just sighed long sufferingly, making us both laugh.

"What kind of beasts?" I inquired, tilting my head to the side as curiosity took over. "Besides horses, I know Calix mentioned those, and something about a menagerie?" I furrowed my brows, still unclear about what he meant.

"I'll show you soon, how about that?" Lilith offered, looking excited at the thought, so I quickly agreed, wanting to know everything I could about this kingdom that would be my home—that I had once only dreamed of visiting.

Most of us had grabbed spots around the bar, but those who didn't stood around and behind us. Even with their king among them, the people here mostly left him to his own devices, clearly used to his presence. I found it fascinating. There were a few who smiled and nodded or said hello, and he indulged every one of them who wished it with conversation for a moment.

I downed my second drink quickly and Ilta insisted I try the astroshots next. We got two each—little glasses full of a dark, glimmering liquid.

"Take it down all in one go. Ready?" Ilta prompted. She was so bubbly and happy, and with her blonde hair and bright blue eyes, she reminded me a bit of a doll that came to life. I nodded with a large smile I couldn't contain, having more fun than I could ever remember having.

"Ready!" I confirmed, and we downed the first shot. I coughed as it settled, but quickly gulped down the second as well. Ilta and Priscilla both laughed at the grimace on my face, but Delia and Harpina began to drag us onto the dance floor. I stumbled off my chair thanks to a major head rush and steadied myself with Priscila's help.

On the dance floor, we twirled around with each other, bodies moving to the beat. We laughed and smiled so hard my cheeks hurt as I spun round and round. When Eryx stepped in and took my hand, he led me in a swinging dance that left me giggling and out of breath.

"You look much happier than before." He observed with a soft smile.

"I am." I blinked in surprise at the truth of those words. Life had been wretched and awful and hard all my life, I never thought I'd see the day I laughed and danced with no worries in my mind. Like the world had lifted me up to the sky and let me stay there—a star rising amidst the darkness.

"I'm glad. I know things in Dusk were hard. No one deserves that, and I hope you can find happiness here." Eryx said sincerely. There was something trustworthy and almost brotherly about him. Having cried all over him in his hawk form, and him being there for me in one of my darkest moments—I felt like we'd been friends forever, as opposed to just getting to know each other.

"I'm here if you ever need anything." Eryx promised. "I hope you know that. You're one of us now." He spun me out with a smile until I was caught by a wall of muscle. I blinked up, seeing a flash of silvery white and purple, and knew immediately who I was pressed up against. His hand went to my lower back as I crashed into him, and he held me against him, not letting me go even once I was steady.

"Dance with me?" He purred, leaning down to speak into my ear.

"Yes, my King." I shivered, aiming for a joking tone, but it came out too breathy and low—too accidentally seductive.

His eyes darkened as he held me against him and began to move. The beat of the music became sultry and entrancing, and I swayed against him, letting the music guide me. My arms came up around his neck, as his hands spanned my back and hips. We spun together; our bodies aligned perfectly, my ass brushing against his covered cock on more than one occasion. His fingers dug into my hips in response, a low growl rattling his chest that did nothing but excite me further.

I was too drawn to Calix to resist, and with so many drinks clouding any rational thought…any notions of holding back fizzled away. Feeling him against me, I was desperate to know what his body would feel like with nothing between us. I wanted to know his lips on mine—to find out if they were as pillowy soft as they looked. If his chest was as firm, if his abdomen was as defined, if his cock was as big as it felt against my backside—bigger than I'd ever considered possible.

He gripped my hips, pulling me further into the cradle of his body. My arms twined backward around his neck, and my fingers slipped into the soft strands of his moonglow hair. His arm bound around my waist and helped me grind against him. We both let out a breathy moan at the contact, the large length pressing against me a delightful tease.

"Fuck." Calix growled deeply, the vibration shaking my own chest. "What are you doing to me?"

"I think the question is, what are you doing to me? Is this some Fae magic? Are you entrancing me?" I whispered back, my head tilting backwards onto his shoulder, looking up into his eyes. They were so intense, with blue, green, and pink overtaking and mixing with the purple until an aurora was looking back at me.

"If it is, you must be using it as well." Calix protested, his hands gliding down my hips to my thighs, fingers running along the bare skin he found there before he inched his fingers back upwards, inching my skirt up with them. "Every time I'm near you, I find myself wanting nothing more than to get closer."

I could certainly relate—even when we clashed in Dusk, I had fought the urge to get closer to him. Even when my mind told me to fight and rage, my body wanted something else entirely.

His hands continued their path upwards, skimming along my waist until they finally glanced off the bottom of my breasts. I inhaled sharply, wanting nothing more than for him to continue, to feel him cup my breasts in those large, rough warrior's hands, to savor the feel of him squeezing and pinching. I whimpered at the thought, arousal flooding my meager little panties. I was thankful that my swaying meant I at least got some friction from the movement of my thighs.

I hadn't taken Fae senses into consideration, however, and Calix growled as he scented my arousal. I moaned, shivering as his cock throbbed against my ass.

"Nox, help me." Calix moaned, an agonized noise that sounded as if he was truly in pain. "You're a temptress sent from the Otherworld, aren't you?"

He spun me around, my front now pressed to his. He ran his hands over my thighs, sliding them sensuously up until he gripped the back of them, his fingers surely leaving imprints behind as he lifted me up. I snaked my legs around his hips—my dress hiking up to my hips with the movement—and as I settled against him, I felt his cock press up against me. My breath hitched— my panties were all but soaked through and useless, so only his pants provided any kind of buffer between us. The cloud leather pants he wore conformed so perfectly to his body that I could practically feel every bump and vein along his length.

Calix moved quickly, and a wall was suddenly at my back as he pressed me into it. The darkness of the bar shadowed us, preventing others from watching as he ground his hips against me like we were still dancing. His forehead came down on mine, moonglow hair falling around my face like a curtain, keeping us in our own little world.

"Calix—" I whined, lifting my hips upwards to meet his. He growled, his fingers digging hard into my hips as he helped me meet his thrusts.

"You smell so fucking good—like starlight, vanilla, and raspberries." He moaned. "Wearing my colors, and this tiny little dress, grinding this luscious ass against me—tempting me beyond anything I've experienced in over four hundred years."

Calix reached a hand up into my hair, gripping it tightly and pulling my head back to look into my eyes. I was panting, anticipation so thick it was like a third entity between us—on edge like I might fall any moment and never stop falling. The beat of the music pulsed around us, luring us both further into this spun-up state.

"You shine like a star in the darkness, Asteria. When you're in a room, it's like my eyes go right to you." Calix confessed, with an agonized strain to his tone.

"I know the feeling." I breathed, reaching for him and caressing down his shoulders, his chest, hoping to ease whatever pained him, to show him I wanted this just as intensely.

Calix moaned, leaning into me, the hard outline of his cock grinding against me and sending shockwaves through my body. Someone called his name in the distance, and I watched in awe as he lifted his hand, darkness spilling out and covering us. Each time I saw his shadows was just as remarkable as the last—I wanted to be enveloped in his darkness, wanted us to be lost in our own little world. One where if I was a star, he was the darkness I shined against. I would dance amongst the darkness and claim it for my own.

His lips came down towards mine as I inhaled the scent of night and fire, eager for him to close the distance, our hips rocking together and the ecstasy I knew was just out of reach…

But as his lips touched mine with the lightest, softest touch—he wrenched himself away. He dropped me to my feet as I stared at him, completely bewildered.

"Calix?" I prompted softly, as I touched his shoulder. I didn't even realize my hand was shaking, too concerned with his own. His whole body was trembling as he looked down at his hands, which were flexing opened and closed, like he was fighting himself.

"I'm sorry." Calix whispered. "I'm so sorry, my réalta, but I can't."

In a blink of an eye, it was like he'd disappeared, he was gone so fast. My hand was left hanging in the air, and I slowly dropped it, mystified and…*rejected.*

It was a new, strange feeling for me. Women had often rejected me as friends, but this was different. Men usually reacted to me like Cyrus and Soren had, I'd never had a man literally run away from me before. I swallowed hard, trying to hold back my pathetic tears.

Things had been going so well, maybe *too* well. I'd been happy and carefree for the first time ever, and now it was all ruined.

"Asteria." I looked up to find Harpina there, sympathy in every line of her face. Great, now my humiliation was public. I was going to have to disappear forever after this.

"Come with me." She insisted softly, linking our arms together, and bringing me to a quiet table in the corner. Lilith joined us along the way, but Ilta was laughing and dancing with Baach, while Eryx was spinning Priscilla, and to my surprise, Callisto, around. I hadn't realized the Resistance leader was here, but she must have shown up at some point. I'd obviously been too consumed in Calix to notice.

Lilith set a drink down on the table for me, and I immediately picked it up and slammed it back as fast as possible. She took my hand, squeezing gently.

"Asteria, Calix—" Harpina grimaced, leaning forward. "This isn't about you; I promise you that."

"What do you mean?" I whispered, staring down at my empty glass. The drink wasn't helping me control my feelings. I knew better—stay away from Fae men, stay away from any sort of feelings beyond friendship. I could already feel stirrings of *something* for him, something that was deep and expansive, and that was a dangerous line to teeter on. Feelings could too easily become love, and that was something I couldn't afford. No matter that I was free now, I knew how this world worked: love was for the Fae alone, not humans like me.

"I haven't seen Calix drawn to anyone like this in a very long time, if ever." Harpina informed me sadly. "He's struggling to stay away from you, and it's clear there's some sort of feelings there. But Calix only has sex now on holidays when the king must participate. And even then, if he could prevent that, he would. He stopped having any kind of relations voluntarily twenty-one years ago."

"What? Why?" My eyebrows scrunched together in confusion. Calix was sexy beyond all belief, he was a king, he was the most powerful Fae in Celesterra—he was the definition of most eligible bachelor. They told me he used to sleep around, and he'd seemed perfectly willing and able—at least up until he ran. Why would he avoid sex?

"Because twenty-one years ago, Calix got his soul mark." Lilith informed me softly, like she was trying to soften the blow of her words. Soul mark. He had a soul mark. Which meant…he had a soulmate.

A *soulmate*. Oh. Oh, Old Gods, I felt so stupid. Of course.

"He doesn't want to do anything that'd be disloyal to her, whoever she is." Lilith continued, eyeing me, waiting for a reaction as I sat there still as stone, my eyes slammed shut. "It's difficult for him. He doesn't know who she is, only that she has to be a Fae female somewhere on the continent. There's been times where he's been attracted to a woman and struggled against his urges, but he only gets it out of his system on holidays."

"But the chemistry between you two—it's hard not to feel it when you're both in the room." Harpina said, and I opened my eyes to look back at her. She looked at me like she thought I was moments from falling apart. "I don't think he's struggled to refrain like this before. It's not fair to you either, and he knows that. He doesn't want to lead you on when his soul is tied to another's."

"Of course." I mumbled. Lilith pushed me her drink, and I sat there nursing it, Harpina and Lilith watching and waiting for a reaction to some kind. But I'd gone numb—of course the gorgeous Fae king had a soulmate out there. That rare and precious thing all Fae wished and hoped for. Who was I to think I could have someone like him? Who was I to get between soulmates?

"I'd like to go home and sleep." I admitted, and they both nodded, their brows furrowing with concern as they stood to help me back to the palace. To the wonderful room Calix had given me.

"That might be for the best. You have training in the morning with Titan, don't forget." Harpina, ever the warrior, reassured me. She seemed excited for me to begin, and I was too, but still—that wasn't what I wanted to focus on right now. When we arrived back, they helped me change, as my limbs seemed to be beyond my control at the moment. My mind stuck on Calix. On him—and the unknown, beautiful Fae woman that owned his soul.

CHAPTER 26

THE next morning, Delia dragged me out of bed, not letting me wallow in my aching body and pounding head. She gave me a cup of steaming liquid, some medicine she promised would help. True to her word, I felt better moments after finishing it. Thoughts of everything from last night still spun in my mind, but I shut them down, refusing to revisit them.

I made my way out to the training field, Delia showing me the way before leaving with a jaunty wave and a smile, wishing me good luck. Titan was already on the field, swinging a blade as he sparred with one of the men. When he spotted me, he called it off and slapped the other man on the shoulder, who nodded and walked off.

"You're going to be fighting Fae for the most part." Titan abruptly began, wasting no time. "We're stronger, faster, and have magic at our disposal. Training you on strength is only going to go so far, it can help you when learning to master wielding weapons, but it will do you no good as a strategy in a fight against a Fae." He explained as he walked up to me.

My eyebrows scrunched at his words, which just echoed the concerns I'd had since I learned I would be able to train to fight.

"What am I supposed to do then?" I asked, throwing my hands in the air. "How do the humans here fight if the Fae are always going to overpower us?" My head tilted to the side as Titan gave me a sly smile.

"You outsmart them. You use your cunning. And based on how you handled Cyrus and the royals in Dusk, you've more than got that covered." Titan nodded, and my cheeks heated at the compliment.

"I don't know about that." I confessed, uncertain how much of that was based on any cunning. "I got lucky that Cyrus was so obsessed with me that he couldn't see what was going on under his nose."

But Titan was already shaking his head, his square jaw jutting out in protest. "You don't give yourself enough credit."

"Prince Kian caught me, remember?" I put my hands on my hips, unsure exactly why I was arguing this point so hard. Maybe it was because I felt like I didn't do much of anything yet. Titan snorted a laugh though, surprising me.

"That's only because he was already watching you." Titan admitted, causing my brows to fly upwards. "We'd sent him a message that we needed you. With the intel we got from him about Cyrus and you, Eryx's observations, and of course, Liv's prophecy, we told him to keep an eye on you and see if you'd be willing to work with us. Calix said you weren't ready when you first met. He didn't even *know* it was you at that point. Liv drew him a picture later, and when he realized he'd already met you—"

My body seemed to release a tension I hadn't known it held, realizing that Calix hadn't specifically sought me out the first time we met. Our meeting— our chemistry—hadn't been the result of them plotting to grab me because of Liviana's prophecy. I wasn't sure why that was so important, only that it was.

Titan shook his head, laughing, "Well, let's just say that night Calix spent a while drowning his sorrows over his perceived failure to convince you."

"Failure?" My head reared back. "It wasn't his fault. I thought Night Kingdom and all Fae were monsters. That wasn't on him."

"I know. All of us know that." Titan softened, his eyes becoming distant. "And you would have been right once upon a time. There were no kingdoms humans were safe in before. I can't even say what it was that changed Calix. It started not long after his mark came in." That got my attention, words from last night ringing in my ears about Calix's soul mark—undeniable proof I had to stay away from him, that he was not meant for the likes of me. A king and a human former-slave? I nearly snorted at the ridiculous thought.

"As the years passed, I watched Calix change. He told me he could feel some of his soulmate's feelings, sometimes in his dreams, and this feeling of unfairness and anger filtered through. It took him a while to pinpoint what those feelings were surrounding, but when he started balking at slavery here, it became clear. Whoever she is, she obviously doesn't agree with the practice, and eventually, he couldn't take it anymore, and abolished slavery here. It was a huge shake up, of course, but he was able to get the lords and ladies in line.

The nobility was used to the way things were, but when Calix laid down the law, they eventually came around. It helped that they already trusted him. There's no one in this kingdom who doesn't love our king."

Titan looked softer than I'd ever seen him as he spoke about Calix. "You really do love him, don't you?" I whispered.

"Of course, I love that boy like my own son." Titan smiled. "I practically raised him out here in the training yard. Him, Eryx, Baach—the three were always thick as thieves, even back then. I trained them all, the little prince, and his spare heir friends."

"Wait—" I paused, my eyebrows rising. "How old are you to have been training them as children?" He laughed slightly at the shock on my face.

"Much older. I'm the oldest Fae in Celesterra." My jaw dropped open, my mouth silently forming the word "wow". I was speechless. I'd known he was older, but there was older, and then there was *that*. He looked no older than maybe twenty-five, thirty years old maybe. It was one thing knowing Fae were immortal, another to meet the eldest Fae in Adamah.

"Which is why I know you have it in you to be a great warrior." Titan clasped my shoulder, smiling softly down at me, towering over me like a giant. "Human or not. I've trained more boys and girls, men and women, than any other. You have that spark in you, girl. One that burns bright. It's time for you to wrangle it and use it to your advantage."

Titan stepped back, and his soft, encouraging smile transformed into a ferocious, battle-ready grin, showing off those sharpened canines. "Now, let's begin."

I smiled widely, bolstered by his words. He showed me the different stances. Where to put my feet. How to form a fist. How to block. How to kick, and how to move my body so I didn't lose my balance after. We worked on repeating movements that would help me evade a stronger opponent. Repetition, Titan said, was the key for my muscles to begin forming those moves instinctually. He promised that my strength would build up with every punch thrown or kick landed. I was exhausted and sweating profusely by the end of our session, and I hadn't even picked up a weapon yet.

You'll get there." Titan laughed as I whined about the lack of weapons. "You're a natural at this, Asteria. Your body was built to move in this way. I've seen a lot of people come and go in this yard. Humans and Fae alike, and you move more fluidly than any human I've trained before."

"Maybe the gods really did choose you." He whispered, eyebrows rising, and I was fairly sure he hadn't meant for me to hear him, but the words struck me hard.

I didn't follow the Fae gods, and they'd already singled me out to Liv, what else could they want? I was helping with the war—did they wish me to be able to fight? I wasn't sure, but I felt chilled at the thought of the Fae gods interfering in my life.

I COULDN'T STOP thinking about it as I thanked Titan and headed off back into the palace. I'd just reached the door when Calix appeared. I inhaled sharply, memories of last night flashing in my mind. He stared at me, and his mouth opened once, twice, but no words came out.

I found myself unable to form words either, so I just nodded once and moved to pass by him, but as I came level with him, he caught my arm, stopping me in my tracks.

"Do you—do you want to learn to ride a horse?" The previously smooth king blurted out. I raised an eyebrow at him, wondering what brought that on. Especially after the way he left last night. "You'll need to know how to ride for battle. I figured now's as good a time as any."

His eyes had a hopeful sheen to them, despite the way he shrugged dismissively. Despite myself, I couldn't bear to snuff that hope out. I sighed, my aching body protesting any more physical activity, especially horseback riding. I'd only just gotten rid of the soreness our ride here had caused, and then I'd spent the night dancing, followed by a morning of training for the first time.

"I'd like that." I nodded, giving him a small smile, regardless of the way my body screamed at me to stop.

Calix led me across the expansive grounds, to the other side of the palace. We were both quiet, unsure of what to say in the wake of last night. I was determined to forget about him—well, forget about him in any sexual or romantic way. That was never going to happen, so I had to shut it down.

But just being around him made that difficult. I swore it felt like every inch of space between us vibrated with the need to close it. When a piece of hair fell into his face, I wanted to reach over and caress the strand before righting it. I had to shake myself several times just to prevent myself from drifting towards him. He had a soulmate and was not for me—no matter how badly my body wanted to climb his.

I'd never had such a visceral reaction to anyone before, and it was seriously the last thing I needed right now.

Calix cleared his throat, looking over at me in a way that seemed almost shy. Embarrassed maybe? I couldn't tell what it was exactly.

"Lilith runs Cosmic Dust Stables as part of her duties." He explained as we walked, filling the silence. "She's very proud of the horses we have here. She's bred them to be the very best. War horses are her specialty, along with ones bred for speed."

"And what about you?" I couldn't help asking. "Do you ride often? I can't imagine I would if I could fly, but then again, I haven't seen a dragon once since arriving. You seem to fly as rarely as Cyrus did." Calix barked a laugh, surprising me.

"I actually shift often and go flying." Calix chuckled. "Liv often joins me as well. My other sister, Ndrita, you'll meet her sometime soon, I'm sure, but she lives in Keris. Her husband is the Lord there. She flies with us whenever she visits. Keris isn't quite as ideal as Tairngire for flying, so she always takes advantage when she arrives."

I was taken aback by the excitement and pure joy on Calix's face as he spoke of flying, and even more so, of his sisters. It was clear he loved them and missed Ndrita when she wasn't around.

I wondered how old she was when their parents died. Calix was one hundred and twenty, and Liv had just been born—how often did Fae typically have children? King Astraeus and Queen Stelara had six children, but I knew King Aelius and Queen Aurelia only had the one.

"Tairngire's location is said to have been chosen for its cliffs." Calix continued, breaking my train of thought. "My ancestors found it was perfect for taking off and flying over them, hence the name Dragon Cliffs."

"And will I ever get to see said dragon form?" I couldn't help but coyly ask, looking over at him with raised brows.

I wanted to know if his dragon form looked anything like the dragons I dreamed of. To see a dragon in person—it would be a dream come true.

"You will." Calix laughed joyfully. His eyes cut to me, a smirk forming on his lips, "What do you say to me—" He licked his lips, and I zeroed in on the motion. "Taking you for a different kind of ride?"

One of his eyebrows rose with his smirk. I couldn't believe him—he literally ran away from me last night, yet here he is making sex jokes.

"Pfft! You couldn't handle it." I sniped back at him. His chuckle in response was deep, and I did my best to keep my eyes forward, I couldn't stand to see that playful gleam in his eyes right now.

"Tonight." Calix suddenly proclaimed after a moment of silence. I looked over despite myself, and saw he looked entirely serious now. "Flying at night among the stars, it's an experience you won't forget. I promise you that."

His eyes bore into mine so intensely that I felt trapped within his gaze, completely unable to look away. At least until he dipped his head downwards, and I watched silvery white strands sway with the movement, the breeze coming through tossing them in front of his face and back again. When he lifted his head, his face was painted with regret.

"Calix—" I began, swallowing hard, suddenly sure where this was heading.

"Asteria, I owe you an apology." He didn't let me deter him, and his voice was so contrite, I couldn't stand it.

"You don't. Really." I insisted, walking faster toward the stables.

Calix grabbed my arm, stopping me in my tracks. I closed my eyes for a moment, taking a deep breath as I gathered my courage, and my dignity, before looking back up. I couldn't help the draw I felt toward him, nor could I stop myself from being swept into his orbit every time I looked into his eyes.

"I'm sorry, Asteria. *Truly*. I shouldn't have drunk so much my inhibitions were affected. I should have known that around you—" Calix paused, swallowing hard. "Fucking Nox." He ran a hand through his long hair, and I watched it trail through his fingers.

"I can't explain the way I feel about—or—or toward you." He struggled with his words, leaving me a bit in awe that it was *me* this powerful Fae king was stammering over. "I should have the willpower to keep things friendly between us. Because that's all it can be, Asteria. Somewhere out there is my soulmate, and a man is only as good as the way he treats his mate."

He laughed softly, shaking his head, "That's what my father always told me. And I strived to ensure I was nothing but loyal to her—whoever she is. But Nox." His eyes barreled into me, like they were stripping me down to my soul. "You test me in dangerous ways. Since the very day we met."

I couldn't deny that I felt the same.

"I'd like us to be friends still, though." Calix concluded with a wince. I nearly laughed—friends? How in the Otherworld would we be able to manage *that*? But what choice did we really have? And, well—he looked so wretched talking about this that the part of me that wanted nothing more than his happiness (and where had *that* come from?) had me nodding with a slight smile.

"I'd like that." I told him softly, cursing myself internally.

Shy smiles graced both our faces as we continued our walk to the stables. As we rounded the corner, my lips parted in shock at the size of the stables in front of me. I heard Calix chuckle and dragged my eyes away from the building to look at him.

"We're outfitting an entire army plus the rest of the city." Calix explained, mirth dancing in his eyes. "Most of the horses in Tairngire get stabled in one of three places. Either here, or in one of two estates in Starshine. Those estates have large stables where they rent out stalls. Some of the other estates have stables as well, but they're strictly private and much smaller. Further out of the city there are other, larger stables, but it's impractical for the people here to use those. We offer free stabling for our residents as well, so most people use the stables here."

"That's very generous of you." I raised my brow, a smile growing across my face. I couldn't imagine how much money he must have to be able to offer such things freely and not care about the loss of it.

"Horses are essential. It seemed unnecessary to charge people for something like that." Calix just shrugged modestly. He wasn't wrong. Horses were the best mode of transportation outside of wagons or carriages, and even those required horses. They were necessary for anyone wanting to go farther than walking distance.

I looked up at the stables as we approached. Next to the palace, which was a near glowing white, with pink, purple, green, and blue shining within it when you looked closely, the stable was quite the opposite. It was black but made to look like cosmic dust, interspersed with the same colors as the star opal—the same colors found in the galaxies above—only done in smaller amounts that circled and swirled into the dust motif. A large sign reading "Cosmic Dust Stables" hung above the large barn doors.

Rings stretched for miles behind the stables, with posts delineating different areas. Some people were out there now, and I could just make out that trainers were calling out different instructions.

Walking through the double doors, I found that the stalls expanded down the stable's corridor, and it was open at the other end, where another set of large double doors were pushed open to the rings. There were walkways leading off to the left and right, where additional stalls were housed. Calix led me to the left, and as we passed, I counted five more long rows this way.

Calix brought us to the farthest row. Each stall had a name plate in front of it, and as he led me through, I looked idly over the names of the different horses kept here. We finally came to the end, and there was a larger stall here with a pair of horses inside instead of just one. My eyes dipped to read the sign in front: Elatha and Arianrhod.

Calix opened the stall door and two large Faethren Horses stood up from where they rested against one another on the ground, nickering as Calix approached. He spoke to them in a low voice, running his hand down their noses in greeting. His long white hair covered his face as he rested his forehead against the horse's. He was smiling as he pulled back, white teeth and those sharp canines flashing as he looked over to me.

"This is Elatha." Calix introduced. "He belonged to my father before me." Faethren horses were named after the Fae as they tended to live just as long as they did. Some of the horses were even rumored to have lived thousands of years. They couldn't be bred either, they were considered a gift from the gods who created them and had to be born naturally—which naturally made them the rarest breed of horse there was.

"And this is Arianrhod. She was my mother's horse." Calix said sadly, his voice betraying the pain he still felt all these years later at her loss. "They're mates, these two, and while Elatha accepted me fairly quickly after my father's death, Arianrhod hasn't accepted another rider since."

I tilted my head as I looked at the female. She was beautiful, with a gleaming silver coat, and a gorgeous lilac making up her mane and tail. It was quite a contrast to her mate, whose coat was a deep, dark blue, nearly black, and his mane and tail were a strikingly vibrant green. That tail swished now as he watched his mate approach me.

"Why don't you to try to approach her?" Calix suggested, running a hand down her silver back. I sent him an incredulous look; certain he'd lost his mind. Faethren horses were notoriously picky about their riders, and so expensive, only the Fae could ever afford to ride them.

"Are you joking? These horses are for the Fae, not humans. And if she hasn't accepted a rider since your mother—"

He chuckled, nodding to the horse, who sniffed in my direction. "She's curious about you. Just pet her. Let her meet you. If she likes you, well—"

Something incredibly sad shaded his eyes. "It would be nice to see her take a rider again. I think she'd enjoy it too, despite how picky she's been."

The smile he shot at me had the ability to melt a person completely. He was much too gorgeous for his own good—or my own good. I rolled my eyes and huffed but approached the horse slowly. She nickered at my outstretched hand, then bumped her nose into it. I let my hand pet down her nose, marveling over how soft she was. They were truly nothing like other horses. Most horse breeds had coarser hair, but a Faethren's coat was more like soft fur, despite their coats not appearing any different at first glance.

After a few moments, Calix stepped out and came back with bridles for the horses. I watched as he secured them, then handed me the reins for Arianrhod's. I gulped but took hold of them. He looked so happy at the horse's reaction to me, that I couldn't bear to disappoint him.

"You said they're a mated pair, right? And they belonged to your parents before?" I asked, nervously. He tilted his head at my question, his brows furrowing, but after a moment, his brows smoothed as he figured out what I was struggling with.

"Ah." Calix nodded. It was all he said before he saddled both horses and led them out to the ring. I waited silently, hoping more of an explanation was forthcoming. When we reached the ring, Calix finally looked over to me. "I don't know, Asteria. Truly."

Our eyes connected and it felt like the world around us ceased to be in that moment. Arianrhod should be his mate's horse, not mine. I swallowed hard, wondering why he even wanted to attempt this. Maybe, whatever this weird chemistry between us was, the horse was able to feel it.

Either way, nothing could happen. I reminded myself of that over and over until I had the will to look away. Calix cleared his throat and helped me mount the horse. His touch burned into my hips and along my leg where he showed me how to swing it over the horse. Maybe horseback riding was a bad idea after all.

Calix mounted Elatha and began showing me what to do. How to use the reins, my legs, and sounds, all to make the horse react in different ways. Faethren horses were said to be very intuitive to their riders, which would hopefully make this easier. We went around the ring several times, Calix showing me how to sit correctly in the seat, how to post correctly when riding. I didn't realize so much was involved in just riding a horse.

But as I rode, I couldn't help loving the feeling it gave me. It wasn't flying, but the freedom when the horse ran across the ground was something special. When Calix suggested leaving the rings for the trails, I agreed eagerly. We wound through the woods and out towards the cliffs, where we took a break.

Looking out over the water, I couldn't help but think of all the differences in this kingdom compared to Dusk.

"Can I ask you something?" I bit my lip as I turned to face Calix.

His eyebrow hitched up, a smirk crossing his face. "Now I'm afraid to hear it, if you're asking permission."

I huffed at him but smiled slightly as I asked, "Why is your kingdom so much more...*magical?* So much brighter? Dusk was so different."

"You know the kingdoms were created to be balanced." He sighed heavily, leaning into Elatha and petting down his mane. I nodded, urging him to continue. "Our magic, and the magic of the kingdoms themselves, works the same way. The gods imbued the land with their gifts, and when the kingdoms are completely balanced, the land, and its magic, flourish. But when the balance isn't kept, it becomes chaos. When that happens, magic gets harder to use, plants will struggle to grow."

"Is that what's happening?" I pushed; my eyebrows scrunched together as I contemplated it. I knew the kingdoms were kept going with a delicate balance, but I didn't realize it was *that* delicate. Calix looked troubled too, which didn't bode well.

"It is." He confirmed heavily, his eyes shifting from their usual violet shade to a darker amethyst. "Kingdoms like Dusk, they've grown corrupt. They no longer give the gods or the land its due reverence, and their lands shift to chaos the more power hungry they grow. Slowly, their magic wanes, and the more magical flora and fauna disappear as they begin to grow more mundane or find another place to live. It's part of why they must be stopped. Even though freeing humans is a large part of my goal, it's hardly my only one."

Calix looked at me with hardened eyes, but I could see him practically beseeching me to understand beneath it. "The further they shift to chaos, the more the rest of Celesterra will be impacted as well."

"Wait." I held up my hand, alarm pulsing through me. "Are you saying it could what—bleed into your kingdom?" The very thought was horrifying. This place was full of beauty and wonder and magic, the idea of it all disappearing...

But Calix nodded slowly, his lips turning down. "It's only a matter of time if things continue this way. They have to be stopped and actions taken to bring the continent back into balance. Otherwise, we could lose everything."

His tone was almost tortured at the thought of it, and I couldn't blame him in the least. Pain speared through me at the thought of losing all of this. I'd only just found it.

"How do we fix it?" I begged, hoping there was a plan in place. He smiled slightly at me, a look of wonder in his eyes, and I realized my slip. I winced, wishing I hadn't said *we*. Not with all we were trying to suppress.

"We end the corruption in the other monarchies." Calix growled lightly. "They begin giving the land what it needs, praying once more to the gods, and begin to act as the rulers they're meant to be, treating all peoples as they should be."

"That's it?" I asked skeptically.

"That's all we know, anyway." He admitted, and my heart sunk. "If there is more, I'm not aware of it. It may not seem like much, but it will be much more difficult than you think. Can you imagine King Astraeus or Cyrus co-operating?" He raised his brows, and it was clear the question was rhetorical. We both knew they would never.

This was why they only used their main power in Dusk, I realized. Their magic was fading. They may only have their lightning left. Their land wasn't as beautiful or magical as the Night Kingdom, because it had already faded too much. *Old Gods*. That couldn't be good. If it had already gotten to that point….

"How long? How long before it's too late?" I asked hoarsely, struggling to imagine this amazing place I'd just found, stripped of everything that made it what it was.

"It's already been happening for years." Calix told me grimly, and he reached his hand out to squeeze my shoulder briefly. "We've been slipping slowly toward chaos. We have maybe a couple years, at most, before Dusk is lost to itself. And if that happens—" His jaw worked back and forth, and darkness began leaking from his hands as he flexed them. "Dawn is Dusk's balance, so they're in just as bad a situation. Once both are completely out of balance, the rest of the kingdoms won't be able to maintain balance either. We'll all slip into chaos."

Calix nodded slowly at my horrified expression. "The kingdoms *have* to be in balance with one another. One kingdom slips to chaos, and we all fall, one after another." His voice took on a bitter tone. "They've doomed us all. Sunset and Sunrise have already shown signs, as well, and while Day and Night have been doing better, I've seen the signs here too. We don't have long to change things now."

Things began to click into place for me. I whipped around to face him fully from where I'd turned to look over the cliff.

"This is why you said you're not at war—not yet." I realized, my eyes widening. "You're planning to be, though, on a much, much bigger scale than the attacks the Resistance has been carrying out. What are you going to do? Depose them? Put monarchs in place who aren't corrupt, to begin healing the kingdoms?"

Calix looked at me for a long moment before he closed his eyes with a sigh. When he opened them, the colors in his eyes were swirling once more. It seemed to happen anytime his emotions ran high.

"I'm not sure yet." He confessed, and that scared me most of all. If he didn't know—what hope did we have? "That's what remains most frustrating for me. The gods choose the rulers, meaning I can only do so much. I have to abide by the gods' wishes, or my own kingdom will become unbalanced as well." The hopeless desperation in his eyes slid into me like a knife.

"Fuck." I said, staring at him. Realizing exactly how tricky his task was. My task too now, I suppose. I'd already signed up for freeing humans, I wasn't going to back away from a complicated situation. Not when it threatened this place that offered me a home, friends… freedom.

Not when this man looked like the weight of the world rested on his wings—shoulders didn't seem big enough to carry this burden. And I could see why—he had a beautiful kingdom, full of magic and wonder and happiness. My eyes narrowed at the thought. It had to stay that way. I wouldn't let this place become anything like Dusk. *Never.*

Calix seemed to read the thoughts spinning around in my mind, and his eyes turned heated as a smirk turned his lips upwards once more.

"There it is." He declared, the heat in his eyes setting me a bit off balance myself.

"What?" I tilted my head a bit in confusion. He swaggered up towards me, the few feet between us rapidly closing, and he reached out, brushing a lock of hair behind my ear, making my breath catch as his fingers skimmed my cheek.

"That light in you." He murmured, the aurora in his eyes captivating me as it danced through his irises. "I swear it's like it burns deep inside, and whenever you feel strongly about something, it rises to the surface. Like a star in the darkness, you shine. Stars aren't *just* beautiful, you know." He smiled, and to my consternation, I felt a blush tint my cheeks at his reference to me being beautiful. Something I'd heard a thousand times and shouldn't be making me blush, but said in that husky, sexy voice of his, it took on significance in a way it never had before.

"Stars, when the time comes, explode. The force of it can take out planets. When that light rises in you, my réalta, I imagine a star going supernova, taking out everything for miles." Calix's voice was low and filled with a promise he couldn't fulfill. I could feel an ache begin low in my body in response.

I stepped back, pressing my thighs together as I cleared my throat, hoping to distract him so he wouldn't notice.

"What does that mean? Réalta?" I asked, hoarsely. He gave me a wicked smile, not at all helping with the ache, as his eyes slipped over my curves, and I knew without a doubt that he was aware of what he was doing to me. But after a moment, he seemed to remember himself. Shaking his head, he indicated for me to mount back up before he turned and did the same. His flirtatious mood instantly vanished, in favor of a resolute, cold mask.

We should probably avoid spending time alone in the future. It was clear there was something between us, and we both had to ignore it. His mate would come one day, and the fact he was trying to be completely loyal to her before even meeting blew my mind. I couldn't imagine being celibate except for a couple times a year on Fae holidays. The kind of strength he must have, the discipline, and here I was—ruining everything for him.

THE RIDE BACK was quiet, both of us evidently thinking deep thoughts. Mine were torn between the horrifying truth I'd learned about the balance of the world, and—*him*. I needed to find a way to get rid of this attraction to him, but even more importantly, we needed to find a way to stop this world from sliding into chaos, before it was too late for everyone.

Lilith was waiting when we returned, with an invitation to tour the menagerie for me. I accepted happily, eager to leave my haunting thoughts behind. I waved goodbye to Calix, who took Arianrhod to return to the stables. He smiled widely as he watched me excitedly bouncing at the chance to see all the exotic animals he'd said were kept at the menagerie.

"Have fun!" He called, chuckling as he walked away. My eyes couldn't help following him. Or…well—following his ass, anyway. Those pants should be illegal. By the time I realized what I was doing and snapped my eyes back to Lilith, she was watching me with something like pity in her eyes.

"Don't." I groaned, burying my face in my hands. "Don't say anything." Her hand touched my shoulder lightly, and I looked up, her forest green eyes meeting mine.

"Let's go. I'm sure this will help distract you." She smiled softly, seeming eager to help.

She was right—the menagerie was more than just a distraction though, it was absolutely amazing. It had been built separately from the palace and sprawled out far behind where the stables resided on the property. I was sort of in awe of how much space it actually took up, part of it even utilizing the cliffs, with some animals making their homes in hollowed out portions of it. Magic was used to create different environments for each animal that matched their ideal home.

Lilith had all sorts of animals in so many different colors and sizes, but there were some I loved more than others. I could certainly leave the creepy ones, anything with more than four legs was just too many in my opinion. My favorite might have been the spotted rozeaffery, a strange creature with a giant neck that stretched to the trees. It was a pretty shade of pink that I couldn't help but love. Or maybe my favorite was the Plutoa Cat. It was an ice blue color, with long fangs and a sleek, muscular body made for hunting prey. Pointed ears pulled back in a snarl when we came up to its enclosure. It was love at first sight.

I knew the jungles of Sunrise contained some animals like this, but I'd so rarely left Sonmathion, I'd barely seen anything this world had to offer—and Dusk was losing everything that made these kingdoms so special. I hadn't realized how big this world was until I left home, until I'd come here more specifically. Now, I wanted to see everything, experience everything—especially if it was at risk of fading away.

I had to drink up as much of this world as I could. Soak in the pure *life* and immerse myself in all of it.

"Calix gave me permission to start it about two-hundred years ago." Lilith explained, and I turned to her, interested to hear how this place came about. "My affinity for nature, and particularly with beasts, allows me to easily find animals who were hurt or ostracized for some reason from their packs or families. I started taking in so many animals, Calix decided I needed a dedicated area for them." A sweet smile graced her face as she remembered. "Most didn't want to return to the wild once healed, and those who were cast out didn't want to be on their own."

"So, all the animals are here willingly?" A smile twitched at my lips. I should have known. Beastmaster. She wouldn't keep animals here that didn't want to be—balance of nature and all that.

"Of course!" She nodded earnestly. "We call it a menagerie because people can visit. The animals enjoy being admired." She smirked slightly and I couldn't help matching it at the thought of them preening for visitors. "But really, it's more a rescue and habitat for them than anything. Any who wish to return once they're healed, are free to do so. Though, as you can see, we create large enclosures for them where they're safe and happy. They have room to roam, and I visit them all daily. I do have people who help me maintain everything, of course, and they visit often as well." Lilith looked so proud of her work here, and I couldn't blame her.

"Faunus has given me a great gift for helping his creatures, I cherish it, truly." Her smile shifted from pride to something softer. Something like peace. Serenity.

I was a bit jealous of that, honestly. I had never known peace, not a day in my life. I wondered what such a thing felt like.

Faunus was the Fae's god of beasts. All animals fell under his purview. He and the Goddess of Nature, Florus, worked hand in hand. They were said to be brother and sister. Created to work together. If Lilith had been singled out by them to be gifted her powers, I could certainly understand why she took such pride, and found such peace in it. Fae took nature and the balance of it seriously, and after my conversation with Calix, I was finally beginning to understand why.

Though it did make me wonder. My own gods, the Old Gods, were said to have been shoved aside by the Fae's gods. But if that was indeed the case, how were the Fae gods gifted control of things like the nature of this world?

"What does your animal form look like?" I couldn't help but ask Lilith, shaking more serious thoughts from my head. She smiled, something slyer than I imagined the tranquil, nature-loving Fae could conjure, and then she—shifted.

I gasped as a willowy female body rapidly changed until there was now a gigantic wolf in her place. And I do mean *giant*—the thing was taller than I was. Its fangs dripped with saliva as it sat back on its haunches.

"Uh…wow." Was all I could manage as I blinked at her.

She was beautiful, still. Forest green eyes looked back at me, surrounded by black fur shot through with blood red.

"My parents were both able to shift into wolves too. It runs strongly in my family."

I shivered as her voice echoed in my head. I'd heard rumors the Fae could speak telepathically while in their animal forms, but I'd never known for sure. The feeling was decidedly strange. Not quite invasive, but sort of like someone walked into my house without knocking, even though I didn't mind the visitor. Unexpected and a tad off putting at first.

"That's amazing." I marveled, looking over her wolf form with wide eyes. "I wish I could shift into something fun like you guys."

What I wouldn't give to be able to turn into a dragon and fly the skies, to stretch my wings and soar as far and as high as I wanted. To be able to breathe fire and flambé assholes like Cyrus without blinking. It would be indescribable. As much as I wished I could shift into a dragon, I would honestly take anything—humans were already so powerless compared to the Fae, and this was just another thing I didn't have in comparison.

Lilith laughed softly at my complaint as she shifted back into her Fae form. Her large, muscular lupine form slimming and narrowing until a Fae woman stood before me once more.

"You're perfect just the way you are." Lilith countered, obviously a joke made in response to my whining, but they hit me harder than I think she intended. Years of being sneered at by other females had its impact. To think that before Emmie and Pris, I'd never had female friends, and now I had Lilith, Harpina, Ilta, and Delia, who were quick to invite me into their circle. It was a bit overwhelming, but I'd never been happier.

Turns out, having friends is great. Who knew?

But I did wonder if the only reason we were becoming friends now was pure circumstance. Would they have scorned me like Verin and the other girls of Sonmathion had we met in a different way? It wasn't fair of me to think that when they were friends with other humans already. Still—

"I mean it, you know." Lilith insisted. "We wouldn't want you any other way." She must have read something of what I was thinking on my face. I sniffed, throwing my arms around her, and she hugged me back while I mumbled my thanks into her wavy hair. "I'm glad you're here, Asteria. Truly. And I have a feeling that things are bound to get more interesting now that you are."

CHAPTER 27

"Get out!" A glass shattered on the wall beside me, and I jumped as another glass hit the other side.

"Emmie—" I attempted, but couldn't even get another word out before I had to duck a shoe. *Fuck*.

"Get! Out!" Emmie screamed again, and I quickly fled through the door, pressing my back against it as I closed my eyes.

Eris must have heard the commotion, her room being right next door. She came and sat down beside me.

"It's not your fault." Eris sighed heavily, leaning her head back against the wall. "She's lost, Asteria. I'm trying to help, but she doesn't want to see me either. She actually accused me of being jealous of her place with the king and taking her away because of it." The incredulity in her tone is fierce, and my heart drops at the knowledge of how far gone she really is.

"Fuck." I mumbled, burying my face in my hands.

"Yeah. Fuck." Eris chuckled wryly. The two of us sat there until Emmie finished screaming herself hoarse. While we may never be best friends, we were at least united in our desire to help Emmie.

"I'll have to think of something. Some way to get through to her." I said mostly to myself as I thought about it. Eris sighed as she stood, heading back to her room.

"Let me know if you do." She offered, looking resigned, and I hated it. There had to be something we could do. At least the other humans who'd left Dusk, Raziel in particular, were recovering well. Priscilla and I had gone to see them before I left to visit Emmie, and everyone seemed in high spirits,

340

grateful to be out and finally free. Emmie was the only one clinging to her chains—what made it even more heartbreaking was she didn't recognize they *were* chains.

I made my way back to my room and showered before heading to dinner. It was being held in the casual dining room tonight, and Delia showed up to help me get ready and show me the way. We chatted about my trip through the menagerie, laughing about the different animals living there. When we reached the dining room, Delia had an excited smile on her face, and I cocked my head, wondering why she was so excited to go to dinner, but she just pushed me through the doors.

I understood immediately, my jaw dropping as I took in the room.

It looked nothing at all like the rest of the palace and was instead designed to look like a giant tree. A trunk came out from the middle of the table, reaching up to branches that stretched across the ceiling and fell down the sides of the walls. The table itself matched the trunk, made of a light wood, all its swirls and knots showing, the edges uneven but smoothed down. The chairs were made of the same wood but had green cushions that matched the color of the leaves falling down the walls. The bottom of the walls were covered in all kinds of flowers. The room didn't look like it belonged here at all, looking more like how I imagined the homes of the dryads of Weathrian.

The others were watching my reaction, smiling and laughing as I looked around, fascinated. All except Calix, who sat at the head of the table and watched me intently.

"What do you think?" Eryx called out as I walked forward, mesmerized.

"It's—it's incredible. How is this even…" I couldn't form words. It seemed so out of place, yet somehow so natural. Eryx pulled a chair out for me, one directly next to him and Calix, and helped me into my seat with a smirk.

"Calix's family built the palace to have *all* aspects represented." He replied vaguely, a sly smile on his face.

I narrowed my eyes at him, "That doesn't explain as much as you seem to think it does."

Harpina rolled her eyes and reached for the food being brought out and placed on the table by their servants. Paid servants, I had learned, not slaves. They weren't even just human, but Fae as well. It was apparently quite a cushy job, and one many applied for whenever there was an opening. It was even more amazing to see than this room, in truth.

Liviana glared at Harpina but turned to face me. She was across from me, next to Calix. I was still trying to avoid looking at him and that inscrutable look on his face.

"The palace was designed to be a showcase of celestial power, but our ancestors wanted to honor all the gods as well." Liviana informed me. "They built rooms scattered throughout the palace that are dedicated to them, each god having their own room that's designed in a way to represent and honor that god's power. This one is for Florus, clearly."

I sent her a thankful smile for taking pity on me, and she returned it before she swept her silver hair over her shoulder and began to dig into her food. Her hair was more like liquid silver than white, unlike her brother's, whose was a tad whiter, reminding me more of the moon. Paired with her silver seer's eyes, it was almost unnerving, but her beauty prevented it from truly being so. Thinking of her explanation, I went completely still, before I looked at Calix.

He was watching me with a smirk, like he realized exactly what had occurred to me. I leaned over to him slightly, whispering, as moot as that was with Fae hearing.

"When she says all gods, does that mean—" I raised a brow and gave him a look. His smile widened as the rest of the table roared in laughter.

"Would you like me to show you the room dedicated to Hedone?" Baach wiggled his eyebrows at me as I turned to glare at him, but he just laughed joyfully.

I looked around the table, at the sly smiles they all shot at me, that let me know there was indeed a room dedicated to the god of sex. Ilta caught my eye down the table, where she was biting her lip and looking between me, Calix, and Baach. I turned back to look at Calix and found him glaring at his friend.

"You have a sex room?!" I hissed at him, and his eyes shot back to me immediately, smoldering with heat, even as the room erupted in laughter once more.

At least until Titan cleared his throat, "Enough of that. Eat, girl. You're going to burn all that food off training in the morning."

His gruff voice instantly brought the rest back in line, and I admired that ability immensely. I watched his eyes cut over to Calix in concern, but the king beside me just gave a winning smile to the man who was basically his father figure. My lips twitched, thinking of him flashing that smile at Titan as a child as he tried to get away with doing something he wasn't supposed to.

Oh. That *was* what he was doing, wasn't it? He wasn't supposed to be flirting or pinning those smoldering eyes on me. He had a mate out there somewhere, and his friends—his family—were making sure he didn't do something he'd regret forever.

Me.

That thought bowed my shoulders, and I tucked into my food to avoid looking at Priscilla, who was shooting me concerned looks from down the table. When she wasn't doing that, her head was tilting toward Callisto with rapt attention. Ilta was too busy flirting with Baach to pay much attention, and Lilith and Harpina were arguing once again. The softer, nature-loving Lilith and the harder, battle-loving Harpina seemed to butt heads constantly, though it was done with love. Eryx was caught up in conversation with Liv, and Titan was ignoring everyone as he pounded down more food than I could eat in an entire day.

But Calix—we seemed to be having the same struggle. I couldn't keep my eyes from him, every other minute, I'd feel the pull to look over at him—to take in that silvery white hair that I wanted to run my fingers through and see if it was as soft as it looked, to see those eyes that filled with all the colors of the night sky when he was emotional. I wanted to see if he was the serious, reserved king at that moment or the playful flirt—or even the loving friend when among his people.

We both pointedly ignored any time we caught one another glancing over, our eyes meeting. Even though the instant our eyes locked it was like a spark catching—fire roaring in my veins. Looking away felt like a crime, but it had to be done. I tried to focus on the conversations around me, and everyone tried to include me, but my mind was firmly stuck on the man beside me.

When I looked up, Liv was smirking at me with this *knowing*, in her eyes. I blushed, and studiously kept my eyes away from the sexy king beside me. I deserved a medal for that alone.

"We should totally do it!" Ilta squealed in happiness, clapping her hands together as she absolutely beamed at Baach. His cheeks were almost as red as his hair as his hazel eyes lit up at her smile.

"Do what?" I leaned forward, curious, and Ilta turned that beaming smile my way.

"Baach suggested we host a ball to celebrate your arrival!" She cheerfully replied. My lip started to curl, remembering the last ball I attended. I felt a hand land on my shoulder—Eryx—and I looked up at him, feeling my rising disgust recede.

"It won't be like the balls you attended in Dusk, I promise." He whispered quietly to me, and I pushed all those messy feelings about my time in Dusk away.

"Oh no, Asteria." Ilta's smile dimmed, and I hated myself a bit for that. "It will be nothing like that dreadful place." Ilta sniffed, chin rising, "The balls here are so much fun! You'll love it, I swear." She aimed her puppy dog eyes at me as I ignored Calix and Eryx snickering beside me.

"She's right." Delia added, leaning further over to see me down the table. "You'll have a great time, it's not anything like Dusk." She was backed up by the others and when Pris caught my eye, she gave me a hopeful look I could only sigh deeply at.

"Okay." I sighed in defeat. "Do I need a dress or is one I have good enough?" Ilta's squeal made Lilith cringe, making me wonder if her Fae hearing was amplified by wolf hearing.

"We'll all get new dresses!" Ilta exclaimed. "It will be so much fun! We can take you shopping in Moonglow, it's the best shopping experience a girl can have. Right, Liv?"

"It's my favorite thing about this city." Liviana told me, looking more excited than I'd seen her yet. "You definitely have to let us take you, Asteria!" I helplessly nodded my agreement and the two of them instantly began talking styles, cuts, and colors as Harpina rolled her eyes.

"I'll make sure it's a night to remember." Baach promised Ilta, his eyes still glued to her, and I watched a soft blush take over her cheeks.

I couldn't help the small smile as I watched them all. I'd never imagined having so many people in my life—and especially didn't imagine caring about them. But once my heart had cracked open for one person, it seemed it couldn't be locked back up again—the floodgates were open, and they all streamed right in.

I had never been this happy when I was alone though, even having Soren in his limited capacity as a lover was nothing like this. Years spent with only my dreams to keep me going and losing myself in my fantasies left me with a bitterness I wasn't ever able to shake. Loneliness gnaws on the soul, seeking to dim its light. But now, all these people—even the Fae I once hated—had pushed that loneliness away.

For the most part, anyway. Watching Ilta flirt with Baach, I found myself strangely longing for—someone—to have a person in my life in a romantic capacity beyond just sex. I had *never* wanted something like that before, and had shut down any inclination for it long ago. Love was for the Fae alone.

Except in Night Kingdom, humans were equal with Fae, allowed everything they were—including love. And now I found myself *yearning*. I nearly snarled at the thought, I wasn't a girl to sit around pining for some moon headed man of darkne—...*someone*—not anyone specific, of course. That was not me, was the point.

"How about that ride?" Calix whispered huskily into my ear, causing me to jolt in surprise. The smirk on his face made me glower at him, but I couldn't help the excited trembling of my hands or the smile twitching onto my face at the thought.

"Come on, my réalta. Let's get you into the sky." Calix's smirk transformed into a genuine smile as I squealed in happiness—my eyes rapidly widened to the size of the dinner plates on the table, my hand coming up to slap over my mouth like it could contain the embarrassing sound. The others laughed, Baach nearly falling into Eryx as he doubled over in laughter, but Calix just smiled warmly at me, and something in me *melted*.

"Flying is one of the best things in the world, and I can't even imagine not being able to do it." Calix said quietly. "I know you love flying as well, and you've been kept from it for too long. Come, let's get you up where you belong."

I cursed myself as tears pricked my eyes, but I reached out and grasped Calix's outstretched hand. His fingers curled over mine, warm, but calloused from years of wielding a blade and hard work other kings refused to bother with themselves.

Those same kings would certainly never allow a human to ride on their back. I couldn't explain how thankful I was for this opportunity, but he seemed to know implicitly. He lifted his other hand, sliding his index finger under my eye and brushing away the single tear that had escaped. No words passed between us. There was simply an understanding—one between two people who felt they belonged among the sky. There were other things in that stare—wishes, hopes, and dreams, along with the crushed realizations of never having any of them. It felt like it lasted an eternity, but finally, Titan pointedly cleared his throat, and we waved our goodbyes as we walked out the door.

Calix led me down the sparkling halls towards one of the many back doors, though this one was just as grand as the main entrance. Only instead of the phases of the moon, it had a swirling galaxy in sparkling purple and green etched into the black door, even the runes here were done in alternating purple and green. The guards posted here opened the doors for us and Calix led me past the back gardens and onto where the cliff stopped and spilled out to a sea of stars.

The aurora was shimmering in the air—pink, purple, green, and blue strands gleaming and swaying through the night sky, while the stars glittered radiantly—brighter and numbering surely thousands more than I'd ever seen. I'd loved the night sky all my life, and I'd never seen it look so ethereal that it took my breath away as it did now.

"The magic of my kingdom." Calix said quietly, looking over at me and watching my reaction. "It makes the nights more beautiful than anywhere else, with more stars, more glimpses of other worlds, and the aurora is a constant here instead of just appearing once in a while like in other kingdoms."

"And now I can fly among them?" I asked with a large smile as I gestured to the twinkling sea of stars filled with dancing bands of colored light.

"Oh, yes." He enthused, his smile growing. "I can't wait for you to experience this. If you think you loved flying before, you'll be hounding me for rides every day after this." His laugh was filled with joy, and I wanted to swallow that joy whole, wanted to take his mouth with mine and experience what that emotion felt like on his tongue—because he seemed to nearly glow with it in this light. The shadows played around him, as they often did, darkness clung to him like a lover, but it only seemed to enhance the beauty he so clearly radiated.

"Let's go, then!" I shook myself from my thoughts, eager to be up in the sky.

Calix smirked as he began walking backwards with a swagger in his step, though I wasn't sure how he maintained it when moving in reverse. He paused quite a distance from me, and then—it began. I watched in awe as he began to shift, rapidly taking up much more space as an Otherworld damned *dragon* replaced where the beautiful Fae king just stood.

It was—fucking intimidating, to be honest, but he must have sensed that somehow, as he rumbled in what I distinctly felt was amusement. How I could tell that's what it was, I had no idea, but I brushed it off as I took him in. He was truly massive—like his wings, he was mostly black with purple interspersed throughout. Long, membranous wings shot out and stretched before curling back into his bulk, giving me a glimpse of the scalier side. He shifted until he was leaning down, his leg and wing positioned to allow me to...*climb.*

I swallowed hard and reached a trembling hand out, gasping as it connected with his scales. They were warm to the touch, but not uncomfortably so. His huge head turned toward me, and he made that rumbling sound again, his lips peeling back and exposing giant teeth that could snap me in half with one bite—but I had no fear. Even I ran my eyes up his body and to his head, taking in the sharp horns there. To my amusement, they actually formed a crown across his head—each one tipped with purple like jewels dotting the spikes of a crown.

I looked down and met his eyes, inhaling sharply—just like with Lilith, his eyes remained the same color. Large purple irises stared back at me, slitted and double lidded, making them seem much more alien, yet somehow it still seemed like him—like Calix. That thought gave me the nerve I needed, and I planted my foot, using my hands to boost myself upwards.

When I reached his back, there was a sort of natural dip behind the neck that I took advantage of, swinging my leg over and sitting down. I marveled over the fact I was astride a dragon, let alone that I was astride Calix. I'd analyze that thought later. I ran my hands over his heated scales, a purring noise whistling out from his maw that made me smile and continued petting his scales.

"Hold on." Calix firmly instructed, his voice echoing in my mind as he shifted upwards. A row of spikes ran down his neck and ended just before my seat, and figuring that's what he meant, I grabbed onto the ones closest to me. With a powerful beat of those giant wings, he was launching over the cliff, and we were sailing through the air. I held on for dear life, my legs burning at the stretch—he was considerably wider than a horse. But it didn't take long before any discomfort was a blurry memory.

I gasped as we flew higher, and the stars surrounded me completely. I reached out a trembling hand, thinking of my dreams with Luna, of the darkness that reached for me, of dancing among the stars. And as Calix swooped gracefully through the sky, it felt like I truly *was* dancing among them. I could feel tears streaming down my face, but I couldn't summon even a shred of embarrassment.

This was everything I'd ever wanted, to fly up among the stars and be free—and here I was, doing exactly that. It was beyond anything in this world or any other. Majestic. Amazing. Incredible. Unfathomable. No words could truly describe the feeling that moved through me, the feeling of belonging—of...*peace*.

I held out both my arms as Calix glided smoothly through the skies, like I'd spread my own wings to fly. I could vividly imagine the weight of wings on my back. I focused so hard on it, that it was like the feeling became *real*. It felt like that weight was truly there, but they were struggling. They wanted to break free and fly—but couldn't.

Because I didn't have wings, no matter how much I wished for them. But this—this was more than I could have ever hoped for. No matter how much my skin twinged, and my back ached—I was accustomed to that pain after all—no matter how real it felt that I had wings that wanted to burst free and fly in that moment, I would appreciate what I had. And that was a king who let me fly on the back of his dragon and experience the amazing joy of flight for myself.

CHAPTER 28

I SLEPT like the dead that night, for as amazing as flying on a dragon was, it exhausted muscles I didn't even know I had. Then Titan and Harpina, who had decided to join Titan in training me, worked those exhausted muscles to their breaking point. By the time I was done, I was forced to take a nap just to be able to get through lunch. I wasn't used to so much physical activity, but I had to acclimate to it if I wanted to be part of the Resistance and the coming war.

I didn't have magic, super strength, or speed like the Fae—I couldn't go to war on a hope and a prayer. I needed to know how to fight. Titan assured me that he would get me to a sufficient level of skill in time, and Harpina promised to teach me some dirty tricks females could use while fighting. Once I got to that point, anyway—I had to manage holding a sword for longer than a minute without my muscles screaming first.

After lunch, I decided to wander around the palace to familiarize my-self with the areas I hadn't been to yet. I stopped to examine the art on the walls, which seemed to be depicting the Otherworld, especially Tartarus for some reason, when Calix walked around the corner—stopping short as he spotted me.

"Asteria." He smiled, walking towards me, and it was only then I noticed Ilta trailing his steps. "What brings you over here?" I was in a part of the palace that contained offices, so I had no real reason to be here.

"Sorry." I winced, ducking my head so my hair hid my face from him. "I just wanted to explore a bit." Old Gods, maybe this was a bad idea. Cyrus would have been—

"You don't have to apologize, you're free to explore as you wish." Calix insisted, looking somewhat bemused by my apology. *Right,* Calix and Cyrus were two very different people. Cyrus had instilled a fear in me that was hard to shake, but I had to stifle that instinctual reaction. I was free now, and Cyrus couldn't touch me. I would repeat that to myself until I stopped acting like the scared mouse I certainly wasn't.

"If you aren't busy though—" Calix began, a hopeful gleam lighting up his eyes. "I could show you the place I told you had to be experienced in person. My meeting this afternoon was delayed so I have time if you do." He looked genuinely excited at the prospect, but Ilta looked between us with an indecipherable expression on her face.

I bit my lip, knowing it wasn't exactly smart to be alone with him, but—I was too curious to see this mysterious place. Curiosity won out over caution.

"That'd be great." I replied, and Calix's face lit up with a smile that made my agreement completely worth it—the man could blind a girl with that thing.

Calix brought me out to the stables, where we saddled up Elatha and Arianrhod. I was pleased I'd get some more practice riding, no matter where he was taking me—though after riding on a dragon, a horse just couldn't compare. But I would take what I could get, anything to experience that thrill of flying through the wind, completely unfettered.

I followed Calix's lead as he led us over to the east side of the palace, opposite to where Cosmic Dust Stables sat. Moving out past the palace grounds, we came to a small river that had a bridge arching over it, leading to the other side. The bridge was made of some kind of gleaming gray stone, with specks in it that sparkled in the sun. We led the horses over the bridge, their hooves clopping loudly on the stone, and were immediately enveloped into the woods. The sound of hooves was replaced by rustling leaves and bird calls, and my next inhalation came with the scent of wood and faint floral notes.

The forest itself was made up entirely of Darkelm trees, stretching high to the sky with thick black trunks, their branches extending out like they were drunk—more squiggles than straight lines, branching out every which way. They were topped with red leaves that looked like blood against the black wood.

"They change color throughout the year." Calix informed me as we trotted along the path carved through the woods. "Since it's the Harvest season, their leaves are red, but they'll shift to silver for Zima, and then into green for Pranvera and in Sommer they'll become a shining gold." I looked around, trying to picture the different colors.

"What's your favorite?" I couldn't help but ask, curious which season brought the best view of the forest.

Calix paused, his brows flying up in surprise. "I don't think anyone's ever asked me that." He barked a laugh, but then took a moment, giving the question some consideration.

"Silver." Calix nodded, his gaze seeming to look somewhere far off, and I wondered what he was seeing in that moment. "When the trees turn silver, the forest looks like a blanket of stars from a distance. With the prophecy—" He stopped abruptly, shaking his head. "Anyway, silver is my favorite, even if I prefer Pranvera and Sommer as far as weather goes." He smirked, trying to shift the conversation, but I was stuck on what he hadn't said.

"What prophecy?" I prodded him, but Calix just shook his head, and it was clear I wasn't going to get answers right now. I knew the royals all had birth prophecies, gifted to the parents by the Oracle prior to their children being born, but Liviana also spoke her fair share of prophecies, so it could really be anything.

"We didn't have these back in Sunrise." I offered, looking around at the Darkelms, hoping to nudge the now deathly silent king into talking once more. "We mostly had shatay trees, which always had green leaves."

Calix nodded, head turning slowly to look at me. "I've been to Sunrise many times, the capital anyway. It's well known for those jungles, and for good reason."

"I didn't live near the jungle." I clarified. "That's mostly all up north. I lived on the coast in a little village that surrounded a vineyard." Speaking of Sunrise brought my parents to mind, and the many questions that would forever be unanswered—how were they doing, were they okay, did they miss me? I'd tried not to think of them at all since Placement Day, and I suddenly felt terrible about that. I thought it would make it easier, just to bury it and move on, but this place, and these people, had been ripping open all the seams I'd stitched around my heart, until every single thing I had buried in there came roaring out.

Calix seemed to sense my shift in mood, concern shining in his eyes, and it felt like he was staring straight into my soul.

"Tell me about it." He urged softly. "About your home." He somehow understood intuitively that I was struggling, but his words left me equally choked up.

"It wasn't home. Not really." I confessed, before it all spilled out of me in a torrent. I told him about growing up in Sunrise, about my parents, even about the girls in my village and Soren. By the end, I was red faced and embarrassed to have unloaded so much on him, but Calix just smiled softly at me.

"Thank you, Asteria." The aurora was back in his eyes, and I couldn't help wondering what I'd said to stoke such emotion in him. "For trusting me with your past. I know it's not easy, but I'm honored that you shared it with me."

I looked down, letting my hair hide my face as I tried to find words to respond, but after spewing out so many, I'd apparently run out. I just nodded, and Calix let me be, riding along in silence as I gathered the pieces of myself back together. He was too good at figuring out my emotions, somehow knowing exactly what I needed.

As we trotted along the path, a few bugs had flown into my face here and there, and I'd swatted at them as I'd been talking, but now that silence had overtaken us, the bugs seemed to nearly triple in number—all of which had apparently decided to target my face. I sputtered as I tried to get rid of the rapidly increasing number of bugs, but for every one I swatted, three more appeared.

"What in the Otherworld?!" I shrieked as I almost fell off the horse trying to dodge them.

Calix's chuckle was distracting, deep and throaty, sending a shiver through my body. "They're starflies. It's strange, they normally avoid people." His purple eyes were sparkling with dark laughter as he watched me try to get rid of them.

I gave him a look, letting him know exactly how unimpressed I was by his leaving me to deal with them on my own. As one landed on my arm, I jumped in the saddle—thank the Old Gods Faethren horses don't spook like normal ones. I looked down at the insect that assaulted me, and paused as I finally got a good look at it, realizing it was actually quite pretty. Unlike the gross bugs I'd dealt with in Sonmathion, these had long gossamer wings in a shining silvery color, their bodies layered with a sparkling refraction of light that gave off the appearance of millions of colors. It looked like the refraction of a diamond or a star opal, with a multitude of colors hidden within, leaving me riveted by their beauty.

"See? Nothing to worry about." Calix exhaled breathily, and I swung my head towards him. The reverence he showed was certainly more than the situation called for, and I tilted my head, disturbing a few of the starflies in the process and causing them to flutter around my head.

"I've never seen them act like this" Calix watched me, wide eyed, as he brought his horse closer to mine. "They're usually only drawn out at night when the stars are high in the sky. Legend says they were created by the Goddess Asteria herself and she made them out of pure starlight. Supposedly, that's why they only come out at night because they're drawn to the stars. Like calling to like."

Calix reached out towards one of the starflies on my shoulder, but only succeeded in scaring them off—the starflies all flying off at once. We both watched, mesmerized, as they flew away in a sparkling conflux of color, disappearing into the thick red leaves of the Darkelms that hid them away.

"Why would they act like that then?" I asked him, the experience was utterly bizarre, but I couldn't deny learning that creatures who were supposedly created by my namesake liked me and felt—kind of unfathomable to me, in a good way. I had never been allowed to learn much about the goddess growing up. We were only taught the basics about the Fae gods, and anything beyond that, like the many stories collected in their vast mythology, was not permitted. Fae gods weren't for mortals after all. But I'd always been curious, and learning about my namesake was something special for me.

Calix shook his head, silvery white hair shaking back and forth and stealing my attention for a moment. I would have assumed the starflies would have been more attracted to him—King of Night and its skies, with hair the same sheen as their wings.

"I have no idea. Maybe they can tell you're named after their creator. Who can say?" He shrugged, but his eyes seemed too intent, looking from me to the tree that the starflies had disappeared into. It didn't seem like he was dodging giving me the answer—he seemed truly astounded by what had just happened.

"Well, I've always been drawn to the stars, maybe they can sense that. Like calling to like, as you said." My admittance had Calix's eyes back on me and away from the trees.

"Is that so?" He rumbled, his brow riding in tandem with the side of his mouth as he smirked.

"I used to sneak out of my room at night to go watch the stars." I nodded with a soft smile, thinking back on those nights. "They were—so unlike anything else in this world. They weren't just shining specs of light in the sky to me, but something perfectly free. They could roam the sky at their leisure, never forced to the ground. They were able to avoid all the trials and tribulations of life on Adamah, and I envied them for that. I would have given anything to trade places with one, even for a night—just to spend that time dancing around the sky and lighting up the world."

I bit my lip, ending the stream of wistful thoughts spewing from me, and wishing I could swallow them back down. They symbolized weakness—a representation of the years I spent under slave masters, where freedom had been a dream. Before Calix somehow managed to deliver exactly that. It was embarrassing how often I spent dreaming of a different life. My mother always chastised me for getting lost in dreams, and I didn't need this tantalizing king to know how pathetic I truly was.

A finger lifted my chin upwards, and I was immediately caught in Calix's intense gaze. The aurora was beginning to bleed into his purple irises as he stared at me with an expression I couldn't begin to unravel.

"I understand. More than you might think." Calix admitted, a growl lining his voice, matching the fierceness of his expression. "I may not have dealt with the same thing, but I've spent plenty of nights flying the skies, wishing I could just stay lost in them. There, nothing else mattered but the sky and the stars and the moon. I could leave everything else behind and just *be*."

It was difficult to look away, a fire catching deep inside that urged me to dig my claws into him and until I found his heart in its cage and grasped it— making it *mine*, and mine alone. I blinked rapidly; the urge was so savage—it took me more than a moment to bury it deep down where I kept everything else I couldn't deal with.

I could have sworn his canines had lengthened, looking more like full fangs as his lip curled up and he inhaled deeply—a moan rattling in his chest. I could imagine what he was sensing from me at this moment—I nearly sighed, another ruined pair of panties thanks to King Calix.

I forced myself to shake off the strange occurrence, pulling back and offering him a shy smile. After a moment, he managed to break himself out of whatever primal surge had overtaken us, but I ruminated on the words that prompted the sudden spike of arousal, and realized that Calix, of all people, actually understood and felt similarly—not thinking me pathetic for my musings. It filled me with a rush of unexpected warmth. Not just lust or the breathless kind of wonder he often inspired, but something deeper—something dangerous.

We continued on our way, directing the horses down the beaten path, but I kept feeling the distinct sensation of Calix's eyes on me. After what felt like an eternity, he finally brought his horse to a stop, and I followed suit, dismounting Arianrhod. I looked up at the trees surrounding us, wondering what exactly he was hoping to show me. He smiled secretively, like he knew something I didn't—which, I supposed, was true.

"Come on." He tilted his head to the right before walking in that direction towards what looked like a thicket of trees.

He pushed aside the red and black branches, revealing a small path that he stepped onto, holding back the branches so I could follow.

"This isn't what I want to show you, but since it's on the way, I figured it would be a good time to visit." Calix said as we walked into a large clearing, my eyes widening as I took in the area.

"What is this?" I breathed, as we walked toward a giant stone statue. Three people were depicted, one of them holding a large bowl that was filled with—some type of water? But not any water like I'd seen before.

"This is our altar, where we come to pray and where we host most of our celebrations." Calix informed me quietly, and I looked over at him with wide shocked eyes. It was illegal for humans to see such a thing in all of Celesterra.

Calix chuckled, "We don't forbid humans from attending here, in fact, most of them have converted to follow our gods…since they found out the truth." He finished softly.

I opened my mouth to ask what he was talking about, my brows drawing together, but he walked up to the largest statue.

"This is Erebus, my ancestor, one of the two kings of the gods, alongside Earendel." He informed me reverently, and it was clear Erebus meant a great deal to him. "Erebus is the god of darkness. Here, his idol protects the Night Water. This water comes directly from the Otherworld, holding the essence of darkness itself within it.

My mouth fell open as Calix grabbed my hand and pulled me forward to get a closer look. The water was indeed dark, but the black depths glittered, and purple and green swirls shimmering within it, making it look like galaxies swirled around the bowl. The essence of darkness may be contained in it, but that couldn't be all it was.

"How in Tartarus does water from the Otherworld exist in our world?" I asked, feeling breathless with wonder as I looked over at him.

"That is knowledge left unknown." Calix smirked with a lazy shrug of his shoulders. His wording caught my attention, after months of trying to riddle out Cyrus and his family—I knew doublespeak when I heard it.

That knowledge was deliberately left unknown. And if I had to guess, well—who better than a descendant of Erebus to keep the god's secrets?

I blew out a heavy breath. I supposed I couldn't be mad if he was keeping the secret for a literal *god*.

I looked at the other two figures depicted in the statue, curiosity rising. "Who are they, then?"

"This is Nox," Calix smiled widely, pointing to the statue of a male on the right. "He's the god of night, the one who has dominion over my kingdom. Erebus is his father, meaning night is part of darkness." Catching the confusion on my face, he explained further. "Think of it sort of like how our kingdoms work here. Erebus is the king, so he handles the high-level tasks, while Nox is like a lord who oversees some of the king's domain.

I nodded—it still sounded a bit strange, but then, I was used to the nebulous Old Gods, who had no specific names or roles.

"The only part of night Nox doesn't rule is the stars. *That*—" Calix smiled widely, eyes locking on mine. "Is obviously left to your namesake: Asteria."

He led me over to the statue on the left, depicting the goddess I'd wished to know all my life. I breathed out, long and deep, examining her. *Asteria.* The goddess was depicted with beautiful, perfectly symmetrical features, wide round eyes and full lips in a heart shaped face, curtained by long, flowing hair. A body blessed with rounded curves, and only a light, clinging dress to cover them. I couldn't help wondering where the sculptor had gotten their inspiration from. The goddess's hands were out with her palms facing upwards, and little stars seemed to almost bounce in her hand—even in stone. Inexplicable wonder filled me as I devoured her likeness.

"We pray to all three here." Calix said softly, like he didn't want to interrupt my inspection of the statue. "The Blessed Trinity: Darkness, night, and stars." I turned to face him, and he was watching me with a soft look on his face. His angular features, with his sharp cheekbones and strong jaw, made him fierce and stunning, a face you wouldn't expect could contain such softness—yet he managed it. His eyes shined in the shadow of the forest, and I cleared my throat before I could be pulled under their spell.

"Why would humans convert to the Fae religion?" I asked, before I allowed myself to get sidetracked further. It seemed unreal to me when the Fae gods had abandoned us, giving the Fae immortality and magic and leaving mortals with nothing. As much as I'd always wished to know more about Asteria, the bitterness clanged through me. An ugly, uncontrollable type of rage that cut deep inside filled me at the thought of humans worshiping those who left us to our fates, at the hands of those like Cyrus.

Calix gave a long, tired sigh. "Because what you know of them is false, Asteria. What you need to understand first, is that humans are not native to this world." He looked so earnest, yet his words made no sense. "Many, many years ago, the Fae sent the Wild Hunt to bring back creatures they could use as their slaves. Humans were found and brought back to this world. The Old Gods you pray to? They never existed here. They are whatever memory remains of the gods worshiped in the world humans originally came from, passed down for generations."

All the bitterness and rage evaporated, leaving me a hollowed-out shell on the inside, nothing but numb in the wake of his declaration.

Calix grabbed my hands, squeezing them and bringing my attention to the fact they were trembling. My lips parted, but no words came out of my suddenly dry mouth.

"I know this is a—shock." Calix said hesitantly.

I laughed incredulously, the empty sound foreign to my ears. "A shock? You just told me everything I've ever known is a lie. We're not even from this world? How do you know this?" My words came faster and faster, hysteria spilling out in increasing volume.

I couldn't comprehend the knowledge. I'd never been very religious, never participated in the few religious practices dedicated to the Old Gods my village had held, but still—knowing they didn't even exist here? That we'd been brought here from another world, just to be slaves? That familiar rage roared back up in me. Swamping my senses until it was all I could see—light flashing behind my eyes and my blood rushing like a glittering firestorm in my veins.

"This is why we're enslaved?" I demanded. "We were taken and…and *bred* for this purpose by the Fae. This is why we don't have immortality or magic. We weren't abandoned by the "new" gods at all. They'd always been the *only* gods here." I laughed harshly, but Calix squeezed my hands once more, looking down at me intently.

"Yes, but you and me?" Calix growled, grabbing my attention. "We're going to stop them from using humans as slaves, my réalta. I may not be able to return humans to whatever world you originally came from, but the gods of this land? They accept all, not just their children, and they will surely guide us as we dismantle what the Fae of millennia ago put in place."

I looked up at him, witnessing his sincerity, his promise. This Fae, he wasn't like the others—something inside me had known he wasn't from the beginning. I had never trusted Cyrus, but Calix, it was all too easy to trust him. He had spent years freeing humans, helping them out of the terrible situations they'd been enslaved to. He was the only one worried about the balance. He was nothing like the others.

"Yes, we will destroy all of those who don't agree with our plans." I hissed, the ferocity in my tone so at odds with the otherwise silent, peaceful clearing. If the gods truly could hear me, they would mark my vow: I wouldn't stop until all the humans were freed.

Calix slowly smiled, a vicious, malignant thing, like he actually enjoyed the bloodthirsty determination and fury blazing through me. His own inner monster coming out to play with mine. "Yes, *we will.* We will topple this world to its knees, and then, we'll build a better world for all in its wreckage."

My skin prickled, hope overtaking me like a fever at the picture he painted. I could see it, the two of us cutting a bloody swath through the kingdoms, until all those who would stop us lay in ashes.

"Now, come along." Calix shook me from my imaginings. "What I have to show you will be worth stowing that rage in your eyes away for later." My eyes widened, surprised that he could actually see the rage that coursed through me.

He laughed slightly. "Oh, yes, I can see it, I can see everything." Calix looked at me intensely, his thumb coming up to trace along my cheek. "You are like no one I've met before. That rage, it's beautiful, Asteria. It tells me you're going to fight, and fight fiercely. You are…devastation, and you're going to bring that fire down on our enemies."

He was right—my rage now had a focus, and I would funnel it all into our purpose. Into seeing the Fae ruined as I liberated this world and saved it from falling to chaos. But first, I had to ignore the tension that sparked and burned between us as we stared into one another's eyes, drifting closer to each other.

Calix looked down at me and the beautiful aurora swirling in his purple eyes arrested me. Moonglow hair fell into his face as he leaned down towards me, the singular braids on either side doing little to hold the full weight back. His hand squeezed mine tightly, dragging me into him before both his hands abandoned their current positions to grab hold of my hips, as my hands flew to his shoulders, feeling the solid strength of them. We were both breathing heavily as our bodies collided, and I let one of my hands snake up to his silvery-white locks, finding to my satisfaction that they were indeed as soft as they appeared.

"My réalta." Calix whispered, his eyes sweeping shut as his forehead pressed to mine, and I breathed him in, night and fire consuming me. But reality was a cruel mistress, and it crashed into us hard, both of us remembering at the same time as the mesmerizing pull between us shattered. Leaving us hastily stepping back and clearing our throats. Calix looked at me, opening his mouth—only to promptly close it, turning toward the horses and walking straight to them. I took a deep breath, chastising myself internally, and followed.

WE MANAGED TO jump back onto our horses and ride on without incident, and before long, we reached a spot where the path abruptly ended. I looked around, confused, but Calix was already dismounting. I followed suit, watching as he swung the hanging branches away with his magic. I was so jealous of that ability—while the royal Fae all had their own special powers that regular Fae didn't have, it was that magic that ran in all Fae and enabled them to do things like move objects out of their way or summon what they needed, that I truly envied. And now I knew they were blessed with it because they were born here, children of their gods.

While me and my kind? Our ancestors were taken by the Wild Hunt from some other world, one likely without magic since we had not a drop of it in our blood. But I could still feel the magic around me, like a taunting caress against my skin, letting me know it was there to be used, if only I'd been a Fae with the ability to wield it.

"This way." Calix smiled widely, before disappearing through the brush. I followed, stopping short as I cleared the trees. My breath left my lungs in a whoosh of air as I finally saw what he brought me out here for. Understanding why he wanted me to see this in person as I gawked in amazement.

"What—" I couldn't even form a proper sentence. The Elysium in front of me...

An oasis stood before me, with what looked like a waterfall—only it wasn't that at all. Those were...

"This is Nova Falls." Calix told me, a proud, excited look on his face as he watched me take in the beauty of his kingdom. "It acts like a waterfall, but it's made entirely of stars. They come into being at the top." He pointed up to the spot where, had this been a waterfall, the water would have flowed over the edge. "And when they reach the bottom, they become nova's, exploding into a burst of color as they hit the bottom, creating the iridescent rainbow banding across the surface here."

It was unlike anything I had ever seen—more magical, more beautiful, more entrancing. I followed the flow of what must be millions of shining stars as they cascaded down into a pool of—not water, I realized, but Night Water. The same Night Water that came from the Otherworld, only in a much larger pool than what the statue of Erebus held.

The stars twinkled into life at the top before falling in a glittering curtain and when they hit the water, they burst into a dazzling beam of colors—pink, yellow, orange, green, blue, red, purple, every color you could think of. It created an effect where a band, a prism of color was always there, floating above the water where the stars continuously fell and exploded into a super-nova of color.

Calix began to drop his things, his sword hitting the ground, followed by his belt—but then he was taking off his jacket, and my mouth went dry as he grabbed the bottom of his shirt and pulled it over his head. My eyes immediately roved over all the bare skin on display.

Perfection.

Muscles covered in miles of gorgeous pale skin covered in tattoos I'd only caught glimpses of before. The cut of his abs grabbed my attention, and I swallowed hard as I looked over each ridge and muscle, until I reached the trail of silvery white hair leading down to his pants, and I could feel saliva fill my mouth as I took in the defined V of his hips, pressing my thighs together in an attempt to quench the rising ache.

I tore my eyes away, but only succeeded in bringing them higher up, to defined, bulging biceps I wanted nothing more than to grip as he covered my body with his own. Shaking my head, I focused on his tattoos instead, iridescent black and purple ink, forming dragon scales that covered his chest and followed across to those gripable biceps. His forearms had bands of silver circling them, made up of runes I couldn't decipher, and on the side of his neck the phases of the moon were inked in a circle, with the full moon in the center of them. Inside the full moon was a rune of some sort, and I'd seen the same tattoo on many of the warriors in the training yard.

Calix turned around, and I got an eyeful of his gloriously broad shoulders that led to a muscular back and flowed down to a narrow waist I wanted to wrap my legs around. But then I spotted the tattoo on his back. No—not *just* a tattoo. In the middle of his upper back was an upside-down crescent moon, with stars falling from underneath the curve, and the rays of the sun inked on the top of the moon's curve. Even though he'd clearly expanded the design, with the aurora of the night sky dancing across his shoulders—the mark stood out as different.

For two reasons, both of which felt like a punch to the gut, making my heart physically hurt.

Reason one: That was the illuminated black ink unique to soul marks. A physical reminder that Calix was not for me to drool over, that he belonged to some Fae, one likely from another kingdom where they treat humans like cattle, considering he hadn't found her yet and they'd mentioned her upset over slavery helped Calix see the light. I hated that it sounded like she might actually be decent, at least in that respect.

Reason two: That tattoo, his *soul mark*, was the exact same design as my necklace, down to the number of stars and rays of the sun. My parents had found that necklace, clearly dropped by a noble, and it was made of star opal, a gem native only to Day and Night Kingdoms.

How in Tartarus did I end up with a necklace depicting Calix's soul mark—was this world truly so cruel? The gods? Was it something his soulmate had made and lost, or was it just a common design for those among the southern kingdoms?

Either way, I was glad I stuffed my necklace in my bag when we left Dusk, and he hadn't seen it. I obviously couldn't wear my necklace around him, not when things were so intense between us. Wearing a reminder of his soulmate around my neck would just be—too much.

An item I'd found so precious and loved so deeply, the only thing I had from my parents aside from an ugly knife, and now it was ruined.

Calix was about to take off his pants, and as much as I wanted to see what was about to be revealed, his mark was a sobering wake up call.

"What are you doing?" I forced out, my voice strangled. He twisted his head back to look at me, a smirk playing on his lips.

"You can't swim with your clothes on." Calix countered, raising a brow as he pushed those pants down and—Old Go—or I suppose, Nox? Either way. That *ass*—what I wouldn't give to sink my fingernails into it as he pounded into me… Muscular and thick, I could bounce a coin off that thing. I quickly looked away as he turned. He should know better than to tease me. If I saw his cock—my restraint might just snap completely.

His sultry chuckle echoed, followed by the sound of splashing water.

"It's safe to look!" He called out, and I peeked an eye open, breathing a sigh of relief, or maybe disappointment, when I realized the dark waters completely concealed anything below the surface.

"Come on in! The water's perfect." He smiled seductively at me, and I steeled myself, cursing internally.

"That water is from the Otherworld, what if it does something to humans?" I hedged, peering into the water suspiciously, but Calix just laughed.

"Plenty of humans have come here, and they've never had any problems." He raised a brow, lazy amusement on his face as his arms moved back and forth in the water, my eyes dropping to the flex of his muscles as he did.

I sighed, going to remove my top. But as I began pulling it up, I noticed his eyes were glued to me. I cleared my throat and raised a brow at him.

"What?" Calix smiled innocently. "You watched me, it's only fair." I glared at him, but decided this might be the perfect chance to turn the tables on him. He had known I was watching and deliberately put on a show for me, and now only smug amusement filled him in the aftermath.

Two could play that game.

I pulled my top over my head, revealing my bustier, or what passed for one in Night. It was a Fae creation I loved that had no straps and nothing around the back or sides, able to hold my breasts up with only minimal material covering the front that pushed my breasts up perfectly—even if it barely covered my nipples, leaving plenty of space for cleavage to be shown off. Magic definitely had its uses. I began to shimmy out of my cloud leather leggings, making sure my ass swung side to side as I revealed my panties, a lace material with a brief triangle in the front and a brief strip that settled between my ass cheeks all that accounted for the back.

Calix watched me with a hungry, almost feral, look in his eyes. His hands squeezed into fists repeatedly, like he was trying to stop himself from reaching forward and grabbing me.

I smirked as I sashayed into the water, I certainly wasn't getting completely naked with him—that seemed like a recipe for disaster. My bra and panties may be a brief barrier, but it was one I needed. The water was warm and strange, feeling almost like a hug around my body, as if the water conformed like a cocoon. I looked up and found Calix still watching me, and knew I needed to distract us both.

"So how does this whole water from the Otherworld thing work? I know what you said, but shouldn't it be impossible for anything from the Otherworld to be in our world?" I prompted him, my thoughts on his doublespeak from earlier still circling. I was too curious, especially knowing this pool of it existed here as well.

The entire area was beautiful beyond measure, feeling like I stepped into another world. One somehow even more miraculous than the rest of the kingdom I now lived in. But I didn't understand *how* it was here.

I finally dragged my eyes away from the falling stars I'd been focused on and found Calix looking at me intently, enough that I knew he was deliberating telling me something.

"What are you hiding?" I narrowed my eyes at him, and he sighed deeply, tossing his head backwards and closing his eyes, cursing softly.

"The knowledge isn't something I'm supposed to share. Only a few people know of it." Calix confessed, and I tilted my head to the side as he lifted his head back up, lavender eyes finding me immediately.

"What about the others? Titan, Harpina, Eryx…" I trailed off as he began shaking his head.

"Only a few of my most trusted know of it." Calix admitted softly. "Both my sisters do, as they are part of House Erebus, they are also entrusted to guard this knowledge. But outside of them, only Titan, Eryx, and Baach know." He smiled wryly. "And that's only because when we were younger, they followed where they shouldn't."

That definitely sounded like them. Still, his explanation only made me thirsty for this forbidden knowledge. "What is it? I promise I would never reveal anything you tell me."

My promise was as soft as it was unfair. I should really let it go, but he looked on the verge of trusting me with such a precious secret and I—I desperately wanted that trust from him.

He bit his lip, and *oh*—to be that lip. *Fuck*, I really needed to get laid soon, this was torture.

"I don't know why I trust you so, but I can't help the feeling that I do—maybe more than I should—but my instincts have never led me wrong before." Calix spoke slowly, like the words were torn from him without his consent. A gentle warmth spread through me, like a Sommer's day, knowing that the trust I gifted him was reciprocated, even if it was despite ourselves.

"Day and Night Kingdoms are different from the other kingdoms in a few ways. Erebus and Earendel, the gods our kingdoms first descended from, are also responsible for the Otherworld. Specifically, Earendel oversees Elysium, and Erebus oversees Tartarus." I listened with wide eyes, having never heard this before.

"I thought the Otherworld was overseen by Arawn? Isn't he the god of the dead?" I asked, thoroughly absorbed by the new history I was learning.

"You're right." Calix smiled, looking down at the waters of the Otherworld as he explained its origins, before looking back at me with glittering eyes. "Arawn oversees the Otherworld in its entirety. He's responsible for judging the souls and making sure they're receiving their deserved afterlife—whether that be in Elysium or Tartarus. But Erebus and Earendel put something of themselves into the creation of those two realms, so they have a tie to them as well. They assist Arawn in some capacity with their respective halves of it, but truly, as they're the kings of the gods, I think Arawn must do most of the work." His words were teasing as he looked at me with a conspiratorial smile that I couldn't help but match.

"The Otherworld has three realms within its borders—Elysium, Tartarus, and the home of the gods themselves. But they had to have ways to cross into this world, and to do that, they needed to create portals to them. Day was tasked with the responsibility of guarding Elysium, while Night—"

"Was tasked with protecting the portal to Tartarus." I finished, realization dawning on me as my eyes blew wide. I tried to process such a realization, that the Otherworld was accessible—and from here—but how did one even process such a thing?

Calix nodded, his face grim. "Yes. King to king, the responsibility is passed down. We are charged to protect and defend it, to ensure none find it or cross its borders who are not invited."

Calix watched me, eyes scrutinizing as he continued. "To protect these realms, the kings of Day and Night, were gifted additional powers, ones relating directly to the Otherworld." He sighed heavily, his shoulder slumping, like the weight of whatever he was about to divulge dragged them down. "I have another ability, more than just the darkness." He looked away, and I hated the shame that shone on his face.

"Calix, whatever it is, it doesn't matter to me." I reassured him quietly, even though I feared putting that thought—that truth—into words.

"It will." He argued in a stern tone. "I'm not a good man, Asteria. I've tried to be better when it comes to humans, but that has only made me a monster in other ways. And none of it erases the terrible things I've done, including using that power."

I tried to interrupt, but he spoke right over me. "I use the ability to make people feel the pain of Tartarus. All I have to do is send that power at them, and they'll be trapped in that torture until I stop it. A true agony, beyond anything that could be felt in this world. And I've delivered that onto people at a whim."

He swallowed hard, and the desolation on his face made me move. I ignored whatever tingle of fear knowledge of such a power existing arose in me—I knew Calix wouldn't hurt me. I just focused on him, approaching him and throwing my arms around his shoulders, uncaring that he was naked, and I was nearly so.

"You're one of the best men I know, Calix." I assured him as his arms came around me and clutched me to him, burying his face in my neck. I pet his hair, as his body shook.

"I'm one of the worst you've met, I promise you." Calix let out a wry laugh. "You've only seen the good—the man I am around my people, my friends and family—you haven't had a chance to see the other side of me yet."

"I know the worst man I've met, and you're nothing like him." I fought back fiercely. He may believe that about himself, but I knew better. "We're all made up of multitudes, Calix. We all make mistakes, all have regrets. If you used to use that power on your enemies—well, *good*. They deserved it." Calix let out a guttural laugh, stiffening like he hadn't meant to do so. "We all make choices when it comes to life or death. You've been actively trying to do better by humans—"

A harsh sound was breathed into my neck that had me gripping his hair tightly.

"Trying to do better—" Calix snorted disdainfully. "And yet I slaughter any who get in my way. My *own* people. It doesn't matter that I do so in the name of protecting others, there's so much blood on my hands, my réalta, it will never wash away."

I could practically feel the self-loathing thrumming off him. I sighed heavily, and only then realized the magic in the air around me was more noticeable. The land was thrumming with it. And so was Calix. He felt like a sensual wash of power over my skin, one that begged me to play with it, leaving goosebumps in its wake as I shivered. The feeling was too inviting, like it wanted me to grasp hold of it and never let go.

"Maybe not." I finally allowed, trying to ignore the heady magic around me. "But you're working for something important, Calix. What you're doing will save not only the humans here, but the Fae too. The whole world is at stake, not just us. And you've saved so many already. You—you saved *me*." He pulled back to look at me, our eyes clashing, and I tumbled deep into those jewel-toned eyes.

"Even outside saving me from Cyrus." I admitted quietly. "My rage was the only thing that kept me going for years, but you've given me so much more than you'll ever know."

"Like what?" He whispered, as caught up as I was, our bodies drifting closer until my legs wound around his waist and his hands gripped my hips tightly. The scent of night and fire invaded my scenes, making me want to moan at the taste of it.

"You saved me from a lifetime of having my choices taken from me, either by the Fae, or men in general." I smiled slightly; Calix hooked on my every word. "You've given me time to discover who I really am. I was barely a person before—just raw anger, an exposed nerve, and it was only recently I found myself facing an onslaught of feelings I'd never dealt with. I had no idea what to do or who I was under all that, and now I have the time and space to figure that out."

"You've given me a place I could actually call home. A place filled with friends and happiness. You've helped me find a focus, a purpose." I whispered, my hands still gripping his hair, and I knew I should pull back, as our lips came so close to touching…

A snap in the forest around us broke our trance, and we both pulled back as we realized how close we'd allowed ourselves to drift once more. Calix looked away as I unwound myself from him and got out of the water, leaving me torn between watching the stars fall and watching his hair fall in front of his face as he looked away.

I had meant every word, and I hoped he knew that. I had lived a half-life for too long. Rage had overtaken me for years.

That's the thing about rage—it's ravenous. It doesn't still and lie down silently when you can't express it. No—when you're forced to hide that rage, it just turns its focus inward…and begins devouring.

Pieces were lost, eaten away; just little bits here and there. It started with hope, and it ended with happiness—dreams were the only thing left in the end. For some, dreams might have been the first to go, but not me. I held strong to my dreams and refused to let them go, even when the hope was gone that they'd ever amount to anything, I had gripped them tight and shoved them down into my soul for safekeeping.

This reprieve, this focusing of my rage—it let it simmer silently for the first time in my life. While hope, happiness, and joy, along with every other good thing I'd forgotten how to feel, somehow regrew in the spots where they had withered, my rage didn't turn on them again.

Everything was different now. This land—I could feel the resonance of it, how the magic practically jumped up and begged to be used, how the magic of night lingered all day, sending out its tendrils across the kingdom. And that magic made me feel more at home, more peaceful, than I had ever been.

Sunrise had never felt like home, nor Dusk.

But here, with a land of balanced magic, a king who cares for all peoples, and a group of people to laugh and have fun with—my rage allowed itself to be pushed aside. It didn't eat away at me now, sated and sleeping like a cat curled up in the sunshine.

Rage was ravenous though, and it still hungered—only I was no longer its target. Not when it was now allowed to look to those who'd been forbidden to it before: those Fae who owned humans, who used them, whipped them, locked them up, or tortured them—those who planned to butcher humans to make weapons. Fae like Cyrus, who would use forbidden magic that would not only have devastating consequences for humans, but for all of Celesterra.

The fate of our world was at stake. Our continent was crumbling, even as outside luxury pervaded it. It was a smokescreen. Without the magic, without balance, everything was lost.

Cyrus had taken too much of me, he would not take all of this too.

My rage noted all of this, calculated the risks and benefits—and it hungered. Cyrus once promised me ruination at his hands, I planned to repay him in kind. I would bring such darkness down on him, that my rage would blot out the sky with it.

As Calix and I redressed, I looked back wistfully at the stars falling behind me—what I wouldn't give to see this all the time. I would have to make plenty of trips in the future. Once dressed, we mounted up and made our way back to the palace. Part way there, Calix turned in his saddle to face me.

"Thank you, my réalta." He spoke quietly, like he was afraid to talk to me after what had just passed between us.

"What does that mean, réalta?" I pressed him, curiosity too much to bear. I'd never been given a nickname before, and every time he said it, a warmth rushed through me.

Calix smirked slightly, looking back at Nova Falls, before his eyes caught mine once more, and like the fire that lived inside him had arisen, those eyes heated into liquid pools.

"It means star in the ancient Fae language." Just like that, he stole all the breath in my lungs. *My star.* He did say I reminded him of a star before, and with my name—but he didn't call me *a* star, no, he called me *his* star.

I swallowed hard, and after a few minutes of riding, where I tried to get my emotions regarding this king of darkness and fire under control, I looked over at him.

"What's the word for darkness in the ancient Fae language?"

Calix looked at me, bemused, a smile twitching on his lips. "Dorchadas."

"My dorchadas." I smiled widely at him, and Calix, to my eternal shock, blushed. Those angular cheekbones dotted with red as he looked down, but I didn't miss the small smile he tried to hide.

I smirked, pleased to have made him feel even a smidgeon of what him calling me his star made me feel.

Two could indeed play that game.

CHAPTER 29

"AGAIN!" Titan barked once again, and I huffed, out of breath as sweat dripped off me. I looked to Harpina for a reprieve, but she just smirked at me, her amber eyes alight with glee as she watched me dying. Okay, dying might be a bit of an exaggeration, but the two of them were running me ragged.

I'd been training every morning, without fail, for weeks. Since going to Nova Falls, Calix and I had been skirting around one another, both of us had opened up to one another, and we'd both felt the distinct shift between us—from lust to something deeper. But we had to keep our hands off one another, so distance it was. In the wake of that, I'd spent a lot of time with the others.

Titan and Harpina covered my training in the mornings, Lilith covered my horseback riding in the early afternoon, and Ilta covered history with me after that, teaching me about all of the kingdoms and their histories, politics and battles. She was insistent that having this knowledge would be necessary long term. Then there were the times I met with Callisto, and we'd go over plots and plans for the Resistance, planning our next moves. I never felt more accomplished than I did after one of those meetings.

"Again. Once more, Asteria." Titan shouted gruffly, I looked up at Titan, begging him for mercy with my eyes, but sighed heavily when none was forthcoming—then chastised myself for wasting all that precious air. I followed his direction, slicing my sword through the air until it hit my opponent's sword. Eryx grinned back at me, my opponent for today. They switched it up often, so I wouldn't get used to just one style of combat.

I thought it was nuts at first, but I had to admit I could see how rotating had benefited me. I didn't grow complacent, expecting the same moves or speed each time, it kept me on my toes, and kept me moving. Considering I was slower and weaker than those I would be fighting, that was essential for my survival.

Swords clashed, Eryx clearly not putting his all into it. I grit my teeth in anger, hating my deficiency. I swung harder, faster, chasing his blade as he brought it up a fraction slower than mine. It was enough. My blade caught his and it flew out of his hand. Eryx's eyes widened in surprise as I brought my blade to his neck, panting, but with a smile on my face as I heard clapping and whooping in the background. A slow smile spread across Eryx's face, and as I brought the sword down, he bowed with a flourish.

"Well done, Asteria." Eryx congratulated, with that smile that always reminded me a bit of an innocent puppy—despite his ability to shift into a hawk with razor sharp claws. He swung an arm over my shoulder, and I jokingly pushed it off, waving a hand and scrunching my nose.

"Yuck, you stink." I teased, making him chuckle.

"Oh, come on, even my sweat smells amazing." He jokily boasted. "Ladies would line up for this experience you know." I raised an eyebrow at him before bursting out laughing, the faux offended look on his face cracking as he watched me.

"Okay." I gasped for breath, my giggles stealing it all. "Whatever those ladies want you to believe."

He opened his mouth to argue back, when we both noticed Priscilla waiting, talking to Harpina and Titan. Eryx swung his arm back over my shoulder as he guided me to her.

"Congratulations, Asteria!" Priscilla smiled widely. "That was amazing!"

I'd thought it sounded like more than two people clapping and yelling. I smiled back at her, pride in myself still foreign but wonderful all the same.

"Thanks, Pris. What brings you out here?" I asked, cocking my head. The training yard was not a typical destination for my peaceful friend—she preferred to leave the fighting to others.

"Callisto needs your help." She smiled ruefully. "She's trying to untangle a plan in her mind and needs some insight." I shrugged in response; it was a common enough occurrence over the past few weeks. Callisto was working on so many plans, so many ways to free humans, and I was anxious to help in any way possible—being able to focus all my rage made me feel a million times lighter.

Still, I was getting anxious, wanting to *do* something.

"Thanks for your help." I kissed Eryx on the cheek, and he squeezed me back lightly.

"Anytime." He promised, and I knew he meant it too. Eryx was like how I imagined an older brother in a lot of ways, and while he may be playful and fun, he was also hundreds of years older than I was and an accomplished warrior—not to mention spymaster. After what had happened to me in Dusk, he seemed to feel the need to look after me.

"Thank you both. I'll see you two later!" I nodded to Titan and Harpina, who nodded back, Harpina with a smirk, and Titan with his usual grim expression. He never lightened up in the training ring, but he did during dinners. Calix always held "family dinners" at least three times a week. The other days were reserved for larger affairs, where residents of the palace and city attended—more like feasts than a dinner. Calix felt it necessary for his people to see him and feel included.

I admired that about him. After getting used to King Astraeus and Cyrus, it was hard to reconcile a king who cared so much about his people, but he very obviously did. Outside of those dinners, we also spent weekends going into the city, to bars and restaurants, enjoying ourselves and getting away from politics and the looming war for a night—but beyond that, it let Calix's people see him and his advisors among them. It was sweet, the way he wanted his people to feel on equal footing with him.

How they ever could be, next to the most powerful Fae alive, I wasn't truly sure, but Calix was determined to make them feel it anyway.

"Training seems to be going well." Priscilla smiled as she linked our arms together and headed toward the war room. Callisto was usually found there, and increasingly, so was Priscilla—despite her distaste for war and fighting.

"It has been." I admitted, biting my lip. "But I can't help feeling like I'm—" I struggled to verbalize what was bothering me. "Not reaching my full potential."

"How so?" Priscilla asked, eyebrows furrowing,

"I don't know." I sighed heavily. "My body is just—" I groaned, aggravation in every line of my face. "I've always had this feeling, like my body doesn't…fit? It's hard to explain, but I feel like it's holding me back. Like I could do so much more, if only I didn't feel like I'd been stuffed into skin too tight for me." I knew it sounded crazy, and the way Priscilla raised her brows at me, bemused, I could tell she thought so too.

"Never mind that." I shook my head, dismissing it. "What have you been up to, missy?" I raised my brows, wiggling them up and down, enjoying it way too much when her mouth dropped open.

"What is that supposed to mean?" She demanded indignantly, causing me to laugh.

"I *mean*—" I emphasized, drawing the word out. "You've been hanging around the war room an awful lot for someone who claims to be unable to help in the war to come. Could it be a certain resistance leader whose Siren Song has you there so often?"

My teasing made Priscilla's cheeks blush bright red, her eyes skittering away to the left. *Nailed it.*

"Are you happy?" I asked softly, dropping my teasing as I looked at her intently. After everything she had been through, everything Princess Daneiris had put her through, Priscilla deserved nothing but happiness. She stopped outside the doors to the war room, turning as she threw her arms around me unexpectedly.

"I am happy." She confessed, warmth suffusing her tone. "It's—it's new. It's not really much of anything yet, to be honest. But—after what happened." Priscilla swallowed hard, and I had the sinking feeling there was much more to her story than she'd told me. "I didn't think I would ever want another man again."

My eyes closed, pain running through me at the confirmation that my sweetheart of a friend had been brutalized by the monsters in Dusk. I didn't know who—and I would never force her to tell me—but I would ensure every Fae male in Dusk, outside Kian, suffered for it.

"I never considered—" Priscilla's voice dropped to a hush, "I never considered a woman before, but there was just a—a spark between us. Nothing has happened, but we've been spending more time together."

That pretty blush graced her cheeks once more, and I could see why Callisto would be interested. I didn't share her preferences, but Priscilla was a beautiful, doe eyed blonde who had a sweet, innocent appearance. More than that, she was genuinely kind, in a world that didn't leave much room for kindness. Given what had happened to her, I could hardly comprehend the strength she had to maintain that kindness after everything.

"I'm just happy that you're happy, Pris." I smiled widely at her, hoping she could see my sincerity. "Whatever makes you happy, I'll support. *Always*."

Tears rose in her eyes, and she hugged me once more, whispering her thanks in my ear. I hugged her back tightly. She had been one of my first true friends, and I wanted her to know, no matter what, that I was here for her.

We parted, and I brushed away her tears before we opened the door to the war room, entering to find Callisto with a horde of people around her. She was directing chaos. People were every which way—grabbing and unrolling maps, going over documents, speaking quietly to one another, or yelling across the room to others. I blinked at the madness until Callisto looked up and smiled fiercely.

"Asteria, good, Pris found you!" She waved me over. "I could use you."

I walked over, running my eyes over the boards situated around the room with details and people's portraits added up, then moved to the map table littered with figures. If our enemies ever saw this place, they'd have a field day. Luckily, Calix was powerful, and his reputation preceded him, so despite the attacks, none dared take the battle to Night's borders, let alone deep within them to its capital.

"What's going on?" I inquired, looking at Callisto and taking in the near manic look in her eyes. At least until Callisto's caramel eyes spotted Priscilla beside me and that mania seemed to fade, replaced by a much warmer feeling.

Callisto was beautiful for a human, with light brown skin that shined with health and thick, curly black hair that bounced as she moved. Her face had a pixyish look to it, sweet enough one wouldn't expect her to be the hardened leader of the human resistance. She wore all leather today, and it hugged her in all the right places—I caught Pris trailing her eyes up and down her body, and I shot a smirk over at her, causing her cheeks to heat.

"We're getting rumblings about a possible alliance between Dusk and Sunset," Callisto explained, leaning over the map and moving a pegasus figure to Sunset, placing it beside the phoenix figure on the capital of Biarma.

"They just arranged the alliance with Dawn." I began, my brows furrowing. "They haven't even finalized the actual marriage yet, right?" I looked down at the map, trying to visualize Cyrus's play—because I had no doubt he was behind this.

"You're correct." Callisto nodded sharply. "The wedding for Prince Cyrus and Princess Zerlina is set for a couple of months out."

"He should be waiting for that before moving on to the next alliance, unless he's so sure it won't be stopped that he's not worried about securing it first." I thought aloud as I stepped around the table, Callisto and several other's eyes following me.

"We know what he wants: more power and control. He needs to wrest control from his father, prevent his siblings from usurping him, and fight Calix and Night's forces. We know he plans to use blood magic to amplify his magic and make superior weapons, but even with that, he's not ready to move against Calix. He knows he can't stop Night, even with Dawn's help. He's not a fool, and he knows he's severely lacking against us at the moment. But he's impatient, and his pride has been damaged, his control threatened. I've seen what he's like when that happens."

I shivered as the memory of that day flashed through my mind. The way he took his loss of control and sought to exert control over *me* to assuage it. I shook my head, pushing the memory back down deep.

"Calix took me, and this is him reacting. He's not ready to move forward based on the blood magic alone yet, so he's trying to desperately pull in more allies so he can move now." I realized. I looked up at Callisto, and she was nodding thoughtfully.

"Do you think he wants revenge for taking you?" She asked, a bit skeptical. "Not many Fae would bother for a human, but if this is pride talking—" She moved her head back and forth as she considered, her curls bouncing with the movement, before she raised her brows expectantly at me.

I fought back another shiver as I thought about Cyrus. That last day in Dusk Kingdom was a creeping specter that refused to stay buried where it belonged. The anger, the excitement, the *glee* on Cyrus's face as he attempted to take me. I thought back to how he fought everyone to keep me—even risking his precious alliance in the process. Paired with his need to dominate…

"He'll want revenge, yes." I swallowed hard, forcing the words from my mouth. "Cyrus needs to feel like he's dominant in all things and he won't take being defeated by Calix well. But he—he won't stop until he gets me back, either. He went to great lengths to keep me with him, and I have no doubt his obsession is unchanged." I blew out a breath, closing my eyes.

"This is a man who tortures humans for sport. I saw his dungeon, and none of what he did was simple information gathering. He took…*pleasure in* it." I wrapped my arms around myself, trying to block out the memory of his face.

Callisto had a sympathetic look on her face when I opened my eyes. I appreciated that she didn't draw attention to my struggle when she continued. "So, we need to find a way to disrupt this alliance before it goes through."

"Yes, we absolutely do." I nodded firmly.

I wouldn't let Cyrus amass more power. *Never*. My rage stirred, wanting to rise up and act—but I promised it the time would come. *Soon*.

WE DISCUSSED STRATEGIES for close to an hour before we called it. Calix was due to take court with the influx of lords and ladies coming in. Baach had arranged the ball Ilta had talked him into throwing, and it would be happening later tonight. The timing worked out well as the Festival of Faunus was next week, so everyone coming would get two big events out of one trip. I'd asked Baach why he bothered with the ball when the festival was coming up, only to get a near hour long lecture on the differences in party types and court politics.

The girls were all excited for the ball, regardless. Talking about the dresses we'd all found or purchased, the jewelry we'd wear, shoes, and hair—everything that went into preparing for a grand ball. Even Eris seemed more excited than usual, wearing a slight smile as she spoke about her dress. I was glad she seemed to finally be loosening up some.

My only disappointment was Emmie. While she'd finally come out of her room, she refused to speak to us. Eris promised she just needed time, and the healers Calix sent, ones who specialize in the mind, promised that was the case. I wasn't so sure about that. They had urged me to see the same healer, to talk about my experiences in Dusk, but I refused. I couldn't bring myself to vocalize what had happened, and I didn't want strangers analyzing me. I'd opened myself up quite a lot since leaving Sunrise, but that was a step too far for me.

Running upstairs to change, Delia and Ilta joined Priscilla and I as we made our way. They helped me change out of my training clothes and were able to whip me up a beautiful hairdo and apply makeup in what seemed like mere moments. My dress was gorgeous. It sat off the shoulder with long sleeves. Dark blue ran along the sweetheart neckline before shifting to silver, both colors equally glittering.

We quickly made our way down to the throne room. I had yet to attend a proper court session, despite having an open invitation. My previous experiences had made me wary, but I was curious about Calix's lords. Plus, Aibeck and Siria would be attending, and I hadn't seen them since we were all rescued.

Eryx was waiting at the entrance to the throne room, and I smiled when I spotted him. He knew my reservations about attending, and his support meant more than he'd ever know.

He smirked when he saw us, a hand going over his heart dramatically. "Well, if I'm not the luckiest man in all of Celesterra, to be escorting the most beautiful women of the land to court today."

I gave him a dramatic curtsy in return, "We thank you, kind Sir, for your assistance with this most perilous of undertakings." My lips twitched up into a smirk as he laughed, and I heard Delia try to smother her giggling in her hand.

"Of course, fair maiden." He extended his arms, and I took one, while Delia took the other. "Shall we, ladies?" The sparkle in his blue eyes was teasing, but I watched as his eyes roved over Delia with more intention than the rest of us. My eyebrow quirked at him, and he quickly tried to cover it with a boyish smile.

Priscilla rolled her eyes at our antics. "I'm going to wait for Callisto. She should only be a moment. We'll meet you inside."

I looked over at her, but she smiled and waved me off, so I nodded, and we made our way into the throne room. Every time I thought I'd seen everything there was to see of Night Kingdom, I was surprised once more. My jaw dropped as I glanced in every direction, trying to take it all in.

"Amazing, isn't it?" Eryx smirked down at me. I nodded, speechless.

The ceiling was—not there. Instead, it was open to the sky. Leaving the hall bright and sunny at the moment, but it would allow the night sky to glimmer above us after dark.

"There's a spell." Delia whispered, leaning her head around Eryx and toward me. "It prevents the elements from getting in. It's like there's still a ceiling, even though there isn't."

"Incredible." I murmured. My eyes shot to the floor, which was a sparkling onyx color. The walls were uncovered, so the star opal shone all around us. Except, of course, for the tapestries that hung here and there, showing past kings and battles, locations like Nova Falls, or celestial events. Columns were scattered throughout, glittering star opal with dragons crawling over and around them. The dragon figures were black with silver detailing, and quite striking against the color-streaked white of the opal columns. Down the middle of the throne room, there was a rug leading up to the dais in a swirling purple pattern.

As we walked forward, I looked up to the dais, and my breath caught in my throat. On it sat a throne that was larger than life. The throne was built into a *dragon*. An entire dragon sat perched on the dais, crafted of course, but looming up over the area. The entire dragon was made to look like the night sky, black with stars twinkling within it. The throne built into it was outlined in jewels, and matched the dragon's eyes, which were both made from amethysts which glowed a light purple, more lavender than amethyst— remarkably similar to the eyes of the king who sat on the throne.

Beside the throne, banners came down from the ceiling bearing the Night Kingdom's sigil, a crescent moon with stars within in a circle, and dragon wings coming off either side, done in the same shimmering purples and blacks that the throne used, I noticed. While above the dragon throne, black stone, the same as the doors to the palace, was a permanent banner, the phases of the moon written across it in silver. The same stone continued down the sides, outlining the dais, and the silver etched out falling stars from top to bottom.

Eryx led me forward still, or I likely would have come to a dead stop as I gaped around. I gave him a thankful smile as he led us over to the right of the throne.

"Should I be so close?" I asked him worriedly, my brows furrowing. "Shouldn't this spot be exclusively for you and the others in his court?"

Eryx smiled gently down at me, "*You* are part of his Highness's court now, Asteria."

The truth of that made me blink rapidly. I hadn't really thought about it, but he was right. I didn't have an official office like he did, but I was part of it, nonetheless. Everyone had welcomed me so readily, having me join them for dinners and nights out. They'd taken me into their friend group, beyond just their court. I wasn't sure I could ever express how thankful I was for such a thing, but the gentle, understanding look on Eryx's face made me think he already knew. If we weren't in court, I would hug him for that alone.

Instead, I gave him a smile and then turned to watch the others file in. Baach came over to stand beside Ilta, who took her place next to me. I was waiting for those two to quit flirting and get on with it, but Eryx caught my gaze and smirked.

"Those two have been doing this for years. Don't get your hopes up." He teased, shaking his head.

"Why don't they just tell each other how they feel?" I whispered, raising a brow. "It's so obvious they like each other."

I caught Eryx's quick glance at Delia, who was chatting with Lilith, who must have just arrived. I raised both brows at him, a smirk growing, and he narrowed his eyes at him.

"We live long lives, Asteria, we don't need to rush these things." He answered, eyes skittering past me.

"That's bullshit." I whispered back.

His lips twitched but he just shrugged, "Sometimes it's easier to keep the status quo, instead of taking a risk."

I supposed that made a sad sort of sense. I could well understand holding back feelings, though I did it for a different reason. But if they'd spent hundreds of years with things one way, maybe they were afraid to change it. Afraid the other wouldn't feel the same, and things would be irrevocably altered. I thought about it as everyone prepared for the king's arrival. I didn't want things to change with Calix, but perhaps that was inevitable. After all, when he found his soulmate, things *would* change, whether I wanted them to or not. Would I even have a place here then? Or would Calix want me as far away from her as possible?

I tried to bury that thought as Calix was announced, the herald calling out, "All rise for His Royal Highness, King Calix Orpheus Atarah Erebus. King of the Night Kingdom. Lord of Tairngire, the City of Shadow & Starlight. Lord of Darkness. The Dragon of Dreams and Nightmares. Keeper of the Gates. Protector of the People."

I raised a brow as I took in the many titles and names I'd never heard before. The City of Shadow and Starlight was a beautiful way to describe Tairngire, and perfectly fitting I thought. But all those titles were quite a mouthful. Eryx smirked, but it was Baach who leaned over and whispered, "He hates all the titles. We like to fuck with him and add new ones sometimes. The last one we added in honor of his protection of humans. He won't argue, just because it means so much to him, but he'll cringe at the additional title nonetheless."

I shot him an incredulous look, and he slowly smiled. "What? We need to get our fun where we can."

I rolled my eyes, but my lips twitched, giving me away. Baach bumped my shoulder with a smile, as I focused my gaze on Calix walking into the throne room.

He was dressed more formally than I'd ever seen him, with a long black coat that had moons, stars, and dragons in silver brocade down the arms, while the rest was crisp and plain. Each button down the front was a phase of the moon, creating the effect when buttoned of all the moon phases atop each other. A royal purple cape was affixed to his shoulders, covering one at a slant and held with a broach of a dragon made of onyx and amethyst. A belt hung around his waist, holding his sword. The black blade hidden by its sheath, but the silver handle showed prominently, a dragon with its wings spread out making up the hilt. A crescent moon on the dragon's back and stars for eyes, both made of the signature star opal.

A crown sat on his head that made my mouth run dry—it was beautiful. Black metal with points coming up and ending in stars made of star opal. The points leading up to them were covered in purple jewels. The phases of the moon went around the base of the crown, also in star opal. Swirls made of silver and dotted with jewels of purple and green surrounded the moon phases on the crown. It was magical and masculine at the same time—it fit him perfectly.

He made his way down the aisle to the dais, where he climbed the steps and sat in his celestial dragon throne. He looked regal and beautiful, his silvery white hair falling around his face. His angular cheekbones and equally sharp jaw gave him a brutal, fierce air as he looked out on his court, but his soft lips and brilliant purple eyes softened him a bit.

"They'll present all the Lords and Ladies of the kingdom, and then open up the floor for everyone." Harpina whispered in my ear, and I jolted, not having seen her arrive. I knew vaguely that Titan and Harpina had followed Calix in, along with Liviana, who now stood at his side. Ilta had also left us to make her way up to the dais to take notes. She was now standing beside Titan, who gripped the hilt of his sword as he stood at attention with several other guards. But I'd been so lost in Calix, I'd barely noticed anything else.

"Princess Ndrita Luna and Lord Sterling Nuit of Keris." The herald called out. Calix's sister. I knew she was older than Liviana, but younger than Calix. Unfortunately, I hadn't heard much else about her yet. A pale skinned woman with silvery white hair, slightly blonder than her siblings, and blue eyes that had just a hint of purple to them, came forward and curtsied. Beside her, a man with tan skin and dark hair shaved back on the sides with the rest tied in a ponytail, bowed. He looked like a warrior, with muscles straining against his jacket, a sword on one hip and daggers on the other.

"Sister, Brother, welcome back to Tairngire. It's been too long." Calix smiled down at them, his face softening.

"It has been, your Highness. My Princess was all too eager to return." Lord Sterling smiled at his wife, who returned it warmly, before turning back to her brother.

"As much as I love Keris, the skies for flying in Tairngire can't be beat." She smirked at Calix, who returned it.

"You have that right, Sister. We'll go flying as soon as we're able." He nodded, and the two bowed before moving to the side again.

"Lord Polaris Ratri and Lady Zillah Nyx Khors of Eirne." The two who stepped forward I would have assumed were brother and sister if I wasn't aware they were married. Both had light blonde hair common in Night Kingdom, though Zillah's had a tinge of silver to her long, straight hair, her pointed ears sticking through it on either side, with jewels added to decorate the points and she had dark blue eyes, whereas her husband held a hint of green. Polaris had the same sharp cheekbones and jawline as Calix, though his face seemed shorter and squarer in comparison.

"Your Highness, it's wonderful to be back. We're immensely looking forward to the ball tonight." Lady Zillah bowed.

"Any party hosted by Baach is one we want to be at." Lord Polaris smirked, making Calix laugh joyfully.

"I hope it lives up to your expectations, Lord Polaris." Calix smirked back at the lord.

It made me wonder about these parties, I'd thought balls were fairly standard, but clearly, I was missing something. I looked to Baach in question, but he just winked at me, his smile twinkling with mischief.

"Lord Ciaran Tolze of Corbenic." The lord stepped forward, and he was truly the opposite of the lord and lady before him. Where their skin was moon pale, Lord Ciaran's was an olive tanned color, his hair was dark as night with the shadow of a beard dusting his face. A sharp nose and high cheekbones made him look quite intimidating, and he quickly greeted the king and moved along, all efficiency.

"Lady Jasira Hanwi of Mael Duin." As Lord Ciaran walked back, he passed Lady Jasira, and I saw the way his eyes immediately focused on her. Her wavy blonde hair came just past her shoulders but was full of volume and she had bright green eyes that shone like emeralds. Like me, the apples of her cheeks were more prominent than her cheekbones, giving her heart shaped face a sweet appearance. Those emerald eyes met Lord Ciaran's and held, and felt like I was intruding just looking at them—but they quickly looked away and the moment was broken.

She curtsied as she arrived before the dais, and I realized—

"There's no Lord of Mael Duin?" I asked Eryx, who looked down at me.

"Calix lets her rule her own land." He smiled, pride shining on his face. "He doesn't see why a woman should have to marry and let her husband take over. Jasira inherited the title from her father, and she's now determined to keep ruling herself. She's very proud to be the first ruling Lady, and she hopes it will inspire other women to begin doing the same and not feel forced into giving up control."

I smiled widely, that was a Lady I could respect.

No wonder Eryx was proud of his king, by the Otherworld, I was too. Remembering Lady Shirma in Dusk, who'd been forced to marry or lose her lands, I was even happier. The idea that a woman couldn't rule just as well as a man was absolute bullshit—I can guarantee we'd do better. Just look at Cyrus, driven by pride and greed—Tartarus, I could do a better job ruling than him.

"Lord Kyler and Lady Aisling Daram of Lyonesse." The two came forward and I looked them over as they spoke with Calix. He had dark silver hair that shone black in certain lights—he clearly had some royal blood in there, even though it wasn't direct. His eyes were like chips of ice, glowing such a light blue they were almost white. Lady Aisling was joking with Calix, but did a quick scan of the room, and spotting me, she winked a jade-colored eye with a smirk, taking me aback. Her hair was the deep red of a berry wine and was half up in braids while the rest fell down her back and framed her face. They were both clearly warriors, with weapons strapped over their court outfits—I even spied a dagger strapped to her thigh in the slit up her dress.

They finally bowed and made their way to the side after a few minutes of discussion with Calix, and the herald called out the final pair to be introduced, "Lord Rhidian and Lady Alora Asman of Segais."

Lord Rhidian reminded me of Titan instantly, with the same dirty blonde hair, strong nose, and square jaw, though Rhidian's wasn't as prominent. His eyes, however, were golden in color as opposed to blue, and while he was large and definitely well-muscled, with broad shoulders that stretched his doublet to its limit, he was still smaller than the massive Titan. On the other hand, his wife stood out as being clearly from a Northern kingdom, likely Sunrise or Sunset, with light brown skin and almond shaped eyes that slanted upwards. The gray of those eyes looked like a storm in a bottle, contrasting how kind she appeared, with a sweet smile on full lips that led to a pointed chin.

When they made their way back into the crowd, I took a moment to look around. There was a good mix of Fae and humans, and I swore I could feel the magic in the air. I inhaled, closing my eyes. It was like a heartbeat, coming from the kingdom itself. Strongest where Calix was, but spots all around the throne room sparked with it. *Magic.* Night magic. That resonance I'd been feeling was stronger now. With so many Fae of the kingdom surrounding me, I could feel the magic of the land like a second beat in my chest.

I'd always been able to feel magic around me, but never like this. It was usually faint, more an awareness than anything. This was something else, something that couldn't be denied. I wasn't sure why—or how—but it was stronger than ever. Like I could reach into the land itself and pull up that power for myself.

I jolted, my eyes springing open and the feeling seeping away slightly, leaving only that strange feeling—like something sparkled in my blood—that I usually only felt when particularly angry. Eryx's hand was on my shoulder, and he was looking down at me with concern clear in his eyes.

"Asteria, are you okay?" He asked worriedly, and I shook my head, eyebrows scrunching slightly.

"Of course, why wouldn't I be?" I countered, brushing off the weirdness.

Eryx's eyebrows flew up. "You've been standing there for a while with your eyes closed. Calix is just greeting the last few people and then court will be over for the day."

My mouth parted in shock, looking around to verify what he was saying. Had I been that lost in it? It appeared so, as I could see the line that had formed of humans and Fae bringing concerns forward was almost done. Lady Alora stepped out on the floor as the last person in line reached the dais—distracting me from the bizarre occurrence.

"Your Highness, I've received word from my contact in Sunset Kingdom." Lady Alora informed the king as she stepped forward. Calix sat up straighter in his seat and I caught Callisto's head whipping towards the Lady of Segais.

"Please, Lady Alora, what have you learned?" Calix inclined his head, all hard lines and strained muscles. His fingers flexed on the arms of his throne, and I squinted. It was hard to make out against the darkness of said throne, but I could just see the wisps of shadow coming from his hands.

Lady Alora bit her lip, "They spoke of an alliance being brokered with Dusk, your Highness. One which would add to the existing alliance Dusk and Dawn are in the process of solidifying."

"We're aware of such." Calix nodded. "We're already working on several plans."

"That's not all, my King." Lady Alora continued. "Prince Cyrus has apparently traveled to Sunset himself to discuss the alliance, bringing his betrothed with him. While he was there, he spoke of—a human, one I believe is here. Cyrus has apparently put a bounty on her head, anyone who can return her to him is being offered an incredible sum." Lady Alora's disgust over Cyrus's actions was as obvious as her apology for having to relay it—but I could barely focus once her words reached my ears.

It was like my vision tunneled, and I looked over to Calix, whose gaze unerringly met mine. Darkness exploded out around him, and the gasps of the court sounded so very far away. Calix's throat bobbed, and the darkness slowly shrank back to him, until only faint wisps remained.

I couldn't breathe, however—Cyrus had put a bounty on me. I'd known he wouldn't give up, had even said as much earlier—but this…I couldn't handle this. A ragged breath finally left me, and then they were coming fast and hard. Everything seemed so far away, a haze descending over my vision.

The feel of someone shaking my shoulders, the blurry form in front of me—their mouth was moving, but I couldn't hear a word. I wouldn't go back, I *couldn't* go back. I would do anything necessary to ensure it. I finally had a bit of peace, of happiness, but the rage I'd lived with my whole life was a familiar friend, and it now shoved aside the panic and fear in favor of itself.

It allowed me to breathe, for my vision and hearing to return. Eryx, Delia, Baach, and Ilta were surrounding me, and Priscilla was eyeing me from across the aisle with understanding and sympathy in her eyes. Harpina was blocking us from view, I realized, ensuring none could see me except for those on the opposite side of the aisle, where Priscilla stood with Callisto. They'd all stepped in to stop me from being totally humiliated.

Affection for them rose within me, only second to the fire scorching through my veins, demanding to be let loose on the man who thought he could leash me like a dog—and I would ensure it was unleashed when the time came.

I would take great pleasure in the destruction of Cyrus's entire world, and only once he was left in the ashes of its ruination would I grant him what he deserved—maybe I could convince Calix to use the power of Tartarus once more, so I could unleash agony like he'd never known upon him.

Exactly as he deserved.

CHAPTER 30

AFTER the intense ending to court, I was eager to get back to my rooms and decompress for a moment. After assuring everyone I was fine, multiple times, and another few assurances were given to Calix directly when his worry seemed too great, I fled to my rooms and threw myself onto the sofa.

The velvet rubbed against my cheek, and I focused on that feeling, slowly brushing my cheek back and forth until my breathing was under control once more. I heaved a sigh and turned around, so I was on my back, facing the ceiling. My eyes traced the intricate architecture, picking up details I'd missed before. The white columns had engravings of stars and moons on the edges, outlined in a faint silver. *Huh.*

It wasn't enough to distract me, unfortunately. I pushed myself up and headed for the balcony. Leaving the door open, as I knew Delia would be here before long to help prepare me for the ball, I took a seat on one of the comfortable lounge chairs. There was a little table next to it with a pitcher of sparkling lavender colored wine, kept fresh with magic I envied. I poured myself a glass and sat back, taking in the view.

Having seen Priscilla, Eris, even Ilta and Delia's rooms, I knew I'd for some reason been given the best view. My balcony looked out over the Dragon Cliffs, the sea and sky stretching out for miles. If I looked down, I could see the pool behind the palace, and the cabanas set up around it for lounging. If I looked in the other direction, the bountiful gardens greeted me, maybe not as elaborate as Queen Stelara's, but all the more beautiful for it—and certainly more charming. Everywhere I looked there were wonders to behold.

It was all so different from Dusk Kingdom, and that's what I needed to focus on. I sipped my wine, letting the bubbles tickle my throat and relax me. I watched the sun slowly sink down across the sky. Sunset. But that thought just led back to the alliance and the bounty Cyrus put out on me.

No. I shook my head. I wouldn't let him take the sun from me. It was *mine.* Well, as much as the sun could be anyone's, but I wouldn't let him ruin my love of the sky. Sometimes it felt like the only piece of *me* truly remaining. Since Placement Day, I'd gone through so much, changed so much, that I wondered if I were to return to Sonmathion, would my parents even recognize the woman before them?

The small village girl I'd been with had thought she knew the world, but she had been so wrong—about so many things. I'd closed myself off to the world, taking the cruelty of my peers, the looming deadline that was Placement Day, and my loneliness, and I created armor from them. Convincing myself it was what I wanted, and not what I was stuck with due to the circumstances—but I knew better now.

I wished I could talk to Calix. My instinct always led me right to him when I had something to talk about. It was clear my instincts were broken. Even if my chest physically hurt at the thought of keeping my distance from him, I had to—we both did. Somewhere out there, his soulmate, his perfect match, his *Queen*, waited. And he would find her, I had no doubt about that.

He'd spent so many years being loyal to the idea of a woman he'd never met, then I came along and ruined everything for him. Maybe that's all I was good for. Ruination. Destruction. Cyrus seemed to unravel at the seams with me there, and Calix was now struggling to keep things between us platonic, and not fuck me up against the closest surface.

If it was just sex, that would be easier, but I couldn't lie to myself. I wanted—more. I wanted everything from him—and everything *of him.* I wanted to be able to go swimming with him in the Night Waters and not worry about wrapping my legs around him as he confessed his fears to me. I wanted him teasing me as we rode our horses through the fields. I wanted him inviting me to ride him in dragon form simply because he knew how much flying meant to me—and then I wanted to ride his other form. I wanted all of it.

But he wasn't for me, and the sooner I got that through my thick skull, the better off I'd be. An agonizing ache pulsed in my heart, and I reached up, rubbing the area as if that would help. It felt like someone tearing my heart to pieces to even think about it—the thought of Calix with another woman made my blood flush with rage, rising fast and furious. But it quickly fell, replaced by a desolation so vast, I was shocked to discover I had such a well of feeling inside me.

I took a giant swig of my wine, letting the sparkling berry taste soothe a bit of the pain. I didn't know how to convince my stupid heart that Calix belonged to someone else, and if I couldn't do that soon, I would be lost.

"Knock, knock." A sing-song voice interrupted my thoughts, and I was so relieved to get out of my own head, I turned to Ilta with a huge smile. She looked even happier than I, practically floating on air as she made her way to the chair on the other side of the small table. With a wave of her hand, the pitcher lifted, pouring the sparkling lavender wine into a glass, and then floating it into her hand as she sat back. Lifting it to her lips, she sipped it down and let out a satisfied hum. I watched her, bemused, until she finally turned to me.

"What's got you so happy?" I teased, and Ilta giggled, her wide blue eyes doll-like on her delicate face.

"I was complaining about having no one to escort me to the ball tonight. A bit loudly, you see, right beside Baach." She smirked as I rolled my eyes,

"Let me guess—" I raised a brow as she nodded happily.

"Baach offered to escort me!" She squealed and I couldn't help but laugh, my head falling forward as I did.

"I'm happy for you. It's so obvious the two of you like one another. I don't know how long you've been trading looks for, but—"

"Oh—" She interrupted, "I'm not sure if he does like me, not like that. He offered as a friend." Her face fell for a moment before she shook her head and forced a smile on her face. "But this is a good step! Right? Attending together, dancing close, who knows what may happen?"

"Ilta." I tilted my head toward her, incredulous. "Baach likes you—trust me. I've seen the way he looks at you. You're gorgeous, fun, and sweet, he would be lucky to have you." I dropped my voice until I was faux whispering. "And I'm pretty sure he knows that too." Ilta bit her lip, looking out at the view as the moon rose into the sky.

"Do you really think so?" She asked distantly, more serious than I'd seen her. I leaned over, placing my hand atop hers.

"I do. The two of you look at one another with stars in your eyes." I smiled teasingly, and it had the desired effect, a giggle breaking through her pouting lips. She brushed her hair back over her shoulder, light blonde interspersed with honey swishing backward.

She pursed her lips as she appeared to consider something. I brought my glass up to my lips and took a large sip, sure I would need it for whatever she was about to say.

"Calix and you look at one another that same way." She broached, soft and tentative, but I stiffened nonetheless, feeling the words like an accusation. She reached out, interlacing our fingers together and squeezing. "Since you've come here, Asteria, you've become such a good friend, I can barely remember what life was like without you here." She smiled at me as she winked, before growing serious once more. "The situation with Calix—it's complicated, I know. But I have faith that things will work out just as they're meant to."

I opened my mouth, but words wouldn't come. I cleared my throat before trying again. "How can you be so sure?"

"The gods have a plan for us all." Ilta replied, squeezing my hand in support once more. "Look at all that has happened to bring you here, and from what Liviana told us, there's more to come for you. I can't believe the gods would do all of this, only for your destiny to leave you unhappy. I don't know what may happen, I don't know if Calix will find his soulmate, or not. There's so many questions, and no answers. I know Calix is a good man, despite what he thinks. I know he thinks himself half a villain, for what he's had to do, for the things he's done in the past. And yes, to some, he's the monster they claim he is, but he's truly a good man. A loyal one—and I know he won't ever be disloyal to those he loves. But he also can't deny whatever this is sizzling between you two. So, I have to believe the gods have a plan for you both, and that in the end, you'll find happiness."

I let out a shaking sigh and jumped in my chair as I heard a soft, "She's right, you know."

Delia smiled kindly from the doorway, where she leaned against the frame. "Sorry, I didn't want to interrupt, but it's important you know that she's correct. The Goddess Ziva is there for you. Don't hesitate to reach out if you need her. Fae or human, it doesn't matter, the Goddess of Love works to ensure all our happiness."

I wanted to believe that, but it seemed like a fairytale. I was already happier than I'd ever been, aside from this thing with Calix. I couldn't ask for more than that.

I stood up, Ilta following suit, and we followed Delia inside, both honoring my silent cue to let talk of Calix and destiny rest. Delia turned her head to smile back at me. "I have your dress, Asteria! You aren't going to believe this."

"Oh! Let me see! Let me see!" Ilta bounced on her toes.

"Don't you need to go get ready yourself?" Delia raised a brow at our excitable friend, while I tried to contain my giggles.

"Of course!" Ilta rolled her eyes. "But I can spare the time to see her dress!"

"Or you could wait to see the complete masterpiece." Delia chuckled, and Ilta tipped her head side to side as she contemplated.

"Okay, you have a point!" She skipped over to me, leaning down slightly to kiss my cheek, and then whispered in my ear. "Make Calix swallow his tongue."

I burst out laughing and Ilta smiled, pleased with my reaction, before she floated out the door once more.

"Sometimes I wonder how Ilta manages to be a ball of sunshine all the time." Delia confessed as she shook her head fondly.

"You're fairly sunny yourself there, Delia." I countered, raising a brow at her.

"Nothing like that!" She laughed. "I like to stay positive, and I believe you get more done with magic than iron, but that's different than the natural bubbliness Ilta possesses."

"True." I nodded, conceding her point. "Still, the two of you are—different, somehow. Lilith and Harpina, even Callisto—"

"They're all warriors." Delia interrupted with a small smile. "While Ilta is trained, it's not her favorite. Me, on the other hand? I never learned to fight. I think something about training, learning how to kill, hardens you a bit over time. Or maybe they were always more serious, and that helped them gravitate towards it." Delia shrugged, "Who knows? But they all have other sides to them. Just wait for the next holiday—you may discover something new about yourself as well." She wiggled her brows at me, causing me to snort out a laugh.

"It's next week, right? The Festival of Faunus?" I asked as I sat down for her to begin my hair.

"It is." She nodded, beginning to weave small braids into my hair. "You're going to *love it*. The holidays here are always amazing—the kind of event you never forget." Her reflection winked in the mirror.

I smiled back at her, but bit my lip, debating asking my next question. "Do you normally—participate?" I swallowed, trying to wet my suddenly dry mouth, as a blush lit the apples of my cheeks. "In the—orgy?" I practically whispered the last word, to my horror.

I wasn't inexperienced, and by the Otherworld I love sex, but I wasn't *orgy level* experienced. I'd had minimal partners, and I couldn't imagine having sex in front of hundreds of people—especially when my friends were counted among them.

"Of course!" Delia giggled, shaking her head like I was crazy. "You have nothing to worry about, I promise. Plus, I'm sure you'll get a warmup tonight." Her smirk promised debauchery, something I never imagined crossing her innocent doe-like face. Old G—Nox? I still hadn't got the hang of that. But—*fuck*! Literally. Was I expected to...

Delia could clearly see my thoughts spiraling, and she grabbed both of my shoulders. "Asteria! Calm down." She laughed lightly. "I promise you'll be fine. You won't ever be required to do anything you don't want to. *Never*. It's completely consensual. You'll never be forced into anything; I swear on Nox."

"I know." I acknowledged, nodding as I let out a puff of breath. "It's just—new. That's all." Delia nodded sagely, and I decided to focus on watching her. The two braids she wove on each side were made to slant sideways and then to disappear into the curls of my hair. Delia brought half my hair up, including the braids, and made a voluminous ponytail, while the rest lay curled against my shoulders. My hair normally fell to my waist, but the large curls meant it now fell to just below my breasts. My makeup was quickly applied until my skin shone and my eyes popped.

Delia took a small diadem out of a case, and I inhaled sharply at the sight of it. The diadem was made of silverium, the glittering silver metal from Day Kingdom. A crescent moon made of star opal sat in the center, propped up by a line of actual stars made of star opal on each side. Diamonds accented them the entire way up and lined the bottom of the piece as well. She placed it gently on top of my head, and I blinked in the mirror.

"It's a crown." I breathed shakily.

"It's a diadem." Delia insisted. "All the ladies will be wearing one. It's not a true crown, like the king will wear. They're common at formal events like the ball tonight." I nodded, appeased I wouldn't be alone.

"It's gorgeous." I whispered, wishing I could wear the necklace from my parents to match it. And wasn't that something? I once thought having that much star opal was incredible and once in a lifetime. Now, I live in a palace made of it, and wore even more on my head.

"Calix thought you'd like it." Delia smiled gently, a twinkle in her eye.

"Calix?" I repeated, my head tilting to the side.

"He picked out everything for you, well, he and Liv did anyway. She didn't trust him with the task." She giggled lightly. "They want you to feel at home here." Delia met my reflection, her expression both comforting and sympathetic.

I breathed in deeply. Okay, I could handle this. The jewelry I was wearing was a gift from the king—the man I couldn't have. Easy—I nearly rolled my eyes at myself. But I couldn't help the thump of my heart against my ribs at the knowledge that Calix had picked out these beautiful things for *me*.

Delia draped a matching lariat necklace around my neck, a crescent moon falling between my breasts, with stars dotted from the moon to the intersection of the y-shaped necklace. The earrings she secured were upside down crescent moons, with stars dancing below it that dangled down to my chin. The last piece of the set was a bracelet that had two separate rows of diamonds that were crafted in a swirling pattern, with shooting stars made of diamonds between the two rows, their trails done in beautiful lines of silverium.

My heart was surely going to beat right out of my chest—or burn up in the fires he stoked within me. Calix wanted me to wear these—he picked them out, just for me. I didn't have time to pick that apart right now, no matter how raging fire and sparkling light tore through my heart and soul at the knowledge. I shoved it all down, not letting myself hope for the impossible.

Delia led me over to the giant closet, where a bag was hanging in the middle. She reached inside, and I got my first glimpse of the dress Calix had selected for me. It was—*Oh. Nox.* This was…

Delia just smiled knowingly as I gaped.

The dress was like a supernova, an entire galaxy transformed into a dress. Made of swirling colors from teal to green, sapphire to purple, pink to red, with splashes of orange and yellow. It appeared as if stars existed within it, sparkling brighter in some spots than others. The voluminous skirts were folded over slightly in some spots and fell to the floor dramatically, with an illusion of colors moving this way and that, like the cosmos were moving over the dress.

The dress was strapless, and a sparkling starburst sat just under my breasts, surrounded by a glittering purple that made it pop. From there, the fabric cinched together at the waist and then curved out and down, where all the many colors swirled.

It was breathtaking—absolutely the most magical dress I could imagine. This was a dress for a celestial queen, one who ruled over the night sky and its stars, not a human. I could feel tears building, but Delia quickly admonished me not to ruin my makeup, and I burst out laughing instead. She helped me into the dress, and to distract myself I decided to tease her.

"Will you be attending with anyone tonight? Eryx, perhaps?" My innocent tone clearly didn't fool her and she faux glared at me for a moment.

"Why would Eryx escort me?" She asked, acting indignant. "I'm perfectly fine by myself. I'm sure he's already attending with someone else anyway." I rolled my eyes. These immortals, they were truly hopeless.

"I have a feeling he's not. Maybe you could ask him to dance." I hinted, but she looked horrified at the thought.

"If anything, he should ask me!" She declared heatedly before leaning down to fix my skirts, mumbling to herself. "Ask him to dance. Pfft. I don't ask men to dance, they ask me." I tried to smother my smile as I listened to her go on.

"I'm just saying." I tried again. "Maybe drop a hint to Eryx you'd like to dance." She stood up straight, looking at me critically.

"We'll see. Now, what do you think?" Rolling my eyes at her evasion, I looked at the completed picture in the mirror.

As beautiful as the Fae, Cyrus had once called me, but now, *now* I actually felt it. Looking at the woman in the mirror, I saw no trace of the bitter girl who buried her feelings and heart behind an ice wall, refusing to care to avoid being hurt. The simple girl in a simple frock whose best day was escaping to stare at the stars and invent stories that took her far away from her reality—a reality where her life would be spent as a slave. Freedom was a concept I'd reached for, but never dreamed of actually achieving.

Before me now was a gorgeous, confident woman. One who laughed with friends and cared about many. Who was free of slavery and had total control over her life—free to make her own choices. A woman fighting to free those still trapped in the chains the Fae kept us all in. No simple girl in a simple frock, but…a courtier in a beautiful gown. A woman who no longer wanted to hide her beauty, but one who *wanted* to look good—both for her own pleasure and to catch the attention of a Fae king, even when she knew she shouldn't. A woman who no longer hated every Fae, assuming they were all the same, but who wanted to grab a Fae king and hide the two of them away in his shadows all night.

I swallowed hard, processing all the changes within me since I left Sunrise, taking in the woman who stood before me and the image she presented now.

"I can't imagine it's possible to look better than this." I meant it. My skin was flush with health and my curves were full and pronounced from eating good food regularly and training daily. My sky-blue eyes were wide and clear, with a sparkle to them I couldn't recall ever seeing before. My heart shaped face was genuinely smiling, plush lips split wide as white teeth shined back at me. The apples of my cheeks aglow with a glittering blush. I was no longer withering under the confines of slavery, freedom letting me shine like the brightest star.

"You look absolutely breathtaking, Asteria." Delia smiled warmly, a hand clasped above her heart, watching me wistfully.

I spun in the mirror, admiring the effect as the colors seemed to spin within it, giving the appearance that they were moving.

"Thank you, Delia." I choked up for a moment, throwing my arms around her in a quick hug that she returned, before stepping back and clearing my throat. "You go finish up getting ready. We're all meeting in the waiting room beside the throne room, right?"

"Yes, we'll be announced at the start of the ball." Delia confirmed with a nod. "Calix, Liv, and Ndrita will be the last to enter." With another quick hug, Delia was off.

I passed nobles of all kinds as I made my way down to the meeting spot. Most nodded in acknowledgement to me, a sign of respect among them, so different from the nobles of Dusk. Humans there were part of the furniture or part of the wall, not to be acknowledged as one of them.

Of course, some people leered or eyed me with lust, but I let that roll right off me, deciding to take it as a compliment. It had always rankled when people paid more attention to my appearance than who I was as a person, but now, I couldn't help the burst of confidence it gave me. I knew I looked amazing tonight, and I wasn't mad about that fact being acknowledged.

Maybe because I hoped one person in particular would notice.

I swung my hips with more intent than I normally did as I sauntered into the little room off the throne room. Instead of using the grand hall where we normally had feasts, balls were held in the throne room itself. It was apparently converted when balls were thrown, adding tables and chairs, along with a dance floor. The room was massive, centered in a wing directly off the central structure of the palace so the ceiling could remain open. I was actually excited for the ball now, knowing we'd be dancing directly under the stars.

When I entered the room, I immediately noticed Baach and Ilta speaking quietly and giggling together in the corner, their long red and blonde locks swaying together and blending as they bent towards one another. Her turquoise dress was heavily beaded with shimmering purple, creating an incredible contrast. Baach most certainly noticed, his eyes straying down every few seconds. Her eyes, on the other hand, kept tracing over his form, clad in a forest green suit with long coattails. I smiled at them both, happy to see progress being made with them.

On the other hand, Eryx cut a vision of a boyish devil. His dark navy suit was quite sharp and contrasted against the boyish flop of hair falling into his face. He was watching Delia like a stalking predator. She, of course, was studiously ignoring him. She did look beautiful, so I could well understand his inability to take his eyes off her. Her light pink dress was embellished with crystals, the color complimenting her light brown hair and eyes.

"Well, well, look at you!" Harpina whistled as she came up and grabbed my hand, twirling me around as I giggled wildly.

"And look at you!" I smiled teasingly. "I've never seen you in a dress before." She looked slightly embarrassed, but it didn't last long before she sniffed and lifted her chin.

"I make anything look good." She winked, but she wasn't wrong. Her silk dress was a perfect match for her amber eyes, falling to the floor in a slink of body-hugging fabric. An overskirt, with so much gold embroidery that it shimmered more gold than amber, was affixed to the waist, allowing her to don a ball gown while still showing off the body she'd toned from years of fighting.

"Asteria, you look fabulous!" Lilith gushed as she approached. She was clad in a sage green gown that was designed to mimic leaves, while beside her, Priscilla was wearing a red ball gown with black embroidery. I nearly choked up again seeing Priscilla dressed up for a ball she could actually attend.

"You look like a Queen, Asteria." Pris whispered, awe in her voice as she took in my dress.

"And you don't?" I laughed incredulously and Priscilla smiled widely, before disbelief crept into her expression.

"Can you believe this? It feels like this can't be real sometimes." Priscilla said quietly, and I knew exactly how she felt.

"It's surreal." I agreed. "But it is real, Pris, and we'll make it a reality for everyone else too." My promise was more ferocious than the occasion currently called for, but it was heartfelt.

Priscilla laughed quietly, shaking her head. "Something tells me our specific circumstances are going to be unique." She raised an eyebrow as she pointedly trailed her eyes over my dress, my diadem, and I ducked my head, cheeks flushed. "But I do believe if anyone can achieve it Asteria, you and Calix can." She bumped my shoulder with hers, her faith in me, in our goal, warming me down to my bones.

Everyone looked incredible, but in comparison, my dress was much more elaborate. And while I chatted with everyone as we waited, I was half paying attention, trying to figure out why Calix put me in such a gown.

Callisto snuck in at the last moment. Wearing a white gown that dipped low in the front and back. Priscilla's eyes were instantly glued on her, unable to move anywhere else. I elbowed her with a smile and barely got a reaction. Lilith met my eyes over her, and we both bit our lips to contain our laughter, but Harpina didn't bother, letting out a boisterous laugh.

"Pris, if you look at Callisto any harder, she's going to catch fire." Harpina snorted as she flipped her hair back, the wine-red curls laced with gold jewels that made her hair glint in the light.

"I'm doing no such thing." Pris refuted, going bright red as she glared at Harpina, crossing her arms and looking pointedly elsewhere. I glared at Harpina, who was clearly getting in the way and not helping, but she just shrugged, unrepentant.

By the time we were called in, Eryx had somehow convinced Delia to let him escort her, which necessitated me hiding my smirk from the two of them. Those of us without dates went together, pairing up and linking arms. The herald announced us as we entered, but my eyes were instantly focused on the sky and not the packed crowd around us. Even the fountains overflowing with an array of lavender, blue, and pink drinks didn't catch my attention as the sky did. Nor the flower arrangements in all the colors of the aurora that decorated the space. Even the giant crystals that were set up around the edges of the room, looking like—*Nox,* pure star opal, completely uncut. They were gorgeous, and at any other moment, would have all of my attention—but nothing could compare with what was above me.

The open night sky shined like millions of diamonds were scattered across it. The aurora was in full swing, the green, purple, blue, and pink lights dancing across the sky in undulating waves. The moon was shining brightly, giving the space most of its light. I wished more than ever to fly through the sky again, to be embraced by the darkness and shine amongst its lights—maybe Calix would indulge me later…

"Now presenting, His Highness, King Calix Orpheus Atarah Erebus," The herald called out, continuing with Calix's list of titles before introducing his sisters. "Princess Ndrita Luna Erebus Nuit and her husband, Lord Sterling Nuit of Keris. And Princess Liviana Chandra Atarah Erebus." Titan and several other guards followed the royal family as they entered the throne room. Everyone in attendance made admiring noises around the room. I, however, inhaled sharply, freezing in place.

While the princesses looked beautiful, Princess Ndrita wearing a light blue gown that brought out her eyes, and Liv wearing dove gray with a ruffled skirt and a bodice dotted with crystals, it was their elder brother who stole my breath.

Calix was wearing a black and purple suit that looked like it had been poured onto him, his biceps and shoulders straining the fabric and the band around his middle accentuating his narrow waist. He looked strong, fierce, suave, and sexy, all at once.

The black suit jacket was outlined in purple with embroidery in the same color around the edges, moons and stars within the scrolling designs. While stars and fire—like a supernova exploding—trailed up his arms from wrists to elbows. Magic had to be in the design, the way it seemed to come to life, much like my dress.

A purple silk shirt was underneath his jacket, revealing a hint of his muscular chest along with it. Black pants matched the jacket, but I didn't let my eyes linger long in that area. His crown resided atop his head, jewels glinting among the black, and as he made his entrance, he gave the moment its proper drama—large dragon wings sprawled from his back, somehow the perfect addition to his ensemble.

As the music began, Calix swept Liviana into a dance, Lord Sterling doing the same with Princess Ndrita. They swirled around on the glossy black floor that reflected the night sky perfectly, making it look like they were truly dancing among the darkness of the night sky, sweeping over the aurora before twirling amid the stars. It was its own kind of magic, and one I desperately wished to partake in.

"The first dance is always just the royals, then everyone else can join in." Lilith whispered to me. I nodded my understanding as the music continued. I let my gaze linger around the room, watching the nobles and the citizens of Tairngire and beyond who'd come tonight.

I spied Aibek and Siria, who were hiding out from the Dusk Kingdom after their escape. I made my way over to them, curtsying. "Lord Aibek, Lady Siria. I just wanted to express how thankful I am that the two of you are okay. I didn't get a chance to see you after our rescue."

"Asteria." Siria smiled softly, "It's nice to finally meet you, I've heard so much about you. And thank you, we've been busy trying to get as many of our people over the border into Night as we can. The temporary camp isn't far from our estate, but it's difficult nonetheless to smuggle them over without Dusk interfering."

She rolled her eyes, and I couldn't blame her. The fact that they couldn't stay in their own home as it was in Dusk Kingdom was clearly frustrating for them. I knew there'd also been several skirmishes with Dusk while getting refugees across—Cyrus's commander having taken up a post in their palace as he patrols their lands. One of the many things we'd been working on plans for.

"I admire your willingness to go back to help your people. I can't imagine many rulers in Dusk would do the same." I told them honestly, and Aibek smiled mischievously.

"That's because most of the rulers in Dusk are a disaster." He rolled his eyes and I tried to stifle a laugh.

"You're not wrong." I agreed, tipping my head to the side in acknowledgment.

"Calix tells us you've joined with the Resistance. Based on Princess Liviana's visions, I have to say I'm thankful for it. It sounds like you will be able to make quite the difference." Lady Siria smiled at me, hope sparking in those pink eyes of hers. I could feel the pressure of those hopes, those expectations, laying firmly on my shoulders. All because of a prophecy none of us understood.

Lord Aibek put an arm around his wife's shoulder, "Don't put so much pressure on the poor girl, we don't want her to crack."

I chuckled, his tone making it clear he was joking around, but before I could open my mouth to respond, they both straightened and bowed their heads. I turned, skirt swirling, and came face to face with the one I was trying to forget about. I swallowed hard, dropping into a curtsy.

"Asteria." Calix's voice was a sensual rumble that touched every inch of bare skin I had. Goosebumps formed in their wake, leaving me sensitized to the touch, shivering as he continued. "Would you do me the honor of dancing with me?"

I wasn't sure it was a good idea, but I couldn't very well refuse the king, could I? I gave him a large smile and bowed my head, dropping my hand in his. He led me to the dance floor and immediately spun me around to him, taking my waist with one large hand that spanned across my back, with his other interlaced with my own.

Our eyes met, and the heat in both of our gazes was definitely not fit for courtly consumption. We began to move, Calix sweeping me around the dance floor, leaving me feeling lighter than air as my dreams clashed with reality, finally dancing among the stars that stretched out above and below me. That I didn't make a fool of myself was entirely thanks to Ilta and Delia, who had taken it upon themselves to teach me the court's dances, with Baach as my practice partner, over the last few weeks.

"You look—ethereal, tonight. You outshine every star in the sky, my réalta." Calix whispered, his lips tugging up on one side, like he was fighting a smile, but couldn't quite manage it. His eyes lingered over my body, and when they snapped back up, I was consumed in those purple irises. His hand tightened around my waist, bringing me a bit closer than was strictly proper.

"Since you picked out my outfit," I smiled coyly. "Does that mean you're truly complimenting yourself?"

His head tipped back slightly in a laugh, and several people looked over in surprise. I sometimes forgot that he only showed the more playful, fun side of himself to his close group of friends, while others mostly saw his hardened exterior.

"What can I say?" He began in a husky, sensual tone. "I have an instinct for what looks best covering your body, my réalta."

The way he purred the name, the aurora slowly expanding in his eyes, his tight grip, and the expression of forced calm that was clearly trying to bank the heat in his expression—all of it told me exactly what—or *who*—would look best covering my body. I couldn't disagree. The thought of him between my thighs…

He surprised me, dipping me backwards and leaning so close to my face, our noses nearly touched. My leg went around his thigh automatically, anchoring him to me.

"Tell me, my dorchadas," I murmured as I tightened my leg around him. Our bodies aligned as he slowly lifted me, causing my breasts to press against him, tightening my hand around his neck as my body slid down his. I bit my lip to hold back a moan before I leaned in to whisper in his ear. "While this dress is gorgeous, I think you and I both know what would truly look best on me. Darkness does become me, does it not?"

I raised my brow as my lips tilted up in a sultry smirk. A low growl echoed through his chest, wisps of darkness greeting me as his control slipped. I inhaled sharply as he used the hand on my lower back to pull me tightly against him. His shadows slid subtly into my dress, causing me to gasp as they stroked down my body, skirting over my nipples and down between my thighs. All the while I was held tightly enough against him that I was able to feel exactly how turned on he was. What dangerous ground we were on.

Dangerous, but thrilling—and wasn't that the best kind?

"Hmm." Calix hummed in a growling voice, more dragon than Fae. "It does appear that the darkness suits you." I felt said darkness caress my skin and I shivered in his arms. He smirked at me, eyes exploding with color now. "What a shame I can't see my essence slipping over every part of you right now, my réalta."

My hand tightened further on his neck, in what to a human would be a bruising grip, and his head inched down slightly, his eyes focused on my lips. I pressed myself against him, gasping as his shadows circled my clit. The smirk on his mouth proved he enjoyed my reaction, and I leaned into his ear to whisper.

"Why not go for a more direct route? I want *my* dorchadas to be touching me." I bit his earlobe lightly before pulling back, in time to watch Calix's eyes slip closed. But then Eryx was there, slapping a hand on his king's shoulder.

"Mind if I cut in?" Eryx insisted, pulling at Calix's shoulder.

Calix's eyes blew wide, and the wisps of shadow dissipated completely. I could see the regret staring back at me and closed my eyes momentarily to avoid the hurt it caused—but it didn't help. I'd seen the regret on his face plain as day. He hadn't meant to do more than dance, and once again, we'd been unable to help ourselves when together.

Calix stepped back, bowing politely to me. "My apologies, Asteria."

And then he was gone. I stared after him until Eryx cleared his throat. The sad understanding on his face was too much, but he seemed to realize that. The man who was there at my worst, who witnessed my complete breakdown, he just took me in his arms and let me rest my head on his shoulder as we swayed.

"Liv's prophecies have never been wrong, you know." He murmured a moment later.

"What?" I asked, lifting my head, confused on where that had come from.

Eryx smiled slightly, blue eyes lightening. "She's never been wrong. And she saw *you*. She may not be able to tell us much, but she said you were important. That the future of our kingdom rested on you."

I snorted at that, still not sure how that could be, but he leveled me with a look before continuing. "This thing with you two—I know it's difficult. For both of you. And it's not fair to you. That's probably what aggravates me the most about it. Calix explained how difficult it is for him, but I told him to think of you. You aren't some pretty girl he can fuck and toss aside while waiting for his soulmate."

I flinched at the description, but Eryx shook his head, a slight laugh escaping. "He decked me for that, *hard*. Said it had nothing to do with that, and to never refer to you in such a manner again. So I know he cares about you, truly. But he's torn, between a fate set out for him and the future he desires. None of that is fair to you, and I just want you to know, we're all here for you, Asteria. Regardless of our king, my brother he may be in all but blood, but we're here for *you*."

Eryx's face was set in serious lines out of place on that boyish face, those puppy dog blue eyes looking older and wiser somehow. I couldn't help the tears that came to my eyes as I threw my arms around him. He hugged me tightly, kissing the top of my head. I wondered vaguely if this is what having an older brother was like, one who'd look out for you and protect you.

I got my waterworks under control and smiled shakily at him. "You're the best, Eryx."

"I know." He winked back at me.

"Pfft." I pushed his shoulder and he jokingly fell back, making me laugh. As he did, Baach swooped in, taking my hand and twirling me in circles.

"Dance with me, Asteria!" Baach's boisterous demand was matched by his mood, and it was infectious. I laughed as we twirled around the dance floor. I could feel eyes on me as I smiled widely at Baach and Eryx as they passed me back and forth between them. I spotted Calix leaning against a column, talking to Lord Rhidian, but his eyes were glued onto me. I let a smirk play on my lips in response to his drilling stare, trying to ignore how sexy he looked as he leaned back—all long, hard muscles and moon white skin.

I ended up dancing with most of the Lords. All except Lord Ciaran, who seemed reluctant to let Lady Jasira leave his side. The way they looked at one another told me there was definitely something going on there, but it was none of my business. Still, that part of me that had been brought to life in Dusk Kingdom, that needed to know everyone's secrets, still lingered there, urging me to find out.

Lord Polaris and Lady Zillah pulled me into a three-way dance between them. They joked and laughed and drank a ton of wine—frankly, they were a ton of fun, completely unlike the nobles I'd met in Dusk.

"Come on, Asteria, another dance!" Lord Polaris smiled, shaking the wine bottle he'd swiped off the table and chugging it back.

"Mercy!" I begged, laughing. "My poor human feet need a break."

I laughed them off as I went to grab a bit of food, somehow ending up near where Calix was talking with several of his lords, Lord Rhidian and Lord Kyler on either side of him. The three large, light haired and muscular men made quite the sight together, and I tilted my head to the side as I appreciated it.

"They're something, aren't they?" An amused, musical voice broke my drooling, and I whipped my head around to find Lady Alora's sweet smile aimed my way.

"They certainly are." I returned her smile. "You're a lucky lady."

Lady Alora laughed, a sound like tinkling bells. "Asteria, right?" I nodded in confirmation, and she inclined her head. "How are you settling into life here in Night? I know the situations are very different, but I grew up in Sunset, so I'm well aware of the challenges of moving to a new kingdom."

She seemed genuinely interested, and while Cyrus had fostered a suspicious edge to me in Dusk, I just couldn't picture this woman doing anything with ill intent, so I returned her smile.

"Honestly, while there's been a few adjustments, I'm happier here than I've ever been anywhere else." I admitted.

Her smile grew as she linked her arm through mine, leading me to a table where another lady sat. "I'm so glad to hear that. We were all relieved when His Highness found you and got you out."

That took me aback for a moment. Why would they care? It took me a second, but then I remembered—the prophecy, right. "You know of the vision Liv—uh, Princess Liviana, had?"

"Don't worry." Lady Alora bumped my shoulder with hers. "We don't worry much about all that." She waved her hand, indicating my slip was no big deal, which was a relief.

"But yes." Alora continued, nodding. "We're all aware of the prophecy. At least, the nobles and resistance are. It was such a relief to hear the one who can help change the tide had finally arrived."

She seemed to sense my struggle with that concept, placing a hand on my arm while handing me a glass of pink wine. I shot it back and a husky chuckle caught my attention. I looked up to see the lady across the table watching me.

"You look like you need to relax." Lady Aisling, Lord Kyler's wife, smirked at me, and I couldn't help my wide-eyed nod of eager agreement.

"The—after party of sorts is starting soon." Lady Aisling chuckled, raising a brow.

"What after party?" I asked, not having heard about it. I jumped as a body slammed into the seat beside me. Baach grinned unrepentantly at my glare.

"The one we're dragging you to after this. The girls have your outfit covered, so you just run along with them, and they'll bring you down. I did promise I'd show you the room dedicated to Hedone, didn't I?" Baach winked before he was off. No doubt making sure everything was prepared correctly—he took his job of Master of Ceremonies very seriously for being as playful as he was. Ilta appeared out of nowhere, like Baach had summoned her, and urged me to go change.

"Did he say we're going to the sex god room?" I swallowed hard.

"Oh, I have to see this." Lady Aisling laughed, tipping her head backwards. "Come, Alora, let's join these ladies, I have a feeling this is where all the fun will be!"

Sufficiently ganged up on by half the Nox damned kingdom, I allowed them to shuffle me out to a side room. They'd made it into an impromptu dressing room, and they'd brought tons of options for us all to choose from.

I couldn't believe what I was seeing. Lacy scraps of nothing, leather bands that barely covered a thing, silk that draped provocatively. Every piece was a dedication to Hedone. These were outfits worn to get fucked. There was no getting around that.

A pair of hands landed on my shoulders, interrupting me from my wild-eyed perusal. I'd known the Fae got up to a lot that humans weren't privy to but—*damn.*

"Come on, don't you want to drive the king wild?" Lady Aisling raised her brow as I turned to her. "I saw you two and it's clear the sexual tension is ready to explode. This will just help you tip it in the right direction." She winked, and while I appreciated her enthusiasm for getting me laid—

"I can't. He has—" I protested, my face falling. I ducked my head to hide it, but a gentle finger under my chin lifted it back up. Lady Aisling was smiling softly, emerald eyes glowing.

"Leave the morals out of it tonight." She advised; her words gentle despite their message. "He might have some stupid idea of being loyal to a person he's never met, who could be fucking anyone, anywhere right now, but life's too short, even for immortals! I say—"

"Aisling!" Harpina's voice was like a whip crack, which suited her new leather ensemble quite well. "Stop causing trouble."

"I'm not! I'm helping my new friend." Aisling sniffed, offended. My lips twitched, and I bit my bottom lip, trying to hold in a smile.

Aisling *was* just trying to help, but Harpina was loyal to Calix beyond his being king—they had been friends for centuries, trained and battled together—of course she would help him uphold his vow.

But as a smirking Aisling ignored her and pulled a dress off the rack for me, I couldn't help matching her smirk with my own. Maybe a little trouble *was* called for…

CHAPTER 31

Tʜᴇ group of us made our way towards the mysterious room dedicated to Hedone. *A Nox damned sex room.* I had no idea what to expect, but I assumed it was different from the brothel Cyrus owned, though I wasn't sure how. Still, all dressed up in this outfit, I felt powerful and sexy as we walked the palace halls.

Our path took us past an open area that contained a lagoon. Columns lined the walls with vines and other flora wrapping around them, surrounding the sunken pool of sparkling blue water. A strange bird-like creature with teal green and purple feathers wandered about, and lounging on one of the beds surrounding the lagoon was a griffin. I identified it immediately by its lion head and eagle's body. It lifted its head, shaking its mane as it called a greeting to Lilith, who went up to pet it.

Griffins were said to be wild and ferocious, but Lilith absentmindedly pet it like a house cat. She caught my incredulous look as she rejoined us, and the griffin put its head back down to resume its nap.

"He needs extra care than the others, so I've been letting him stay here until he's fully healed mentally." Lilith told me, and sympathy rose for the griffin. They may be ferocious, but it appeared even they weren't immune to mental trauma.

I wanted to inquire about what had happened but was distracted by the women around me discussing the men who'd be attending and what they wanted to do with them. My cheeks flushed pink, making me immensely grateful for the mask I was wearing.

It was black and silver lace with beautiful lines swirling all around it, giving it an elegant edge. The mask covered the area around my eyes and down to my nose and matched my lace dress wonderfully. The dress was also black, with just a hint of silver on the edges—black definitely seemed to be the color of choice for the after party. It was honestly barely a dress at all, as it ended at the very tops of my thighs. Thankfully, the lace was tightly knit in the skirt so it wouldn't expose the areas barely covered by the equally lacy undergarments I was wearing.

The top of the dress, however, was a much looser knit, showing more skin than I was used to as it peeked out from the lace. The front dipped low, down to my navel, and the back had a matching dip that reached to just above my ass. My nipples were covered by a spell, of all things, one that held my breasts up and covered the area strategically. I had to hand it to these Fae, they were inventive!

My favorite part of the dress had to be the long bell sleeves, which stopped at my hand on top but underneath, draped down to the floor—it made me feel both sexy and elegant at the same time. The lace had celestial patterns, which I absolutely loved, and the only other adornment I wore was a necklace—one that dipped low, a star falling just above where the v of the neckline met at my navel.

We came to a plum-colored double door engraved with runes in that language I couldn't decipher.

"Dedications to Hedone." Lady Alora smiled reassuringly at me as Ilta came up on my other side, linking our arms with an excited smile.

"You're going to love this, trust me." Ilta tossed her head as the doors opened, her blonde hair flying behind her like some goddess come to life.

I felt much like one myself right now, as every eye in the room turned to watch our entrance. The masks may cover part of our faces, but it seemed fairly obvious to me who was under them. Still, they did give one the strange confidence of being anonymous. My hips swayed as we walked in, my dark hair a contrast to Ilta's light, but there was someone with even lighter hair I was keeping an eye out for.

That would have to wait, sadly. This was—something else. The room was dark and sensual, plum walls with black velvet in a damask pattern across them. Crystal chandeliers containing candles hung from the ceiling, the only light source in the room, leaving it in a dim, sultry light. Black velvet lounges were scattered throughout space—some round like an ottoman but large enough for two or more people to spread out on, and they certainly were.

Everywhere, people were engaged in all sorts of acts. Some were having sex out in the open, while others were on their knees, sucking someone off or eating someone out. Hands roved over sweaty bodies, and the scent of sex was heavy in the air, arousal permeating the space and mixing with the incense that was lit in every corner.

We stopped at a table holding glasses of red bubbling liquor that fizzed with small sparks. I inspected the glass in my hand curiously, and Aisling laughed, tipping the glass up towards my mouth.

"Drink it. It's great for enhancing sexual experiences." She assured me, and I raised a brow at her.

"It will make me—" I hesitated, but she was already shaking her head.

"No, it doesn't *make* you do anything." She smiled slowly. "It just makes everything—*more*." I looked suspiciously at the glass but finally shrugged, downing half the glass to dull my nerves.

"Have you never watched others fuck before?" The redhead smirked, her eyes scanning the room.

"I have." I admitted, thinking back to that night at the brothel. "But it was—different. It wasn't so many people, for one."

"I imagine it must be intimidating." Aisling chuckled. "Many humans aren't used to the ways of the Fae when they arrive here, despite living among them. So many humans are stuck living half-lives because the Fae of other kingdoms treat them as other. They don't get introduced to the ways of this world, instead they're kept in the dark and hidden away." She sighed heavily. "Calix is doing an amazing thing, you all deserve much more than the other kingdoms offer."

"I never could have imagined half the things I've seen since arriving." I agreed, nodding, but it was undercut by the giggle that slipped out, the drink already hitting me.

"Well, don't waste it! Go take someone for a spin. I have to go grab my wayward husband before Kyler finds the wrong redhead." Aisling rolled her eyes as my shoulders shook in laughter. "He needs to wait for me for that." She winked before taking off to find said husband—and possibly another redhead to join them.

I noticed only then that everyone else had already disappeared. Ilta was likely with Baach somewhere, and I would bet Eryx went after Delia.

Harpina—well, who knows what she may be doing in that leather get up she was wearing. Lilith I could still see, talking to someone across the room, but Lady Alora was long gone as well. Pris and Callisto had both begged off coming, and I desperately wished for them as I found myself alone—even Eris would have been nice, but she went straight to bed after the ball.

I steeled myself, taking a deep breath. I could handle this, no problem. I made my way through the room, wandering around tableaus of people engaged in all kinds of sexual acts. As I wandered, the music began playing a slow, sensual beat, a threesome I passed thrust perfectly in time to it. I twitched a brow—what skill it must take to coordinate.

I sipped my drink as I observed the two men fucking into the woman at perfect pace, feeling my body heat more and more the longer I was here. If the drink was supposed to help, I didn't think it was needed. I remembered vividly what had happened in the brothel and being here just cinched it—watching any kind of sexual acts turned me on. Made me long for the feel of a thick length pounding into me, or Tartarus, I'd settle for a cock in my mouth right now—something, *anything*, to ease the ache building steadily in me.

A few men eyed me as I passed, inviting and sensual, but I didn't want them. My desire was fixated on one person. I entered a corridor of sorts, except there were small rooms off it on each side, sheer black curtains pulled closed on some, but others were wide open, inviting people to look in. I kept walking with just a few peeks inside. This "sex room" dedicated to Hedone was no mere room, more of an underground orgy *wing* than anything else.

I wondered how often they had these parties, but I was distracted when I realized the room I had entered was filled with a bunch of contraptions hanging from the ceiling. I recognized Lady Alora immediately, who was strapped into one, squealing and moaning as her husband, Lord Kyler, pounded into her. Her breasts swaying as his hips moved at inhuman pace. My eyebrows practically flew off my face—I hadn't expected to see sweet Lady Alora being pounded in public in some—was that a swing?

I tilted my head as I took it all in, pacing in a circle around the grouping of swings spread out around the room. A chorus of shouts and moans and the rhythmic slapping of skin on skin filled the room over the beat of the music. *Fuck.* I rubbed my thighs together, feeling my arousal leaking down the inside of my thigh.

I moved into the next room and nearly wept in relief to find more wine. Nox knew I needed liquid courage to get through this. I paused with the glass halfway to my mouth as I caught the familiar scent of night and fire. *Calix.* He was here, and close.

I tossed the green drink I'd grabbed down and turned, letting my hips sway as I strutted through the room. Here, people were having actual conversations, but more often than not, women were sitting in men's laps as the men's hands tweaked nipples and rubbed their fingers through soaking wet folds—in full view of their conversational partners.

I stood corrected—there was a woman perched on another woman's lap who was being felt up as well, and a male who had a man and a woman on each leg. Then there was the man in the middle of the room, who instead of having his partner in his lap, had him on his knees before him, his cock down his throat as he lazily thrust into it. It was definitely equal opportunity here, which was admittedly nice to see.

"You look lonely, would you want to join me, my Lady? Someone as gorgeous as you shouldn't be alone on such a night." A masked man asked, looking me up and down as he licked his lips. He was Fae, his pointed ears poking out through his dirty blonde hair, with a strong jaw and nose, and his eyes were a pretty shade of green. An idea struck me, and I decided to play, hoping it would work. I swayed over to the man, a smile teasing at my mouth, when a hand suddenly clamped around my waist and pulled me back into a *very* hard body. The scent of the night sky and blazing fire overtook me immediately.

Calix.

Found you.

A part of me I hadn't even known existed sat up and practically purred in pleasure that I managed to entice him out and over to me. The idea of another man touching me made him jump up to stop it. That part of me was the one who ground back against the very hard bulge I felt against my ass. A smirk pulled at my lips still, but for a much better reason. I imagined this was the same satisfaction fishermen felt when an ornery fish was reeled in.

"The lady's with me." Calix barked at the man, who held his hands up in surrender. I tilted to the side and turned my head so I could see him. His scowling face glared at the man who invited me over, his hair as white as the moon with eyes the purple of an aurora in the night sky as fury bled through them—the man wasn't going to argue with his king.

Calix kept his hand around my waist, leading me over to a dark gray oversized velvet chair. Another man was sitting in the one kitty corner to it, and he raised his brow at Calix. Clearly, Calix had abruptly halted their conversation for me, and a pleased smile spread across my face.

Calix sprawled out in the chair and grabbed his glass full of red fizzing liquor, knocking it back in one go, while his other arm shot out and grabbed me—pulling me down onto his lap.

"Are you trying to torture me, my réalta? This dress is nothing but a scrap of lace." Calix murmured in my ear, his voice a low rumble that instantly made wetness seep down my thighs. His nostrils flared and he let out a pained groan. *Right, Fae senses.*

"Not any more than you're torturing me, my dorchadas." I whispered in his ear as my hand came up to play with his hair. He buried his head in my neck, nipping slightly and causing me to moan and squirm in his lap. I could feel him hard beneath me, but his damn restraint was still holding him back.

The drink had done wonders for me, for I no longer cared about the consequences, no longer cared that he would inevitably hurt me—I only cared about one thing.

"Calix…" I whined, rubbing against his covered cock until he grabbed my hips, halting me. He was panting heavily now, and I just needed to push his control a bit further until it snapped. It was only then I noticed the man across from us was sitting back and watching, amused. Calix lifted his head and growled at the man, who only smiled wider.

"Asteria, this is Nithe." Calix informed me begrudgingly. "One of my spies, and a distant cousin." Nithe's hair was a dark tumble to his shoulders, while his eyes were pink like Siria's. It was an interesting combination, but good looking though he was, he was no Calix.

"Pleasure to meet you, Asteria." Nithe smiled widely, all charm and grace—perfect for a spy. It gave me an idea, one that had my newly discovered sultry, teasing side applauding. I fluttered my lashes as I smiled, reaching out my hand to Nithe.

"Pleasure's all mine. Hopefully anyway." I winked at him, my voice a sexy rasp that surprised even me.

Nithe threw his head back in laughter, shaking it slightly before he took my hand, kissing it instead of shaking. Calix's hands tightened on my hips to the point of pain, but I relished it, rubbing my thighs together to relieve the ache it caused.

"Is this your plan then? Show me what I can't have and rub it in my face?" Calix pouted, so I turned to face him and gently traced my fingers over those pouty, soft lips. A thrill ran through me at finally getting to touch him in such a way. He nipped my finger and I moaned longingly.

"Who says you can't have it?" I smiled slowly, rubbing my ass back and forth on him, and he bit his lip, but as he threw his head back, a moan finally slipped out before he could stop it. It sounded like victory. All that pale, exposed skin called to me, and I leaned forward, nipping along the column of his throat until he lifted his head.

I leaned back against him, winding my arm back around his neck and burying my hand in his silvery white hair. Calix swore loudly, his hand sliding across my stomach, tracing upwards to the deep v of my dress. His fingertips trailed up the expanse of bare skin, before he brought both hands up to cup my breasts, squeezing them with perfect pressure. His hands on me felt like Elysium, and I moaned, tossing my head back against his shoulder. When he let go of my breasts I was disappointed, until he used those hands to pull the lace covering my breasts to the sides, letting them spill out into the air.

"Nox damn me, your breasts are fucking perfect, Asteria." Calix groaned in my ear at his first glimpse of my naked chest. Those large hands of his nearly covered my plentiful chest entirely as he reached up and got his first handful of my bare breasts. After a few moments of appreciating them, he spared two fingers on each hand to roll my nipples between them, pinching them.

"Fuck." I moaned, my head falling forward. Calix chuckled huskily, making me shiver in delight. He released my breasts, watching them bounce as he licked his lips, while Nithe sat forward, watching avidly. Calix ran his hands down my curves, and I arched up into those magnificent hands, wanting them to touch me everywhere.

"So responsive, my réalta." Calix murmured, his cheek brushing mine. "I wonder if you're so responsive everywhere."

I turned my head until our lips were a breath apart and that new side of me was now in full control, coming out in a sultry whisper. "Why don't you find out, my dorchadas?"

His eyes closed for a moment, and I wanted to scream, or possibly cry— that was always his cue before he ran. I braced myself for disappointment, but thankfully, I wasn't the only one drinking the inhibition lowering alcohol tonight. "I can't have sex outside holidays, but that doesn't mean I can't…*bend the rules* a bit."

"This ought to be good." Nithe chuckled, and I think we'd both momentarily forgotten he was there, and just as quickly, we forgot once more. It was just us, in our little world. The haze of the room and its atmosphere, the drinks we'd imbibed, all of it combined to create this needy, desperate feeling, like I might explode if Calix didn't put his hands on me.

Calix slid his hands along my body until he reached the bottom of my tiny skirt, hiking it up and exposing my lace panties. He situated us so my legs were on either side of his, and then spread his own legs. It took mine with him, spreading me wide for him, while also keeping his sadly still covered cock lined up against my ass. It was perfect.

His finger snapped my panties with a single twist, the pieces of lace fluttering to the floor. Both men inhaled deeply, but I was only focused on one. Calix inhaled my arousal like a drug as his eyes feasted on the sight of me—somehow making me even wetter, when I was already sure I'd never been as soaked as I was right now.

"Fuck, you're perfect, my réalta." Calix praised, making me smile, pleased that he liked what he saw, and even more pleased when his fingers slipped down the outside of my cunt, caressing my skin while dancing around where I needed him. He spread his legs a bit more, leaving me spread out and exposed for his perusal—only I didn't feel exposed, I felt set free.

"What a pretty little cunt." Calix cooed, and I preened until his hand came down and slapped it, ripping a gasp from my lips. His mouth found my neck and I felt his smirk against it before he sucked the skin between his teeth. I tilted my neck to give him better access, as I lifted my hips to try to get him to *touch* me. Tartarus damn him, did he not understand how badly I needed it?

He chuckled, a silky, promising thing, and then his fingertips were sliding through my wet folds. I moaned as I arched into him, chasing his touch, and he began to run his fingers up and down my slit, circling my clit each time he moved upwards. "Fuck, you're so wet for me, my réalta."

"Yes." I whimpered. "Please, please Calix." I begged—*begged*! I couldn't even feel shame over it, I wanted, *needed*, him too badly.

Finally, he let two fingers play at my entrance before sinking inside. Long, thick fingers that could reach places my own never could. I couldn't stop the noises coming from my mouth as he began thrusting his fingers in and out. The wet sound was almost embarrassing. It was so loud, but I couldn't summon it—in fact, with Calix's whispered praise in my ear proving how much he loved it, I somehow found it even hotter.

His thumb began circling my clit, earning him high pitched moans of his name in response.

"That's it, baby." Calix murmured, thrusting harder and hitting a spot that made me positively *sing*. It had never felt like this before, and I thought I might float out of my body as he sent me to heights I'd never known. "Good girl. I want you to cum for me. Can you do that for me, my réalta?"

Oh, I could see the playboy prince of years ago now, breaking through as he pleasured the human he was forbidden from touching, and was finger deep inside anyway.

"Yes, *fuck*—yes Calix, *please*!" My hips rose to meet his thrusts, craving more. He obliged me with another finger and the stretch had me tossing my head as I moaned my gratitude.

His other hand came up and twisted my nipple before moving higher and grabbing my neck. He wrapped his massive hand around it and squeezed, cutting off just a bit of air—just the right amount. It spiraled me higher, my body quaking, my blood sparking as light flashed behind my eyes as they fluttered closed.

When I dragged them back open, my vision was darkening in spots— *no*—that wasn't my vision. Strands of shadow were floating around us in a haze of darkness, while others creeped up my body, caressing and stroking it. The shadows circled around my nipples until they were acting like his fingers, pinching and soothing. The darkness was like another hand to him, another way to touch and take.

"Fuck, look at you. Dressed up like my own slutty little doll, eager to be played with. Do you know how badly I want to sink my cock into this tight little cunt? How badly I want to stretch you out until you're left gaping open when I'm through with you." Calix's voice was low and dark, making goose-bumps spread across my skin. His words elicited reactions from every part of my body, like I was nothing more than a sensitized nerve, as my arousal dripped down my spread open thighs.

"Please!" I writhed on his lap, pushing against his cock before thrusting up to meet his fingers. "Yes, I need you—I need you inside me. I want to feel you fill me up."

He groaned loudly, his forehead falling to my shoulder, moonglow hair falling over his face until he lifted his head back up, his eyes meeting mine in a collision that I swore shook the world. "You have no idea. *None*. I want to grab your hips, hold you down, and drill my cock into you until you lose your voice from screaming. Until you beg me to stop because it's too much. I need to feel you around me, surrounding me with your tight heat." He growled, and pressed a soft kiss against my cheek that was so at odds with his words. "You're my own personal Tartarus, Asteria. A temptation I want nothing more than to succumb to."

My heart pulsed, like it wanted to both expand and shrink at the same time. His words were as sweet a torment as he claimed I was. But thankfully, desire swept me away before I could ruminate too long.

"Then do it, please. Let me feel you. I want you, so badly. Please!" I babbled, words flying from my mouth with no thought, pure lust and unfulfilled desire fueling them. My pleasure was building, and the thought of him actually fucking me was an image that nearly made me cum itself.

A shadow slithered south, breaking off into two wisps of darkness until they circled around where his fingers were thrusting into me, and they sank into me, joining his fingers. I gasped loudly as they expanded inside me, until I was being stretched and filled to the limit. The fullness similar to an actual cock as they joined his fingers in fucking me. I moaned as I tossed my head back, my orgasm approaching ever more rapidly now.

"Nox, you are an exquisite sight." Calix admired, eyes riveted on his disappearing fingers, shadows laced around them every time he pulled them out. "Otherworldly in your beauty, but even more so as you let me drive you to the brink. As you moan for my shadows like a lover. Letting them fill you and stretch you out the way my cock should be doing."

He wasn't wrong. I wished it was his cock, but I would take the shadows. The cool sensation of them was indescribable and the way he could control them was the true Otherworldly thing here—the way they mimicked his length inside me, the way they stroked my walls as I contracted around them.

"So fucking sexy. Like my own little fuck doll, who will let me fill her with shadows until she cums." Nox, his words were too much—this was a man who knew what he was doing, and he did it *well*. It was a crime against nature that he'd been near celibate as long as I'd been alive.

A twitch of his fingers had more shadows blanketing me. They caressed every part of me, and it made me so over sensitized, that when he flicked my clit, I flew over the edge, screaming his name as I came with a sob. He groaned my name as I clenched around his fingers and shadows, and his lips found my neck before trailing up to my cheek. His fingers stroked me as I came down from my high, only pulling out of me once I stopped twitching around them.

I watched as he brought them to his mouth, where he licked every drop of me off his fingers. I couldn't help myself, and I grabbed his face, kissing him. He hesitated for only a moment before grabbing my hair and pulling me harder into him. His lips met mine in a battle for dominance, but his tongue slipped out and met mine in a sweeter dance.

His hands skimmed over my body and had me shivering in delight. My mouth chased his when he pulled back to look at me, something in his eyes shifting before he descended once more, our lips and tongues saying everything we couldn't. He shifted me on his lap until I was kneeling on either side of him. His shadows danced over my body, further enticing me, and I realized, keeping me from view—which was sweet of him.

My hips slotted against his, my cunt still drenched and surely getting all over him as we ground against one another. I could feel the outline of his cock through his leather pants, and I thrust against it as we devoured one another's mouths. He pulled my hips tighter against him, and I could feel myself rapidly spinning towards another orgasm as his cock rubbed against me, hitting my clit perfectly.

My tongue explored his mouth like a new frontier, wanting to know and experience everything there was about him. The way he kissed me with brutal longing left me with the impression he felt much the same. When we finally parted, both panting as we stared at one another, I could see shock bleeding into the aura in his eyes—

Oh. My eyes widened as I realized the drink was wearing off. And now—I hastily moved so I was no longer straddling him. My body was crying out from the loss, but I pulled down my skirt and moved my top to cover my breasts once more. I swallowed hard, watching as Calix readjusted his straining pants as he watched me in turn—the length of him long and thick as it stretched down the side of his thigh. *Fuck*, I nearly whimpered.

We were both coming out of our lust induced fog now and as Calix stood, I eyed him warily, waiting for his reaction.

"Nox." He muttered, running a hand through his hair. "What have I done?" The look of abject pain on his face *hurt*. I could see it all over his face. His belief that he'd betrayed his mate.

A dull pain throbbed in my chest. Of course, he would be concerned for the other half of his soul. Never mind that he hadn't even met her yet, he was a good man, despite what he thought, and he was loyal to his core. He'd made it very clear before this was a line he wouldn't cross, and a combination of drink, atmosphere, and the sizzling chemistry between us had pushed him right over it. But to my surprise, he cupped my cheek, kissing my forehead.

"Forgive me." He whispered, and then in a cloud of darkness, he was gone.

Leaving me with pain in my chest like someone was squeezing my heart in their fist, and my eyes filling with tears I furiously blinked back.

CHAPTER 32

Calix POV

Looking up at the sky, I would have given anything to be able to spread my wings and take flight, clearing my mind among the stars. But no—Baach and Eryx were determined to keep me grounded, badgering me like my mother had lovingly done once upon a time.

I loved them like brothers, truly, but if they didn't shut up soon, we were going to need to stage another attack just so I could let my pent-up aggression out—a little bloodshed was exactly what I needed right now.

"What were you thinking?" Eryx demanded, pacing back and forth. I hadn't seen him this angry since the day he took revenge for his parent's deaths.

"He wasn't." Baach snorted, leaning against the rail of the balcony. "Or his cock was doing all the thinking at any rate."

I shot him a glare, but he just chucked, brushing me off. I wasn't in the mood for his blithe remarks, as much as I generally enjoyed them. A dark mood had followed me since I'd left Asteria in the Hedone room. The drinks may have lowered my inhibitions, but I couldn't blame them, not really—that was all me. My desire for Asteria was beyond anything I had experienced in four hundred and twenty-one years of life.

Before my soul mark, I would have taken her and kept us both in my bed for a week, until neither of us could walk and we were nothing but sweat and cum. I hated the disloyal part of myself that fiercely resented not being to do so now. I wanted her with a passion that blazed like the fires of Tartarus—there was no putting it out.

And yet my soulmate was out there.

"Obviously, he wasn't fucking thinking!" Eryx roared, and I eased my white knuckled grip on the railing to turn to face him, surprised by the venom in his voice.

"What is the big deal, Eryx?" Baach protested, shaking his head. "They're both consenting adults.

Eryx scoffed, shifting his ire to Baach. Despite our many years together, or maybe because of them, we could still pick at one another like children on occasion. "The big deal is that Asteria is going to be the one left hurt here. She's been through enough. She deserves better."

"You're right." I agreed, quietly. He whipped back to face me, incredulous.

"Then why, *the fuck*, did you do that?" He spat at me, and I had to admire the way Asteria drew people into her orbit. She didn't even seem aware of it. The way people always told me I had a natural charm that drew others in, kept my lords on side and cooperative, my friends and family close—she had that same natural charisma in spades. Asteria had blown into our lives, and already had my entire inner circle ready to fight for her—even against me.

"Do you think I enjoy this?" I grumbled back at him. "That I want to be torn in half this way?" I turned back to face the sky, trying to calm down so I didn't deck him. My rage was an inferno that could spark out of control and consume everything in its path. A dragon's rage was a ferocious thing to behold, and not something I would ever unleash on my family. I could feel the fire rise inside, begging to be released.

I cracked my neck side to side, desperately wishing there was someone to fight. I needed to get a spar in soon, or I was going to explode. I nearly snorted—beautiful brutality is what my enemies had dubbed my skills on the battlefield, but I saw no true beauty in battle. Just a necessary relief from the pressures crushing me from every side.

"Cay, you've been controlling your desires for years, why do you need *her*?" Eryx pressed, his anger diminishing a bit.

"Why does the sky need the stars?" I mumbled to myself, but Fae hearing meant the other two had no issue hearing me. Baach let out a low whistle, both his brows flying upwards, but Eryx just looked dejected.

"Look—" I continued, pushing off the railing. "I get you're unhappy, and that you're protective of Asteria."

"She's like—like a little sister, almost. Sort of like Liv." Eryx confirmed, and I smiled softly, the first one that had crossed my face since I last saw Asteria.

"I'm glad." I told him honestly. "She deserves nothing more than to have someone truly looking out for her. I know how loyal you are to those you love, and it's a relief to know you're there for her."

Eryx raised a brow, shaking his head. "This isn't just lust, is it? You wouldn't care about me looking out for her that way if it was. You've never acted like this before, Cay. It's a bit concerning, considering."

"For me more so than anyone." I admitted, knowing if I could trust any with the truth of this, it was these two. "I don't know how to explain it. You know, words like always, forever—you'd think they'd mean more to us immortals, since we live so long—we should take those promises more seriously than any other."

I shook my head, looking at the stars again, but they only reminded me of Asteria—my réalta.

"But the truth is, it just makes them easier to forget. Time stretches like a yawning void, and what felt so desperate, so necessary, fades over time. Passion shifts to familiarity, then into boredom. Like the Darkelm leaves change color every season, our viewpoints, our emotions, do the same, and over the length of years we have? Those promises end up falling by the wayside. When I discovered I had a soul mark, I realized I *never* wanted to forget. Never wanted to be one of those who found his mate, only to—years later—no longer appreciate them, this gift I was granted by the gods themselves."

"Then why—" Eryx interrupted, shaking his head with a furrowed brow—frustration radiating from him.

"Because despite the promises I've made to myself, the mere sight of Asteria washes everything else from my sight. The sound of her voice drowns out that of all others. The thought of her sparks a fire in me that burns all others to ash." I declared passionately, shocking Eryx into silence.

"Damn." Baach, of course, didn't know the meaning of silence. "Is it really that intense?" He looked unsure, eyes shooting between Eryx and me.

I nodded, fisting my hands as shadows danced around them, my mixed-up emotions summoning them without my notice.

"If that's the case, then you need to make a decision, Calix." Eryx put a hand on my shoulder. "Things can't stay this way. You have a mate out there, and it's clear how much that means to you. Asteria deserves better than you running hot and cold on her. So figure your shit out."

Easy for him to say. How was I supposed to make such an impossible decision? I couldn't stay away from Asteria, circumstances didn't allow it, and being around her meant my control slipping entirely. The thought of not seeing her sent a sharp lance of pain to my chest, and I attempted to rub it away, but it lingered.

The thought of my mate only added to it. She was somewhere out there, and here I was, dishonoring her. What would happen when I found her? This was a mess, that was certain. I'd wanted a mate since I first discovered the concept of them. A woman who wouldn't be with me just for the crown on my head—to get one of her own. The number of women who had thrown themselves at me hoping to be queen was uncountable, so I'd kept away from serious relationships, not trusting the motives of those who approached me.

Fighting and fucking were great outlets over the centuries. The pressure on me was intense, even back then. Learning how to be a good king, raising my sister, my birth prophecy—every person in the Night Kingdom knew that one day my queen would come thanks to that prophecy. That she would bring light to my darkness, and together, we'd bring this land into a new age. They knew I would be responsible for great change, which probably helped when it came to my abolishing slavery. But it also meant tons of women who yearned to be the one the prophecy spoke of. I'd learned to keep my exploits to a night only—okay, or a week—but never longer.

And loneliness lingered underneath it all. The thought of a mate to chase away that loneliness, to love me for all that I was, to support me, to help me rule, to bring in that new age together—it was indeed a light to my darkness, keeping me going in a whole new way once my mark came in.

And now—I didn't know what to do, how to handle this. For once, I was at a complete loss.

So, I spread my wings, and took off into the sky, leaving Eryx and Baach to bicker on the balcony. I let my body shift into my dragon form, hoping flying would help me empty my mind as I let my rage bubble out, my flames shooting across the sky.

But as I flew through the stars—all I saw was her.

CHAPTER 33

"**U**GH!" I grunted as I punched with all my might.

"Again!" Titan nodded. I readjusted my fists and then aimed for the pad he was holding.

"Mmfh." I shook out my fist after that one, flexing my fingers. Titan was watching me with a raised brow.

"What's with you today?" He questioned with a critical eye. "You're letting your aggression overcome your instincts."

I gave him a pouty glare he was completely unimpressed by. I threw my hands up in the air and turned away, unraveling the tape wound around my fists. I was letting my mind trip up my body; it was as simple as that. Since the night of the ball, when Calix and I had crossed that line—he'd been ignoring me.

Dodging me whenever possible, I only really saw him during meetings. With the information from Sunset about the alliance and Cyrus's plans, we had to make a move to show Sunset why it was a bad idea to mess us up. Calix managed to avoid my eyes in meetings too. It had been four days, and my patience with him was quickly drying up.

Harpina put a hand on my shoulder, and I looked up at her. "What's going on, Asteria? You and Calix have both been weird for days."

While she said it without any heat or accusation, I couldn't help feeling like it was there anyway. Harpina had been against whatever this was between us from the start. I knew she was trying to protect us both, but still, I couldn't exactly confide in her about this without proving she was exactly right.

"I'm fine." I forced a smile. "Just anxious about the meeting today." That was true enough. We'd been going in circles with the information, and I wanted a plan of action—wanted a chance to unleash the rage that bubbled inside me.

She looked me over, narrowing her eyes, as she tilted her head, inspecting me. "Come with me."

I followed her, still in my training gear with cloud leather leggings and an armored corset made of dragon scale with straps about two inches wide. The armbands I wore came up over my elbow and had finger holes to allow for full range of movement. Harpina was in her full black leather armor, sword hanging at her side as she marched through the palace gates.

The gates were reinforced stained glass that depicted a crescent moon and stars, with a dragon twining itself around the moon. The reflection of the sun against it was striking, but its beauty was amplified at night—the magic of this kingdom enhancing everything after dark. My earlier thoughts of battle with Dusk sparked my curiosity as I eyed the gate.

"What would happen if an enemy ever invaded?" I asked Harpina as we walked. "There are no walls or fortifications around the palace."

"Is that so?" She smirked, amber eyes lighting up as she looked back at me.

"What do you mean?" I cocked my head, narrowing my eyes at her.

She shook her head, red hair flying back and forth. "Calix's ancestors wanted this city to be beautiful, to showcase the wonder and majesty of the magic that imbues this land."

I could well understand that. I remembered Calix's pride when he showed me the city for the first time, as I gaped at the magnificence of the kingdom laid before me. Now, as we exited Shadowgleam District, Harpina led me to an arching bridge that led from Shadowgleam to Starshine, extending across the edge of Moonglow District to connect them, with several staircases along its length so you could depart in different areas.

Harpina continued as we walked onto the bridge, its path a shining pearlescent pink while the barriers on each side were light gray stone accented with onyx handles and rails down each side. "But just because they wanted to showcase its beauty, didn't mean they were fools. They built defenses that could be raised if the city ever came under attack. Underground, there are giant barrier walls that can be erected in moments around both the city and the palace."

"Where?" My eyes widened in disbelief.

"They wouldn't be very good defenses if they were easily spotted, now would they?" Harpina smiled, showing too many teeth. "There's also a fortress built into the Etheralta Mountains. Though shared with Day, the mountains on our side must be protected, nonetheless. The miners live there now, but in the event of an emergency, everyone knows they can flee the capital and head there. It's built to hold the entirety of the city within its walls."

My mouth dropped open in shock. That had to be a huge fortress if it fit the entire city and didn't even get in the way of the star opal mining operations.

When we reached the end of the bridge, it sloped downwards and left us at the beginning of Starshine District. Harpina headed towards the area full of apartments that I'd noticed upon my arrival here. I looked around as we walked, taking in the architecture so unique to this city, or maybe the kingdom. The swooping lines and curves instead of hard edges were a favorite of mine, and I loved the way they seemed to make the buildings flow more naturally, more in tune with nature.

We left the main road, turning onto a side street that snaked around several corners before inclining up a small hill. Halfway up the hill we came to a stop outside a tall building that was teal and bronze, with swooping lines making up the front. The door to the building was surrounded by glass that extended up half the height of the building, with a burst of metal lines in bronze running across it.

"What are we doing here?" I asked Harpina as we entered, giving her a side eye. Her face was grave when she looked at me, making me frown in confusion.

"In Sunrise, you didn't see much of what went on with the Fae there, and it wasn't until you went to Dusk you saw how bad it can get. But even then—" She swallowed hard, eyes closing momentarily as if to brace herself. "You haven't truly seen. What was done to you and your friends, it was horrible. I would never think to dismiss or belittle that. That isn't what I'm trying to say."

She took my hands in hers, squeezing hard, as her eyes beseeched me—maybe for understanding, maybe for grace. Either way, I nodded slowly, still very confused but willing to go along with it, and she let out a soft sigh. She led me by the hand to a door on the 5th floor. Knocking, we waited for whoever lived here to answer. The door opened slowly, only being shoved wide when they spotted Harpina.

"Harpy!" The girl smiled, and it took everything in me to not react. She had been…*maimed*, was the only word I could think of. She was missing an eye, a glass replacement sitting in its place now. One of her arms was also missing and deep scars ran from her shoulder, across her chest and down, disappearing below her shirt—like an animal had clawed deep.

"Tesha!" Harpina smiled widely, hugging her quickly. "How are you doing?" The girl smiled wider than I would have been capable of in her circumstances.

"Oh, the usual. What brings you here?" She gave me a curious look as she waved us inside and I forced a smile on my face as we stepped into her apartment.

"I was hoping you'd be willing to talk to Asteria here about your experience." Harpina looked over at me. "She was from a small village originally, so though she saw the occasional whipping and heard rumors, it was only more recently she experienced firsthand how corrupt some of the Fae have become. She's blaming herself for some actions despite them not being her fault. I want her to get a more well-rounded view of what is actually happening out there." *How in the Otherworld?*

"You make it sound like I don't understand the way humans are treated by Fae. I've lived with anger over it my entire life. You think I'm blaming myself? I'm blaming Cyrus for what happened." I put my hands on my hips as I faced off with Harpina.

"Asteria, come on." She shook her head. "You think I don't see the way you blame yourself for Emmie? Or for trusting Cyrus not to hurt you? You may be angry, sure, but you're placing the blame on yourself more than you're willing to admit. And as long as you do that, you're going to be focused on the wrong things."

"Oh?" I scoffed. This was why I avoided friends for so long, they were able to see too deeply. "And what should I be focused on?"

Harpina was smiling, and so was Tesha, and I looked between them, confused. "Harpy likely brought you here for two reasons. One, to help you see the bigger picture, and two, to get you to admit that what happened isn't your fault." Tesha gave Harpina a fond look. "A lot of humans live with that same rage you do, but we're forced to hide it deep. By the time we get here, we're so used to it, we bury it all, letting it fester. Sometimes, it just takes someone rubbing you the wrong way to let it out. Admitting the truth will help you come to terms with it a lot faster."

I looked bewildered at Harpina, who shrugged at me with a smirk. "You've been twitchy and anxious about what's going on with Dusk but won't admit it."

I took a deep breath as I collapsed on Tesha's sofa. She gave me an understanding look and smiled softly. "I get it, trust me. It took me months to admit what happened to me, and that none of it was my fault. I was assigned to Dawn Kingdom. I'd grown up in Dun Ailinne in Day Kingdom, a city that had plenty of punishments dished out that I'd witnessed. Still, I wasn't prepared for the brutality in Dawn."

Tesha swallowed hard, her eyes shifting down to where her arm would have been. My heart bled for her. My scars were all internal, but she had been maimed in vicious fashion. I couldn't imagine the pain she had experienced.

"My twin sister and I had been separated, and I was desperate to find her. I ended up sneaking around the castle, mapping a way out so I could escape and somehow get myself to Sunset Kingdom so I could look for her. But I got caught." Her voice was hollow, sending chills down my spine. I'd been looking for a way to escape too, and it brought to vivid light what could have become of me if things had gone differently.

"King Tariq was sure I was a spy, and despite me swearing I wasn't, they didn't believe me. I explained about my sister—" A tear fell down her cheek, and she brushed it away quickly. "They tortured me for information. I had never experienced anything beyond a lashing before, and this was much worse than that. They brought in the commander of their armies to help—he shifts into a large bear. He's the one who did this." She gestured to her chest where the deep scars lay—explaining why it looked like an animal had clawed her.

I was horrified. I had seen humans who'd been tortured in Dusk, but in a limited capacity. Nothing like the extended torture she went through—and nothing like being mauled by a bear shifter.

"But then, they brought out my sister." My heart sank into my stomach as realization dawned. Tesha nodded gravely. "They were still certain I was a spy, so they contacted King Tieran, claiming they had a traitor spy and that my sister likely was too. It was enough to hand her over, and they dragged her out, torturing her in front of me. When I couldn't tell them anything they wanted to hear, they killed her and made me watch. That fucking commander came in, shifted, and sliced her open."

My eyes closed in horror. So, it wasn't just Cyrus. I knew King Tariq was just as corrupt, but this was well beyond that. I didn't have words for this. I'd lived with my rage all my life, knowing humans were cattle to the Fae, unable to be free, to make their own choices, being whipped and degraded—but I could never have envisioned the brutal torture and forbidden magics being used on us. They had to be stopped.

Liviana's visions indicated I would help accomplish that—*somehow*. I wasn't sure how exactly that was possible. I was only one human—but I was determined to find a way. Tesha's story only firmed my resolve. Harpina was right, in my anger, I'd been focused on Cyrus—but this was so much larger than that.

The whole world was at stake if we didn't fix the balance. That would start with getting rid of assholes like Cyrus and Tariq and freeing the humans everywhere.

"I screamed and screamed when they killed her, called them all sorts of filthy names, and it enraged the commander. He tore my arm off in retaliation. The king looked at him like a misbehaving child. He merely sighed and ordered them to stem the bleeding, so I didn't die before they got their information." She sneered at the memory, and I joined her, still unable to believe the lack of empathy these Fae had.

"If it wasn't for King Calix, I would be dead. He raided the place, saving me and a bunch of others." Tesha smiled fondly. "I owe him everything. Unfortunately, with my arm and my eye—" She hadn't mentioned how she had lost her eye, but given what she *had* shared, I could only assume the details were gruesome. "I'm not able to fight. I help the Resistance in other ways though. Namely, taking in those who are too hurt, either physically or mentally, to get on their own two feet right away. I help rehabilitate them and integrate them into society here. For many, they're untrusting and twitchy for a while, and it helps to have a human being the one to help them. Someone who's been similarly affected, and not a Fae."

I had hated all Fae before and could certainly imagine the difficulty many would have around Fae when first arriving here. I still hated many now— those corrupted ones leaning towards chaos, or who were already all in—but I had slowly realized Fae were just as complicated as humans during my time in Dusk. There were terrible ones like Cyrus, but then there were ones like Kian who helped get me out. If there hadn't been, I would have likely been one of those who wouldn't let Calix help them.

"But what happened to me wasn't my fault." Tesha reached over, grabbing my hand. "And what happened to you wasn't yours." My hand shook, her words stirring up all sorts of feelings I didn't know what to do with. I knew she was right, that Cyrus was the one at fault, and it made me angrier that I'd take on his guilt as my own. It brought angry tears to my years as I tried to bury the fire rising.

"Say it, Asteria." Tesha whispered, and I raised watering eyes to meet hers.

"It's—" I choked, the words not coming. I tried again, clearing my throat. "It's not my fault." It felt like the words were ripped from my soul and as the tears fell like rain, Harpina and Tesha were there, holding me steady through it.

"It's okay to feel however you do, Asteria." Harpina promised, wiping my tears away with a sad smile. "I just didn't want you to take on that blame when it doesn't reside with you. You'll get your chance to make Cyrus pay. That I know. But humans all across Celesterra need you. Liv's prophecy tells me one thing, that you're the key somehow. And you need to think of all the humans out there that are being hurt, not just those in Dusk."

I opened my mouth to argue, but Harpina shook her head. "I know you were, that you wanted to free them all—but I don't think you had truly realized how bad it's gotten. Things are tipping more toward chaos every day, and the more it does, the worse those corrupted Fae get."

I nodded my understanding, because she was right. The admittance that I wasn't at fault for what had happened set something free within me—released a burden I hadn't known I was carrying. And while Liviana's prophecy still mystified me, if I was somehow going to free the humans, then I had needed this. This was bigger than my own vengeance. I would still take it, that was certain—but I had to keep the big picture in mind.

I THOUGHT ABOUT it the whole way back, and as we headed to our meeting, I was bolstered once more. My rage simmered just under the surface, wanting to unleash. My mixed-up feelings of wanting to help all the humans enduring such torture across Celesterra, and my own fury over blaming myself for Cyrus's actions, were difficult to sort through. I wished I could take my rage out on those it belonged to. Unfortunately, the objects of my ire were far away. For now. Planning an attack was going to be the closest I got today.

I stopped dead in my tracks upon entering the meeting room. When Eris looked up and spotted me, she smiled larger than I'd ever seen her.

"Emmie?" I whispered; afraid I was imagining things.

"Asteria." Emmie turned to me with a smile. Her bubbly nature was much subdued, but I supposed that was to be expected after everything.

"You're…here?" I hesitantly questioned, not sure what to make of it.

"I figured it was time to stop wallowing and time to do something." She nodded firmly but my eyebrows furrowed.

"I thought you were angry we took you from King Astraeus?" I questioned, cocking my head.

Emmie sighed deeply, ducking her head as blonde curls fell into her face, hiding those brown eyes I hadn't seen a light within for too long. "I was at first, but I realized what a fool I've been. I'd allowed myself to be swayed, let him get into my head, and when I realized, I was too embarrassed to face you all. I want to help in whatever way I can. King Calix says you're planning to invade another kingdom shortly. I want to go with you and help."

I raised a brow at her and looked to Eris, who nodded. "I trained her to protect herself when we were growing up. We'll have to keep her out of the thick of the fighting, but Calix swore with our plans it'll be fine.

I nodded; Eris would know her capabilities best. I'd been surprised when we began training that Eris was so good. When she told me her father had taught her to fight, I'd been insanely jealous. No one in my village would have dared such a thing. I had always wanted the ability to protect myself, but at least now, I could.

I gave Emmie a smile and laid a hand on her shoulder. "I'm so glad you're with us for this."

She pulled me in for a hug and I sighed in relief. Knowing she was going to be okay was a huge weight off my mind. I turned to Calix and Callisto, only sparing a brief look at the former. If he wanted to ignore me, then fine, I had other things to focus on. Namely, planning this invasion into Sunset Kingdom and the rescue of as many humans as possible.

Calix avoided my eyes, but leaned forward over the table, hands gripping the edge tightly until his knuckles whitened. "You'll notice we have several additions today. For those of you who are newer here, my lords and ladies join our ventures from time to time. Usually, they rotate who joins me, or sometimes two will come at a time, but since they're all here for the festivities, they all decided to grace us with their presence." He smirked as he looked around the table, eyeing the nobles.

"Except they can't all join us on this mission. If something were to go wrong, we can't have every single lord and lady of Night captured or killed." Harpina crossed her arms, raising a brow at Calix.

"Agreed." Calix nodded sharply. "While they'll all join the planning, half will stay here. Aibek and Siria won't count toward that number, since they're from Dusk, it won't impact the running of the kingdom." Lord Aibek and Lady Siria both nodded in acknowledgment, and the vicious little smile on Siria's face nearly made me smile—she absolutely wanted blood for what was done to her. Cyrus had targeted them and seen to their capture; she deserved some retribution as far as I was concerned.

"Rhidian, Kyler, Aisling, Ciaran, Jasira, Polaris, Zillah, Sterling, Ndrita, I thank you all for your loyal service. It warms my heart the way you all seek to support me and the people of this continent." Calix spoke sincerely, his eyes lingering on his sister. She smiled softly, giving him a small nod. I hadn't had a chance to really interact with her yet, but the love between them was obvious.

"Sister, as you're technically my heir should anything happen to me, you and Sterling will stay here." Calix commanded.

Ndrita immediately opened her mouth to argue, endearing me to her immediately. "The gods haven't chosen me as your heir, which means the power may not go to me should something happen. I should be there."

"I need you here." Calix shook his head. "We have plenty of people to go with me, but few who can run Tairngire with the authority you can as an Atarah Erebus. Rhidian, Kyler, Aisling, and Ciaran will join me, while the rest run things here." Everyone nodded, except Ndrita who crossed her arms and narrowed her eyes at her brother. My lips twitched in amusement, and Calix's eyes shot to me for all of a second before skittering away. I would have thought I'd imagined it if I couldn't feel the burn of his gaze so thoroughly.

"We'll plan to hit Biarma after the festival. We'll enter from here and here." Calix pointed to two spots around the capital of Sunset on the map. Using his magic, the little figures on the map slid over to them. "We'll have two main groups. The one hitting the front gate around the capital will cause mayhem in the streets. Save any humans who are willing and get them out."

Heads nodded around the room. Callisto picked up the thread and continued the explanation. "That team will distract everyone, and the guards will converge on them, leaving the path as clear as possible for the second team. They'll enter from the back and sneak into the palace. From there, splinter teams will go and place the documents containing the intel Asteria obtained detailing Prince Cyrus's plan to use blood magic and weaponize iron."

Everyone turned to me, and I smiled wryly in acknowledgment. Hopefully, my information would convince Sunset not to ally with Dusk, but either way, we'd at least put plans in place to counter it.

"Asteria, Eryx, Harpina, Callisto, and Emmie, you'll be with me inside the palace. With the distraction, we should only have a handful of guards to deal with, but every human will be paired with a Fae just in case. That way each pairing will have the protection of magic in addition to blades." Calix looked at each of us as he called our names, but his eyes cut back to me for a moment after, and our gazes locked. I forcibly moved my eyes elsewhere—he couldn't ignore me and then stare me down, dammit.

"We'll split into three smaller teams. Each team will be assigned the room of either King Tieran, Prince Vesper, or Prince Zakat, and will be responsible for delivering the documents to it. We'll meet back up outside the palace at our entry point." Calix said, using his shadows to roll out the map containing the palace's layout and place figures on each room we'd targeted.

"For those of you on the ground outside—shock and awe. Use your powers, use whatever you have. The bigger the distraction, the more time we have." Callisto added, looking anxious for the task ahead. Nods and grunts of affirmation passed around the room.

"Asteria, you'll be with me, and we'll hit Tieran's room." Calix surprised me, and I whipped my head back to him. He was already looking at me, and I could see the worry in his eyes. He may have been ignoring me, but I knew it wasn't for a lack of care, and my anger melted away. He was in an impossible situation, and I knew I hadn't made things easy on him—I'd in fact made them quite hard, when he was just trying to do the right thing.

"Eryx, you'll take Callisto to Vesper's room, and Harpina, you'll be with Emmie and take Zakat." Calix continued when he tore his eyes from mine. "Ensure you're back at the meeting point quickly—we won't have time to waste."

He turned to look at those who'd be on the streets of Biarma, stirring up chaos. "Remember, only kill Fae if you have to. Or if you can tell they're a Nox-damned corrupted piece of shit—Tartarus, those you can take pleasure in."

Vicious smiles lit up the warrior's faces, and I rolled my eyes, but still smirked at them, a bit pleased to see it. I enjoyed training, but a true battle was something I'd never experienced, except from the other side. I vividly recalled my first meetings with Calix. I'd been terrified and aroused—and confused by the combination. Now I'd be facing my first real test since learning how to fight. And Nox knows, I lusted for a chance to set this world on fire—I just hoped I wouldn't let everyone down. The prophecy loomed large, and I worried that I'd prove it false when I actually got out there.

Calix didn't seem to worry at all, a bright light in his eyes at the thought of battle—even though he wasn't going to be out on the streets this time. He was well known for his skill on the battlefield, and having witnessed him slaughtering people, I could say beautiful brutality was indeed a perfect description of it. He moved like a dancer, making an art of watching him as he fought savagely.

We spent several hours going over all the logistics. Tomorrow was the festival, and we'd be leaving for Sunset two days after that. It would take nearly two weeks to reach Biarma while dodging patrols and lookouts along the borders and using magic when necessary to cloak us. Titan would command the army going into the city, while Calix would oversee the smaller group of us going into the palace.

When we finally broke for the night, I looked to Calix, but he was already leaving, keeping his eyes firmly away from me. I sighed, heading to my room. I found Delia and Priscilla waiting for me, and I eagerly accepted the wine they handed me.

"How was it?" Priscilla asked, since the two of them wouldn't be going on this mission, they'd decided to skip this meeting to instead help Baach with preparations for tomorrow. I sighed heavily, downing my wine, before tossing my head back on the sofa.

"Calix won't even look at me, let alone talk to me. Aside from that? Just swell." My sarcasm made them chuckle and I glared at them, pouting, until Delia bumped my shoulder with hers.

"I know things are difficult with him right now, but there's always tomorrow." She wiggled her brows at me. I furrowed my own brows, unsure what she meant.

"Asteria!" Delia laughed incredulously. "The two of you are playing some Tartarus-damned game and you didn't even remember there's only a few times a year Calix *must* have sex to appease the gods?"

My eyes widened and I jolted forward. Pris doubled over in laughter at my reaction, but I was too focused on Delia to care. "The holidays." I whispered. I couldn't believe I'd forgotten.

"Yes, the holidays." Delia smiled smugly, nodding. "Calix will have to participate in the orgy tomorrow, though he doesn't have to take multiple partners. He just needs to take one, to return the energy to the gods and the land. I can only imagine *who* he might be interested in doing so with." Her heavy sarcasm was not appreciated, and I glared at her as her lips twitched into a smirk. I let out a deep sigh, a sudden nervousness overtaking me.

"What if—" I licked my suddenly dry lips, "What if he chooses someone else?" My voice came out much smaller than I'd intended.

"I don't think you have anything to worry about there, Asteria." Priscilla reassured me, putting her arm around me. "But you should be focused on what you'll do after."

"What do you mean?" I shook my head, confused.

"Can you handle it?" She asked softly, sympathy in her eyes. "Having him once, then never again? Knowing you will never have him truly? His soulmate is out there somewhere, and he's doing a good thing by not starting a relationship with someone else in the meantime. It can only end in heartache for all involved. But it's clear there's something going on with you two. I just—I want you to be careful." I hated the spark of pity in her eyes.

I didn't need pity. Yes, there was chemistry between Calix and I. Would I have liked to pursue something if he didn't have a soulmate? *Yes*, but he did. I knew I couldn't have him, but if I could just get him out of my system, maybe that would solve everything.

The thought rang hollow in my own head—and even more so in my heart. I couldn't lie to myself very well, apparently.

Fine. Did it hurt that I wasn't enough? That he had some great, destined love out there? Of course.

Still, there was a reason I'd never allowed myself to fall in love with *any* man. I certainly wouldn't be doing so with a man fated to love another. Wanting to fuck him, even having *some* feelings for him, wasn't the same thing.

Love was nothing more than a shackle people willingly donned, binding you to one person and giving them the power to break you. I'd spent enough of my life as a slave to recognize that trap for what it was.

CHAPTER 34

I LOOKED at Delia, completely bemused as she explained to me what I'd be wearing tonight.

"Come again?" I cocked my head, blinking quickly in confusion.

She giggled, the sound echoed by Ilta who was here to help her get me ready. It was apparently a two-person job for the night. Judging by the supplies laid out in front of me, I could well believe it.

"The Festival of Faunus not only celebrates the Fall Equinox, but it's truly a celebration of Faunus himself, with nods to Flora as well." Delia explained as she pointed to my vanity chair. I rolled my eyes but did as requested, sitting down for her to start doing my hair. "Faunus is a wild, animalistic god. He oversees beasts after all. Tonight is a celebration of nature at its core. The whole reason we have orgies on our holidays is because the release of so much sexual energy feeds the magic of our land, and thus feeds our gods—it's all part of the cycle of nature. So, we dress up in honor of it."

"Still—this is—what is the paint for then?" I was hopelessly lost on this point. The two laughed, and Ilta smiled widely.

"The paint has two purposes." Ilta began, looking mischievous. "The first is to celebrate all of the colors of nature. And the second, well, this isn't any old paint, this paint is infused with magic." I raised a brow at her, looking at Delia, who nodded in confirmation before Ilta continued. "In the light of the stars, this paint will glow—it's quite the sight during the orgy."

She winked at me, and I considered the sight of that—everyone naked and glowing. Nox, this was going to be an experience.

"Plus, it's quite fun." Delia added, Ilta nodding eagerly along with her. "Just let us take care of everything, you'll look amazing!"

I sighed but gave up fighting it. Delia placed a pair of large horns, with brightly colored blue and purple flowers at the base of each one, on top of my head, and secured it so my hair covered the band. My hair was left down and wild, while my makeup was bold and dramatic. Purple and blue shimmer dusted my lids, and my eyes were outlined in a dark kohl that swept out toward my temple. The colors brightened my eyes while the kohl made them pop.

My lips were painted a bright purple, and I looked at the two of them, aghast at their choice, but they swore that everyone would be doing their makeup like this. I swore then that if this turned out to be some elaborate prank, I was going to pay them back tenfold.

They helped me into my outfit, a little semi transparent silver dress that had purple and blue underneath, making it appear iridescent, shimmering with color. It had a sweetheart neckline and elaborate swirls down the front. The skirt was longer on the sides, with tulle making it appear wider and strips of other colors added in.

They had a matching pair of fake wings to go complete the ensemble. They were an iridescent mix of blue and purple, and when I put them on, I couldn't help sighing wistfully, wishing they were real. I smiled wryly at them, shrugging. "Well, I've always wanted wings."

Ilta clapped her hands joyfully as the two of them celebrated turning me around on the idea. With horns, flowers, and wings in place, I just needed the paint. They cracked open several jars—blue, purple, and green paint inside. They each took a brush and began pairing swirling patterns on my legs, arms, and chest.

It felt mad, but when Priscilla, Eris, and Emmie all showed up with the same sort of ridiculousness, I felt better. At least I wasn't being tricked somehow. Priscilla even went so far as to paint her hair, shimmers of every color of the rainbow now replacing her blonde tresses.

Ilta came back wearing a flower crown, and she continued the theme across her face, vines and flowers painted from her temples to down under her eyes and across her cheekbones. A floral dress in bright pink, blue, and yellow cut in at her stomach, just a thin line running from her breasts to her skirt, which barely hit the top of her thighs.

She looked like spring personified. And if Ilta was spring, Delia was fall itself. Autumn leaves and flowers were braided into her hair and a burgundy, orange, and green colored slip covered much more skin, at least compared to Ilta's.

WITH NIGHT NOW fallen and the moon high in the sky, we made our way out to head toward the forest full of Darkelm trees. Stepping out of the palace, I swore I could feel the shift in energy—of magic. Chills broke out over my skin as it caressed me like a phantom wind.

The stars were high in the sky, and my skin illuminated as their light washed over me. I looked down in wonder, appreciating the effect of the paint as we entered the woods. I could hear those deeper in the forest immediately—music, laughter, and shouts echoing. We sped our pace until we reached the spot Calix had shown me, the stone altar of the Blessed Trinity rising high above the festivities.

This was how the Fae partied.

A giant bonfire roared in the center, a maypole set up around it where women were dancing and swaying. Torches filled the space, providing light, while a circle of drummers surrounded the dancing women, a pounding beat filling the air as flutes, violins, and other instruments joined the cacophony. But it sounded strangely—*right*.

The area was completely crammed full of people drinking and dancing, letting nature take over for the night, their souls let loose in the presence of Faunus. He was the wild god of beasts, after all, and that wildness filled the people celebrating. I suddenly desperately wanted the same, wanted that wild untamed feeling for myself, to experience the freedom of being swept into the frenzy. So, we made our way over to the Fae handing out drinks, magic filling the glasses with a swirl of their fingers. I downed my first drink quickly and grabbed another.

Everyone was wearing similarly wild ensembles, with wings, horns, flowers, and leaves, while paint was splashed over any bits of bare skin. Nature dominated in the outfits tonight, reminding me of the natural dryads of Weathrian or the colorful pixies of Chromatos—or at least, what I imagined them to look like, though the pointed ears of the Fae were more akin to the Elves of Gemaria. And their sharp canines were reminiscent of the Vampyres of old—whose bloodlust grew insatiable, until the gods were forced to destroy their own creation to save the others.

"Once Calix arrives, the festival will truly start." Harpina explained as she and Lilith appeared at my side. I blinked rapidly, taking them in. Lilith looked like a goddess of the forest, with green leaves and brown twigs mixed in with the curling horns atop her long curly brown hair. Her dress was forest green, with thin straps that left her shoulders bare, but the sleeve began again lower down, covering her biceps. In contrast, Harpina was the personification of fire, with orange and yellow leaves and a crown of flame around her head, blending perfectly with her deep red hair. Her lightly tanned skin was complimented perfectly by the red and orange dress she wore, so different from her usual armor.

"You guys look amazing!" I gushed, smiling widely. Harpina took my hand and spun me around, letting out a low whistle. I laughed merrily, already feeling the drink.

"You look like a true Goddess of the Stars." Harpina complimented, a smile softening her face. "Something tells me you'll match perfectly with a certain someone."

She raised a brow, and my stomach swooped at the thought, while my heart ached at the idea. We'd hardly seen each other since the night of the ball, with him avoiding my eyes until today's meeting.

The crowd went silent before I was forced to respond, and I sucked in a gulp of air as I spotted why—*Calix*. Harpina was right. Large, dark horns jutted from his pale hair just as mine did, and he was covered with purple, green, and blue paint. It was all over him, thrown atop the dragon scale tattoo on his chest, covering the soul mark on his back, and making the runes around his forearms nearly indecipherable.

But I could still make out the defined abdominal muscles running over his stomach and the thick biceps I longed to grab hold of. I swallowed hard, saliva filling my mouth as I looked down. His pants were slung low, showing off the deep v of his hips and the light trail of silvery-white hair that disappeared where I couldn't follow.

"Oh, it's starting!" Lilith yelled, grabbing my arm as she hauled me forward, closer to where Calix was about to address everyone.

"People of Night!" Calix called out, a large smile on his face, and the crowd cheered loudly. "Tonight, we celebrate the Festival of Faunus! We honor the God of Beasts and his sister, Florus, the Goddess of Nature!"

Callisto and Priscilla crept up on my other side and my eyes widened as I took in Callisto. She'd turned her hair blue, with ringlets fading in an ombre of dark to light blue. She was dressed like a mermaid, with a sparkly blue top that was more like a bustier, covering only her breasts, and a small sequin skirt that was designed to be triangular in shape, mimicking a mermaid's scales and fin. Her stomach was bare, and a scale pattern was painted on it, using blue, purple, yellow, and green paint, which was also in swirling patterns down her arms and legs.

"Wow." I mouthed at her, and she smiled widely, then pointedly looked me up and down.

"Damn." She mouthed back at me, and we both giggled, before returning our attention to Calix.

"The four fires have been lit!" He roared to the cheering crowd. "In honor of the Sommer and Zima Solstices, the Pranvera and Harvest Equinoxes—the balance of nature is everything to our world, and it is up to all of us to uphold it. Tonight, we will battle! We will spill blood in sacrifice to Faunus! Shift into your animal forms, let the beasts loose! Then begin the hunt through the woods—the gods will select our prey for the night. Whoever sacrifices the glowing beast in the name of Faunus first will win the title of Beast King of the festival and bragging rights for the next year!" Calix amped up the crowd with a charisma that left me awestruck, as everyone around me screamed and hollered in bloodlust laced with joy.

"They spill blood?" I asked worriedly.

"Oh, not like that—minor blood spilled in battle. We're encouraged to fight and prevent each other from winning the hunt. Everyone wants to get to the prey first." Lilith answered, her eyes lit with a strange excitement. She clearly wanted to win herself—bloodlust shining in feral eyes.

"The gods really select an animal to kill?" I couldn't help but be skeptical. I'd learned my own gods weren't even real here—an idea, a fantasy, from another world.

"Faunus does." Lilith confirmed with a nod. "Calix and his sisters won't be able to change their forms—the dragons are the only ones who stay in their Fae forms, they're just too large for the woods. But the rest of us will shift when it begins, so be prepared."

I nodded, curious and wary in equal measure as we moved with the crowd. The Fae participating in the hunt began forming up along the starting line, while the humans joined on the sidelines, eager to see the spectacle. I looked around and finally spotted Calix, looking like a god himself as he took his place in the line. His eyes connected with mine for a moment, and a charge ran through me—I swore I could see his eyes darken from this distance.

There was something—feral, wilder—about everyone tonight. Him included. It made me want to tear into him and taste that wildness for myself. Maybe the magic in the air had affected me more than I realized, as that thrilling bloodlust seemed to be fogging my own head. I wished I had the ability to shift into an animal myself, to experience that firsthand.

The Fae all began shifting into their beast forms, giving me a glimpse of how distinctly other Fae truly were from humans. I spotted the giant red and black wolf I knew was Lilith, and beside her was a gray panther with curling white horns on its head, exactly where Harpina had just stood. Eryx flew overhead in his hawk form, his brown body highlighted by orange feathers down the middle. While a yellow and white fox slinked ahead, next to a light pink swan and a deer with brown and turquoise spotted fur—Baach, Ilta, and Delia.

Liviana and Ndrita were still in their regular Fae forms, near Calix. I'd heard about some of the lord's and ladies' beasts to be able to identify them. The black lion with razor sharp spikes down its back and the graceful gray and lilac gazelle were Lord Ciaran and Lady Jasira. The white leopard with gold spots and large bear with white fur on its body and silver legs and arms nuzzling one another were Lady Zillah and Lord Polaris. Lord Kyler was a furred creature that seemed both feline and canine at the same time, with a silver and navy-blue mane and a tail of pearlescent bushy fur, while Lady Aisling shifted into a red and green scaled creature—one with incredibly sharp teeth. Lord Rhidian was the large yellow gorilla and Lady Alora the much smaller lemur with pink stripes over her teal fur. Lord Sterling was a bird of prey, one with wings like a bat, but he seemed abnormally large for a bird. I imagined Ndrita enjoyed him being able to fly with her though.

It was then I saw Titan, and his form was certainly interesting. He was some kind of bull, but one that walked on two legs and not four, with huge horns curling up toward the sky and claws like daggers. He kept close to Calix, and I had no doubt he'd try to stay by his side for the duration.

All the assembled Fae yowled and howled so loudly, I had to cover my ears to avoid going deaf—but when Calix raised his hand, they went unnervingly silent. We sat in that silence for a moment, until Calix opened his mouth, letting out a roar that belonged to his dragon, not the gorgeous male form he was currently in.

I was shocked, not having known he could access parts of his dragon without shifting, but I didn't have long to process that fact, as Calix's roar was a signal to let the beasts loose. They took off, and the sound of pounding paws, gnashing teeth, and fluttering wings filled the air in a rush of madness.

That's what this night was about, I realized—the madness of the gods and nature itself. It wasn't the kind of chaos the world could slip to if the balance wasn't maintained. No, this was something else—something purely wild and free. And I rejoiced in it.

The sounds of battle floated to us on the breeze. Beasts ripping their teeth and claws into one another, spilling blood in honor of Faunus—and Florus. The twin gods of beasts and nature were the wildest of the gods, and this night encompassed their spirit in its purest form.

We walked through the forest, Priscilla, Callisto, Eris, Emmie, and I trying to move quickly to keep up with the action. We rounded the first great bonfire, representing the Pranvera Equinox, and made our way through the trees, the bonfires marking our path, until we rounded a bend and the fire for the Zima Solstice sparked in the distance. It was there I saw him.

Calix looked like a god of war, a god of death. In Fae form, he battled with vicious looking beasts that tried to tear into him, but he used his claws to fight. Another way he could summon aspects of his dragon form without shifting fully—I supposed it made sense, since the royals could all manifest wings in their Fae guises.

I watched, completely transfixed, as Calix moved, his muscles flexing as he grabbed an animal that leapt for him in midair. Catching it by the throat, he growled at it, exposing razor sharp teeth that made me gasp in shock, and then threw the beast into a tree. Another animal pounced and as he grabbed them, they rolled in a tangle of limbs, Calix landing on top and slicing into its shoulder. He stood in a swirl of movement I could barely keep up with, rushing another beast and taking it down with ease.

Then he was off, rounding the next bonfire as we passed drinks back and forth, watching the bloody hunt unfold. Calix caught my eye when he turned a corner, winking at me. My eyes widened in surprise; the spirit of Faunus was surely riding him, considering he'd been dedicated to ignoring my existence lately.

We made our way to the last bonfire—the largest of them, as the Festival of Faunus marked the night of the Harvest Equinox itself— where animals were engaged in fierce battle ahead of it. None had made it to the fire itself, and to my complete shock, there stood a gigantic, glowing stag—penned into an area to the right, where the beasts had herded it. Though similar to the ones I wore tonight, its antlers were shining in the darkness, while its fur almost looked like starlight with the way it was glowing.

Every single Fae here was trying to get to it, fighting one another and stopping them from moving forward. I watched as a hawk swooped down and used its talons to rake across the face of another animal. A polar bear rushed someone, claws out. A gazelle sprinted forward, only to be taken down by a leopard. A strange black and white creature was being strangled by a lemur's tail, and I laughed watching sweet Alora make this Fae flail beneath her.

Calix was in the midst of the frenzy, but even he could not stop the monster of a wolf who leapt forward, sailing over the heads of many and crashing down on the stag, teeth buried in its throat. Everyone went silent, and then Lilith's howl filled the air as she released the animal from her teeth.

The others howled and roared, acknowledging her win before they began shifting back. I ran forward and threw my arms around Lilith before anyone else could reach her.

"Congratulations!" I kissed her cheek and she smiled widely, her face flushed as she accepted everyone's praise and acknowledgment.

Calix smiled widely as he came over, looking quite pleased with himself despite his loss. "Thank you, Lilith, you just won me a lot of money."

"You bet on me winning?" Lilith narrowed her eyes at him, but there was something strangely vulnerable in her eyes, like she couldn't believe her king would bet on her. Calix threw his arm around her, pulling her in for a one-armed hug.

"Of course I did. I know my Beastmaster, and she's Faunus's favorite." He chuckled warmly, and Lilith blushed, ducking her head to hide her pleased smile.

"Now, let's go celebrate the Beast Queen!" Calix roared, and the cheer that went up in response was deafening.

WHEN WE RETURNED to the altar site, the clearing was set up for music, dancing, drinking—my nerves flared, and my heart sank as I remembered what came after the hunt. First, they'd pray—and then…*the orgy.*

Nox. Tartarus. By the damned Otherworld! Fuck! I couldn't help the litany of swears that went through my head as I tried to grapple with what was coming.

Thankfully, Ilta was suddenly there, and she grabbed my hand, squeezing hard. "Breathe. It's going to be okay."

I took deep breaths as she led me to the altar. Ilta had been gods sent to me since my arrival, but now more than ever, I appreciated her bubbly yet calming presence. Her smile was wide and was obviously excited.

"This is the best part, and I know my king." Ilta assured me, an almost smug, knowing look on her face. "You have nothing to worry about, trust me! Just enjoy yourself."

She was right, I knew she was. Things I was unfamiliar with made my emotions swing all over the place, the anxiety of the unknown taking root. But I knew better than to let that fear control me, so I took the drink Harpina shoved into my hand, downing it and then immediately taking another from Delia, who laughed delightedly. I turned to watch as Calix, Liviana, and Ndrita stepped up the statues of the Blessed Trinity.

"Tonight, we dedicate to the gods." Calix began, and the entire crowd quieted to a hush. "While we honor the gods of beasts and nature tonight, we do not forget those whose dominion we serve—the Blessed Trinity." Looking to the sky, he directed his next words to the gods directly.

"We dedicate ourselves to you: Erebus, Nox, and Asteria. Darkness, Night, and Stars. This blood, we dedicate to you." Calix broke open the skin of his palm with one of his claws, before letting them disappear, becoming fingers once more. He dripped the blood into the bowl of Night Water Erebus's idol held.

That was it—a quick dedication, because the rest of the night had been blood spilt in honor of Faunus. Now, the party could truly begin. Music began pounding in the background, and Ilta grabbed my hand, dragging me to the maypole. We both grabbed ribbons and I laughed as we danced around it.

I let go of all my worries—for one night, I could experience freedom in a new way. The beat of the drums infused my being, and I swayed and skipped and threw my hands in the air as I danced. I lost myself to it, like a haze took me and swept me away.

Eryx grabbed me, twirling me around, and I laughed as we moved, swaying to the beat. He grabbed my hands, moving us in a circle before Baach appeared, stealing me away and tossing me in the air. I let out a squeal that had him laughing loudly, then doing it again.

Priscilla was there next, and we locked our hands together as we swayed our hips, lifting our arms in the air and swaying them in tandem. Callisto brought us more drinks, and we kept one hand clasped in the other's while the other held our drinks, sloshing liquid around as we tried to dance and drink at the same time—making us both crack up laughing. Priscilla, my loyal friend, who was there for me at my lowest—a surge of emotion overtook me, and I threw my arms around her in a loose hug. For a moment, we just swayed together like that.

But then Lord Polaris was there, and he dragged me into a dance with him and his wife with a roguish wink. Even Lady Zillah was watching me with a predatory gleam in her eye, scanning my body. I laughed, recognizing their intent—but I had other plans for tonight.

They passed me back and forth between them as we danced, until Harpina tore me away and brought me to join the maypole once more. We danced around the circle, ribbons fluttering like my wings in the breeze.

I inhaled, and the scent of night and fire greeted me. It was already in the air with the scent of night magic and the bonfires, along with the darkness of true night all around us—but this was different. The scent was infused with something purely masculine, the promise of passion and ecstasy, and a hedonistic thrill ran through me.

I turned, and there he was, prowling toward me. I'd never seen that look on his face before, like he was…*unleashed.* He grabbed me around the waist, pulling me hard against his body. I melted into him as I placed my hand on his chest, swaying against him.

He growled, moving us further away from the fire to a spot with a bit more privacy. His hands on me burned with a pleasant heat—one I wanted everywhere—and the sizzling heat of him surrounded me as we danced. We moved in sync, our bodies instinctively flowing, like we were always meant to do so. My arms wrapped around his neck, as his went around my waist, and I let out a breath, dizzy with the feel of him against me. I let out an incredulous laugh—because this feeling rising inside me, it was incredible.

I'd never before experienced anything like this. It was—*pure life.* It was breathtaking, exhilarating, and I breathed in, like I could gulp that life down and keep it with me. Fill myself with it so I'd never feel so empty, again. I'd spent most of my limited time on Adamah living a half-life, and now that I'd had a taste of what true life felt like, I could never go back to that bleak emptiness again.

Even the feeling of my skin being too small for my body, that cramped feeling I always tried to stretch out, dissipated in light of the pure ecstasy encompassing me.

The feeling was incredible, and I resented my past self for trying to stay safe behind her walls. What was the point of a life lived safely?

Life is meant to be risky. It's meant to challenge you. Safety means stagnation, and I'd been stagnant too long. You can't grow if you're staying stagnant—and what is the purpose of life if not to grow? To learn and experience—love, heartbreak, friendship, joy, but also hatred, rage, envy, and pride. Life was all of it, and you had to accept the good with the bad to fully live.

Life is more than simply surviving, I now realized. The unknown of it may frighten us, but it was always worth the leap.

Calix twirled me around, and the smile on his face stole all the breath from my lungs. He had so many pressures on him, so many things to deal with as king, that he was forced to be hard and unyielding. But this was Calix as he was truly meant to be. Not the serious king and commander—no—but a being of laughter and love and joy. That light in his eyes as the aurora danced along with us, the smile blinding in its brilliance, and the relaxed slope of his shoulders as he threw caution to the wind and let the wild magic of the land ease his burdens—this was Calix in his truest form.

My smile widened even further, until my cheeks hurt—but I couldn't help it. Dancing out here around the fire, celebrating Faunus and all the gifts he'd given, I had never experienced joy in such a way, and it spilled onto my face, needing a release.

Calix nearly stumbled when he looked at me, his eyes growing wide. He looked slightly stupefied, actually, but he recovered quickly. He wrapped an arm around my waist, pulling me into his body once more, and I crashed against his chest with a laugh as he swung us around to the beat. His eyes shone with warmth and happiness as he smiled down at me.

"You are absolutely breathtaking when you smile like that." Calix murmured, his thumb brushing at the edge of my mouth. He looked at me so intensely, that I could feel the heat bleeding into my cheeks.

Unlike Cyrus, or any other before him really, Calix's compliments weren't pandering, or suggestive, or manipulative—and they were genuine. His were the only compliments I'd ever coveted.

I knew much of the happiness I felt now was because of him—maybe a bit because of all the alcohol I'd consumed—but I tried not to focus on that right now. Nor did I want to focus on the inevitable, for us. Even outside his mate, I was human, while he was Fae, my life would be a mere blip compared to his.

But those weren't problems for tonight, so I pushed all those thoughts away, focusing only on the positive. On the way it felt to be in his arms, not on how he'd avoided me. Instead of how hurt I'd been when he left me in the Hedone room, I instead focused on the joy of dancing with him.

I wrapped my hand around Calix's neck and leaned into him, as one of his hands snaked down my ass and to my leg, pulling it up around his waist. I gasped as the move pulled us further together, until I could feel the thick length of him through the layers between us. He pressed into me with a low growl.

I rubbed myself against him, letting go of all the reasons this was a terrible idea—I no longer cared. Calix had saved me. He'd given me freedom in a way I'd only ever dreamed was possible before. He's been helping me find myself, giving me the space and the tools to figure out who I am without a master. And the attraction between us, well…it was absolutely explosive.

We both knew it, both tried to ignore it, tried to fight it. Him, for the sake of his unknown soulmate. Me, for the heart that would surely be dam- aged in the aftermath, knowing his heart was destined for another, and that this attraction between us could lead to nothing. But now, with the festival loosening everyone's inhibitions thanks to Faunus's wild spirit and copious alcohol, with Calix actually required to participate in the orgy and gift his sexual energy to Faunus—it felt like an inevitable collision was about to occur.

I looked around quickly, spying other couples, and some three or four- somes, scattered around the area. Everyone giving into the sultry drumbeat and the magic in the air, dancing degrading and turning into grinding, hands leaving shoulders and waists and slipping under clothes.

I knew every Fae holiday ended in an orgy, but this was the first I'd witnessed one. The magic of nature and the gods themselves demanded sex and pleasure in return for their gifts. The sacrifice of the flesh, given freely to the gods. I'd heard rumors, of course, but humans weren't allowed to attend unless personally invited by the Fae. And in my backwoods vineyard village? There was no chance of that happening.

This was an experience I would never forget, not only for the soon to be naked, glowing bodies intertwining, but Calix himself was a memory to last a lifetime. I'd imagined riding my dorchadas in many ways, and as Calix's eyes raked up and down my body, I knew he felt the same. His pupils dilated, swirling with the colors of the aurora, encompassed in those gorgeous purple irises. The night sky I'd always loved so much reflected in his eyes.

I ran my eyes down the rest of his body, letting myself look at my fill of every sensational inch of him. His hands roved up and down my body, glancing at the sides of my breasts as they spread down my curves, over my waist, out across my hips, and down over my ass, where he squeezed both hands around it—and then those hands began back up the same tortuous path. I let my own hands wander over his broad shoulders, across his pecs and to his narrow waist, feeling every ridged abdominal muscle. I was finally feeling every glorious inch of him, until I came *so close* to where he desired…that he growled viciously when I moved my hands back up to retrace their path.

I let a smirk play over my lips, and that seemed to be all he could take. The sexual tension between us. The game we'd been unwittingly playing—tugging and pulling back and forth. The magic of the holiday. The sensual beat of the drums. The energy surrounding us as others began to slake their lust. Or maybe my glancing touches. I couldn't say which it was that finally drove him over the edge. Maybe none. Maybe all.

His lips slammed down on mine as our bodies fused together, only his pants and my panties separating us. He ground against me, and I could feel how soaked I was, the slightest friction tearing a muffled shriek from my lips. His lips took possession of my own like they were always meant to do so. Dominating and brutal, yet sensual and lush; it was a dichotomy that only made me rub myself against him harder—my arousal ratcheting up until I was practically mewling against him, begging for more.

His tongue played with my own, caressing and chasing, taking control of me and my body—and I let him. It wasn't the way Cyrus had wanted to control my body. No, this was a willing, mutual surrender. One highlighted as I ground my hips against him, and he moaned in pleasure into my mouth.

When he kissed me, I felt the world stop, stutter, and restart. Like one of the stars at Nova Falls, falling and falling, only to die a fiery death and spark back to life, born anew. It was madness, chaos incarnate, yet also somehow *right*—like I'd found balance I'd been missing my entire life, until this moment.

I was a star forged a new, lighting up the world in its glow. Calix looked at me like he saw that exact same thing. Like I was the Draco star that we navigated by, he looked at me like his world now oriented around me. For tonight, I'd allow myself to believe that.

Calix slid his hand down my thigh, trailing his fingertips softly, until he reached my knee, where he bent it, indicating he wanted me to lift it. It was the only leg currently touching the ground, so he boosted me up, until both of my legs were wrapped around his narrow waist. His hands immediately went to my ass to support me as he walked us over to the closest tree. Faunus wanted his pound of flesh to happen against nature—a tree, the ground, it didn't matter, so long as nature was able to soak up that energy.

My back slammed against the tree as Calix pressed me into it with his body, his hips flush against mine and my breasts against his chest. His hands grasped my face as he kissed me desperately, and I kissed him back with just as much desperation. The desire for something I could never truly have filled me, but if this was all I could have of him—then so be it. I would take every single bit of him I could get. He was as addictive as the eclipse drug that addicts would take to reach artificial ecstasy—only he was the real thing.

He may be saving himself for his soulmate, but he didn't seem to be suffering from this. No, it seemed more like a release. He held himself back daily, and his slip the other day had rocked him—I could tell by the look on his face afterwards. But the holiday gave him a pass to truly unleash all those pent-up feelings, and he was taking advantage of the opportunity to give me a taste of what could be. It would have to be enough. He tries so hard to be faithful to a woman he hasn't even met yet. Whoever she may be, I truly hope when he does find her, she understands how phenomenally lucky she is.

Like Calix could tell where my thoughts had gone, he pulled back, his lips leaving mine, now gentle hands lingering on my cheeks. He was panting hard as he stared into my eyes, and we both paused—it felt like the whole world must have paused, no other sound or movement reached us.

"Asteria." Calix growled roughly, and the sound sent a flood of arousal to my core, the rumble moving through my own body.

"Calix." I returned breathily, and his eyes closed momentarily, like he was savoring the sound. When he opened them once more, I was granted the vision of the night sky, the aurora a banner across it.

His darkness began leaching out of him, spreading around us in a haze of shadow—like he wanted me just for himself. He may have to share me with Faunus tonight, but no other. There was none I wanted, of course, none but him. Still, he covered us in darkness, keeping me to himself.

He made the shadows thin enough for us to see out, letting us witness the others losing themselves to the enchantment of the night. I recognized the faces of our friends, in the midst of being lost to their own lust, the magic of

Faunus invading them and taking over—but they still surrounded themselves around their king—for whatever protection that might offer.

Callisto was splayed out between Priscilla's legs, while Delia's breasts bounced where she raised herself up and down on Eryx's cock. Baach had Ilta bent over as he thrust into her, and Titan was doing the same to the man he had laid out on the ground.

Calix looked at me like I was a goddess, his eyes wide and worshipful, a deep well of feeling laid within him, struggling to get out. No one had ever looked at me in such a way before. *Only Calix*. And I mourned what could never be between us, even as I embraced the wild lust scorching through me.

"I have wanted this since the moment I met you." Calix ground out through clenched teeth, every word a struggle. His hips swirled against mine once more, and I gasped my need, clutching at his shoulders and trying to pull him closer to me. I wanted less talking, more skin. Immediately.

"So have I, so let's not wait any longer." I murmured through my panting. He began to open his mouth, but I put a finger against his lips to stop him. "I know." I shut my eyes briefly and opened them only once I forced out my next words. "I know this is a one-time only deal. You're loyal beyond anything I've ever known, Calix. Your soulmate is one lucky woman."

"I wish—" He started, conflict and pain a living thing in his eyes. "Nox, I wish we could have this." His brow furrowed so hard it looked almost painful, and his hands tightened on my flesh, like if he just held on tightly enough, he wouldn't have to let me go.

"Whoever gets to keep you, will be the luckiest man in the realm, Asteria. Soulmates are supposed to be our perfect matches, but I can't imagine any-thing beyond you. I feel like a disloyal ass for even saying that, for disgracing my sacred bond in such a way, for admitting to you how much I have—" Calix clenched his jaw, cutting off whatever words may have followed.

When he did continue, the words were no less gut wrenching, fighting their way through clenched teeth. "But you have gotten into my soul some-how, my réalta. It shouldn't be possible when my soul is reserved for someone else, but it is—and I don't know how to get you out."

His impassioned words ended with his fist biting into the tree behind my head. My heart tore and bled, but it also lit with that fire only he could make burn within me. I slowly grabbed his hand, kissing the bloody fingers that had punched into the wood. His forehead crashed against mine, and I let my fingers snake up to his face, caressing along those sharply defined cheekbones.

"It seems only fair, since you've gotten into mine as well." I let myself admit that painful truth I'd been trying to deny—that this was more than simple lust. That Calix had snuck past every defense I ever built, until my heart darkened with shadows and burned with fire—belonging in the claws of his hand.

"But I know, despite how much we both want this, that you're too loyal, too honest, too *good*, to act on this beyond tonight." I smiled sadly but set my expression into something resolute as I continued—like my soul wasn't crying out in protest. "We will honor the gods and give the magic back to them and the land. We'll allow ourselves this night to pretend, and tomorrow, we'll pretend like our world hasn't changed. Like *we* haven't. We'll go on, knowing we can't have this, that you're meant for another. No matter how much it hurts us both." I nodded firmly, and he looked at me with awful devastation across his lovely face.

His enemies saw him as this brutal, ruthless king—and he certainly was that. But one look into that expressive face, and I knew that brutality would only ever be wield *for* me, never to me. No matter what the future held. The same way he wielded it for all of those he'd saved. Only, for me, it was personal in an entirely new way for him.

Calix softly caressed my face, and I did the same to him. We just took each other in—in mutual agreement, and agony, about what tonight was. We both soaked up this contact, cherishing every moment we had, swallowing the pain we both felt. The unfairness of this world never ceased to astound me. I forced myself to push it all away, for now. I focused only on Calix, on the need he fostered in me. I ran my hands down his chest, and then ran them back up and behind his neck, using the leverage to pull his mouth down to meet me. At the movement, his cock twitched, hitting my clit at just the right angle—

And then…we ignited.

The sweetness melted away in favor of wild abandon. I was sure the fire nearby must have sparked and begun consuming us both. Frenzied heat and desperate desire suffusing through and taking over—or maybe it was Calix's own inner flame—maybe this was what it truly meant to have a dragon between your thighs. I had never felt more powerful in my entire life than I did at this moment—the sheer power of the being before me…and he was just as lost to the wild passion between us as I was.

Calix's mouth descended on mine once more, devouring and possessive as his lips took mine, his tongue entering my mouth at my first inhalation. His hands did not stay idle, ripping my dress right down the middle, and leaving me in tiny panties that'd be easily ripped away. His lips parted from mine only for his eyes to roam all over me.

"Nox, look at you." His growl of appreciation rocked through me with a shiver of anticipation. "I swear you glow brighter than anyone here." The awe in his tone was overwhelming, but a glance confirmed he wasn't wrong. For some reason, I was glowing brighter than the others painted up, including him. "My réalta." He breathed, his eyes glued to the areas with no paint at all with just as much admiration.

With paint the only thing covering his torso, I had easy access to his chest, but I wanted access to everything. I grabbed onto his waist, trying to get the buttons open. But I wasn't the only one wanting to touch, and Calix's palms grabbed full handfuls of my breasts. Squeezing them before switching to squeeze the hard nipples standing out in the night air. A moan ripped out of me as his mouth descended on the hard peaks, sucking them into his mouth as his tongue played against them.

My head fell back against the tree, but I forced my eyes to remain open, not wanting to miss a moment of this.

"Fucking perfect." He groaned around my nipple. "You're fucking perfect, my réalta." He continued fondling my breasts but got to his knees and began kissing down my stomach. I buried a hand in his hair as he ripped my panties off, hunger in his gaze as he licked his lips.

"My dorchadas—please," I moaned, desperate for him. The energy around us all consuming—the wildness of Faunus spread through me, leaving me a wet, wanton mess.

Calix's growl was my only warning before his face was between my thighs, his tongue licking a swipe up my cunt that had me gripping his hair tightly. He descended on me like a man possessed, his tongue moving quickly as he licked every inch of me. He sucked my clit into his mouth before gently scraping his teeth over, wrenching a scream of pleasure from my lips.

His fingers were gripping my thighs, keeping them spread open—but he slowly inched them up on one side. When he reached the apex of my thighs, he spread them through the wet mess he'd made of me, before spearing me with two fingers. They entered me in a hard thrust and I let out a strangled moan. "Calix, my dorchadas, please, please, please."

He pulled back, making me want to scream in frustration. A wicked smirk graced his face as I pouted back at him. "I love hearing you beg for me."

He shot up and took my lips in a fierce kiss, biting my lower lip and pulling back slowly before releasing it. His fingers were still thrusting inside me languidly, but as he returned his mouth to my cunt, they began to speed up. His mouth joining the action as he licked up my slit before circling my clit. I thrust up into his face, but he used his other hand to hold my hips down against the tree. "You taste so fucking good. By Nox, I could eat you forever."

His voice was husky and delightful, and while I shivered and moaned, I just managed to get out a few sultrily spoken words—wanting to push him further. "Yes, please my King."

Calix pulled back, his eyes blazing as he looked at me. A wild look crossed his face as his smirk turned wicked.

"Good girl." He cooed, fingers twisting and spreading inside me, his shadows slithering up my legs before breaching my entrance.

"Calix—" I whined as darkness filled me to the brim, shadows fucking me just as thoroughly as his fingers as they swirled around.

"*Very* good girl." He praised, latching back on to my clit, and then I was screaming his name as I came, my walls clenching around the combination of fingers and shadows. "You're absolutely dripping for me, baby."

Calix slowly eased off me as I panted against the tree. He stood from his knees, once more towering over me—and I so loved his height. It felt like he consumed my whole world as he leaned over me, taking up my vision entirely.

"My réalta." He murmured, ripping his belt from his pants with a fierce snap. "I have to have you." I gulped as he tore off his pants, leaving him in all his naked glory.

"You're beautiful." I whispered honestly, as I took in the sculpted form in front of me, leaving me in no doubt he'd been designed by the gods. It was no stretch to believe he had the blood of Erebus in him. Descended from the king of gods, the god of darkness, and he looked the part, a statue of perfection come to life.

And then I looked further down. I inhaled sharply, fierce want consuming me, and a fresh rush of wetness dripped down my thighs. His cock was perfection—long, thick, with a slight curve to the left—bigger than I thought I could take, in truth. But by the Otherworld, I'd certainly give it my best try. Cyrus had opened my eyes to what the Fae were dealing with, but this was a monster of a different sort. Calix grasped his cock, stroking it once, twice—until I let out a pained, wanting moan.

He chuckled darkly, a smirk on his lips that peeled back to reveal sharp fangs—and they were definitely *fangs* now, not just sharpened canines. "You want my cock, my réalta?"

"Yes—" I nodded desperately. "Please, my dorchadas, I need you." I squirmed against the tree, wanting him inside me *now*.

"Beg me again, my réalta." He commanded, his eyes slipping over my body like silk. "Show me how much you want me." His finger came up under my chin, and his lips softly caressed mine—not quite a kiss, but a tease.

I smirked. Even desperate as I was, I was more than down to play his game—and I knew just how to make him break for me.

"Please, Calix, my King, I need your cock. I need to feel you inside me. Need to feel your huge cock stretching out my tight little cunt." My sultry whisper was like a Siren Song, Calix's eyes going wide and blazing with an internal fire—his dragon awakened.

And then he was on me. Desperate, fierce kisses verging on violent in nature as we crashed together. He grabbed my ass and lifted me, my legs automatically shackling around his waist. He fisted his cock and looked down, my eyes following his, as he slid it through my cunt, spreading my lips wide as he got his cock wet. I moaned repeatedly at the feeling as his thick head bumped my clit again and again.

Calix groaned, his forehead leaning against mine, before he began kissing down my neck. He brought his cock to my entrance, and the stretch around his girth was intense, light flashing behind my eyelids. But I quickly adjusted, Calix watching me all the while to gauge my reaction. When he saw I was ready, he gave one swift thrust, bottoming out inside me. I let loose a scream at the intrusion. His cock was a beast—larger than anything I'd ever had inside me. It was magnificent.

I could feel how stretched out I was, my poor cunt trying to adjust to his size as Calix trembled, trying to stay still and give me a moment to do so. His hands dug into the tree on either side of my head, fingers flexing as he waited. My walls fluttered around his length and we both shuddered.

"Move, please." I gasped out, needing more. Calix growled deeply, more dragon than Fae, and slowly pulled out. He thrust back in, and I tossed my head back with a loud moan, the feel of him filling me absolutely divine. The stretch of him perfectly riding that point of pain that became pleasure.

He began speeding up, fucking me harder and faster. I wrapped my arms around his neck and burrowed one hand into his hair. He grabbed onto my hips tightly as he thrust into me, the sound of skin meeting skin filling my ears, along with the sound of his cock breaching my cunt—I was so wet that you could *hear* it.

His lips collided with mine as he sped up to a speed only a Fae would be capable of. The sweet edge of pleasure and pain enhanced as he tweaked my nipples and bit down on my neck, sharp fangs barely retracting, and surely leaving bloody dots in his wake. There was a feral look in Calix's eyes that I wanted to lean into.

Our kiss was a messy, magical thing. The feel of him inside me felt more right than anything ever had. I screamed and moaned my pleasure to the sky, when it wasn't muffled by his mouth.

"So good. I knew you would be. Better than anything I've ever felt." Calix muttered against my lips, his tongue flicking out and meeting mine before pulling back and looking at me as his hips hammered into me. He looked down and watched as my breasts bounced with his thrusts, and a purely male look of satisfaction filled his face as I tumbled over the edge of ecstasy with no warning—my orgasm taking me with a brutal scream ripped from the depths of my soul.

I was left twitching and moaning weakly, shook by the intensity. I'd never experienced an orgasm like that—I had clearly been missing out. But then Calix pulled out of me, leaving me empty. My desperate whine was met with an amused look, but he grabbed my hips, turning me around.

"Grab onto the tree." Calix instructed as he bent me over. I smirked, looking back over my shoulder. He growled as he lined himself back up and thrust in hard. I yelped as he smacked my ass, squeezing the globe afterwards.

"Fucking Otherworld. You are Tartarus damned *enchanting*, do you realize that?" Calix hissed, anger riding the desire in his voice. His sharp thrusts hit something deep inside me, each thrust making sparks explode behind my eyes. The angle making him feel even larger, like he might rip me in half if he wasn't careful.

"Enchanting?" I managed to gasp out. He grabbed both my ass cheeks, squeezing them as he thrust into me, the sound of his balls hitting my ass and his cock thrusting into my dripping wet cunt, were mesmerizing. He looked up as I swung my gaze around.

He curled over my back, kissing his way up my spine before he captured my lips in a fierce, messy kiss. When he released my mouth, he grabbed the back of my neck, holding me there as he began a punishing series of thrusts that had me seeing stars.

"Yes." His growl was even more animalistic, like a contained roar in his throat. His wings burst out of his back, and I screamed as he took me on the wildest ride of my life.

"You have completely fucking enchanted me. It shouldn't be possible." He grumbled with every thrust, and I just held on for dear life. "I should be able to resist. But I can't. You're a fucking Siren come to tempt me. And you feel like fucking Elysium. Like your cunt was made to take my cock—and my cock alone." A possessive snarl was followed by a hard thrust that made my whole body shake, a scream ripped from my throat as I sobbed in euphoria.

The feeling of magic rose, growing more intense, like the world around us was fully alive as it fed off our sexual energy—off everyone's. I'd forgotten thousands of others were also having sex here right now. Calix's shadows making it seem like we were alone, but no, we weren't, and like he could sense my thoughts, he smirked, letting the shadows around us dissipate.

And just like that, I was nearly overwhelmed by the orgy in full swing around us. Naked people were everywhere I looked, bent over, on their knees, on their backs, held up in the air—there were so many couples, threesomes, foursomes, and more grouped together. The middle of the field was a free for all of people fucking on the grass.

The energy was so intense, and that feeling only rose higher as Calix fucked me into another world. My head dropped, hanging down as he gripped my neck. At least until he pulled me upright, arching my back as he pulled me against his chest.

His angle changed, fucking up into me as his hands gave my ass one last hard smack, making me moan loudly, before they immediately went to my breasts, grabbing them and squeezing. His fingers going to my nipples to pinch and pluck them—twisting them until I screamed. Pleasure and pain twinning together and making my arousal drip down my thighs, and his.

"Naughty girl." He growled in my ear before nipping my earlobe. "You like it when I'm rough with you, don't you?" His voice was a silky whisper, drawing me under his spell. I nodded eagerly, wanting more, and he chuckled darkly. I shivered at the promise in it. He dragged his hand down my stomach, to my clit. I was already clenching down on his length, trying to stave off my orgasm, wanting to prolong this.

"You think you can keep your orgasm from me?" A hand came down hard on my cunt, smacking it and glancing off my clit, making me jolt in his arms. "No—your orgasms are *mine*, my réalta. Now, cum for me, and when you're done, I want at least six more from you tonight."

A thrill went through me, knowing this wouldn't be the last one… but I gulped. Usually, I was too sensitive to go again right away after cumming, but I already had once and somehow found myself able to continue with no recovery. Calix himself an aphrodisiac that kept me aroused beyond what I'd thought possible. The thought of seven more orgasms, eight total, in *one night…*

A sharp pinch of my clit had me screaming loudly as I came. Wetness dripping down his cock as I exploded, shivering and twitching as he caressed my stomach with gentle hands. Calix kissed along my neck until he tilted my chin towards him, kissing me with an achingly soft touch, his tongue running teasingly over my lips.

❧ ❦ ❧

WHEN I FINALLY sagged into his arms after I was spent, he pulled out. Still hard, his cock now shining with my arousal, he smirked at me, clearly not ashamed in the least. But then he was dragging me to the ground, my legs over his shoulders.

"Calix—" I gasped out, but his lips took mine and his tongue invaded my mouth. He pulled back, meeting my eyes as he thrust into me, filling me up as I cried out.

When he was completely sheathed inside me, he leaned up and pushed my hair back out of my eyes, his own swirling with colors, fascinating me as I followed them. "You're so fucking beautiful, Asteria."

Tears filled my eyes at his sincerity, the word holding more weight coming from him than it ever had. He began slowly thrusting, in and out, gentler than before as he worked me back up. Tartarus, this man knew what he was doing—when to go hard, when to mix pleasure and pain, when to go soft and gentle. He seemed to just intuitively know what I needed.

He swore loudly as my walls clenched down around him, and he hit that spot deep inside that had me swearing in turn.

"I swear your cunt is magic, my réalta. I've never felt anything so good." He shuddered, and I could tell from that alone that he meant what he said.

Over four hundred years, and *I* was the best thing he'd ever felt. I tightened my arms around him, pulling him to me until his chest was pressed against mine. I kissed him, pouring all of the passion I felt for him into it, letting the wall I'd been trying to keep my feelings behind fall, and letting them unleash over us both.

He brought my legs down from his shoulders and wrapped them around his waist. He pounded into me hard and fast in the haze of desire that overtook us. I scratched deep gouges into his back with my nails, but they instantly healed. I growled, wanting to mark him in some way. Calix laughed, a feral light shining in his eyes that I knew must be staring back at him from mine.

He leaned down and bit my neck hard, causing me to let out a loud cry as I quivered around him. I could hear the same sounds echoing all around me—the screams of pleasure, the slapping of skin against skin, moans, groans, grunts, and growls. The energy hummed loudly, and I could feel the magic seeping into all of us. Like the god of beasts wanted to see us all become just as wild as his creations. The magic of Night was like a blanket across the grass I was splayed out on.

I arched my body into Calix's, a whine leaving my throat involuntarily as my nipples scraped against his chest. I let my hips continue rising and falling to meet his, the harsh thrusts sure to make me extremely sore later—and yet, I could only feel satisfaction from that knowledge. And an urge for more.

I grabbed Calix by the shoulders and threw all of my weight at him, pushing us up. He let out a delighted laugh as he grabbed my hips in a bruising grip, but I had him where I wanted him.

With him sitting upright, I adjusted so I had a knee on either side of him, his cock still spearing me open. Calix looked down with a smile, and reached out to run his fingers over where he stretched me open.

I began bouncing up and down, Calix meeting my downward thrusts with his own upward ones. His hands helped me along, tight on my hips and keeping us at a frantic pace. I felt my orgasm quickly approaching and switched up my movements, grinding back and forth and letting my clit brush against him on each forward grind. We both groaned in pleasure as our lips fused back together. Calix took control and moved my hips back and forth as he grinded up into me, swiveling his hips in a circle as he did, and earning a loud shriek ripped from my throat in return.

I managed to extract my tongue from his mouth, loathe as I was to do it. I bit into his neck, his rough shout lost in the chorus of people fucking like animals. When I tasted blood I pulled back, looking at Calix, both of us dazed, lost in a haze of pleasure and magic.

His mouth crashed back into mine, tasting the blood on my lips. He bit my lip, hard enough a bead of blood rose up, and he swiped it away with his tongue, a smirk growing on his face. I leaned forward, chasing the taste on his tongue, combining our blood.

Our hips ground against one another's, and Calix looked down with wide eyes before his hand went to my stomach, pressing down on it. I moaned as it hit something that felt fucking exquisite.

"You have no idea how fucking sexy you look like this." Calix groaned. "Look." His voice was awed, and I realized he was pressing on where the outline of his cock was clearly seen against my stomach. He was so deep inside me that you could see it every time he pressed in, my stomach expanding with his length. He moved his hips forward, and it stood out even more, Calix pressing his hand against it as he thrust into me even harder.

The scream I let out was more of a bellow, and Calix chuckled, looking up at me with the night sky in his eyes. Something sparked and I felt truly rabid as I looked at him, wanting to wrap myself in him and never let go. I wrapped an arm around his neck and pulled him in for a messy kiss, raising and lowering my hips faster and faster, grinding on him every time I came down.

Calix tossed his head back with a groan, then grabbed me by the hair with one hand and consumed my mouth fully. Every drop of passion we felt pouring into each other through this kiss.

"Nox," Calix whispered, looking dazed when we paused for air. "I've never seen a better sight than this. You above me, split open on my cock, and riding me furiously. So damn sexy." His hands roamed over my skin, grabbing my breasts and squeezing before pinching my nipples and twisting.

I moaned desperately, riding him at a fever pitch as his hands touched every inch of me. When I was least expecting it, he shoved us back, so I was once more on my back before him. He grabbed my thighs and spread them wide as he thrust into me hard, watching his cock disappear inside me.

"So fucking tight, you feel like Elysium." Calix rumbled, his voice low and smokey. "Hot and wet and fucking perfect. And all mine—mine to fuck, mine to use how I will."

"Yes!" I hissed, my hands roaming his shoulders, wanting to touch every inch of him I could as I felt myself rising higher and higher. My agreement caused a dark light to enter his eyes, and Calix smirked before he slipped a finger down to rub my clit, his hips crashing against mine, and the sound of his cock entering my wet cunt filling the space. He looked at me and for a moment it felt like we would truly consume one another until nothing was left.

I felt him shudder, his biceps quivering as the fists on either side of my head held him up. I wrapped myself around him, taking his mouth before whispering against it. "Cum with me, my dorchadas."

"My réalta." He breathed into me, and I let go, my orgasm coming quick, fast, and intense. Lasting longer than I thought one could. My whole body shaking and quivering as I felt his cock throb inside me, followed by a wet spurt filling me up.

Calix collapsed on top of me when he was finished, and for several minutes, we just stayed as we were, wrapped up in one another. But then the energy in the land around us rose once more, and I flexed my legs around his waist, while he experimentally thrust into me in small strokes.

Before I knew it, it was like we'd never stopped, our tongues and limbs tangling, and tiredness fading away as the gods and the land provided energy. I wasn't sure how exactly I realized that was what was happening, but instinct told me to trust it, so I gave myself over to it.

When Calix turned me on my hands and knees, I arched my back like a cat and leaned into it. His cock rammed into me from behind and I let loose a moan so loud it might as well have been a shout. He began fucking me hard, with steady, intense thrusts as he grabbed my ass.

"I've dreamt of nothing more than being inside this tight little cunt, feeling the way you clench around my cock." Calix growled, running his hands over my curves. "Letting me stretch you out and make a space for myself inside you, until you want no one but me." I moaned at his words, eagerly agreeing.

I pressed back into each thrust, and when his hand came down on my ass, I moaned in encouragement. I felt Calix lean forward as he placed a kiss on the back of my neck. I felt his smirk against my sweaty skin. "Just wait, my réalta."

He pulled back up and began thrusting at a speed no human could match, so intense and all-consuming I felt like I might shatter apart at the seams. I shook with each thrust, and each time he pulled out, I missed the feel of him filling me.

He smacked my ass hard and I felt wetness drip down my thighs, sneaking out past his cock the volume was so great. The sound as he fucked into me was obscene, the wet gush of fluids from repeated orgasms on top of my arousal, but he just groaned in pleasure and somehow fucked me harder.

Calix grabbed my neck, letting his fingers trail along the skin of my throat, before slowing tightening his grip. He lifted me by that hand, until my arms and legs were dangling, held up only by his cock and his hand.

"I regret not taking advantage of the sex swings in the Hedone room when I had you right there." His murmur was made for seduction, silky and luxurious, dangerous and tempting. If I wasn't already full of him, I would have thrown myself at him.

I was lost in the haze of pleasure, and Calix held me in midair as he thrust into me over and over again. His balls slapped against my ass as his other hand came down, making my ass red with every hard slap, while his hand slowly tightened until breathing became more difficult.

Calix worked my body up and up, spiraling toward an orgasm of epic proportions. Darkness suddenly crept in, shadows slithering over my skin. I felt them cup my breasts and I arched into them, but then I felt one at my clit, circling and pinching as the ones at my breasts were doing. Several shadows held my thighs even further apart, while others stroked my back and hair. But it was the ones cupping my ass, with one rogue shadow slipping to my back hole that I took issue with. Except I couldn't speak, could barely breathe.

"Relax, my réalta. I've got you, I promise." His soothing whisper did indeed have me relaxing, and it was that moment that the shadow took advantage of as it slipped into my ass, a hole I never intended to make use of in such a way.

The odd feeling was one I quickly adjusted to, however, and with all the overwhelming feelings his shadows and cock worked in tandem to stoke within me, the extra feeling of fullness, of being stretched and fucked, was too much. Calix had the gall to chuckle darkly, squeezing his fingers tighter around my neck, a shadow pinching my clit before slapping it, and the shadows at my breasts doing the same—Calix timed the slaps perfectly to the moment he let go of my throat—

I wasn't prepared for the rush of breath—or the sensation of being slapped directly on my most sensitive areas—and I fucking *exploded.* My cunt clenched around his cock, squeezing tight as I convulsed, and my arousal rushed out of me in a way I'd never experienced before, like a dam bursting. The orgasm was more intense, more sensitized, than any orgasm before it.

"Calix, fuck!" I whined as I continued to convulse, my orgasm going on and on.

"By the Otherworld." Calix groaned, sounding just as out of it as I was, wonder and awe lacing his tone as I felt him cum inside me, his body shaking as he leaned over my back, wrapping his arms around me as he lowered me back to my hands and knees on the ground.

I wrapped my arm over his, his lips finding my neck and kissing it lightly. We were both completely unraveled. "You are a wonder to behold, Asteria. That was, hands down, the hottest thing I've seen in my entire life." He paused for a moment. "We really need to try that sex swing."

I chuckled huskily, my throat still feeling like fire had scorched through it. I didn't bother mentioning this wasn't going to continue past tonight, I didn't let any of those intrusive thoughts in.

I just leaned into the warmth of the dragon behind me, radiating heat like a furnace after all of our activities.

Eventually, I felt Calix's cock thicken where it was still buried inside me.

And we lost ourselves to the magic of the night once more...

CHAPTER 35

MY thighs burned—I loved Arianrhod, and I loved riding her, but two weeks in, and I was really starting to wish we were flying. I'd been excited at first, having never seen Sunset Kingdom before. Even if I was going under not—the *best* circumstances. But now, all I could focus on was the burning in my thighs from riding every day for two weeks straight.

After the Festival of Faunus, things had been—weird. Calix and I, everyone really, had spent the night fucking in the woods, giving our energy to the land and the gods. I knew the second Calix pushed me against that tree, that I was heading down a path I would come to regret later.

Calix was loyal, and I vividly remembered the horror in his eyes when the influence of the drink cleared the night of the ball, and he realized what he'd done. Every time he'd given in to this attraction between us, it was with the influence of something else—or at least, with a justifiable reason like the festival.

I knew when it came to it, he wouldn't choose me.

Not when his mate was out there.

Even if he wanted me, and I knew he did, he wouldn't do that—to either of us—me or his mate. Not when he couldn't give himself to me fully with them out there.

"You're perfect, my réalta."

I shook my head, telling myself to bury the memory. Words said in passion didn't count, everyone knew that.

Still, it was hard not to remember the way he'd felt between my thighs. The stretch of him inside me. The feeling of his lips caressing my throat. His fingers playing my clit like an instrument.

The morning after, I woke in Calix's arms, spread across his chest. He must have been awake for a while, but he was just watching me, running his fingers through my hair. I hadn't moved for a bit, wanting to enjoy the feeling before it disappeared. Clutching the moment like it wouldn't dissolve the moment I acknowledged it.

He'd smiled at me, a lazy, smug thing that had made me narrow my eyes at him before he chuckled. He helped me up, leading me to the pile of clothes prepared in advance. Apparently, losing clothes was common enough they'd started bringing piles of clothing for after their orgies.

He'd helped me dress, and then kissed me on the head, holding me to him. The look on his face when he'd pulled back…the combination of *want* and *grief* had been staggering. Until Callisto had appeared with a request to get back to work, our deadline to leave rapidly approaching.

I LOOKED OVER to him now, where he rode Elatha, the horse's green tail swishing quickly back and forth. He got antsy when he was away from Arianrhod too long, and Calix was well aware of that, riding with me often to keep him calm. He usually took one of his warhorses to battle for that reason, since Arianrhod had refused a rider for so long. But now, with her having chosen me as a rider, Calix was able to take Elatha instead. Calix was riding beside Titan now, the two of them going over plans for the army on the ground as they rode.

Calix and I had been strangely fine since the festival. Both of us were adults, and though we both knew we wanted the other, we equally knew we couldn't have one another, so we went on as we had before—as friends, if nothing else.

We were able to talk and laugh as normal, and talking to him was just so *easy*. It felt like it shouldn't be, but the fact of the matter was, I could talk to Calix for hours and never get bored, it was quite the novelty.

Calix fell back from Titan, waiting as I pulled up beside him.

"Elatha was making his displeasure with my traveling companion known." Calix teased, sending me a grin I couldn't help but match.

"I can't blame him, I *am* a much better traveling companion after all. Elatha just has good taste." I winked, throwing my hair over my shoulder dramatically. Calix threw his head back in laughter, making me giggle.

"There's no doubt about that." Calix murmured, no longer teasing. His eyes heated intensely, and I was forced to look away. He usually banked that heat quickly, and watching it happen always made my chest ache.

"I can't guarantee how long that'll be the case." I said, while trying to massage my thigh. "Any longer and my legs are going to give out—I won't be quite so pleasant then." Calix raised a brow at me, amusement all over his face.

"We're close." He assured me. "We should be there within the hour, and you can stretch your legs."

He wasn't wrong, as just half an hour later, the first signs of Biarma could be spotted on the horizon. We'd navigated up the coast, following a straight path north. Except for where we skirted around Asphodel, it was nearly a straight shot to Biarma.

I could see the rounded top of the palace from here, standing out against the kapok and ipe trees surrounding it. We halted, and Calix and I brought our horses over to Titan and Callisto.

"You're all set?" Calix asked, looking his father figure over, a tightness around his eyes that told me he was worried. Except for Calix himself, Titan was the best fighter we had. He likely had nothing to worry about, but rationality had nothing to do with love.

Titan nodded stoically, ever composed in front of his army. "We're good to go, your Highness."

"We all know the plan, your Highness." Callisto bobbed her head in agreement. "They'll make sure to cause a big enough distraction to lure out the guards. Are we all ready for our parts in this?" She looked over us critically before looking to the group behind us.

She narrowed her eyes, and I followed her eyeline to Emmie. I looked back at her with a questioning expression, and she leaned over to me. "I know she's your friend, but this turnaround of hers happened suddenly. I'm not sure she's stable enough for this."

"We've already come all this way, and she seems fine." I shook my head. "Plus, she'll have Harpina with her. We all know the plan, it will be fine." I hoped if I said it confidently enough, it would make it true. But the truth was, my nerves were all over the place, and from the look Callisto gave me, she could see right through it.

We found a place to make camp, where our reserves would wait, just in case. We tied up our horses since we'd be going on foot from here. We split up into our two groups, and Calix, Eryx, Harpina, Callisto, Emmie, and I all made for the back route leading to the palace.

We snuck through the capital, using magic to hide ourselves when needed, cloaking us in the shadows. Looking around Biarma, I wished we had come for some other reason. While it wasn't as beautiful as Tairngire, at least to me, it was colorful, gorgeous, and lively. It was dominated by architecture with arches and mosaic tiles, and the palace was a sprawling thing, wide instead of tall. It was made up of rounded roofs that reminded me of globes, shining in the sun.

As we crept closer, the abundance of jungle plants grew heavier. The plants were the only barrier around the palace, no true wall protecting them from the outside. *Their mistake.* Though, as we reached a lagoon at the back of the palace, surrounded by jungle plants and flowers, with teal and orange—the kingdom's colors—decorating the space, I was taken aback by how inviting it was. Large arches that came to points at the top were repeated across the walls that led into the palace, covering three sides of the lagoon.

We waited until we heard the alarm sound, signaling the attack, and then the echoing sound of many boots hitting the ground. The guards running off to protect the city. Some guards would have taken the royals to a safe room, based on the protocol Sunset had in place, leaving their bedrooms wide open.

"Okay." Calix whispered, turning to us. "According to the map, King Tieran's room is to the right from here, Prince Vesper's to the left, and Prince Zakat's straight down the middle. Follow your maps, keep quiet, and be quick." He looked over all of us critically. "Ready?"

"Ready. Let's go." I nodded as everyone agreed. I looked at the others, especially Emmie. "Be safe." Emmie just gave me a look that I couldn't quite read before Harpina shuffled her away to the middle arch. Eryx gave me a quick nudge in farewell before he and Callisto disappeared to the left, leaving me with Calix.

He grabbed my hand and began pulling me along. He summoned darkness to cover us, shadows that let us see out, and prevented others from seeing in. Creeping through the palace, I tried to ignore the beauty of it and not look around. We had a job to do.

We stayed against the walls, turning corners carefully. Only a stray guard or two was left, and we just waited for them to turn before slipping past them.

My heart beat quickly in my chest, and I'm sure my palm against Calix's was sweating. We followed the map and got to the hall containing the bedroom of King Tieran, but unfortunately, two guards still stood in front of it. Calix let go of my hand and took out his sword, giving me a look. I unsheathed my own and nodded to him, preparing myself for what may come.

Calix immediately sent out his shadows to take the guards prisoner. They hovered in the air, mouths gagged as they looked at us with wide, scared eyes. I winced, hating that I felt awful for them. These men participated in slavery; I shouldn't care.

But I remembered the guard who tried helping me in Dusk, who armed me despite the fact it would have meant a death sentence if anyone found out.

"Can't we leave them?" I begged, tugging on Calix's sleeve.

He looked back at me with furrowed brows, but his look quickly changed to a sympathetic one as he looked into my eyes and saw the battle I was waging with myself. He reached up and moved my hair behind my ear, the gentle action so at odds with the fierce look on his face.

"We can't be seen here." He whispered, ducking his head toward mine. "They'll remember us, Asteria. This is the only way." My face fell but before I could ruminate on it, Calix turned and beheaded them with one quick slice. I turned my head to the side as the blood sprayed. Calix grabbed my chin, pulling my head back to face him.

"Now you see the monster everyone else does." He growled, his teeth grinding and his eyes growing hard, shoving down the pain in them.

"This isn't you being a monster, Calix." I argued, shaking my head. "It's doing what we have to. Just because it hurts, doesn't mean it's not the right thing. Stop moping." He let out an incredulous chuckle at my words, but I meant them.

I grabbed his face in my hands, forcing him to look at me. Aware of the time passing that we desperately needed, but this needed to be said. Calix was just as important as our plans.

"Some might think you a monster, and maybe you are." I shrugged, carelessly, emphasizing how little that meant to me. "But if so, it's to battle worse monsters. Those who enslave humans and treat them as disposable resources. Who torture and kill them for no reason. Maybe you have to become a monster to kill a monster, I don't know. But if you are one, then you're the monster I want on my side, protecting me."

Calix swallowed hard, his throat bobbing. His eyes were shining as he looked back at me. "I'll always protect you, my réalta. No matter what happens, no matter who might be part of my life, I'll always do whatever it takes to protect you. *Always.*"

My heart beat even faster now, and I licked my suddenly dry lips, while his eyes followed the motion. The fire that always simmered between us began to burn, but the sound of boots scuffing the floor, not too far away by the sound of it. They eventually reached us. We both jolted, quickly breaking apart and slipping inside the king's bedroom.

It was thankfully empty, as predicted. Multicolored lounge pillows and large poufs laid across the floor over rugs with intrigue designs. The warm sun came through in shafts from the windows—which were actually pointed arches in the wall, only these were covered with a screen made up of small rising suns and geometric designs. They left the room half in shadow as the sun slotted through it. Potted plants surrounded every corner, overflowing and giving the room a wild feel. A divan against the largest arch in the wall was covered with papers that piqued my interest.

To my great surprise, the bed was round, sitting on a platform with several layers of yellow and turquoise fabric looping above it sort of like a canopy, and draping down. Teal silk sheets with orange pillows graced the bed, and instead of a traditional headboard, a round mosaic with a Phoenix in the middle took its place. But it was the desk against the other wall that we needed.

Calix pulled out the folder we brought, containing all of Cyrus's plans with blood magic, and put it dead center on the desk, where the king couldn't miss it. I let out a sigh of relief with our task completed, now, we just needed to get out. Calix grabbed my hand and we made for the door. Only when we opened it, I shrieked, and Calix pulled me back by the waist and slammed the door closed.

Guards, an entire battalion of them, awaited us outside the door. They threw magic at us right away, but Calix's quick movement prevented me from being hit. They crashed against the door, shouts and the sound of weapons clanging rang in my ears.

I panted, leaning on my knees to catch my breath and calm my heart rate from the scare. When I stood up, I had to hit Calix's forearms to get him to let me go, as he was still clutching me tightly by the waist. I pulled my sword back out, since Calix already had his in hand, and I noticed his magic holding the door closed as he began seeking out another exit.

"There's only one way out." I reminded him, panic rising. "You saw the map as I did."

"Fucking Tartarus!" Calix swore, anger furrowing his brow. "Stay behind me. I'm going to bring the door down and send out a wave of shadow to knock them down. It'll give us the advantage. You've been trained how to use that sword, now's the time to use it." Calix grabbed my shoulders, giving me a hard nod, but I saw the fear in his eyes. Not for him, but for me.

So, I did what I could to help ease it. I swallowed my panic, firmed up my stance, gripped my sword, and put on my game face.

"Let's do this." I nodded firmly.

He smirked at me, giving me a sultry once over. Clearly, he enjoyed the sight of me ready for battle. He kissed my forehead tenderly, and in the next moment, the door fell, and Calix charged into the hall. I stayed behind him as promised, and watched as a blast of darkness knocked the guards down in one fell swoop.

I stabbed my sword down into the chest of a guard who didn't get back up fast enough, then quickly turned and raised my sword to block the blade of a guard who charged at me. I parried his blow, and he looked surprised, and I determined I would prove the flaw of believing a woman can't handle a blade fatal—I used his surprise to dance around him and take him out at the knees, kicking the back of them and causing him to fall to knees in a hard thud. I took the opportunity to slice my sword across his neck from behind, watching in satisfaction as he gurgled blood, before falling face first to the floor, dead.

Another guard was up and barreling toward me, so I went on the offensive. I swung, and he blocked my blade, so I increased the speed of my thrusts, and eventually got a hit. Calix was working through the guards much faster, but I kept at it, blocking, striking, parrying, thrusting. It was like a dance, and I just had to not miss a step. Finally, I was able to get in a strike down his chest that opened him down to the naval, and he fell to the ground. I was panting with exertion while Calix was already taking out the last guard.

Calix turned to me, his eyes wild and fierce, and looked me over carefully, checking for any injuries. I nodded to confirm I was okay, and he grabbed my hand, pulling me along as we ran through the halls. My nerves were rising though—I didn't like this at all, my instincts screaming that something wasn't right.

"How did they know where we were?" I asked Calix as we ran, shaking my head.

"I don't know." Calix admitted pensively, swinging his head back to look at me. He had a grave expression on his face, and I liked that even less. We turned a corner, and I gasped as I stumbled back in shock. Calix steadied me, but squeezed my hand tighter, and I could feel the anger in the way his fingers tightened around mine. I swallowed hard, shaking.

No—this couldn't be real.

It *couldn't*.

But it *was*—

"Darling, I've been so very worried. Yet here you are. With my enemy no less." There Cyrus stood, surrounded by what had to be at least 50 guards. My heart felt like it was going to beat out of my chest as Cyrus's smirk drilled into me.

"She's not your darling. She's not *your* anything." Calix hissed at him, and Cyrus raised his brows, amused, as he turned to him.

"I'd be careful how you speak to me. After all, I have something you may want." Cyrus taunted, a smile growing across his face.

"Doubtful." Calix snarled. His face was…I could really only describe it as murderous. He partially shifted, his teeth growing into large dagger like fangs, and I could hear the gruffness in his voice that surely resulted from the fire billowing low in his throat.

Cyrus just smirked, that amusement never leaving his face, which made my heart sink into my stomach. He knew Calix was more powerful, which meant he had something up his sleeve to remain so confident. And that he somehow knew to be here, knew what he'd face…

He motioned someone forward and I gasped as Harpina was dragged out in chains. She looked as murderous as Calix, even chained up. She glared at Cyrus like she could burn him with a look. Calix growled low, and it should have been a warning Cyrus took seriously. The fact that he didn't, made me incredibly nervous.

I couldn't go back. *I couldn't*.

Looking at Cyrus now, remembering as he held me down, as I screamed and fought—I thought I might throw up. My hands shook, and Calix squeezed mine hard, centering me back to reality.

"Iron chains." Cyrus smiled, delighted by the reaction he was getting.

"How?" I murmured, my brows furrowing as I tried to figure out what had happened, how he was here. Cyrus smirked at me, and it took everything in me not to flinch back. I wouldn't give him that power.

"Oh, you'll love this, my dear. Come here, girl!" Cyrus smiled widely, and I watched in horror as Emmie stepped through the guards. She gave Cyrus a smile, and I was sure I was going to throw up now. Emmie turned to me and glared. She glared—at me. At *me*.

My heart shattered. I let them in, I let *her* in. I had been firmly against forming attachments, but I grew weak. I let her weaken me to her friendship, and now, *now* she was stabbing me right in the back. I should have known better—should have known her miraculous turnaround was bullshit.

"I told you I wanted to stay with the king!" Emmie spat at me, like everything was my fault. I supposed to her, it was. "I was happy there. I had everything I could possibly want. And you ruined it!"

"Emmie, he's a fucking monster!" I argued, trying to appeal to her logically, but it was useless. What had happened to the girl I first met?

"Who cares?" She scoffed. "So he kills some humans—even some Fae? What does it matter? As long as I was living in luxury, safe and sound, that was all that mattered." It was at that moment I realized I never truly knew her at all.

She smirked at me, like she could read my realization on my face. "I told you when we met, Asteria, you can never trust *anyone* at court. You were so easy, too. So unaware of how the world worked. I knew Cyrus wanted you, and you would give me access to the royals. I refused to live the life of a damn slave forever. I deserved more! I deserved jewels and fancy dresses instead of having to deliver them to others. I wasn't made to scrub pots and do laundry." She tossed her blonde curls over her shoulder, a smug smile crossing her face. "I was born to be taken care of. And that's exactly what King Astraeus did. Exactly what *you* took me away from."

"You see, Asteria? She knew to take advantage of what was offered. You could have had that too, but instead, you refused me at every opportunity." Cyrus snarled, his voice dark with resentment. "Emmie had been given an enchanted pen by my father. Anything written with it would go right to him. It made it oh so easy to get information on what you were up to."

Fuck. This was all my fault. If I'd just left Emmie to Astraeus, our plans wouldn't have been exposed. How much did Cyrus now know? Were the rest of Calix's operations now at risk?

Cyrus looked at Calix, a fake smile lingering on his mouth. "If you want Harpina back, you'll hand over my slave without a fight."

Calix roared, his face a furious snarl as fire blew out of his mouth with a lick of flame. "Asteria isn't a slave. She's a free human."

"You're outnumbered, old friend." Cyrus chuckled, raising his arms to indicate those with him. "You can't kill all of us before I kill Harpina."

Harpina managed to work her gag out of her mouth as Calix fumed silently at Cyrus. "Kill them fucking all, Calix!"

Cyrus's head whipped over to her, but that was all Calix needed to hear apparently. Darkness came from him in a rush, and a wall of it formed—a wall of shadow between me and everyone else—including him. My heart rose that his first thought was to protect me, but fell in the same breath that I was trapped behind a wall as they fought.

I could still see through it though, and I put my palms up to it, wanting to see what was happening. I was struggling to breathe, the idea of going back with Cyrus too much to contemplate. All of my worst nightmares were coming true before my eyes.

Cyrus here to take me back.

A friend betraying me.

Another friend in mortal peril.

And the man I lo—the man I cared for, who'd saved me, who'd given me freedom, readying to fight to the death.

This was exactly why I hadn't wanted to care about anyone. This is what happened. Still, as I watched Calix launch himself into the mess of Fae guards, I couldn't find in myself to regret it. I finally knew what it was to *live*. I'd already sworn to myself I wouldn't go back to living a half-life again.

Living was infinitely preferable to existing, and I would embrace all the pain of living to experience the joy it offered.

I watched Calix, and he was—*Nox*, he was *amazing*.

This was a man who gloried in violence. He'd told me before he wasn't a *good* man, and *no*, looking at him now, I knew he was correct. He wasn't *good*. He was fabulous at killing and he did it with no reservation. Blood coated his skin, staining his silvery white hair red, and I gloried in the sight of it. Never had I imagined a man could fight so fiercely, and certainly not on *my* behalf.

But here Calix was, cutting down person after person, without a care for the lives of the ones he put down, as long as I was safe. So no, maybe he was not a *good* man, but he was a *great* one.

Here was a man who stood against a continent, who defied every known convention of his people because he saw the wrong that was slavery and was determined to fix it. A man who raised his two younger sisters once their parents died, who treated his friends like family and took people into their group without hesitation. He empowered people, giving them the tools they needed to be their best, free selves.

I would take a great man any day, over a good one. There was no room for worrying about being good when battling against slavers. There was too much underhanded dealing and bloodshed for that.

Was he a monster? My dorchadas was a *dragon*.

All the Fae could be considered monsters, Calix more than many, maybe—but a dragon stands far above the others. Fierce and protective, he was everything he should be. He couldn't be contained in such simple terms.

Could *I* even be considered good? After all, I schemed my way out of Dusk, I learned how to kill in Night—and as Calix focused on the men in front of him, I was the one left to handle the guard sneaking through. He somehow cleared away the darkness that Calix erected to protect me. And then the guard's hand reached to grab me and landed on my waist, but I spun, and his grip faltered—I felt no compunction about spitting his throat open with my dagger.

But now I was in the open, grab-able. I had no idea what magic that guard had used to clear away the wall of darkness, but I couldn't focus on that. More guards were already rushing at me, so I pulled my sword and charged at them. They froze for a moment, not anticipating that I would fight back.

After all, slaves weren't allowed to even hold a weapon, let alone train. Calix had given me that. If he was a monster, then there was no such thing as a good man. A monster who empowers the weak is the kind of monster I want on my side—one who fights like a monster to protect, instead of harm. Cyrus was the kind of monster who wanted to cause harm. He wanted me back, wanted me to be his, and that, I could not allow.

I hacked and slashed, spinning left and then right. But I was fighting Fae much stronger than me. Titan's words came back to me, how I had to be more cunning when fighting opponents much stronger and faster than I am.

I backed up, into a narrower side hall. It gave me less room to move, but it also forced them to face me one at a time instead of several at once. It allowed me to take a few down before I truly started to flag against their strength.

"Calix!" I called, hating to distract him, but left with little choice.

"Oh, Calix looks a bit busy at the moment. Don't you think?" I squealed in shock as Cyrus picked me up from behind. His hand covered my mouth, and I kicked out, trying to fight him off. His fist crashed down on my head, and it instantly fell forward, the pain crippling.

"Asteria!" I heard Calix bellow, his scream laced with rage and desperation. I barely managed to lift my head, looking up to see a blur of silvery white. It took me a moment to identify it as his hair as he swung towards where I was. The sight of him charging forward was the last thing I saw, as darkness descended over me.

CHAPTER 36

DARKNESS was all I knew. It pervaded every sense. It was all I saw; all I could feel. I could practically taste it on my tongue. The scent of it was in my nose. The whoosh of darkness moving around me was the only sound that existed.

But I'd always been comfortable in darkness—even if I longed to feel the sun on my face after a while.

I wasn't sure how long it lasted, but eventually, I seemed to float away. This darkness was different, better. It sparkled and shined, and when I looked up…I smiled. *Luna*. She unfurled from her balled up position and flew towards me, nudging me with her snout when she arrived. I reached out and pet a hand down her head. She made a mournful noise and nodded her head to indicate the darkness around us, using her snout to urge me to go to it.

Confused, I shook my head but followed her direction. My hands began to glow with starlight, and I reached out—sure enough, the darkness reached back, or tried to. There was something—something strange. Like the darkness was more…hesitant? I could feel emotions beginning to come through, and it seemed as confused as could be. Rage, grief, anticipation, desire, fear, regret, sadness, love. It was overwhelming. The darkness slid around me, not able to touch with the barrier, but then it just—slinked away.

I gasped awake. My whole body hurts. The feeling of my skin being too tight overtaking everything for a moment. I went to stretch it out, but my limbs wouldn't move. I tried to pull my hands down, and nothing happened except a hard pull on my wrists. I forced my eyes open. Everything was blurry, but I was just able to make out my legs—

Spread open and cuffed to a bed.

Panic rose, and I looked up to find my wrists cuffed to the bed as well. Thankfully, I still had my clothing on, but I was spread eagle on someone's bed and—

"You're awake." I froze. That *voice*. No—*no*.

Memories came back to me in a rush. The mission in Sunset. Sneaking into the palace in Biarma. The fight. Calix. *Cyrus*. Emmie—*by the Otherworld*, Emmie had betrayed us.

Betrayed *me*.

The first person I had trusted in my new life and looked at what happened. What hurt the worst was that she was right, she did warn me not to trust her. Or anyone.

But she was wrong, I knew that now. Despite her betrayal, I was finally in a good place in my life, surrounded by people who cared about me. Or—I *was*.

I refused to consider that I wouldn't be again. I had to get out of here, somehow. This wasn't going to be my life. A slave to *him*. A slave to *anyone*.

Never. Again.

I was free. Well—okay, I was currently a captive, sure. And Cyrus probably considers me his *slave*—but no, I wasn't. I never would be again. I just had to have faith. Faith in my friends. Faith in *Calix*.

My king may be torn on his feelings, but I knew he had them. The way he called me *his* star in the ancient language—

Calix would come for me.

Swallowing any trace of panic so Cyrus wouldn't get the satisfaction, I let my rage take over, forcing myself to meet the gaze of my captor. Lightning flashed in blue eyes I once thought hard to resist, until I learned who he really was. Until I met a king who truly was hard to resist.

"Cyrus." I snarled, fighting against my bonds, but he just laughed merrily.

"Oh, my dear." Cyrus smiled condescendingly. "I would wipe that look off your face." The merry smile faded into an awful expression that spoke of his own rage, along with his embarrassment, his want. I had to be very careful. Cyrus was clearly deranged, and I didn't want to make this worse.

I stiffened as he leaned over me, flashes of him forcing me down, freezing me in place, my breath growing heavy and fast. Cyrus smirked, like he could scent my fear—and he probably could, I realized. Fae could smell many things, and I kept forgetting that little fact.

"You're at my mercy now, Asteria. Calix—" Cyrus growled. "Isn't here to save you. You're mine. You've always been mine, and it's time for you to accept that."

His mouth crashed down on mine, and I tried to keep my lips closed. When he forced them open, I savagely bit his lip until he jerked back with a snarl of outrage. He reached up and grasped my neck, starting to squeeze as I tried to gasp for air, but he was completely blocking my airway. I tried to move my arms to bat at him, but only succeeded in rattling the chains.

"Cyrus!" A voice yelled from the doorway. Cyrus looked down at me, face still twisted into a snarl, as a familiar voice called his name again. I never thought I'd be so thankful to hear Zerlina. "Cyrus! You—oh for Tala's sake! You brought *her* back?"

Cyrus turned his twisted fury to the doorway, releasing my neck. I gasped in air, following his gaze to where my surprising savior stood. Zerlina had her hands on her hips, and she was glaring fiercely. She was clad in a red and gray gown, still wearing the colors of House Bathala despite the fact she was marrying into House Tynan. *Interesting.* Seems things weren't going well—not that I was surprised.

"*What* are you doing here?" Cyrus growled out at her.

"Your mother wants to have lunch with us." Zerlina huffed, shaking her head. "You scared the slave away who was supposed to tell you, so, here I am." Her voice was dry, her dislike of her task more than clear as she threw her arms in the air in exasperation. "Let's go, my *dearest* betrothed."

Her sarcasm made Cyrus snarl, and he whirled around, stalking toward her. He grabbed *her* by the neck, and it was obvious Cyrus had gone over the edge. Where before he might have feigned civility, now he went straight for brutality.

"Watch your fucking tone, Zerlina." Cyrus demanded, lightning crackling around him. "If I didn't need this alliance with your father, I would choke the fucking life out of you. *Happily.*" Zerlina just smiled widely at him, looping a leg around his.

"Try it." She purred, while he pressed himself into her.

Ew. This was definitely some demented flirting. Maybe they were perfect for one another after all. Actual monsters—spoiled, privileged assholes, who thought mortals belonged to them and used them as they would.

Watching them made me sick, so I turned my head away. Unfortunately, that meant I didn't notice when Cyrus approached the bed again. He loomed over me once more and unwanted fear rattled through my bones.

"I'd say be good, but you're not getting out of these chains until I'm ensured of your loyalty." He smirked down at me.

I cleared my sore throat, my voice more a croak than the strong tone I'd prefer. "What if I have to go to the bathroom? Or eat? Drink water? Are you going to leave me to die of dehydration?"

"Don't worry, I have someone to watch over you." Cyrus chuckled, and my blood ran cold. "You'll have to wait to go to the bathroom until I'm back to watch you, but she'll help with food and water." He waved a hand to the doorway, and I snarled as Emmie appeared.

"You remember our deal?" Cyrus nearly purred as he asked Emmie, who nodded meekly. It looked like she'd been crying, her eyes puffy and swollen. She'd gotten exactly what she wanted, what in Tartarus did she have to cry about?

Cyrus left me with Emmie, who came and sat at my bedside. I glared at her, and she glared right back, neither of us speaking for an extended period of time. I was left to ruminate over her betrayal, and hoping Calix, Harpina, and everyone else were all okay—that they'd gotten out alive, and that they'd hopefully be coming for me.

"This is all your fault, you know. If you had just been happy with what Cyrus gave you, none of this would be happening." Emmie finally said a while later, her tone gratingly superior.

I ground my teeth, rage sparking at her ridiculous words and uppity tone. "Be happy with being a slave? With being used? At the mercy of a fucking monster? No thanks—I have more self-respect than that. Something you clearly lack."

"Oh, so superior." Emmie laughed wryly. "Yet it was you who was just fucking a man who has a soulmate, a man who's tried so hard to be loyal to her. You had no problem ruining that, did you? Maybe you just wanted a king, was that it? You weren't happy with the Crown Prince, you wanted more. But the king chose me, and you couldn't handle it." She sniffed, squaring her shoulders.

I wanted to claw her eyes out.

I stiffened, my chains rattling loudly in my ears. "You have no idea what you're talking about. I could care less about his title. And do you honestly think I wanted to care about a man whose soul is literally tied to another? No, of course I fucking didn't! I can't help how I feel. You should understand that, if you're in love with an awful, corrupt soul like King Astraeus. Who you only got chosen by because Cyrus manipulated things to have you spy for him. Oh! And he's a married man, isn't he? Yet, you had no issue with *that*."

Emmie glared at me, her fists curling, and I felt a sick sense of pleasure at angering her.

"You have *no* idea." She hissed, "You think you've had it bad? The beautiful Asteria, whose princes and kings will do anything to have." She scoffed. "Some of us don't have the luxury of being singled out for such things, we have to slave away for years, to reach any kind of safety, and some don't even get it then. You even had the luxury of growing up in a little village, where the Fae barely bothered you. Do you know how rare that is?"

"Yes." I whispered, my heart sinking for whatever had led her here— twisted her mind into thinking *this* was the answer. "I do. I met a woman in Night who was in Dawn too, and she was brutally tortured. Her eye taken out, her arm ripped off, her sister killed in front of her—I've seen what Cyrus and King Astraeus are really up to. The humans they torture and kill. I've seen the laborers in the streets of Evenfall, the brothels full of women who didn't want to be there. I've had Cyrus attack me and try to force himself on me."

"What?" Emmie interrupted, looking shocked.

"Oh, yes, you dutifully handed me back to the man who tried to rape me. *Thanks ever so.*" I snarled at her.

She looked uncomfortable, and I hated the part of me that was thrilled at that. A hateful part that wanted her to hurt for the pain she caused me.

"In Dawn, we had nothing." Emmie eventually said, pushing a curl behind her ear. "My parents worked in the palace, but we weren't allowed out of the slave quarters when not working, which meant children like me and Eris couldn't leave. Ever." She went quiet for a moment, and I did feel a twinge of pity then. "We had one outfit a piece, and they were falling apart, raggedy and dirty, only allowed to be washed once a week—if you were able to fight to get it into that week's load. It wasn't always possible. I would go a month sometimes wearing the same dirty thing."

She looked at me then, tears glimmering in her eyes. "I swore to myself I'd get better for myself one day. I'd find a way to turn some Fae's head and get *more*." Emmie scoffed, narrowing her eyes at me. "And then there you were, getting exactly what I wanted, and not appreciating it one bit. Then, when I finally did get exactly what I wanted, you ripped me away from it. To *freedom.*"

The sarcasm in her voice had me furrowing my brows at her in confusion. She sounded disgusted by the notion but—

"After all that, why wouldn't you want to be free of them?" I shook my head. I didn't understand it. I could maybe understand her feelings about me, sure. If she was deluded enough to want the attention of these horrible slavers, that's on her. But to spurn freedom?

"Why would I want to have to work and take care of myself when King Astraeus would have taken care of me forever?" Emmie shook her head, tears filling her eyes.

"Because it wouldn't be forever, Emmie." I explained, not understanding how she didn't grasp this. "It would just be until he got bored. Or someone told him you were sleeping around to open a spot for a spy just like Cyrus did. Astraeus so easily cast his bedmate of many years away at the slightest suggestion. One who he seemed to actually care about."

"He wouldn't have." Emmie protested, tears beginning to fall. "But now he...he—" She gasped for breath between tears, and I wanted to roll my eyes. All of this just because she wanted someone else to take care of her. She couldn't have found someone else to do so? Someone in Night? If she was truly that desperate. It was absolutely ridiculous. I couldn't blame her for finding a way to survive while enslaved, but once free—crawling back to slavery? No, that I'd never understand.

"He's replaced me!" Emmie wailed out, dramatically, and I couldn't help rolling my eyes now.

"Of course he did." I scoffed, truly floored how this cunning woman could be so blind. "Did you think you were special? We're their *slaves*, Emmie! Wake up!"

She raised her head, brown eyes glaring at me like everything bad that ever happened to her was *my* fault. "He wouldn't have if you hadn't torn me out of here. But Cyrus promised if I watch you, he'll ensure his father takes me back."

She wiped her tears away, but my heart sank in my chest. "Emmie, if he's telling the truth, and that's a huge *if*—he'd do it by hurting whoever he's with now."

If I thought the idea of an innocent being hurt would change her mind, I was in for a rude awakening. She just shrugged—shrugged! Like she couldn't care less.

"Eris would be ashamed of you!" I spat, glowering at her, absolutely disgusted. I couldn't believe she'd fooled us for so long. "What did you tell them about our plans, Emmie? She's just as involved as the rest of us. She did so much to help you and you'd turn around and betray her too? Get her captured?" Emmie's shoulders stiffened and she glared back at me, but she stayed silent for a while.

When she finally spoke, her voice was quiet, "I'll do what I have to do."

I shook my head at her but said nothing. There was nothing more to say.

When Cyrus finally came back, it was *almost* a relief to see Emmie go, to get away from the strained silence between us—only then I was stuck with him. He sauntered over to me, sitting on the side of the bed.

"Are you going to be good so I can let you out of these chains?" He drawled, raising an eyebrow.

I opened my mouth to tell him to go to Tartarus, but I had to be smart here. I needed to find a way out, a way *home*. Because that was what I had now, a true home, and I was desperate to get back. The first step would be getting out of these chains. I wouldn't get anywhere if I was stuck, chained to this bed.

I gritted my teeth, resigning myself to what I'd have to do to get out of these chains. I let myself slump in them, like I'd given up, and looked up at Cyrus from below lowered lashes.

"Yes, Prince Cyrus, I'll be good." I hated the words slipping past my lips, but the defeat in my tone made him smile widely.

"Wonderful! Now, just know, if you do anything stupid like trying to run, or contact Calix—" Cyrus said sharply, his blue eyes flashing as he narrowed them at me. "I can guarantee you won't like what happens afterwards."

"I know. I won't." I admitted, not caring in the least. I wouldn't let it get to that point. I wouldn't make a move until escape was assured. Cyrus looked at me critically, but the front I put on must've worked—or maybe he was just desperate to believe it. He pulled a key out of his pocket and reached up to unlock the cuffs around my wrists. When both my wrists were free, I brought them together and rubbed at the sore, red spots where the chains had continually rubbed at the skin.

With my legs free, I swung myself up to a sitting position on the side of the bed, holding my wrists as the pain radiated. I arched my back, trying to stretch out the pain of being stuck laying down for so long on a bad angle, and the feeling of my body not fitting the way it should. I may be used to that pain, but adjusting to it didn't make it less bothersome.

Cyrus grabbed my chin, jerking my face up suddenly. His eyes held a challenge in them, and I knew I wouldn't like what was about to happen. When his mouth came down on mine, it took everything in me to resist fighting, knowing I had to act submissive. For now.

I didn't know what had happened after Cyrus grabbed me. Harpina had been chained up, and the last I saw of Calix was him fighting his way towards me. I didn't know if the rest had been caught, and I couldn't imagine Calix letting me go easily. I remembered vividly how he screamed when Cyrus grabbed me. What had happened? How in the Otherworld had they over-powered *Calix*?

The only way to get answers was Cyrus. I would give in to his kiss if it meant a way to find out about my friends. If it meant being out of chains so I could find a way to escape.

Fuck his threats—he didn't know how much of a threat *I* could be.

Liviana said the gods told her I was needed, that I was a lynchpin in freeing humans from slavery and bringing balance back to Celesterra. Which meant I had more worth than Cyrus would ever have. The thought made me smile.

Cyrus made a pleased rumble, and then I remembered what my mouth was occupied with in reality, far from where I'd disappeared inside my mind. He'd thought the smile was for him? Ugh. *Men.* As if I would ever. But I supposed it helped sell my submission.

I thought back to my last kiss before this, to Calix. Nox, he must be beside himself now. But that night—by the Otherworld, it had been *perfect*. I'd never experienced sex like that before. He made me feel like I was fucking goddess, and I'd barely been able to walk the next day after spending the night with him between my thighs. My cunt *ached* afterwards, stretched and used in the best way possible.

What I wouldn't give to be back there now. To have him be the one kissing me. In this moment, I couldn't care less about the complications, about his mate and my weak heart that wanted him anyway—I just wanted him here. I wanted to experience that all-consuming feeling that overtook me when we kissed, like the world was somehow turned upside down the whole time, and when he kissed me, it was finally right side up.

I was brought back to the present as Cyrus bit my lip. He pulled back with a nasty smile that made me think he somehow knew my thoughts, but he just stood up and walked away. I watched him, confused, and he looked back at me with a smirk.

"Did you honestly think I would give you the satisfaction of getting fucked after what you pulled?" Cyrus chuckled as he turned and leaned on the doorframe. I almost laughed myself, the mere idea that he could delude himself into thinking I wanted that was hilarious. "You're going to have to earn it, my dear."

I would rather stab my eyes out.

CHAPTER 37

ᗝAYS passed in a blur. Confined to Cyrus's rooms, I was slowly going insane. When he'd left the first time after chaining me up, I went to sneak out the door, only to find myself hitting an invisible wall. Cyrus had returned later, smirk firmly in place.

"Let me guess, you tried to leave?" He tsked, slowly prowling closer as I tried to back up. But before I could, he grabbed me by the shoulders in a painful grip that had me wincing. "You know the wonderful thing about blood magic, Asteria?"

I felt my blood freeze in my veins. Oh fuck.

"It allows us to do so many things. Things they tell us are impossible. But *nothing* is impossible." Cyrus grabbed my hair, yanking it back and forcing me to look up at him. "I'll tell you a little secret. All it takes, is *sacrifice*."

I looked back at the doorway, where strange magic had stopped me from leaving, horror filling my soul as my eyes closed in pain. I knew his plans, but this was confirmation he'd already begun. "You sacrificed humans."

"You knew I would, didn't you?" Cyrus laughed, reaching up to caress my cheek. I tried to turn my face away, but he forced me to keep looking at him as he touched me. "It turns out you were a better spy than even I knew. We'll have to address that, we can't have you going through my things again."

His voice hardened, and I cursed Emmie—she'd told him *everything* then. Our advantage, gone. All for what? Her to be spoiled by the king? Only to get here and find she didn't have a place with him anymore. It would be tragic if I wasn't so furious with her.

"In the meantime, I've placed a ward around the room tied specifically to you. You can't leave until I allow it." Cyrus gloated, and it dawned on me exactly what he'd done. Even if someone came for me, I wouldn't be able to get out of the room.

I wanted to fall to the floor and cry in frustration, but I wouldn't give him the satisfaction of seeing it.

That had been the first day, and things hadn't improved since then. I'd only seen a few people, including Emmie, who didn't talk to me, and I didn't talk to her—a mutual cold shoulder. Cyrus let a few slaves in to tend to things in the room for him, but no one else. I wondered if Kian knew I was here. If he'd reached out to Calix to get me out once more, or if he considered my usefulness at an end now that Cyrus knew about my spying and information gathering.

Boredom was killing me. After spending my days training, going to meetings, and going out dancing and drinking, this sudden stop of everything was horrible. I hated it. I hated this room. I hated this kingdom. I hated *him* most of all.

But it was better to be alone than having him here. It was my unfortunate luck that Cyrus entered once more. I was reading a book on the sofa, trying to lose myself in fantasy, and he came in to intrude on even that.

"What are you reading?" Cyrus asked, sounding almost amused. I stiffened, his moods ever unpredictable.

"A book." I answered shortly. He snorted and came over, ripping the book from my hands and flipping it to the cover.

"Forbidden Love and Other Tales." Cyrus read aloud. His eyes shot to me as he threw the book on the table. "Ah, a smutty romance. So, you do feel lust—you just refused to give in to me specifically, is that it?"

"You know why." I murmured, swallowing hard. "I told you over and over. A man who owns me is not a choice, it's forced no matter which way you look at it. You can't consent to a person who *owns* you. Women have been taken advantage of in every level of this society, from slaves to queens. I refuse to allow myself to be degraded in such a way."

I knew the words were dangerous as they left my lips, and I was proven right as those lips were then split open. Cyrus backhanded me, *hard*. His ring splitting my lip and causing blood to hit the velvet sofa I was slammed back against. I looked up at him with wide eyes, my hand going to my mouth in shock. I'd known he was capable of horrible violence, but he'd never unleashed it on me before.

Cyrus smiled cruelly, pulling me up until I was standing in front of him. He leaned in and licked the blood off my lips. I tried to flinch back, but he held fast. When Calix had done the same, I'd found it sexy, but the same action from Cyrus left me wanting to bathe.

He raised his hand, and I flinched as I watched it fly toward me. It hit me harder this time, sending me to the floor in a heap. My head rung from that one, his Fae strength causing more damage than from a human. Cyrus grabbed my chin, forcefully, turning me to face him from where I sat on my knees, panting.

"Degraded? Let's see about degrading you, shall we?" Cyrus purred, making me exceptionally nervous. I was incredibly right to be, as he undid his pants and pulled out his cock. I backed up on my hands, hitting the sofa with a bump.

He smirked as he sauntered over to me. He grabbed my chin once more, squishing my lips together, as his fingers bruised my jaw. "Open that mouth."

I shook my head desperately, clamping my mouth closed.

"Open, or I'll knock out your teeth and force your mouth over my cock." Cyrus cooed. I looked up at him with wide eyes, but he only smiled, with a sick, excited look on his face that made me want to vomit. "Those wide eyes only make me imagine you looking up at me as you suck me."

I quickly looked away and he chuckled. "Open. Now. Last chan—"

A loud banging at the door had him tossing his head back with a groan, but I nearly wilted in relief. I had no idea how I was going to get out of this. The lack of options bore down on me. Trapped. I was completely trapped. I needed to get to Night Kingdom, but I couldn't even leave these rooms. Trapped inside with a man eager to take me against my will.

Tears fell from my eyes, no matter how hard I tried to hold them back. I let my head fall back as I gasped in a breath. Only thankful Cyrus had already stuffed his cock back in his pants and went to answer the door, so he couldn't see me. The tears were half terror and half relief.

At least we were interrupted. *For now.*

Maybe the gods truly did look out for everyone, and not just the Fae. Maybe attending the Festival of Faunus had made them pay more attention. If so, I'd go to the altar and pray to them every damned day if they got me out of here.

I vaguely heard Cyrus arguing with whoever was at the door, before he left with them, slamming the door before him. I collapsed in relief. Sitting on the floor crying wasn't going to accomplish anything though, I had to force myself up. Find a way forward.

Standing, I shakily made my way through the room, only to shriek as the wall—*opened*. The fucking *wall*! I'd never noticed a seam there for a hidden door, but it must have existed.

"Asteria?" My jaw dropped. Whoever I thought was about to come through that door, I couldn't have been more surprised by who did.

"Soren?!" I shrieked, cringing at the noise and hoping no one heard.

"Asteria, thank the Old Gods!" Soren sighed as he rushed toward me, pulling me into a hug. I hugged him back tightly, a little numb from what had just happened, and a bit from seeing him here.

I had just enough presence of mind to notice his hugs no longer felt as they once did. He was once my lover, but I no longer felt the same desire as I once had when he touched me.

"Soren, what in Tartarus are you doing here?" I whisper-shouted as I pulled out of his arms. I truly never thought I would see him again, and yet here he was. In Dusk. In Cyrus's rooms.

"I'll tell you on the way, come on, we have to get you out of here." He insisted, taking my hand and pulling me to the wall.

"Soren—" I tried to protest.

"Come on, quick." He cut me off, and I rolled my eyes as he yanked me, knowing it was futile.

I let him try to pull me through the wall and wasn't a bit surprised when I couldn't go through. The hand holding mine got stuck in the ward, and it stopped him in his tracks. He looked back, his jaw dropping as he tried to pull his hand through again, but connected to mine, it wouldn't budge.

I sighed dramatically, letting go of his hand, and watching as Soren's went smoothly through. I raised my eyebrows at him. "You think I haven't tried leaving?"

"What in the Otherworld is this?" Soren demanded.

"Cyrus put a fucking ward around his rooms that stops me from leaving." I rolled my eyes. "It's the result of blood magic. It's—well, it's a long story, frankly. Now, why don't you tell me what you're doing here?" I put my hands on my hips, the resolve on my face letting him know he wasn't getting out of this.

He sighed, running a hand through coppery red hair that was longer than I remembered it, now down past his shoulders instead of the shoulder length style I had once run my own hands through. It reminded me of Baach, and the ache I felt at that thought…I missed my friends more than I could say. Seeing Soren didn't seem to make up for that as it once might have. In fact, his hair, which I once thought was beautiful, now seemed ordinary. His green eyes not as enchanting. I much preferred silvery white hair and purple eyes, as it turned out.

"I'm here to get you out, Asteria. Get you to safety. Far away from Dusk and Night and whichever other horrid monsters might think to take you." Soren explained, his voice hardening in a way I wasn't used to. I furrowed my brows at him.

"Night isn't full of monsters." I automatically defended, glaring at him. His incredulous look sort of pissed me off, despite the rescue attempt. He opened his mouth, so I rushed to continue. "How did you know I was even here? In fact, how in Tartarus did you escape your masters?"

Soren cringed, looking uncomfortable. "I didn't escape anyone. Queen Aurelia sent me."

"The queen of Day?!" I hissed at him, my mouth dropping open in shock.

He nodded solemnly, and I noticed a reserve about him that had never existed before. "She wants to help you, Asteria."

I looked at him suspiciously. No Fae royal would randomly help a slave they didn't know. Well—I supposed Calix was the exception, but still. There was something off about this whole thing.

"I swear. When I arrived in Day, she immediately took me in her service. I was so nervous, but she said she saw me with you and wanted to help. She said we needed to get you out of Dusk, and then, when we found out you'd been taken by Night—" Soren swallowed hard. "She was devastated. We tried and tried to find a way in to save you but—"

"I didn't need saving in Night. I was happy there." I told him firmly. I didn't know what this queen was up to, but it couldn't be good. Manipulating Soren into taking me—

"Happy?" He hissed, as his eyes widened incredulously. "They're murderers!"

"You don't know what you're talking about, Soren." I argued, shaking my head. "They aren't that at all."

"Oh, I suppose you're going to tell me I imagined the attacks they've been launching on other kingdoms?" He raised his brows expectantly.

I shook my head with a deep sigh. "For the greater good—freeing humans. That's why they always disappear, they aren't being slaughtered to pieces, they're being freed. He saved me, Soren."

My voice softened without my notice as I thought of Calix, my eyes unfocusing for a moment as I imagined him here in front of me. "Calix is a great man. He helps his people and treats everyone equally. He helps set humans up with new lives, and gives amazing support for those who've been badly traumatized—"

I trailed off, realizing I was babbling. I looked up at Soren and he was watching me with a strange look in his eyes, his brows furrowed together. He was slow to speak, and when he did, I finally recognized the emotion brimming in his eyes. Defeat. "You're in love with him."

"What?" I gasped, my mouth dropping in surprise. "Absolutely not! How could you even—" I paused, shaking my head, not wanting an answer to that. "No, I'm not in love with *anyone*." I stressed, refusing to believe that the warmth that heated my blood and the thrill that made my heart pound was *love*. "Now, I don't know how much time we have, and I don't know why your Queen wants me, but I'm going back to Night."

"Asteria—" Soren whispered, looking pained as he reached out for me— just as we heard boots coming down the hall. We looked at one another, wide eyed. Soren grabbed me in a hug and not knowing what would happen, if I would ever see him again, I hugged him back hard.

"Be safe. Please. I'm not giving up on getting you out of here, no matter where you go after." Soren promised, and his face was full of a mixture of resolve and longing as he disappeared into the wall and closed it behind him.

I let myself collapse against it, unsure what to make of what had just happened. Not that I had long to ruminate on what the Queen of Day wanted from me. I remembered her from Placement Day. She'd *seemed* kind, giving me a smile when I thought I would descend into a pit of rage and helplessness. But I'd since learned that seeming kind meant absolutely nothing. Emmie had seemed immeasurably kind and look how that had turned out.

CYRUS SAUNTERED BACK into the room, Zerlina storming after him. As much as I disliked her, I let out a small sigh of relief. If she was here, he would hopefully be too preoccupied to deal with me, in theory, anyway.

"You're a damn fool, Cyrus! All this over a little slave girl? You've lost your damn mind." Zerlina screamed behind him. "Think of what's to come, I beg of you. We will be King and Queen, we'll have a legacy that will last millennia, and you're going to throw it all away over property that'll be rotting in the ground getting picked apart by maggots in a blink of the eye!"

I blinked, not much appreciating that disgusting description, as true as it may be when comparing our lifespans. I jumped as a bolt of lightning flashed in the room. Oh, Nox, that wasn't good. Zerlina even looked a bit scared now, backing away with wide eyes as Cyrus advanced on her, his eyes completely consumed by lightning.

"Zerlina." Cyrus growled as he cornered her. "You will never understand what it takes to be Queen." She flinched, earning a smirk from Cyrus. "Do you not understand this is about so much more now?"

"Like what?" She spat at him, though her voice had dropped to a whisper. I clung to the wall like I could disappear into the same spot Soren had appeared from.

Cyrus chuckled, something sinister in it chilling me to the bone. His fists landed on the wall on either side of Zerlina's head, and her proud chin tilted upward to look him in the eye. I had to give her credit, that took guts.

"The fact you even have to ask, proves my point, my darling betrothed." Cyrus chuckled harshly before his mouth dipped to hers, and I scrunched my nose in disgust watching the two of them. Desperate to disappear entirely and to tell them to shut up and go away—but self-preservation kept my mouth clamped shut.

Especially as Zerlina's legs went around his waist, rucking her skirt up, and she ripped open his pants. She pulled out that dreaded cock and impaled herself on it. My lip curled, they had to know I was *right* here.

Cyrus thrust into her hard and fast as Zerlina held onto the wall for dear life. I tried to find something else to look at as grunts and moans filled the room, along with Zerlina's sniveling little comments about how much she hated him—but it was impossible. My eyes kept going right back to the disaster happening before me.

As they did now, when Zerlina let out a particularly high wail, and I flinched to see Cyrus already looking at me. His eyes roving over me as he fucked into his betrothed. I glared, but he just smirked, blue flashes of lightning in his irises letting me know his control was on the edge. I knew not to push him now, so I just looked away instead.

But feeling his eyes on me was unsettling. I looked back at him with narrowed eyes, but was unfortunately just in time to see them both cum. *Gross.* The way Cyrus watched *me* as he came wasn't lost on any of us.

"You've got to be kidding me!" Zerlina shrieked, earning an eye roll from Cyrus, who clearly couldn't care less about her complaints.

He just kept eyeing me, licking his lips as he stared at mine. I shivered—how close it came to him shoving his cock in my mouth against my will was chilling. I needed to find a way out of here.

Before it was too late.

CHAPTER 38

I EXPECTED Soren might come back, but two days later, I still hadn't seen him. It was starting to make me anxious, jittery—which Cyrus was beginning to notice. That was the very last thing I needed when I couldn't explain what was happening.

My inability to connect to the outside world was starting to truly get to me. Cyrus had blocked all the windows magically so I wouldn't be able to find a way out through them. I needed to see the sun. Feel it's heat on my face like the old friend it was. I'd taken to trying to take small naps during the day just to see Zhu and feel a bit of the sun in my dreams. Dreams had always been there when reality failed me.

At least at night, I could sleep and see Luna. It was somewhat painful, reminding me of the dragon I most wished to see right now. I wondered where he was, if he was struggling to find a way to get me out. Cyrus still hadn't told me what happened the day he took me, blowing me off completely when I asked him. So dreaming was a bit bittersweet.

But at least I got to dance among the stars, feeling more at home, more at peace, then I should have been able to. Only one thing was missing—the darkness didn't come for me anymore. I called to it, tried reaching out, and nothing. It was gone, only the true darkness of the night sky remained. Leaving me feeling more alone than ever.

I'd spent so much of my life alone, and for the very first time, I'd found people who I *fit* with. The people of Night Kingdom—Calix, Ilta, Delia, Eryx, Baach, Lilith, Harpina, Titan, and Callisto, along with Priscilla, and even Eris—they'd filled a hole I hadn't even realized was empty.

I'd loved my parents, truly, but we'd never been able to connect the way I did with my friends. They were happy to continue slaving away, while I wanted to tear it all down. We were too opposite to ever find common ground. In Tairngire, I finally found the family I'd always wanted.

Only to have it all torn away.

I should have known, nothing good happened to me—not for long. The gods must have realized their mistake and set out to fix it. It still didn't stop me from praying. Which is what found me on my knees now, collapsed against my bed.

"Asteria, Nyx, Erebus, I know I'm not Fae, but if Calix and the others are to be believed, you won't mind. I'm begging you, *please*, let me get out of here. I don't know how much more I can take of this." I prayed, voice breaking as I quietly sniffled. The daily threat of being violated, getting hit and thrown around, cut off from everyone and everything I loved, even the precious sky—I was cracking at the seams.

I wondered if my prayers were answered when later that day, the secret door opened once more. A whoosh of breath left me as I jumped up.

"Soren!" I cried, throwing myself at him, hugging him around the neck. "I wasn't sure if you'd be back."

Soren hummed as he hugged me back. I'd forgotten he did that, and a sense of nostalgia came over me. Not a longing for something, but a fond memory of the past you can look on with joy, without wanting it to happen again. When I finally pulled out of his arms, he rushed to reassure me.

"We're trying to find a way around the ward. I promise, none of us have given up on you, Asteria. Not the queen, and not me." He swore fervently as he moved to brush a piece of hair behind my ear, the look in his eyes all too familiar. I stepped back, putting space between us—not wanting him to get any ideas. I didn't forget his last words to me, his profession of love. Or what he thought was love.

"What exactly does the queen want?" I demanded, and Soren sighed deeply, a trace of frustration crossing his face.

"She wants you safe, that's as much as I can say right now." He replied, shaking his head. "She wants to talk to you directly." I crossed my arms over my chest, finding it wholly strange that Soren was so dedicated to the queen of Day. What had happened to him since Placement Day?

"Then once I'm out of this Tartarus damned kingdom, she can come visit me in Night." I asserted, staring him down. He cocked his head to the side, a frown forming on his face.

"Why do you want to return there so badly?" Frustration lined every syllable, and his eyes turned pleading as he begged for answers. In truth, I couldn't blame him. He wasn't the only one much changed since the day we parted.

I sighed heavily, uncrossing my arms and looking to the side. "Everyone I love is there. My family is there."

Soren flinched, and I winced as I realized how my words sounded. "I didn't mean—"

"You *are* in love with someone." Soren murmured, sounding defeated. His shoulders slumped from the new soldier's posture that he must have learned in Day Kingdom. I flinched at his words, shaking my head in denial.

"That's not it at all. Soren, the people of Night, they're amazing. You'd love them." I raised my brows at him. "They saved me, took me in, and made me one of them." I smiled softly at the thought of them all. "I just want to go home."

"Isn't that sweet?" The cooing voice made me freeze, turning as the door opened wide. Cyrus walked through with a malicious smirk on his face. "And who is this?"

Soren's emerald eyes widened, shooting over to me before he tried running for the secret door. but before he could get there, Cyrus had him by the neck.

"No!" I screamed, rushing Cyrus, only for him to use his other hand to backhand me, sending me to the floor. I raised a hand to my mouth, pulling it back to see the blood trickling from the corner. Energy rushed through me, the fear for Soren a living thing.

"What is this?" Cyrus questioned, shaking Soren by the neck. "Ahh, I remember you. You're the one who kissed my Asteria at Placement Day, when I found her." He chuckled sinisterly. "I should have known. You whored yourself to Calix quickly enough, why not whore yourself out to this one too."

He tossed Soren to the ground, red faced and panting, holding his neck where it would surely bruise. I tried to crawl over to him, only for Cyrus to step in front of me. Soren froze, Cyrus's magic holding him in place as his wild eyes met mine, terror brimming in his gaze—a terrible part of me felt relief I wasn't the only one.

I looked up at him, fear running through my veins like blood. My rage ignited like a volcano erupting, sparking my blood and making me stretch and curl my fingers as the horrible feeling of my skin being too tight became unbearable. I swore I could feel a strange weight on my back, pressing me down, before it was quickly gone.

"I didn't touch him. Not since Placement Day. Let. Him. Go." I demanded, hoping against hope he'd just write him off, but Cyrus merely raised his eyebrows.

"I don't think so." Cyrus chuckled as he slowly crouched down over me. "You've been a defiant little bitch since the day I claimed you. You belong to me. You're *my* property. No one else is allowed to touch you." He leered at me, looking me up and down. "Not without my permission anyway. But you'll have to earn that privilege back."

I winced at the incredulous look Soren sent me, but I turned my gaze on Cyrus and glared back at him. "The fact I'd rather die than be stuck here with you should tell you something, Cyrus. This desperate act isn't very attractive."

I knew the words would incite his anger but deemed it worth the feeling of victory as the words registered in his mind. The look on his face was priceless. Lightning hit the ground next to me, charring the rug, and I jolted back. I swallowed hard to clear my rapidly drying mouth, and I couldn't help but wonder if I might have just sealed my death.

"You fucking whore." Cyrus seethed, his hands trembling from the force of his anger. "You're nothing but a slave who should be kissing my fucking boots! If I can't break you down nicely, well—" He sneered nastily. "Let's try something a bit more *exciting*, shall we?" A cruel grin overtook his face as lighting gathered at his fingertips. Fingertips he pointed—Right. At. Me…

I shook but braced myself. If I was to die or be tortured, I wouldn't give him the satisfaction of seeing me flinch. He wanted my fear, my tears, my timidity. I would give him *nothing*.

I blanked my face and squared my shoulders, which seemed to only enrage him further. He moved his hand, and—

An incredibly fast blur took Cyrus down before I knew what was happening. I gasped as the two rolled, and I caught a glimpse of who stopped him.

"Calix!" I cried, tears filling my eyes as I took him in. Silvery white hair was long and flowing, braided back from his face on the sides, purple eyes narrowed and seething with color, darkness bleeding out from him—out of control as his emotions rioted. Armor covered every bit of him except his head, and his black bladed sword was at his hip, the silver runes hidden in its sheath.

I'd never seen a more wonderful sight in all my life.

My heart pounded as his eyes met mine, and it felt like everything would be okay, now that he was here. Everything would be right in the world—his eyes alone soothing me from the terror I'd been experiencing. Making the week spent here seem like only a moment in comparison to the entirety of our time together. It couldn't stack up in comparison.

"Calix." Cyrus growled, lips pulling back in a snarl. Calix matched his growl with a roar that shook the windows. "You shouldn't have come. She's mine." Cyrus hissed at him, but a winged horse could not compare to a dragon, and he knew it. "And now you and all of your people will pay for taking her."

Calix laughed wryly, shaking his head in a taunting manner. "I wouldn't be afraid of you even if you *could* equal my power. But we both know you don't. And no amount of stolen power will make up for it. Asteria doesn't belong to you. She's free. Completely her own." His face hardened, and a combination of darkness and fire licked every word he spoke next. "Know that I am going to make *you* pay for every single time you laid a finger on her."

His voice was pure menace as he faced Cyrus. the promise of death lingering on every word, yet all I felt was the promise in them, heating my entire body. No man had ever tried protecting me before. Not Soren. Not even my father, whose best attempt was handing me a forbidden blade. Certainly not Cyrus. Calix and our friends were the first. But not even Eryx, Baach, or Titan would do *this*.

"Oh, I don't believe it." Cyrus laughed, shaking his head and cackling, "You've fallen for her, haven't you? You absolute fool. I heard you had a mate out there somewhere. I wonder what she'll make of your love for a slave?"

Calix's eyes met mine over Cyrus's shoulder, and we both stilled as the accusation settled. My heart was beating so fast I thought it might be visible in my chest, but there was no time to consider what he was saying. No time to entertain the idea that maybe—

No.

Not. The. Time. Asteria.

I looked to Soren to see his reaction, only to find him—*gone*. He'd disappeared. The door in the wall was left open, and the man who'd opened it to supposedly save me was long gone. *Coward.*

"You always did love to run your mouth, Cyrus. But I mean it, I will kill you for touching her. And I'll enjoy every moment of it." Calix swore, letting loose a breath of flame at Cyrus. But then lightning was cracking towards him, and Calix dodged to the side, his darkness exploding through the room.

It was so dark that I couldn't see my fingers in front of my face. I'd never seen Calix use it to blot out an entire room completely before, but I found the darkness comforting, despite the circumstances.

I could hear two forces colliding but couldn't see what was happening. Okay, now I was a little peeved about the darkness. Fae could see just fine in this, I was sure. *So unfair.*

Lightning started cracking throughout the room, lighting it up enough for me to see what was happening. Streaks of blue white parting the black in staggered bolts. It was—beautiful, in a devastating way.

Not that I could focus on that. Not with two powerful Fae males trying to kill one another mere feet away.

The darkness tried surrounding Cyrus, but he had used some sort of spell to protect himself. I could see shadows dart toward him, only to bounce off, while lightning was sent at Calix, only for him to be somehow faster each time, the bolt hitting where he'd just been. I could see the frustration mounting in both of them.

They seemed to both give up on using magic at the same time. Calix was vastly more powerful than Cyrus, what had the blood magic given Cyrus access to—what was making it possible for him to fight Calix this way?

What else could he do with blood magic?

It was a chilling thought.

As chilling as the sight before me. Calix and Cyrus rushed one another with screams of rage. They collided, now using their bodies to try to take the other down. Thankfully, Calix definitely had the upper hand.

He fought with his entire body. Fluidly. He moved like a dancer, smoothly moving from one move to the next. A fist into Cyrus's cheek while he bent back to avoid a similar fate, then swinging around to take out Cyrus's legs, who managed to save his balance and get up just in time to avoid being pinned. Cyrus went after Calix in a flurry of punches that were all blocked.

Blood spilt a moment later, and I watched Calix flip a dagger with a smirk. Cyrus's chest was sliced down the middle. It quickly healed, but Cyrus was enraged. It made him sloppier, his form suffering from the way he went after Calix with pure fury. He had his own dagger in hand now and used it to try to stab Calix with no success.

Blows went back and forth, and back and forth, making me nearly dizzy I was watching so closely. Calix managed to land a slice down Cyrus's face with the dagger, and I wanted to cheer from the sidelines, but I refrained, purely so I wouldn't distract him.

Except then Cyrus pulled something out of his pocket, a vial of some sort. Calix cocked his head, only to widen his eyes as Cyrus threw it down and muttered something. My own eyes widened as I realized what was happening—blood magic. Calix was already moving toward Cyrus to stop him, but halfway there, he froze in place.

His limbs completely locked up mid-movement, and the darkness around us dissipated completely.

Oh, fuck.

Cyrus knew Calix was going to win and used his forbidden magic to gain the upper hand. I rushed to my feet, terrified he was going to use this moment to kill Calix.

Only—

He wasn't there.

I looked around, certain he wouldn't have left, only to freeze myself when cold metal licked my neck. An arm banded around my waist, pulling me back into a body I wanted to set on fire, not be pressed against.

I snarled, but Cyrus dug the blade further into my skin, not quite cutting it, but coming close. The pinch of metal was all too real as I swallowed hard, regretting it a moment later when I felt my throat being nicked against the blade.

Calix unfroze quickly, the magic not enough to hold him for long. His last movement followed through only for there to be nothing there to hit, and he whirled around, rage bristling off him as he spotted Cyrus holding a dagger to my neck. I looked at him helplessly, apologetically.

"Now, Calix. You're going to leave. And you're not going to bother me and my pet again." Cyrus stated confidently, making me want to rip his face off.

"Never." Calix snarled back, and I could see in his face that he wouldn't leave. He wouldn't leave *me*. Not to this fate.

"Calix," I pleaded, my voice rough with fear and a million other emotions. "Don't put everything at risk for me. *Please.*"

He knew what I meant. If Cyrus killed him here, the Resistance would fall and the world with it as it fell to chaos. We couldn't let that happen. This was bigger than all of us.

"Yes, Calix," Cyrus taunted mockingly, grating on my nerves. "Leave. Don't waste your life and all your little plans on this whore."

Calix's jaw was grinding so hard, I wouldn't be surprised if he broke a tooth. "If you think I'm leaving without you, my réalta, you're delusional. You didn't think I came alone, did you?"

The smirk on his face spoke of complete confidence, and I let it fill me with confidence, despite my shaking limbs.

"Drop the blade, or I plunge this one in your heart." Eryx's voice was colder than I'd ever heard it. Cyrus froze, a rough snarl coming from his mouth as he realized Eryx had come up behind him. "Let her go. Now." Cyrus shook in fury at Eryx's demand.

"If I can't have her, no one can." Cyrus promised, sounding completely unhinged. My heart dropped in my stomach, the strange certainty of the end hitting me a moment before I felt it.

Pain—like I'd never felt before as the knife slid across my throat, slicing it open. I barely registered the roar of my name, the fear and desperation in it, as I fell to the floor—only to be caught by familiar hands. Eryx lowered me down as I choked on my own blood. His hands went to my neck to try to stem the bleeding.

"Calix!" Eryx shouted; his face panicked. I managed to follow his eye-line to where Calix and Cyrus were fighting once more.

"Hold on, Asteria. We'll get a healer. Just hold on for me." Eryx begged, his voice shaking, and I wanted to tell him it was okay, but blood filled my mouth and stopped any words from forming.

I could feel death approaching. I wasn't ready. Not at all. I still had too much to do. A world to save, a people to free. So many people I didn't want to leave behind—those who'd experience the very pain I'd kept my heart closed off for so long to ensure I'd never experience.

But now, death reached out, like an old friend—one eager to say hello. I felt it in every drip of my life blood spilling out. Facing death was somehow simultaneously more and less frightening than I'd imagined. Seeing colors blur together where I stared at the ceiling. Sounds fading out. I existed for an extended moment in a peaceful sort of place, disassociated from the agony, but raw terror quickly filled my heart despite it.

Whispers reached my ears, lapping one over another—fast—too fast to make anything out. Until a man's deep voice became clear over the others, and I somehow knew exactly who it was.

Arawn, the god of death, was whispering to me.

I guess the gods really do pay attention to everyone after all.

CHAPTER 39

Calix POV

THE blade flashed across her neck and everything in me froze in a moment of pure terror. Everything good and light and wonderful that she'd brought into my life over the past few months, withering before my eyes.

The twinkle of eyes as blue as the sky when she laughed, a sight more and more common the longer she'd been in Night. The blush that would take her cheeks when she'd look at me and her thoughts were clearly somewhere very interesting. The laughter and playfulness she seemed to naturally bring out of me. The way she seamlessly fit into my life and my family.

There had been agony too. The torture of trying to stay away from her, despite every single atom of my body being drawn to her—keeping my hands off her was a study in futility. The idea of my mate had always been one of intense longing, but when she came into my life, I was ashamed to say that longing began to ebb away.

My Asteria was a force of nature trapped in a woman's body. She would do great things for this world, as the gods had foreseen. So why were they allowing this to happen?

No. I couldn't lose her. Not now. Not *ever*.

My heart thunked against my chest like only my armor was containing it from ripping out. It was no longer mine, and maybe it wanted to make its way to its true owner.

I had tried so hard to prevent this. Yet my inability to stay away from her had made it inevitable.

The moment Cyrus took her, using some of the darkest magic imaginable, I had let loose on the remaining guards in Sunset, slaughtering them brutally in retribution. Asteria deserved a better man than me, that I knew. But I was finding, to my surprise, that I was too selfish to let her go.

I knew I had a responsibility to my mate. The dreams I'd been having, where I became darkness incarnate—I could feel her there. Like on the other side of a barrier. All I could make out was a glowing figure on the other side. I tried desperately to reach her every time, but to no avail.

Years of waiting loyally for the day I found her, my *fated mate*, completely ruined in a few months with Asteria.

But how could I deny the pull I felt to her? The feeling was so similar to what mated pairs had described—but it was an impossibility. Everyone knew only Fae could mate with Fae.

This insistent pull between us left me absolutely stumped. Irate, even. It felt like she had a rope around me and was steadily pulling me in. I had a soul mate out there and couldn't entertain it—or that's what I told myself.

She made me weaker than I'd ever been. I'd been a pillar of strength for my people since Father died, yet a mere woman broke me down, made me weak, made me *want*. Keeping my hands off her was hard enough, but the night of the ball, she had set her sights on me.

And she was—Nox, she was *everything*. I wanted her with a passion I couldn't deny. And it wasn't just how absolutely gorgeous she was. No, it was everything about her. How she tried to shut herself off from the world, only to open herself up to me and my family, becoming one of us so easily. How Eryx and Baach became like big brothers to her, how the girls swarmed and circled around her like she was their sun. Her kindness and compassion were limitless, but she preferred to hide them under the veil of her rage to protect herself.

That rage in her had festered for years, and now it was a boiling fury she had to let out. With a focus now, she could put the rage aside. And those moments where she just *lived* were miraculous. The passion in her is more than enough to match my own. The way we came together at the Festival of Faunus—it wasn't only the best sex I'd ever had, it was transcendental.

It was the moment I had realized how fucked I truly was. How much I need her, how we fit together so perfectly, how she looks at me and doesn't see a villain, only a savior. She makes me believe I could be more than just the brutal king who slaughters his way across the continent. She made me envision a home filled with children—ones with black and silver-white hair and that—that was impossible.

I couldn't hurt her. I couldn't hurt either of them. My mate or Asteria. I was stuck and had no idea which way to turn.

But then she was taken, and I was ready to burn the world down. And luckily, I could do just that. I'd shifted into dragon form and laid waste to the retreating soldiers who were following after Cyrus, letting my fire cleanse Adamah of those who'd separate me and Asteria.

I needed my réalta back. I refused to rest until I had her in my arms. The thought of her being back in the hands of the one who assaulted her—it made fire rise in my throat and darkness bleed out from my fingers. She was *mine*—and I refused to allow her to be hurt like that again.

When we arrived back at Night to plan, we'd gotten everyone together. Asteria had touched the lives of so many during her time here, everyone was eager to get going and rescue her. Thank Nox for Kian. Without him, who knows how long it would have taken. A week already seemed an eternity.

When I mounted up to leave, Elatha ornery without his mate, I snorted. "You and me both."

I froze as I spoke those words. Asteria wasn't my mate. She wasn't Fae. Fuck, mixing them up could only lead to disaster. What was I thinking? *I wasn't.* I could only think of Asteria and what Cyrus may be doing to her. My hands tightened on the reigns as fury overtook me.

"Calix!" I'd been jolted from my downward spiral by Priscilla, who ran over to me, panting. "Take this. Asteria's parents gave it to her on Placement Day. She loves that necklace. She used to wear it all the time in Dusk." She shrugged lightly, but I could see the strain weighing down on her. Asteria was her best friend, her own savior.

"I'm not sure why she hasn't worn it lately but take it. Use it as a reminder of how important she is. I don't care if she isn't your mate, the two of you clearly have feelings for each other, so pack away thoughts of a woman you haven't even met yet and get back the woman who'd do fucking anything for you." Priscilla raised her brows expectantly as she held out the necklace.

A smirk crossed my lips; it was the first time I'd ever seen Priscilla so demanding, and that it was in defense of Asteria made me glad. She deserved a friend like Priscilla, who'd fight even a king on her behalf. Unlike Emmie, who'd sell her out to get back to a corrupt one.

I took the necklace, holding it up to take a quick look, only to freeze in shock. Starlight and darkness engulfed my vision for a moment—leaving me with a haze of confusion and the desperate driving *need* to find her.

"Where did her parents get this? Why give it to her?" I asked Priscilla forcefully, who looked confused at both my questions and intensity.

"I don't know." Priscilla admitted, shrugging. "Her parents said they found it, and they kept it for years instead of selling it. Considering it's made of star opal and silverium, they could have gotten a lot for it too."

That was an understatement, but I didn't care about selling price—I cared about why and how Asteria had a necklace made from the gem of my land—in the *exact shape of my soul mark.*

I clasped the necklace around my neck so I wouldn't lose it, gripping the pendant on and off the entire way to Dusk. My nerves were already completely frayed. We had one shot to rescue Asteria. We had to make it count.

Thoughts of the necklace plagued me, but I put it aside as we reached Evenfall. Titan gave me the nod and I shifted, my form twisting and altering until I could feel the heft of my dragon form. I would take no chances with Asteria's life. This was no regular battle, where we went in to get out any humans we could and cause some chaos on the way. So instead, I took flight, watching from above as Titan rallied the armies behind me.

I flew above the trees for a moment until Evenfall came fully into view. The main gate of the city was closed, and soldiers covered it from all angles. A growl formed in my throat as I let my fire gather. These were men keeping my réalta a prisoner, they would get no quarter. Before they even had time to hear the beats of my wings, I opened my maw and let fire reign down on them. Screams filled my ears as the scent of charred flesh hit my nostrils. Usually, I mourned having to take the lives of guards who merely served under the orders of their corrupt lords and kings. *Not today.*

I let loose another breath of flame and flew straight toward the palace, letting my fire clear the path to Asteria. Titan and the army would be right behind me, but I beat my wings harder, desperate to get to the palace and find her. I left a trail of scorched bodies and buildings in my wake until I reached the black monstrosity Astraeus called a palace and shifted back quickly, letting myself fall lightly to the ground for the last few feet.

The palace guards watched me with shock and horror lining their faces, gripping their swords with nervous, sweating palms, I was sure. I drew my blade as I let my shadows out to play, blanketing them in eternal night. I spun my blade as more guards came from the left and was quickly hacking into any man who dared stand between me and Asteria. Eryx, Bach, and Harpina appeared around me and quickly joined the carnage. Between the four of us, there was little resistance left, and impatient, I used my shadows to snap the necks of the remaining few.

I normally preferred to fight more honorably, letting the men have a chance to live, but today was not a normal day.

We stormed the palace, and I let my darkness and blade work in tandem as I took out any who dared to stand in my way. A large guard stepped forward, daring to smirk at me. "King Calix, we were told to expect you. All this for some slave, huh? Bitch must be one great piece of ass to have two nobles fighting over her."

A snarl ripped free as my fingers turned to claws against my will, the rage that rose in me at his words too great to contain. I let a hiss of fire escape my mouth, causing the man to flinch back warily. I smiled slowly, taking the moment to put my claws away so I could swing my sword. "You don't get to talk about her, you don't get to even think about her. You are a pathetic man working for a Fae who's lost his damn mind, helping him hold an innocent woman captive. I'll take great pleasure in killing you for Asteria. You can go to Tartarus knowing that your death was in that former slave's name."

I relished the look of horror on his face as I swiped my sword at him. He barely blocked it, and as I struck again, he parried, only to be distracted by the shadows tripping his legs. He grunted as he fell back, and I swiped my sword down his stomach, opening him up. He screamed as his innards began to spill out. I stood above him, smiling, listening to his cries as he begged for a death that wouldn't come fast enough.

I kneeled down over him as I summoned my other power, the one I told Asteria I hated using. I despised the power much of the time, but this time—I thanked Erebus himself for gifting me with it.

"This pain?" I hissed, grabbing his face with one hand to keep him looking at me, as I began to let the power of Tartarus flow through me and into him. "This is what you'll get to experience for the rest of eternity. I wanted you to know what you have to look forward to, what you could have avoided had you not been stupid enough to assist with holding her. Keeping her from *me.*" I growled and left him to his screams as the flames and wretched agony of Tartarus consumed him from the inside out.

I wished him a fucking eternity of misery.

We fought on, fighting any in our path as we made straight for Cyrus's rooms, where Kian said Asteria had been locked up since arriving.

The thought made my blood boil, darkness rising around me as the shadows leaked out. I let them cover me as I entered the room, but it wasn't enough. My powers failing me for the first time in my life, when it was of the utmost importance they succeed.

And now, I stood facing the woman I had tried so hard not to love—only to feel my heart rip in half the way the knife ripped open her throat.

"NOOOOO!" I bellowed, the world shattering around me. "Asteria!" I tried to launch toward her as she fell to the ground, her blood spilling out much too fast.

But Cyrus was immediately on me. We battled once more, but desperation was now driving me, and whatever magic he was using had exponentially increased his effectiveness. Still, he was a sloppy fighter, and I had to get to my réalta. My light. My love.

It was then a bright flash of light exploded through the room. I instinctively held up my arm to block my eyes, Cyrus and I both freezing as we watched what was happening—or trying to through the blaze of light.

Fear overtook me once more. I couldn't see Asteria through whatever the blinding light was. It began to fade after a moment, and I could only pray she was okay, that I had time to save her, to get her a healer.

"Erebus, Nox, Asteria, I beg of you, please save her." I prayed, hoping the gods, my ancestor, answered me now. Liv saw her in her vision, which meant she couldn't die—right? She just couldn't. There was more for her to do, and I—I couldn't do any of this without her.

"I'll do anything. *Anything.* I know she is not the mate Ziva and Hedone chose for me, but she has managed to make me hers regardless—without a bond, without anything outside of who she is. I love her fiercely because she is fierce. She's a dragon at heart, with starlight in her veins, and a soul that calls for darkness. I could not imagine a more perfect woman in all the kingdoms. Please, grant me this, and I will forever be your grateful servant."

I felt a breeze sweep through the room, brushing against my cheek and shoulder. Like a delicate hand trailing down my cheek, while a larger hand clasped my shoulder the way Titan might.

The touch of the gods was a delicate, rare thing, one I wished I could savor, but my terror over Asteria was still thick in my throat. The light faded and a moment later, Cyrus ducked into the secret passageway. He skittered away like a rat from a sinking ship, but I couldn't focus on detaining my enemy now.

A ragged gasp drew my attention.

Asteria!

CHAPTER 40

AWE filled me as I realized exactly what I was hearing. How I knew it was Arawn speaking to me, I wasn't sure. Maybe only the confidence of the dying, recognizing he who would oversee them forevermore. But I knew what I was hearing—ethereal whispers coming from another place, certainly not of this world.

I listened to his whispers, confused by his message. It didn't seem possible.

As the god of death whispered in my ear, time seemed to slow and stop—only to immediately start again and speed up in a dizzying rush once his voice faded away, the whispers of so many others fading right along with him.

I felt it then—through the agony, the burning heat, the feel of my blood and life ebbing out of me...

I felt it—the oppressive feeling I'd always carried with me. All my life, that ache, like my skin was too tight, had followed me. My body trying to break out of the shell holding it together—*yes*, it felt just like an invisible shell had surrounded me, pressing down and holding me in. I felt that nebulous shell now—and then, I felt it *crack*.

The sound was deafening. A mighty roar whipped by my ears as that invisible chain binding me cracked in two and fell away.

Light blasted out of me, and I winced, expecting to lose my eyesight as the overly bright illumination blinded me—but I didn't. Instead, I felt the life that was seeping out of me...stop.

I could feel the jagged slice across my throat, and the pull as it began to quickly knit itself back together. I blinked quickly, shock running through me as I spat out the blood in my mouth. A ragged gasp fought its way past my lips, and I began gulping in air, finally able to breathe once more.

Panic began to stir, not quite taking root—confusion was too heavy. My body, that moments ago was bleeding out on the floor, seemed to somehow be infused with life. The toll of blood loss reversing itself moment by moment.

I pushed myself to a sitting position. Eryx, whose slack face and gaping mouth would have made me chuckle under other circumstances, was instantly there to help. Despite his shock, he was there to support me, grabbing my arms and steadying me. I sat there for a moment, panting. Immeasurably grateful for his help.

I reached up, feeling for my neck. Blood came away on my hand, but no wound greeted my searching fingertips. The skin was smooth. Unblemished.

What. Was. Happening?!

I looked up, seeing Calix frozen as he watched me, paralyzed from a storm of fear and shock, but I couldn't focus on that. Not as I realized—as I realized I could now feel so many different things. That nebulous feeling I always felt—my skin feeling too tight, my body wanting to take up more space—that feeling had been correct all along.

I *was* being held inside a too tight shell. My skin never fit me right because it *wasn't* right. Feeling like there was something always just out of my reach…

I didn't want to believe it. Because it meant that everything I knew about myself was a lie. True panic started to take root, clearing its way through the shock and confusion and *awe*—

I couldn't lie to myself. I knew now what it was that had been locked up inside me, screaming to get out as it rattled its cage…

Magic.

Magic flooded through my body. I could *feel* it. It was a riotous force within me. Too long held back, it had finally snapped its chain—and now bared its fangs.

I raised my hand as I noticed the magic crackling at my fingertips. I brought my hand in front of my face and cocked my head to the side as I took it in, the bright light that had washed over me whenever it had held back the magic, *my* magic, all this time had broken—that light was now playing over my fingertips. Like it couldn't help but play now that it was free.

It was beautiful, like millions of little stars dancing around my fingertips. Flitting around one another in a swath of sparkle, like I'd shaken the night sky upside down and dumped the stars out of it and onto my hands. Just like in my dreams, I realized with a jolt. Starlight infused my hands then, making them glow in the darkness.

It was *real*. I gasped in a breath—it was all real. Whatever had held back my magic when awake, it didn't affect me as much at night, allowing me eventual access to it. Allowing me to bring stars to my command.

Wonder and awe crashed together with desperate panic and more confusion than I'd ever felt.

It was then I noticed the other changes in me. My skin, the faint illumination—it wasn't just the magic. Or maybe it *was* and that was why all the Fae had that slight illumination to their skin when one looked closely. Either way, the illumination traveled past where my new magic played, continuing up my arm, to my chest—

"Asteria." Calix's breathy exhale sounded a million miles away, even as I yearned to go to him. To look into those purple eyes and find a port in this storm.

But I couldn't.

I could feel the tremble in my hand as I lifted it. Bringing it to my ear, I started at my ear lobe and gently ran it upwards. Up, and up—and where a smooth, rounded top used to be—a pointed tip met my fingertips.

The world seemed to tilt and shift. Everything I once knew about myself crumbled to stardust. My breathing picked up in panic as I faced the reality of what was happening. It didn't make sense. I *couldn't* make any sense of it despite what was happening. I knew what this was, what I was. But it couldn't be, it wasn't possible. And yet—I knew it was undeniable. The feeling like I was stuffed into too tight skin was gone. The wrongness I always vaguely felt, like I was smothered and suffocating in some nebulous way—It was gone too. Everything clicked into place with heart wrenching awareness.

Fae.

"I'm Fae." I breathed out, looking up and connecting with those purple eyes I dreamt of, my breathing too quick and on the verge of hyperventilating. But once my eyes locked on Calix's, it felt like something snapped and then locked into place.

His eyes were wild, looking at me so intensely, like he had never seen anything so astounding in all his long life. His silvery white hair swished around his face as he moved quickly, kneeling before me, and taking my face in his hands. His eyes roved my face like it might disappear from right in front of him. His fingers stroked my cheeks with a heartbreakingly gentle wonder.

"You're more than that, my réalta." Calix murmured, and his voice still sounded like he was out of breath. Like his awe, his surprise at what was occurring had stolen the breath from him. His eyes shined brightly, water building up in them as they fluttered closed for a moment, only to open quickly so he didn't miss a moment.

The feeling of—*of home*—of safety and love and life, like darkness and stars made manifest, filled my lungs. All of it hitting me as Calix looked into my eyes.

When he opened his mouth, I didn't think anything could shock me more than the discovery that I'm actually, somehow, in some way I couldn't fathom—*Fae*—mere moments ago. But what I was feeling between us, some instinct I always followed where he was concerned, told me what was coming would change my life forever—and I could barely handle what was already happening. Part of me wanted to cover his mouth and stop the words I could already feel in my bones.

In my *soul*…

But speak he did, his whisper full of wonder and happiness—heartbreaking relief.

"You're my soulmate, Asteria."

And I could only crumble.

CHAPTER 41

S ITTING among my ladies in waiting, listening to them chatter about nonsense, like who will marry who, I nearly rolled my eyes. Thank Hyperion, I had much more decorum than that. But still, I wished to tell them marriage wasn't all it was made out to be.

They were taught from an early age that a good match was the only thing for a woman to aspire to in life. I had believed that lie as well, up until I actually got married, that was. I was considered one of the *lucky ones*. One of the ones who received a soul mark by the grace of the gods—and had the good fortune to find my mate quickly.

And he was the king of Day Kingdom no less! Oh, I'd been so overjoyed. My entire family was. As a cousin of House Bathala, the ruling family of Dawn, I'd always wished to find a way to gain more power. I'd grown up looking at it from a distance, and ruing the fact that a chance twist of fate saw my despicable cousins upon the throne, while I was left with nothing.

My father had told me that good daughters don't have ambition. They don't reach for more than they're given.

But I had never wished to be a good daughter.

I wished to carve my own path. While my father wished to use me to take power of his own—the hypocrite. When men wanted more power and schemed to get it, they were considered smart and politically inclined. When a woman did it? We were overreaching, not staying in our place.

I had hoped my husband would be different. As my mate, I'd assumed he'd understand the desires of my heart and see them accomplished with a smile.

What a fool I was.

I learned my lesson quickly. I'd managed to find ways around my husband though, playing the delicate queen, all the while scheming to achieve some semblance of power in Day.

Until the Oracle.

Until the prophecy.

Everything I did now, it was for her.

I spent years slowly working to get others on my side. Some scorned me for not giving Aelius a *true*, god's blessed heir to the throne. There was only Arien in their minds, and that's how it had to stay—for now, anyway.

But I worked hard, as did my son, to ensure the court split down the middle. I knew not all would follow a woman, so this was the safest bet. When the time came, and I knew it would, they would be ready. Aelius hadn't the faintest idea what was going on in his own court—exactly as I'd intended.

Once, I would have relished having so much power over this kingdom. Now, I just longed for her to be here.

Everything I did, I did for her—my daughter, my heir.

Waiting for Soren to return was excruciating, my nerves rising the longer it went without him returning. When a knock came, and one of my guards announced Soren's presence, I stood quickly—wanting to shoot up out of my seat, but forced to maintain my royal air.

"That will be all today, ladies." I smiled demurely at my ladies. "I'm afraid we'll have to cut this short." Despite my efforts, only about half of them were loyal to me. My husband continually put his own people around me, and I couldn't let them find out what I was up to.

Soren stepped into the room once they'd departed. So human, so young—I'd seen him on Placement Day, desperately panting after her. I knew immediately I had to get him on my staff. It was a blow that she hadn't assigned to Day, but not one we hadn't expected. It didn't mean we couldn't bring her here.

We had to. But as Soren entered alone, my heart dropped, my hope flickering out like a candle in the breeze as my posture wilted like a flower in despair.

"My Queen, I'm sorry." Soren dropped to one knee, bowing his head. "She doesn't want to leave Night Kingdom. I wasn't able to get her past the magic Prince Cyrus had in place, but King Calix showed up to rescue her. They seemed—*close*."

The jealousy he was trying to hide was ridiculous, though understandable. Still, this was something I needed to figure out. "Rise. What do you mean she wanted to be in Night?"

My tone left no room for misunderstanding. I didn't care how uncomfortable he was, I needed the full report. Soren sighed, running a hand through his hair as he stood.

"She claimed that they aren't monsters, that King Calix isn't what we believe." Soren stated hesitantly.

I snorted, not a very queenly thing to do, but still—the man had gone mad 20 years ago, suddenly shutting down his borders, letting no one in. Not even trading! Then, the attacks started. He never attacked Day, of course. He'd never risk the scales balance in his own kingdom tipping to the wrong side. But it seemed obvious he was trying to conquer the continent.

At least, that's what we'd thought at first. Only, he killed random Fae, took humans, and ran. As Soren explained what she told him, I let out a shaky breath, slowly sinking into my chair as I took the information in. If this was true, then she was safe.

Safe.

My head dropped as I shook, relief more potent than any I'd ever known filling me. I still needed to meet her soon, but this was wonderful news. Though we'd have to deal with Calix's plans later. Hyperion, what was he thinking?

"I stayed in the tunnel, listening to the battle between King Calix and Prince Cyrus. I knew you'd want the full report, and I saw—" Soren gulped, and my nerves ratcheted back up.

"What?" I demanded.

"Prince Cyrus slit her throat." Soren struggled to get out the words, his voice hoarse and his eyes haunted. I brought a hand to my own throat, horror clouding my vision as my heart broke into pieces. I opened my mouth, but Soren rushed to speak over me. Normally I'd not allow such behavior, but now—

"But then a bright light exploded out of her—" Soren exhaled, awe shining through his remembrance, and my breath caught in my throat. "And her neck healed completely. I caught a small glimpse of her after, and her ears—"

Soren struggled to speak, so I opened my mouth once more. "Were pointed."

Soren nodded, wide eyed, and I waited for him to connect the dots, while my heart stitched itself back together, knowing that she was okay, that she was *whole*—

"You knew she was Fae." Soren gasped, and I nodded silently in confirmation. "How? Why do you want her here so badly?" He finally dared to ask the question he'd kept on the tip of his tongue since the first time I informed him of his mission. I'd had him training from day one to help her.

"You're dismissed for the day. We'll discuss this later." I told him sharply. I could tell he was unhappy, but he wisely held his tongue. I had more important people to discuss this with, and joy was now cautiously rising as I struggled to believe it was finally happening—and trying to keep my hopes reasonable. She didn't know me, barely knew herself, and I needed to remind myself of this every time my giddiness grew out of control.

I swept out of the room, the white double doors that led out of the parlor opened for me on command. My dark purple dress dragged along the floor as I made my way to the railing that overlooked the training yard, finding Arien right away.

Despite his young age, Arien was born to be a General. Natural talent and pure determination ensured he was more than fit for the job, yet his appointment to the position caused some discontent with those my husband favored, who thought him too young and inexperienced—who resented him for not being Aelius's heir.

It wouldn't matter when the time came. Their words wouldn't mean a thing to our side. He'd been trained all his life for his purpose, and the time was finally coming soon. Excitement filled me, even if there were now complications with Night's involvement, but we'd figure it out.

I waved down at Arien, and he quickly stepped away, taking the nearby stairs quickly but strolling toward me to avoid any undue suspicion. His gold armor shone in the sun, and as always, pride filled me at seeing him in the role he'd taken up—I couldn't wait to see him fully step into it.

"Mother." Arien greeted me with a nod, a smile tipping one corner of his mouth upwards.

"Son, I have some wonderful news. Come with me." I smiled widely and urged him along through the halls. Arien followed me into the library, I knew it was usually empty this time of day, and I frequently used it for clandestine meetings. Now in private, I laid out everything I'd learned from Soren for him.

Joy, pure *joy*, spread across Arien's face.

"It's time. Finally." Arien murmured, inhaling sharply. He took my hands, squeezing, and I smiled gently at my second-born as tears filled my eyes, nodding in confirmation.

"It's time."

CHAPTER 42

Cyrus POV

Tap. *Tap. Tap.*

My teeth set on edge at the wait. I suppose he felt the need to show-case that a king doesn't run when a mere prince calls, but my jaw ground back and forth against the insult. I forced myself to swallow it down—*for now*.

Tap. Tap. Tap.

This was too important. I could not allow myself to look a fool, to look weak—this would show the entirety of Celesterra that I was no such thing. That I was in control. Strong. Impenetrable.

Tap. Tap. Tap.

I'd spent years crafting my image. Building up my resources. Implementing my spy network, one person at a time. Creating certain alliances and enemies within my father's court that would ensure my rise to power.

Tap. Tap. Tap.

I stilled my leg as I realized my foot was nervously tapping against the marble floor. I couldn't afford to show such a weakness, especially not here. Not after I'd been made a fool of.

Fury blazed inside me once more.

How had this happened? All my careful planning, years of setting up plans, and it all began to crack apart due to a woman. A human, I'd thought. Insignificant but for what I wanted out of her.

Sex. Worship. Obsession.

She was meant to want those things from me, to feel them *for* me. Instead, I'd somehow ended up ensnared in *her* web instead. She refused to let me touch her, making me salivate after her—while she would rather fuck Calix of all people! I couldn't let this stand. I *wouldn't*.

Not only had a seemingly human woman rejected me, but she wasn't even human! How had I been fooled when seeing her in her full Fae form had made it blindingly obvious she was always meant to be Fae—I would never live this down. My reputation had to be salvaged. And while Asteria may have healed from my slitting her throat, the end goal still remained—I would not allow anyone else to have her.

She was mine. Fae or not.

Though, it did explain my obsession with her. She was something new, something that had never existed before. And that was likely why she had been hiding as a human. King Aelius would never stand for such a thing. The Fae were always beautiful, and that was the one part of Asteria that couldn't be hidden away, her Fae features too fair to belong to a human. I'd known the second I saw her where she belonged.

And that was in my bed—tied up and helpless as I did what I would with her. I could imagine tying her up spread eagle to my four-poster bed and spending the entire day eating her cunt until she begged me for mercy—but I wouldn't give it. I would thrust my cock into her while she cried and begged me to stop.

It's what I had imagined when I locked those cuffs around her wrists and ankles, spreading her on the bed for my pleasure. I should have just fucked her then, not given in to the thrill of torturing her with anticipation.

I cut off that line of thinking for now as I felt myself growing hard, shifting slightly to relieve the growing ache in my cock. Asteria should have been here to service me. That was her purpose in life, not to warm Calix's bed, not even to follow the gods' plan for her.

No—she existed to please me, that was all.

Oh, I knew my soon to be wife would have argued against me keeping her around. Zerlina was a jealous one, which I admittedly liked. I wanted women fighting over me for the pleasure of gracing my bed. She would have come around though, once I made some truths very clear to her.

I stood as the doors opened and a line of guards parted to reveal their liege. I first saw the gold tipped shoes hitting the white and gold marble floor, then the flowing blue robes with a golden brocade, until I raised my eyes up and found golden hair and sky-blue eyes.

Asteria's eyes.

A roaring din of wrath rose within me, but I forced it down. This meeting was too important. I bowed, gritting my teeth as I always did when forced to do something so beneath me. "King Aelius. Thank you for agreeing to meet me."

"Prince Cyrus." Aelius nodded, regally, his nose in the air like he was doing me some great service by gracing me with his presence. "I can't say I wasn't surprised. It's not often a royal from another kingdom asks to meet with me, and informs me they'll be alone, without guards, to share a very important bit of news that no one can find out." He sat down across from me and leaned back, an amused smile upon his lips. "All very dramatic."

I forced a smile, wanting to send a bolt of lightning into his damned blue eyes, both from his words—and so it didn't feel like looking into *her* eyes. "It's extremely important, and I think you and I can help one another."

"Have we not already agreed to do so? If you find my heir?" Aelius raised an inquisitive brow.

I barely refrained from rolling my eyes. "A tentative alliance with my father, yes. I want one with *me*." As I expected, Aelius's eyes sparkled at the news.

"Is that so?" He asked as he took the seat across from me. "And why would I cut the king out of this? You are a mere prince." He leaned back, relaxed as I could be, and I took a mental deep breath so I wouldn't spear him with a bolt.

"My father won't rule forever. The time is coming for me to take my place, and when it does, I intend to take out Night Kingdom completely. All that land will be available. Including the places that border your own kingdom. Even the remaining parts of the Etheralta Mountains." I raised a brow at Aelius who smirked in return.

"Hmm. An interesting proposition. However, Night Kingdom is our balance. We'd risk chaos." Aelius challenged. I smirked at him, hardly believing that was his rebuttal.

"What's wrong with a little chaos? I doubt you're unaware my kingdom has been leaning that way for some time, and we've suffered no ill effects at all. It's a children's story, in truth, meant to make us all behave." I explained, rolling my eyes and mocking the idea. An act, of course—the gods were as cruel as ever—but Aelius didn't need to know that. The gods may be a problem, but we would remake this world, force them out of the picture somehow. They deserved it after all—everything I did was for the best, and yet my powers waned.

At least there was blood magic to make up the difference.

"It's an awfully big risk for me." King Aelius chuckled, shaking his head. "I don't see how it could possibly be worth it."

"Because I'm going to kill your heir for you." I smiled, running my tongue over my sharpened canine. I took satisfaction from the way Aelis jolt back in his chair.

"What did you just say?" Aelius replied, going completely still as he stared at me with hunger in his gaze.

"Oh, yes, your heir. I found her." I smirked as his face grew cold; anger obvious in the set of his mouth—the same way Asteria's looked when she tried to hide hers.

"Is this some kind of joke? Women don't receive the blessing from the gods." Aelius insisted, glaring at me.

"The gods certainly can—and they will, just to fuck with you. They've never chosen a woman before, but lucky you, it was your heir who was chosen to be the first." I told him merrily, sarcasm clear. The gods who gave me my magic only to take it away were at fault for this too—the battle for the future of Celesterra was coming. I could practically feel it in the air. I would ensure they were brought a reckoning—once I ruled the continent. Not that my allies needed to know my plans. They certainly wouldn't agree to the full picture.

"No, I will not abide a *woman* inheriting my throne!" Aelius shook his head as he slammed his fist down on the table.

"Something tells me that's why your wife hid her." I told him dryly. The man still wasn't putting the picture together. This was the King of Day? Oh, this would be too easy.

"My wife?" Aelius questioned, cocking his head to the side. I fisted my hands, hating the similarities I spotted between them. Hating her—yet needing her all the same. She was the only one to ever see the rage within me and match it with her own. How could she have turned her back on that? Did she not realize how rare it was? "You think she was aware of this atrocity?"

Aelius's words brought me back to the present, but it was worth it. I couldn't help the joy I felt at needling him along the path to answers. I leaned back in my chair, exuding the casual arrogance I was so good at performing. "I would say so, considering your heir is—"

"Who?" Aelis demanded, slamming his fist down again. His demands made me want to slam my fist into his face.

I laughed, pausing for dramatic effect. He was right where I wanted him, and now—for the push.

"The heir is your daughter." The words dropped into the space heavily, but Aelius scoffed.

"I don't have a daughter." The King of Day scoffed, rolling his eyes. "Merely a son. A useless waste of a firstborn." Aelius sneered, and the division between them was a good point to note for later. I wondered how deep his wife's deception ran.

"Except I wager he isn't your firstborn." I countered. I knew what I saw— that light that surrounded her, that brief glow right after her own magic faded away—that was unmistakable. "This heir was born on the Sommer Solstice, twenty-one years ago, and has black hair and sky-blue eyes. Your wife must have hidden her with a spell, knowing what you'd do. She hid her away as a human, where you'd never have a chance of finding her."

Aelius grew increasingly agitated with every word, and I eagerly watched him descend into a mad temper. Every step away from rationality was one I could use. "War is coming, King Aelius, and if you join me, she'll be on the opposite side. We'll get our chance to take her out once and for all."

"The human you were said to be obsessed with?" Aelius raised a brow, looking me over critically.

I bristled at the accusation, snarling at him. His guards shifted as if to rush forward toward me, but Aelius raised a hand to stop them from leaving their posts. I forced myself to calm down, until I found the words to argue against him. "She was no human in the end. Fae, the entire time."

"What is her name—"Aelius narrowed his eyes at me. "This monstrosity the gods thought to call my heir?" He glowered at the thought, and I was pleased to see it. Everything was going to plan.

I let the pain I so looked forward to bringing her fuel me, a cruel smile growing on my lips, thinking of my plans to return every ounce of humiliation she brought me as I fucked her bloody.

"Asteria. Asteria Faelynn Zagreus. Or, I suppose I should say...*Asteria Faelynn Earendel. Crown Princess of Day Kingdom.*"

Want More?

Get Exclusive Bonus Content!

Scan the QR code below to sign up for my newsletter and you'll receive a welcome email with a password to a locked page on my website that contains some awesome bonus content—exclusive to my subscribers! You'll have access to never-before-seen art, including a depiction of the climax, and NSFW art, along with bonus and deleted scenes! You can also sign up via my website at **www.rachelfallonauthor.com**!

The Star Queen Chronicles will continue

in Book 2

Installments of The Star Queen Chronicles

Book 1: Of Darkness and Ruination

Book 2: Title to be Announced

Book 3: Title to be Announced

Untitled Spin Off

RACHEL FALLON is a writer and cat mom from Massachusetts who's been obsessed with making up stories all her life. Always one to daydream and with an incredibly active imagination, she's spent her life making up stories in her head and watching them play out like movies.

A huge lover of fantasy and romance, she's always read stories and watched movies and tv shows where the two are intertwined, even dating back to childhood. She craved the chance to tell her own story full of fantasy and romance, and the rise of romantasy opened the door to her dreams. After a prolonged period of being unable to write creatively as she once could, a decade later saw the ability return, and she began writing stories online to get used to writing once more. The encouragement she received and several requests for her to write her own novel inspired her to actually give it a shot. While working her office job full time, she made room for writing (and of course reading) whenever a moment could be spared. She found quickly that this story just flew off the page, and the expansive world of The Star Queen Chronicles was begging to be told!

Acknowledgments

To my grandmother, though she may be gone, without what she left me I would never have been able to accomplish this dream. May your time in the Otherworld allow you to travel the world as you wish, and may you look down and see your granddaughter achieving dreams she never thought possible. *Thanks to you.* I love you, always.

To my mother, thank you for every bit of support you have given me, I could never have done this without that. Thank you for allowing me to follow my dreams, for teaching me everything that brought me here. Thank you for encouraging my writing as a child, you helped build the foundation this novel sits on. I love you!

To my cousin Bobbie and Aunt Betty, along with my dear niece, Jordyn (though we cover her ears when needed—I hope when she's an adult she can appreciate this fully). Thank you all so much for always being my cheerleaders! You've helped give me the confidence to keep going and publish this novel. Your unyielding faith in me means more than you'll ever know. I love you all so much!

To my dad, thank you for everything. I know you'll likely never see this, but I spent too many years as a daddy's girl to not thank the man who shaped so much of who I am and how I think. You're more amazing than you'll ever know. I love you.

To my amazing editor, Loren Sorensen, I can't thank you enough for coming in at the last minute and editing my novel! You knew this was on a time crunch, and lengthy to boot, and you took it on anyway. Without you, I would have been lost. But you understood my characters and directions, and helped me to make this what it is now! Becoming a great friend in the process. Thank you from the bottom of my heart!

To Rena Violet, my incredible artist, who designed the cover, hardback, map, interior, and graphics—I knew the moment I saw your work that you were going to be my artist. The vibe was just right, and I knew you would create something special—and I was absolutely right! Every bit of work you've done for me has been so gorgeous, and perfectly suited for this book. I can't thank you enough for bearing with me as I figured this all out, and creating a masterpiece that will surely bring many more eyes to my work! Thank you a million times over!

To my PA, Margie Barr, you have been so, so amazing! Helping me put everything together for this has not been easy, and I know I've had a million questions, but you've been there every step of the way! Thank you so much for taking me on and helping to ensure that I did this thing right! I truly would be lost without you, so thank you!

To Danielle, thank you for being there and letting me vent to you, cheering me on, and helping me whenever I was stuck. You helped me find the name for this entire world, and Adamah will forever live on thanks to you! And all in all, thank you for being a wonderful book friend turned real life friend!

To Meghan, thank you for being such an ardent support, for reading and rereading my manuscript, letting me vent, helping me find solutions to my problems, helping me with graphics, and so much more! You helped me through my editing meltdown, when I needed someone to listen more than ever. You've helped share my work and the love you have for it just lights up my heart. You're an absolute gem darling, and I don't know what I'd do without you!

To Emma and Renee, I have no words for how amazing you two are! I'm so happy this book has brought us together! Thank you for all of your help! It was a huge undertaking that you took on for pure love of the story to help me, and it means the world to me. This story is going out into the world in thanks to the hours of effort you put into proofreading and I will forever be in your debt.

To the girls in the Baby Authors group on Instagram, you have all been so supportive and amazing! You've given me direction when I was lost. You've answered all my inane questions and helped me figure out how to do this publishing thing! I couldn't have done this without all of you!

Huge thank you to the authors who have spared a kind word, advice, or more for me! Briar Boleyn, Nisha J. Tuli, Erin Mainord, Fay Bec, Charlotte Mallory—thank you all so much! <3

To all the girls who spent years making me feel less than—you gave me the knowledge of how to fight back, how to rise above, how to move on, and how to show the world that I'm more than you will ever know. I'm a Queen at heart, despite your nastiness. But you helped me build my characters, and without your venom, I would never have been able to write them so authentically to my experience. So—Suck it.